ENTWINED

BRUTES OF BRISTLEBROOK
BOOK THREE

REBECCA QUINN

Cover by Artscandare.

Editing by Jessica Ryn and Andrew H.

ISBN: 978-1-923196-03-2

Read Also

CONTENT NOTE

Hello lovely Quinnksters,

We're back for the third and final book. AHHHH! It's finally done. It's finally here, and I'm so, so grateful to all of you coming back to see out this series with me.

This book has been one of the hardest and most rewarding things I've ever done in my life, so thank you for giving me the space to bring it into this world.

Firstly, I would like to gently direct everyone to my website, rebeccaquinnauthor.com, where there is a list of all tropes and content warnings for this book. Entwined is about as dark as Entangled, but it deals with a new and wide range of scenes and situations that readers may find triggering, so I would encourage everyone to look those over before you continue on.

As with the previous books in this series, I've tried to be as comprehensive as I could with that content list, but please, if you have any questions or concerns, or believe anything should be added, contact me at rebecca.quinn.author@gmail.com

I take all notes about content very seriously.

Secondly, on the above note, I'd like to specifically call out the fact that this book deals with content around the trafficking of women, with the various ways people respond to trauma, anxiety, PTSD, and mental health in general. It deals with the difficulties women face in trusting men, and the fears and dangers rife with that decision-making process. While this book has a lot of lighter moments too, its underlying topics are serious and are handled as such.

Your mental health matters, so please be kind to yourself and seek support if you need it.

Finally, this book also deals with a range of BDSM scenes and dynamics. As with the previous books, please be mindful that this is fiction, and shouldn't be taken as instructional reading. Liberties are taken for the sake of the story, events are dramatized, and relationships and dynamics move faster in fictional, apocalyptic worlds than they do in life.

In fiction, kink is seamless, there's no poop in the chute, first times aren't the uncomfortable equivalent of two bodies making awkward small talk, refractory periods are myths, characters *just know* how to make their partners feel good, and they already know exactly what to do for aftercare.

Must be nice, right? If you're inspired to try any new kink, please communicate extensively with your partner, research non-fiction, reputable sources of information, and always, always, keep things safe, sane, and consensual (or insert preferred kink acronym of your choice).

Okay, Becky's safety lecture is complete. Now go and have some fun!

Lots of love,
Becky Quinn

It's a hard thing losing a vibrator you love.
Not so easy to move on, you know?

Maybe one day I'll commit again,
but for now, I'm in my fling phase.

So this dedication is for me,
and for my arsenal of dildos and vibrators
that would make even Jasper blush.

Why choose, baby.

PART ONE

FAMINE

CHAPTER 1

EDEN

SURVIVAL TIP #86
*Don't let your fear of being alone
turn you into someone who makes it a reality.*

"Traitor!"

Another man from Red Zone spits at my feet, and Lucky yanks me behind him. Shouts crash around us in furious waves. We're encircled by armored men and women . . . and some of our own people.

The Sinners only left us with one weapon each, but one weapon is more than enough to tear me apart.

"How could you do that to Heather?" Jennifer demands.

I'm shoved from behind, then someone grabs my shoulder, and I whirl around to see Sloane staring at me in confusion. In *hurt*. "Were you working with them? Shit, Eden . . . Make it make sense."

"I—" I stammer, and her fingers dig in hard enough to bruise.

"Remove your hand or forfeit it, Sloane." Jasper's voice blows in like a winter wind from behind me.

We're on the brink of the forest and the city, where the Sinners dumped us minutes ago with a final warning to behave. The moon's feeble blue light paints everyone in wan, miserable hues.

Sloane's jaw flexes, but she drops her hand. Ava moves in and squeezes her arm.

"Heather trusted you." Ava is hard-eyed and unforgiving as she adds bitterly, "We all did."

Heather's furious, betrayed eyes slice my memory.

My stomach churns, acidic with shame and adrenaline . . . and anger. This wasn't supposed to happen. If my lies were a tangled mess, Alastair somehow twisted them into a noose. Intangible, unlike the one that silenced Sam forever—but surely enough to kill all the faith our people have in me.

The faith my brutes have in me, too.

I glance at the woods, at all the shadows that infect the trees—at the endless, endless loneliness of them. My palms turn clammy.

"It wasn't like that," I insist, and my pulse pounds in my throat. "We had a deal. Alastair promised they'd take it all down from the inside. That he'd free the women and children. I couldn't leave them to Sam. It was their only chance."

My eyes catch on Beau as he bandages a man's bleeding arm, and he sends me a reassuring smile that doesn't quite reach his somber eyes.

It doesn't reassure me at all.

"He *swore* he'd free them," I finish shakily.

A reedy man from Red Zone scoffs. "And you believed him?"

"Fucking idiot," a woman mutters, and I flinch.

My stomach is sulfurous. Their anger, miasmic. It clogs the air, and all the panic and fear I'd held at bay tonight threatens to thunder through my composure.

Where is Dom? He took the lead with Red Zone before. I stood my ground with Alastair, but it's starting to shake under my feet, and I can't see him anywhere.

I *need* to make them understand. Communication, Jasper told me, and I've been working on it. If I can only talk to them calmly, I can fix this. Somehow, I can *fix this*.

"This is her fault!" someone shouts.

"What are we going to do about Bentley?"

"We have to get them back!"

The frightened, angry voices bleed together, and the jostling gets worse.

Lucky steps in close beside me, his eyes on the mob and every muscle hard, and Jasper's cool hand slips up the back of my neck in a possessive gesture that makes me shiver.

They're . . . not letting me go.

I bite the inside of my lip at the immediate sting in my eyes. That's what this means, right? They won't make me be alone again? *They won't, they won't, they won't.*

Soaking in their strength, I turn toward Arthur, Bentley's warm-faced second-in-command.

The scarred, scored-out city sign towers behind him in a belated warning.

CYANIDE IS SUICIDE
STAY OUT!

Arthur's broad features are set and serious now, his armor damaged and dusty.

It doesn't look like a costume today.

My hands tremble as I lift them, and I force them to steady. "We survived. We're alive, and they're not coming after our homes anymore. I understand you're angry at me—God knows I deserve it—but Sam is dead and . . . and at least Alastair can be reasoned with."

Oh, God.

Can he be reasoned with? I have never felt so outplayed. So incredibly outmatched.

In veiled promises tonight, he told me he'd keep the women and children safe—when we were at his mercy and there was no reason at *all* for him to do so. That's *something*. And Alastair could have killed us, but instead he let us go, and . . . and . . .

I try to slow my rapid, panicked breathing.

Sure, he let us go, but with nothing except a single ephemeral promise of taking more in the future. More we don't *have*. He didn't just defeat us, he humiliated us and crushed us beneath his boot.

He took *everything* from us.

From *me*.

Alastair wants an empire.

And I think I just gave him one.

Arthur glances around at the mob with a grave shake of his head.

"We didn't secure any food, any medicine. Our people are injured . . . and we lost Bentley. We have children, teenagers, to protect. His nephew . . . You don't understand how much Bentley does for us. We *need* him."

Soren. My heart slices open a little more when I think of his haunted eyes and the worship in them when he talked about his uncle.

Alastair's promises for safety apply to Heather and Bentley too, surely. If they're collateral, he won't hurt them. He can't. Right? Even after Heather tortured him?

Oh, God. *Heather.* Whatever her reasons, she put herself at risk instead of me again.

And I let her.

I swallow my nauseous guilt, steeling myself as I cast around for a solution. *Any* solution. "You could all come back with us to Bristle-brook. We could . . . you could consolidate there."

"And sleep where?" Ava breaks in. When I look at her, her eyes are dark with distress. "And eat what food? We didn't secure any of the resources *we* needed either, Eden. Or did you forget our people are starving back home?"

Sloane curses. "Should we go back in? How the fuck are we supposed to go back like this?"

"Getting our asses kicked once wasn't enough for you?" Beau mutters as he secures the man's bandage. "We go back to the Den, we die."

"If we go back home with no food, we die, asshole," Ava shouts, her voice breaking.

I open my mouth. Thankfully, nothing comes out. I feel like I could throw up. Jasper squeezes the back of my neck, and I press back into the touch like it might hold me up.

We're all in ruins, and I can't see a way out.

"I'm sorry," I whisper to Arthur, and the words feel dredged up from my soul. "I'm so sorry."

"We can't feed ourselves with sorry."

I nod, taking the hit, and Arthur meets my eyes. "You need to make this right. We expected a fight, not an ambush. I need to get things settled back home, but . . . expect us. We need a plan, and you owe it to us to help."

"Maybe . . . we can come back with—"

Arthur shakes his head. "Your people aren't welcome inside our walls again."

The acid crawls through my veins, and I bow my head in acceptance.

The same man who spat at me shoves the visor up on his helmet. "That's it? She's a traitor. She should get the same as Aaron."

Lucky's head snaps in his direction. "*Try it.*"

The promise is a lethal growl, and my heart trips over itself. I've caught glimpses of Lucky's dark side, but right now, it's unsheathed. His hand moves to his holster, but the Sinners took his pistol. It doesn't matter.

When he's like this, Lucky *is* the weapon.

Beau stands up, casually tucking the roll of bandages away in his medical bag. Moonlight glints off his scalpel when he pulls his hand back out, and new fear prickles down my spine as the chorus of angry shouts takes on a fevered pitch.

The Red Zone man's lips twist. "She shouldn't get special treatment just because you like the way she—"

Lucky grabs him, dragging him close.

The man's sudden, sour fear clogs the air.

"That's enough," Jasper cuts in.

He releases my neck, and chilly goosebumps flicker over my skin at the loss. He walks over to lay a steadying hand on Lucky's back, but Lucky ignores him, still glaring into the man's helmet. The thin man's shaky breaths rattle around in the metal.

"*Enough*," Jasper repeats, pitched lower this time.

It takes a long moment, but Lucky's grip loosens, and the man stumbles back into the crowd with a panicked rasp.

Jasper eyes the dirty, agitated faces around us with cool disdain. "You all should pause to exercise some logic. The only thing you should be saying to Eden right now is *thank you*."

Arthur frowns, and his troubled voice lifts over the mob. "How do you figure that?"

Jasper turns to him, raising one brow. "Eden freed Alastair, yes, but if she hadn't, we still would have attacked the Den. Aaron still would have betrayed us. Our plan still would have been compromised. Only it wouldn't have been Alastair who discovered us, it would have been Sam . . . and we would all be dead right now."

Only the waiting trees creak in the night wind, and there's a sudden hesitation in the crowd. For the first time since the Sinners left us outside their city, everything is still. Struck silent by Jasper and his biting rationality.

He continues, each point a silken anvil hammering against my ribs. "*Eden* didn't decide to attack the Den. *Eden* didn't bring Aaron in on strategy discussions. The only thing Eden changed about how tonight was executed is *who* was executed—and you'll note, it wasn't us."

The wind picks up as Jasper's words catch somewhere deep in my chest. He doesn't think this was my fault.

I stare at the lean, bladed planes of his jaw, utterly confused.

It *is* my fault. I've made such terrible mistakes. I've lied and hid and disobeyed orders. I betrayed them all so horribly the guilt could crush me.

Still, my mind works its way around his words, looking for dents and weak spots. It's too reductive. Too simplistic. It ignores too many facts. And yet . . .

Is there truth in it anyway?

On the edge of the crowd, Sloane nods to herself, and her gaze lifts to mine. Her regard doesn't have any of the warmth it had yesterday . . . but it doesn't hold contempt, either.

Some of the mob's edgy tension bleeds into discomfort, but Jasper's anger isn't as easily contained. He stares coldly down the hushed people all around us. "Thank her for your lives. Her judgment you're so quick to condemn is all that saved you."

I release a long breath, staring at the sharp, clever man as he defends me. He's showing nothing of his usual elegance. He's mussed and filthy, and pale cement dust has settled into the furious lines of his face . . . and he's never looked more beautiful.

Jasper believes me. He *trusts* me. I don't know how he cut through tonight's mess so cleanly, but his brilliant mind somehow found the best of me, deserved or not.

It's something *family* might do.

I duck my head so I can swallow down my tears . . . because it's my family I've hurt.

Alastair is cold and ruthlessly devious. Maybe Jasper's right that Sam would have killed us. Maybe Alastair *is* better than a rapist and a thug, because I truly don't believe that he's either.

But that doesn't make him *good*.

I freed a monster to destroy another monster, and it's only now, after he's swallowed Sam whole, that I truly consider what that means.

Alastair just absorbed Sam's people. His weapons. His power.

His *strength*.

The more dangerous monster won tonight.

And now it's my family who will be left to deal with him.

Heated fingers twine between mine, and I look up at Lucky. He squeezes my hand hard, and I grip back just as fiercely, my throat closing over.

I love him. I love them both.

God, how are we going to survive without the Sinners' resources?

Tonight was supposed to solve all our problems. Somehow, it's only created more.

"That might be true," Arthur concedes, "but it doesn't change anything. Aaron was one of yours, and we're still without a leader or any of the medicine we came for. We still have Sinners on our doorstep, threatening every single person inside."

He wipes the sweat from the back of his neck. Despite his words, the fight seems to have left him. It seems to have left all of them.

Weary worry slumps their armored shoulders, and their angered attention is no longer on me. There's so much fear and confusion in the way they turn to one another for comfort that my horror grows for a different reason.

These people aren't aggressors. They aren't evil.

They're terrified.

My eyes find Beau, and he gives me another one of those quick, reassuring smiles that still doesn't warm his eyes.

Arthur picks up his pack, moving like he's wounded deeper than flesh. God, they have teenagers to protect—*dozens* of them.

"We need to get back to Red Zone. They need us there. But we'll . . . we'll talk." He looks around at his people, waving for them to move, and adds softly into the stale air, "We're going to need all the help we can get."

"We'll figure something out. For *all* of us," Jasper insists in a low voice.

My stomach roils.

The people of Red Zone begin to bleed away until ours are the only ones left standing on the cracked road out of the city.

Finally, I see Dom.

He stands just outside the group, on the brink of the shadowy trees, and he's far enough back that he seems . . . other. His skin is waxen and pale under the moon's sallow light.

I follow his gaze and realize he's staring at Jasper, seeming lost in dark, awful thoughts.

I replay Jasper's words in my head.

Eden *didn't decide to attack the Den.*

Eden *didn't bring Aaron in on strategy discussions.*

That acid eats right through my stomach this time, and I can taste my own guilt. Again and again, I see Dom's shoulders collapsing in defeat as he knelt beside me.

"Dom," I breathe, choked. "Please. He didn't mean . . ."

His eyes flick over to me. Their usual gold is dulled, rusted and oxidized. He shakes his head, then turns back into the forest.

And the darkness swallows him whole.

Chapter 2

Lucky

I force my fingers to uncurl from my rifle.

The last person from Red Zone disappears behind a crumbling building. They're heading back to their base, but it's taking too much effort not to start spraying bullets. They threatened *Eden*. *My* Eden. I only just got her back from the Sinners and in one night she was at their mercy *again*.

All at once, I see the walls of the med bay closing in while I wait and wait for her to come home. I feel the gun at the back of my head while I watch Alastair threaten and manipulate her. I smell the sweaty mob of angry Red Zoners as they shove toward her.

I'm so sick of being so fucking *helpless*.

My arm is wrenched behind me. My pinned arm screams in painful protest as I struggle, the joint straining at a brutal angle. Jasper's hand wraps around my chin and forces my head back against his shoulder.

"Be still, Lucien. You and Jaykob can thrash about like apes when we return home if you wish to wrestle. With me, you will behave." His lips brush the shell of my ear as he talks, and he inches the arm behind my back higher.

I grunt in pain, breathing hard, but I stop moving. After a

moment, I lean into the strain until my back arches from the sharp-sweet hurt, and goosebumps ripple over my skin.

The miserable, angry panic doesn't subside, though.

My eyes search out Eden, the way they have ever since I realized she was at the center of tonight's firestorm. Again and again. She's always in the middle of it.

Her long hair is windswept, strands flying free of her braid, and she's white as bone, but there's no other mark on her. She's not filthy like me or Jasper. She's not covered in blood or bruises. There's no sign at all of how close she came to dying tonight.

We *all* could have died tonight.

I almost had to watch it happen, too. Fuck, the bomb. I nearly killed Jasper myself. Stupid, stupid, *stupid*. *I* was stupid. Careless. What is wrong with me? This isn't a game. What if I'd lost them tonight? It was a mistake to come out here. I don't know what I'd do if—

"Ah!" I cry out as Jasper wrenches my arm higher, and I lift onto my toes to ease the pressure.

"Rein it in, sweet boy," he tells me gently, so at odds with his vicious hold.

Eden doesn't even look at me. Her guilty eyes are glued on Dom as he sweeps into the forest.

Look at me. Look at me, look at me, look at me. I need those eyes on mine. I need her to never be out of my sight again.

I need to be more careful.

"I *can't*," I choke out. "Please. Let me go to her. I need to . . . I have to *do* something."

My brain is clouding over. I can't move. I'm useless again. Impotent. Weak.

"Houst—"

Jasper releases me before I can even finish my safeword, turning me so he can look at me. His grip is fierce against the side of my face.

"Lucien, this wasn't your fault."

"I don't care about fault. I just need everyone to stop being in danger for like two fucking minutes." My chest feels too tight to pull in air properly.

The rest of our group is heading for the trees, and Eden trails behind them like a hesitant duckling. It only takes seconds to come up behind her, and she glances at me distractedly when I take her arm and drag her into the trees.

Ava slows for a minute, checking on her, but I don't have it in me to reassure her right now.

Eden tugs back against my grip. "Wait, Lucky. I need to talk to Dom. He's devastated. Do you think I should—"

I yank Eden into my chest and kiss her hard. Her soft lips give under mine. She's pliant. Warm. She makes a surprised sound, and I drive her back into a tree, sinking deeper into the heat of her mouth. Tasting her. *Needing* her.

Ava can stay or go or film the whole thing if she wants to, but I'm not stopping.

I rip at the buttons on Eden's pants. Her zipper. It's when I start wrenching the fabric over her hips that she turns her head away from my kiss with a gasp. I move my mouth to her neck and shove her clothes down past her ass. I suck on her pulse, hard enough to bruise.

She's here. She's here, she's here, she's here.

"*Lucky*?" She grabs the front of my kit, but trails off on a snaking moan.

I bury my fingers into her pussy, rubbing her slippery clit with my thumb. She's too worked up, the same as me. Her cunt is as hot as her mouth, and she grinds her hips down over my hand.

My cock *throbs*.

I kneel down and yank her boots off, vaguely aware of Jasper moving up to guard the trail behind us. A flashlight bursts to life, and our tangled nook between the trees brightens.

Eden pants above me. Her eyes are dark and dazed with lust behind her glasses, her lips bruised red and still wet from my kisses.

Her eyes are finally on *me*.

"I get you're worried." I rip her pants the rest of the way off, and she needs to clutch the tree to stay upright. "I get that there are five of us." I jerk her pale legs apart and lean in to bite her inner thigh. Eden flinches, but her breathing snags on a gaspy moan. "I get that Jayk is jealous, and Jasper is confusing, and Beau is dramatic, and Dom is hurting." God, I can smell her. I can see how wet she's getting. My fingers are bruising her hips, and easing my grip takes so much effort. "I get that the low-drama guy can usually wait."

I meet her eye, and I let all the fear and worry and that fucking helplessness show.

"But this isn't a Dom moment, Eden. I need you, too. Please don't make me wait."

Tears gather in her eyes, and she shakes her head. "Oh, Lucky, no." Her hand finds my hair, and she strokes it back off my forehead with heartbreaking tenderness. "You get any moment you need."

Tears prick my eyes too, and I tear open the front of my pants to free my cock.

I surge to my feet, lifting one of her legs as I go, and I fuck into her. She's a wet vice. Hot and plush and it doesn't matter that the angle is awkward. It doesn't matter that I'm loaded up with gear and that bark is scraping her ass. She's squeezing my dick with perfect little shivers, and her arms are all around me. She's *with* me. Wrecked with adrenaline and fear and soaking my cock like a good fucking girl.

"What were you thinking?" I whisper in her ear as I fuck her desperately. "You offered yourself up to them? You don't do that, beautiful. You don't ever. Fucking. Do. That."

I kiss her neck, her cheek. Anything I can reach. She grinds back over my dick, gasping and panting in my ear, meeting my thrusts with the same fervor.

But her hands are gentle on my neck. Soothing.

"You're no one's sacrifice, okay?" I tell her urgently.

My whole body is lit up, fighting pleasure and fear, my cock slick in her snug pussy. Eden doesn't say anything, so I take her harder—until it hurts. Pine and sex spiral through the air around us. Ancient scents. Like witchcraft. Like vows.

She cries out. "Yes. Yes, yes, okay. I— Lucky, I'm sorry."

I'm shaking like a leaf. I'm going to come.

Eden's hands find my hair, and she drags my head back from where it's buried against her throat until we're looking at each other. Her cheeks are dark red now, and her pussy is gripping me hard. I rest my forehead against hers.

Her glasses fog up.

"Just let me fucking keep you safe. Stop doing things on your own. I'm here now. I'm with you. Do you get that?" I kiss her again and taste brine. She's crying. Or maybe I am. "I'm here. Just let me help."

"I will. I swear, Lucky. No more secrets. I'm here."

Eden cries out again as I squeeze into her. She comes hard around me, in scorching, fluttering pulses I want to drown in. I yank her hips into place so I can ride it out with her, so I can bury myself deep and explode to the feel of her breaking over me. I come hard, groaning, soaking her in me, breathing her in as I claim every gasp and moan and shivery sob as she comes down.

Finally, her toes touch the ground, and my shaking has eased to a tremble.

I glance at Jasper, who looks back at just the same moment. A dark, feral hunger prowls his eyes. He turns back to study the darkness, but his grip on his rifle is white-knuckled.

Eden's fingertips brush my lips, and I look back at her.

"Are you okay?" she asks, still trembling and breathless. "Did that . . . help?"

We're both half-dressed and freshly fucked, and our whole group is probably ready to pluck out our eyeballs with rusty pliers for making them wait after the night we've had.

This might not be my classiest moment.

"There's not much a quickie can't fix, right?" I tease, trying to summon a wink.

Eden's fingers move from my lips, and she tugs my beard.

"Ow!" I swat her hand.

"Be serious, Lucky," she scolds, her eyes soft.

I let the smile die. It's easier than it usually is, to let it fall. Eden sees through it anyway, and I don't want to pretend with her.

"It helped. I'm just . . . I'm really glad you're okay," I tell her.

Eden grimaces, and I pull her in for another hug. I still feel the need to chain us together for the next twenty years or so—but even minus the shackles, it feels good to have her close. Maybe if we stay this way, I can make sure she doesn't fall into a den of vipers, and she can make sure I don't do anything stupid.

I don't know where any of us go from here. How the hell we're going to get Heather back, or fix the Sinners problem, or how we're going to make it even another month without food—but even if I need to drag her off to a cave and feed her fresh kills by hand, I'm keeping this girl safe.

Ugh. These primal instincts are gross.

I wonder if this is how Jayk feels all the time.

Eden rests her head against my chest, and I bury my hand in her hair.

I just need to keep her close.

CHAPTER 3

BEAU

S *lap.*
The mosquito zips from under my hand, and I glare as it buzzes off to join its asshole friends. That speedy bastard got me yesterday, I'm sure of it. Now word of the delicious Beaumont snack-sicle has spread and there are hordes of the little suckers soaring in from every swampy ass crack of the forest to get their slurp.

Our trip so far has been hot and wet, I'm so covered in bites I'm about ready to peel my skin off, and now dusk has them flocking for another feast. I have had *enough*. This blood bank is closed. Happy hour is *over*. That legion of tiny flying vampires is going to have to get their Bloody Beaumont somewhere else.

Slap.

Another mosquito flits off, unsquashed.

Son of a bitch.

Apparently unconcerned by the airborne infestation, our exhausted group is gathered around the fire. Once again, everyone's focused on their own meal, quietly tearing into their remaining rations. No one mentions what happened back at the Den. No one mentions our breakneck pace, or Heather, or Alastair's threats of *more,* or Red Zone's expectations. Not one of them mentions how, each night, our portions get smaller and smaller as we try to conserve rations.

We all know it's about to get a whole lot worse.

Standing back and watching the group, I try not to stare at their food like the little match girl through the window. I hit the end of my rations at lunch, and my stomach has been kicking up a loud protest all day. I don't want to think about how long it might be before my next meal.

As if to top all that off, it's been rudely hot for fall, the civilians are spent and defeated, Jasper's been clucking around like a fretting hen, Lucky's snappish and downright rude, and Eden . . . Well, *Eden* seems to be holding strong for everyone. *Eden* seems just *fine.*

Not sure that she'd think to tell me if she wasn't.

So, it's not even my fault I got through my rations so fast. I'm a stress eater, and this last week? This week has tested my patience to the end of days.

And then there's Dom.

He's nowhere to be found. Again. No, sir, once again, *I'm* left reading maps and deciding where to camp and who's on watch. Because Dom has gone running off by himself. To "fish." *Again.*

He hasn't said two words about what went down, or how we lost a whole pile of weapons and all the meds I brought with me. Hell, he hasn't even tried to talk to me about a plan. But sure, he's *fishing.* Used to be I'd drag him off to spar and we'd bounce ideas while he beat my ass into the dirt . . . but it's been a long time since we did anything like that.

Maybe that's the problem.

I'm not sure who Dom has to talk to these days.

My stomach cramps, and I scowl down at it. I'm *hungry,* that's all it is. Dom will be okay. Of course he will. He'll figure it out.

By the fire, Jasper polishes off the last of his meal, and my vision hazes dizzily. This is getting serious. I am *faint.* From the woodsmoke, maybe, or maybe from the hunger.

Slap.

Another mosquito corpse drops into the leaves under my feet.

Or *maybe* I'm dizzy because of the massive *blood loss* from these good-for-nothing, blood-sucking *swamp demons*. I'm not having it. I'll be damned if these tiny bastards eat better than me.

I scowl down at the splattered body. Damn it, nothing is going right, not for days. We should get back to Bristlebrook tomorrow night—and as far as I'm concerned, we can't get there any sooner. Food and rest will sort everyone out, my mama was right about that.

"Here." Eden pops up by my elbow, appearing out of the smoke like a mirage.

I flinch. "Holy flaming hell."

My senses aren't what they should be. My body is *eating* itself.

Eden lifts the bundle in her hands higher, her eyes big and serious behind her glasses. She's closer than she's been since the Den, and she looks . . . good. *She's* not sweaty and lumpy with mosquito bites.

She's prettier than she has any right to be.

She's pretty enough to hurt.

I edge backward.

"Ah, sorry, darlin', I was just in the middle of . . ." I glance around, realizing I'm not in the middle of anything, actually.

Around the fire, the group is starting to break up and move toward their packs, getting ready to make camp for the night. Jasper stretches out like he's settling in, though, and Lucky hovers a few feet away, leaning against a tree and not even bothering to hide the edgy way he's watching Eden. We've been traveling for days, and he hasn't so much as let her pee without inspecting the bushes first. Poor guy is having a rough time.

So, it's not that I've been *avoiding* Eden. Lucky's just needed her more.

In fact, I bet he needs her right now.

When I catch his eye, I glance back at Eden significantly. Lucky frowns at me behind her back, then points to her. I shake my head minutely, and he glares and points harder.

Eden glances over her shoulder, and Lucky brings his hand up to rub the back of his head. He looks up, inspecting the tree canopy, nodding to himself casually.

"I'm sure you and Lucky need to talk some more," I say, edging backward.

She looks back at me and purses her lips. "Lucky and I have talked plenty."

Her braided hair is draped over her shoulder, and sprigs of lavender are worked into the plaits. That braid would be perfect for tugging. She has gorgeous hair. I could wrap it around my wrist and scrape my nails along her scalp just the way she likes it. She'd make that sound again, like she's breaking apart.

But like it has every night since we left Cyanide, the urge is chased by something else. Something sore and sorry and tinged with—

No. *No*. Eden is kind-hearted to a fault. She's been through so much. You'd have to be a real asshole to have a problem with a girl like that after all she's had to face. She's fine. *We're* fine.

I back up some more.

We're absolutely perfect.

Eden peels back the corner of the package, a determined light in her eyes. Jerky and dried apple peek from the cloth. "Come sit by the fire and have something to eat with me."

I stop in my tracks.

The jerky is sweating in the heat, the apple shriveled and curled at the edges, but my stomach goes into revolt, ripping out a roar so loud it ripples the trees. It's a *banquet*.

It's a trap.

I lick my lips—just to check I'm not drooling over my chin. "I'm not taking your food, pet."

"I could last another week on what I have left. You need to eat," she insists.

It takes my starved, sluggish brain a minute to catch up. She has more than *this*?

I frown. "How could you have a whole week of rations left? We'll be back at Bristlebrook tomorrow. You should be almost out."

Eden raises a brow over her glasses. "I'm used to living on much less than this. Don't worry about me."

My stomach swoops . . . and lands hard. She's deliberately eating less than she needs. She's still worried about where her next meal is coming from.

And between Alastair clearing us out, us not securing any food, and the fact that we have dozens of hungry mouths back home . . . she should be.

A pointed smile quirks her lips before I can comment. "Rationing is also much easier when you don't try to eat all your feelings. Some of us prefer to talk those through instead."

My back hits a tree, and I splutter. "I do *not* have feelings!"

"Of course not. So, there's no reason you shouldn't come and eat with me." Eden's smile firms, and she steps in whisper-close. "And *talk*."

She smells like lavender and lies.

"Why are you pushing this? There's no problem here," I insist, forcing a smile.

But Eden doesn't relax. Her eyes search my face, growing graver as she takes in my smile.

I grit my teeth behind my smile. "I'm. Not. Mad."

"You're mad," she repeats slowly, watching me. She lowers the food. Her throat works delicately as she swallows, and the hurt in her rips at my heart. I'm familiar with every expression turning through those eyes. I woke up to them for weeks. Watched them as she told me everything—all her secret thoughts and feelings.

Well. Almost all of them.

"I said I'm *not* mad." I run a hand over my head, looking back over to Lucky for help, but he's still examining the trees like he's shooting for a career in dendrology.

"It's okay, you know. If you are. You have every right."

I look back down at Eden, and her soft, serious expression. It breaks my heart. I know I should hug her—just wrap her in my arms and make it all better. My mama always said that a man who makes women cry is no man at all. I'll be damned if I'm ever the one to upset Eden.

I reach out for that hug, but for some reason, I find myself patting her shoulder awkwardly instead.

She looks at my hand with a dubious expression, then back at me. "Beau . . ."

The air is starting to sour, and I can only guess it's the smoke. And the heat. It's an uncomfortable day.

A mosquito starts buzzing around my head, and I grit my teeth.

Then I force a smile for Eden. "No, darlin'. I have no reason to be mad at you. You were going through a lot. Who am I to judge your choices, right? I wasn't even there. I mean, I was next to you, afterwards. For weeks. Living with you. You could have trusted me. But everyone's allowed privacy, and I can respect that."

Eden sighs. "Beau, that's not—"

Sweat starts gathering under my arms. Why is it so damn *hot* today? "You've beaten yourself up enough. We have plenty of other problems to focus on. Doesn't seem right to keep living in the past. What's the point in all that?"

"Because you clearly have some valid—"

That mosquito just won't *quit* it. "Look, it probably wouldn't have made a difference if we knew about your alliance. I mean, we could have strategized around it, sure. Changed our plan. And we probably would have used Alastair effectively, if we'd known. Maybe stopped him from taking every advantage we have, claiming our home as his, and making it so that everyone from here to Alabama is going to live with Sinners' boots on their neck. Maybe we wouldn't have to worry about slowly getting bled dry by *tithes* we can't pay to people who don't even deserve the dirt off my shoe. But there's no use speculating now. It's done with. We're alive."

Eden turns dead white.

Finally, stiffly, she whispers, "That isn't all on me."

Slap.

Another mosquito corpse hits the ground as I get the asshole, but two more take its place. They won't leave me alone, just biting and buzzing and pestering. They're getting under my damn skin, and I can't escape them.

God, her face.

I *am* an asshole. This is exactly why I shouldn't be talking to her right now.

There's too much panic closing in around my chest. No, her not talking to me isn't the reason for all of this. Or not the only reason, anyway. A whole set of dominos crashed into each other to get us here, starting all the way back when we decided to let Sam go free.

It's just that this situation is too big—and with Dom MIA, I don't know how we're going to fix it. I don't know if we *can*.

How do we stop an empire from forming?

How do we stop ourselves from being at the bottom of it?

I rub the back of my neck, swallowing hard. "You're right. You're right, it's not."

She doesn't say anything as she watches me swat two more of the flying bastards.

Finally, I edge out around her. "We're just fine, Eden. I promise. Don't you worry about a thing. Eat something, okay?"

"Beau."

There's a scold in her voice I don't particularly feel like hearing. Not while I'm hungry and being eaten alive by every mosquito in the forest. *That's* why I'm cranky. *If* that's what I'm feeling.

I need to leave before I say something I regret.

I turn right into Dom's chest. "Ah."

His eyes are summer storms, amber lightning behind rain clouds. But he's not looking at me. "You're not eating your rations?"

Eden flushes a dark pink, and her determination staggers under his gaze. "I—I haven't been hungry."

My mouth closes, and guilt swirls in the sick hollows of my stomach. Does she really have a whole *week* of food left? How many meals is that? I could eat a horse, and I've licked up every crumb I had.

I eye Dom. His empty hands. I try not to let the disappointment show. "You, ah, didn't catch anything?"

The corners of his mouth flatten, and it is no wonder at *all* that he didn't catch anything. I'd swim in the opposite direction too at that sorry face.

"Eat your food, Eden," he orders quietly.

He pushes past us, right as she whispers, "Yes, sir."

The words fall off her lips like a promise.

Dom pauses as if struck, and from beside the fire, I see Jasper's head lift to glance between them. But I can only stare at her. At all the shattered hues in her eyes, and the apologies tucked between them.

She's bleeding for him.

Dom's head cants, like he wants to turn back . . . but he doesn't. "I'm taking first watch."

I clear my throat, looking between them. "Katherine had first watch, Dom. Dom—"

He doesn't stop, and I blow out a frustrated sigh, trying to mentally rearrange the schedule as Eden's eyes press painfully closed.

It all makes my stomach hurt. Whatever my problems with Dom and this mess over Eden, I still love him. We've been friends for too many years for a few bitter months to ruin it. And in all the long, long years of being by his side, I've never seen him hurt like he's hurting now.

Eden's throat cords delicately, and she takes a long breath before her chin lifts again. I've seen her do it a dozen times this week already. I wonder if she's let herself fall apart yet. I wonder if she needs to.

I can't help myself.

"You haven't talked to him? Not since . . ." I let the words die.

Not since he realized she went behind his back, ignored his orders, undermined his authority, lied about it to *everyone*, befriended and romanced him, and then paved the way for his humiliating defeat at Alastair's hands.

Not since she betrayed him.

Eden looks away. "I don't think Dom wants to talk to me right now."

At her quiet words, my stomach hollows out further. I'm empty of everything that usually fills me.

"I'll fix him," I promise. I'll figure out what to say to him. How to say it. But something has to give. This is bigger than any fight.

Eden wraps her arms around herself. "Be gentle with him, Beau. Please. He needs you."

"He needs you, too," I find myself saying, and she stares at me.

I don't blame her. I made it damn clear I didn't want Dom ruining their relationship. I was so sure he'd break her sweet heart.

Instead, she broke his.

I meet her eyes, and it comes easier when I add, "Don't abandon him now, darlin'. You need to make it right. We both do."

With a last look, I start walking toward the others. I need to fix tonight's schedule and leave a message for the cameras so Jayk knows we'll arrive tomorrow. We need to think about how we can help Red Zone and all the kids there who are now so much worse off because of us. We need to think about how we're going to pay whatever price Alastair is going to ask from us when we're just about as bad off as we can be. All the things Dom usually handles and hasn't even asked about.

It's wrong. Bad in a kind of way I don't know what to do about. No matter how things go to hell, no matter how many cities burn or who we lose, Dom always has a plan.

I don't know what our world looks like where he doesn't.

As I pass Lucky, he crosses his arms over his chest and gives me the same shitty, unimpressed look he's been giving me since we left Cyanide. I know he eavesdropped on every last word. Jasper may be looking back at the fire like it contains the world's secrets, but he's no better. They're as nosy as each other.

Lucky's sour expression makes me slow. "*What*?"

The night's too hot for a fire. This close to it, sweat starts trickling down my spine. The mosquitos are hovering around the flames, gathering in swarms.

Lucky's eyes track over me with something real close to disgust.

"You better pull your head out of your ass sometime soon or you're going to lose her." He kicks off the tree, and mutters, "You're acting like a shit."

Slap.

I watch him walk off, watch him tug her into the hug I couldn't give her, and I scowl as I turn toward our group.

This will be fine. It will all be fine. I'm sure I'll get over it.

Eventually.

CHAPTER 4

EDEN

Maybe we wouldn't have to worry about slowly getting bled dry by tithes we can't pay to people who don't even deserve the dirt off my shoe.

I sink into Lucky, stinging over Beau's words and how acutely they echo my own fears. Accepting my weight, Lucky presses me into his chest, and I settle into the nook of his neck. Just for a moment. He's damp with a light sheen of sweat, but he smells perfect. Like the wood fire and pine and *home*.

"Forget him. He's not even a proper cowboy, you know. Doesn't know how to ride off into the sunset or anything," he whispers into my hair.

I huff a laugh, though my chest aches heavily as I try to pack away the worries we can't do anything about. Not right now. "Oh? How about you? Will you take me there?"

He considers that. "Well, maybe not on a horse. But I bet I could work out some sort of slingshot situation."

That startles an actual snort out of me, which makes him wink, dimples teasing both his cheeks. The ever-present worry that's been shadowing his eyes since we left Cyanide vanishes in a happy *poof*. I give him a light shove, but my hand lingers on his chest.

"Much as it pains me to interrupt your rousing seduction, Lucien, I've found one of Eden's misplaced meals."

Jasper's wry tone is like a pebble sinking through a quiet pond. There's gentle affection in his dark eyes as he watches us—and a touch of quiet longing that he isn't even trying to hide anymore. But concern paints somber lines beside his mouth, and my 'misplaced meal' is in his hands, my pack open at his feet.

With a sigh, I resign myself to wasting more resources. I didn't lie. I truly haven't been missing the extra food; I know what I can survive well enough on, and it's much less than their generous rations. Watching Beau, watching all of them this week, it's become painfully obvious that they don't understand it—we are burning through our stores far, far too quickly.

I'm cursing myself for being surprised. Why should they understand? They've had more than they need for so long. It makes me itch with the need to hunt and trap and grow. I've been in such a fog for weeks, sinking into their assurances and authority like they had all the answers to every question.

But they don't.

I've been lax, and this isn't how I survive.

This isn't how *any of us* survive.

Still, I'm woefully outnumbered. Lucky and Jasper have both been on my case about eating more, and now even Dom has pulled himself from his viscous silence to demand the same.

And I can't ignore any more orders from Dom, I just can't. Not now. Not yet.

I settle on the ground in front of the fire, and it's not until I notice how motionless Jasper has fallen that I realize I sat by his feet. Orange light glows over the empty seat on the log beside him.

He recovers smoothly, handing me the tiny ration pack, but color slashes his high cheekbones.

Lucky drops obnoxiously between his legs a moment later, forcing Jasper to widen them. I'm confronted with his warm, firm thigh, very much in my space. Lucky's eyes laugh at me over the bridge, and Jasper buries his hand in the back of his blond hair.

I pull out a strip of jerky and tentatively lean into Jasper's leg, watching as he tugs Lucky's head back. "Rediscover your manners, beautiful boy."

The shiver that wracks his body is delicate, entrancing. They move so seamlessly together: they could have done this a hundred times or more. The jerky is tacky and bland, but they have a flavor I need to taste.

"Sorry," Lucky says, not sounding sorry in the slightest. His smile becomes roguish. "Mind if I spend some time between your thighs, oh lord and master?"

"So mouthy." Jasper's gaze slides to mine, assessing. "We've been telling you to eat all week."

He doesn't sound reproachful, only curious, but my cheeks still sting.

I examine the jerky. "You made some . . . suggestions. I took them under advisement."

"*Suggestions*?" Lucky crosses his arms over Jasper's thigh, leaning over with an incredulous laugh. "Beautiful, I will force-feed you like a baby woodpecker if I have to."

Jasper regards me as he toys absently with Lucky's hair, and I avoid his gaze.

"You need us to order you to do it, is that it? Want me to drop my voice a few decibels? Eat gravel for breakfast and turn my arms into tree trunks?" The quirk of Lucky's lips becomes sly, and he leans confidingly over Jasper's knee. "Would it help if you called me *sir*, too?"

"You—" I gasp.

That was an *accident*!

The sting in my cheeks becomes a burn, and I stick my middle finger up at Lucky. Right up at him. I've only flipped off two things in my entire life. My "last notice" gas bill and now my officially-least-favorite boyfriend.

Jayk would be proud.

Long fingers twist shiveringly through my hair an instant before my head is wrenched back. On his other side, Lucky receives the same treatment. The pull of the strands at my roots is sharp and hot, but I'm too trained now for it to feel anything but good. My neck strains in a perfect arch, the grip and angle somehow neater than the way Jayk or Beau arrange me. Like Jasper is taking his show horse out for dressage and not a dusty, reckless ride.

"Play nice, children," he scolds, sounding amused. "You're being rude. Apologize."

Jasper has us in each hand like unruly puppies, and my eyes meet Lucky's.

"I'm sorry, Lucky," I offer, obedient.

I'm rewarded with the slight scrape of Jasper's nails against my scalp, and my shiver is everywhere.

Lucky laughs softly. He tries to twist away, but Jasper's grip grows crueler, pinning him against his thigh. He shoves him down, until Lucky's face is just inches from mine and entirely at Jasper's mercy. We're so close, all tangled up, and I can see the heat rising in Lucky's cheeks as he fights and loses. The fog glazing his eyes as the humor slips away.

"Sorry," he works out huskily. "Sorry, sorry, sorry."

Jasper makes a soft, approving sound, deep in his chest. "Good boy." His eyes are dark burning coals as he adds casually, "Now, kiss and make up."

I suck in a jagged breath, startled. We're still in camp. Yes, everyone's gone to bed, but it's not *private*.

Jasper doesn't seem to care.

My hair screams as he drags Lucky and I toward one another. We're not show horses, or puppies. We're his toys, his dolls, and he's going to make us do whatever he wants. Whatever *pleases* him.

When I realize that, I melt into his touch. I want to please him. I want him to drag me and take me and use me.

I'll be Jasper's doll.

A hot, liquid ache throbs through my abdomen. It squeezes my core. Lucky's face is pressed closer to mine until our noses brush and my whole vision is overtaken by his heated, glowing blue eyes. Jasper adjusts his grip, angling my head to tilt me under Lucky, right as he pushes Lucky down.

I *am* liquid now. Slippery and wet.

Lucky's lips slide over mine, parting in a fan of hot breath. Jasper's grip leaves no room to move, to maneuver, so he sinks in like this. His tongue teases my lips apart, and then Jasper makes a lost, helpless sound and pushes him deeper, holding us so that we can do nothing but explore one another. Nothing but breathe each other's breaths and swallow each other's involuntary sighs and moans. Lucky licks along the inner rim of my mouth, his beard brushing my skin, and I suck on his tongue until I feel him shake.

And all the while Jasper's cruel, cruel grip locks us messily together.

He doesn't lift us for a long time—not until I'm a trembling, hungry mess—and my lips come away bruised and wet with Lucky. He pulls us away by our hair and my whole scalp, my whole body, burns with vicious fire. I want those tiny, nasty prickles over every inch of my skin. I want to feed the sensation, because everything about it is *ravenous*.

Jasper's thumb starts making soothing tracks along my hairline behind my ear.

"Very good," he murmurs thickly.

I dare a glance up at him through my glasses. His eyes are hooded. His lashes, veils. The thin curtain shrouding something darkly, deathly depraved.

I don't want him to stop with a kiss. I want him to drag my mouth over every inch of Lucky. Over every inch of *him*.

My gaze drops to Jasper's lips, and my mind turns over every moment of the night I arrived at Bristlebrook. Jasper and Beau catapulted me into my first ever non-solo orgasm that night, and the memory is a lusty mist of lips and hands and teeth and delicious embarrassment—and I *cannot parcel out what he tasted like*. Which mouth was his and which was Beau's. Did Jasper even kiss my mouth?

God, I want him to.

God, those lips.

For a moment, the steady path of his thumb staggers.

"Eat your food, Eden," he says, and I'm so distracted by his cool, beautiful hands and those perfect, bee-stung lips that it takes me a moment to catch up.

It's what Dom told me to do. My eyes narrow on the tiny self-satisfied tuck of his smile. It's *exactly* what Dom told me to do.

It *is* a cabal.

"Yes, *sir*," I mutter tartly to him and ignore Lucky's laughing eyes.

The ration pack is twisted between my knotted fingers, and it takes effort to unwind them. Was this all a ploy? Turn me limp and pliant and agreeable to every decision they want to make? Even the unsexy food-centric ones? Even the *wrong* ones?

I feel them both watching me, and I tear off a strip of jerky. I fight back a scowl. This is a mistake. I pop it in my mouth anyway.

They watch me with the intensity of malnourished guard dogs. The awful sound of my own chewing fills my ears, and I swallow the too-large chunk of the sweaty meat, just to make it stop.

It catches in my throat.

Coughing delicately, I try to dislodge it, but Lucky's face has already turned bone white, his eyes snapping to mine in raw panic.

"No, Lucky, don't—"

Gunshot-fast, he yanks his canteen out of his pack, then leans back over Jasper's thigh to shove it against my lips, tipping it up urgently. I open my mouth with a muffled squeak so I don't get doused, then choke on the stream—in earnest this time.

Droplets splatter on Jasper's thigh, and he hisses, flinching back.

"Eden? Eden, are you okay? What are you doing? You have to take smaller bites than that," Lucky lectures anxiously. "Can you breathe? Eden, I need you to breathe."

I shove the canteen away before he drowns me. My eyes water, and I try and fail to hold back my glare.

Don't snap, don't snap, don't snap. He's worried. It's sweet. Remember it's sweet.

A fit of coughing overtakes me, and I struggle to find air.

No. It's not sweet. I'm going to kill him.

Lucky has been glued to my side since we left Cyanide. Just *hovering* like an overzealous sheepdog over his idiotic flock. A tiny flock. A flock of *two*.

Thankfully, my flock-mate and I seem to be of a similar mind.

Jasper stands abruptly, and Lucky collapses to the ground. His mouth compressed in feral displeasure, Jasper wedges his boot under Lucky's chest and kicks him onto his back with one blunt, brutal shove. Lucky lands hard, gasping. He stares up at Jasper, his eyes wide and stunned . . . and Jasper moves his heavy boot to rest against his vulnerable throat.

My lips part.

Jasper looks unrefined. In Lucky's uniform, his hair falling over his forehead, free of its usual, elegant curves, his mouth curling in disgust, he looks vengeful. Lucky is helpless underneath him, his delicate Adam's apple at the crushing mercy of Jasper's boot.

It's difficult for me not to notice how hard Jasper is. The disgraceful, pretty flush in his pale cheeks.

I don't know what it says about me that I'm more intrigued by Jasper than I am worried for Lucky.

"You are treading very close to a line you do not want to cross, dear boy," Jasper warns.

Lucky's throat bobs against the dirty rubber, and to my surprise, his mouth sets into a mulish, unhappy line. Jasper studies him, then uses his boot to tilt Lucky's chin up and waits for those reluctant blue eyes to lift. "I know, love. I'll give you what you need very soon. But I won't tolerate you suffocating Eden in the meantime."

He doesn't wait for a response. Jasper rakes his hair back into its neat, studied curve and examines me next.

"Eden, I think it's time we had a talk. Would you take a stroll with me?" He says it casually, like he couldn't crush Lucky's larynx with a simple shift of weight, but his dark eyes etch their way into my skin, and they're not casual at all.

He wants to *talk*.

I try not to let apprehension take me. I've been waiting for this—for another "session." For Jasper to start prying open my secrets and unpacking every reason I locked them down so tightly in the first place. He'll be kind, I'm sure of that much. I know he wants to help. But even Jasper's kindness *hurts*. Being alone with him is like walking barefoot and naked into an inquisitor's chamber. I'm invariably left emotionally bloody. A shaky, distraught mess.

So it takes far more effort than it should to nod.

Jasper removes his boot from Lucky's throat and steps over him without glancing down. He offers me a hand, and I'm so startled that I stare at it for a full thirty seconds before I shove my half-eaten strip of jerky into one hand and slip the other into his grasp.

His fingers close around mine—gently, but they might as well be thumbscrews. The casual contact is riveting. Merciless. He leads me toward a moonlit path, but my attention is torn, caught between the glancing touch and the abrupt flood of anxious thoughts.

I wonder where he'll start his dissection. On my lies? He's read my journals. He knows how I felt about "A&M" and my messy battle between obedience and my own certitude. Will we go over the position I've left us in? Or maybe he'll dig in deeper. He knows my fear of being cast out. How that frigid, dark expanse of lonely nothing haunts every decision. He knows my engulfing, bilious guilt.

So many delightful emotional entrails to slip around in.

The back of my throat grows hot, and I'm suddenly on the verge of tears. I don't want to cry in front of him, but a disapproving word will shatter all the composure I've forced myself to build this week. My fingers grow sweaty in his hand, and I try to gather myself.

I'm a prisoner on her way to the gallows, my executioner at my side. Jasper's steps are fateful, resonant . . .

And accompanied by a light musical patter.

"*Lucien*." Jasper stops, turning, his hand squeezing a brief silent command for me to do the same.

Behind us, Lucky's eyes widen innocently. "Hm? You want me to walk five steps behind you, pookie?"

Shadows coalesce around us, and Lucky's dimples bloom.

Jasper arches a sharp, unamused brow. "I don't recall inviting you."

"Okay. Rude."

"It's a private conversation. We are allowed those, are we not?" Jasper bites out. Lucky opens his mouth, but Jasper cuts him off. "I seem to recall you pestering me: 'Have you spoken to Eden? When are you speaking to Eden? Do you want to hang out with Eden?' Consider this me accepting your offer, *dear*. Now, shoo."

Lucky's offended expression almost draws a smile out of me. He glances between us, taking in my resigned expression, and sighs. "*Fine*."

It was the only outcome, but my heart still sinks. Around Lucky, Jasper is lighter. Indulgent. Around me, he's thawing frost.

We start toward the shadows again, and still . . .

Tap, tap, tap.

Lucky is still strolling along at our heels with a far too cheerful bounce in his step. He winks at me, and I roll my lips in to hide a smile. My heart flutters too fast, and that cheeky glint in his eye does something warm and smoldering to my insides. I need to calm down. I feel like an anxious flame—a hearty gust right now will either snuff me out or start an inferno.

Jasper hesitates, then keeps walking, pausing only as we exit the camp to pick up a length of the coarse rope we've been using for our tents on rainy nights.

I peek at his glower and wonder where Lucky finds the nerve. Surely, anyone sensible knows you can't melt an entire avalanche with dimples alone? Then again, there's still dirt on Lucky's throat. *Anyone sensible* clearly doesn't include overdramatic masochists with absentee survival instincts.

Mine, however, are delightfully intact.

The rope is coiled around Jasper's wrist like a dangerous promise, and the dread in me deepens. Ropes are a hard limit for me. My wrists are still pink with fat scars from where the Sinners restrained me, and it throws my mind into bleak, glacial nights tied beside Heather.

Lucky, on the other hand, brightens considerably the longer he eyes the coarse length of rope.

I toy with the leftover jerky in my left hand, debating with myself. I might as well have something in my stomach for my upcoming emotional surgery. I lift it . . . but can't bring myself to take a bite.

Jasper's eyes are back on me, and I ignore, ignore, ignore.

But I also lower the jerky.

I'm not eating it, darn it. I've had all I need for today.

The path begins to widen out, and Jasper squeezes my hand again in the silent *stop*. I slow, and he inclines his head. "Just one moment, sweet girl. Let me deal with him."

Then the polite calm breaks, and he turns to shove Lucky against a tree. He wraps his hands in his kit and slams his mouth over Lucky's. My hand flies to my throat at the sudden punch of violence, but Lucky's already making a raw, needy sound deep in his chest. Jasper captures his hands, pinning them over his topknot and scraping them against the bark.

Their mouths are a battle. Fierce and beautiful, soft and punishing, and the flickering, anxious flame in me billows higher. I can't take the press of their bodies. It hurts how much I want to be between them. But if I were between them, I wouldn't be able to *see*, and they're scalded into my brain. Bubbling into my veins. My nipples tighten painfully, and I need to wrap my arms over my chest to try to make them stop.

Jasper begins wrapping the rope around Lucky's wrists above his head. It's intricate, and without meaning to, he's somehow creating art from the crude cord. He captures Lucky's lower lip between his teeth, and I suck mine jealously into my mouth as Lucky lets out a broken groan.

Suddenly, Jasper pulls back and flips Lucky so his face is pressed into the bark. He grinds his hips against Lucky's ass, and it's me who whimpers this time. At the sound, the muscles of Jasper's back tighten. He ties off the rope swiftly, then steps away, pulling Lucky back by his collar.

I look between them, and when Lucky staggers around, his wrists bound tightly in front of him, his hair half undone, he looks just as confused. Jasper takes the long tail of the leash, then walks back toward me with a polite nod, as though his pupils aren't blown, and his mouth isn't smeared slick and rubbed red from Lucky's beard.

He tugs Lucky along behind him, and they both walk past me.

Haltingly, I follow—and try not to let my dizzy brain cross my feet underneath me.

It only takes a few more steps before Dom comes into view, leaning back against a large boulder, his gun at the ready. When he sees Lucky being walked, one sable brow lifts.

Lucky is less pleased to see Dom. He digs his heels in. "Hey, no. No. Jasper, I was just walking the same way! It was a coincidence." Jasper yanks his rope sharply, and Lucky staggers forward, spluttering. "Okay, mostly a coincidence. You can have privacy. I was just going to keep watch—if you're talking, you'll be distracted. You're outside camp, so you should have someone watching your back, that's all."

Jasper places the long end of the rope in Dom's hand. "Mind this for me, please."

"*Jasper*. Come on, don't—" Lucky backs up hard, his wrists straining, and I wince in sympathy. "This is so unnecessary."

Dom's arm strains, holding him in place. His gaze shifts between Lucky and Jasper, then lingers on me. He sighs, then starts dragging the rope in, wrapping it around his thick forearm. Lucky curses as he slips forward.

"Half an hour, then I'm shooting him," Dom warns. "I don't want a pet."

I flinch. Dom's eyes find me again, and for just an instant, they lose the full, tarnished sheen and turn molten again. He grimaces and looks back at Jasper.

"I don't want *your* pet."

It must be my overactive imagination, that dip, the emphasis on *your*. I'm not Dom's anything anymore. If I ever was.

"Jasper. Sweetie. Lover. Baby. Hey! No! I didn't sign up for G.I. Jackass. Hey, where are you going?" Lucky tugs at his ropes, looking incredulously at Jasper's retreating back.

Dom tugs back. Hard. "G.I. *what*?"

The small, satisfied smile on Jasper's face is positively chilling, and he holds out his hand again. "Come now, darling. The babysitter's sorted. Let's take a stroll."

CHAPTER 5

EDEN

SURVIVAL TIP #104
Remote crannies of the woods are excellent places to be murdered.
Also for other things.

W e're holding hands. I don't know how it happened. At some point over the last few minutes, Jasper's grip shifted from polite assistance to . . . this.

I count to five and glance down again, just to make sure I have it right. That his fingers truly are tangled between mine. Messily. Like legs. Sheets. Silk, like the ones on his bed. The bed I slept in the night of the bond-fire, beside Lucky, when we were both too drunk and ill to make it far from the bathroom. The bed with the cage under it, which, as a concept is downright *appalling*, and—

"A pretty night."

My eyes snap up from our entwined fingers, and I feel myself flush.

"I—" I glance around. Starlight dapples over mossy rocks and a soft gurgling sounds from the wide cave, telling me there's an underground water source nearby. There's bear scat by the entrance, but even from here I can see it's chalky and flaking. Too old to be a concern. Bright flowers are pocketed between tree roots, and the balmy breeze is fragrant with their earthy sweetness. "Yes. It's . . . it's lovely."

He's drawn to a halt, and I'm not quite sure what he's waiting for. He still has my hand.

His thumb starts coasting along the inside of my wrist, and I tear myself free before he notices the full-body shudder the simple touch erupts in me. It's embarrassing, and it doesn't help me brace for my inquisition.

He's studying me, waiting, and sweat springs up under my arms. I can feel his attention tingling the back of my neck. Words and excuses and reasons and anxieties are bubbling up in me. I'm going to projectile vomit every thought I've ever had all over him, and he won't need to say a word. He already has me primed and prepped. We both know I'll spill every secret.

The bastard.

I stiffen my shoulders. I should just get this over with. If I slice myself open first, then he can get back to stitching me together again all the sooner.

I spin back to face him, and quickly adjust my gaze away from his face to fixate on the incongruously bright yellow flower pin he always wears these days. It's safer than his face. Because his face has a way of soaking in moonlight like a pearl, and his eyes . . .

"I'm sorry, okay? I'm *sorry*. I should have told you what A and M meant. I just . . . I knew, I *knew* it was unforgivable—letting them go, I mean. Dom was so clear. You all were. I went behind your back. I lied. I kept lying. By omission, maybe, but I know it's still a lie. Dom is right to hate me. And Beau. Oh, God." My voice catches.

The night is too beautiful for how much these confessions hurt.

I shake my head. "The way they look at me now. I could have cost us everything. Maybe I did. Alastair wants to *rule*, and I don't think he'll be shy in taking it. He certainly wasn't with us. And I *did* cost Heather everything. She's at the mercy of the man she hates more than anything, and *I* did that, Jasper. Me. And we just *left* her. Her and Bentley. Oh, those teenagers needed him, and you saw how worried Red Zone is. Do they have enough food? They're going to ask for our help and . . . and Jasper, I don't know what help we can *give* them. What are we going to do when Alastair comes knocking? We have nothing left."

Jasper is so still, and I can't bear it. I look up, and his eyes *are* doing that thing. If his skin is lustrous with light, his eyes gather darkness. They're nebulous, unfathomable . . . and kinder than I deserve.

My words grow wobbly and hot. "I was just so afraid those women and children would be forgotten. That Heather would murder Alastair, and that we'd never have another way in. And *then* I was afraid that I was wrong anyway. That they truly were with Sam, and I'd doomed us all—and even if I hadn't, it wouldn't matter, because I was *lying,* and you would be in your rights never to forgive me. I was terrified I might be exiled for putting everyone at risk, the way Sam was exiled. That I would be alone. That I'd never . . ."

Jasper's hair eddies over his forehead, and I stutter to a halt, watching the perfect swirl with wet, stinging eyes.

"That I would never see you again," I finish in a damp whisper.

Jasper gives a small, pensive nod. When I don't say anything else, he walks over to me, and when he steps into my space, I tilt my chin up to watch him warily. He touches my cheekbone with the pad of his thumb, then traces the single track of my tear down to my jaw with the reverence of a Renaissance painter.

"Anything else, darling girl?"

I swallow, confused. "I don't . . ."

He nods again, and his gaze travels my face. His thumb rubs my tears like he needs them on his skin.

"You will always be welcome in my home, Eden."

I tense, trying to stop the bitter waver of my lip. "Well, thank you for saying that, but—"

"*Always.*" The word is a whipcrack. Fierce and painful in its implications.

I fall silent, trying to battle the confusing glare I want to give him. He can't promise me that. There are a thousand variables. In our relationship. In *all* my relationships. The other men are his closest friends. Lucky is the love of his life. He can't say things like *always* to me.

His grip tightens on my face, almost painful, and he pins me with his pitiless gaze. "*Always,* Eden. With the men or without. Lie, kill, steal my every heirloom. Shatter my heart into a thousand pieces if you must, but you will *always* have a place at Bristlebrook. You will always have a safe place to land, no matter how bad things get. You'll never be alone again. Not if I have anything to say about it."

His face says that he has many, many things to say about it.

My lips part, and I mean to speak, I do, but all that comes out is a hitching, pained gasp. A few tears squeeze treacherously from the corner of my eyes, and they pool in the curve of his hand.

"Jasper, I . . ." I can't get any more words out. My mouth is shaking too much.

It's the kind of promise I used to dream of as a child. Something rare and precious that seemed reserved for lucky children from doting parents. Something *unconditional*. It's not something reasonable people offer. There are always limits.

But Jasper's gaze refuses reason.

He means it.

He holds my eyes until my disbelief melts into confusion and relief, and I sob again, because I can't help it. Because we haven't kissed, that I know of. Because we've been in each other's orbit, and in each other's heads, but somehow, I haven't told him that I—

He makes a lost sound, then his mouth is hot on my cheek and his tongue is dragging over my skin. Over my *tears*. He groans helplessly as he tastes me, and I shudder, everything zeroing in on the unexpected contact. He kisses my cheek, the corner of my eye, taking every tear as if they belong to him. Scorching. Open-mouthed. He nips my cheekbone, and I fall into him.

His arm catches around my waist, and he breaks contact to bury his face in my hair. "Eden, Eden, Eden," he murmurs.

My breath catches again, but I don't think I'm crying anymore.

It takes a moment, but I find a place against him. He's taller than Lucky by a few inches. He's more slender than Jayk. Not as broad-shouldered as Beau, or as rock-solid as Dom. But I find the perfect spot to rest my head, just below his collarbone. My hands settle along the lines of his back. His find their home with less caution. In the curve of my hip, around the nape of my neck.

It's funny, how I feel made for him, too.

Jasper sighs. "Eden, you have spent most of your life alone, making decisions for yourself. From what I've gathered, you worked around your grandmother and your husband's rules more than you ever worked with them . . . because they couldn't be trusted with that control."

I stiffen in his arms, but he just squeezes my nape, like he knows. He knows how unsettling it is to be summarized in just a few pitiful sentences.

Gently, he continues, "A few weeks of submission with anyone, no matter how you feel for them, is not going to overcome a lifetime of learned behaviors and distrust. Particularly not when you're spiraling." His voice becomes acerbic. "No matter how much Beaumont would like to believe in the healing power of his phallus, his overwhelming white-knight complex won't quite do the job on childhood trauma."

I strangle on a scandalized laugh, pulling back far enough to give Jasper an appalled look. "That's— No, Jasper. Beau has been wonderful. He's right about the position I've put us in. I shouldn't have lied. He was nothing but kind and understanding and—"

His nose wrinkles in mild disgust. "Right up until you showed a hint of fallibility? Of humanity? I am fond of Beaumont, Eden, don't misunderstand me, but I'm about ready to ask Jaykob how exactly one performs a *swirly*." My mouth drops open, and Jasper's eyes catch a twinkle of silvery light. "Perhaps spending time with his head in a toilet will familiarize him with the nature of his opinions."

This time I do laugh, though I can't help a twinge of guilt. Beau did deserve my honesty, my past notwithstanding. But this side of Jasper is entrancing. A little wicked. It reminds me of his curling paperback annotations, declaring that Dracula seems 'sorely in need of a period-appropriate interior decorator.'

Seeing me study him, Jasper's expression softens, becoming something gentle and full of secret nooks. Something intimate. His lashes shadow us together.

"I didn't mean to make you cry tonight," he murmurs. "I had just thought that we might . . ." Jasper's lips twist ruefully, and color trails sheepishly into his cheeks again. "It's my own fault. I suppose our interactions are usually rather charged."

My mind trips over his blush. Falls hard. On its face.

This remote glen suddenly looks different. Less like the gallows or a sadistic scene carefully chosen for how well the leaves might disguise a pool of blood.

He didn't bring me here for an interrogation.

He's *blushing*.

Heat floods my face in what must be some kind of sympathetic nervous response.

"You—" I stop. Try again. "We were with Lucky. We could have—"

Jasper's eyes crash against mine like dark matter, too full of mass and meaning. "I plan on spending many, many nights with the both of you." My mouth turns dry. "But you and I need time also. How I feel for you exists outside of how I feel for Lucien . . . and it needs different things."

His hand traces around my neck, along my collarbone. His fingers dip into the hollow where my pulse hammers.

"I've worried that we're too similar for our own good," he murmurs. "Too reserved."

It's a thought I've had before, wondering whether we're doomed to our own orbits. Whether by circling Lucky we'll only ever shine on him and never one another. Wondering if my past with Henry, and his with Soomin, has left us too skittish and bruised.

"Too cautious." I nod, mulling that over.

Hesitantly, I bring my hand from his side up his chest. I reach up and push back the hair that's fallen across his forehead again, the sweet lock that always teases me. I tuck it into its place, where I know it won't stay long, and marvel at how silky soft it is.

"Lucky's not cautious. He makes it easy." It's my turn to smile.

He catches my wrist on its way down. "Lucien has his own delights and challenges. He might be a masochist and beautifully free with his affections, but he's also a brat, and he has little patience for my rules. You might never delight in pain, but you don't test me the way Lucien does." His mouth dips closer to mine, and his eyes darken as I shiver. "And the way you respond to me, Eden . . ."

He bends my arm behind the small of my back, bowing my back, and every part of me turns soft.

"The way you *submit* . . ." His voice edges toward raw, almost a snarl. Liquid, lascivious things whirl between us, and my head dips to the side, exposing my throat.

"It's like going to church."

He breathes against my skin in sharp, hungry pants, and I want to rub and squirm against him. If he were any of the others, I would. But Jasper is holding me still.

So I'll be still for him.

He kisses my fluttering pulse, so lightly.

"We'll work it out," he says, mostly to himself.

My heart squeezes and my head spins, and I whisper, "I know we will. I want it, Jasper. I want *you*."

Jasper's shiver takes me over too, as we're pressed so close together. His grip on my wrist eases, and the next moment, he's cupping my face.

"I'm going to kiss you, darling girl."

I suck in a sharp breath. His thumb is on my too-large lower lip, pulling it down, parting it like he's entitled to entry. And he is.

He's so perfectly beautiful, and his lips are hovering a millimeter from mine when I pull back just slightly.

"Wait, I need to . . . Jasper, is this the first time?" His brow lifts, and I'm too urgent, too scrambled when I ask, "That first night, with Beau. Did you kiss me then? I was never sure who it was, and I need to know if . . ."

"That *night*." His voice isn't silky anymore. It's not refined. "That night ruined every attempt at sleep I've had since you arrived. *Yes*, Eden, we kissed. I took your throat, your pretty breasts. I had tasted every sweet inch of you I could reach. We *kissed*." His upper lip curls, and his eyes narrow. "There's little similarity between me and your disreputable doctor, my girl. In the future, I expect you to be able to tell the difference between us—even if you were blindfolded."

My breath shivers over his mouth. "Yes, Jasper."

His lips tease mine, and he delicately licks the deep Cupid's bow. "Study me carefully, Eden. I'm going to kiss your cunt exactly like this when I get you home."

My mind misfires.

His mouth slants against mine in a pitiless, studied claiming. Whatever he says about his reserve or caution doesn't apply to this kiss. There's an inherent cruelty in the way he does it, the way he luxuriates in the sharp pinch of teeth and the following licks of heat. The way he leans into pressure, and his nails bite too harshly, even while he stokes nerve endings I never knew existed. I'm dizzy and sizzling with it, my heart beating wildly, adrenaline-drunk on the whiplash and wondering if the next slide of his mouth will hurt or cause that hot, liquid swirl through my abdomen.

He kisses me until I'm clinging to him hopelessly and he chains my hands behind my back. He kisses me until I cry, and I gasp his name into his mouth. He kisses me until he groans into my throat and tells me I'm perfect, I'm beautiful, that he needed my limits list yesterday, and that my essay on submissive-dominant safety is overdue. He kisses me until, if I had enough air, I would say the words beating against my skull.

I love you.

CHAPTER 6

DOMINIC

SURVIVAL TIP #311
Pets are a liability, best to set them free.
(Or drown them in a sack.
It really depends how much you like them.)

Lucky yanks sullenly against his tied wrists.

I tug back on the rope. "Easy, boy."

We've done rounds twice, and I've rechecked the trip alerts around the camp. Everything's quiet.

"Cute. You're really cute. But my fingers are turning numb. You need to let me out," Lucky complains for the five-hundred-millionth time, wiggling his fingers at me.

Almost everything is quiet.

I glance down at his hands. They're tanned, a bit dirty, but they're not swollen or blue-tinged—they're not even reddening around his bonds. The tools might be less than ideal, but Jasper ran the shibari masterclass at Darkside. It's expert work.

As usual, Lucky's talking out of his ass. Typical subbie wheedling.

He's standing beside my boulder awkwardly, and, sure, I could move over so he can sit next to me, but that would give the pest the impression I want him to stay.

And right now, I need to think.

I go back to watching the trees, but I only see Aaron scowling at me. Heather tracing the line of Alastair's throat with her knife. Eden in the forest, telling me we could get Alastair and Mateo to switch sides, her eyes like gravestones. Mary Beth's face when I barked at her for carrying the axe. Bristlebrook's empty inventory list. Aaron staring at the battle maps, taking notes. Eden stepping up against Alastair, her hands shaking behind her back, while I was on my knees.

My knuckles are white on my rifle, and I force myself to unclench my hands. One rifle. One clip to get us to a home where our people will already be starving.

The Sinners might have stripped us bare, but there's only one person responsible for fucking us that night.

Suddenly, Lucky's ass is on mine. I don't know how, since his hands are still tied, and this boulder is huge, but he's somehow monkey-crawled into my single square foot of personal space and is shoving his ass into mine like he's trying to link cheeks.

I let out a long, low sigh. "Lucky?"

"Yeah, boss?" He settles his shoulder against mine comfortably. The butt cheeks nestle in closer.

Uncomfortably close.

"Can you at least pretend you're house-trained?" I ask tiredly.

Lucky shoots me a grin, but it sours and dies when he joins me in staring at the trees. Like he sees anything but greenery as well.

I look at him, then away.

I'm not curious. I'm not. He, Jasper, and Eden have been stuck together all week and it's . . .

I rub my hollow chest. It's none of my business. I have too much to think about already, and Eden's love life isn't my concern. It never has been.

But I hear myself ask, "You don't like them being alone together?"

I'm not asking about her. I'm asking about him. If he's going to squeeze cheeks with me, then we're in personal questions territory.

I wouldn't have picked Lucky for the jealous type, but I've never seen him in a relationship before. Not a serious one, anyway.

Blond brows fly up, and he gives me a puzzled look. "What? No. No, they need to do their thing. Read books. Stare pensively at each other. Develop matching frown lines. Just . . ." He huffs, and his eyes track back to the trees. "They should just do it at *home*. Behind your scary moat. In a panic room. Preferably surrounded by an ancient booby-trapped labyrinth that only I know the path through."

Right.

"Indiana Jones style?" I deadpan. "Or Pan's?"

He considers that, then shrugs. "Jones, but David Bowie could fondle his balls on the way if he wants."

I study the side of his face. The anxious tap of his foot against the rock. It drags me out of my own shitty spiral.

"Jasper's not the same man he was five years ago, Lucky. He can handle himself." My throat feels like crushed glass when I add, "Eden can, too. They're not stupid."

Lucky sighs suddenly and rubs his tied hands over his face. His fingers bury themselves in his hair. "I *know* that. I do. They'll be fine. They *are* fine. I just . . ." He peeks at me sideways between long strands of his hair that have pulled free of his bun. There's lavender tucked into it, and it peeks from his kit, too. Purple everywhere. "I just need them to stay fine. You know?"

Eden had lavender all through her hair, too.

The wind kicks up and it's too hot for this time of year. Another mosquito darts around my head, and I glare at it, daring it to try me. It does, and I slap it down.

Its squished little body doesn't make me feel any better, though.

I sigh. "They don't need us, Lucky."

It's Lucky's turn to study me, then suddenly, I'm having lavender tucked behind my hair too, like I'm a milkmaid and he's an overenthused stableboy. Like he's not trussed and being babysat by his former CO like a sticky-fingered, armed toddler.

I cock a brow at him, and he gives me a half-smile. But his blue eyes are unusually serious.

"We all need each other, Dom. All of us."

I stare at him hard, the scathing replies sticking in my throat.

It reminds me of standing in front of my old man, shoulder-to-shoulder with a scrawny sixteen-year-old Beau as we got our asses handed to us.

The first few weeks after he landed in military school were rough. He was soft as underbaked apple pie, cursing his mama and the rest of the world for catching him with that fake ID and sending him off to get straightened out.

I was the too-serious golden boy protégé with a sideways rod up my ass—and I took it on myself to do the straightening.

Stupid.

I don't know exactly what it was about him that pissed me off so much. Maybe it was his floppy hair, or his whining, or how his sisters teased and hugged him for fifteen whole minutes when they dropped him off, or the dumb accent that only comes from a lifetime of living in *one* place.

Whatever it was, he was in *my* class, *my* dorm, and he was too soft to survive the hard rules I lived by. So I beat his ass, shaved his head, and ran him ragged every day until he finally stopped whining. It took him less than two weeks before he snapped and flipped me over a table.

We fought.

I broke his nose.

He gave me a concussion.

And my dad wanted to take the rest out on my hide.

I remember standing bloody and ashamed in his office after the principal was through with us, wanting to die on the spot at the disgust and disappointment in his face. How he ripped us up for over an hour for breaking protocol, for disgraceful behavior, for shaming him, for setting a poor example, and two dozen other things, and I didn't say a single damn word.

How he finally ordered Beau to tell him what happened.

And how Beau drawled in that annoying accent, "Walked into a door, sir. I'm real clumsy sometimes."

To my dad. *My* dad. Colonel Slade himself.

And all for some asshole who'd made his life hell for days.

For that one moment, Beau had my love for life.

Not that it meant anything to my old man. He just sent Beau away and sat me down for his final, disappointed words under the glinting glare of his medals.

"You're nothing without your team, Dominic. A good team can elevate a mediocre leader. A good team will function even with*out* a leader. But a bad leader . . . a bad leader will get a good team killed."

His Medal of Honor shone the brightest on his wall, proud and centered over his desk like a halo.

And he didn't flinch when he said, "I always knew you were mediocre, Dominic, but today, you were a bad leader. And sometimes, the best thing a bad leader can do is walk away."

Those words ring in my ears, jarring and jumbled and sounding of nowhere—of no place that could ever really be called a home. They tumble in with Lucky as he continues to talk, waving around his tied hands. He's a good man. We have a good team.

They don't need me.

Eden doesn't need me.

She was incredible up against Alastair, deft and clever. Humbling herself to salvage my shitshow. I knew she was smart, but watching her fox her way out of the box we were in was impressive as hell.

She's a good judge of character.

She knew I wasn't making the right call with the prisoners, so she fixed it herself. She knew I was furious about it, and she didn't trust how I'd react enough to speak up.

She knew I was lacking, just like my father did.

So now, just like with him, I say nothing to Lucky. I just listen to him chatter about every kind of bullshit until the moon hangs low and we're eventually replaced for our watch.

CHAPTER 7

EDEN

SURVIVAL TIP #76
Nature can harm or heal.
Just like lying, wicked women.

It rained overnight. It's sweltering again today, of course, but between the sticky heat, and the mud, and my soggy socks, it's been a miserable final day of travel.

Though, soggy socks or no, I don't think I'm having the hardest time of our group.

Beau swipes the air again, and I nibble on my lower lip, torn. He glares around him, a deep scowl painting his face. Over the last few days, I've quietly handed out lavender around the camp until everyone is more or less mosquito-free. Even Dom has some tucked into his kit, after his impromptu bonding—bondage?—session with Lucky.

But Beau . . .

Fiery red welts cover his face and neck, even the backs of his hands. Beside him, Dom swerves to avoid getting smacked, his jaw tight.

As I bend over to gather some echinacea, Beau's eyes catch on me, then skitter sideways before I can make eye contact. He scratches absently at the back of his neck as he pivots away like he never saw me.

I yank the pretty purple flowers out by their roots, long past fed up.

I know I screwed up, but this silent treatment is *infuriating*. We won't be able to fix anything—with us or the Sinners—unless we can talk.

Beau is a *child*. I hope he enjoys his mosquito bites. I hope he gets *swarmed* by them. I hope they bite him between his shoulder blades. On his butt cheek. Between his *toes*.

I stare at the sludgy crevasse I've created in the mud and straighten.

That's enough echinacea for now.

I clean off the clumpy roots as I trail behind the two of them, once again dropping to the back of the group, trying to convince myself that I'm not trying to delay the inevitable. We're close enough to Bristlebrook now that I'm recognizing landmarks, and my feet keep speeding up despite myself. Then slowing down. Then speeding up.

I'm a mess.

I haven't seen Jayk since I left for Cyanide and he stayed to protect the civilians. He needed time to think, and he's had two weeks. Surely, he's made his decision by now.

Speed up.

God, what if he's decided he doesn't want me? What if he's decided that this whole sharing-me-with-multiple-people business *is* all too much, and I'm not worth all this awful, soul-tearing struggle?

Slow down.

No. I know Jayk loves me. I wrote him the letter—it was a *good* letter.

He has to choose me.

I'm speeding up when I see a sprouting of feverfew and veer to gather that up too, though my boot squelches deeply into a muddy puddle. I ignore the brown slurry that trickles into my sock—feverfew is a fantastic find.

However Jayk feels about me, I'm going to find out very, very soon.

If it doesn't change when he hears what I did.

Low, dark laughter lures me from my thoughts, and I look over to see Jasper's lips still dusted with it. Lucky is walking beside him, his head tilted intimately, with this happy, dazzled smile that squeezes my heart.

Lucky has been helping me fill out the—frankly terrifying—limits list Jasper gave me, and it's been a nerve-racking experience. It's *seven pages long*, and it's . . . comprehensive, covering everything from kinks and specific toys to dozens of acts, to how I do or don't want to feel, what concerns or phobias or triggers I might have, to what I want aftercare to look like. Many things I've already talked about with Beau, and even Jayk—but also plenty I haven't. Plenty we haven't needed to.

And Lucky smirked his way through the entire blasted thing.

Their shoulders shift together with each step, and Lucky glances back to check on me. While debating whether or not to just pluck the leaves now, I wave an exasperated hand at him to keep on. The attention is sweet, but it's nice to finally be more than fifteen feet apart.

Slap.

Beau curses, and to my surprise Dom breaks his silence to snap, "Would you *shut it*?"

I pull a final bunch of feverfew and follow quietly. Their backs are to me, but when Dom turns through the sparse trees, I see he's pinched with irritation and paler than usual.

"It's these heinous flying freeloaders. They won't leave me alo—" Beau stops midway through an air-swipe to frown at Dom. "Well, you look like a soup sandwich."

"Just sick of hearing you bitch about the wildlife," Dom says, ducking under a branch.

Beau's frown deepens. "Dominic."

"*Beaumont.*"

My heart crunches like gripped paper. It's the same words, but offbeat—like someone missing the punchline of their favorite joke.

"Fine." *Slap.* "Son of a—" Beau stops himself with visible difficulty. "*Fine.*"

They walk in silence for a few minutes, and I harvest a few leaves from my flowers as I step over branches and listen to the low murmur of Jasper and Lucky up farther ahead. Sloane calls back from the front of the pack, telling us to make the final turn toward Bristlebrook.

"We should talk about what to tell people when we get back," Beau starts, and I edge as close as I dare to catch the lowered words. "Then we'll need to put together a supply plan."

"You do that."

Beau holds the spindly leaves of a tall bush back for Dom. "Come on, Dom. We had a bad run. You need to un-fuck yourself so we can fix it. You have a team here."

Dom pauses, then says quietly, "It's not my team. Not anymore."

The words ice my stomach.

"Now, you don't mean that. We'll *fix* this—we just need a plan."

Dom walks past him without a word, and Beau stares at his back for a long moment, his tanned jaw working. He drags his feet after Dom, and I squeeze past the bush to follow. "You know the civs are going to be mad as all hell that we left Heather behind."

The feverfew leaves crumple in my fingers. The sap spills over my fingers, and I wipe it off with shaking hands, knowing from experience that my skin doesn't like the mild irritation.

The hatred in Heather's eyes still spits at me from my memories.

Bentley's panic.

Oh, God. What are we going to do when Red Zone contacts us? We can't go back into Cyanide again. We can't take them in either, not the way we are. We're worse off than they are.

But it's still our mess.

My mess.

What if Alastair is still giving them trouble? How much more is he going to demand from them?

Dom's calm doesn't waver, but when he looks back at Beau, I can see the deceptiveness of it. The deadly fins and lashing tails deep under the still surface.

"Heather's out there taking the heat for all of us because of bad leadership and bad calls. We've lost most of our arsenal. The weather's going to turn, and we don't have enough rations to see us through. We're all going to starve." The words hang like a noose. "You want to tell them something? Tell them that."

Beau eyes Dom uneasily.

"Maybe I'll . . . paraphrase." He grabs Dom's shoulder and pulls him to a stop. "Hey, seriously, you look like shit."

Dom tips his head back. "Just a headache. It's your fucking accent."

I hover by the prickly bush and try to make it look like I'm not actively stalking them. But the thread of discomfort in his voice has my fingers itching to check him over.

Beau beats me to it.

"Have you had enough water?" He pulls his canteen from his pack.

Dom presses the heel of his hand between his brows. "Save the lecture, *doc*. I've heard it before."

Beau shoves his canteen into Dom's free hand anyway. "One of the most common causes of—"

"I'm hydrated, asshole. I drank my damn water." He tries to shove the canteen back at Beau.

Beau doesn't take it. "The Sinners swiped all my meds, so this is the best we've got. Drink up, princess."

I clear my throat. "I can help."

Two heads lift in unison, and I shift from foot to foot. There's pretty much no way to hide that I've been peeping through the bushes at them.

Dom's jaw flexes as he turns to keep walking. "I'm fine."

His clipped voice stings, but I blurt, "You're not, though."

His footsteps falter, his heavy muscles bunching, and my voice catches as I add more softly, "You're not, sir. Please let me help you."

So slowly, Dom turns back to look at me, and his eyes find mine. My mouth goes dry at the force of them. It's like getting hit by flowing lava, fierce and hot and glowing gold.

Oh God. I called him *sir* again! What is *wrong* with me? The man is in pain. I need to be *muzzled*.

Beau's gaze rolls between us, his brow knitting in confusion.

Then he rubs the back of his neck, avoiding my eyes again. They settle instead on the flowers in my hands. "What is that?"

"Feverfew." Grateful for the distraction, I stumble through the bush, ignoring the sharp pricks—there's enough of those around already—and stop in front of him to show him. "It's perfect for headaches, but he can't eat the raw leaves. They'll cause sores in his mouth. I can make him a tea when we get back to Bristlebrook."

"But what *is* it? A lot of these herbal remedies have side effects, Eden. I don't think this is a good idea." Beau's white teeth bite down into his lower lip, and I force myself to forget the way they dug into my skin when I came.

I blink, offended. "I wouldn't give him something that would hurt him. Unless he has allergies to—"

"How do you know he doesn't?" His voice is burred and prickly with irritation. He crosses his tanned, corded arms over his chest. "We'll still have some actual medicine back at Bristlebrook. They're very sweet, but you can put your flowers away, darlin'."

Dom's tense expression takes on a vicious edge. "Fucking *enough*, Beau."

Slap.

Beau curses under his breath, scowling around himself at invisible mosquitos.

Sweet? Ooh. This man!

I glower at Beau as that solicitous condescension rubs against everything raw and irritated inside of me. It pokes at my vulnerabilities like a scalpel.

But things are different now. *I* am different now.

Something was seeded when I broke our deal, and it grew roots when I fought back, when I spoke up, as I've grown. That same *something* held me up in Cyanide, and it's now stubbornly butting up against my guilt and shoring up all those soft places inside me.

I've apologized for my mistakes, and I *will* make up for them—but I don't deserve this from him. I'm no one's emotional punching bag anymore. If he has a problem with me, then he needs to use his words, even if I have to drag him kicking and screaming into an adult conversation.

And if he won't, then I'm spraying sugar water on his clothes and letting the mosquitos have him.

"We can't rely on modern medicine forever, Beau. We're going to run out. It will all expire eventually. Or be used. Or stolen." I refrain from stamping my foot. Like a lady. And—ladylike—I hiss, "Maybe consider that you aren't always right for a change!"

He rubs his head like he's the one with the headache. "Mouth sores, Eden? Sounds swell. Tell me, do you *want* him to suffer?"

Anger fizzes in my veins. "No, you patronizing—"

Dom's hand falls from his face, and he glares at both of us. "Can it, both of you, I'm *fine*. Move out."

We both whirl on him. "*You're not fine.*"

My mouth snaps shut at the same time as Beau's, our words echoing through the trees. I tense and feel Beau do the same. He presses against my shoulder, hot and heavy, and I realize we've ended up side by side.

I can't look at him.

He hasn't touched me in over a week, and even this—this pathetic, glancing graze of skin—is swallowing my anger in seconds. It becomes something aching and lonely. After weeks of drowning in his scent and talking every night, this distance between us is *wrong*.

Beau doesn't look at me either, so I try to ignore the heat of him and focus on Dom.

On him, at least, we can agree.

Dom is stone-faced, braced and standing against us. He's different today. Every gentle curve of humor has hardened, and the strength he was starting to yield is newly callused. Dom is too proud—he's always been too proud—but these new defenses look impossible to chip.

I fixate on the stiff, invulnerable line of his mouth, and, abruptly, I want to cry.

A scorching lump lodges deep in my throat when Beau's hand hesitantly brushes my waist. "You should have some of the flower tea. Maybe it . . . maybe she *can* help."

His voice is husky, suddenly uncertain, and I have to swallow my own lump down.

Is this better than his pain? To have Dom back in his relentless leadership role, arrogant and uncompromising . . . and hating me? Will he cut me down the way he used to, like a tank pressing down every soft roadblock in its way?

Maybe it is better. I'd rather hurt for him than let him bleed.

"It will help you, sir. Please let me help you," I whisper, desperate for him to hear everything under it.

That serious mouth firms in dismissal.

My heart buckles, and my trembling fingertips brush the rigid corner.

Right as the forest explodes in a deafening roar.

CHAPTER 8

EDEN

SURVIVAL TIP #8
Shoot first.

I'm yanked into hard arms, and the forest spins dizzily, shuddering with chaos all around us. My head is still whirling when I realize I'm on the ground with Dom crouching over me, his rifle drawn and ready. Beau is still in the open, his weapon up, and muffled shouts ring from all directions.

"What the hell was that?" Ava yells from somewhere ahead.

Katherine snaps, "Was that a bomb?"

Another boom sounds somewhere to our distant right, and Beau and Dom both swivel to face it. With shaking hands, I lift my glasses from where they've fallen around my neck and shove them on. Even then, I can't see any immediate danger.

"Are you okay?" I push myself up between Dom's legs, looking him over while my heart storms against my throat. He's still smeared with sweat and dirt, but I can't see a mark on him.

He glances down at me with an unreadable expression. "Still fine, pe— Eden."

The hairs on the back of my neck prickle to life.

Beau looks back, urgent divots between his brows. "It's Bristlebrook. Someone's set off the tripwires."

Bristlebrook? My heart stalls.

Jayk is at Bristlebrook.

Dom lowers the tip of his gun. "We need bodies over there *now*."

Beau nods once, like they haven't just been bickering like school children.

Up ahead, Sloane shouts for orders. Dom brings his whistle to his lips. It's piercingly loud, and moments later there's a crunchy rush of boots on dying leaves.

Suddenly, a rapid pelt of blistering gunshots echoes through the forest, and my breathing picks up. It has to be Jayk firing. He's so quick to shoot. It's almost certainly nothing. A deer skating too close to the property, maybe.

Beau's eyes flick to me, and for the first time in days, they linger, clouded with worry. "Get up, darlin', we need to move. No one fires like that unless they need backup."

Dark and grim, Dom starts moving toward the trees. "Or unless they're the problem."

It's not Jayk.

I scramble to my feet and chase after him, my stomach hitting my feet. Not again. For a moment, the trees are clogged with smoke, and I'm watching the barn glow black and orange.

Fear makes it hard to breathe. Not Jayk. I can't. Not again.

A second round of shots explodes up ahead, thudding with my erratic heartbeat, and I'm fighting memories of Jayk's barn being lost to flames when Lucky's voice splits the air.

"*Eden?*"

I pull up hard, looking back frantically, but the rapid gunshots swallow the sound. I can't tell where it came from, but he sounded *raw*. He's on edge already; he can't take much more.

I take a few steps back in the direction I last saw him, and Beau curses. "Lucky!"

"Eden? Eden, where are you? Fucking answer me!" Lucky's fear tears me apart, even as more shots pump panic into the air.

Dom hesitates, his molten gaze torn between me and the echoing firefight. "Eden, *move*. He can handle himself."

No. He can't.

"*Lucky?*" I call again.

Beau stalks back to me and grasps me around my waist, but I

shove off him, searching the greenery. It's too loud. There's movement everywhere. I just need them to *stop* and breathe, and I need to *think*, and—

Suddenly the gunshots stop entirely.

The answering silence is thunderous.

Uneasy goosebumps shiver down my arms as the leaves fall too still around us, and Beau's jaw squares worriedly.

"Lucien, perhaps we should listen to Dominic—"

Tension rushes out me, and my heart lifts.

"Don't even try me right now, Jasper. Get your weapon up and hit five o'clock," Lucky snaps.

Is he closer? He sounds closer. Beau pulls me along again, but I still can't see Lucky. Our group starts appearing through the trees, and Dom's screaming whistle spurs them to speed on at a ground-eating pace. He shouts orders as they pass us, like 'due west to Bristlebrook' and 'hold cover' and 'hang fire—only on command.'

I yank out of Beau's grip again, straining for any flash of golden blond. "Lucky?"

"Eden?" There's a sharp note of relief in his voice this time.

Lucky shoves through a copse a moment later, his eyes black with fear. When he sees me, he drops the nose of his gun into the dirt and bends at the waist to suck in air. "Fuck. *Fuck*."

I rush over to him, and he drags me into a fierce hug.

"I couldn't see you. You weren't there, and—"

"I know. I'm okay. They had me. We're okay," I whisper to him.

A cool hand squeezes my arm, and I glance up to see Jasper's intense eyes.

"Eden, stay with Lucky. Lucky, bring up the rear—you have our six. Everyone else, *move*," Dom snaps.

They tear through the trees at speed, and Lucky lets me separate enough to jog in front of him. I don't have a gun anymore, not since the Sinners dumped us outside of Cyanide with only a single weapon each, but my little knife is squeezed into my palm, and my demon is starting to wake.

If Jayk has so much as one scratch on him, I'm carving out eyeballs for my next soup.

My thoughts are a furious, fearful jumble, and I can't make sense of any of it. It *doesn't* make sense. We left the Sinners back in Cyanide. Alastair couldn't be here so soon, and I'm not sure why he would be.

For a moment, I wonder if it's Red Zone, as if my earlier thoughts summoned them, and they're here already to demand a solution to the problem we made, but I shake the thought off as soon as it comes. There's no way they could have arrived ahead of us, either.

So who the hell is attacking us?

Lucky starts to slow, whistling for us to follow suit. Jasper keeps close to my side, his face set and cold as winter.

Split, ravaged soil spills from the ground ahead of us. Trees are collapsed in haphazard heaps with blackened trunks and missing chunks, and round blast wounds scar the bark up ahead.

Arrows pepper the trees alongside them, and I squint in the dusk light.

Arrows mean Bristlebrook. Arrows mean the Valkyries are here.

"Stay low and keep behind cover where you can," Lucky mutters.

Our group seems to be following that advice. Whether by instinct, instruction, or training, Jennifer and Sara are almost crawling up to a dense thicket. Ava is crouching behind a decaying, obliterated log, and Sloane is beside her. Katherine and Jo are rounding the far left, farther back.

Dom and Beau are only a few feet in front of us, arguing in low voices. Dom breaks to gesture to Jennifer and Sara to . . . go around the blast site? I'm not quite sure, and I only spare a moment to curse the fact I never advanced far enough in my training to learn their shorthand. Jennifer did, though, and she and Sara change direction.

Dom looks at us and gestures sharply to Lucky. Lucky shakes his head, and Dom gestures again, his eyes blazing with more life than I've seen from him in a week.

"I have her, Lucien," Jasper begins, and Lucky's jaw hardens.

"I have both of you, right here. *Safe.*" He gives Jasper a fierce, cold look. That edginess is back in him, ground into something brittle and sharp. "I'm not going anywhere without you. He can go fuck himself."

I glance at Dom, feeling his impatience, the frustration. "Lucky—"

Lucky punctuates his speech by flipping Dom off, but his gaze is already back to anxiously tracking the trees around us.

Dom stares at the gesture, and I watch the fire inside him slowly suffocate. Then he nods to himself, his face draining again into that same stony calm.

"It's okay, Eden," Lucky whispers, as I try to work out why Dom's expression unsettles me so much. "Just keep your head down for me, okay?"

Beau continues arguing. I can't make out a word from here, but Dom doesn't say another thing. His gaze drops to his gun. It doesn't take long before Beau throws up his hands up with a disgusted scowl and . . .

Ice slams into my veins.

Beau is climbing on top of a thick, fallen oak, utterly exposed.

I push up from my hiding spot, but Jasper grasps me around my throat and yanks me back into his chest. In my ear, he murmurs, "I'm afraid you're staying here, darling girl. I've grown rather fond of you."

I'm sure he means it as a joke, but the implication that being exposed could mean *death* while Beau is doing a perfect impersonation of a human target outline is enough to stall my heart.

Beau glances down at Dom from his vantage, and I wait for Dom to make a move, to take over, but he . . . doesn't. He's still staring at his gun—grim, dark, and resolute. Waiting.

Beau gives him an impatient look, then swings his wary attention back to the trees. His grip on his rifle is loose, deceptively casual, as he calls, "I think you'd best introduce yourself, stranger."

A bullet shreds the air, and I strangle a scream as it hits a tree high above his head, gouging a violent hole in the bark. Beau doesn't flinch. Instead, he turns in the direction of the shot.

"What the hell is he doing?" I hiss.

"He's pinpointing where they are," Lucky says distractedly, edging up to peer in the direction of the bullet. "So the others can close in from behind."

"Do they know to do that?" Jasper asks, and Lucky shoots him a guilty, stressed look before shifting forward, his rifle up.

My heart hammers in my chest. This is why Dom wanted Lucky to go—to cover Beau.

Instead, he's here. Protecting me.

"Lucky . . ." I whisper shakily.

A rough, twangy voice chases the bullet before Lucky can respond.

"Well now, we got another country boy. You always welcome guests into your home with explosives? And *arrows*?"

His accent is suffocatingly thick.

Snorts and whistles accompany the question, and my muscles tense into stones. Something is wrong here; this doesn't feel like the Sinners.

In quick reply to the stranger's complaint, an arrow slams into a tree somewhere near the voice. My heart leaps viciously. *Yes!*

Maybe our people don't have military training, but they have brains.

"Identify yourselves, or those tripwires will be the least of your trouble," Beau drawls back casually.

He's *threatening* them? Urgency stumbles through my veins. I'm pummeled with images of Beau crashing off that tree, a violent, bloody hole ripping his perfect face apart.

Get down. Get down, get down, get *down*. I am going to *kill* him for this.

Jasper's arms tighten around me. "He'll be fine, sweet girl."

"He could be *shot*."

Lucky gives me a quick look. "He's in his kit. That'll take the worst of it."

"And if it's a headshot?" I ask sweetly, but my voice trembles too much to hold the snark.

Lucky flashes me a dimple. "Yeah, that would be bad."

Jasper's hand slams over my cursing mouth as the stranger's drawling voice kicks up again. Anger, hot and bright, bubbles through his words.

"You invite us here, try to blow us to high hell, and you're tellin' me to identify *my*self? Boy, who the fuck are *you*? Give me one good reason why I shouldn't put a bullet between your eyes right this god-given second."

"Shit," Lucky swears, his smirk dying.

He steps toward Beau, lifting his rifle, then stops to look anxiously back at me and Jasper.

My lips go numb, and Jasper's grip over my mouth turns painful.

Dom is so still, staring at his rifle like it holds the world's secrets.

I meet Lucky's torn gaze.

Go, I beg him silently. *I need him, too. Help him.*

Beau fires into the air, and I nearly rip out of Jasper's arms at the sudden burst. My knife hilt digs painfully into my palm, but it's a good kind of hurt. If they won't watch out for him, then I will. I know I can do it now. I've killed for him before, and for Heather, and for *myself*. I'm stained red to the bone now.

I'll kill all of them if I need to.

"Let them work, Eden. Trust them. I know it's impossible, but trust them," Jasper urges, somewhere between coaxing and commanding.

Trust. The man is standing in the open like a sacrificial *lamb*. I don't know our attackers. I can't trick them, or poison them, or talk my way out of this.

This is another chessboard entirely.

I glare at Lucky, tears stinging my eyes, and he turns his attention back to the trees, shame clenching his jaw under his tight beard. He doesn't move to help Beau.

"Invite you here?" Beau calls skeptically. "You must be mistaken, stranger. This is our home, and we're not too fond of outsiders these days. Consider this your official un-invitation."

A frigid silence bites through the sweltering heat.

Lucky curses, training his rifle in the direction of the strange voice —not that it will matter from here. We're too far away from Beau and Dom. He doesn't have an angle on these people.

Jasper releases my mouth, pulling me into a crouch.

"Get ready," he mutters.

Dom shakes his head, ashen and angry, still hunkered behind the oak Beau is standing on. He looks at Lucky for a long moment, then pulls the whistle from his pocket and brings it to his lips.

His golden eyes meet mine, bridging the distance.

"You need to learn some manners," the chilling voice replies to Beau.

Run, Dom mouths to me.

I roll up onto the balls of my feet, poised to move.

"Stop! *Stop*, you idiot fucking assholes!"

Dom blows the whistle.

It's shrieking, wild, and gunshots begin splattering the air like bursting balloons. I curl into Jasper, watching Beau as he twists, as he drops down beside Dom with a heavy thud and then pivots back around, leaning up over the oak to fire at the intruders.

Still hidden behind its cover, Dom stares at Beau hard, then swears and slams up beside him, joining the firefight. Bullets explode into their fallen tree cover, then past them, into the forest around us. One screeches past me and Jasper.

"Fuck!" Lucky swears, running forward.

A bullet flies past his head, and he swerves, then slides low over the loose leaves, skidding in until he lands on Beau's other side. He starts shooting, too.

Jasper starts pulling me in the opposite direction.

"Do you have shit for brains? Stop!"

A whistle starts screaming in short, earsplitting bursts, but it's that *voice* that makes me catch my breath.

"*It's Jayk*." I grip Jasper's kit, dragging back against his pull. "He wants us to stop."

Jasper stops trying to drag me away, sharply examining my face. He tilts his head, listening, and that rogue lock of midnight hair falls over his forehead.

"Are you sure it's—"

"Cock-sucking sons of bastard asshole mother*fuckers*! *Stop*!" the voice bellows.

Jasper sighs, then gives me a quick nod.

I look a question at the others, and he nods again, his grip loosening. He moves toward them, but I drag him low until we're both crawling through rotting leaves and moist mud.

"Ah! Fuck!" This voice is higher—Jennifer, maybe? "Fuck, *fuck*."

Beau pulls back, dropping back behind the oak, swearing. He catches sight of me and Jasper and hisses, "The hell are you doing?"

"It's Jayk! You need to stop!" I whisper-shout. Twigs scratch my arms as I crawl, and I'm encrusted in dirt and loose leaves.

Beau squints at me like he doesn't understand. Next to him, Dom's back flexes with each pounding shot.

"Doc? A little help?" Someone else nervously shouts from the same direction as Jennifer. Sara was with her. It must be Sara.

"Was that a *woman*?" a man's voice calls from somewhere else.

"There's a whole lotta woman out here, baby boy. Come say hello!"

Jasper makes a surprised sound in the back of his throat, and it takes me a second to place Ethel's creaky voice.

Jasper and I finally make it to the oak tree. Lucky pulls back, his face draining white when he sees us so close, but Dom continues to fire. There's an odd smell in the forest, like gunpowder and adrenaline.

Beau swears again and slings his rifle. He quickly checks his hollow med pack, then his eyes lift to mine. "I need to help Jen." He looks to Jasper next, his eyes reminding me of every deathly cold night I ever spent in these woods. "Get her somewhere safe. Now."

I grab his arm, burning with frustration. "Beau, *listen to me*. For once, please, you have to—"

"STOP!" Jayk shouts, and this time the accompanying whistle goes on and on and on until the gunshots start to fade and even Dom yanks his gun back over the oak and pulls back behind its cover.

The silence that follows is broken only by Jennifer's pained gasps. Beau hesitates, still crouched to take off after her.

"Reapers?" Jayk calls out, his voice like an anvil, and Beau's eyes sink closed in recognition.

Who are the Reapers?

There's a beat of silence, then, "Well, well, well. It's King himself. Finally decided to show the fuck up, huh?"

"Jayk?" Sloane's distant, incredulous voice soothes some of my worry. "*You* invited these asswipes?"

"They weren't supposed to come *here*!"

The drawling voice—a Reaper's?—breaks in. "If I'm going to make a deal with a man, then I'm makin' it to his face. Man to man, the way God himself intended."

I frown. A deal? Oh, God. What deal has Jayk made? And with *whom*?

Jasper matches my worried look, but Dom . . . Dom's jaw is set tight. He meets my eyes again and holds them.

But he stays silent.

My gaze narrows on him.

Jayk's voice takes on a snarl. "How did you even find us, Sawyer? You—"

"Are you in charge, King? Or is it fancy Mr. Southern over there? I don't want anyone wastin' my time. You better believe we're going to be askin' reparations for this whole mess," this Sawyer man shoots back.

My eyes stay locked with Dom's.

He shakes his head minutely, almost a warning, and it finally hits me. Why he's been so quiet, why he's let Beau take the lead this whole way home. He's not going back to his old self.

He doesn't think he can do this at all.

I shoot to my feet and glare at him as I insist, "Dom is captain."

Right as Jayk confidently says, "*I'm* in charge."

My eyes widen, and Beau wrenches me back down behind the oak. Did Jayk just say . . . ?

"Shoot! They *do* have women!" someone yells excitedly. "She was right!"

I frown.

"Well, which is it? King here or this Dom fellow?" Sawyer asks, when no one says anything.

Jasper is watching Dom, his eyes shadowy graves, as Lucky checks him over for holes. Beau's heart thunders against my back, but I don't look away from Dom. Tears burn my eyes, and I shake my head again as my heart hollows out.

Don't do it.

This time, Dom's eyes fall away first.

"Dom," I whisper.

He shakes his head and stands slowly, like it hurts him to move. But his voice is sure and resonant when he finally speaks.

"Jayk is in charge. Dom has officially stepped down."

CHAPTER 9

JAYKOB

SURVIVAL TIP #216
Diplomatic solutions don't involve bullets.

Fuck. Fucking motherfucking *fuck*.

"Did you forget to bring bullets?" Kasey whispers dubiously. "Wasn't that your whole job?"

I shoot her a glare as I pat around my toolbelt like I might have stashed a spare mag next to my wrench. Nothing. Of course there's nothing. I only have my rifle.

We were out checking the hydroelectrics, trying to work out if we can upgrade the thing, when Jada bolted out of the McMansion, shouting about seeing men approaching on the cameras. The forest blew up like the Fourth of July while everyone else was getting into position, but like the dumb asshole I am, I didn't have my shit with me.

I'm naked as a fucking newborn.

"Well, which is it? King here or this Dom fellow?" Sawyer calls, the same smug Reaper prick I radio-called two weeks ago.

How the hell did they find us? Captain Dickwad is going to blow a gasket.

Hovering beside Kasey, Jada gives me a nervous look. She's unarmed, too.

At least the shots have stopped.

Kasey throws a bee-sting punch into my shoulder. "Dude! Bringing bullets is like Soldier 101! We're going to die. I'm using you as a human shield."

I run a hand over my head, trying to think. "Un-bunch your panties. I'll talk to them." She winces, and I scowl. "I can talk!"

Kasey and Jada exchange a look, and Kasey adds delicately, "Are you sure that's a good idea? Remember last time?"

Last time.

Fucking *fuck*.

That radio call was a shit tornado.

I stand up. "They're talking, not shooting. They want something."

If they want something, maybe a deal is on the cards after all.

I just need Dom to stop acting like he knows everything for two seconds. A lot of shit has changed these last two weeks, and he has no clue what's going on. I need to break him into the new order. But doing that mid-combat? Getting the CO to stop acting like he's the only one who's ever had a single bright spark go off in his skull is never going to happen. I'm going to have to wrestle control out of Dom's cold, dead—

"Jayk is in charge." My head whips toward the captain's voice as it blasts through the forest. "Dom has officially stepped down."

I frown.

What kind of bullshit game is this?

I'm still staring when Kasey whacks my leg. "Is this you talking? Or did you forget how to do that, too?"

I flip her off and give Jada a hard look. "Get her back to Bristle-brook and lock her in a bathroom."

Kasey's eyes widen in outrage, but Jada is already dragging her backward. I whirl around and push out into the open. It's bullshit doing this without a kit. I have the mag I already loaded, but that's, what, thirty rounds, max?

Talking. Gotta talk. We need this. I can't afford to fuck this up again.

I stop between a bunch of narrow trees that won't stop a strong breeze, let alone a bullet.

At my two o'clock, a handful of arrows litter the trees. At least the civs are on the ball.

"Pack your heat away and show yourself, Sawyer." I rub my dusty, sweaty tank, wishing I remembered to shave. Or shower.

I leave my rifle over my shoulder as four men appear out of the forest, materializing from behind trees and bushes and a mound of displaced soil.

And I stop worrying about looking like a meathead.

All four of these assholes look like they just stepped out of Bumpkin Magazine. They're loaded up in more denim than a normal human should own, battered boots and T-shirts, and caps with stupid, cheesy slogans like "Part-time farmer, full-time charmer" and "No farms, no food, no future" and "I'm real good at f_ _ _ ing" next to a stalk of corn that belongs in a porno.

Every one of them has a shotgun slung over their shoulders and pistols at their hips, and it only takes a look to see *they* didn't forget their bullets.

But I relax anyway.

They might be standing like their dicks don't fit between their legs, puffing their chests like it doesn't just make them a bigger target, but their nerves are blood in the water. They're so bunched together that one spray on full auto would take them out.

My thirty rounds might be enough after all.

A dark-haired man with a proud handlebar mustache breaks from the flock. He knocks back his cowboy hat, then tucks his thumbs in his belt.

I fight the urge to remove his smirk with my fist.

"You the King?" he drawls, holding out his hand to shake.

The old name throws me hard, and it takes me a second to recognize the voice from the radio call.

I scowl at him. "The fuck are you doing here, Sawyer? I don't remember giving you a location."

Sawyer doesn't drop his hand, but his eyes harden under the brim of his hat. "You know, it's awful rude to ignore someone tryin' to introduce himself."

The men behind him shift casually, easing their shotguns over their shoulders and stroking pistol grips, and the little nicks and dents in the metal tell me they're not just for decoration. I still think I can get my rifle around before they get off more than a shot or two, but I don't reach for it.

It's bullshit that they showed up here, but hope has me starting to sweat bullets. The larder is coming up on empty, the hunting team hasn't caught shit worth writing home about in a week, and supply runs have turned up shit-all, and even though I keep slipping Kasey a chunk of my rations, she's so thin I could use her tibia as a toothpick.

The Reapers are sitting on a gold mine of agricultural land. It's the difference between life and death for us, if they'll play ball. I still have a scar from where they shot me the last time we tangled with them, though, so I'm not counting their chickens yet. These fuckers don't like to share.

And ain't that cute.

We have something in common.

I fight the urge to look for Eden and step into Sawyer's space, slapping my hand into his. He narrows his eyes on me, and I bare my teeth in a smile, squeezing his hand.

I can be diplomatic. As long as the buddy-buddy cock crew doesn't decide to actually watch my back for once and put one between the asshole's eyes, we can work this shit out.

Sawyer doesn't release my hand.

He squeezes harder.

I stop smiling. We're about the same height, and his calluses and functional muscles say he hauls ass doing real work rather than pounding it out at the gym, but he has to be able to see I could crush him.

He grins lazily again, and I clench my fist around his until he grunts.

If he won't cooperate, that's fine.

I'll *make* them play ball.

Sunlight is starting to die, but the air thickens around us, dense and wet and hot with challenge. A fat bead of sweat rolls down his forehead, pooling in one bushy brow. It springs up under my arms. Down my back.

His palm is compressed white around mine, and the vice grip bites brutally into my skin. Veins throb in my forearm as I hold him steady, and the fucker still *doesn't let go*.

Try me, his face says.

Arrogant. Dick.

Like I haven't handled every two-bit bully and smug, privileged asshole I ever came across. Like I can't see when someone thinks they're better than me.

If I back down now, we're not getting shit from them. We need a deal, but if they think they own us, that they're *stronger* than us, then we might as well bend over, 'cause we're getting fucked without lube.

Sawyer steps into me to get more leverage and I clench my teeth, pushing him back.

There's a muttered "*cavemen*" behind me, and a sigh I've heard in too many sessions from another smug, privileged asshole.

Jasper could never get it. He's always got everything he ever asked for. He doesn't know how fast it can all slip away.

He doesn't know how to fight with his teeth.

The trees rustle, and then Sawyer's hand is dropping from mine to his holster, his eyes training on whoever's stalking over to us. I smirk, linking my hands behind my head.

Pussy.

Dom falls in beside me in his full battle rattle, and I don't bother acknowledging him. If he was going to piss on my parade, he'd have done it already.

"Unless you want to waste time looking for a hand job next, maybe you can answer the question: the fuck are you doing here, Sawyer?" I ask. Diplomatically.

Farmboy stares hard at me for a long moment, then sniffs and shrugs, lazily scanning the tree line. "You want to make a deal, don't you?"

Before he can answer, somewhere to my ten o'clock, a woman makes a high, pained sound, then snaps, "Fuck, Doc. Gentle!"

I stiffen as Sawyer's curious gaze lingers on that patch of green, and the urge to punch him returns. I don't want him curious about her, or Eden, or any of our people here.

He absently rubs the hand I crushed into bone dust.

"You hung up on me," I grit out, loud enough to swamp the sounds.

The memory burns. I barely got out my offer before he shut down the radio call.

"Eh, I prefer to do things the old-fashioned way, don't I, Cole?" He waves a hand at the pretty boy wearing the "No farms, no food, no future" cap and a cocky-ass grin.

This Cole guy nods agreeably, his eyes bright with humor. "Sure do. Gentleman-like."

Gentleman-like. Yeah. My fucking specialty.

"More old-fashioned than a HAM radio?" I mutter. "Did you bring the food at least?"

If they've brought some stock with them, maybe we can make a deal right here right now. It brings me right back to the same problem I had two weeks ago, though—I have no goddamned clue what to offer in exchange.

Fuck. *Fuck, fuck, fuck*.

Something tells me they ain't here for the posh prince's art collection.

Sawyer gives me a tense look. "Does it look like I brought—"

Beau bursts through the trees, and the men behind Sawyer snap into action, slamming their guns up toward him. Jennifer is in his arms, bridal-style, her pants torn around her bloody, bandaged left calf. Her face is white with pain, and my brows crash down.

In my peripherals, I see Eden shoot to her feet. She yanks Jasper's 9-millimeter from his waist and levels it on the Reapers, set and cold and *furious*. Her hands shake a little.

She's remembered to switch the safety off this time, though.

My pulse trips over itself at the sight of her. She's back. She's safe.

Sure, she's also a filthy, murderous mess, but fuck if it doesn't make me want to pick a fight with her first.

Miss Manners ain't playing nice today.

"Eden," Jasper hisses, like she isn't mostly protected behind the oak Beau was swinging his dick on earlier. I debate shooting him just to stop him drawing attention to her.

Lucky keeps his trap shut for once and covers her exposed side.

I dart a look at the Reapers to see if they've clocked her, but they're still focused on the doc and Jennifer.

Idiots. *They* aren't armed.

Eden is the threat.

Sara cuts out of the trees behind Beau, circling wide, her gun drawn, and her movements smooth and confident. While the Reapers snap around to track her, Katherine leans around a tree behind them, her rifle trained on their backs.

Jo skids in to crouch a short distance away, and Ida and Ethel close in with their bows drawn a moment later.

It's too much movement, too much danger all at once, and everyone's too armed. This is how shit goes south fast—I don't know what the fuck Beau was thinking, jumping out like that.

I ready to swing my rifle around, waiting for these assholes to explode, to *react*.

And they do.

. . . Like idiots.

All four of them drop their weapons, their eyes widening like they're staring down a unicorn's asshole and not a bouquet of Berettas.

The sweaty, bearded one with the "full-time charmer" cap pulls it off his head. It crumples between his hands.

"Well, I'll be," he breathes, his eyes shining.

The porn-corn hat guy turns to stare at Katherine, then he slaps his friend's shoulder. "Oh my word. Look, Buck, there's another one. They're everywhere!"

"I see her, Pete!" Something close to awe dawns on Buck's face, and he wrings his "full-time charmer" cap. "They're all so pretty. I never thought they'd be so pretty."

Eden gives him a sharp look.

Their weapons are on the ground; they're not even trying to defend themselves.

I look around at the civilians—lethal, armed to the teeth—and down at myself, who they were ready to beat to a pulp. I don't get it.

Even Sawyer's punchable smirk has been traded for puppy eyes. They fix on Jennifer's pain-drenched face as Beau storms toward the group.

"Oh, shoot. Miss Ma'am, are you okay?" Sawyer asks anxiously.

The pretty one, Cole, darts a look at his friends, then snatches his cap off too. His hair is in the kind of mess that chicks always lose brain cells over, and he runs his fingers through it. For some stupid reason, he throws Sara some shy smile, like she's not about to light up his brain matter like a busted lava lamp.

Even stupider, her rifle dips away from him. Like it *worked*.

Everyone's losing their damn minds.

"No, she's not okay," Beau snaps as he approaches. He looks over my shoulder at Dom. "I need to get her back to Bristlebrook. I'm in the red on supplies. I can't do shit out here."

My mood instantly fouls as he ignores me. Not like it's any surprise he's not taking my lead. He was always going to side with his bunker buddy.

Beau used to send anyone who questioned the captain's authority off for a prostate exam with the ice-fingered old dinosaur on base, Doctor Grimblefode—he was invasive, had the grip of a car compactor, and the twisted technique of a torque wrench.

I shudder.

Fucking Beau.

Fucking Grimblefode.

That old asshole might have had his hands on my jewels too many fucking times, but he isn't here now, thank fuck . . . and Dom isn't taking over this time.

He looks at me.

"What do you want to do?" He meets my eye, the same way he did when I rolled on up to the regiment, and adds, "*King*?"

I glare at him under the ridge of my brows—more out of habit because he says my name with none of the old mockery the shitbags used to fire it off with.

He's . . . calm.

What the hell is his game here? Since when does he take a back seat?

"This is ridiculous. You know that, right? He can't just take your job," Beau mutters to Dom. He adjusts Jennifer impatiently, and her injured leg jostles. She lets out a yelp, then a string of curses so foul even our old squad would have flinched.

Blood pools under the bandage, and I scowl at him. "Go fucking fix her. What are you wasting air looking at him for?"

Beau rolls his eyes, but I'm already turning to Sawyer. "You're coming with us—keep your shit holstered and hands where we can see them."

It doesn't matter what Dom's doing. If I have to jockey dicks with Beau, Jasper, and all the Reapers, then I will. If I have to do the touchy-feely bullshit, then I will. I *can* be patient.

Eden needs food.

Everyone here needs food.

I turn toward Bristlebrook, but Beau doesn't move. "You really sure you want to bring the trigger-happy armed strangers home for tea? Around Kasey? Around *Eden*?"

Blood leaks down Jennifer's leg, and Beau's *still* looking at Dom like he wants to push him to step in. I pull out Ryan's pocketknife and run it between my fingers.

I'm still patient.

But I'm not the only one the doc is pissing off.

Sawyer's frown vanishes in a furious *poof*. "We don't hurt women."

No one says anything, but Jennifer's pained breathing fills the forest.

Sawyer rubs the back of his neck. "Well . . . except for that one time." He clears his throat and adds, "We're real sorry, ma'am."

Bearded Buck swipes at his wet forehead, muttering, "Why're all the ladies out here where they can get shot at, anyway?"

There's a loud snap as Jo replaces the magazine on her rifle.

These assholes are going to get *themselves* shot, and we'll never get our food.

A hot wind blasts through the trees, snagging and swirling leaves across the earth. New, sweltering sweat breaks out along my scalp.

I can do it. I can be patient.

So. Fucking. Patient.

"The fuck does it matter if they come back with us?" I ask Beau impatiently. "It's not like they haven't crawled up our asshole already." I flick my knife and roll my eyes. "Besides, if they can't even avoid a simple tripwire, then they're too stupid to be a problem for us."

Sawyer rounds on me, his mustache twitching. "Did your mama drop you on your head? You come beggin' to us and you still want to measure dicks?"

He's in my space again, breathing *my* air, and I'm done.

Patience is overrated.

I shove him back. "What did you say about my mama?"

He blocks me hard, a snarl on his lips, getting up in my face. "You have any clue how much good we could do for you, you little shit? You think I don't remember how you came onto our land and stole from us? You're scavengers. Poor, pathetic—"

Broke. Trash. Jaykob King, trailer park royalty.

I'm raising my fist to knock his lights out when a sudden, brutal *bang* blisters the air, and the dirt explodes at my feet. I throw myself back, and Sawyer trips me up as he does the same. Clods of dirt and burst leaves spray us in a damp confetti as we hit the ground, rolling.

"Oh my God! Jayk?" Eden's panicked voice filters in. "Jayk? Are you okay? Oh *crap*!"

"The hell was that?" Cole shouts. "Sawyer? You good?"

I shake my head, and dirt sprinkles down. Sawyer grunts, lying next to me.

"Eden, give me the gun."

"Holy shit, she actually shot Jayk. Nice."

"I'm *sorry*!"

I'm pulling myself to my feet, swiping up my dropped pocketknife, when delicate hands start tugging under my elbow. "Jayk, I'm *so* sorry! He was in your face, and I panicked—I *swear* I didn't mean to pull the trigger."

Eden's face comes into focus, white to her lips and all big, frightened eyes. She smells like lavender.

"You just shot me," I say, dazed.

Misery fills her face, and I snort incredulously.

"Sugar, if you want to make me bleed, at least take my clothes off first."

Her lips tremble, and I wrap my hand around the back of her neck and yank her in for a fierce, hard kiss. It breaks under me, and I only get a second of the hot, wet slide of her mouth before I hear someone give a low whistle.

I pull back to glare at Sawyer. But it's the pretty one, Cole, who ignores me to check out Eden.

"How you doin', pretty lady?" he asks gently as he helps Sawyer up. "You don't need to worry about us, but try to lay off the trigger, yeah?"

His little smile looks like a rat's butthole, and my grip tightens on Eden's neck as I remember how Sara lost her damn mind over him. But she just leans into me, and when I look down at her, she's biting the corner of her lower lip and watching me, not fancy-face.

Just me.

I love you, Jayk, with all my heart and never only a part of it.

Heat creeps into my cheeks, her letter hanging between us. Damn it. This wasn't how this was supposed to go.

I had a whole speech.

And she wasn't supposed to shoot me.

A callused, dirt-lined palm thrusts between us, breaking our quiet conversation.

"Earnest Sawyer, ma'am. I am mighty pleased to meet you." The man's handlebar moustache twitches over his sudden grin, his eyes bright with interest as he looks at Eden, and my teeth grind together. "I am so sorry to come barging in like this. We have some Ts and Is to be going over with your menfolk here. Some negotiations that need negotiatin'. You understand. I can promise you we didn't come here looking for trouble." He plucks off his cowboy hat and presses it to his chest. *Earnestly.* "We come from a gentler kind of place. Why, all this mess just took us off guard."

Yeah. He's a regular lady's maid.

"Um, Eden. Charmed," she replies uncertainly, placing her hand in his for a brief shake. "I'm also, uh, very sorry about the, um . . ."

She falters, waving her hand awkwardly at the rent earth and bullet holes.

My brows slam down. "The fuck you are." I yank her back and scowl at Sawyer. "Touch her again and you'll go home wearing your intestines as a necklace."

Eden lays a delicate hand on my arm. "Jayk, I'm sure our *guests* could use some refreshments?"

Right.

Diplomacy and shit.

She clears her throat. "And maybe Jennifer . . ."

Jennifer's leg is still bleeding, and the doc looks ready to take my head off. Guilt stabs me, and I roll my shoulders to shake it off.

"Yeah. Fine." I glance Sawyer's way and mutter, "Come with. We'll get you some . . ."

Ah, shit.

Do we even have anything? Water? Booze?

Cole exchanges a bemused smirk with Sawyer, and my ears burn.

Eden comes to the rescue. "Tea. We'll make some tea."

She squeezes my arm, her fingers cool and firm. Soothing. My blood pressure starts to go down at the contact, and I shrug. "Yeah. Tea. Love tea."

Beau just gives me one more frustrated look, then strides toward Bristlebrook. Dom follows without a word, but he's got that tight, disappointed look he gets whenever I start shit. I scowl, hating that I feel it in my gut.

How did I forget about the talking part so damn fast? I've been managing all of this just fine the last two weeks.

It's everyone else who sucks.

Sawyer's grin turns into a lazy smirk at me, but he inclines his head to Eden in sweet acknowledgement. Then he and the Reapers turn to follow Beau.

Jasper and Lucky lower their weapons, and Ida, Ethel, and all the others begin to fall in for the walk home. I watch them clear out and nerves start chewing at my insides. Maybe I'm in over my head with this King shit. Maybe they were right to leave me in the tool shed. Kasey said it just now—I blow up every conversation I have.

How the fuck am I going to negotiate anything?

CHAPTER 10

EDEN

SURVIVAL TIP #80
People are like teacups.
They break easily.

Bristlebrook looks fearsome.

The red-gold sunset burns over the cliffs and lights up the slow-healing apple tree in a fairy-tale glow, but the civilians are primed for reality, armed and on alert. They're settled behind reinforced metal walls built up on towering wooden platforms, their rifles peeking through careful openings. Bows and guns in hand, they peer watchfully out of tattered and shattered second-story windows. All of them in position, ready and tightly coordinated.

There's an enormous platform built up beside the apple tree, and as the fading sunset shifts, the huge hunk of scrap metal atop it begins to shine with blinding light.

The dry moat that was half finished when we left is now complete, and a barbed wire fence curls around the inner rim like wicked briars protecting a den of deadly sleeping beauties. Hundreds of lethally sharpened pikes at the moat's base dare us to approach. It's too wide to jump. Too densely packed to try to traverse.

The burned-out husk of the barn has been cleared away, and there are rows and rows of freshly turned earth where my garden has expanded fourfold, all carefully protected.

Jayk has been busy since we left.

He signals to the civilians, and it takes eight women to lift a heavy wooden bridge and maneuver it into place over the center of the moat. Two more bridges lie stacked nearby, untouched, though there are two other openings in the barbed wire where they could be placed.

We cross it carefully, silently, but mutters spring up like susurrant leaves as the civilians assess the Reapers. As they assess *us*.

"Who are the cowboys?"

"Did they set off the tripwire?"

"Weren't they supposed to bring back more people?"

"Remember Cassie? Do you think the Sinners still have her?"

"Forget the Sinners—where is the *food*?"

"Where's Madison?"

My steps get heavier with each question, but that name cuts into me with dagger sharpness.

We failed her. We left her behind.

I betrayed her.

Swallowing down the shame that won't help me right now, I flick my eyes over the huddled Reapers as they creep over the singed grass in front of the looming mansion. They're tense, some of their posturing falling away as they take in the fortifications and the distrustful, gaunt faces staring back at them.

Their mutters reach me too.

"What on God's green happened here?"

"Explosives? Look at the windows."

"Look at the pikes! They could skewer a man right through!"

I'm not sure what to make of these strangers.

I'm not sure why just four men would walk into potential enemy territory and still have the confidence to pick a fight with their leader. I'm not sure how to feel about the naked longing in their eyes when they looked at me or the other women.

But apart from the obvious discomfort, there was something in their expressions that reminds me of the breathless, immediate kinship I felt when I first saw Akira and Heather. That sense of something precious not having been lost after all.

There's a danger in that rarity . . . but perhaps an opportunity as well?

They could have fired on me for that stupid, silly mistake with the gun. In that situation, it would have been understandable. Defensive, even. Sam would have beaten me to a pulp.

But they didn't.

They smiled and rushed to reassure me and all but patted me on my little head like I was a stray puppy. It's infantilizing, but I don't think they want to make me into a skin suit, at least. Or lock me in a dungeon and beat me into compliance.

So in apocalyptic terms, they seem quite lovely.

But can they be true allies? Are they like Beau, sweetly chivalrous and just a little rough around the edges, or will their fascination with me and the others sour if we don't play nice? Do they want to get to know the women here as people and potential partners . . . or do they want possessions?

I look around at the chilly, determined faces of the gathered women—women like me, who have kept themselves alive for years.

They don't belong to anyone.

"You sure you want to do this out here?" Dom asks Jayk in a low voice. "Might be better not to do this in front of the civs."

Dozens of cold faces stare at us from every angle, but Jayk shakes his head. "They're part of this. I'm not hiding shit from them. They deserve to know what's going on."

Dom gives Jayk a thoughtful, sideways look, then nods once.

Deanna rushes out of the wide, taped-up sliding doors and runs up to Beau. The primary care physician is lovely, with braided gray-peppered hair and a deep brown face that creases with concern as she examines Jennifer, who is white to her lips. Beau mutters something to Deanna, and they both hurry up the stairs into the house.

Sawyer runs a fretful hand over his moustache, watching them go. "She is going to be all right, isn't she?"

Jayk's snort beside him is derisive. "The fuck do you care? You shoot someone, you're going to fuck them up."

The big-eared man with the mildly pornographic corn hat throws him a defensive look. "You blew us up first!"

"Tripwire." Jayk flicks his knife, shrugging. "You blew yourself up."

He breaks away from the Reapers, and rather than head inside, he walks toward a low stage beside the apple tree. As he climbs the steps, the light shifts again, and I realize this stage and the large shining object atop it aren't part of their defenses.

I stare, dumbfounded, and the others pause beside me.

"No fucking way." Lucky barely keeps his voice down in his excitement, and his anxious cheeks have rediscovered how to dimple. He laughs, tugging my shirt. "Is that really—"

"A *throne*?" Jasper says from my other side, sounding utterly aghast.

It . . . *is* a throne.

Built from welded scrap metal and old tin cans, it's deep and wide and shockingly imposing. The bright silvers catch the sunlight and the dusky ripples of old metal make a rippling patchwork of shadows. It's rough—and surprisingly beautiful.

Jayk turns at the top of the stage, looking down over everyone, the apple tree looming behind him.

Then he sits on the throne.

Lucky steps forward, entranced. "I want one."

Jasper grimaces. "I'm scheduling him another session."

On Jasper's other side, Dom shakes his head and follows Jayk up. He stands behind the throne at Jaykob's right shoulder, crossing his arms. The two of them are striking. Lit from behind and almost terrifying in this brutal, fortified field, they look like old warriors fresh from a reaving. Tried and hardened and ready for violence.

The small hairs along my arms tingle awake.

The Reapers stare up at them, their teasing smiles gone. This isn't a subtle power play, a dance of words like my waltz with Alastair. This is a blunt, shameless warning from a king.

I hesitate, not sure how I fit into this picture.

Lucky doesn't have the same problem. He drags me forward until we're climbing the stage's steps too, and he takes Jayk's other side. I move to stand next to him, but someone grabs the back of my shirt and yanks.

"Ah!"

My legs drop out from under me as I flop gracelessly backward, my butt landing heavily in Jayk's lap.

Oh, son of a . . .

I clutch at his tank, trying to right myself, and he just throws a possessive arm around me, not bothering to help. So, I don't bother to stop my elbows from finding his stomach as I drag myself into a sensible position.

I catch Dom's golden eyes over the edge of the throne, and he gives me a brief, searching look before his gaze cuts away to scan the crowd.

Jayk lifts his free hand, halting Jasper as he climbs the steps. "Don't bother. Go make us all some tea."

Jasper's head tilts, and shadows pool along the sharp angles of his face. "I beg your pardon?"

"Tea. For our guests. Go make some." The smirk on Jayk's face is insufferable, and I hate that even a part of me finds it delicious.

I try to slip off his lap so I can help Jasper, but his hold on me tightens, his hand gripping my thigh.

My body springs to life. The hold, his wild, windswept scent, the raw closeness of him: it's all more than I'd been prepared for. I'd braced myself for the worst. Arguably, walking into a firefight instead of a welcome party *is* the worst. But in another way entirely, Jayk holding me to him like he never wants to let me go . . . well, it's not the worst. Not even close.

Jasper doesn't appear to agree.

His lips are a violent slash, and he doesn't move for a long, pointed moment. Then he pivots and walks to the lodge, but the final look he gives Jaykob promises ice-cold blades and unholy retribution.

"You're in trouble," Lucky sing-songs under his breath.

Jayk relaxes back in the throne, spreading his legs wide. I'm left dandling on his knee while he feels me up like a medieval bar wench, and I try not to mirror Jasper's glare at him.

"You said you wanted to deal, Sawyer, so spit it out. What do you want?" he drawls.

Sawyer stares up at him, grim now. He looks to Cole, the one with the devilish smile, who shrugs one shoulder.

Sawyer runs a hand over his head. "How do you like living out here?"

That distracts me from Jayk.

That question is as locked and loaded as Lucky's bazooka.

Jayk rolls his eyes, but his thigh becomes steel under me. "It's home sweet home."

"Yeah?" Sawyer hooks his thumbs into his belt loops as he frowns at the fortifications. "How homey is it gonna be come winter? You got the stores to feed—" He shoots a questioning look at Cole, who tears his eyes from the house. "Seventy? At least seventy."

Ninety-two, actually—or eighty-nine now, without Akira, Aaron, and Heather.

Sawyer nods. "You got the stores to feed seventy through winter?"

The whispers around us pick up speed, like a rush of startled beetle wings. Jayk scowls, and I settle against him, leaning into his chest. If he's the king on this chessboard then that's fine. I can play this game.

I know what the queen's role is.

Dom and Lucky, and all the women watching here will make sure no one shoots him. There are other ways I can protect Jayk.

I can watch.

Between their caps and clothes and their on-the-nose name, I can assume these people are from the farmlands south of Cyanide. They're full-faced and strong—healthy the way my brutes were when I met them. They have food.

If they're asking questions like this, it's because they want something in exchange.

It takes a beat too long for Jayk to respond.

"We'll be fine for winter. We've got options." When Sawyer snorts, Jayk bends around me to sneer. "We'll take it if we need to."

Cole's hand finds his shotgun as Sawyer's eyes turn to glaciers.

There's an answering click of dozens of guns being refocused, and the air turns brittle.

The cracked, taped-up doors to the sitting room squeak open.

Jasper backs through it with a large gilt-edged porcelain tray. A large, gorgeous teapot sits atop it, alongside a precarious stack of teacups and saucers, and he turns with excruciating care.

The cups rattle as he glides over the lawn, stiff-backed and unheeding of the armed airspace around him. Ninety-odd pairs of eyes watch him as he approaches the throne. His upper lip is curled in dark displeasure, and he doesn't need to say a word—he's seething, and it writhes out of every motion.

He places the tray down with the gentlest care and begins unpacking each cup and saucer.

One.

Then another.

Then another.

Cole's hand leaves his weapon, and civilians shift awkwardly as they wait.

When Jasper unloads the fifth cup, less than halfway there, Lucky steps forward, only to be pinned by dart-like dark eyes.

"Stay, Lucien. Our *King* has given me a task," he says silkily.

There are torture chambers and echoing, cobwebbed dungeons in his voice, and I shiver. The corner of Jayk's mouth lifts further at the silent challenge in it.

Another cup, then another, and then he pours the steaming liquid. The scent of peppermint is sharp and cool, and Jasper makes us wait, taking deliberate care in measuring each tiny cup.

He delivers them to the Reapers, who take the cups and saucers awkwardly where they stand. The bearded one has to shove his pistol back in its holster to hold his set.

Jasper then hands the next cup off to Lucky, who brushes his fingertips over Jasper's as he takes it, then one goes to Dom, who reluctantly uncurls himself from his bouncer stance to accept. He hands a cup to me, and I apologize with my eyes, praying I don't get caught in his ire alongside Jayk.

Then he presents a cup and saucer to Jayk.

Jayk stares at it, then lifts his gaze to Jasper. Everything in his expression tells me he's enjoying this far too much.

"Nah, you keep it. I've got my hands full." He punctuates the drawl by clapping his hand to my ass and squeezing.

The tea in my hand sloshes, and I almost decide to dump it on his head.

In the last two weeks, I've been dwelling on every moment between us—him rubbing arnica into my bruises after our first night, his gruff kindness, his vulnerability when he spoke about his mother.

How on earth did I forget he's an absolute, infuriating *jerk*?

Jasper's eyes linger on Jaykob's hand, then scan my face. He raises one chill brow at me, and I feel myself turn scarlet.

Is he embarrassed for me or himself? *I'm* embarrassed for me. Should I be defending Jasper here? That would be gallant, I suppose. Lucky is watching the exchange like he wants to grab popcorn, but I should say something when one of them is being an ass, shouldn't I?

What *is* the etiquette when your boyfriends are fighting?

I peek at the Reapers, at how Sawyer is watching every moment.

We do seem to have bigger concerns right now.

"Don't insult our guests, Jaykob," Jasper murmurs. The patience in his quiet voice is violent. "You might have the emotional bandwidth of a testosterone-drunk orangutan but *try* to string together enough brain cells to realize we don't need another war right now. Drink the tea. And do let me know if they use words over two syllables so I might explain them to you."

I sip my tea to hide my wince.

On second thought, they're big boys. They can handle themselves.

Jayk takes the saucer in his free hand, trying not to spill the fragile cup. I peek at him. His renewed scowl and the glowing tops of his ears have me fighting a sigh. They all know each other too well.

They go for the throat.

Jasper settles by my feet with a curt, ironic glance my way, and Jayk finally rests the saucer on the thick arm of the throne. It sits at a slight angle over an uneven bump, so he clings to the miniscule handle. It's small enough that even I can't fit my fingers through, but it looks ridiculous in Jayk's large hand. He has to pinch the delicate floral curve between two filthy, callused fingers.

The Reapers aren't faring any better. Pete is holding the saucer in one hand, looking around again at the women, and every time he takes a sip, he sticks his little finger high in the air.

"What were we saying again?" Jayk snaps irritably.

Sawyer lowers his teacup, and the ends of his mustache are damp. "You were saying how you were going to attack us and steal our stores?"

Jayk just nods. "Yeah. That."

"We've got eyes, King. You've mostly got women here. Not exactly a huge risk," Sawyer drawls.

There's another round of mechanical clicks, and Buck startles, dropping his saucer. He picks it up slowly, looking around with wide eyes.

"We have weapons. Training. You think this shit happens by accident?" Jayk growls, gesturing with the tiny cup. Molten peppermint tidal waves over the rim. "And my girl nearly blew your lights out thirty minutes ago. She can do it again, asshole."

Cringing, I sip my tea again.

Ah yes.

A masterstroke of training, that.

This time, Cole pipes up. "You'd put her at risk?"

He looks me over, and I can't help but notice how thick his lashes are. Not as thick as Jasper's obviously. He's also got that slow charm in the way he moves that reminds me of Beau—not that it looks nearly as good on him, of course.

He is kind of gorgeous, though.

Cole brushes his thumb over his teacup, and he smiles. Just a little. "Now, I can't imagine putting any one of these incredible women in danger to wage a pointless war on us." He shakes his head and adds, as if to himself, "No, sir, not me."

Jayk's grip is *crushing*. "Why the fuck are you people here? You have food. We want it. Give it to us, or I'll just kill you right here."

"*Orangutan*," Jasper mutters, and I throw him a reproachful look.

Sawyer just shakes his head. "Don't recommend. Starvation's an awful way to go. We die? You get a boatload of nothing. I have a better offer." Before Jayk can respond, he looks around at all the civilians muttering behind their weapons. "Come back with us. We have enough lodgings for all y'all. *Beds*. And more food than you could eat. You don't need to stay here. None of you need to starve."

All the mutters fall silent. The breeze has died too, as if holding its breath, and I hear every tremble of my cup against the saucer.

Back with them? These *strangers*?

Too many competing thoughts crash through my mind. Too many *memories*. My brutes catching me at my most desperate, offering me safety.

The Sinners, catching me in the dark and stealing me away.

"You want us to come back with you? One big happy family?" Jayk sneers . . . but I hear the hint of uncertainty in it.

I press into him further, feeling uncomfortably hot.

"Perhaps," Jasper muses. When I look down at him, he's staring into his teacup like he can tell our future in it. "Or perhaps they only want some of us."

Sloane scoffs from her seat on the porch. The butt of her rifle rests on her thigh, and Mary Beth sits beside her.

"Not fucking likely," she calls, and there's an instant, thunderous rattle of guns on wood.

The women stand, whistling approval. Graying Patrick stands beside his wife in cold support, and Valerie's kindly face is forbidding as she pounds the butt of her rifle against the slab she'd been huddled behind.

Lucky adds a piercing wolf whistle that makes my eardrums bleed but sends a swell of laughter through the fury.

Jayk smirks as Sawyer's shoulders drop. "I might not be the sharpest tool, but that sounds like a no."

Cole touches Sawyer's arm, and Sawyer shrugs him off. The other two, Pete and Buck, look almost . . . worried.

I frown.

Cole runs his fingers through his hair again, tossing it into further bedroom messiness as he looks up at us. "This ain't about that. We could use you, *all* of you—we have land that needs to be maintained. Crops that need planting and harvesting. Livestock needing tending. Extra bodies would help, and we'd feed y'all in exchange. This is a win-win."

I suppose that . . . makes sense. It's not like we couldn't use the food, and extra help and hands wouldn't go astray when Alastair eventually comes making demands. Maybe we could consolidate enough to help Red Zone, too.

So why does something about this itch at me?

I glance back at Dom to gauge his reaction, but he's granite. A silent guard, his arms crossed over his thick chest, the teacup and saucer placed beside his feet.

He can't be this removed. This is his home.

"How many women do you have back in your territory?" Jasper asks calmly, and I swivel back around.

Cole shakes his head, and Sawyer blows a frustrated breath, "That doesn't matter, we—"

"How many? Versus how many men?" It's a whipcrack, carelessly cruel. Jasper sips his tea again.

"Twelve," Cole mutters. "To a . . . few more men. But that don't mean a single thing, all right? Don't you go making this about something it ain't. We just need *people*."

Again, that nervous tension.

"For the farmwork." I repeat his earlier words, and Jayk's hand tightens on me.

He looks at me from under those pretty lashes, then his gaze skitters away. "I . . ."

My attention sharpens. Hm.

From the sounds around me, I'm not the only one who disliked the non-answer.

"It's not fucking happening," Jayk snaps. "We don't barter women."

Lucky leans against the side of the throne, spinning his teacup on his saucer. "Yeah, that is *so* 1740 of you."

Bearded Buck gives him an alarmed look, then stares, panicked, over at Katherine. Sweat is *flowing* over his receding hairline.

She absently scratches her cheek with her middle finger.

"No!" He insists. "We're not trying to—"

Sneering, Jayk cuts him off. "You haven't stopped eye-fucking everything that breathes since you got here."

"Well, can you blame us?" Pete mutters, looking at me bashfully, and Sawyer smacks the back of his head.

Cole steps up, raising soothing hands.

"Okay, yes. So it's been a while, and these ladies are pretty as a picture, no getting around that. You'd need to strike me dumb and dead not to notice." His smile is staggering, but Jayk's thunderous glare quickly makes it vanish. He clears his throat. "Noticing doesn't make us bad people. We don't hurt women. We want to help."

He seems earnest—determined, even—but there's something else. This is too good to be true. It has to be.

It almost always is.

Maybe I'm too burned. Maybe this is a valid offer. I've never been a trusting person. Good men do exist, and my brutes are proof of that. I just can't shake the feeling that these men are hiding something.

We might be in a terrible position—starving and at the Sinners' mercy—but by now I know that things can always get worse. I'm not trading one monster for another. Not again.

Jasper meets my eyes, and I sense the same pensive caution in him.

Jayk is . . . less cautious. He dumps his teacup on the tilted saucer, and I rescue it at the last moment as he leans back, staring at Cole with heavy scorn.

"No."

Cole's back stiffens, and I see the first flare of real anger from him as he bursts out, "You're starving!" He points at the women up in the music room. "*They're* starving! Are you really willing to let them die because you're worried that we'll flirt with them?"

The air is sticky and uncomfortable, but ice washes through my veins. Around me, I feel Jayk's chest rumble, his powerful muscles charged and furious on our behalf—but I don't need him to fight this battle for me.

"*You're* starving." I don't mean to say it, but once the words are out, they linger on the breeze like a snap of snowfall.

Cole falls silent, a hint of confusion passing over his features. Pete shifts behind him, and I look at each Reaper in turn, strangely composed, even as my chest roils with a chilly discomfort and my wrists burn with remembered ropes.

"Do you think we can't see it?" I ask, not bothering to soften my voice. I list off every red flag I've been collecting like I'm preparing for a bull run. "You've hardly been around women for years. You want to drag us back to your home within minutes of meeting. You talk over and around us like we're children—*stupid ones!*—that need to be kept and coddled . . . and you think we're concerned about *flirting*?"

Buck ducks his head, and Cole pales, flinching at my tone.

"Do you think we don't know what happens if we're caught alone with ravenous animals?" I ask, and finally Sawyer meets my eyes.

He's grave. Expectant. The grim line of his mouth says he already knows he won't like my answer.

"We get torn *apart*."

His eyes close, as if in pain, but I shake my head and add quietly, "If you don't understand that fear, if you can't *respect* it, then you don't deserve to be anywhere near us."

Jayk takes the teacup rattling violently in my grip. His heart pounds against my back, a booming, constant drum.

Then I realize that's not the only drumming.

The civilians are rattling their weapons again, in wordless, vehement agreement. My throat thickens as I take in the solemn, unhappy faces.

My first meeting with Dom, Beau, and Lucky plays in my mind, the similarities setting me on edge. I remember my exhaustion and hunger and bleeding feet. I remember how intoxicating the idea of sanctuary was, of food and protection.

I was lucky.

If they had been a different breed of men, if they weren't so concerned with my boundaries and my comfort, and if they hadn't listened to me when it was all too much, that situation could so easily have ended atrociously for me.

All of us have grown so much since that stupid deal, and I can't regret it, not after what it brought me . . . but I've learned that lesson already.

It's not okay for men to leverage our desperation to fix their own problems. We deserve better. We *are* better.

I swallow hard right as the sitting room doors squeak open again.

Beau walks through, and he's as lovely as he was on that first day. With his square jaw and that soft hair, he looks like a storybook prince. His compassion tempers his stubborn edges, and there's something cozy with romance in the way his eyes find me first in every room—even if lately they're quick to skip away.

Beau is the one who first made me believe I could have a happy ending here.

My heart throbs like a bruise as he makes his way over. He's doubting that now, I know he is. So maybe I'll just have to take my turn in convincing him . . . because I'm not ready to let him go.

Everyone watches him anxiously as he stops on the stage's steps.

"Is the girl okay?" Sawyer asks, his gaze switching between Beau and the door like he wants to see for himself.

Beau doesn't look at him—or Dom either, this time. He frowns at Jayk for a long minute, taking him in . . . and me, on his lap. Resentment burns lines between his brows.

Finally, he looks away from Jayk and says pointedly to everyone *but* him, "Jen will be fine. She needed a few stitches, but as long as she stays off her feet for a few weeks, there won't be any lasting damage."

The tension in the Reaper's shoulders deflates. Buck gives Pete a relieved grin, and I swear I see Pete blink back tears.

"Nice work," Jayk says gruffly, and a strange warmth steals over me. Not the sticky, uncomfortable heat of the day, but something that spreads from the inside out.

There's no mockery or sarcasm in Jayk's voice—it's the same way he spoke to me when I helped him in his barn. He's not flowery, but he's quick to acknowledge people's efforts. He shows gratitude without making a fuss. I'd wondered if he was just that way with me . . . but I should have known better. It's just who he is. There's a reason he's earned the civilian's loyalty.

Beau's brows lift, and he gives Jayk a strange, searching look. He tenses a little, like he's shrugging it off, then moves to stand beside Dom.

Everything settles inside me.

I have all my brutes gathered around me now.

"I'm sorry," Cole says quietly a moment later, and he's looking at me. When we stay silent, his voice strengthens, "Truly, we all are. We don't mean any harm. We heard you'd had trouble here, and we'd had some of our own. So when King called . . . well, we came to get the measure of you. See if we might be able to work something out. We need—"

Sawyer gives him a quelling glare, and he grimaces, faltering. Jasper's assessing glance is razor sharp, and my curiosity piques again.

"Look," Cole starts again, giving Sawyer a hard-eyed look back. "Maybe we could use some extra manpower." He glances around at the armed civilians and rubs the back of his neck. "Womanpower works, too. It's true we have food, but that has some drawbacks, too."

"You also have people who want to take it." The realization is soft in Jasper's voice, and it all clicks into place for me at the same moment.

"The Sinners," I say, mostly to myself, and Jasper nods thoughtfully.

It makes sense. Cyanide is only hours away from the farmlands, and I'd wondered before how the Sinners were feeding so many inside a dead city. Scavenged supermarkets and empty apartments would only hold so much—and it's not like the Sinners have any moral concerns over theft.

The Sinners have been stealing from the Reapers.

Which means they're in the same position as us.

Jayk's eyes burn the side of my face as he stares at me, but I'm too focused on Sawyer. Pete throws a wild, worried glance at Sawyer, who gives me a speculative once over.

Then, shrugging slightly, he exchanges a look with Cole I can't read.

The sun begins to tuck itself behind the trees, and a slow darkness falls over us.

"They're a pest. We've had our ways of . . . of *working around* them, but . . ." Cole shrugs, eyeing Dom's kit. "We wouldn't turn down your skills."

Jayk snorts. "So you *do* need us. Fuckers."

Sawyer scowls at Jayk. "Not as much as you need us. They need us too much to kill us, and we can live on the produce they let us keep. You can't." He rubs his mustache, then raises his brows. "You'll starve without our help. These women will starve."

Lucky splutters an incredulous laugh. He pushes off the throne, disgusted. "If you're so worried about it, why don't you send us enough food to see them through winter? If you're so *good*, maybe don't make deals that put conditions on their survival."

I send him a sideways look under my lashes, the irony of that one stinging a little. He catches the glance and has the grace to blush.

But Sawyer just shrugs. "We didn't say we were good. I just said we weren't *bad*. And they ain't leaving us with *that* much left to spare." With that, he turns, facing the crowd of women scattered through the field. "Look, you don't trust us. I can understand that. So maybe we stick around. You can get to know us—see we aren't such bad guys, when it comes right down to it."

Jayk's muscles turn to stone under me. "You think we're just going to let you into our fucking *house*?"

Hot wind whips our clothing, as if in warning.

Sawyer raises his hands. "Don't get your dick in a knot, King. We'll stay behind your . . ." He frowns at the deep, wide ditch encircling Bristlebrook. "Pike pit?"

"It's a moat," Jayk mutters.

"Right. Behind that." He turns around to face the civilians. He plucks off his cowboy hat, then holds it against his chest. "Any one of you is welcome to join us—for a meal or to live. No one will touch you, not unless you ask. You're safe with us."

Sawyer looks over his shoulder at Jayk, then adds, "Or you can wait until your hunting dries up with the winter, and your vegetables die in the frost, and you start wondering why you're blacking out because you don't have the energy to stay awake."

My breath stalls in my chest, every tiny hair on my arm standing on end at the horrific image. At the *likely* image.

Pete and Buck look around hopefully.

Still, not a single person moves.

Cole lets out a long, disappointed breath, but Sawyer just nods. He puts his hat back on. "You all stay safe, you hear? We'll be setting up real close if you want to come say hi."

He looks us over as the other Reapers awkwardly put down their tea sets and shuffle after him.

Cole hesitates, eyeing us. "There ain't any more of them explosives hiding around here, are there?"

"About a dozen." Lucky's dimples flash dangerously. "Watch your step."

Uneasiness slips into his expression when no one offers more information, and he grimaces, then braces himself as he follows his friends.

We watch them leave in silence. But as the last light winks out between the trees behind them, I only have one thought.

Sawyer is right.

We are going to starve without them.

But if we agree to go against the Sinners to help them, then it's war.

And we could be condemning Heather and Bentley to death.

CHAPTER 11

EDEN

SURVIVAL TIP #131
*You're part of the pack,
or you're part of their food chain.*

B ristlebrook is a mosaic, frozen in place after the Reapers leave. Hard, chipped, and beautiful. I wonder if I should get up, maybe go inside to talk, but Jayk won't let me up.

After a few minutes, Shelby calls from the hollowed-out music room window, "They're gone."

Jayk mutters to Ava to trail them, and she nods.

Right as the mosaic shatters.

"What the hell happened out there?" Emerson snaps, climbing down from her platform and storming over.

She's not the only one. Kasey storms through the front door with a string of curse words I'm sure she shouldn't have learned yet—and there's no doubt in my mind where she learned them.

"You had me locked in a *room*?" she shouts at Jayk.

"You did bring food, didn't you?" Mary Beth asks, her hands knotting anxiously as she looks us over.

My fingers tighten in Jayk's shirt as I open my mouth to reply . . . but nothing comes out. How on earth are we supposed to explain this? We've had a week, and I still don't have a single thing to say for myself.

Jayk stands, dropping me on my feet, and Jasper unwinds himself from where he's seated.

Beau rubs his forehead as he watches Jayk, then cuts a sideways look at Dom. When Dom just stares stubbornly back, Beau huffs in frustration.

Leaving Dom behind, Beau walks to the edge of the stage, his hands spread soothingly. "I know everyone has questions, but it will be easier to explain if we can all remain calm."

"What the hell did you do?" someone spits.

Over the top of her someone else begs, "Is Madison dead?"

I flinch.

The mutterings are breaking into violent shouts. The civilians have swarmed from their positions and are pooling around the stage.

"No one died," Jasper says, cool and a little too sharp to be soothing.

Lucky presses into his side, night and day beside one another, and he gives Jasper a nervous smile. "Hey, don't lie. A whole bunch of Sinners got whacked. That was fun, remember?"

The distress painting the civilians' faces says plainly that they're not in the mood for jokes.

I put a restraining hand on Lucky's arm. "We had some . . . issues." Everyone keeps talking, *shouting*, so I raise my voice, hating the desperate edge to it. "Aaron betrayed us."

"Where is Madison?" June yells back, drowning me out. Fierce and lithely muscular, she looks like she wants to take me *out*.

Deciding a little caution is never a bad thing, I edge backward into Jayk's chest. He's frowning, grim and unsettled.

"Heather was taken captive." Dom's deep voice carries over the shouts in a way mine never could, and I pivot to stare at him.

I didn't expect him to speak up, not after his announcement in the forest.

He uncrosses his arms and looks heavily down at the civilians. "Aaron should never have been there. No one should have been able to break ranks after learning the plan. Cyanide was a failure of leadership at every step—"

"Stop, Dom," Beau snaps, ignoring the civilians as they shout questions and demands. "You couldn't have stopped half of—"

Dom cuts him off. "Cyanide was my op. Everything that happened—*everything*—can be traced back to my mistakes. Mine *alone*." A muscle ticks in his jaw. "Which is why I've stepped down as leader."

Stars begin shyly peeking from the gloaming sky, and my throat closes over.

Dom doesn't blame me for Cyanide. Not for any of it. I should have known he wouldn't hate me for my mistakes. Dom is harder on himself than he is on anyone around him.

He blames *himself*.

Lucky's hand finds mine, and he squeezes it hard. My stomach hollow, I squeeze it back fiercely.

"Heather is Alastair's hostage and collateral," Dom continues with brutal, even calm. "We didn't rescue the targets. Weapons and explosives were confiscated. Bentley was taken hostage too, and Red Zone expects compensation. We also didn't secure meds, supplies . . . or food. We lost."

That draws a beat of deathly silence, and I close my eyes against the blow.

The panic around us is feverish now, and too loud, and they drag at one another like there's somewhere else to go. It makes them look different, this fear. Defending Bristlebrook, they were warriors. But with reality setting in and cold terror stealing the warmth from the air, it's easier to see the shadows under their eyes and the hungry hollows in their cheeks.

God. I need to think of something. There has to be a way out of this.

The Sinners. The Reapers. Red Zone. *Us.* This is all one big chessboard, and we need to start playing a better game.

Jayk shakes his head, taking in the carnage, then stares at Dom with a dark scowl on his face. I can't even tell if it's in blame or concern.

The civilians grow louder.

"What are we supposed to do now?"

"You just *left* Madison there? You son of a bitch. *She* was our leader. Not you."

Jasper raises one cutting hand. "She volunteered. We will of course do our best to—"

"Shut the fuck up."

"How do we get her back?"

"How far away is winter?"

Ida pats Mary Beth's arm with a strong, weathered hand and says gravely, "I'm not sure we'll last until winter, dear."

My gaze bounces from face to face, feeling the panic, the rage. It expands, plumes like the aftermath of a detonation. It clogs the air with choking fear and anger that batters us like stray debris. Kasey's face is gaunt—all wide, accusing eyes.

We can't make a deal. We can't afford not to.

It's hard to breathe.

A stone launches from the group. It falls short and skitters, clattering between Dom and Beau, who swerve apart, and then Lucky is pulling me back, all sympathy winking out from his face, his pulse hammering at his throat. Jasper grabs his rifle, backing up so he's in front of both of us.

Jayk curses, and to my surprise, he rounds on us. "All of you, get the fuck out of here. You're making it worse."

Lucky stares at Jayk. "Did you just give us orders?" He gives me a doubtful look before Jayk can reply. "Can he do that?"

"No! He can't," Beau bursts out. His teeth snap together, and I can practically hear them grind. "He doesn't get to just declare himself—"

"He does," Dom stops him impatiently. His golden eyes flash. "This isn't a fight, Beau. I gave it up. Let it go."

Frustration and worry steal over Beau's features, darkening the glens in his pretty eyes as he looks at his friend.

As much as I'm concerned about Dom too, I have bigger concerns.

I nervously look at the enraged crowd. "Jayk, I don't think . . ."

Jayk's face softens, just a fraction. "Just go inside."

He storms down the steps and Dom gives his back a grim look, then nods at Beau to move.

I hesitate, but Lucky is already herding me off the side of the stage.

The others follow, coming up behind us right as Jayk is swallowed by the mass of furious, terrified women.

CHAPTER 12

EDEN

SURVIVAL TIP #288
*It's easier to cut someone else
than to open yourself up.*

I drag my feet, twisting to try and make sure Jayk's okay, but Lucky harries me until I'm finally inside, like he's herding a recalcitrant puppy. I bat him away as soon as I clear the doorway. Then I draw short, my pounding heart slowing.

The base of the staircase is crowded with furniture and sprawling mounds of clothes. It's obnoxious against the open, elegant order of the house—nothing like we left it—but I only give it one puzzled look before I beeline to the taped-up sitting room windows.

I might not be able to eavesdrop, but I can still creepily stare from the sidelines to make sure Jayk's okay.

On the way, I need to sidestep nearly a half a dozen sleeping bags. I'd wondered where all the tents had gone—Jayk must have moved everyone inside. It's packed uncomfortably close, but they'll certainly be more sheltered in here, particularly as the weather starts to turn.

I tweak the gorgeous, heavy curtains to the side and crack open the sliding doors so I can see outside.

As he follows us into the room, I hear Beau call, annoyance thick in his voice, "Wait, this is all my stuff. Why are all my things out here?"

Ignoring him, Jasper steps in behind me, and I try not to shiver over the casual way he notches his chin on the top of my head so he can watch the scene too. Lucky falls in beside us, and he gives me an amused sideways look when I stick my head through the missing window frame.

It doesn't help much, but at least I can see Jayk now.

The crowd has parted around him in the unfurling darkness, and he's serious as he talks to them. Unsneering. Unsmirking. Un*scowling*.

And . . . the worst of their panicked anger is already fading.

Mary Beth's shoulders slump, and Jayk shrugs as he talks to her. Sloane squeezes the back of Mary Beth's neck under her auburn hair, nodding along to whatever he's saying.

"They're really listening to him," Jasper murmurs, a note of confusion in his voice.

Dom leans against the door frame on the other side, and I push open the door so he can see too. He looks strangely more at peace than I've seen him this last week as he watches them. The harsh frown lines between his brows have relaxed, and I wonder why he looks like this now, when everything is at its worst.

"They trust him," he says, without looking up.

Ida and Ethel are turned toward Jayk, open. Listening.

They all are.

Not with the fearful awe of peasants for a brutish medieval king. His throne is abandoned behind him, and he's speaking to them as equals—and they're responding as the same.

"Eden, I don't think any of this is yours." Beau's confusion travels as he picks through the furniture. He throws something down. "Seriously, why is my shit out here?"

Jayk rolls his eyes, waving Ida off as she pats his cheek, and she throws her head back and laughs. Smiles crack stern faces, and he rubs the back of his neck, glancing our way.

Hope, sweet and warm, slides through me at the affection between them. Jayk is coming into his own here, and it's beautiful—so, so beautiful—in the middle of all the destruction.

Dom finally pulls back, an odd expression on his face. It's almost nostalgic, as though he's seeing something lovely but lost to him.

He lets the curtain drop heavily back into place and turns away.

Painful shards fill my throat at the resignation in him. He's filled with it, like it's swelling his very muscles and somehow deflating him all at once.

It's too bittersweet, too unkind and lovely, that Jayk's strength rises out of his fall.

"Dom. Sir . . ." I whisper, taking a step after him.

He looks back for another pensive moment, then turns for the stairs. "I'm going to get some sleep. We should all get up before dawn to help Jayk. He's going to need it."

"My lamp! It's just dumped here!" Beau storms in, holding his hideous shaded lamp. The fringes clatter against the gilding as he shakes it. "Why would anyone just leave it like that? They could have broken it. This is probably a Douglas family heirloom."

"It most certainly is *not*," Jasper says absently. He's studying Dom. "You're surely not indulging this ridiculous leadership run of his? You did hear him with the Reapers. He's lucky they didn't open fire on us."

Lucky's blond head is still sandwiched between the curtains. "My favorite part was the arm wrestling."

Jasper walks over to sprawl on one of the elaborate couches, careful not to let his boots touch the upholstery. Though I'm not sure it matters—the dirt and exploded glass after the battle for Bristlebrook did a number on the delicate stitching.

He plucks at a stain on the velvet cushion with distaste. "I believe that was a handshake."

"It was?" Lucky looks back, surprised. "Huh."

Beau slams the lamp on a side table, his jaw flexing, but I'm too busy wincing at the memory of the competing scarlet of Jayk's and Sawyer's faces to soothe him.

At the base of one of the massive, curling staircases, Dom stops, his hand gripping the gleaming balustrade.

"I think he did a great job," I offer, then adjust my glasses nervously at the arch look Jasper gives me. "I do! I actually think he made a few excellent points. He found out what they wanted, and . . . and he stood his ground while they were trying to bully us." I frown. "Or seduce us. I'm still not entirely sure which. It doesn't matter. What *does* matter is that Jayk advocated for us, for all the women here, despite what it might cost us. That matters. To me? To them? That matters a lot."

The crowd is starting to break up now, turning toward Bristlebrook.

Beau shoots one last baleful frown at his lamp, then leans against the subtle wallpaper. "We've been advocating for them already, Eden. What do you think this whole damn trip was about? Getting resources, protecting ourselves *and* them. It's the bare minimum, okay? It doesn't make him a leader."

Dom turns abruptly.

Nothing else, just turns . . . but he steals every eye.

Even silent, even resigned, he's still their captain. He has the ability to command a room just by breathing. Maybe it's the perfect posture, or the forbidding breadth of his shoulders, but his presence has a heavy weight.

And right now, there are the makings of a blaze in his eyes, molten embers that could strike a brilliant flare.

"You all need to shut the fuck up." The words are calm, *commanding*, but the simmering anger just underneath feels ready to blow. "Do you have any idea how much work it must have taken to get Bristlebrook into the shape it's in? How hard it is to coordinate that many people for the kind of organized response we saw today?" His gaze cuts the men down, one by one, and his face is chiseled from stone. "I know you don't, because none of you lifted a finger to help."

I open my mouth, then close it when Dom's eyes meet mine, teeming with frustration. He hinted at this before over coffee, how overwhelmed he was. I remember him coming to our door and begging Beau for help.

Lucky turns away from the window, stretching. "I mean, he also managed to build a whole-ass throne out of scrap metal; he can't have been *that* busy."

He flinches back at the way Dom glares at him.

Beau blows out a frustrated breath. "Is that what this is about? If you need more support, Dom, we can do that. You don't need to be stepping down. Don't get me wrong, Jayk is a handy guy—but this is your show."

"For fuck's sake, Beau. Shut *up*." Dom's filthy boots track mud over the vibrant rug as he storms forward. His eyes are searing; they should scald Beau to the bone. "You just expect that all this shit just gets done, but it doesn't. Jayk organized Bristlebrook—that's not just mechanics and building, that takes planning. And the only reason he can organize these civilians like that is because they trust him, just like they trusted him tonight." He gestures around the room, clipped and cold. "They don't trust me, or any of us. Only Jayk earned that. And you don't earn loyalty like that by just being *handy*."

His fingers are curled into fists as he fights for control, and my insides start tearing in two. I believe in Dom as a leader with everything in me. He has a mind for strategy, an appetite for risk, resourcefulness, strength, resilience under pressure—and his compassion has grown in leaps and bounds.

But I also believe in Jayk.

No, he doesn't have the experience yet—or the finesse—but Dom is right. He deserves a team behind him.

Maybe Jayk needs this chance to see who he can be . . . and maybe Dom needs some time to heal.

I glance around at Beau, then Lucky, then Jasper. "Jayk also gave us our first shot at real food by bringing in the Reapers. He managed more than we did."

Jasper lounges back on his couch, and his hair falls over his forehead. He looks at me appraisingly. "The idea was good, I'll grant him that—it's the execution that leaves something to be desired."

Dom rubs a hand over his mouth, staring at Jasper, and I'm glad I'm not on the receiving end of that look.

"I— I don't think that's entirely fair," I say hesitantly. "Not exactly. I think . . ."

Jasper brushes an amused finger over his lips as he watches me stumble over my words, and I narrow my eyes. It feels strange to disagree with Jasper, and stranger still to voice it.

He waits for me, dark-eyed and expectant, and I steady myself.

"Jayk pushed the Reapers, and I think they revealed more than they planned to." I rub my nose under my glasses, thinking, remembering the conversation, the moves like a chessboard. "There's something there. The Reapers and the Sinners are at odds. I'm not sure what to make of it yet, but we have options, so many more than we had before, and that's entirely because of Jayk."

And yes, maybe they're not *good* options, but it's a place to start.

If we can stop bickering long enough to talk about it.

Beau runs a frustrated hand over his face, and it's splotched and red with mosquito bites. "We have a woman laid up with a bullet wound, so I'm not really sure that—"

Whatever thread of calm holding Dom at bay snaps. He storms over to Beau and pushes him against the wall. Beau's mouth snaps shut, and he grips Dom's arms, holding him back.

I suppose that's a no. They're not stopping their bickering any time soon.

I step forward, then hover on my toes, not sure if this is a brawl-I-should-break-up or a brawl-I-can-let-myself-ogle.

"We should really get one of those flippy counters," Lucky says conversationally, dropping into another chair. "Zero days since a fistfight."

"At this rate, let's just make it a painting," I mutter acerbically, and he throws me a wicked dimple.

Civilians trickle into the house, then pick up the pace when they spot the commotion. I sigh as they hurry past and resign myself to watching the tussle. Dom doesn't have a knife this time, and I'm sure he won't shoot Beau.

Reasonably sure, anyway.

"You're an asshole and a hypocrite," Dom growls. His body is a block, a tank ready to crush Beau against the wall. "You keep saying you're supportive and loyal, and I know you think you're *sensitive*, but you need to stop. Jayk isn't taking my job. I stepped down. Treating him like shit won't make me change my mind—just like cutting me out didn't fix anything between us."

The watercolor art behind them looks like it's spilling across the wall.

Beau's jaw squares further, and he unclenches his hands from Dom's uniform with strained patience. "I'm *not* cutting you out." The words come from between clenched teeth. "I needed space for a while, that's all, but I'm here now. Everything is *fine*. I want to hel—"

The last word is garbled as Dom's forearm finds Beau's throat.

"It's not fine, you dick. The only reason you stopped acting like a petulant fucking toddler was because you thought I was *sad*, so you just shoved all your shit to the side again so you could play hero."

A shutter slams down over Beau's face, and he shoves Dom back. "Get off me."

Dom is an erupting volcano, raw and hot in his need to cause destruction. Beau braces, and Dom slams against him again, pummeling him against the wall.

It's almost . . . sloppy, not at all like their lethal sparring sessions. Those I watched mesmerized by their breathless skill and the way they anticipate one another. At the violent, beautiful dance they performed for hours.

This is just a mess of camo and fists and frustration.

Dom kicks out Beau's ankle. He wrenches Beau's tanned arm behind him and slams him against the wallpaper, face-first this time, and spits, "You're not the hero, Beau. You just got lucky enough to grow up with a nice mama and sisters who adored you. A dad who . . ."

There's a rough ache in Dom's voice as he cuts himself off. I remember sitting under the candle-lit apple tree as he smiled over the dearly missed Bennetts.

Jasper leans forward, resting his elbows on his knees as he studies them. His eyes are obsidian scalpels as he dissects them, and I can almost see the notes he's silently jotting down. Lucky winces as he eyes them, kicking his legs over the arm of his chair.

"You think your family made you a good person, Beau, but they didn't." Dom presses Beau harder. "You don't get what it's like to never be good enough, or what it's like to be hurt, because they always protected you. They loved you no matter what. When you fucked up, you just had to flash a smile and they *forgave* you—you've *never* had to apologize. You've never had to work to make it better. You've always had people, Beau, so you don't know what it's like when they're not there for you."

Beau stiffens, then tries to twist to look at him. "Don't, Dom. Don't bring them into this."

But Dom's not giving him an inch.

"You don't get it," Dom snaps. "You never have. You live in the highs and can't fucking deal with the lows. You can't get angry unless I plan a scene for you to work it through. You—"

Pinned against the delicate, painted swirls, Beau's eyes squeeze shut, and suddenly I feel like this is too far. This isn't a tussle.

This is an evisceration.

I step forward, anxious. "Dom. Sir, this isn't right . . ."

But Dom doesn't stop, he grinds Beau's face against the wall. "You never meet people where they're at or try to see things from their side. You never accept an apology—and you sure as hell don't accept criticism. Perfect fucking Beau. Must be so nice up there on that high horse."

Beau slams on the wall hard, then twists with a sharp elbow to Dom's gut. Dom grunts and he wrests his way free, staggering away.

Beau looks at Jasper, who gives him a pursed lip look that offers silent disagreement. Even Lucky's gaze skips guiltily away. He stops, panting, his whole face dark and red as he turns to his friend. "Funny, I don't remember ever hearing an apology from you. Not ever, Dom."

My heart squeezes, torn. Beau has his issues, but so do they—so do *I*. The naked vulnerability and confusion in his face makes me bleed in a thousand places.

His lips press together too hard, and he looks down, breathing unsteadily, before he looks back to Dom. "You're wrong that I've never been hurt. *You* hurt me. You hurt me, Dom." His throat works as he swallows, and he adds more quietly, "And I *still* haven't gone anywhere. I just needed some time, that's all. I want to see your side. I'm not . . . I'm not your father."

Dom is panting hard too, more than the brief scrap warrants, and dark, bitter unhappiness shrouds him like a smog. It weighs down his mouth and clouds his eyes.

Beau, on the other hand, looks like he might fracture apart. He's glassy-eyed and glowing bright, and I feel a rip down my middle, wanting to help them both.

Wanting to hold them both.

Dom's voice becomes hushed, too scored and rough with emotion to survive full volume. "You can't just waltz back on into my life like nothing ever happened. I'm not going to pinch your cheeks and make you a pie just because I missed you, Beau. I needed you *then*, and because you couldn't grow up and talk it out, you just left me alone. You broke something here. And you're breaking it with her, too."

I suck in a sharp breath as the shards in my throat dig inward.

Neither of them look at me, but the energy in the room charges, becomes fizzy and uncomfortable. Gooseflesh shivers self-consciously over my skin, and I look down at my boots. The toes are pointed together, just a little, and I hate that I've tracked this mud in.

My vision goes cloudy again. I'll clean the rug tomorrow, and re-tape the windows, and whatever else needs doing.

I'll fix it.

Somehow, I'll fix it.

But God, how on earth am I supposed to share a room with Beau when he can't even talk to me?

"Did you have a point? Or do you just feel like airing our dirty laundry any old place?" Beau asks tiredly after a long, excruciating silence.

I glance up, aching, and Dom rolls his shoulders back, looking just as exhausted as I feel.

We're not going to make any progress on our issues tonight.

We're all fried. It's been an enormous few months. We all need to rest and breathe for a while, because this? This is impossible.

Dom's fingers dig into his short dark hair, then he releases it, shaking his head. "My point is that Jayk has been doing good fucking work. He's been thinking and acting, and he has their loyalty. Rather than dragging him down for everything you think he's doing wrong, why don't you pull your head in and actually help him. Not a single one of you could do any better. Show some fucking gratitude." He nods at Lucky and Jasper too, and the amusement is wiped from their faces. "That goes for you two as well. You need to stop skipping out on everything that doesn't directly involve you. Pull your goddamned weight."

He's not even angry anymore. It's that same slow, stinging resignation. The frustration and exhaustion that burns enough to blister.

Lucky looks away, shamefaced, and after a long, frigid look, Jasper gives him a long look, then finally nods once, in curt acceptance.

"Well on that note," Kasey says from behind me, "I'm going to practice my knife throwing in the library. You have fun with all that."

Oh, *crap*.

I spin to see Jayk standing just inside the door . . . and he's staring at Dom with a confused, unguarded expression.

My heart tumbles as I realize he heard all of that.

How rare is it for Jayk to get support like that from these men?

"*Knife* throwing?" Jasper leaps to his feet, staring after Kasey in alarm. "Jaykob? Tell me she's joking."

She'd better be.

I walk over to Jayk. It's not until I touch his arm that he startles back to himself. I give him a small smile, a little hesitant. He hasn't been treating me like we're over, but we left things in a strange place, and he's only had the highlights of what happened at the Den.

And I'm not sure how much he heard of that conversation, but even if it was just the last, he has to know we were all talking about him.

He stares down at me, his eyes navy seas, with pirated treasures sparkling in their depths.

"Jayk, you need anything?" Dom asks, and Jayk's head snaps up, and he gives him that wary, cornered-animal look again for an instant before he plasters a smirk over his face.

I'm debating how to approach him when he spins, and the next thing I know I'm being thrown over Jayk's thick shoulder.

No, no, no! I *hate* this!

He gives my ass a resonant *smack*.

"You know what, sugar? I think it's time we went back to our honeymoon suite."

Chapter 13

Eden

Survival tip #333
Cavemen are not hot.
Cavemen are not hot.
Cavemen are not hot.
(Even if they are wonderfully decisive.)

I shriek as the ground rushes up toward my face, then jerk hard as his arm clamps around my waist. Not trusting it, I scramble to balance myself, and my hands land on the firm curve of his ass. My heart clatters around my chest as my fingers flex involuntarily.

Well. Perhaps it's not *all* bad.

"Honeymoon suite?" Lucky asks.

My glasses swing from the chain around my neck and the ground moves dizzyingly under my face as Jayk walks to the stairs.

Nope. I hate it again.

"I thought we were full up on rooms," Beau says, puzzled.

Jayk steps around the edge of Beau's gaudy green armchair and . . . My brain pings on the memory of the last place I saw that chair, and my stomach drops with a sudden, nervous flip.

"Ah." Jasper's silky voice is thick with mirth, and I cringe. "Oh dear."

"Oh dear? Why oh dear?" Lucky asks.

There's a beat of silence. Jayk makes it to the stairs.

"You moved me *out*?"

Beau's roar has the propellant ripple effect of a drone strike, and Jayk finally speeds up.

Crap, crap, *crap*. I cringe into his back, clinging to his belt for my life as I jolt with each step.

The jerk *did* move all of Beau's things out of our room—and if "honeymoon suite" is anything to go by, he moved himself *in*.

Lucky howls with laughter from some faraway, unhelpful distance, and Jasper's amused snort makes me want to strangle them both. Oh God, I'm dead—or Jayk is. It's one of the two and, quite frankly, it had better be him because I do *not* deserve this.

My whole body bounces as Jayk moves, my stomach bobbling against his solid shoulder as he slams rapidly up every stair.

I'm going to be sick.

"You son of a bitch," Beau shouts, and I manage to push myself up off Jayk's butt enough to see all of them standing at the base of the staircase . . . in front of all Beau's things. The lamp. The chair. *All* his clothes. One set of boxer briefs dangles obnoxiously from the ear of a marble bust in the hall.

Jasper picks it off with two pinched fingers and an equally pinched expression.

Jayk makes it to the top of the stairs, and he turns to look down at them over the balustrade like a bull-headed emperor over his subjects. My heart is thundering with a different kind of panic as the room swirls, and I lose sight of them again.

I'm woozy.

I'm caught.

He's holding me like I'm barely an annoyance—a sack of grain he's hauling off to the mart.

Damn it. Why are the others not *helping me*?

"Let me *down*," I hiss, and his snort tells me that's not going to happen.

Squirming, I try to twist out of his hold, but it's like trying to scrape free of a bear trap. I'm going to need to chew off my own waist and claw my way along the floor to escape him—or use my safeword.

I consider it, briefly, but decide against it. I'd much prefer to blister his *hide* over this as soon as I get him alone.

There may be a teensy, tiny part of me that's looking forward to the battle.

I've been restrained and careful all week. I've missed fighting with Jayk.

Even if he is being a particularly enormous brand of jerk right now.

"You don't seem to be getting the picture here—so let me clear it up for you." Jayk leans one arm on the polished railing, lazy with that same insufferable arrogance from earlier, and I tilt precariously against his neck. If he drops me over the edge to my death, I am coming back as a zombie and taking him with me.

"I'm the king of the castle," he drawls. "All of this is mine now. The civilians, your stuffy house . . . and this one, too."

He jostles his shoulder in a shrug, and I jangle about like a rag doll.

This one?!

Asshole!

I beat at his steely ass with both fists. He doesn't flinch, so I try to throw a kick, but the angle is all wrong. My legs just flail about like a pathetic inflatable car wash man, dancing in the wind.

"Jayk!" I shriek, but he just wriggles me into a more comfortable position.

A more comfortable position for *him*.

"I told you I wasn't choosing," I snap.

He shrugs, and I flop again.

"You don't have to choose," he tells me casually. "I'm choosing for you."

Oh, we are *definitely* fighting about *that*.

Lucky's laughter starts to peter out. "Wait. Hold on. Wait, what?"

"Jaykob, put Eden down," Jasper demands, his voice sharp with alarm. "*Now*."

"He's claiming her."

I stop wriggling when I hear Dom . . . but there's absolutely no inflection in his voice. No hint at all to say how he feels about that.

It catches me short, blunting some of my thrilled frustration.

I scramble to pull my glasses back on, and I twist, trying uselessly to see from this humiliating angle.

Jayk *knows* how I feel about the others. My love letter to him was never supposed to be an invitation for him to just *take* me. His hold on me is possessive, though—the definition of caveman. So something has *definitely* been lost in translation.

Something I plan to correct *very* shortly.

But.

Fear pricks me.

Is Dom really going to just . . . let me go?

"You can get pissed off, fight me, I don't care." Jayk pushes off the railing, and I can hear his smirk. "She's mine—and you're going to lose."

"Fuck off, Jayk," Lucky snaps, and there's no humor in him anymore. Every word is edgy and tense. "This isn't a joke. We're doing this together. All of us."

"It's okay, Lucky. I'll fix it," I call back.

But my thoughts are still on Dom. Dom . . . and that dull, empty voice.

Jasper is close behind Lucky, lethally unimpressed. "Jaykob, taking charge of the civilians is one thing, but this isn't what Eden wants. You're making a fool of yourself."

Jayk ignores them, turning back toward my room—our room— and he pauses. "Say goodbye, sugar."

Not. A. Chance.

I lift my head, realizing he's positioned me so I can see them.

Dom is standing away from the others, a shadow in the back. All the rawness, all the combative emotion that was exploding out of him moments ago has been packed away so neatly, it might never have been there.

My adrenaline starts to slow, turning nauseating, like a heart frantically fighting off poison, only to recognize it's pumping the decay everywhere.

He meets my eyes, and his look has the same sad-sweet nostalgia in it that it had when he was watching Jayk and the civilians earlier. He rubs his chest and walks away.

His steps echo like empty gun chambers.

Beau is holding up two of his favorite shirts, but his hands drop as he looks after Dom, all his stunned fury swirling away like water down a drain. Confusion and panic and uncertainty paint his face, the cracks their earlier fight left in him splintering open further.

He looks back at me and Jayk like he's never seen us before.

"Fuck this," Lucky snaps, and he pushes past some of the furniture.

Beau shakes his head. His brow is knotted, creased with distress.

"You can't just . . ." His clothes drop from his fingers, but he doesn't seem to notice. "You can't just take everything! That's my room, that's my . . ."

He falters.

I wait, imploring him with my eyes to finish that, to assure me and everyone that I am still his. That he wants me. That all of this wasn't just a romance of convenience—a silly infatuation with the first woman he'd seen in years, come and gone like a rainstorm rainbow.

I need him to tell me we're stronger than one awful mistake.

"I've been waiting my whole life to fall in love with you," I choke out, and his eyes slam closed like I've struck him. His head turns, his Adam's apple bobbing.

The poison in me becomes distressing. Corrosive. It burns my throat.

Jayk's arm tightens painfully around me, and Lucky begins taking the stairs two at a time. Jasper isn't far behind.

Apparently unhurried, Jayk yanks me over his shoulder and into his arms so he can look down into my face, and I squeeze my eyes closed too, because I know he doesn't want to see this, how much I'm aching for his friends. I know he doesn't get it, and maybe never will.

"I told you they're no good for you," Jayk says gruffly, almost soft. "You don't need them. We don't need any of them."

I shake my head, knowing in every cell that he's wrong, but I'm embarrassed to keep fighting for Beau when he so clearly can't fight for me.

Jayk looks up as Lucky nears the top of the stairs, then starts storming down the hall.

"No," Beau says suddenly, sounding panicked. "No. Eden, wait— Jayk, stop."

But Jayk is already almost at my door.

Fast, furious footsteps echo off the towering walls, chasing us, and he wrenches the door open.

Jasper and Lucky appear at the end of the hall, silhouetted like twin shadow wraiths.

Lucky takes a few steps forward. The light catches him differently, haloing his hair. "She's not just yours, Jayk."

The *just* squeezes me like a hug after Dom, Beau, and Jayk. Lucky gets it. He always has.

"Shut that door and I will lock you in the prison under my bed and throw away the key, Jaykob." Jasper's voice is like the crack of a whip—and upset enough that I squint to try and see his face. "I will put you in a cock cage that will make you weep blood. I will—"

Jayk just smirks. "Try it."

With zero ceremony, he throws me into the room.

Then he slams the door closed behind us.

CHAPTER 14

EDEN

No, you can't lock yourself in a room and avoid all your responsibilities.
Yes, you can have a friend do it for you.

Jayk flicks the lock just as fists slam against the door. Lucky shouts from the other side, and I sigh, stepping forward to unlock it. Lucky has slept beside me every night since Cyanide. He still wakes in a cold sweat, clutching me to him like I'm about to disappear like smoke between his fingers. I'm not locking him out.

But Jayk's not having it.

As soon as I reach for the door, Jayk tosses me back over his shoulder and then dumps me on the bed. I lie there for a moment, stunned, then sit up with a huff—only for him to casually shove me back onto the mattress.

"Stay."

I glare at him from my back, shoving my glasses back on.

"Would you like me to sit and roll over, too?" I ask with a saccharine smile.

He shrugs one shoulder, turning to the heavy side table. "Whatever gets you wet."

I sit bolt upright as he picks the table up, and I try to ignore how his bare arms hardly strain under the massive weight. My cheeks singe with heat.

"It *doesn't*," I splutter, and he throws me a mocking look, all knowing eyes and stupid muscles and that *mouth* and . . .

Darn it!

I squeeze my legs together.

"Let me in, Jayk, or I'm breaking the damn door down!" Lucky shouts, pounding against the door.

Distracted, I shift toward the edge of the bed, and Jayk shoots me a warning glance.

Then he wedges the side table under the door handle.

I resist the urge to throw a tissue box at him. "Jayk, this isn't helping. You can't just lock my boyfriends out of my room!"

He steps back to admire his handiwork.

I force patience. "Maybe we could just—"

"Try to get in now, asshole," he shouts to Lucky, and my mouth clicks shut as I muffle a sigh.

There's a loud bang that sounds awfully like someone throwing themselves against the door, and the wood shudders precariously. Jayk's self-satisfied smirk fades into a scowl. He looks around, then quickly picks up a heavy chest from the corner.

It only takes a moment before he's pushing the chest on top of the side table.

Oh boy.

He wipes the dust from his hands onto his tank, then gives me a brief, smug look. "They're not your boyfriends anymore. You don't have boyfriends. You have me."

Don't strangle him. Your hands are too small, and his neck is too thick.

I lean back and let my fists strangle the bedsheets instead. "You don't get to decide that for me, Jayk."

His gaze runs down the length of me where I'm sprawled on the bed, lingering on the surreptitious clench of my hands. A challenge glints in his eye.

My heart putters in excitement, flooding with the remembered thrill of a dozen fights. A dozen chases. Jayk taunting me into a fury that leaves me limp and airy and freed of all that hot, uncomfortable pressure.

Shivering, I unclench my hands. We can't do that today. I'm channeling Jasper. We need to talk, so I'm staying calm. *Reasonable.*

I'm not going to slake all the frustrated anger of the last two weeks on his cock.

But a prodding, breathless question tumbles out of me anyway.

"If you're not my boyfriend . . . what are you?"

The door shudders again with another collision, but this time Jayk ignores it, sizing me up with speculative interest. He strolls over to the bed, then puts his hands on either side of my hips, looming over me.

And suddenly, he's very, very close.

Jayk is big and heavy and a little filthy. Here, I can see the lazy scruff on his chin he hasn't bothered to tidy. The silky fringe of his lashes. Every tide of blue in his eyes.

Even irked as I am by this whole escapade, I'm only human, and I missed him dearly . . . and the seductive heat of his body is like a siren call.

Tingling all over, I tilt my face toward his.

His lips twist in a slow, mocking curl, every line of his body urging me to come play. "I'm your king."

"Oh, *no*," I choke out, caught somewhere between outrage and horror. "You did *not* just—"

He plants a hard, hot kiss on my mouth. In it, I taste greed and jealousy and a reckless, questing need. When he pulls back, his lips are damp, and his eyes swirl with taunting tempests.

"Feel free to get on your knees whenever you like, Miss Manners," Jayk drawls.

My hand slaps over my lips, and I stare. There's a low flush in his skin, but despite his insufferable teasing, a slight breath of uncertainty sits under the cockiness. A hesitant question that tells me we really do need to talk, no matter how much easier it might be to let him rip my clothes off with his teeth.

He's made a statement here.

I need to make one too.

"Jayk—"

The door shudders again, and I suck in air, startled.

Lucky's voice registers. "We have a sledgehammer somewhere. No, we do. Jayk had one. I've seen it. Jasper, he's stealing her! No, I don't give a shit if he's protective of his tools."

The vulnerability winks out of Jayk's face.

He glowers at the door, then walks over to the tall bookcase.

"Just let him in," I urge, exasperated. "Lucky's allowed in my room, Jayk. I don't want him taking down my door!"

"Would you stop saying that?" Jayk snipes. He examines the bookcase, looking behind it, then nods to himself, satisfied by whatever he sees there. "This ain't your room, it's *our* room. And they're not allowed to touch my shit."

I rub my temple. "Jayk, you just dumped all of Beau's things out of *his* room like they were trash. Don't you think this is a little hypocriti . . ."

I trail off as he starts sliding the massive bookcase toward the door.

His muscles gleam, finally put to real work, and he lets out a low, rough grunt of effort that makes me swallow.

Twice.

I blink. *No. Bad.* This is *bad* behavior.

He threw Beau out of our room, for goodness' sake. He also moved himself in—*without* asking. Then he had the gall to toss me over his shoulder, declare to everyone that I was his property, and now he's *barricading me inside* with him.

It's really . . . It's not . . .

I definitely don't *like* . . .

A sneaky, slow heat begins to curl through me, and the sensible librarian in me slaps it down. *Bad.*

So, so bad, my sexed-up self purrs back, and I sigh, praying for strength.

"I think we need to have a talk about boundaries."

Jayk pauses pushing the bookcase, quirking a confused brow at me.

"God *damn* it, Jayk. You can't just take her!" Lucky shouts, his voice breaking. "She's not a prisoner."

My breath catches as it clicks.

Oh, Lucky.

"Jayk—"

His muscles strain as he pushes the bookcase a few more inches. "No."

"*Yellow.*"

He stops pushing instantly, giving me a sharp look, and I bounce myself off the bed.

"I need to talk to them for a second, Jayk. I'll deal with *you* in a minute," I mutter.

Eyeing me, he crosses his arms over his chest and leans back against the bookcase, abandoning his relentless barricading—and he nods at the door.

"Knock yourself out, then, sugar."

I'm already hurrying over to the door, though there's not a chance I can open it with everything piled the way it is.

The battering barrage at the door stops.

A moment later, there's a neat knock.

"Who is it?" Jayk calls mockingly, and I shoot him a scowl.

"Jasper?" I ask through the door.

"Eden?" He sounds tired, and a frustrated resignation burns through my name. "Can you please just confirm whether you're okay? If you don't wish to spend the night with Jaykob, we'll retrieve you." There's a pause, and even through the door, I can feel that the frosty pressure has changed. "By whatever means necessary."

I bite my lip against a blooming smile.

His concern catches me like a soft net after a panicked freefall . . . but it's the way he leaves the choice with me, without guilt or pressure. I feel myself melting against the wall.

How is it that Jasper acting the gentlemen has the same visceral effect on me as Jaykob acting like a total brute?

I glance back at Jayk, who's staring at the door with low, hostile brows.

Jasper isn't a soldier, but he'd go toe-to-toe with Jaykob if I told him this isn't what I want. And as entertaining as that might be . . .

"I'm okay here for tonight, Jasper. I think Jayk and I have a few things we need to clear up," I tell him, and Jayk narrows his eyes at me.

"All right, sweet girl. We'll see you in the morning."

His voice is so tender, so absent of the wicked edges I'm used to from him that my forehead falls against the wall, and I sigh softly.

"No, just wait. Stop, Jasper, I need to—" There's a scuffle of boots, and then Lucky's voice gets louder.

"Eden, you don't believe him, right? He doesn't get to choose for you. I just . . . I love you."

The vulnerability in his voice splits me like an opening vein.

I lift my head to give Jayk the most irritated look I can muster, and he just gives me a withering one back.

"Jasper, would you kiss Lucky for me?" I ask huskily.

There's no immediate answer, but then there's a soft *thunk* against the door and the sound of hot, urgent breaths. I touch my lips, listening like some debased deviant, fueled by every sound. I hear their clothes shifting together and I know they're close, locked against one another, their mouths a tangle of lips and tongues.

There's a low, broken groan that shudders right through me.

"Fuck," Lucky curses breathlessly a moment later.

My lips tremble under my fingertips. I'm tingling all over, picturing the dazed, dizzy way Lucky always looks at Jasper after a kiss.

"Thank you," I whisper.

"Of course," Jasper murmurs back thickly. "I'll take care of him, Eden."

I know he will.

I take a steadying breath. "I love you, Lucky. I promise that no one"—I glare at Jayk, who scowls—"can change that."

Their footsteps fade as they leave, and I send up a quick prayer that Jasper can do more for Lucky than I've been able to, then turn to face the room.

I have my own battle tonight.

Leaning against the wall, I cross my arms too, and Jayk and I stare one another down.

"Did you really think this would impress me?" I ask, exasperated.

Jayk pushes off the bookcase, the corner of his mouth lifting mockingly. "You really going to pretend like it doesn't?"

He prowls closer, and I bite the corner of my lip, and even though he's being an ass, my pulse starts to dance. Maybe *because* he's being an ass. That dare in his eyes is a promise I want to make.

No, no, no. We're *talking* tonight.

Warily, I push off the wall too, edging sideways.

"You know I'm involved with the others, too!" I hiss. "We talked about this."

He snorts dismissively. "Yeah, Dom seemed real invested. And let's not even mention the doc—that was just sad."

That smacks right over the fresh cuts inside me. Swiveling, I pick up a pillow and throw it at him. Jayk bats it away, and he stalks closer.

"Come on, Eden. You can do better than that."

I scramble onto the bed. "You're being a jerk. Beau and I just . . . we're just fighting. It happens to *couples*. Which we are. A couple. A great couple, even." I shuffle backward as he advances and the soft blankets tangle around my hands. *Too slow, too slow.* "We're a couple, and it will be fine. Dom will be fine. Everyone will be fine."

Jayk lunges forward and grasps my ankle, then drags me down the bed. At the last moment, I slam my hands down, catching the far edge of the mattress with the tips of my fingers to stop my desperate slide. They *strain*, turning white, one by one.

This really doesn't feel like talking.

"Except you. I'm going to wreck you, sugar," Jayk taunts.

He yanks me hard, and my grip breaks with pathetic ease. I shriek, slipping through the sheets and flipping over. Frantically, I kick out with my free foot, catching him hard in the gut, and the breath coughs out of him.

"Nice," he grunts approvingly.

I try to scramble away, but he lashes my other ankle too, catching it in his punishing grip. In moments, he's wrestled my legs open and dragged them around his thighs.

"Oh, you—"

He lets go of my legs as I try to sit up, wrapping one hand around my throat and pinning me to the bed. I cut off, glowering at him, hating that I feel myself wanting to grind into him. Hating that he's hovering high enough above me that I have nothing to grind against.

"You were awful to the others, Jayk. That wasn't what we talked ab—"

Jayk bends down and fits his mouth against mine. It's wet and scorching hot, and he gives me a thorough, filthy kiss that I whimper helplessly into. His five-o'clock shadow abrades my lips, and I suddenly can't stop shivering at the scrape. Giving in, I moan and kiss him back angrily, overcome. I'm too shaky, irritated, *needy*.

When he pulls back, I'm gasping. "I . . . you . . ."

Snorting, he grasps his tool belt and pops it open with one hand. It drops a moment later. I try not to watch, not to notice the hard, delicious length of him straining obnoxiously against his jeans.

"We need to . . ." I swallow against his palm, and it tightens around my neck. My nipples furl painfully in my bra. "Talk. We need to—"

He kisses me again, harder this time, and frees the button on his jeans. I gasp as he bites down on my lower lip, and he sucks away the sting. Squirming, I pant into his mouth.

This isn't *fair*. I break the kiss and ready to scold him, but my mouth turns dry.

His jeans sit low on his hips, low enough to reveal a dusting of dark hair that I want to trace with my tongue. He drags his zipper down, then strokes himself through his briefs, and I watch the outline of his cock against the fabric, mesmerized.

Everything in me turns liquid, and I force myself to remember that he's in trouble.

"We have to . . . we can't just keep having sex instead of actually having a—"

"I think that's enough talking." Jayk bends down and yanks something textured and white out of his toolbelt. His voice is hot and almost breathless with snarky amusement. "Three slaps to stop me, sugar."

Slaps? Why would I need my non-verbals? There's nothing in my—

Suddenly fabric is being stuffed into my mouth with two rough fingers.

Oh, he *didn't*.

Instinctively, I try to bite down, but Jayk casually grabs my jaw with his other hand, pressing my cheeks until my teeth pry open. His fingers force their way past the barrier, filling my mouth.

I try to throw myself to the side, but he lowers his bodyweight onto me, pinning me hard. My jaw strains, and I choke. Panic edges into my indignation, and I try to push the dry rag out with my tongue, but his wide hand is pressing it down, holding it in.

"Breathe through your nose," he orders, watching me closely.

I'm supposed to be breathing?

The panic doubles when I realize I'm *not*, in fact, doing that, and Jayk pauses, panting. His eyes are dark and intent on my face, like deep sea anchors as he waits.

I grip his arms, and those eyes hold enough space for thoughts to wrestle their way back in—to see the bed, the room. To hear Beau explaining traffic lights in his slow, easy accent.

And to remember Jayk's white face in the woods when I didn't use my safeword.

Yellow, yellow, yellow.

My heart racing, I slap his shoulders twice.

His grip gentles, and he tenses, but he doesn't let go yet. He waits a beat for the third, searching my face for the *stop*, but that's not what I want.

I *want* air.

"Breathe, Eden," Jayk demands, tapping my cheek. "Through your nose. Now."

His eyes fill my vision again, demanding and scorching hot, and I drag in a deep breath through my nose. It's bright. Freeing. *Easy.* It smells like Jayk and need and the beginnings of filthy sex.

Why didn't I do this before?

The panic bleeds out of me as air slips into my lungs, and the tension around his eyes relaxes. As if he can't help himself, he grinds his hips up, rubbing himself against me through our clothes, and I can't help my involuntary moan. All the adrenaline in me starts to crash in giddy, daring waves, and I almost giggle into his hand.

Jayk snorts at me, his smirk warmer than usual, and tinged with more than one shade of relief.

"Fucking terrifying woman," he mutters, and I snort, my heart rate spinning into something thrilled and edged with danger.

At my teasing sound, his brows lift, and he looks down at me. "You want to play it like that? I can play."

With one hand wrestling my mouth closed, he leans down and

pulls something else from his tool belt, and I hear the rip of duct tape as he drags it over my mouth.

Duct tape?

He bends down to tear the end off with his teeth. Stunned, I lift my hands to touch it as he sticks down the edges against my cheeks, tight and puckered. And I'm not sure why, if it's the hot laughter in his eyes or my own curious stubbornness, but it doesn't really occur to me to rip it off.

I take another deep breath through my nose, and my pulse begins to skid into an infuriated, pounding beat as what he did registers.

He *gagged* me!

With a *rag*!

"Don't freak out. It's clean," he mocks, then mutters, "Mostly."

I glare at him, and he snorts a laugh at my muffled, livid protest. My nails dig into his shoulders bitterly enough to draw blood.

I might not want to ruin his game, but it doesn't mean I won't punish him for it.

He hovers over me, then squeezes my cheeks again. "You wanted to talk, right, sugar? Let's talk. If you have a problem with me being the only person you ever get to fuck again, tell me now."

Oohhhh. No. I'm going to *murder* him.

I incinerate him with my eyes, squeaking an irate protest into the gag. He nods, a self-satisfied smile on his face as he listens.

"Not a word? Works for me." Jayk's mouth finds my throat, burning hot and rough-bristled enough to scrape me.

I shove at his shoulders, careful not to slap, and he wedges his hips into place between mine. His cock is heavy and hard against me, and I shudder in . . . annoyance.

I arch against him.

Definitely annoyance.

"Yeah, you're right," he continues, far too much amusement in his voice. "You *should* keep doing my laundry for me. Just speak up if you have a problem with that."

"*Asshole!*" I shout into my gag—or I try to. It comes out garbled and squeaky, and his shoulders shake. He is *insufferable*.

I glower at him, and he fucks against me like it doesn't faze him at all. I *know* it doesn't faze him, and it makes me want to scream all over again. I'm edgy. Sparking. *Combustible.* Jayk riles my frustration like he was born to it, and things start loosening inside me. Heating like rising particles.

I've been sweet all week. Contrite and patient and soothing and calm, even though I've felt anything but. And yes, Jayk is being ridiculous. Unkind to the others and *absurd* in dragging me off like an oversexed neanderthal, but that frustration is just the flame to my powder keg. There are barrels and barrels of dormant dynamite waiting to explode.

Because the Sinners *won*.

It was right *there*. It could have been perfect. We could have been fed and safe, and Dom wouldn't have bruises in his eyes, and Lucky wouldn't be an anxious mess. We all lost so much that night. I'm furious, just *livid* and *frustrated* over all of it, but . . . I can't say any of that. The others haven't needed my fury this week. They've needed someone to gentle the storm.

But with Jayk, I don't need to be sweet anything.

With Jayk, we are the storm.

His hair is almost too short to grab, but I snare it in my fingers anyway and wrench it viciously as I squeeze my legs around his waist.

"You're fucking feral, you know that?" he groans, arousal brutalizing his voice. His breaths are hot against my ear, and I can feel him fighting for control. "Three slaps, Eden. Remember it. Give me three, and I'll stop. Gag comes out."

He curves me into him and runs his tongue along my jawline. The wet trail he's leaving is indelicate, careless, but I can't help the way my head tilts back, begging for more. His body rumbles in approval, and he adds, "But I don't think you will. You seem pretty hard up for it to me."

I stiffen under his mouth.

"Guess you just haven't had any good dick since you left," he continues with mock sympathy.

Spitting fire with my eyes, I thrash under him, but his grip on me just roughens as he rides the wave, rolling his cock against me. I drag in air through my nose again as I shudder, and that infuriating smirk returns.

He squeezes my throat. "Don't worry, sugar. I've got you covered.

All you need to do is just shut the hell up for a while and ride my cock like the hot little brute you are."

Brute.

I wrench my face away, and he just grips me tighter, then licks my cheek, tasting me. "You can even keep your prissy little nose in the air and pretend you don't like it if you want." He makes a soft, hungry sound when I shiver. "We both know it's a dirty fucking lie."

Brute.

The word unfurls inside of me.

The reminder and the promise.

He knows I love this fight—he made me confess it to him in a dozen different ways before he truly let me try.

Burning up, I rip out of his grip and glare up at him, wanting him to see all of it—every *brutal* moment . . . but it only serves to kindle a dark light in him. Something bestial and rapacious. He's unkind with his strength, bold and bullying. He grinds his cock against me again and again, careless in using his size to hold me down and use me . . . but he groans in feral satisfaction at the bloody brands I leave down his arms, and he seems lost to his need, unable to tear himself away, even long enough to strip.

Jayk's rhythm begins to fall apart as he fucks against me, and I moan into his hand. It's too muted. Cruelly so. I want to be made of wild things too, but *instead*, my tongue works irritably against the gag, and his body surrounds me entirely. It stokes my frustration higher.

There's a fierce, dark challenge in his eyes that begs me to unleash on him, that *dares* me to break free, and my rage twists into something hotter, determined to immolate him too.

If he's my end, then I plan to be his.

I tangle myself around him, and his teeth cut into my skin as he breathes me in. His body rubs over me, and the growl he lets out is made of caves and claws.

I don't need to pretend anything around Jayk.

I yank him close to me by his tank, and his tattoos ripple as he braces himself over me, letting me lift my hips so I can wantonly rub against his cock, taking over his rhythm. I don't hold back when I moan, and his eyes darken into ocean trenches.

Greedy, I let my hands run over his chest, my broken nails leaving pressure trails along his muscles. Red swirling between the black patterns on his skin in pretty, violent shades, and each line is a delightful fire in my veins. Because I *am* cranky at him, too. For Lucky and Jasper and Beau. For not letting me talk. For *gagging* me.

And I don't need to temper it.

Fighting with Jayk is a wild, reckless kind of fun.

My fingertips play in the hair on his abdomen, and it's starting to be too painful. There are too many clothes between us, and I'm slick and flushed, and I ache terribly. Apocalyptically.

I begin ripping at his tank, trying to tear it off his body, and he can't hide his barbaric grin when I succeed.

Because he loves this fight at least as much as I do.

Jayk's mouth finds my neck, sucking on my pulse hard enough to make me yelp, but I'm too lost in the way he's grinding against me to notice much else.

Until a frigid, metallic slide against my chest makes me gasp.

I try to arch away, but Jayk doesn't let me move as he bites down on the curve between my neck and shoulder. Hot, sharp pain blooms, but I freeze as I catch the dull gleam of his pocketknife between my breasts.

Not *again*.

I make a sound of alarmed protest, and he rolls his eyes.

"Relax your sphincter. I'm not going to cut you."

I know *that*. We've talked about this before. I'm more worried about—

With one sharp flick, he slices my bra right down the middle.

That.

My breasts spill free, and I only have a moment of stunned mourning for my favorite sports bra before his knife is gone and he's cupping my chilled flesh. His hand is searing, and his calluses scrape over my nipple as he squeezes, making a coarse sound of satisfaction.

His teeth find the edge of my jaw and mark their way down my throat, and I arch into the sting. I yank his hair, then cling for dear life, pressing him into my skin. His rough hand flexes around my neck, and my frantic legs climb his, trying to capture his hips.

It's undignified. Embarrassing. Completely vulgar.

But God, I *do* want to ride his cock.

I wriggle up, trying to pull his head down to my breasts, trying to pull his hips between my legs. I groan into the gag, almost choking on it again as I try to catch air. He shudders against me.

His mouth fastens over my nipple, taking my offering, and he sucks brutally hard. I yank and yank his hair, but he doesn't shift. My heart races, and I arch my breast deeper into his mouth, not sure if I'm trying to ease the pressure or demand more.

I whimper again, praying he understands my muffled, unintelligible begging.

"That's it. You're with *me*. Look at me," he growls, his scalding lips pushing against my nipple. My lids are too heavy, my whole body is syrupy and drunk and buzzing. He bites the side of my breast. "Look at me, Eden. Know who's fucking you."

He finally releases my throat, and he yanks my pants down to my boots with two hands. I force my eyes open as he shoves his hand under my underwear.

He finds my clit, and I cry out, widening my legs. I force my eyes open a crack to look at him as he bends his body over me, pinning me to the bed as his fingers work me roughly.

"How many of them did you fuck while you were out there? Did they do you like this?" he demands, and I sob as he takes control of me, the flimsy fabric straining around his wrist. I'm soaking wet, slippery, and there's no finesse in how he's touching me. He's rubbing me hard, racing toward a point, and I grind against his hand, wordless and gasping, the pressure in me painful. "None of them can fuck you like this, Eden."

I splinter apart, turning my face into the blankets as my gag muffles my scream. I squeeze my thighs around his hand to hold him against me as I turn violently oversensitive and pleasure rips through my body, my mind bursting into blinding, obliterating fragments.

Vaguely, I feel him pull back to watch my face. My chest heaves into him with every heavy breath, and I whimper as his touches become even hungrier.

His hand moves between my legs, not about to be stopped by me and my quivering thighs. He slips his fingers down, and I'm soaked, swollen and puffy. My panties cling to us both as he presses two fingers deep inside me. I clench around him, my inner walls still shivering with aftershocks, and moan, weak and defenseless as he continues to touch me however he wants.

Because Jayk touches me greedily. Like my body was made to fall prey to his. Like he's always owned it, and now he's just making sure I know it, too. His lips are wet, and his tidal eyes are swallowed by possessive need as I tremble against his half-bared cock.

Suddenly, he moves the arm he was leaning on to brush a strand of hair off my forehead. A single strand that he tucks back into perfect place when he's just ravaged me like a shipwreck by cyclonic tides.

The touch is so gentle, so wholly unexpected, that I blink rapidly at him, shivering with lust and pleasure and totally confused. These moments with him are too rare, gone too fast, and I want to protect his softness with both hands.

My gag holds me in silent penance, so instead, I brush his cheek with my fingertips, and something moves in his eyes. Something wary and touched in reverence and dipped in his own confusion.

Then he rips the duct tape off in one brutal pull. I yelp at the tearing sting, and he slaps my cheek, grabbing my chin roughly.

"On second thought, I think I like hearing you beg for my cock," he mutters.

I'm still gasping in pain when he kisses me, his tongue jealously invading the opening. He kisses me druggingly, holding me to him as if this time he really can't bear for me to escape. He kisses me until I'm writhing against him again, reaching down to cup his scorching cock. It throbs in my hand, swollen hard and dampening his briefs.

Jayk breaks the kiss, groaning into my neck as I squeeze, and I shiver a husky laugh, teasing, "I think maybe you just like me."

The tips of his ears turn red. "Shut up."

Suddenly, he pulls his fingers out and then rips my panties down the side. I open my eyes enough to see him free his cock. It's straining and flushed, dewed with precum—and I am tingling everywhere, almost a burn, too sensitive to take him right now.

He pulls my boots off as he strokes himself crudely, staring at my glistening pussy, and I make a sound of protest. He doesn't stop, ripping my pants off and stalking around me.

My heart rate jacks up again, and I flip myself over to crawl to the end of the bed on wobbling arms.

Before I've gone two feet, his hands have wrapped around my thighs, and he yanks me back into him. His cock presses along the seam of my ass.

He grabs himself and rubs himself all over me. Messily. Coating me in precum and smearing it into my skin with bruising fingers before he notches his wet, heavy crown at my entrance. My puffy lips part around him, and he starts to push in, breaching my searing swollen walls.

I flinch away. "Wait, Jayk, I'm too—"

"Do the others stop and cuddle you when you whine? You have a safeword, sugar. Use it, or I use you."

He pauses for a single, mocking heartbeat . . . then he snorts.

He grabs both my hips and drags me back against him. Knocking my thighs wider, he fucks inside me with one hard thrust.

My mouth drops open, and my eyes roll back as he fills me thickly. I clamp against the intrusion, trying to shut him out, but he just grabs a fistful of my hair and yanks it back so my back bows, and I gasp sharply, my breath strangling in my throat as he pushes in deeper.

My breasts brush the bed, only enough to tease, and he thrusts into me, rough and fast, sending them bouncing.

I writhe against him, but he uses my hair to anchor me to him as he takes me.

"Yeah, that's what I thought," he mutters, fucking into me hard.

Every oversensitive inch inside me sizzles into delicious life, and my breathing turns shallow. Our bodies slap against one another. I can feel my wetness slicking my thighs, soaking his cock. I'm scalding hot everywhere, then shivering, then too hot again.

"Fuck." He groans. "Fuck, you feel good."

"Jayk, oh, shit. I can't—" I gasp, squirming as he hits every perfect spot inside me, fast and brutally hard.

There's no escaping now. There's no wanting to. The oversensitivity is turning delicious. Euphoric.

He drives into me so ruthlessly my toes curl. Sobbing, I buck against him, wanting him that deep again. His breathing turns ragged, and his other hand bruises my hip, fighting me into place.

"This isn't for you. Stay put, woman. I've been beating myself off to you for two fucking weeks, and I'm done."

God.

I can't help the impossible picture of him stroking his cock, spilling himself to thoughts of me. I clench around his dick, sending him cursing.

His hand abandons my hair and finds my throat again. He wrenches me back, pinning me against his chest, and each thrust becomes punishing. Brutal enough to make tears spring to my eyes. I can feel every inch of his cock. I feel it everywhere as he demands everything from my body.

He said this wasn't for me. He hasn't even touched my clit again. But that look in his eye demands a response.

"You said you're mine," he whispers through clenched teeth. "So you're going to be mine. You're going to be in *my* bed, riding *my* dick whenever I want . . . like my good little queen."

Queen?

I'm too dick-drunk to protest, but it doesn't matter.

That word seems to break him.

Jayk kisses me, his tongue making a mess of my mouth as his grip on my throat turns tight enough to steal my breath. He kisses it out of me, and my vision goes momentarily dark as his thick cock fills me too. I feel him swell and soak me in hot, wet cum, and I'm gasping for air as I come dizzyingly hard, his mouth on mine, sealing a single word into the breathless place between us.

Queen.

CHAPTER 15

EDEN

SURVIVAL TIP #14
Work for peace.
War works for no one.

E very inch of Jayk's scorching, damp chest is pressed to my back. His kiss is everywhere, his stubble abrading my chin, his tongue in my mouth, and I'm chasing shivers all through my body.

But that *word*.

I shove him back, breaking the kiss, and he slips out of me. He immediately scowls at the loss, his eyes still whirlpools of hunger, over-sexed and glassy and focused on my mouth. His brows crash down, and he reaches for me again, but I put a restraining hand against his chest, stopping him in his tracks.

My head spins, but I ignore it. "*Queen*?" Jayk starts to smirk, still watching my mouth, and I poke his chest, right between his pecs. "You're taking this all a little far, don't you think?"

He leans down to kiss me again, and my legs quiver with the effort of holding myself up. I've been walking all day—all week—and my orgasms are still quaking me at my foundations.

"You want a throne too, sugar?" he asks, his breath fanning over my lips. He shrugs one shoulder. "I'll make you a pretty one. With sparkles and shit."

"I—" I can't help but splutter a laugh, torn between cringing at the awful, garish image of a sparkly scrap metal throne . . . and being oddly endeared by the offer. All of this—the violent claiming, the room, the possessiveness—is a statement. It's *sweet*.

His cum slips down my thigh, and I wince.

For Jayk, it's sweet.

Sweat is dewed across our skin, and he's scored with nail marks and new-blossoming bruises. They mark my skin too, in indented pink bites and purpling sucks and possessive red finger marks I want to examine with interest.

I raise my brows at him. "Fine." My hand still on his chest, I start nudging him back onto the bed. "If I'm the queen, then you can obey me for a change. Sit down."

"Not even a please." He snorts as he lounges back against the headboard. He sprawls out in the center of the messy sheets, his massive body obnoxiously making a mockery of the king-size bed. "Bossy."

Rolling my eyes, I crawl on top of him until I'm hovering over his lap.

There, I hesitate.

He's still naked. And . . . soft. My thighs are turning sticky, but I'm still soaking wet between my legs, and this already feels like a mistake. Is there some etiquette around sitting on a naked man's . . . appendage? Do I *move* it? Bat it out of the way?

Jayk yanks me down, and I slam my hands against his chest to stop myself from overbalancing. Avoiding his amused expression, I shift, realizing I can feel him under my ass. Okay. Not a direct crush. Got it.

More hot cum trickles out of me, pooling into the dusting of hair on his thigh, and I close my eyes in embarrassment.

I really should have cleaned up first.

"You good?" he asks lazily.

"Yep, I'm just, ah . . ." I wince, peeking at him. He has to be able to feel that. "*Leaking*."

The smug curve of his lips widens into a wide, self-satisfied grin. "No shit."

My face scalds with heat, but my eyes linger on that grin. It's relaxed and real, and, even dripping with cockiness, he's unarmed. There is no defensiveness in the pretty crease of his cheek, or snarky daggers hidden in the stubble along his lips. There's not a single bitter curl or wary tuck to be found.

It's unbearably lovely on him.

More moisture trickles out of me, and he hums, rolling my hips over him a little, smearing it. I squeak as I slide in our mess, my hands spreading over his pecs.

"Um. Maybe we should have a shower . . ."

He squeezes my ass with both hands, watching the slick join of our skin. "Or you could give me five minutes and we can go again."

"Aren't you the optimist," I say tartly, and his gaze flicks up with a scowl. Sweetly, I smile at him. "Maybe in the *hour* you'll need to recover, we can talk about whatever fit of madness inspired you to tell the others that I'm yours?"

Jayk grabs my hand, yanking me in close to his face. "Thirty minutes, and you *are* mine. I have it in writing, sugar."

Ah, my *note*.

"I'm not *only* yours!" I exclaim.

Oh, he is *maddening*!

His grin turns, his brows edging down again, and I narrow my gaze on him, trying to work out the best way to wrangle his stubborn butt into this conversation. My head is still spinning, and I'm starting to think it's not just the sex. I haven't eaten much today—and Jayk is a workout.

Taking a calming breath, my gaze skims over his chest. His ruined shoulders.

My fingers trace them. "Do you have anything to clean these with?"

He leans back against the headboard again. "It doesn't matter."

Pushing my glasses up the bridge of my nose, I look at him and wait. It's his turn to roll his eyes, then he leans over, twisting across the bed. Yelping, I cling to him to stop myself from falling off. He opens the drawer of the remaining bedside table, and rummages in the untidy clutter inside. I spot lube, condoms, piles of fresh-cut cloth that looks much cleaner than what he stuffed into my mouth earlier . . .

Twisting back, he tosses a few of the cloths down on the bed, along with a small bottle of iodine. I go to reach for them, but instead I'm smacked in the face with a wrapped bar.

"Ow!" I pick it up, realizing it's some kind of energy bar.

"Eat something. I don't deal with swooning broads, okay?"

Despite the callus words, Jayk's eyeing me worriedly, a stubborn-set scowl settling into his face. I know my ribs are sticking out more than they did two weeks ago, and I know that it isn't *great*, but so are his. So are everyone's. This isn't a choice.

It's survival.

Hating the way he's looking at me, I examine the ingredients on the packaging instead, reluctantly impressed. It's incredible. Packed full of sugar and preservatives, it'll last years and years. The calories in that one bar alone . . .

Ignoring the sunken, needy void of my stomach, I raise my eyebrows. "How many of these do we have left?"

"Who the fuck cares? Queens don't starve." He takes it out of my hands and rips open the packaging.

"Queens who eat more than their fair share are pretty awful—"

I choke as Jayk shoves the bar into my mouth. Crumbs spraying from my lips, I pull it back enough to haul in air.

"Stop *gagging* me," I growl, and he smirks.

Unguided by me, my tongue finds a crumb on my lip and sucks it into my mouth. My eyes flutter closed. It's grainy and a little stale, but the sweetness rolls through my mouth and—not to insult Jayk or any of my brutes—but it's the most delicious thing I've tasted in weeks.

Surreptitiously, I swipe for more crumbs and find at least three of the gracefully aged, wonderful specks beside my mouth.

The bar in my hand glistens, a little wet from my saliva.

It *is* already open. It's not like it will last long now. It would be rude, even, to give it to someone else when it's already been halfway buried in my throat.

Jayk tucks one arm behind his head, his bicep thick and darkly patterned in those beautiful, unnerving tattoos. He watches me arro-gantly. "Just shut up and eat. You can give me this cute little lecture when you're done."

Giving in, I take an unladylike chomp and crumble half the bar over my tongue with an erotic shiver. As I eat, Jayk's eyes linger on my disheveled bun, then he pulls at my hair tie. A moment later, my hair tumbles around me, falling around my hips.

A low breath rumbles from his chest.

I eat slowly as his eyes drink me in, sexed but sated, running over my glasses and hair, lingering on my breasts and the wet mess I've made on his abdomen.

The small space between us warms. It's not the exhilarated inferno of earlier, now. He's already scorched me clean of all the hot, sparking frustration that had been weighing on me like residue, and the possessive fire in him seems to have been soothed to a simmer. The warmth here now is cozy, gently crackling in a way that reminds me of the day I spent working with him in his barn.

It's home.

I'm back at Bristlebrook. I'm with Jayk. He still wants me, and everyone is alive. Everything else can be managed.

I take another bite, looking at the haphazard pile of furniture barricading us inside with mild bemusement. When I woke up after my nightmare a few weeks ago, it took me *twenty minutes* of huffing and puffing to push that stupid side table over to the door—it was a miracle I didn't wake Beau up with all the heaving. Luckily for me, Beau tends to sleep like he's been drugged into a coma, his mouth a little parted like he's waiting to be kissed awake.

I haven't seen him sleep for more than a week now.

The energy bar starts to lose some of its sweetness.

There are holes in the room. Gaping, gauged spaces where Beau's things used to be. His medical bag isn't on the couch, and his socks aren't carelessly and offensively piled beside the hamper. Without his armchair and the revolting lamp, all the furniture matches. And of course there's Jayk, stretched out across the bed, right where Beau used to sleep.

It doesn't smell like Beau anymore.

Now the room smells like cleaning products, and sex, and Jayk. And I *like* having Jayk's scent here, I do.

I just . . . wasn't ready for Beau's to be scoured away.

My throat stings.

The last time I arrived back at Bristlebrook, it was Beau who took me to this room and fed and fucked me. Like this, and not at all like this. He set the fire up and fed me cheese by hand and soothed every hurt, inside and out, like it was his duty to cure each one of them. He handled me like I was fragile—and that day, I was.

Beau's confused, wounded expression as Jayk carried me away stamps itself in the center of my mind.

I crumple the empty wrapper in my hand and blink rapidly as I set it on the side table, casting about for something to say that won't reduce me to tears.

At least the food has settled comfortably.

"Is there any cheese left?" I ask, picking up the iodine and cloth beside me and hoping he won't notice the huskiness in my voice.

Jayk watches my hands as I pour out some of the liquid onto a cloth. "Out of cheese. Out of all milk products. Also sugar, honey, and potatoes. The fleabags are getting low on their feed, too."

My head snaps up. Those are *staples*. They should have been stretched for as long as humanly possible; none of them are easily replaceable. Not *quickly* replaceable, certainly.

Especially the cheese.

Ugh, damn it. Maybe this wasn't a good topic after all. No cheese for the foreseeable future is almost *definitely* worth crying over. At least we still have the goats to . . .

Oh no.

I slap Jayk's chest urgently. "No one killed Billie or Baa-bara did they? Oh, God, please tell me Henrietta's okay. Because Lucky—"

"I didn't kill his stupid pets," Jayk mutters, an irritated tic in his heavy jaw. Then he bursts out, "But he's a moron for naming them. They're food. What kind of dumb shit idiot names his food? I don't care if he cries about it, if shit gets real, I'm ganking them myself. You and Kasey aren't going to starve just because he decided to go all goat-daddy on some lamb chops."

Relaxing, I bite my lip to hide my relieved smile. "Thank you for protecting them, Jayk."

He glares at me, looking a little too like a belligerent toddler for me to take him seriously.

"This will sting," I tell him, then press the cloth against the little cuts my nails made in his skin. He snorts, unflinching, because apparently, *he's* a big tough soldier who chews rocks and doesn't feel pain, but I grimace over the marks. My nails are filthy. If we're going to tear shreds off one another, it should *at least* be hygienic.

"Jayk, we need to talk about the others," I continue firmly, and this time, he does flinch. I continue my ministrations as though I don't notice. "You can't just cut them out of my life on my behalf. I told you how I feel about them. I thought I'd explained this."

He's locking up under me, muscle by muscle. I glance at his face, but he's not scowling at me. Not glaring or glowering. That same bold, reckless challenge is in his eyes.

"I heard you, Eden. You didn't want to choose. Now you don't have to. *I'm* choosing."

My hands stop on his skin, and I fight a sigh. "You said that, but I don't—"

"You think you want them. Fine. They want you. I even get that." Jayk's tongue touches his lower lip, and his gaze rakes down my body. He pinches one nipple hard, tugging on it, and I squeal, squirming. The corner of his mouth lifts. "But you don't need them, sugar. Neither of us do. They're ungrateful, moody, petty-as-fuck assholes, and they'll never get you like I do. They weren't here for two whole weeks, and you know what? This place did just fucking fine without them."

I shake my head, pulling back. "No, Jayk."

But he's leaning forward, the lazy arrogance swelling into hot frustration. "I'm done with them. You are too."

I press my tongue against my teeth for calm, then bite out, "I was clear, Jayk. If you choose me, you're choosing this arrangement too. You don't have to be a part of this—it would kill me, but you don't. They're part of the package."

"Bull. Shit. I'm making my own choice here. And I choose war." Jayk is in my space, all around me. "I'm the only one you need, and I'm going to prove it to you. You want to fuck them, go ahead and try. I'm going to be there. They want to drag you off, I'm going to be there. Whatever they do, I'm doing it better. They can fight as dirty as they want. It's not going to matter." There is war in his face, a stubborn, dark readiness for battle. "*You* leave me if you have your panties in a knot. Kick me out on my ass. But *that*? That's *my* choice."

I tip my head back, gritting my teeth. "I'm not leaving you. I'm not leaving *any* of them. I love them."

"They walk out, Eden!" he snaps, his hands snarling in the ends of my hair like a leash. "They *walk*. Dom's been trying to shove you out the door since you got here. Lucky is hanging off Jasper's dick. Jasper's always ready to fall on his fucking sword for the stupidest fucking reasons. The second he thinks it's for *your own good*, he's out. And Beau." Jayk snorts. "The doc is so far up his own ass he doesn't know which way is out. He bottles shit up worse than you do, and he holds a grudge. Looked to me like you were in his shit books. Good luck getting out of those."

"Stop," I snap back, my heart pounding.

I shift off his lap, but Jayk yanks me back against his chest.

"I'm not *like* them. We grew up as trash, Eden, and they throw people out like they're garbage. I won't do that. I don't *do* that. I don't care what the fuck went down at Cyanide. I don't care how dark you need to go. You're *mine*." His eyes blaze, and he drags my hips over him again like an aching reminder. "We can go dark together."

I'm reeling, feeling him stir against my ass, feeling his chest, his whole, huge body hard and hot and all around me. But the anger I thought I'd extinguished finds a new spark. The warmth between us starts broiling, and only the tall, cracked-open window sweeps in cool eddies of air. It was one of the few that didn't shatter when Dom set off the bazooka.

"You *did* walk away from me," I remind him.

His jaw firms in instant disagreement, and I drag in a harsh breath. I don't want this getting out of hand between us, but I need to make him understand.

With shaking hands, I loosen my grip on my cloth and start cleaning his cuts again. He shrugs away, but I grip his bicep and scowl. "Stay still and listen to me."

"Bossy," he mutters.

"You did make me your queen, didn't you?" I mutter back.

Ridiculous man and his ridiculous opinions and his ridiculous throne being ridiculously hot. I huff, sweeping a line of blood gently from his skin.

"You did walk." This time when he opens his mouth to protest, I ignore him. "You walked when I hurt you. You walked because we weren't talking properly, and everything was messy—*I* was messy— and you needed space to think. And you had to do that, and it was okay in the end because now we're doing better. We're learning, Jayk. We talked and gave each other space and we *learned*."

I swallow hard and look at him. "We're all learning, okay? Yes, Dom was wary of me at first. He was worried I'd break Beau's heart— a fear that unfortunately now is seeming quite valid. But he let me in. Dom isn't some giant unfeeling asshole. He was kind to me. He was a friend when you were gone, and I desperately needed someone who wasn't going to smother or coddle me. He put me back on my feet and reminded me that I could be strong."

Jayk stares at me, long and hard.

"I can do that," he says in a low voice. His hands run up my back, hesitant. "I can do all of that."

The cool air picks up, softly billowing the strange, thin curtains that have replaced the old luxuriant velvet.

My heart aches, and I lean into his touch. "Dom was hurt badly at Cyanide, Jayk. Whatever you say, I know you care. He's lost his confidence. He doesn't want to lead."

He pauses, then glares at the ceiling. "*I'm* in charge now. Problem solved."

"Jayk," I scold softly. "He's supporting you. You heard him earlier. He's not the villain, he's a good, good man, and I—"

Jayk flips me onto my back, tossing my glasses askew, and settles between my thighs. "Yeah, feel free to *not* talk to me about him."

His cock is hardening lazily, and he strokes it over the slippery mess he left, rubbing over my clit. My body starts to perk up with tired interest, but I frown at him.

"Bristlebrook," I say steadily, and he freezes.

Pushing off me, he sits back on the bed, watching me turbulently.

I move into a kneel, throwing the used cloth onto the side table. "You're not distracting me this time. Let's go through your other points, too, shall we? Lucky is in love with Jasper, yes, and they're lovely together—but you'd have to be blind not to see that he's in love with me as well. Lucky has *never* walked out on me. He's unbelievably kind, and attentive, and he makes me laugh, Jayk. He brings me so much joy." I point at him across the silken bedsheets. "He brings you joy, too. No, don't scowl at me. We both know he does."

Jayk scoffs, getting off the bed. "I'm taking a dump."

He walks toward the bathroom, and I scramble across the bed to grab another pillow and throw it at his back.

He spins, scowling when it smacks him.

"Don't you leave just because I'm right!" I cross my arms over my breasts. "Mister 'I-don't-walk-out.'"

Jayk stares down at the pillow, then up at me. He rolls his eyes at my terrible impression of him.

"I don't walk out of *this*!" He gestures between us. "Not the *room*. I like you, sweetheart, and you're a hot piece of ass, but I draw the line at shitting in front of you."

"Poop *later*," I bite out. He can be as crude as he likes—he doesn't get to run away. I start ticking the others off on my fingers. "Jasper is an ethical, honorable man, and I happen to love that about him. He made mistakes with Lucky, and he owned up to those and is making it up to him. He's intelligent and compassionate and terrifying . . . and being with him is like being at peace for the first time ever. I can be *still* with him, Jayk."

He leans against the wide bathroom door, starkly naked and unashamed. He's almost too beautiful to look at. Not like the patterned wallpaper beside him, or the expensive, gold-rimmed urn on the cabinet that Jayk seems to have used as a holder for a shabby water bottle . . . but like his throne outside. Jayk is battered and bruised, covered in old scars and new, tatted and rough and broken in by life.

"You're not quiet, Eden. People made you that way," Jayk says in a low, gruff voice. "You're a bottle rocket—and the second we're alone, you go off. You're kidding yourself if you say you don't need that. Two weeks away with them and you were ready to blow."

I lower the next pillow, deciding against throwing this one at him.

For now.

"I love how we are," I tell him, just as seriously. "I love this and you. But this isn't all of me. Just like it isn't all of you. Kasey and the civilians, and Dom, Lucky, Beau, Jasper, all of them, they all pull different things from you as well."

Jayk's brows lift mockingly. "Difference is, I don't need to fuck them."

My hands twitch on the pillow.

"I love them all," I say again, and he scowls, looking away.

"Jasper's calm matters to me. Lucky's joy and empathy. Dom's friendship and strength. Beau's—" My voice breaks, and I clear it, looking at the ceiling for a minute. "Beau matters to me, even when he's being stubborn. I would think you could empathize with him on that. You're as aggravating as he is, sometimes. And you should know, while you're being so quick to sneer at him, that when the situations were reversed—when *he* was here, and *you* weren't . . . Beau fought for you. He helped me find the courage to go after you and tell you how I felt."

Jayk's lips press into a thin line, but his eyes slip away, a tiny crease forming between his brows.

"I'm not giving them up," I repeat again, more softly.

He takes a moment, glaring at the floorboards, then he looks up at me. He starts walking back over until he's at the edge of the bed. "You don't need them. We don't need anyone else."

I open my mouth, then close it, thinking. Putting my glasses back on, I reach up to hold his arm, then I tug him down for a kiss.

When we break, I sigh softly, searching his face. "You're wrong, Jayk. They're family. You know better than to turn family away."

His hand spans over the back of my neck, and his fingers stir my hair, almost tentative. He touches me slowly, and so, so softly over the livid marks on my neck, and I blow out a long, exhausted breath. I rest my forehead against his chest, leaning into him. He still smells like engines and fresh wind.

He doesn't reply immediately, and when he does, his voice takes on a bitter tinge. "I'm not the one with the problem. It's them who have a problem with me."

The slow, hesitant touches don't stop. He rubs strands of my hair between his fingers. "You heard them, Eden. They think I'm dumb as shit. They keep me around to fix what they break and then hang out together for the feel-goods."

The loneliness under that statement bites, and I think of how many years he spent out in the barn—not so very different from my cave.

"Is that what they think?" I murmur. "Or is that what *you* think?"

His hand drops away, and he steps back. I'm about to sigh when he yanks the water bottle out of the urn.

"I already have a shrink, sugar. Don't knock yourself out." He slaps the bottle into my hand. "Drink this."

I give the dented bottle a brief look, then take a sip, deciding the insistence on hydration is definitely a dominant thing.

When I've had about half the bottle, I hand it back to him. "You too."

He gives me a dry look.

"What, water is only for women? It's a hot day, and you didn't even have a sip of your tea earlier," I say snippily, and he rolls his eyes, taking the bottle, so I continue more gently. "You heard what Dom said earlier. Look at what you've done here, Jayk. He's right. You *should* be proud of it." Twining our fingers together, I squeeze his hand. "He respects you. They all do."

Jayk looks away, but not before I see the flush of color in his cheeks. He wipes his mouth and tosses the bottle down, avoiding my eyes, and I drag him back to sit on the bed beside me.

"I respect you, too. I hope you know that," I add. His shoulders roll, uncomfortably hunched, and I smile as he struggles to take the compliment. "And this, too."

I look around the room, all of it neat and in order, and free of bloodstains. The curtains that had been soaked in it have been replaced with white bedsheets, horribly hemmed at the bottom in a way that makes me question if he actually did the hemming himself.

My eyes sting at the sweetness of it. "You did all of this for me. And don't get me wrong, it was horribly rude to throw Beau out, but . . . I appreciate the rest of it. So, so much." I swallow. "I love you, Jayk."

His breath rushes out of his nose, and his jaw works. It takes a moment of struggle, before he finally clears his throat, glancing at me. "Me too. I love you, or whatever."

I bite down so hard on my lip, I'm sure it's going to split. I can't laugh at him now. Not when my heart is thrilling into a kaleidoscope of joy, and he looks ready to crawl under a rock.

But how does the same man who declares *mine* with his whole chest and who stares down a room of men while daring them to try and take me *also* look like he'd rather lick the inside of a toilet bowl rather than say those three words.

When I'm sure I'm not going to burst into a fit of elated giggles, I squeeze his hand and decide to let him off the hook. "Just let yourself be proud of it, too, Jayk. These civilians love you. They listen to you. You've done so much for them."

Jayk scoffs, throwing me a confused look, his brows knitted. "It's not me. I don't know what the fuck I'm doing. It's them. They're the ones picking up all the slack."

My chest warms at how easily he gives them credit—and sighs over how little he takes for himself.

"I'm no expert in leading people . . . but maybe you don't need to have the answer. You just need to be open to hearing it." I nudge his shoulder. "And you *acted* on it. The Reapers, the defenses here, God, don't you see how incredible this is." I smile at him. "You're incredible, Jayk."

This time, the red takes over his ears too, and he starts to look so uncomfortable, I'm sure that if he hadn't walled us up inside, he'd be flying out that door already.

So I let out a little laugh, teasing, "I admit, the whole king thing might be a little . . ." Arrogant. Obnoxious. Entitled. "A little *much*, but they clearly admire you enough to humor it. The others see that, too."

Or they will. Dom sees it, at least. I'm sure of that.

"It's my name," he mutters, glancing at me warily, and I tilt my head, puzzled.

"King?" He shrugs, and it starts falling into place. "Jaykob King."

How did I not know that? I frown at the tangle of our fingers where his hand engulfs mine on his thick thigh.

"I never went by it." He pauses, and his voice is low when he rushes the next words out. "It was a stupid name for how I grew up. It was a joke."

I search the side of his face. "But you're going by it now."

His head lifts, and he looks me in the eye.

"I'm not a joke anymore, Eden." His shoulders straighten, and there's a new pride there. A silent confidence that wasn't there even two weeks ago. "You said I need to believe in myself or whatever. So I'm doing it. I can do this. I'm stepping up for the civilians—and for you." His hand squeezes mine hard, and his face is deadly serious. "It's going to be me in the end, Eden. *Just* me. I'm going to prove it to all of you."

Emotion rises in my throat, making it rough and rocky. I meet his new confidence with my own. "I'm open to you trying, Jayk." My voice firms. "As long as you're open to me proving to you that maybe *I'm* right, and that maybe instead of neither of us needing the others . . . maybe *all of us* need each other."

For what's coming, I know it's true.

At the moment, Jayk thinks starvation is our only problem. I still need to tell him about Alastair's empire and that we're now expected to live under the Sinners' boots. About Red Zone, which will need our help with food and medicine and all the things we can't afford to help with.

We're not going to be able to deal with any of it if we're not on the same side.

He appraises me, his midnight eyes swirling with stars. A cocky smile begins to return to his face, and his hand shifts in mine.

Then he shakes it.

"Good luck, sugar. You're going to need it."

CHAPTER 16

LUCKY

SURVIVAL TIP #156
Sticks and stones may give you a bone,
but a sadist will love and destroy you.

Jasper closes the door behind him, and we're enclosed in moody, secretive darkness. It smells like rich leather and expensive oils. Deep wood warms the walls, and a buttery bronze gleams from ceiling hooks and fixtures. Each tool hangs with exacting precision in neat, ordered rows. His art.

The lock clicks shut, and my breathing slows. The air grows very, very still.

His room is my church.

There's a reverence here that swallows sound. An expectation that has a weight. It's the one place in the world where it doesn't feel right to raise my voice.

Which is probably for the best, anyway, since I just about shouted it raw at Jayk.

That fucking asshole.

I roll my shoulders uneasily, shaking off the worries I don't want chasing me here.

I'm slow to advance inside the room, letting the peculiar peace of this place soften the edges of my restless panic. My pulse quiets to a deep, steady throb, and I trail my fingers along the padded spanking bench.

It soothes me.

Jasper sweeps into the room, his boots clicking on the floorboards, shattering the silence.

"Impact floor, Lucien." I startle at his clipped tone. "Inspection position."

I eye him cautiously as he considers the tool wall, but he's too veiled by shadows for me to make out his face. He seems . . . off. Jasper is a patient predator—slow, deliberate, and lethal.

He's not usually so abrupt.

Jasper unhooks something, and my attention switches to the display, alarm spiking. *Crap.* What did he take? The knives are in a separate drawer, so not those. The masks and canes and crops are still there. So is the shock collar, violet wand, his vampire gloves . . .

He turns, and I only glimpse the dull shine of coiled black leather in his hands before he spots me.

His mouth thins into a ruinous line. "What part of that sounded like a request to you?"

Shit.

I jump into a walk only slightly shy of a run, and his dark eyes have a biting pressure on my back. I'm halfway to the floor before it even occurs to me to sass him.

Jasper is in a *mood*.

Nervous, excited shivers trip down my spine. I'm ready for him to distract me. To hurt me. Whether I anoint these floors with tears or blood or cum, I'll face my reckoning here. It doesn't matter what tools he chooses—in Jasper's hand, even a feather can be as vicious as a blade.

I *want* him to be vicious.

Nothing else has been working lately. I need him to pull me out of my head and back into my skin.

The impact floor has high ceilings with discreet bars and hooks that can be used for suspension. I stop in the middle of the wide, cleared space and hesitate, realizing I'm already in trouble.

Inspection position.

Crap. How do I do that one again?

Jasper's boots echo around the room, and fear thrills through me as he approaches.

Running on instinct, I stand straight, chin up, arms down by my side, my legs together.

I . . . *think* this is it?

It's a military position. I've spent hours standing like this in tidy ranks, soaked in rain and baked by sweltering suns with Dom staring down my uniform for the smallest imperfection. I scour my brain, trying to remember if I learned it at the kink club too. I'm sure there was one crossover position.

My memory sucks, though.

Darkside's mandatory training courses were great for a lot of reasons, but unless the class involved someone trying to fuck or hurt me, my attention to my studies was spotty at best. But the position *seems* right.

Right?

I hold my breath as he stops in front of me, his face shadowed. I can't tell if I've chosen correctly or not.

His soft mouth is terse. "Safeword?"

"Houston," I tell him huskily.

It's the first step in our ritual, one of the little rules Jasper refuses to ignore or bend, and it puts another brick back under me.

But there's no ghost of his usual, begrudging humor at my safeword.

In fact, there's no warmth at all in his face.

Jasper's eyelashes curtain his eyes, but I'm getting better at seeing the things he tucks away . . . and his unhappiness is thick as smog, heavy under his pretty cruelty.

If this is my church, my god is displeased.

My worry spikes, but he starts circling me slowly before I can speak, his skin glowing in the low lights.

He's painfully beautiful.

Jasper's always been dangerous, but today, the threat of him isn't disguised under cool silks and hot tea. He's in his full uniform, and between the dusty malice and that glacial expression, he looks ready to punish and rend. It's only then I see the spiteful bullwhip now attached to his belt, and my mouth goes dry.

That whip is trouble.

The best, most terrifying kind.

I swallow hard, trying to work some moisture back into my mouth. Me. He's ready to punish and rend *me*.

"Is there anything you would like to add to your usual limits?" he asks.

The boot clicks pause behind me.

Shit.

His breath stirs my hair, and the back of my neck prickles in warning.

"Ah . . ." I clear my throat. "Nope. I'm good. Great, even. I think I—"

"Good."

Jasper grasps my wrist, then wrenches it up so my hand is behind my head. His grip is merciless, cruel, and I shudder as he does the same to the other.

The painful pressure is sweet. Just the smallest tease of what's coming.

"You have miserable form, Lucien," he says, his breath hot against my ear. "Are you aggravating me on purpose, or do you simply not care enough to apply yourself?"

My cheeks sting with embarrassment . . . and more than a little lust.

He hasn't used this tone with me since he told me he loved me.

But that unhappiness in him puts me in a chokehold.

I'm about to reply when Jasper knocks out the back of my knee, unbalancing me, then kicks my leg wide. His hand comes up between my thighs, and I tense, heat flushing through me as he adjusts my stance with casual ownership.

Fuck.

"Feet hip-width apart. Hands behind your head. Shoulders straight, chest out," he corrects me. When I don't move quickly enough, he draws my elbows back, sharply. "Chest *out*, Lucien."

My shoulders bunch as I push myself into the exposed, uncomfortable position.

There's a pause as he adjusts me again, then a cool, distracting hand slides over the tense muscles. It traces the slope of my back. His hand barely touches my uniform, but I shiver at the contact.

I know why he's brought me here—and he didn't drag me away from Eden's door for another lecture, or for one of the few hurried fucks we've been able to steal these last two weeks.

We both need this.

"*This* is Inspection." Jasper's boots resume their clicks around me as he assesses every inch of my posture.

He comes into view, and I find myself examining him just as closely.

"You were in Attention. Learn the difference," he advises coldly.

My heart tugs at the familiar, icy mask. I hate that mask. He's worn it for too many years and hid too many things behind it. I don't want him to hide anymore. Not here. Not with me. But I don't know how to reach him when he's like this. I've never been good at it.

I cast about for a reply that won't frustrate him further.

Eden's sweet, teary face pops into my mind. The way she whispered to him during the bond-fire.

The way he reacted.

Clearing my throat, I offer a shaky, "I'll remember, Jasper . . . if it pleases you."

Jasper's gaze lifts, startled enough to be downright offensive. Okay, so I might need a few reminders on details, but I *did* learn all the fancy high protocol stuff. It's not my fault I find it about as interesting as watching my toenails grow.

But it does seem to have an immediate effect.

"Obedience?" He stops in front of me, his head canting curiously. "You surprise me."

He's still beautiful—still cold, severe marble—but the harshness trickles out of his tone. Dark, fathomless eyes bore into me. "No sass for me today?" He steps closer, and I can taste his breath. "Are you going to be a good boy for me?"

I feel his approval like a fist around my cock.

His lips purse again as he hums speculatively. "Won't that be a nice change."

I . . . did that actually work?

Desperate to warm that cool expression, I offer him a hesitant, playful smile. The one that usually makes him stare at my lips like he wants to bite them.

And I take a risk.

"I mean, you are taking your sweet time. Another submissive might call you a grumpy, ineffective sadist who can't recognize the right end of a whip."

He doesn't reply.

Oooh, I'm an idiot. This isn't risky. This is *hazardous*.

My blood pressure rises with the slow, chilly lift of his brow, and I flinch as he reaches up to unbuckle one of the straps on my kit. Standing the way I am, I'm completely exposed to his touch. My breathing gets shallow as those deft, deathly fingers work to strip me.

I can't tell if this is making his mood better or worse.

His bullwhip slithers at his hip.

"I *could* say that," I clarify nervously. "But I wouldn't. Probably. Because I'm being so obedient and all."

There's a long, tense moment where I can't breathe at all.

Then, finally, I see that severe mouth soften, just a fraction. A hint of wry amusement touching its edges.

My legs wobble in relief.

I debate my next words. I could let this happen. I'm sure he'll devastate me, and I'll thank him for it, but . . . that tiny downcast to his expression is wrecking me worse than any whip. "I think I'd rather ask why you look like someone just tied all your favorite floggers into knots."

His hands pause for a moment, then resume their motions. He unstraps the last buckles on my kit, loosening it. There was a time it took him longer, but it's second nature now. A smooth, methodical undressing.

He still doesn't look at me. "This scene is for you, Lucien. And long overdue. I'm quite all right."

Buckle. Zip. Buckle. Buttons.

"Please," I whisper, stung that he'd think I'm so selfish.

I hold still against the tiny jostles. Watch the careful way he hangs my kit, then his own. He starts unbuttoning my uniform, and each inaudible *pop* slowly reveals my chest.

When he eventually looks up at me, there's an unsettled pensive-ness to his dark gaze. A hint of frustrated vulnerability I'm not used to seeing there. "Jaykob's words are . . . bothering me."

A humorless laugh slips out of me. "Yeah, they pissed me off, too."

Jasper's brows lift, and my eyes skip away as that inexplicable panic clouds my throat again. It didn't *just* make me angry.

The throne, I was into. The Reapers, I can roll with.

But Jayk *took* her.

In hindsight, that probably shouldn't have surprised me. He *is* known for his whole "don't touch my shit or I'll clobber your skull into a bloody pulp" thing. We should have prepared something to ease him into it. A heartfelt slam poem, or a "Welcome to the Orgy" card, maybe.

But it *did* surprise me.

I can feel the sting of my broken nails where I raked at his door. The bruises on my fists from pounding on it. Seeing him take her away just . . . wrecked me. And it keeps happening. Every time I let her go, someone steals her away. Sam. Alastair. Fucking *Jayk*. I can't shake this feeling that the next time I leave her, I'm never going to get her back.

The ugly image of bullets bursting into trees around Beau comes back to haunt me. I can still feel the weight on my chest as I let him get shot at so I could cover Eden and Jasper. Dom's disappointment in me.

Fuck, I almost got Beau killed today.

Jasper unhooks the last button, and his hand pauses on my collarbone. I focus on his touch. The room. What's about to happen. I don't need to think of how bad I'm messing everything up right now.

My uniform falls open, and I shiver.

But his eyes stay on my face.

"You're anxious being apart from her. It's understandable, given our recent history," he tells me calmly. I grimace at his first, gentle lash, but he continues, "Are you concerned for her safety?"

"With Jayk?" I ask, surprised. "No. I just . . . I don't know. Lately I've been . . ." I stop, then give him a look. "We were talking about you. How did Jayk upset you?"

Jasper trails his fingers down my chest, over the ridges of my pecs and the valleys of my abs. He eases my shirt and jacket off me, then has me return to Inspection. My head falls forward, and I breathe out hard as my body comes alive. Every cell focused on the lightest points of contact.

He's always softest right before he hurts me the worst.

Jasper gives me a scolding look, but he allows the change of subject.

"Eden loves Jaykob. She loves him dearly." His fingers trail over my abdomen. "Dominic is right that what he's done here is incredible, and this bold statement Jaykob has made . . . perhaps I'm a little concerned that she'll be swayed by it. It's vulgar, for my taste, but Eden . . ." The mystified expression on his face almost makes me grin. "Eden seems to find him charming."

An adorable, puzzled frown appears between his brows, and I stick my tongue in my cheek. He's upset. I can be sympathetic. A good, doting submissive.

I just didn't expect him to be so . . . cute.

His fingers absently trail over my abdomen.

When I'm sure I can keep the teasing out of my voice, I ask, "I mean, can you blame her?"

Jasper flashes me a filthy look. In one swift move, he unsnaps my belt.

"Oh, come on. Dom is busy falling on his sword or whatever, and Beau's all up in his feelings. Coming back to Jayk wanting to toss her into a cave and go to town has got to feel good." I shrug. The wild sparkle in Eden's eyes as he carted her off wasn't lost on me. I get the same feeling when Jasper pulls out his cane. "He has a thing. I get why she's into it."

Jasper's hands get harsher as he rids me of my pants, my boots . . . my briefs. Delicate, sable strands of his hair slip against my legs as he works, and I try not to think about how close his mouth is to my cock.

Or how he might punish me if I dragged his mouth to it.

"I'm not tossing you over my shoulder, Lucien," he mutters, looking up.

"Safety first. I like it," I reply glibly. "Don't want you throwing your back out."

Jasper doesn't react, just nods to that, like he's collecting strikes.

It knocks a few rungs out of my confidence.

I'm naked in front of him as he stands. His cool hand flattens on my heated abdomen, right above my stiff cock. It aches, begging for attention, and I shift my hips a little, chasing his touch.

He ignores me, that pinched crease worrying his brow again. "Eden and I are still finding our way."

He walks around me again as he talks, letting his skin slide over mine. Over my side, over my ass. He draws a finger up my back, slowly enough to send gooseflesh down my spine, then around my bicep . . .

"We've had much less time together—which is my fault, I know— but I don't know if I've made enough of an impression. If she might choose Jayk's idea of forever after all." Jasper's voice becomes soft as his touch lingers on my chest, right over my heart. "One without me in it."

It's murder.

When he finally stops, I'm breathing fast and shallow, and color slashes his cheekbones. But when he meets my gaze again, the naked concern melts me.

"Jasper, anyone who has the chance to have you in their life is going to fight like hell to keep you. Eden isn't going to give you up," I tell him huskily. "I don't care how many ways Jayk can helicopter her on his dick."

Jasper blinks at the image, then the color deepens in his cheeks.

"You were concerned about him storming off with her too," he says defensively. "I believe there was some talk of sledgehammers?"

I let out an exasperated snort. "I'm not worried about *Eden*. The woman's all over me. *And* you."

Jasper gives me a dry look, then walks over to press a button on the wall. The lights brighten, and a narrow spreader bar attached to a thick chain begins to descend from the ceiling above my head. Two wide, padded cuffs dangle from either side.

I eye them, nervous adrenaline kicking low in my stomach. "I . . . What was I saying?"

Jasper raises my wrist above my head. As he fastens the cuff around my wrist, he prompts, "Eden is all over me."

He buckles it tight. "Right." The leather swallows my other wrist. "Don't even try to tell me you don't notice how she stares at you. She gets all cute and stammers. She watches your hands a lot. Oh, and whenever you start on something extra boring, she does that dreamy little sway."

"*Extra* boring?" he asks mildly.

The chains start lifting again, higher . . . and higher.

A breathless grunt of effort escapes me as he stretches me out. I dangle from my toes for a moment, my arms straining, before he drops me a few inches.

Sadist.

He leaves me fully extended, but my feet are flat and stable. I grasp the chains above the cuffs, testing the give and finding none. It holds me in place, but it also lets me stabilize.

Jasper nods once as he looks me over.

We both know I can hold this position for a while. That he likes to deliver it soft. Then hard enough to make me stagger. He likes to wait for me to find my feet again, patient and hard and amused before he does it again.

He likes it when I shake.

We also know that when I inevitably collapse and can't get up, he'll lower me to my knees, and I pray quietly, fervently, that this time he'll fuck me while I drown in the high of the pain.

Jasper unhooks the bullwhip from his belt as he considers me. "I make Eden nervous. That could explain the stammering."

He uncoils the leather, running it between his fingers until the fall drapes over his hand.

"Nervous. Weird," I agree.

A wry smile turns up his lips, and he moves into the empty space beside me, rolling his shoulders. "She is fond of me," he concedes. "I do know that."

He gives the whip a short, easy test swing. The crack snaps in the air like a gunshot. It's deafening. Beautiful.

Terrifying.

"Eden's made herself clear, Jasper. She's not giving anyone up." My restless anger bites at me again. Jayk's smirk is smeared over my mind. The way he slammed the door in our face and Eden's face winked out. "*Jayk* is the problem here. He's being selfish. He's the one who took her."

And I didn't stop him in time.

I never stop them in time.

Jasper's head is angled like he's listening, but he just gives the whip another test swing. Then another. I watch it slash the air again and again, slowly getting faster, testing different types of swing until it whistles through the air. He taps the same hook on the wall three times in rapid succession.

A cruel, calm satisfaction curls over his features.

"Jaykob," he muses.

The next swing is vicious, the black leather licking through the air like a serpent.

Crack.

I feel the breath of it, and fear snaps over me in delicious, horrible shivers. I know the mindless sting, and the awful, thudding depth of this whip.

It's mesmerizing.

Jasper catches the fall in his hand again, then walks over to me.

There's a ripe flush in his cheeks, and an unholy gleam in his eyes. His small smile is heartbreaking. "Jaykob is the problem."

"Uhh." I'm too turned on for this. "You're not going to kill him, are you? Because as hot as I'm finding that idea right in this moment, I feel like that might put us in Eden's naughty book."

Jasper moves in close to me, close enough that his uniform grazes my naked, oversensitive skin in a dozen places, each touch as brutal as a knife. I'm so oversensitive, I worry what a single solid stroke from that whip is going to do to me.

He tilts my chin up, and my lips part, though I doubt I'm that lucky. Jasper is sparing with his kisses during a scene. He finds it amusing to make me beg for them.

My cock throbs, and the empty space between us pulls taut.

His eyes are onyx, heavy-lidded and hot on my face. "No, love, I'm not going to kill him. But he invited a fight—and if Eden craves a claiming, then who am I to deny her one?" The pad of his finger crushes my lips, and he brings his mouth close to mine to whisper, "A prettier one."

I groan, my lids dropping closed at the image. At the millimeters between us.

Suddenly, I feel coiled leather trailing over my flushed, throbbing cock, and my chains rattle as I jerk.

"Jasper," I gasp.

His lips brush over mine, then his tongue traces the inner rim. It's delicate. Filthy. He knows what thoughts he's dragging out of me.

"Jaykob is outnumbered. He won't steal her away again. I won't let him." He slips his tongue into my mouth, hot and silken, drinking my moan—and as his kiss takes hold, and his deadly leather wraps around my cock, so does the idea. Me and Jasper taking Eden this time. Her buried between us, safe and squirming and mindlessly fucked.

Jasper pulls back, and my lips are wet with him.

Dazed, I murmur, "She's ours."

The idea settles into me. Taking her back. Keeping her. It's violent and appealing after weeks of helplessness. Jayk doesn't get to take her. He can't cut us out. He doesn't get to make that kind of decision for her when she loves us too—and we won't let him.

Eden doesn't belong to anyone but herself.

Seeing the change in me, Jasper nods, resolved. Lit and glowing with ruthless, ungodly anticipation.

"Jaykob needs to be taught a lesson in humility." He steps back, pulling the whip wide. "And I have a few ideas on how to deliver that lesson."

The first lash is warming, a kiss, and I close my eyes as my swollen cock slicks in need.

They become hotter, brighter with every stroke.

And even when the pain becomes dazzling, one thought remains.

Jaykob will get his fight after all.

CHAPTER 17

JAYKOB

I s this really what I was fighting for?

I can't do this. There's no fucking way this is going to work—I don't know why I was kidding myself. I need to get away from her.

Now.

It's a thousand degrees tonight, and I've been lying in this stupid four-poster bed for two *hours* trying to get some shut-eye. Eden's welded against my side, snoring like one of those wheezy, inbred puppies—just *sleeping*, like the room isn't a sauna, and sweat isn't dripping off my balls.

Isn't she *hot*?

She *feels* like fucking lava.

I nudge her arm, trying to push her off, but her forehead scrunches, and she curls in closer, her thigh sliding over mine. We glue together at another dozen points of contact. For fuck's sake. She's *stuck*. Peeling her off me is going to be like ripping off a Band-Aid. One shove and I'm going to wax her nipples off.

Like a fucking comedian, a breeze lifts the shitty sheet-curtains I made, and I get a moment of hope before a flamethrower of hot air pumps over me. Sweat pools in my pores.

Fucking. Great.

Nature's got jokes.

I thought having a woman in my bed, especially this woman, was supposed to be . . . I don't know, *nice*. I don't remember our first night making me want to peel my skin off and drown it in an icebox. But we didn't exactly do a whole lot of sleeping that night either.

Before that, I can't even remember the last time I shared a bed with someone for more than a few hours. Getting Ryan settled, maybe, on the cramped fold-out back in the day. I remember piling on blankets, worrying he'd get cold.

It wasn't a fucking furnace, though.

Even her *breath* is too hot.

No. This is a stupid way to sleep. It ain't happening. If this is what it's like, I finally get why most couples seem so fucking miserable.

They're sleep-deprived.

Another fiery gust of air billows over me, and that's it. I don't care how pretty her nipples are, they're done for. It's a real shame; we had a good run. But she's got to go.

I look down, ready to dump her off the side of the bed, when I realize a strand of her hair has fallen over her lips. It flutters like a hummingbird wing. I fall still, watching. It does it again, flickering up with each little breath, then settling back against her soft, pink mouth.

Trying not to wake her, I push it gently off her face, tucking it behind her ear, and her face relaxes, her lips curving up. I feel my lips hook up too, and my heart beats unsteadily.

She looks happy.

Whatever. Maybe this isn't so bad.

Dawn is only a few hours off, anyway.

Hesitantly, I curl my arm around her, and her thigh tightens over my hip. She's *snuggling* me, I realize. She fell asleep after a shower, before I'd even finished with the arnica . . . and now we're snuggling.

While she's down, I rub my thumb over her soft skin. Down her arms, onto her side, and . . . I frown as my fingers dip into each rung of her ribs. I look back down at her face again. The skin is pulled too tight over her cheekbones and jaw. She didn't have much meat on her when she got here, but since she was kidnapped, it's worse.

Damn it.

Fear pricks me, and I scowl. It's been years since I've had to worry about shit like this.

She's thin. Kasey's thin.

My stomach rumbles, and I grimace. So much for *incredible*, and *impressive*, and *all the things I've done*. She wouldn't be so impressed if she knew how bad this was.

And it's all for nothing if we starve.

Eden shifts, dislodging her glasses, and there are red little marks where they've been pressed into her skin. I pull them off her face, then put them on the side table.

I trace the indents they left, the tired circles under her eyes, and pressure crushes my chest.

How am I supposed to keep her safe?

She filled me in on all of it. Cyanide and fucking Aaron. The Sinners, Alastair and freeing him, and the massive question mark *something* they're going to demand from us at some point. Red Zone getting fucked sideways, and the teenagers they're trying to keep alive —the help *they're* needing from us, too.

What the hell am I supposed to do with all that?

There's a loud rap at the door, and I swing my legs out of bed and hurry over. The other assholes wouldn't knock.

"Jayk?" Ava asks through the door.

"What?" I bark.

Eden turns in bed again, and I freeze. Did I wake her up?

When she doesn't move again, I scowl, lowering my voice. "It's three in the fucking morning. Can't it wait?"

"Oh, is it? *Three*, you said? I had no fucking clue. Here I was trying to work out what all that twinkly shit is up in the sky. That explains everything."

I roll my eyes, and Ava's voice turns dry. "We came earlier, asshole. You were busy doing the naked mambo—either that, or wrestling a grizzly. It was a bit hard to tell from the sounds. But hey, if you want me to interrupt next time, I'm more than happy to get National Geographic on board and—"

"The fuck do you want, Ava?" I growl.

"We followed them, like you said. The Reapers. There are more of them—maybe fifty or so. They're camped pretty close, but they're not getting too comfortable. Their shit is still packed."

Fifty?

"What happened to our fucking cameras?"

I only just stop myself from shouting. Fifty is trouble. Fifty is a shit fight if they attack, even with the defenses.

"Cameras are on. They're sitting between them. No visuals."

These fucking cameras. They *used* to work. Hell, we've turned away over a dozen groups before they crawled up our ass. Now every two-bit hick from Pigsville is somehow slipping our surveillance.

Son of a *bitch.*

"They're not moving?" I check, suddenly irritated by how much shit is blocking the door.

It seemed like a good idea a few hours ago, but now I just see our only exit barred. Quiet as I can, I start shifting furniture.

"Nope. They're getting their beauty sleep. Just one guy on watch, and he keeps nodding off."

She sounds amused, and too relaxed, like she thinks this isn't a big deal—like they're too stupid to be any kind of a threat. They are stupid. That doesn't mean they ain't a problem.

"You watch them. Multiple eyes—and backup for them. Any one of them so much as scratches their ass, I want to know about it," I growl, straining to drag the bookcase to the side.

"Done. And if you're busy basting your girl's ovaries again? Should I go to Dom?"

I stop short at the question. At how god-damned tempting it is to say yes.

I'm in over my head.

"No," I snap into the silence. Panic spikes, but I strangle it the fuck out and try to sound sure. "I have this. I can do it myself. Just knock. I'll answer, okay?"

"All righty. You're the king," she replies, and I scowl at how fucking indulgent she sounds.

I slide down the wall when she leaves, taking a steadying breath. How the hell does Dom do this? Maybe I fucked up with this whole king thing. I wanted to make a point. And maybe . . . maybe I wanted to prove that I wasn't just the dumb asshole they kept treating me as. That they need me.

I didn't bank on any of them letting me get away with it.

And I really didn't expect to walk in on Dom blowing sunshine up my ass. *Good fucking work*, he called it. I can't remember the last time I heard real gratitude drop out of his mouth, but he just starts dropping that shit now behind my back?

I rub a hand down my face, looking at the mess of furniture I still need to move from the door.

It hasn't been that rough so far, being in charge. The civs are smart, and we've been working together fine. But this food thing . . . I don't know what to do about that. And fifty Reapers? That shit could go south quick.

If I ain't smart here, I'm going to be in charge of digging out a mass grave for the people I was supposed to keep safe.

I look back over at Eden, and she lets out another loud, dragging snore.

It doesn't matter now. It's done, and I'm not letting her down.

But as I rub my heavy eyes, I can't help but wonder what the cap would do.

CHAPTER 18

DOMINIC

I don't have anything to do.

It's strange. I've showered, changed. Cleaned my room. Made my bed twice. I've done a perimeter check and got shooed away from the surveillance room. Everyone's busy doing their own thing. Normally I'd have a dozen tasks to work through, but they're either covered by civs . . . or they're Jayk's responsibility now.

A steady chatter of voices fills the halls, and I drift toward the kitchen.

"I still think we should go after her," someone says.

I pause with my hand on the door.

"Yeah, with what weapons? Madison's gone up against Cyanide and lost twice now. If she and the Rangers couldn't do it, then there's no way we can," another voice grumbles back.

"No one is going to Cyanide." I recognize Ethel kicking back like a recoil. "That girl can handle herself. We have plenty to fret over here. And I . . ."

"Ethel, sit down," Ida says sharply. "Kasey, bring some water."

Cutlery and bowls clatter inside.

"Is she . . ." Kasey starts.

"I'm fine, quit your nagging," Ethel grumbles.

"Do you think those Reapers really have food?" Kasey asks, subdued. "Maybe they're not *that* bad. Maybe it'd be okay if we—"

"Maybe we should attack them instead," Katherine mutters, and I've heard enough.

I push inside, and everyone shuts up. Maybe a dozen civilians are sprawled around the room, and they could be any gossipy soldiers in any restless, dusty mess hall I've supervised over the years. A chicken is being carved up. Its organs are sitting in a bowl, and Mary Beth's gloved hands are busy cleaning and chopping. Ida is dropping the bones into a large, fragrant pot with a handful of vegetables, and Katherine is making some sort of thin stew.

A whole chicken.

They're stretching it, but the chickens were still laying when we left. Breeding. Rations aren't my area, but is the net benefit of a few meals now really worth losing the supply? We had less than a dozen left.

"Need something?" Kasey asks, the same belligerent set to her jaw I've seen Jayk wear for years.

I don't miss the exchanged glances. The tensing. Mary Beth is already cringing, not looking up from her work.

Ethel looks at me tiredly from a seat beside the breakfast bar.

She seems older and frailer than I remember.

It's a stinging reminder of how badly I've fucked it up with them, so I swallow my disapproval. It's Jayk's call, and he's defused the angry mob. A chicken's a small price to pay.

I shake my head. "I'm going to crash. You need a hand with anything before I go?"

Ida pauses, then turns from her pot to study me. She and Ethel exchange a weighted, puzzled look.

"From you?" Kasey says under her breath. She takes a swig of her water bottle. "*Unlikely.*"

Right. Defusing teenage girls is beyond my expertise.

Sitting on the breakfast bar, Sloane looks up tiredly. "Shut up, Kasey." She glances my way, and she's got the same grim look I saw in the mirror earlier. "We're good here. Thanks, Dom."

I nod to her. Sloane's been almost as quiet as me since Cyanide—and as guilty about Heather. She should hate me for it.

I'm glad she doesn't.

The silent *fuck off* from the rest of them is clear enough, though.

I should take it and go. It's not my call anymore. I'll talk to Jayk tomorrow, make sure he knows they're spitting ideas that'll get them killed, but it's up to him what he does with that. Their lives aren't on my shoulders anymore, and there's a relief in putting down that weight. And I *am* putting it down.

I turn for the door, then hesitate.

God damn it.

I slap the frame in frustration and turn back.

I'll put it down in a minute.

I cast a heavy look around the room. "Starting a fight with the Reapers would be a bad call. We've been out that way before. They might be farmers, but they have numbers—big numbers—and the Sinners wiped our firepower. We can't afford another war."

Then again, making a deal to defend the Reapers would start one, too. There's no way Alastair would let that slide.

We're fucked either way unless we get food soon.

Katherine rubs a defeated hand over her face, and Kasey's freckled nose wrinkles in a withering look.

"What are you even doing here? Don't you have any friends to boss around?" She settles back against the wall and mutters, "Jayk will figure it out."

"We all will," Ida murmurs back, sprinkling some salt into her pot.

Sloane thumbs her lip ring as she looks at me, grim disagreement in her bunched shoulders.

I arch an impatient brow back. She should know better than to go looking for a fight. She saw how Cyanide played out.

Giving me a long look, she just says, "Maybe you should spend less time eavesdropping, and more time fixing your own problems."

There's no heat to her voice, but her words still hit me under the ribs. They heard Jayk's bullshit speech, then. Probably half the fight with Beau, too.

For fuck's sake. Sloane is right. Our team is a mess.

After an awkward pause where no one meets my eye, the conversation moves on, and I take the hint this time and leave, stinging.

But my feet stick outside the kitchen door, and, hesitating, I stare blindly at Beau's shit crammed into the halls. That whole interaction took all of five minutes, and I still have nothing to fill the rest of my night. Nowhere to go. No decisions to make.

Just dead hours stretching in front of me.

Grimacing, I slowly make my way up to my empty room. The house is quiet now, everyone locked away behind closed doors, spending time with their people. I pass Eden's door, locked tight, and I force myself not to slow.

It doesn't help.

Her face floods me, like it does every day. She's everywhere. Her soft, hidden smiles haunt me. Her scent chases me. I still taste her in my mouth, still feel the way she sucked on my tongue like she wanted my cock instead. My body reacts like she's under me again, and I grit my teeth.

She doesn't make *sense*.

She didn't trust me to handle Alastair and Mateo, or enough to tell me the truth before we walked into that shit show at Cyanide—and I get it, why should she? I've fucked up at every turn. But she befriended me. *She* pursued *me*.

Why the hell would she do that?

If she doesn't respect me as a leader, as a *man*, where does she get off looking at me with all those stars in her eyes? Why would she tell me she wants me—or that she thinks I'm *brilliant*—when she can't count on me when it matters?

And why the fuck does she have to keep calling me *sir*?

That wrenching, familiar ache settles into my chest, and I let myself into my room. It's inspection-ready. Crisp and clean, the way I left it. No clutter on tables or loose edges on the bed.

It's . . . hollow.

Lucky's things are all packed and gone, and he's locked away too now, with Jasper. It's a good thing. He was a shitty roommate. Loud. Messy. Touchy.

The silence rings in my ears.

Slowly, I sit down on the larger couch in front of the silent TV. It gives under my weight. Minutes pass, and the walls stare back at me. How did this happen? When did I turn into my old man? Living between battle plans and empty rooms.

The military corners of my bed scream at me from across the room.

What do people *do* with their nights if they don't have a purpose? What if they don't have people to be locked away with? Am I supposed to just . . . sit here? Read a *book*? There's only one in my room—and I was reading it the day *she* came. When Beau made her fall apart all over his lap in the games room. When I let him share her with Jasper and not me.

My empty room stares back at me.

The unwatched action movies and the unopened whiskey.

Pressure closes in on my chest, and I slam to my feet. There has to be something to do. Someone always has a problem, and Jayk's occupied. I'd only be helping him out.

I stride to the door and wrench it open . . . only to stop short.

Beau is sitting in the hall. Still coated in dirt and sweat from the day, he's in his full kit, with his rifle and bag propped up beside him.

A pillow hangs from his filthy hand.

His head tilts up as the door opens, but he doesn't quite meet my eyes. He's examining a stain on the pillowcase.

My throat gets rocky and painful. I doubt words could make it out, even if I could think of anything to say.

"I've been in the med bay with Deanna and the others, and these people, Dom . . . they need food." He stares at the wall, his eyes searching nothing. "I don't know what to do. It's not my kind of medicine. Everything's . . . all of it's such a mess." His breath sighs out, so tiredly, and his head tips back against the wall. "How'd it get to be such a mess?"

The lead that's been in my gut since Cyanide sits heavy and cold. I don't know what to say to that either, because he's right. It is a mess.

But it's been a long time since Beau has talked to me about his messes.

The quiet stretches between us.

"I . . ." Beau's throat bobs, and his voice is low. Too controlled. "I don't have any place to go."

The rocks have jagged edges, and I can't swallow past them.

I don't know what the hell I'm doing anymore.

I snapped today. The two of us have been at each other's throats for weeks now, but that fight . . . that was bad. My own shit has been taking me by the throat, so I shot a bullet into every soft spot he had. It's pathetic.

Weak.

Today, I was exactly who my father always thought I was. I was exactly the kind of man I told myself I'd never be.

But Beau is still at my door, bleeding out in front of me.

He's always at my door, especially when I least deserve it.

Glancing up, I blink hard, then push off the doorframe and hold out a hand to him. It shakes more than it should.

Beau stares hard at it, then ducks his head away.

A moment later, he clasps my wrist, and I pull him to his feet and into a hug. I clasp his back, and he squeezes me back tighter than he usually does.

When he pulls back, his lashes are wet, and he still can't look at me. It rips at my chest. How the hell did we get from Beau standing off against my old man . . . to him standing off against me?

Did I really never apologize to him after Heather? That whole time was a mess. I left him in the dirt, detonated our friendship, and he still picked me up out of the grime when everything blew up in my face.

I'm such a fucking asshole.

I don't trust my voice, so I just nod for him to go inside. He picks up his bag, and I grab his rifle for him, then shut the door, my heart pounding.

Beau goes to put his bag on the couch, then seems to rethink it and puts it on the low coffee table instead. I lean his rifle against the wall and clear my throat—it doesn't budge the avalanche inside it.

Is this where we're supposed to hug it out? Cry on each other's shoulders?

We both face each other, shifting.

He's still holding his pillow, and he presses it between his hands, glancing at the bed. "You want to head-to-toe it? 'Cause just for the record, I'm not sure I'm up for a snuggle."

That startles a snort out of me. "Please. We've been fighting." Rubbing my jaw, I raise a brow at him. "You can sleep on the couch."

He huffs a laugh, then glances up at me with a wry tilt to his mouth. "Right."

For a second, just for a second, it almost feels normal between us —and then he looks down, his smile falling away.

Fuck.

"Go shower," I tell him gruffly. "You stink."

He nods, still not looking at me. "Yeah. I . . . Yeah." Haltingly, he puts his pillow on the couch and snags his bag. "Thanks."

While he showers, I track down spare sheets and make up the couch. It's still hot, but my room doesn't have a fireplace, so I add another blanket over the arm just in case before I get into bed and switch off the overhead light. It's early for sleep, but I don't want to make small talk, and I don't even know where to start with the rest of it.

The running water in the next room cuts off, and the soft sounds of Beau getting dressed fill the space.

It might be awkward as fuck, but at least it's not quiet anymore.

The door opens, and I stare up at the ceiling. Beau hesitates, and I force myself not to look at him. Whatever he was going to say, he lets it go and heads to the couch.

When he's lying down, I flick off the bedside lamp.

Darkness blankets us both.

Minutes tick past, and my eyes adjust. The deeper outlines and shadows of furniture and art taking form in the gray. I hear Beau breathe, the rhythmic *in–out*. His blankets shift with him.

He's not asleep, either.

After these many years, I know his sounds. I've heard them a thousand times, in a thousand places. In hot deserts and crowded kink clubs. In arctic winters, freezing our balls off. In pubs, around friends. In barracks, and bedrooms with women tucked between us. I know his breathing. His kinks. What turns him on. I know *who* does.

And that he's hurting over Eden as much as I am right now.

Beau takes a deep, heavy breath, and I let out my own. The shadows fill with all the things we're not saying to each other.

I tore him to shreds today, just like he did to me a month ago. Told him every stupid, petty and not petty thing that drives me up the wall about him—but I didn't tell him the rest of it. Maybe I never have.

I didn't tell him that he's brave, and kind, and funny. I didn't tell him that for every small thing he gets wrong, he does ten things right. I didn't tell him that he's my best friend. My family. My brother. I didn't tell him that the reason his family forgave him everything was because he's so damn easy to love.

There are too many words I don't know how to say to him.

But there are a few that have been a long time coming.

I look up to the same shadows taunting me, taking another deep breath before I confess.

"I'm sorry, Beau. I'm sorry for everything. With Heather, the Plan, the civilians . . . all of it." The words shudder out of me, hanging in the darkness. "I'm so fucking sorry."

The silence between us almost buries the words. It's tense. Taut. Like holding your straps and waiting for the clearance to jump. A mass tactical drop.

I can't hear him breathe.

Then finally, he does.

"I'm so mad at you," Beau says roughly, hurt breaking his voice. "And I'm mad at her, too. I . . . I can't make it stop this time."

His hurt breaks me too, and I close my eyes. There's no parachute for this one.

"I know," I tell the night.

Beau's breathing gets choppy, and I try to keep mine under control. I always know when he's mad. Don't think I remember him ever admitting it before, though.

Maybe we're both growing up.

"I still love her," he whispers.

Bittersweet pain lances me. "I know."

"You love her, too," he says, and it's not a question.

Love.

She floods me again. Her eyes. The river. The candles in the apple tree. I'm still falling with nothing to catch me.

What would it be like for my nights to be full of Eden and Beau?

You love her.

The hollow ache of the last few weeks becomes something raw, and rough enough that the next words are ripped from my chest.

"*I know.*"

Crash landing.

I'm in love with her.

The words slam into place inside me with the force of a wrecking ball. Brutal. Decimating. They tear down whatever final, flimsy, fucking foundations of myself I had left.

I love Eden. I love her strength and her mind. Her kindness and cunning. I love her so fucking much that she can rip me to shreds, and all I can think about is how fierce she looked doing it. She's not cruel . . . she just doesn't trust me.

Hell, I don't trust *myself*.

The darkness stretches.

What am I supposed to do about this? I'm not fit to be in charge, as a leader or a dominant, and if I'm not fit for that . . .

My chest aches with the same hollow, sick throb it has since Cyanide.

Who am I, if I'm not their captain?

"It'll be okay." Beau's voice is quiet—like he's reading my thoughts the way only he knows me enough to do. "We'll work it out. *All* of us."

I swallow hard, wishing I believed that.

But it is *something*.

I might not know who the hell I am anymore . . . but I know who matters. I know who I need to protect. I can love them, whether we can work this out or not.

I take a deep breath, and Beau's sounds wash over me.

"I love you as well, Beau," I tell him softly.

There's only a beat of silence this time, and I hear the smile in his voice when he replies.

"Love you always, Dom."

CHAPTER 19

JASPER

SURVIVAL TIP #107
The perfect delivery of pain isn't in knowing how hard to hit.
It's in knowing where not to.

I love him.

Lucien settles into Jaykob's throne, sprawling over it with surprising arrogance. Tendrils of his hair curl around his jaw and flushed cheeks like spun gold.

His restless sadness has been whipped free, and every part of him is languorous. Luminous. His eyes. The red-raw lines that blush his back and thighs and ass. The dimples that shine in his cheeks.

It's a contagious glow, one I'm sure he pressed into my skin after our scene. It's been too long since I've had him at my mercy. Unrestrained. Ungentle. Too long since I was able to break him open and taste his tears. And better, now. I can love him properly. He can touch me back. We can be more than just sadist and masochist; we can be something better.

We can just be . . . us.

My heart hasn't stopped its ache since our aftercare. It's a pleasant pain, almost exhilarating. It's as though he's infected me with his fearlessness, filled me with an urge to do more. To take a risk.

My eyes drift to Eden's window, and this time I don't bother to suppress the thrill of need.

I'm done playing nice.

Lucien steeples his fingers, looking down at me where I linger on the grass. "Oh look, a loyal subject. Have you come to bend the knee?"

I raise a brow at him, taking in the lazy tilt to his mouth. The way he kicks one leg over the scrap metal arm. Our bag of questionable supplies sits by the throne.

I climb the steps slowly.

My very skin is vibrant, sensitive, and alive with danger. This is a ridiculous escapade, but I can't blame Lucien for this foolishness.

This one was my idea.

It's rather novel, this kind of willful madness.

I stop in front of him. He's lustrous in the moonlight. He almost looks like a king. That infectious wildness still rides me, and I'm curious enough to indulge him.

Dropping to one knee in front of him, I pull his sprawled legs wider.

Lucien's smile falls away.

This close, his heat surrounds me. His thighs are tense and corded with muscle under his sweats, and his scent, freshly showered and uniquely him, is so much more present than when our positions are reversed. It's a curious feeling to be engulfed like this, by him.

"Does this amuse you?" I slide my hands up the inside of his thighs, and his head drops back. The pathetically thin fabric betrays him, and I can see the outline of his cock as he hardens. "Do you want to play king, too?"

This ridiculous throne is the reason we're here, after all.

He catches his lower lip between his teeth, and he looks down at me through his lashes. One hand finds its way to the back of my head, and he tunnels his fingers through my hair.

I wonder, with casual interest, where he's taking this.

Lucien is potent. Dangerous to me in so many ways. His raw strength is its own weapon, one I know he's relished using on other partners, switching into other roles . . . and yet he holds himself in check, not trying to move me. He only rubs the strands of my hair between his fingers, watching me softly.

Lucien doesn't need to be strong with me.

He doesn't want to rule.

Amused, I lean forward and press an open-mouthed kiss over the head of his cock.

He's hot and hard through the fabric, and his fingers clench in my hair as a groan slips out of him. It's a vicious sound that makes a vice around my balls. I've exhausted myself on him tonight. My arms ache from the exertion of the whip, and I feel every used muscle in my back. My lust should be slaked.

As if it ever could be, around him.

I trail my mouth over his abdomen. I nip his chest between the unbuttoned swathes of his shirt. Collecting the bag at his feet, I lift myself until I hover over him, resting my knee against his balls. Our mouths are a moment apart.

"Under you. Over you. It doesn't matter, Lucien. You'll always be at my mercy."

His eyes glow, and I kiss him. Every inch of his mouth is godless. The brush of his beard. The bitten roundness of his lower lip. The hot gasp of his breath as I press his brutalized back into the rough-cut metal.

I pull back and drop the heavy bag over his lap.

Cans of spray paint and markers spill out. Ribbons and glitter.

If Jaykob wants to behave this ludicrously, then his creation should reflect the absurdity. And if anyone has the skills to assist me in some light vandalism, it's Lucien.

Jaykob will learn: I can play in the dirt, too.

I pluck up one yellow can, called "Rubber Ducky Release" of all things, and examine the directions.

Lucien rubs a hand over his mouth, studying me. "You really want to do this? You're not having, I don't know, second thoughts?" He tilts his head. "Are you feeling okay?"

Stepping away, I try to catch the light from the house and hold the can back, squinting at the tiny typeface. Why are the instructions so *small*? And why on earth are there so *many* of them?

"Jaykob took something of ours. He should hardly be surprised when we retaliate," I say absently. Grimacing, I toss the can down to him. "Show me how to use this."

Lucien catches it, then swings his leg off the arm of the throne.

His eyes widen. "Hey, why do you think *I* know how to use it? Vandalism puts you on Santa's naughty list, you know."

"You're always on the naughty list."

Unimpressed, I regard him through my lashes, but he just winks, then stands, rolling his shoulders. He eyes me sideways, like he's puzzled, then glances up at Eden and Jaykob's window.

I follow his gaze and catch a flash of motion. I freeze, my heart pounding. Are we caught? We need the bag. All evidence. He can prove nothing if we—

The pale curtains flutter again in the light breeze, and I exhale slowly.

Ignoring my own racing pulse, I quickly reassure him. "If you're worried about how he'll respond, don't be. If Jaykob discovers us, I'll make sure he turns his wrath on me."

I won't have that barbarian wielding his club on Lucien.

Lucien's dimples reappear, and he tosses me a knowing, twinkly-eyed look. "Well, aren't you Prince Charming?"

I roll my eyes, but heat tinges my cheeks. He hardly needs me to save him.

Lucien laughs under his breath, then stands, twirling the can in his hands with a practice that tells me he does, indeed, know how to use it.

I scowl. "Why are you resisting me on this? I'm finally indulging in one of your ridiculous little pranks. I thought you would . . ." I trail off, abruptly feeling foolish. "I thought you'd enjoy this."

Lucien's face softens. "You did this for me?"

I purse my lips, staring up at Eden's window. Her tower. Her prison.

Perhaps *I'm* the one who would like to steal her away for a change.

"Hmm. Not for me, then."

I glance at him, frowning, and laughter threads his gaze again as he wanders over to me.

He looks me over, head to toe, then peeks into the open bag on the throne. He winces. "Okay, so, the enthusiasm is great. Ten points. Very proud. But since you still have your training wheels on for this whole pranking thing, I'm going to let you in on something. Every brat knows that there's a line between good fun . . . and just being a dick." He shrugs, and the bared muscles of his chest ripple. "As a subject matter expert, I've got to say—we may be straying into dickishness here."

Tilting my head, I massage my temple as I regard him. "You went on a hunting trip six months ago and left me a note telling me that you'd left five strips of dried fish in my room."

His head comes up, and he laughs. "Oh yeah."

The memory still rankles.

I glare at him. "There were only four strips of fish, Lucien. *Four*. Do you have any *idea* how long I spent searching for the fifth?"

He cackles, grinning fondly.

Sourly, I stroll toward him. "Or perhaps you recall the time you convinced me the new blender was voice-activated? Or when you made three of the surveillance screens continuously run dungeon porn during my shift? Was that not *dickishness*?" I stop in front of him and mutter, "That isn't a word, by the way."

"I was hoping you'd get ideas." At my violently unimpressed look, he shrugs one shoulder, and his smile sobers. He adjusts the fall of my shirt. "Look, the guys on the squad, they used to give him shit about it. Jayk, I mean. The whole king thing, him still living in his trailer— dumb jock stuff, but I kind of got the impression it wasn't the first time he'd heard it."

That gives me pause.

I think back to those years, running over my notes in my head. "That never came up in our sessions."

Lucien snorts. "Jasper, I mean this with love, but do you really think it would?"

I give him a blank look, and his eyes dip significantly toward Bristlebrook, extravagant against the cliff-face. My second home. Then he tugs on my shirt. Silk. Louis Vuitton.

Ah. Right. *That*.

Jaykob has always had deep insecurities about money. Guilt pricks me.

Lucien lifts one shoulder. "Anyway, I told Dom, and he shut it down. But come on, Jasper. You're a sadist . . . you know where not to hit."

I barely have time to feel the sting of that before he starts grinning again. He looks over the ridiculous chair with hearts in his eyes. "Plus, he built a whole-ass throne. That's pretty fucking cool, right?"

Mangled, dirty, overlarge beast of a thing.

But it does have a strange appeal, I'll give it that.

I sigh, toying with the bag. Jaykob taking charge of the civilians isn't my main concern, though I'd be lying if I said I had no reservations, both for his sake and because I still believe Dominic is best suited for the role. I do, however, have an issue with his arrogance, and his willful dismissal of Eden's wishes.

And, if I'm honest, my own as well.

"She's mine—you're going to lose," Jaykob told us.

He is so sure she will end up firmly with him.

Only with him.

Lucien looks back at me, his hair falling like golden gossamer around his face, his eyes soft and understanding, just as they were before our scene. He does understand me, my Lucien.

"We should return to bed then," I say, sighing ruefully.

It appears I'm not cut out for these kinds of adventures after all.

Blond brows fly up. "Oh, no. No, no, no. I didn't say *that*."

At my confusion, a slow, wicked smile creeps across his face.

"I'm just saying we don't have to cut him off at the knees over being in charge." He strolls over to me, then turns me by my shoulders until we're facing Eden's open second-story window. "But we can totally crash his party and teach our asshole friend a lesson."

The curtains flutter again, and I frown, not following.

"I don't understand. He's barricaded the door. We can't get inside."

When Lucien doesn't answer, I look at him, and he grins back, then tilts his head at the window.

It clicks.

"No," I say firmly.

"Yes."

"*No.*"

He laughs. "Come on, where's that adorable sense of adventure now?"

That makes me pause, and I take in the flush of his cheeks, all the sparkle in his eyes that I was looking for earlier. *This* is the mischief he wants to cause.

"I am not scaling a building to impress anyone, Lucien," I splutter.

And he thought graffitiing a hunk of scrap metal was going too far. Love is one thing.

That could get us killed.

Lucien rolls his eyes. "It's romantic."

"It's *absurd*. Only a pure fool entirely lacking in common sense would do something that stupid." I pinch the bridge of my nose, wondering why I thought any of this was a good idea. I should be sipping tea in my slippers by now, if not sound asleep in my bed.

Lucien shrugs one shoulder. "I don't know." His smile softens, and the moonlight glows over him. "Maybe just a fool in love."

My chest aches. Reluctantly, I look up at the window, and the curtains flutter in the wind. Is that what love is? Grand gestures and Neanderthalic aggression?

That's never been me.

Why does no one write of a gentler kind of love? One that burns more quietly . . . but is just as enduring.

I think of sitting before the fireplace with Eden, the soft turn of pages and her slow blushes, and I sigh. I'm too sensible for these games. Scaling buildings and stealing princesses are for the pages in her storybooks. Not for the man who reads them with her.

Whatever tender feelings for her are sweeping me away, they're surely not *that* foolish.

"No," I finally decide. "We'll give them their moment. This *one* moment. Then we'll talk to him like gentlemen."

Lucien's lips twitch, and he spins the can of spray paint again. "So no grappling hooks?"

Irresponsible, wonderful little fool. He was born to love recklessly.

But imagine me, climbing a building.

I *would* have to be a fool in love to consider that.

Laughing softly at the absurdity, I pull him in for a hard kiss. "No, darling boy. No grappling hooks."

PART TWO

CONQUEST

Chapter 20

Eden

Survival tip #250
*If you can trust someone with your peace,
you can trust them with your life.*

Calm takes me.

I putter easily through the kitchen, fetching a mug while the pot simmers, the ingredients now packed away. The supply list sits on the counter, my scribbled recipes for stretching rations detailed in the margins. We're almost out of most staples, and the meager plot of potatoes we planted before I left still have months before they're ready. I need to go foraging soon. What I collected on the route home will barely touch the sides.

Only, I'm not sure any amount of foraging is going to cut it.

We might have time before Alastair comes knocking or Red Zone needs our help, but we're starving now. We need to solve that problem first, or we'll die before either of those two problems arise.

I just don't know what the solution is. If we start eating the chickens and goats, then we lose eggs and milk, which are the only things sustaining us right now. Jaykob has already been sending the civilians out to nearby towns in search of food, but the Sinners have hollowed out every town they've approached.

Maybe we can go out farther? Push harder? But even then, it would be weeks before anyone could return.

Which leaves the Reapers.

Even if we did trust the Reapers enough to leave Bristlebrook and put ourselves at their mercy, they would want us to help defend them against the Sinners.

Which is just wonderful.

We can save ourselves from starvation only to be murdered by Alastair for treason shortly after.

Sourly, I stir my pot.

Should we just contact him? The idea of begging Alastair for help after everything grates, but if he truly wants to lord over us, then maybe he'll give up some of their food until we can plant enough to get on our feet.

Some of the Reapers' food, I remind myself guiltily.

But Alastair's voice rings in my ears. *"Of course the women and children stay here. She's going to ask for our food and medicine again next, I imagine. It must be hard to see, watching your betters have everything."*

I don't think Alastair plans on giving at all.

He got what he wanted from me . . . and Alastair has only made promises to take.

I sigh. I don't know what the answer is, but I feel better having something cooking. It eases something inside me—some long-standing anxiety that there won't *be* a next meal.

It feels like taking charge, even if only in a small way.

My empty stomach cramps hungrily, and I eye my pot. It's a congealed, fatty shade of brown, with a thin sheen of oil on the top. My Save-Your-Life Slop recipe, coming right in time. And okay, no, maybe it doesn't look appetizing—and it smells . . . *interesting*—but that rusty color is perfect. The preserved fat is *life*.

I smile proudly at it.

Dawn isn't yet breaching the treetops, and the house is still snuggled asleep. For the first time in too many days, quiet sinks into my bones. No one is hawking over my every move. There are no thick, expectant silences as they wait for me to eat, no tension sharp enough to snap bones, no being torn in five different directions.

My body is deeply rested, the overlarge T-shirt I shouldn't have stolen wraps me like a hug, and I can finally enjoy a moment alone.

Through the cracked, poorly glued windows, the forest is a blanket of green. Ida and Ethel are keeping watch on one of the towering defensive platforms—their occasional lazy movements and the soft sway of the trees break the stillness. Even the babbling pot's low chatter feels familiar and comforting, reminding me of pebbled brooks and the dappled waterfall that used to run near my cave.

The deep quiet feels like an old friend. One I grew to loathe during my long solitude.

For years, I woke up to chilly cave walls and deafening silence. I used to crave the company of morning bird trills and the fat bellows of bullfrogs. I used to sit with my feet in the rippling water, just to feel like I was part of its noise.

Because silence like that can be suffocating.

I found an abandoned toy bear on the side of the road once, and there were days when I used to press its heart-shaped stomach over and over, just to hear an unnaturally cheery woman sing to me. Day after day, she kept me company.

Right up until her voice began to stutter and melt.

Until even she fell quiet.

Now, this silence is as strange to me as sound used to be.

I flick the burner off when the liquid starts to churn up thick, bubbling clots. Lately, my life is fierce and loud and messy. Painful and wonderful, vivid and awake, and I love it, for the most part. But for all that my old life was painfully lonely, it was also . . . serene. I miss having time to think.

Maybe now, here in this quiet, I can finish plotting out more recipes. Or work out how I'm going to convince everyone to start playing nice with one another.

I tuck my makeshift supply list into the front pocket of my shirt and scoop out a heavy ladleful of slop. Breathing in the fragrant cloud, I steady myself in the silence.

Maybe I'll do all that.

Or maybe I'll just watch the sunrise and let myself enjoy the moment.

Slowly, the tension bleeds out of me. I don't need to be afraid of the quiet anymore. It's only a brief respite from the noise.

When I finally open my eyes, Dom is leaning against the wall, watching me. His dark hair is still damp from a shower, and red shirt clings to his chest. He's . . . so unbelievably beautiful.

I have no idea how long we've both been standing here, but I don't feel the urge to move. His presence curls around me—the stillness not exactly restful, but strangely intimate.

It's the longest we've been alone together since Cyanide.

I offer him a tentative, welcoming smile, and the gold in his eyes warms before he murmurs, "Good morning, pet."

His voice is low—adding to the quiet, rather than stealing it away.

Pet.

"Eden," he corrects, so softly. "I mean . . . good morning, *Eden.*"

My chest fills with sweet, gentle pressure, and I look down, swallowing delicately. I didn't think I'd ever hear that word out of him again. Not for me.

I'm not sure it could hurt more, that it's only by accident.

But still, he's here . . . and I don't want him to go.

Reaching down to the cupboard, I pull out another mug, then ladle him a cup too.

His eyes flick to my hands, but he doesn't move any closer. He doesn't leave, either. After a moment, his eyes fix on my face, and it takes every effort not to fumble under his intense attention.

And it . . . confuses me.

What *does* he want from me? He walked away from Jayk's challenge last night. From *me.* I'm not sure he could have been much clearer.

I sneak another look at him—only for his eyes to pierce me through. For just one second, I could swear I glimpse a sharp, golden . . . *wistfulness.*

Then he looks outside, his throat working, and my heart squeezes.

Maybe it isn't so clear.

His words from yesterday ring in my ears: *Cyanide was my op. Everything that happened—everything—can be traced back to my mistakes. Mine alone.*

He doesn't blame me for Cyanide. He blames himself. I don't know where that leaves us, or if he still feels anything like what I still feel for him. But whether he does or he doesn't, I can't let this go on.

We need to talk.

Flushing, torn, I stare down at the slop, and a small bubble bursts over the surface. He must be starving. Debating with myself for a pulse-pounding moment, I eventually pick up both mugs and walk over to him, frissons of tingling energy licking down my spine as we get closer and closer.

When I reach him, his scent envelops me—a spicy, sippable scent that sits on the back of my tongue.

Strangely nervous, I try to breathe it out.

After a long, confusing moment, Dom takes the mug from my hand. His fingers brush mine, and those pinpricks of energy intensify, prickling all over my skin.

He shocks my system awake.

It reminds me of every coffee date we had while I was learning to spar. Of every time he battled with me for hours over what to do about raiding parties, or about which section of the defenses needed to be built first. Of his dry humor, and the way he'd sometimes stare at my mouth for just a little too long.

The silence becomes confusing, warmed in the tiny valley between us, and I look up.

Tender, liquid gold runs over me.

Slowly, Dom takes a sip from the mug, the usual hard line of his mouth soft and full. Something flickers over his expression, his lips tightening as he glances down at the cup—in gratitude, maybe? His eyes lift to track over my face, and he pushes off the wall with a nod of thanks.

And he walks out of the kitchen.

Disappointment cuts into me, bladed and miserable.

Idiot. Silly, blushing idiot. Say *something, you—*

"You coming?" Dom calls.

At the quiet offer, relief thrills through me, and I rush to follow him out onto the deck.

We're going to talk.

CHAPTER 21

EDEN

Outside, the sky is finally thawing from a dispirited blue into a ripe blush, and Ida raises one hand in a brief hello before she turns back to Ethel, fussing over her in her seat until Ethel bats her away.

Dom settles into the porch swing, his large body taking up more than half of the seat, and after a hesitant moment, I sit beside him. He angles himself toward me, and his knee brushes my thigh. Every inch of him is firm, heated . . . gorgeous.

Stop, Eden.

Clearing my throat, I firmly stare out at the forest. It's better than staring at his thighs, which feels like my only other option at this point —and my God, I'm a *problem*.

My foot taps on the deck. *Keep it together, woman. You have so much groveling to do before you should even* dream *about his thighs.*

But I can't help it.

Dom's presence has always been a physical thing to me. Something weighted and significant, like he makes the very air denser, *electric*, just by sharing it.

The mug is hot and full in my hands, and I let the scald ground me.

I shouldn't make this about us. It isn't fair. It's about *him*, and all the reasons he's wrong to take this on himself.

The image of Dom on his knees has scarred me. I can't sleep without seeing the defeated slump to his shoulders, or the *hurt* in his eyes when he realized how deep my lies ran.

He rocks us, very slowly, but my peaceful morning is different now. Charged.

There's an odd lack of anger in him that I'm not sure I deserve. The roiling thunderclouds around him have settled into something heavy and thoughtful. Something I don't know how to penetrate.

My stomach churning, I sip my slop, trying to work out exactly what I want to say. The hot, greasy liquid in my hollow gut is *not* sitting happily, but I drink more anyway.

Beside me, Dom drinks as well.

When we take our fourth matching sip, I work up the courage to glance at his face—only to catch his grimace.

A *grimace*.

At *my* slop.

I stare at him, aghast. "You hate my slop?"

Dom eyes me over his cup, calculating. "I like having slop with you."

A small, offended squeak escapes me as he takes another wincing sip.

"That's not the same thing."

He casually looks out at the forest, but there's a sneaky, reluctant humor in the hard edges of his face when he shrugs. "*Nope.*"

The twinkling lightness on him is unexpected, *mesmerizing*, and just like that, my choked indignance turns into a laugh.

He's *teasing* me.

The slow swing suddenly feels like I'm flying high.

"Well," I mutter tartly. My ears feel strangely hot. "You don't need to suffer through the slop if you want to spend time with me, you know."

The rocking pauses, suspended, then resumes.

The strange, soft curve of his lips deepens. "Good to know."

A low flush of confused heat rolls over me. He *wants* to spend time with me?

God . . . *why?*

I clear my throat. "The Reapers. Do you know where they've settled? We need to talk to them. There has to be a compromise, one where we don't need to leave with them. Do you think if we just gave them some advice, maybe some weapons, that they'd—"

"It's not up to me anymore, Eden," Dom breaks in quietly, and the amused tuck of his mouth has vanished. "You'll have to ask Jayk about that."

My throat filling, I look back over at him, studying him the way he's been studying me—*wistfully.*

I want to be worthy of his trust.

I want to protect him from all the ways I wasn't.

"Jayk told me he loves me," I confess, staring down into the mug. "He wants me all to himself."

The slow sway doesn't stop this time, but I feel Dom's attention sharpen.

Swallowing, I look out at the shadowy trees. At the pink and orange streaking out from behind them.

"I told him no, of course. That I was in love with . . ." *With all of you.* Awareness breathes between us, and I hesitate, then stumble on. "I told him that I couldn't do it. I wouldn't choose."

Dom takes another sip, letting me speak, and his face is impassive, giving nothing away. The morning is already muggy and sweat begins to prickle along my hairline.

I would give anything to know what he's thinking.

"He's sure he can convince me to choose him—or that he can fight anyone else off, one or the other," I tell him, sighing irritably. I tuck my knees up to my chest under the large shirt, putting my empty mug to the side. "It's hard, you were right. I don't want everyone at each other's throats, but I just feel . . ." My chest swells. "Things with me and Jasper, they're different now. I can finally just *be* with him, and it's . . . he's so . . ." I trail off, smiling. "He's been wonderful. But God, you know how he and Jayk are on a good day. This is going to be a nightmare. Not to mention that Lucky's been anxious. Jayk pulling this caveman act isn't helping."

Still angled toward me, Dom leans forward, his elbows braced on his knees as he looks cryptically over our battlements. Orange sun filters over his face until his deep olive skin glows, his dark hair almost seeming to catch alight.

And I still can't make out a thing he's thinking.

But he's still quiet. Thoughtful.

"I don't think Jayk will have to worry about Beau, at least," I continue softly, my throat sticking. "He's so angry with me, Dom. He can't even look at me. God, I don't even know where he is right now. All his things were just *gone*. I'd hoped that when we were both back here, he'd finally have to talk to me, but he's been so frustrating, and *stubborn*, and he . . . he walked away. He's been making these jabs, and I . . ."

He just gave up on me.

Hurt blooms in my chest all over again. All of this is a mess. Every one of *us* is a mess. But Jasper was right. There is a family here, and I can *see* it now—what we could all look like together if we could get past all of this. But I don't know if it's possible. I don't know if we can ever get there, if I'm the only one fighting for it . . . and when they're all so busy fighting each other.

I look at Dom, sun-caught and quiet.

Or when they're not fighting at all.

"He's staying with me," Dom finally says, glancing back at me briefly. "Beau. Snores all night, too. Sounds like a chainsaw."

"He is?"

Beau talked to Dom. They're actually talking. After their fight yesterday, I wasn't sure whether they would be able to forgive each other.

I bite my lip against the surge of emotion.

A family.

Maybe I'm not the only one fighting for it after all.

"That . . . I'm glad." I nod, and a smile breaks free that quivers a bit too much. "That's . . . that's good. You need each other."

When Dom glances back up at me, he doesn't smile back. "He'll figure it out, Eden. He lost everyone he ever loved once, and he loves hard. He's not about to lose you, too."

All his strength is sun-warmed and hazed soft, and it takes me a minute to realize it's because my eyes are misting up. This time, I need to duck my head, pressing my forehead against my tucked knees as I try to catch my breath.

I didn't realize how badly I needed to hear that until the words were in my ears.

Beau and Dom are working things out. If they can do it, then surely Beau and I can, too.

"What is this, Eden?" When he finally breaks the silence, his voice is rough. Carefully controlled. "Why are you telling me all this? About Jayk, and Beau, and . . . What is this?"

I swallow hard, then shore up my courage.

"Rule six, sir."

The husky words might as well have been a slap considering the way he flinches. Tension sharpens every angle of him, and I rest a gentle hand on his thigh, but I can't stop now.

"You told me to talk to you when I was upset, or if I need something, so I am. *Rule six.*" My voice is firm. "And that's why I need to tell you that you're wrong. About Cyanide. About all of it. That wasn't your mistake, okay? There wasn't anything you could have done."

Dom grimaces at his half-full cup and sets it aside. He stands up, jostling the swing. Caught off guard by the abrupt change in him, I drop my legs off the seat to steady it.

"Drop it, Eden."

My heart thunders. He said it calmly enough, with no bitterness or judgment, but his shoulders are anvils again. All his sneaky humor is gone.

"No."

My reply comes out sharp, and tension simmers between us. I grip my thighs to stop my hands from shaking when I look at him. The razored intensity under his calm reminds me of the way he was last night, his control right before he snapped at Beau.

I stand up, too, smoothing down my shirt. "No, sir. I won't. I'm the one who lied to you. *I* went behind your back and freed Alastair, even after we talked. You did everything to protect us." Dom shakes his head, and I try to swallow the frustration in my voice. "It was on *me*."

Dom turns back to face me, leaning against one of the posts on the porch. The sunrise is breathtaking behind him, a melting pot of pinks and oranges and purples.

His face is lethal. "Why?"

The single word is an unexpected gunshot, and I press my hand against my stomach, stepping back. "W-why? I don't . . ."

"Why did you lie to me?" His question is clipped. *Short*. "Why go behind my back? Why not come to me later?"

My hair falls around my shoulders as I shake my head—it's a helpless tangle, one I never would have allowed before I met my brutes.

It's only with them that I've learned how to be messy.

"It's complicated," I start. Panicked memories of Day Death, of police sirens and screams and pretty deputies who should have known better, burn the back of my eyelids. "I made a mistake, I—"

"You didn't trust me."

I falter, staring at him.

Dom's lips hook up on one side, but it's a dark, humorless kind of smile.

"You didn't tell me, pet, because you knew I wouldn't listen. You didn't trust me." Finally, I see the bitterness, but he's only looking inward when he says softly, "And why should you?"

This time, it's my turn to stiffen, and a balmy gust of air buffets us both, stirring me. No amount of morning peace and quiet tree lines can compare to the bright, livid way I wake up around these men.

My anger sparkles, bright and alive.

Another thing they taught me.

I lift my chin. "You're wrong, sir. I do trust you."

At *sir*, Dom's eyes flare like solar storms.

"Bullshit." He pushes off the post, looking down at me, and my eyes widen at the sudden loom. "You raised your issues, told me what you learned while they had you, and I didn't listen. I didn't anticipate Aaron. I let major breaches get past us, damn it. And what about later, Eden? If you really trusted me, you'd have said something, but you didn't."

"I almost did," I snap back.

The morning is already heating up, becoming moist and sticky. Starting to feel lightheaded, I tug the T-shirt back from my chest to give myself some air. As he prowls forward, hard-eyed and certain, there seems to be less and less of it.

"At the bond-fire," I splutter, edging back around the porch swing, "before my room and the blood and . . . I was going to tell you."

I was going to tell him more than that. Under the candlelight and wrapped up in his arms, I almost told him everything.

I wish I had.

"You were afraid."

Lionlike and intent, Dom presses forward, and I back up, my breath quickening.

"I'm *not* afraid of you."

His arm slams up over my head, and I realize I'm pinned against the wall. He doesn't have a hand on me, nothing at all to stop me escaping, but that's the last thing I want. There's a light sheen to his lips now, like he's wet them, and I need their taste. I can feel my pulse throbbing in my neck.

Throbbing everywhere.

No, I'm not *afraid* of Dominic.

The golden eyes staring down at me are fierce, and all my arguments line up in my head, like soldiers waiting on the battlements to return fire.

But his next shot is delivered softly, and oh so perfectly on target.

"You were afraid I'd make you leave," he says.

My breath catches.

My arguments waver, momentarily caught by how deeply he's considered this. Caught by the memory of endless, rolling trees and too-quiet birds. By the desperate press of that damn toy bear's stomach.

His lips compress like I just confirmed it.

"I did that. That deal . . ." His hard exhale falls over my cheeks, and he looks up like he's searching for something. The sky churns behind him before his eyes block it out. "You should never have had to worry about being alone. There's a difference between compliance and submission. I don't know if we managed to land on the right side of it, but there should never have been a question."

"*Sir*—"

"Stop calling me that!" Dom's resignation snaps, and he crowds me against the wall, but I don't flinch. *I trust him.* His voice lowers to a growl, and the hurt spills free. "I fucked up with you from the moment we met. That isn't a leader worth a damn, Eden. I'm not a good dominant. I'm not a good man." His lips twist. "I'm mediocre. At *best*."

He pulls back, and I press a hand against his shirt to stop him. I know he could pull away, but he doesn't. To Dom, my gentle pressure acts like a chain, and he stops still.

His firm, heated muscles press against my knuckles.

"You didn't make me afraid of being alone, *sir*. My mother did that. My ex-husband. My whole damn life. *You* didn't. This is a different world. People don't risk themselves for others. They just don't. But you *did*, no matter how begrudging you were at first. Over and over again, you did it for me and all these people. You kept me safe. You came after me. Do you know how—" I break off, remembering too much.

There are too many people who left me behind. Too many people who pretended to be good and weren't. I look up at him with every memory of them playing in my mind.

"Do you have any idea how rare you are?" I whisper. "You don't have to be perfect, Dom, but there's nothing mediocre about you. You are nothing short of exceptional."

Something gleams in his eyes, and his throat cords.

I flatten my hand against his chest, and his heart pounds under my palm.

"That deal . . . I won't pretend it was the best idea, or that it was handled perfectly, but we've *all* learned from it. This is my home, now. You're my . . . damn it, you became one of the best friends I have. And maybe I didn't trust you back then, even after I was taken, but you took the time and you *earned* it. All of you. You earned my *l*—"

His gaze flashes at me in warning, and I cut off the word I know he doesn't want to hear right now.

That he might never want to.

My heart rips, and I glare back at him hopelessly as my throat begins to burn, wishing I knew the right words. "I betrayed all of you. If I was worried about being cast out, it was because of that."

Dom's bitter smile becomes sadder. He doesn't need to say it, I know he doesn't believe it. Of course he doesn't.

"You—" I begin, frustrated. "*No.* You don't get to just *do* that. You can't just decide that everything is your fault, or . . . or that my bad actions are *your* responsibility. It's infantilizing!"

That seems to catch him off guard, and Dom pulls back with an incredulous snort.

"Do *not* snort at me," I snap, poking his chest.

A dark winged brow cocks up as he looks down at my finger, but this is too important, and I'm not in the mood.

"I'm not a perfect person, Dom. My choices aren't some derivative of yours. I have plenty of flaws of my own, and they were *raging* while I was listening to Heather hurt Alastair and Mateo. I was terrified of what it could mean for the women and children if they died, and I *did* bring that to you because I *do* trust you. It's not your fault I didn't abide by your decision, sir—and you shouldn't have to worry about being betrayed by the people who are supposed to support you."

He pulls back, but my hand shakes on his chest, my fingers digging into his shirt. "I do trust you, Dom. I just . . . took too long to realize it. And, God, I really thought Alastair would free the captives. I thought I knew better but . . . I didn't. He lied. He took Heather, and Bentley, and we have no food, and that's . . . that's on *me.*"

Dom's breathing hard, and the air around us is too hot, too dizzyingly thick, to be able to catch it.

"Sam would have killed us, Eden." He's bitter honey, resigned and dark. "I let Aaron see the plans. Jasper is right—we'd still have been betrayed no matter who was in charge, no matter how much you told me."

Dark strands of hair sway and curl around his ears. It's longer than I'm used to seeing.

The military cut bleeding out.

"A mistake," I repeat, watching him with hot, wet eyes. "*One.*"

Dom's eyes flash in rigid, instant defense. "It's years of them. Drop it."

He turns to stalk away, but desperation rips through me. I catch his arm, and his bicep flexes under my grip.

"No. Rule six, sir. I'm talking to you. You can't just—"

His arm snaps around my waist in a hard band, his mouth an inch from mine. "*Forget* the rules, Eden." If his words were a single gunshot earlier, this is a barrage, quick and battering. "They don't matter now."

The sliding door slams open, but fear catches me like a riptide, and I can't let this go. Even if he doesn't want me, even if it's not to save us, I need him to understand that all of this, the situation we're in, doesn't rest on him alone.

I know what dark places feel like, and I'm not leaving him alone in his.

"You're our captain. We still have the Sinners to deal with, and now the Reapers? We need you," I insist, tears edging my voice, and he shakes his head with a scoff that has too much of a cut.

The sun breaks over the trees, and Dom is intense, burning just as bright. Just as wickedly hot.

"And here I thought you were happy for Jayk," he snipes, and it's a wide shot.

I press closer to Dom, frustrated. "*Don't* bring him into this. It isn't about him. Jayk can do anything he sets his mind to, but he doesn't *want* this, not really. He's only doing any of it because he doesn't feel like any of you respect him."

"Is that something a good leader does? Makes their team feel small?" He's a violent blaze, barely contained.

Heat blossoms in my cheeks, those electric shivers start prickling over my skin. "So, *work* on it. Fix it. You can bring them together, sir."

His hands travel over my hips and down to grip my ass, dragging me hard against him. "I told you to stop calling me that. Now. I haven't earned it."

The snark comes out of me this time. "If you don't want to be my dominant, *sir*, then maybe you should stop ordering me around."

"Okay," a familiar voice breaks in. "I think that's enough."

Ignoring it, I bite my lip, searching Dom's eyes as they darken unhappily.

Selfishness curls through me. I want him to be okay, more than anything, but I do want *us* to be okay, too. We haven't even had a chance to be something yet, not really, but it's always been there, waiting.

Even when we were friends, *sir* danced between us.

"Do you really want me to stop saying it?" I ask him. My chest is too tight. The implication is too big, and it drowns everything else out. "Don't say it if you don't mean it, because I will stop if you ask me again. If you don't want this, you need to tell me."

Dom looms over me like a volcano about to blow. His eyes are flaring, igneous, and . . . *torn*.

Angry, fearful tears fill my throat.

"Do it, then." I shove at his chest, but he catches my wrists as my eyes blur.

"No."

"Do it!" My tears spill over, scalding my cheeks. "Tell me it's done."

"You don't trust me!" he roars, and I stare at him in shock. He drops my wrists, and his voice is as hard as a brick. "Trust is *everything*."

My knees hit the porch before I realize I've decided to kneel, and Dom freezes.

I settle back onto my heels, tucking my chin, and the minutiae of the position comes to me like breathing. Like air. The pretty posture, the open wrists. The porch wood bites into my knees, and it reminds me of church pews and penance.

The position usually feels like peace—a safe place to slip into and the world goes quiet.

Today, I find a different kind of strength in it.

Today, it feels like defiance.

The hot wind batters us, and it throws my hair into something wild and witchy. Dom's golden eyes are locked on me, his lips parted. I'm not entirely sure he's even breathing.

The next tear that slips down my cheek is a challenge.

"Say it again, sir. Tell me again how I don't trust you."

But it's not Dom who answers.

"No, darlin'," Beau breaks in, firm and clear. "I don't think either one of you should say one more word. You two are in a time-out."

CHAPTER 22

EDEN

SURVIVAL TIP #352
Trust isn't something to prove.
It's something to earn.

B eau's voice is like a chisel through glass, and the spell around us shatters. Sounds and smells and the world rush back in—the house waking up, the screeching birds, Jasper and Lucky strolling past the apple tree. It all springs back to life and makes me suddenly, awfully aware of where I am and what I'm doing and . . . and *Dom*.

Golden, glowing like fireflies, Dom's eyes are stuck on me. They're tracing over every inch of me—my face, my hands, the T-shirt pooled around my thighs, and the press of my legs against the porch. His wide, callused hand is white-knuckled on the swing.

But he's not saying a word.

I duck my head, pressing my lips together to suppress a sob.

A wide palm touches my back, like I'm a horse to be soothed. "Hey now. It's okay. You're okay."

Tears scald my cheeks, and I lift my head to glare at Beau. He's on one knee beside me. The tanned column of his throat peeks out from the collar of his shirt, golden and gorgeous in the sunrise, and there's more kindness in his face than I've seen since Cyanide. He and Dom smell like the same spicy shampoo.

And it *hurts*.

It hurts to kneel in front of Beau, in the form *he* taught me in *our* room when everything with him was wonderful. It hurts that it's not wonderful. It hurts that I'm feeling every porch splinter digging into me and not my soft rug and his hands adjusting my body.

I don't want Beau to pack away his anger just because I'm upset. I don't want this to rot because *he* has a big heart.

If I won't be held accountable for my actions, how can I trust that they'll be accountable for theirs?

"Tell him," I demand of Beau, my voice too watery. "Tell him it's my mistake, not his. I'm the fuck up here. You believe that, right? That's why you're not talking to me, isn't it? So tell him." He's too blurry, and I can't help my sob this time. "Tell him all of this is my fault. I trust him. I do. It was my mistake."

Beau's lips part. As he watches every expression cross my face, his brow crumples . . . and something pensive and curious sinks into his.

"*Damn it*, Eden," Dom snaps. He releases his death grip on the swing so abruptly it clatters against the wall. "No. I'm not doing this. If you want to whip your own back, then you do it on your own time."

He turns to storm down the porch steps—maybe toward Ethel and Ida who are doing a terrible job of looking like they're not eaves-dropping—but Beau drags his eyes away from me to growl, "Quit it, you stubborn mule." He points at the porch swing. "You sit your ass on that chair. *Now*. No, shut up, Dom, I don't want to hear it. You're not running from this."

Dom's boots pause, and I wait for them to leave. For him to *go*.

But he doesn't.

The porch creaks as he walks back over and sits heavily back on the swing.

I lift my glasses to swipe at my wet cheeks, infuriated that they're betraying me.

This morning's peace is wrecked—tossed into a whirlwind and pulverized—and I'm suddenly . . . vulnerable, here on my knees. Over-exposed and lacking the fight I found with Jaykob. I'm not sure what I was hoping for here.

I sniff wetly and meet Beau's eyes.

"Just tell him," I whisper. "It's okay. It's really okay to hate me for hurting him."

I do.

The morning light picks up all the fractures in his hazel eyes, and there's a pained pinch between his brows as he shakes his head.

"Oh, darlin'," he breathes. "I don't hate you. I couldn't ever."

It surprises me. More than it should, maybe, but I've seen how he is—how he shut Dom out for weeks and how he's been avoiding me, and after last night I just . . .

"Damn it," I choke out as tears flood me again.

He doesn't want me to leave.

He doesn't hate me.

I pull back, gasping, as the relief of it hits me, and he raises his hands.

"Oh, no. No, no. Easy, pet," he murmurs. "Easy. Come here. On your feet now. Come on."

Tears drip off my chin, and I shake my head silently, but his hands run up my arms anyway. Testing. Soft. Giving me plenty of room to move away.

He edges closer when I don't, and he pulls me gently to my feet. I press my forehead to his chest, curling into him despite myself.

"There you go, darlin'." His lips press to the top of my head, and his hands begin a quiet, soothing rhythm up my back. "Breathe for me, come on."

I hate that I've missed this. I hate that his kindness has a way of puncturing my anger until all I want to do is expire in his arms.

I breathe him in, drenching myself in him, needing to be marked by all the warm and subtle threads of Beau that Jayk erased from my sheets. Needing the sunshine on his skin and the heat of him against me.

Dom sits dark and brooding in his chair, watching us like a bottled storm.

Beau's hand presses against my neck, tilting my head back, and his forehead finds mine.

"You don't kneel like that, Eden," he tells me, his voice roughen at the edges.

"I—"

His grip tightens. "*No*. You hear me? You don't do it to make a point. You do it when it fills you. When it makes you more, not less. You . . ." He sighs, and his eyes travel over my face. "Do you remember your lessons?"

Delicate heat fills my cheeks.

I remember giggling on my knees beside our bed while Beau grinned down at me, correcting my form. Almost every night, after my painful journaling and the awful memories that accompanied it, Beau distracted me with comforts and sex and laughing lessons—from "Primal 101" and "Submissive Fundamentals" all the way to "To Brat or Not to Brat: The Delights and Dangers of Funishment," as he called it. He played professor for "The Art of Charming Your Soft Dom with Role Play and Affirmations," and yes . . . in the last nights before Cyanide, we had begun "High-Protocol Basics: How to Ruin the Rule Sticklers." With jibes and eye rolls, he walked me through every formality he'd clearly never cared about. For Jasper. For Dom. For *me*.

Do I *remember*?

I exhale against his lips, my chest aching. "Every second."

The colors in his eyes fracture further, and the pad of his thumb traces the corner of my mouth. "Kink isn't supposed to be a gotcha, darlin'. It's a tool, sometimes useful—in getting things out, or working things through, but . . . it can't fix fundamentals."

My throat pulses.

I pull back from Beau, wrapping my arms around my waist as I stare out at the sunrise. It's crude and beautiful, flaring over the dark forest.

Lucky breaks free of Jasper from under the apple tree, laughing, and his eyes light on me. He grabs Jasper's arm, and I smile softly, aching at the transparent joy in them.

"Trust isn't something you prove, Eden. It's something you earn." Dom's words are heavy behind me; for all their gentle delivery, they have the force of an anvil.

"So *let me*," I insist quietly, watching as Jasper slips Lucky's hand from his arm and tucks it inside his.

"You're not the only one who needs to earn it."

That catches me, and I turn back.

Dom is sitting on the swing, braced on his forearms. He's drenched in scarlet and the gold in his eyes is intent and intense, but I was right. The wistfulness is back.

His voice is the deep rumble of shifting earth when he says, "I'm sorry for shouting at you, pet."

This time, he doesn't take back the endearment, and my throat burns with unbearable relief. With *joy*.

He *wants* this.

Beau lets out a long, shuddery breath. His gaze is far more hesitant when it meets mine. "I . . . I'm mad at you. I'm mad about so many things, and God, Eden, I could just *shake* you."

A hard, disapproving sound punches out of Dom, but God. I breathe in sharply, smiling, and the early morning air is fresh and bright in my lungs.

What a relief it is to finally hear someone *say it*.

He's stopped trying to run. *Beau* has stopped trying to run. The three of us are here now, and this thing between us is beating like an injured heartbeat. If they're talking to me, if we can try. If there's even a *chance* . . .

My heart expands, pressing painfully against my ribcage, and I throw myself at Beau. His eyes widen an instant before I wrap my arms around his neck, and he catches me up, swinging me into his chest.

My lips press against his ear as I whisper, "*Thank you.*"

His mosquito bites are livid and raw on his neck and arms, and I resolve to give him the lavender after all. Lavender in his hair. Lavender oil. All my lavender, if he wants it.

He squeezes me back, almost painfully, and his huffed laugh is choked. "For being angry with you?"

My hands slide down his arms as I pull back to look at him. "For being honest."

He sobers at that, his mouth tightening a little, but he doesn't unleash any of the things he could say right now.

I feel like I'm trying not to spook a wild horse—one which will bolt at a wrong word. So I hold my tongue, too, and bury everything else I want to say.

I miss you. I'm sorry. I'm mad, too. Please talk to me.

It seems to work. Beau takes a deep breath, and nods, accepting it with that same strange, thoughtful expression on his face.

Then his gaze dips—and those brows shoot up.

"Is that my shirt?" he asks.

Beau walks us backward until he sits beside Dom, settling me on his lap like it's where I belong. My feet naturally fall into Dom's lap, and Dom looks down at them like they're something strange and unexpected.

Beau tugs at my clothes, and I blink.

His . . . shirt?

I look down, finally remembering pulling Beau's old shirt from one of my drawers this morning. Back when Beau was living with me, I wore his shirts to bed most nights, and when I found it in my drawer this morning . . .

I shouldn't have put it on. It just felt like the next closest thing to having him with me.

I really hadn't thought about him catching me in it, though.

"Oh, I'm sorry," I stammer, heat flooding my cheeks.

Dom wraps his hand around my leg, drawing it onto his lap, then the other. He leaves his hand loosely cuffing my ankle, and the calluses on his hand burn against my skin.

"You're wearing my shirt," Beau repeats, dumbfounded.

I give him a panicked look. "I— Jayk missed a few things, and I just— I'm sorry. I'll give it back, of course."

"Now?" Dom asks, dry amusement making cracks in his intensity. He leans back against the swing, stretching his arm over the painted wood as he watches us.

I shoot him a quick scowl. "I . . . *no*, I'll wash it first, *then* I'll—"

A smile breaks over Beau's face.

"Just keep it, pet." He laughs.

My stammers die on my tongue, the words lost. He's been so angry lately—so tense and quick to avoid me. But his smile is beautiful. It's warm and brimming with a tilted, unexpected affection. It's nights of aftercare. It's him kissing my fingertips after I cried.

He finally meets my eyes, sobering.

"Keep it," he repeats. "It looks better on you, anyway."

I'm too raw from my conversation with Dom. My fight with Jayk. From Jasper and Lucky trying to pull down Bristlebrook itself to get to me.

Tears sting my eyes, and I blink fast, trying to hold them back.

"Oh no, not those." Beau's hand finds the side of my face. His thumb wipes at a tear. "Not those. Not over me."

I press my cheek into his hand, desperate for the touch, and he doesn't let me go. Soothing, soft, he just strokes my face until my shaky breaths finally even out and, shyly, I look up at him through my glasses.

"Good morning, darlin'," he says softly.

This time, my smile up at him is warm and genuine. "Good morning, Beau."

His eyes search mine, then he finally bends down and gives me a gentle, lingering kiss on my cheek. Dom watches us like he can't see anything else, like the sunrise is dirt and this is all he woke up for. His hand tightens on my ankle. Caught with emotion, my lids slide closed, and I breathe my brutes in—their spicy shampoo and the way they mix together.

If we could just stay like this. We could be so good, all of us.

We just need to stay *like this*.

Does this mean we're going to try? I open my eyes again, and Dom is still staring at me.

Does this mean he is?

"Ooh, this is cozy! Scooch. I want in."

"You sit your ass on me, Lucky, and I'm kicking it off the porch," Dom warns, and I look up in time to see Lucky jump up—only to skid to a stop in front of us, an affronted pout already forming.

A laugh huffs out of me, my emotions crashing in.

"Mind his back, Dominic. He's still recovering." Jasper's more measured footfalls follow up the newly repaired steps, and he somehow looks icy under the fanning warmth in the sky.

It's belied by the whimsical yellow flower nestled behind his ear.

"Recovering?" I ask sharply, looking Lucky over in concern.

He winks back, an easy looseness in his colorful shoulders I haven't seen in weeks. They're decorated in livid red gashes, and his skin glows—*he* glows—like they're some vital medicine for him, and not terrifying strokes of violence.

"On a scale of one to ten, how much detail do you want?" he asks. "One being like—I just want to know that you're feeling good enough to tap dance and giggle over daisy chains. Five being like—he strung me to the ceiling and whipped me till I came on the floor, then fucked me in my mess until I just about passed out."

I tilt my head, my blood rushing in horrified, fascinated ways. "What is ten like?"

"I don't need to hear about ten," Beau breaks in, rolling his eyes.

Jasper strolls up and leans against the post, adjusting his cuffs. "Ten is if you choose to watch." His dark eyes find me. "Or participate."

Ah. Right.

Whipping.

Watching me, Dom snorts, and I frown at him, then smooth down the front of my shirt.

"Thank you for the offer, Jasper. I'll consider it," I say, then add pointedly, for Dom's benefit, "I'll consider it seriously."

Lucky laughs, then bends in for a quick, enthusiastic kiss that makes electric sparks shoot down my spine. He snags my mouth, pushing me against Beau as he makes himself welcome with pure, unselfconscious joy—and enough heat that I squirm.

He rubs his nose against mine as he pulls back, then grins.

"Glad to see you made it out of the tower. If he left you in there any longer, I'd have been appropriating some swords and armor from Red Zone so I could start slaying ogres." His smile sours. "Jayk is the ogre. In case you missed that."

I'm still blinking up at him, taken aback by the ease with which he kissed me in front of everyone. Comfortable. Like this is fine with him, and he expects it to be fine with everyone else. Bewildered, I glance around.

And no one is acting like it *isn't* fine.

Elation, bursting bright and sweet, almost makes me laugh, and I beam at him.

Lucky blinks. Eyeing me warily, he starts touching his face.

"What, do I have something? Can't be food. Not like I've eaten."
He considers that, glancing at Jasper. "Well. I've snacked."

I shake my head, my throat sticking with bittersweet happiness,
and I lean back into Beau's chest, allowing myself to enjoy his warmth.
The smell of Dom's shampoo on his skin. Cautiously, Beau's hand
brushes over my hair.

Jasper hasn't taken his eyes from my face, and they're unusually
kind.

"You're quite all right, Lucien. You did well," he murmurs. "Very
well."

Lucky's gaze slips between us, baffled, and he scratches the back of
his neck. "Uh, good, I guess?"

Dom picks up his half-empty cup of slop from beside the swing.
"Here. Eden made breakfast."

I frown. That was *his* cup. He should drink the whole thing.

My empty mug rests beside him too, and my morning slop
assuaged my hunger more than my last week of rations put together.
The thick, gelatinous goop has a way of sticking against my insides like
it's growing in my gut, filling me more by the moment.

Lucky perks up, swiping the mug. I try to stop him, but Dom still
has me chained at the ankle, and Beau at my waist.

"Oh, but it won't be hot," I protest.

"Don't care. I'm so hungry I could eat the ass out of a skunk."

Dear *God*.

Lucky slugs back the slop like it's a straight shot—and spits it out
just as fast. He hacks like a cat with a hairball, then turns, bending over
the side of the porch like he's going to throw up.

"Whoa, easy, Lucky!" Beau calls, and his tentative hold grows
more sure as he's distracted, fitting under my breasts more naturally.
"Breathe. Through your nose."

"It's *in* my nose!" Lucky retches again, and Jasper touches his
shoulders, bemused.

Dom's shoulders start shaking, and I glare at him. Then at Lucky's
back.

"It is *not* that bad!" I insist.

Lucky coughs, then gives me a watery-eyed look over his shoulder.

"Is it poison? Is this what you gave the Sinners? Why are we letting Eden cook?"

Dom's silent shaking breaks into loud, snorting laughter, and he leans forward, like he needs to brace himself.

I glower at him, but the tension between us seems to have dissolved somewhere between Lucky's gags and his *giggles*.

I nudge him with my foot. "You drank it! It was *fine*."

Dom's thumb presses into the hollow behind my ankle.

"Baby cakes, I'm not being dramatic when I say I wish it *was* skunk anus," Lucky replies, straight-faced.

This, from the man who I saw drinking from a sweaty *boot* at the bond-fire.

"Okay, hand it over, Lucky. I need to try this," Beau decides, reaching out a tanned arm. "Jasper? You game?"

Jasper eyes the mug, then glances at me. I look at him hopefully.

"I . . ." he begins, his voice strained, but Lucky covers the top.

"No *way*. It's nuclear waste—and you owe me so many more orgasms before you die. I won't let you." He drops it into Beau's waiting hand. "You have fun though, Beau."

"Gee, thanks."

Jasper rubs his mouth, hiding a smile behind his hand as Beau pulls the mug closer to examine it.

"Do you drink it or eat it?" Beau asks dubiously.

"You want me to get you a spoon?" Dom replies, dry as dust.

Lucky bends over the mug. "I think it would melt the spoon."

My indignation releases in a reluctant giggle, and I give up, relaxing back against Beau as he sniffs it.

They start bickering, and I tuck my chin in, smiling as I settle back to watch—and I'm suddenly warm, all the way through.

It's not just Lucky who seems freer this morning. Jasper isn't masking quite so carefully today, and his quiet pleasure reaches out to me as much as mine seems to be reaching him. I can't even find a hint of jealousy in me about it. I *want* him to have endless nights with Lucky. With me. Endless days just like this, all of us laughing and together.

Across the porch, Jasper gives me a gentle smile back, so much knowing in his eyes. And I know he sees it—how impossibly lovely this moment is to me.

He sees so much, from his quiet shadows.

The morning's peace might have been broken, but it's been mended into something far more beautiful.

Right now, I'm just . . . happy.

"Oh, fuck *this*," someone snarls.

CHAPTER 23

EDEN

I'm suddenly wrenched out of Beau's arms. My glasses fall around my neck, and the world spins around me in a dizzying storm. Seconds later, a hard, hot mouth is splitting mine, and I'm locked against the wall. I arch against the man, gasping, but he's buried between my thighs, rocking his cock against me. He's only in his boxers. Gripping his bare, scratched-up shoulders, I tear my mouth away on a shocked moan.

"Jayk!" I snap, breathless.

"What the fuck?" Beau jumps to his feet. "Give her *back*."

Jayk sucks on my throat, hard enough to leave a hickey, and lawless heat throbs deep in my pussy.

"They were just saying good morning," I hiss, as his hand grips my ass.

Jayk rubs me against him until I shudder. "They can say it without putting their hands all over you."

"They can put their hands wherever I *want* them to put them." I rake my nails down his chest, but I can't help the way my hips shift over him when he finds the most brutal, perfect spot. I'm already too worked up.

"She's not your fucking toy!" Beau snaps.

My head falls back, and I crack my eyes open just in time to see Beau wrench Jayk off me. Jayk whirls around, pushing Beau back, and I drop, staggering, onto uncertain legs.

Lucky swoops in to hold me up with a private, reassuring dimple.

Beau's face is filthy with anger, but Dom shoves between them, shoving a hand against his chest before he can take a swing at Jayk. Dom gives him a harsh, quelling look, then frowns at Jayk.

"Enough. You know the score with her. She wants to share." A grimy irritation snaps at his words, and he glances back at Beau, sharing his disapproval. "This shit isn't helping anyone. Pack it away."

Beau scoffs hard.

Jayk folds his arms over his chest, all sleepy, smirking annoyance as he switches his attention to Dom. "You know, it's like you already forgot—you're not in charge anymore, *Cap*. And Eden ain't yours to worry about."

Lips flattening, Dom holds Jayk's gaze, and I wait, almost dizzy.

Tell him he's wrong, I silently urge, tense and watching. *Tell him I'm yours, too.*

But the reminder seems to cool his temper, rather than inflaming it. Carefully neutral, Dom lifts one heavy shoulder. "Yeah. You are in charge, Jayk. Hope you're ready for it."

Disappointment crushes the fragile spindle of hope in my chest.

As if sensing it, Dom glances at me, and he hesitates, his jaw tightening like he's frustrated.

"No." Beau's face flashes wicked dark. "*No*. You don't get to just build yourself a throne and call yourself boss, you ungrateful asshole."

"The fuck do you care if I step up? Not like any of you do any work," Jayk sneers, his chest pressing into Dom's staying palm.

"Told you talking to him was overrated," Lucky mutters to a tense Jasper.

Beau matches Jayk's expression, all the anger from last night bubbling up like it had been sitting just beneath the surface, waiting for some heat. "You don't win friends, or any fucking respect, by shitting all over everyone, Jayk. You just have to play the villain every goddamned time."

Jasper straightens off the post, his expression turning back to marble, and the switch up crushes me. "Beaumont, de-escalate. Step back. You're not in the right frame of mind to have this discussion. We can handle this like *gentlemen*."

I eye Jayk, tattooed and all but naked, scowling at everyone. Beau glaring over Dom's shoulder.

I think we're past gentlemen.

They're all brutes.

"Should have just scaled the building," Lucky breathes, and Jasper throws a scowl in his direction.

"I have respect," Jayk snaps at Beau. His shoulders draw back and some of his sneer drops. "I have it from everyone who matters."

There's a thorn under that one, and it pricks me hard.

"Oh, Jayk," I murmur, hurting for him, and Lucky studies me, then looks at Jayk with a thoughtful frown.

But Beau's handsome face only grows more scathing as Jayk's anger cools. He moves forward, but Dom catches him again, dragging him back with a frustrated growl.

"*Stop*, Beau. Not like this. He's not the one you're mad at."

"The hell I'm not. This isn't *right*." Beau looks over Dom's shoulder, his gaze all hot, sulfuric anger. "You think we're going to follow you anywhere? You can't just take *everything*, you bastard. You don't fucking deserve any of it, and you're hurting people. You don't deserve my room. You don't deserve to replace Dom, who has never been anything but a fucking great captain to you. You sure as fuck don't deserve Eden. You ruin *everything*. We were all having a good time until you showed up."

"Beau," I breathe, horror filling me as something bitter and dark breaks over Jayk's expression.

"Holy shit, man, chill," Lucky says, shocked.

Jayk just nods like this is nothing new. He looks at me.

"Him?" He searches my face, his eyes deep, depthless seas. "Really?"

Aching, I sigh. There's so much hurt here, between all of them. So many unkindnesses that they're so quick to pile onto one another.

Dom starts talking to Beau, hushed and firm.

"He's wrong, Jayk. You deserve everything," I tell him steadily, and his shoulders loosen. But before he can relax too far, I add, "But you could have joined us. This doesn't have to be a fight."

"Sure, sugar. We could all join a boy band and start a secret handshake." Jayk's mouth turns down, bitterly. "Wake up. This isn't a family, Eden."

"Enough. Do *not* put your insecurities onto her, Jaykob." Jasper steps forward, his eyes flicking over Jaykob with quiet, eviscerating contempt. "You're not the only one who cares for Eden. This *is* her home, and we *are* her family now. I don't appreciate you implying otherwise. And I certainly don't appreciate you impeding her ability to be with who she chooses."

Jayk eyes Jasper head to toe, his thick muscles flexing as he stands at full height. "You plan on stopping me?"

"If I must."

"You couldn't last night."

Jasper stiffens, his chilly mask cracking. "*Last night*, you behaved like an immature, musclebound meathead. I'm not sure in what world you thought kidnapping a recently kidnapped woman was a brilliant idea, but as usual, you display the emotional capacity of an enraged hippopotamus. Do you have any idea the effect that could have had on Eden? That it had on all of us?"

As Jasper glances at Lucky, his cracks split wide open.

There's so much livid concern, so much worry in him, that I squeeze Lucky's arm, hearing the echoes of Lucky battering at my door. Hearing his broken whisper, *"I need you, too. Please don't make me wait."*

Lucky grimaces, avoiding my eyes.

God. What is happening to us?

They're *all* splintering.

"You're wrong, Jasper." Dom turns from Beau to look back at him, heavy and serious. "You saw how Jayk was there for Eden after we got her back. More than me, more than you, more than anyone. He helped her get through it. He's not crossing her lines with these stunts, he's helping her to find them. He knows what he's doing." Dom nods his chin at me. "She trusts him."

Jayk sends an uncertain frown at him, but the others aren't having it.

"Be that as it may, Eden's lines aren't the only ones that matter here. Jaykob's actions affect everyone," Jasper bites out.

Beau huffs incredulously. "Jayk *wasn't* with her more than anyone." Mosquitos whizz around us as the day heats, and his skin glistens, damp with sweat as he scowls at Dom. "*I* was there. I was *living* with her—every day, I was there, helping her through her nightmares, through her triggers, helping her figure out all of you and *your* damn problems. *Being there* isn't enough. It doesn't mean she'll share anything at all about what she did or how she felt. She might love you—but it doesn't mean she trusts you."

Hurt throbs through his every word.

Understanding pierces me, jagged and hot, and a sharp whistling starts up in my ears.

That's why he's mad.

He and Dom are a matched pair, after all. They might handle it differently but it all comes back to the same thing.

Trust.

All five of my men are clustered together like explosive material about to be set off, and Jaykob widens his stance, every line of him set in pure defense.

Jasper is glaring at Dom. Beau's heart is breaking over me. Dom is set off against them, and Jayk with everyone. Where did the morning go? How on earth am I supposed to fix all of them, when half their problems have nothing to do with me? And the ones that do . . .

Beau can't even look at me right now, and I finally understand why.

I just have no idea what to do about it.

Lucky looks between Jasper, Jayk, then Beau, Dom . . . and me. The sunrise is in full storm, drenching Bristlebrook's battlements in brilliant light, and his hair glows around his conflicted face.

"What?" Jayk snaps at him, noticing. "Stop looking like an injured puppy. It's pathetic. You want to take a swing too, then just do it."

Fire flashes into Lucky's eyes, and he lets me go. He doesn't jump into attack, not like Beau, but his cloaking humor falls away.

The anger is bare, deep, and very, very serious.

"You know, I want to take your side, Jayk. You just make it really hard."

Jayk scoffs, and Lucky's face hardens.

"I'm not your enemy, asshole. I've been trying to be your friend for years."

"Don't scoff at him, Jaykob. He's right." Jasper steps in sharply, and Jaykob matches the step. Jasper's lip curls in distaste. "Beaumont may have been out of line in his expression, but he's not wrong in his sentiment. If you intend to lead, Jaykob, you will need to reevaluate your approach." He tilts his head at me, though he doesn't look my way again. "With all of us."

Beau dives in again, then Dom.

I take a step away, hugging myself as I watch them.

The whistling increases until their arguments fall away, but it takes me a moment to realize it's not in my head.

It's Ethel, her emergency whistle screeching between her lips. It takes another blast before I see Ida racing down from her platform. She begins urgently trying to pull back the heavy wooden bridge that spans our dry moat, and I scan the trees, not seeing anything that would spark her panic.

But Ethel keeps blowing her whistle in harsh, urgent shrieks.

"Um, everyone?" I interject, but they're not paying attention.

Ida struggles with the bridge, trying to pull it away—but it was made thick and large, long enough to span the moat. Even if it is only wide enough to fit people walking across in single file, it's incredibly heavy. I'm not sure if one person can so much as shift it.

No matter how Ida pulls, that bridge doesn't budge.

I step forward, squinting . . . but the trees remain a distant blur of still, peaceful green.

The small hairs on the back of my neck prickle to life.

"Don't act like you're some hero, Doc. Ever think maybe she didn't talk to you because she knows you sulk like a fucking toddler and leave every time someone hurts your feelings?" Jayk sneers.

Ethel's whistle screams in the distance.

The trees begin to move.

"There's something happening!" I snap, but the men are too absorbed in one another.

Windows slam open above us, and civilians begin pouring

through the front doors, rifles in hands. Finally, the alarm starts going off, blaring through the speakers.

My temper fries, and I whirl on the others. "I said—"

"*What?*" Beau snaps, and I don't even have it in me to flinch at the harshness of his voice.

Instead, I push my glasses back up my nose. I no longer have to squint to see the civilians leaning out of windows or manning every looming defensive platform, or to see every rifle gleaming in the morning sun.

I don't have to squint to see the threat that has appeared from the forest.

There, lining the inner rim of trees all the way around Bristlebrook, stands over fifty Reapers. They're armed and dirty, loaded down with heavy bags and pack mules.

Sawyer and Cole stand at their head, right in front of our defensive dry moat, all their camping gear in tow.

I guess we just figured out where they want to stay.

I take a deep, steadying breath, and point in their direction.

"We have company."

CHAPTER 24

BEAU

SURVIVAL TIP #303
Forget hunger.
Anger will eat you alive.

"Oh, fuck." Lucky's anger drops away as he stares at the Reapers closing in on us.

"Get the rifles, Lucky. Now," Jayk orders, jumping off the porch.

The air is clogged with heat, and, as I follow, I just can't shake the rage off anymore. All I can see now is more people to spit it at.

"Did you know there were more of them?" Jasper asks Jayk as he follows, alarmed.

Jayk scowls, darting a glance at him. "We've been watching them. I'm handling it."

Jasper slows, staring daggers at his back before he lifts his voice. "That would have been helpful to share, Jaykob. *Why* did they bring so many men? Did you think—"

Jayk waves him off, nodding to Ava up on her high platform.

"What are we doing, Jayk?" she calls, lined up beside Mary Beth, alarm pinning her tone.

"Give me a frag in case I need to blow the bridge," he mutters, nodding at the bridge in the center of the moat.

The one in front of Sawyer.

"Hold," Jayk shouts as he storms past the platforms. "No one fire a single goddamn shot or I'll pull your intestines out your asshole and make you skip rope."

I'm close on his heels, and Dom looms like he's ready to muzzle me. Dom, who's buddying up with *Jayk*—the asshole stomping all over him. The asshole who took my room out from under me. Who threw The Plan 2.0 out the window right beside my favorite shaded lamp—the *new* Plan that I so graciously included him in, too.

But no, Jayk doesn't give one flying hoot about any of that. Even when I used Eden's ass as a notepad and sent her to him dripping and desperate, he wasn't grateful, though that has to be about the most generous gift one friend can give another.

I'm a great friend. Who does he think he is? Saying I cut people out of my life. Going around and calling me petulant. Unforgiving. *Stubborn*.

He's just dead wrong. I've never been stubborn a day in my life, and anyone who tells me different is a filthy liar.

Dom eyes me sideways, and I ignore him, my hands shaking with unshed violence.

Eden follows along behind us like a tentative foal, and I rub my fingertips together guiltily.

They're still coated in her tears.

Damn it, I can't. This has to stop. I need to figure it out. To . . . to breathe or do *something* to calm the hell down.

I don't ever want her tears on my fingers again.

A civilian hands me her rifle as I pass, and I mutter my thanks, but the Reapers aren't grabbing for their weapons. They're unloading tents. Cooking kits. They have fold-out chairs like they're setting up for a church potluck. The sweltering sun glints off Jayk's stupid throne, and my resentment *burns*.

Yeah.

None of this is calming me down.

As we approach, Sawyer parks his ass in one of the chairs, right in front of the bridge. His wide-brimmed hat shades his eyes, and a grin crawls out from under his mustache. A flannel-wearing Reaper tosses him a hard crust of bread as Cole dumps himself in a neon pink fold-out beside him.

My stomach snarls at the sight, hollow and vicious. After a bare slurp of thin bone broth last night and a lick of Eden's nail varnish slop this morning, I'm ready to shoot him for the bread alone.

For a moment, I think I see a flash of long, dark hair behind one of the tents, but when I look back, the spot is still.

One by one, Lucky tosses the others their rifles, and we fall into line.

Jayk gestures, and we stop in front of the moat, armed and ready. Only one narrow, heavy bridge separates us from the army of Reapers.

Leaning back in his lawn chair, Cole's doubtful eyes travel over Jayk's mostly naked body, scarred and scuffed, his hair still standing up—probably from Eden's fingers.

A mosquito twitches around my ear.

"You have a problem with clothes, King? 'Cause I've got to say, if anyone was going to come walzin' out of that house in their sleepy clothes, you wouldn't be my pick," Cole drawls as he rifles through his pack, finally tugging out a jar of . . . is that home-made jam?

My mouth waters.

Jayk shoots him a glower, but he addresses the boss. "Get off our lawn, Sawyer. This isn't what we talked about. You got a whole fucking forest to cozy up in. You don't need to block us in."

Sawyer takes the jam from Cole, then flicks open his pocketknife to scoop out a generous chunk that I'd shred eyeballs to suck down. Eden shifts forward, watching the jam too, and a pang of worry works through my anger.

She better be eating more.

I rub my fingertips together again. I'll check on her, make sure she's fed at least.

"Well, shoot. That ain't very hospitable." Sawyer tips back the brim of his hat to wink. "How're you all supposed to get to know us if we set up all the way back there?"

He smears the jam over his corner of bread, and I slap and miss the mosquito.

My temple throbs, my muscles aching with the need to punch, and trap, and shoot. I shake my head, but it doesn't shake the urge.

"Jesus Christ. Eden, Jasper? I'm leaving you for jam." Lucky groans.

"Fickle," Eden breathes beside him.

"You want jam, pretty lady, just march your fine behind over that bridge. We'll make sure you're fed." Cole swipes the jam back off Sawyer, and he frowns as he looks Eden over. The mosquito lands on my ear. "You look like you haven't had a proper meal in a good while." He smiles, slow and suggestive. "These boys not taking care of you right?"

My vision hazes out.

The gun is kicking back before I realize I've fired a shot. The jar explodes in his hand, and both men haul up to their feet.

There's a rush of sudden clicks as the safeties of at least fifty guns are flicked off, and a shuddering grumble behind us answers as the civilians lock into gear.

"Fucking idiot." Dom snatches the rifle from my hand, giving me a condemning look as he tosses it down, and I give him an alarmed one back, shaking.

My pulse throbs in my neck, my vision coming in spots.

The Reapers shout, and I raise my hands, as Jayk talks them down. They're trembling.

What did I do?

My heart drums in my ears, and my head spins dizzily as memories flash. My rifle on the ground. Jayk flipping someone off.

Eden's arresting gray-blue eyes watching me with concern.

Anger still thrums through me in hot, draining bursts—but shaky fear suddenly flashes alongside it as I latch onto those eyes. I love those eyes. I love them bright and sharp. I love them fogged with need. I love them watching me from the next pillow.

What sort of man gets mad—really, *truly* mad—at the woman he loves?

But I am.

My mama always said, a man who makes his woman cry is no man at all.

But I *did*.

It's like admitting it last night broke the dam. There's so much of this anger in me now, strange and unfamiliar, and I . . . I don't know how to handle it. And maybe shoving it all down wasn't the healthiest way, either, but it had to be better than *this*.

"Fine, fine. Weapons down, boys," Sawyer calls back, reluctantly sitting down. "He's protective. I can understand that."

Eden lifts her chin, her gaze cutting back to the Reapers. "I'm not interested in anything you have to offer, sir." Her voice is tart when she adds under her breath, "I have more than enough to satisfy me here."

"Don't call him that," Dom mutters.

The Reapers go back to unpacking, all their tents and pots and pans—the blankets they won't need in this forsaken weather. Hell, there are *three* mules laden with food.

The tension around us unwinds . . . but mine only coils tighter. Heat is frying the early day and sweat beads under my arms. The mosquitos are too loud. My chest is clenching like someone's taken a bite from it.

What's happening to me?

"You're doing fine, Beaumont. Try to breathe. Focus on that," Jasper murmurs, suddenly beside me. He's composed and so barely audible, still focused on Sawyer, that no one so much as glances our way.

I tuck my hands in my pockets and step back as I breathe, trying to cool it. I can *always* cool it—this time might just be a little harder is all. This time . . .

Fuck, I don't have it. Not last night with Dom, or this morning with Jayk, and not now.

I almost got us all shot.

Jayk crosses his arms over his chest. "We need to get in and out, Sawyer. You wanna be friends? *Move your ass.*"

Dom paces along the moat, scanning the Reapers as they set up.

It's all a blur.

I'm mad.

Sawyer lifts one shoulder. "No can do, King." He nods at the sole remaining bridge. "We're behind your pike pit—"

"Moat."

"*Pike pit.* We're staying. Any one of you is welcome to join us for breakfast or dinner or anything in between. We'll be happy to have you." He kicks a cool box. "Anyone here like sausages?"

"It's a siege." Lucky grimaces. "You're *starving* us out."

"It is *not* a siege." Sawyer has the grace to look like he means it. Absently, he takes a bite of his sweet, slathered bread, and my rage spikes again. "We're not here to hurt anyone. We just can't go home without you is all. We need your help. Just think of it as . . . I don't know. Aggressive friendship."

Lucky's head tilts, a dimple springing to life in his cheek. "Okay, then. Gimme some of that bread, bud."

Lounging in his pink chair, Cole grins back. "Come over here and share it with me. Show all your pretty friends you can trust us."

"I'd trust you more if you stopped calling them my pretty friends," Lucky replies dubiously, and Cole snorts.

"This is an attack," Jayk snaps, his own anger making him dark. Aggressive.

Damn it, it's no way to be.

"Easy," Jasper murmurs to me. "Go back inside if you need to. We can talk soon."

I shoot him a glare, but there's no condescension in his quick glance. Only compassion.

Through a garbled mouthful, Sawyer declares, "Now don't be ly tha. We're all fronds here."

Lucky throws him a pointed finger. "Yeah, friends don't besiege other friends." He shrugs. "You know, just a little motto I have."

"Friends don't let their friends get all their food raided by Sam and his asshole cronies," Cole counters.

Sam.

The image of him swinging by his neck pummels me. Eden standing off against Alastair.

Dom on his knees, defeated.

Alone.

God *damn* it. Anger roils in my gut, oily and slick.

This morning, I woke up thinking *maybe*. Dom and I were talking, our mess was all out there. It all felt possible. And then it was like that with Eden, too. She was pretty as a picture, wearing my clothes, draped over me like a dream and being sweet as anything. I told her I was mad, and she *thanked* me. In fact, right up until Jayk ripped her out of my arms, I was feeling light enough to float—like I might actually be able to get a handle on this whole *angry* thing without turning into someone my mama would be sad to know.

Everyone was together, and she was happy, and I just . . . believed in it. That we could all do it.

That I could pretend this isn't eating me up.

But playing make-believe on a pretty morning doesn't change that she doesn't trust me. It doesn't change that just weeks ago, Dom was at my door, begging for my help, and I turned him away. Because I was *mad*.

I look over at Eden, and she flinches like she can feel it.

I'm mad.

At her, and at myself, for not being better at this. I'm mad that none of us have been trusting each other, and I don't see an easy way to start.

When Sawyer's eyes narrow, flicking from one of us to the next, I realize I've crossed my arms. Eden's staring at the ground between her feet, breathing too carefully, and Lucky steps in close beside her.

"What?" Sawyer prompts.

Jayk looks at us, then rolls his eyes like I'm in control of any part of myself right now. "Sam's dead. Alastair's playing the evil overlord now."

Color drains out of Cole's face, and Sawyer stops his lazy lounging, the confidence crashing out of his smirk.

They exchange a look, until Cole stammers, "What are we going to do about—"

Sawyer looks at us, and Cole cuts off. He stands, then kicks his chair over with the same aggression that burns in my bones. Turning away, he links his hands behind his neck.

Behind them, Reapers start muttering, and I struggle to pay attention.

"We can't. We can't do anything. We—" Sawyer rubs a hand over his moustache, staring at his back. "It changes everything. Cole, you know he's going to—"

"What?" Jayk mimics Sawyer, and my teeth lock together in irritation at his pettiness.

"Do you have a satellite phone we can use?" Sawyer asks urgently.

Jayk frowns, glancing at Dom's back before he seems to catch himself. He scowls.

"We have a radio, but like you said. You're staying over there."

We do have a satellite phone, gathering dust from the early days when we were trying to reach embassies and allies, but it's too valuable to hand over to anyone. The radio works to talk with anyone around here just fine.

Her hand pressed to her stomach, Eden tentatively asks, "Isn't that better? Sam sent the Sinners after you, but maybe Alastair will take a different approach? Maybe you can work something out with him. Something that doesn't involve fighting."

Is she *still* defending him?

Alastair is a snake.

"Sure, maybe the Reapers can be like us and just have to *hand over* enough food to beggar them instead of having it stolen by force," I mutter to Jasper. "Won't that be so much better."

But his reply is clipped and cold. "She's trying to avoid a war, Beaumont. You're mad at the wrong person."

I flinch.

Sawyer shakes his head, then pushes to a stand. "Look—" He glances between us, and I can see his mind ticking as he decides what to say. "Look, Alastair's no better. He's the one who *led* most of the raids on our land. He's fucking smart, and he's made it clear he has no problems killing us if we get in his way. At least Sam was dumb as bricks." He starts pacing, then stops and looks at Jayk. "This is bad. We . . . we're just farmers. We have a lot of land, King. A lot of food. But it all means nothing if we can't keep it." He shakes his head again, and he looks at Jayk seriously. "He's going to attack us, and if he's in charge, he won't hold anything back. If you won't let us use your radio, then just . . . can *you* call them? Our people? Please, just . . . just tell them that he's coming."

I see her take the hit. Eden pales, her hair falling over her face as she ducks her head, and my worry for her starts washing through the anger.

She really is beating herself up over this.

And here I am adding to it.

Sweat pools along my hairline.

"You're not going back?" Jayk grinds out. "Don't they need you?"

Cole turns back around with a bitter scoff. "There ain't a damn thing we can do to stop them. Why the hell do you think we're here, King? We need you. We need you yesterday." He waves a hand at our defenses. "We need *this*."

Buck and Pete are moving slow as molasses as they build up their makeshift fire, but even caught up in my own mess, I can't miss how they look at each other over the tiny flames.

They're afraid.

God *damn* it. Maybe they don't deserve this anger either.

Dom turns back around, giving Sawyer a hard-eyed look that reminds me of rapid deployments and barked orders. He should never have felt like he wasn't our captain.

The sweat starts trickling down my spine.

"Why bring so many men?" Dom asks Sawyer bluntly, but I barely hear him.

Eden's head comes up, and she gives Dom a piercing look. Jayk's head turns to him too.

Maybe . . . maybe I do cut people out.

Sawyer and Cole exchange a tense look. Eden steps forward, her sharp gaze traveling between them before it flicks up to scan the Reapers.

I haven't talked to her in a *week*, not really. How much space is too much space?

. . . *Am* I the problem?

Cole sucks some jam off his hand, but it doesn't look half as casual as he seems to be aiming for. "Insurance. King here didn't seem like the friendliest sort. Thought some backup might not be such a bad idea."

"But why so many?" Dom walks over, his red shirt demanding blood. Telling them to stop. "You needed fifty-three men to face a handful of us? I know Jayk didn't tell you our numbers."

That makes me refocus.

Jayk pauses, a crease marring his forehead. "No," he confirms slowly, flicking his gaze back up to Sawyer. "I only mentioned the five of us."

"All Ranger-trained," Sawyer counters, his mustache twitching.

Cole grimaces, his pretty face buried under the worry as he picks crumbs off his lap.

Jayk's shoulders pull back, his face darkening. "Didn't mention that either."

"You knew we had women here before you even left. How long did it take you to get here? A week?" Dom drills him with his gaze. "The tents. The amount of food. You brought a donkey. You were ready for us. How?"

Sawyer's eyes skitter away, but he shrugs. "It's a mule, actually. His name is Cherub."

"Is she here?"

This time, when Eden breaks in, it's not careful or polite. She sounds damn near as demanding as Dom. The burned grass crunches under her feet as she edges forward.

Sawyer and Cole both fall quiet, staring at her. *Caught*.

She glances at them for a moment, then nods, continuing to scan the Reapers.

"Akira?" she calls. "I know it's you."

Shock pins me in place.

Jasper freezes, and Jayk's head whips around, looking for her as Lucky snorts in horrified laughter. Dom's eyes sink closed briefly, his shoulders dropping again.

Suddenly, Buck squirts some oil on their firepit and flames flare up. Pete falls back with a surprised shout.

"No. What? No. Yes? Really?" Lucky eyes Eden up and down, then follows her gaze. "Wait, really?"

Eden brushes her long hair out of her face, giving him a patient look. My shirt hangs concerningly on her fragile frame. "Who else knows exactly where we are, who we are, and how many people are here? Didn't you hear the man yesterday? 'I never thought they'd be so pretty,' he said. They had to know there were women here if they had time to imagine what we'd be like." She looks back at Jayk, terse. "And Akira went out with you to repair the cameras, so they were able to avoid those. She's the only one who knew all of that. She told them to come in force so they could pin us here."

I stare at her, stunned.

She just put all that together.

In *moments*.

Cherub brays loudly, tugging at his rope tie.

"Come on out, Akira," Cole calls with a shrug, but I barely register it.

I'm too busy looking at Eden. Her shoulders are steeled like they were when she faced Alastair. Her chin tilted up, and her sharp, clever eyes calmly staring down the small army against us.

Who is this girl?

Because she's not the same woman who sobbed in my arms after we saved her from the hunters. She's not the woman who foolishly followed me and Dom into the woods and nearly ended up with my bullet in her skull. She's not the woman who wept her heart out in the shower after we finally got her home.

I know she's brave. I'm not blind to her heart or her kindness or how she wants to help. I know she's smart, and proud, and resourceful.

But this is different. This woman is angry.

And *devious*.

Akira walks out from behind the tent where I spotted her earlier, her dark hair swinging. She doesn't acknowledge any of us. Cole reaches out a hand, which she ignores, though she gives Sawyer a tight, nervous nod. He smiles back in a tight, neutral sort of way.

When I last saw her, she was undernourished and dead-eyed, heartbroken over losing some Sinner who got what he deserved. Now, she's glowing with health and softly feminine in floral.

As she hesitantly appears, loud, furious mutters start up behind us.

Jayk's mouth twists. "You miserable sack of shit."

The nervousness in her face dies. "Call me whatever you want—I don't owe you anything."

She glances at Eden and hate sparks in her eyes. I've never hurt a woman in my life, but that look makes me want to pluck them out.

But Eden steps forward again, just as fierce, and a bemused Lucky has to tug her back from stepping right into the barbed wire put up around the dry moat.

Christ, the woman needs her eyes checked.

"You brought armed men here? Kasey is here, Akira. She's fourteen," Eden bites back, unfazed by the lethal look. Her hair fans about her like a crown. "Hate me, I always understood that, but these women did *nothing*."

Sawyer whistles low. "You weren't kidding, Kiki. They don't seem to like you much."

"I don't have anything to say to her. I don't need to explain myself." But her mouth twists when she looks down at him. "I only did what I had to, same as anyone. I *survive*."

Eden's brows drive down at that, something flickering over her expression.

Jayk scratches at his chest, watching them. Sawyer and Cole just glance away like they're checking out the civilians, then at their camp being set up, like they've decided this fight isn't worth getting in the middle of.

Eyeing Eden, standing off against Akira like two battle queens about to wage war . . . I might agree. Eden's formidable like this.

When *she's* mad.

The sun beats down on me like a punishment. Mosquitos storm me like a plague, and my stomach's in unrest. If I've been wrong about everything, how am I supposed to know what's right now? Is she a liar, or am I just a blind fool? None of the others seem to have any trouble forgiving her.

What am I missing?

Why does it have to be so hard?

Eden lifts her chin, shaking Lucky off. "The civilians aren't going with the Reapers. They don't trust that easily. Not like you seem to." Her expression softens. "You didn't have to leave Bristlebrook, Akira. It was dangerous, going to them."

Akira waves a swift hand. "I'm doing just fine. I was doing fine before you showed up, and I was fine after. These women? They'll be fine, too, as long as they don't start shooting at the men here who can actually help them. It's *you*, Eden. You want to play the hero, but you're really just a devious, murdering bitch. They should leave you in the dust before you get them killed as well."

The sudden, sickening echo of that word is like a bare-handed slap.

Devious.

Eden's hands clench, but she only nods. Like she believes it.

Like she *deserves* it.

And suddenly . . . the injustice of it rattles me. Eden's standing there, *compassionate*—being her kind self to a woman who painted her room in blood. Eden, who only schemed and lied and killed to *save* herself. She killed to save me, and I know how much that cost her.

I don't know what I'm missing. I don't know why she didn't trust me, but suddenly, I'm real sure she's not the whole problem.

She might not even be most of it.

Jayk's hand snaps to his rifle, but Dom grabs his wrist, and for once, I wish he wouldn't. For once, I'm in agreement with Jayk. He *should* be mad.

Eden deserves better.

"Don't you call her that again. Don't you even think it." Just this once, I let all that filthy hot rage pump through me. "Eden's a survivor—and a better person than you could ever be."

Jayk gives me a sharp, surprised look as I fall in beside him. But finally, he nods, and our shoulders press together as we glower at Akira.

Jasper sighs. "I'm putting you both in joint anger management."

Sawyer points at me, sniffing over his mustache. "Hey now, I'm not threatening your ladyfolk. You don't threaten ours."

Neither of us reply, but he nods like we're in agreement . . . then he stands up. "Okay, then. Time to clear a few things up."

He walks to the edge of the long bridge spanning the moat—the only one left.

The only way in.

The only way *out*.

"I want y'all to hear me!" Sawyer booms toward the civilians. "There's a lot of talk about numbers and who said what, but we're only here like this to keep ourselves safe. We don't mean you any harm, not a moment of it. We need each other—"

Cole hurries up beside him, tugging his shirt back, a rueful smile flashing over his face. "For work. Protection. Not . . ."

Sawyer's eyes widen, and he slaps Cole's shoulder. "*Right*. Not for nothin' . . ." He coughs. "Not for anythin' *unsavory*."

Cole nods, and Sawyer nods too.

"If any one of you choose to come with us, you can get your mouths around as much of this as you can handle!" Sawyer spreads his flannelled arms wide, stepping back to gesture at Pete and Buck as they sweat over their fire.

As we watch, Pete throws down a few thin cuts of meat onto the pan Bucky's holding over the flames . . . and I suck in a sharp breath as the scent invades my lungs.

Bacon.

Jayk grunts beside me.

Holy mother of all things delicious. They have *bacon*.

I've never been so hungry in my life. So hot and bothered and miserable. Worse, I think I might even deserve it. I swallow down another lungful of that snapping, crackling fat like it's an actual taste, watching it crisp up. Forget waterboarding or limb removal. *This* is torture.

Realizing all eyes are on them, Pete and Buck blink at each other, startled, then straighten up. Pete swipes off his cap, giving a little wave, and Buck smooths down his thinning hair with a winning grin.

"The food, he means. The . . ." Cole laughs, giving up, and he throws the civilians a slow smile. "I'm sure you ladies would appreciate the food, is what we mean. It's a real nice spread. Just like my mama used to make. Meat, grain, oats, cheese . . ."

Lucky wraps both arms around Eden's waist, and she gives him a dry look. But I don't miss the way she's looking at them. Worried. Thoughtful. *Considering*.

I glower at Cole. Cheap and petty tricks. Smiling, playing up that Southern charm like that. Talking about *cheese*. Any man with half a brain should know that won't work.

"I think the point of the matter is, we could all do with some more friends. So if that sounds good to any of y'all, just come on over this bridge here and you'll be welcome. We'd love to have you." Sawyer finishes with a tip of his hat, then strolls back to his seat.

There's a long, curious silence behind us.

"We could just shoot you," Jayk says.

Sawyer turns, giving him an even look. He brushes a hand over his mustache. "I really don't want it to come to that."

Jayk stares at him, his muscles locking up as he draws tall. Considering.

My hand flexes, ready to reach for my rifle.

Then Jayk grimaces, shaking his head.

"Fall back." He gestures at all of us to move.

The others begin to peel away, but before I turn, Sawyer brushes his hands over his jeans and blurts, "Wait . . . uh. Wait one second?"

Jayk and I look back at the same time, and Sawyer looks between us. "How's the girl? The one that got shot."

I pause, my anger spiking again as I think of her injuries. So many little hits of it that I can't get a hold of.

"Jennifer's on bedrest. She's in pain. We don't have pain meds like we used to," I bite out.

Most of my meds were taken at Cyanide.

The weathered lines tighten beside Sawyer's eyes, and he nods. He seems to think that through for a moment, then he reaches down and rummages through his pack. Next thing, I'm catching a bottle against my chest. I check the label, and surprise shakes my anger loose.

Shit. It's pain relief. Heavy-duty, shelf-stable.

It's gold.

I look up sharply, shocked, and he buries his hands in his pockets as he shrugs. "Just get her fixed up? And maybe you can tell her I'm real sorry?"

I stare at him for a minute, rethinking everything. Did they come here to bully or beg from us? Are they villains or not? Is there even such a thing anymore?

I feel the ghost of Eden's tears on my fingertips.

Maybe it's just that this world is making villains out of all of us.

I nod, and relief touches his features.

"And our people? You'll contact them, too?" he asks, and I grit my teeth.

"We'll call them."

When I turn back, Jayk is shouting at Sloane to double the watch, and the civilians are all talking a mile a minute. The Reapers are lounging, laughing, *eating*. The other guys walk behind Jayk, following his lead, and Eden is right by his side.

I follow them all more slowly.

My anger ebbs back into low, smoldering embers, but I feel . . . drained. Hollow and ashy. Like a wildfire has ripped through me and razed me to the ground. It doesn't feel good. Worse, it feels like it could happen again.

Eden throws me a worried look over her shoulder, and my throat sticks. I don't want to be mad anymore, but pretending I'm not isn't fixing a damn thing.

I think . . . something needs to change.

I slap another mosquito.

And this time, I get it.

CHAPTER 25

JASPER

"What do you need?" Dominic is stuck to Jaykob's side as they storm through Bristlebrook's front door.

Eden's soft T-shirt flirts around her thighs, hiking precariously as she scales the porch stairs. Women jostle her on all sides as she follows behind them, and I grip Lucien's arm as boot after boot comes down hard beside her bare feet.

Careless, *clumsy* little sheep.

Every civilian not still outside appears to be swarming at our new commander's heels, clogging the entryway with their incessant questions and suggestions. I push closer, edging around Sara, but it's too late. Eden's thighs and vulnerable toes and long, loose hair have disappeared entirely between the sweaty, shoving bodies.

She's been devoured.

Jaykob doesn't even look back. "Someone get me maps."

"On it!"

I tear my eyes from my search as Lucien slips out of my grasp.

Oh no.

"Lucien. Stop. Lucien, don't leave me alone with . . ."

He flashes me a pair of maddening dimples before vanishing

inside, and I bite down on a hiss of irritation. I squeeze through the doors after him, but he's already gone. I've lost him, too.

The last of my good mood blackens.

People swarm around me like locusts, and I begin edging toward where Jaykob and Dominic are looming, their heads and shoulders above the crowd.

This day is a budding disaster.

To think, this morning I woke to Lucien's fingers on my skin. To nothing but his dimples and our cocoon of blankets. To slow kisses and the prickle of his beard against my chin. This morning, Eden looked peaceful. I had her private happiness, my friends all together, and for a brief, beautiful moment . . . we were almost a family.

No longer.

Now we have Jaykob at war with all of us, Reapers sitting on our doorstep, and I'm suddenly fighting an accidental elbow to my kidney and a mouthful of a strange woman's hair.

My temper purrs.

"What are we doing?" Ava asks, stomping on my foot as she follows Jaykob, and I shoot a wicked scowl at her back. "Are we just letting them sit there?"

"Jayk! We just hit the last of the rice!"

The call from the kitchen elicits a chorus of concerned shouts, but I'm busy eyeing a woman dumping her dirt-drenched behind into Beaumont's favorite chair.

Utterly repulsive. All of them.

But at least the chair can't get any more hideous.

"I say we shoot first. We can take 'em." Ida slings her rifle, and Ethel runs a weathered thumb over the sharpened head of an arrow.

Beaumont finally trails inside, but he lingers at the back. He's ashen and grim enough that I keep one distracted eye on him.

He's worrying me.

Mary Beth wrinkles her freckled nose. "Don't you think the Reapers seem kind of sweet? Maybe we should just go with them. If I have to eat one more bowl of broth . . ."

"We don't have to *trust* them. Let's just go over so we can eat. We can always stab them after, right? If they suck?" Kasey flicks her knife open—one so like Jaykob's I need to take a second glance as I attempt to edge past her.

"Oh, sure," Ava says darkly, stepping into my path. "Who needs the fortress we just spent a month building? Let's just expose ourselves. We're *stuck*, okay?"

I'm stuck.

The witches are *everywhere*.

They press against me on all sides, and I hold myself still, fighting my growing, vinegared annoyance. My once-pristine home is cluttered with their belongings and Beaumont's carelessly discarded furniture. Someone's lime-green bra is under my foot, and the trail of dirt leading down the hall seems to return so often, I can only assume it's their preferred aesthetic.

And by far the worst of it—I cannot escape the smell.

There are too many bodies overwhelming Bristlebrook's delicate air filtration system, and no amount of long-expired bargain basement perfume is making my home more breathable. Every inhale reeks of stale gardenias and body odor, and my stomach *aches* with hollow hunger.

But.

I am calm.

I press my tongue to the back of my teeth, forcing myself to appear pleasant. Empathetic. The mask I used to wear for my sessions. This isn't the civilians' fault, after all. Their concerns are valid. Their presence, necessary. The Reapers are still a threat, even if they aren't firing on us directly, and these women's voices are important.

But.

I'd be lying if I said I hadn't fantasized about tossing the lot of them out on their repulsive, hollering behinds so I can pour myself some tea and enjoy my apocalypse in peace.

"Everyone shut the hell up. I can't hear myself think. I'll tell you when I know what the fuck I'm doing," Jaykob bellows, barreling toward the sitting room, and people part around him.

Then I spot her.

He has her.

I watch Jaykob acerbically as I inch through the crowd, keeping my hands raised so I don't accidentally brush something I shouldn't.

He has Eden squished under his unwashed armpit, and my ire becomes wrathful. He's done it *again*, claiming her like she's a medieval wench with no choices of her own. Just like he claimed Bristlebrook, like it's a town for plunder and not my childhood refuge. And she, for some godforsaken reason, is *indulging* it all, allowing him to grind her lovely hair into his sweat.

My eyes narrow on them.

Beaumont has been wrong in many things lately, but I fear this is not one of them. Jaykob is out of control, and despite his unfathomable sway with the civilians, nothing in his behavior leads me to think he's equipped to handle the Reapers.

But Dominic still stands behind him, and he seems determined to keep up the charade. As if his captaincy isn't melded to his very bones.

I finally pop free of the pack as Ava throws a hand up. "Jayk, stop. We can keep shit moving out there, we both know that, but this is your place, and we need to know . . . are you all thinking about joining up with them? Because if you are, we need to make our own plans."

Are we thinking of handing them over to the Reapers, is what she means.

She shifts, then grimaces. "I get it, if that's what you have to do. I know we need food—I know there's Red Zone and Alastair to think about too—but we need to think about ourselves. I don't speak for everyone, but for myself . . . I don't know those men. I'm not going anywhere with them."

The women fall quiet, and I pause as Jaykob turns toward her and takes in the crowd. Beaumont glances up from his silent brooding to look at him too.

My eyes find Eden. She's quiet and dignified, nodding minutely at Ava's question. I'm suddenly certain, just by that silent agreement, that were we to turn our backs on these civilians . . . she would go with them.

She *is* them.

Abruptly, my empathy stops feeling like a mask. These women have all fought hard for themselves for far too long—far harder than we've had to. They shouldn't have to fight any longer. Despite how their presence grates on me, we'd be less than men if we weren't willing to fight for them also.

This is their home now too, after all.

Jaykob's brows lower, and I brace myself to do damage control.

"Look, stay or play nice with them, that shit ain't up to me. You want to trade your ass for some bacon, knock yourself out. I don't have a collar around your neck. But this?" His shoulders bunch, and he glowers as he gestures around the room. "Stinks like ass. I've taken shits that look better than our options."

I stifle a sigh.

He might have all the tact of a drunken trucker but, all around me, the women relax and—for a moment—I'm grateful for him. I'm not sure they would have trusted my pretty promises.

They need this obnoxious honesty.

My gratitude lasts right up until Jaykob hauls Eden back against his side.

Ava snorts, glancing over the crowd as tension unwinds its stranglehold from the room. She shrugs. "Okay, fine. Then how about you all use your Ranger magic to figure that whole siege fuckery out, and we'll go on doing all the hard work. Keep everything running. Make meals out of wishes and air. Make sure our new friends don't shoot us while you're playing with your maps. You know, the little things."

Jaykob's scowl deepens.

She smiles sweetly back.

"This *is* hard work," he finally mutters.

"Of course it is, dear." Ethel pats his arm.

"You're doing a wonderful job." Ida nods, and Eden hides a smile behind her hand.

"Are they, though? I'm still hungry," Kasey grumbles, tugging at her tank.

Ethel lets out a tinkling laugh and waves at Kasey to follow her. "Come on, my girl. Let's see if those Reapers will take pity on a poor old granny and her goddaughter, hm? I bet we can find one fool who'll give up a bread roll without us crossing the pit."

"*Moat*," Jayk growls at her back.

They filter out, either back to the gym where the majority have set up their sleeping quarters, or back out to woman the defenses. The room drains of gardenias and knobby elbows until only the five of us remain.

It's painfully tense, until Lucien slides off the banister, his arms laden with my parents' rolled maps. "What did I miss?"

"You want to attack?" Dominic asks Jaykob, unreadable.

Jaykob looks back at him, then snatches the maps out of Lucien's hand and strides into the sitting room. He releases Eden suddenly enough that she staggers. I quickly move in to steady her, and my hand slides under her arm.

My skin tingles where we touch.

She looks up at me, startled, and her bright eyes are like a punch of lightning. I can't stop my fingertips grazing over her wrist, or what the feel of her does to me.

Awareness breathes between us.

Her skin is so silky soft. So unbearably fragile. I let my fingers skate over her skin, enjoying her little shivers too much for such a fleeting touch. There's still so much newness with this, a thrill in being close enough to see the sweet part of her lips. This polite distance between us is agony.

But I'm an experienced enough sadist to appreciate the torture.

I step closer to her, and she sinks into my side like her own weight is too much for her alone. Unconsciously, like a breath. Like allowing me to touch her is intrinsic and immutable, as core to her nature as pretty tears or her vaguely concerning obsession with cheese. She lets me hold her up, and despite the others raging around us, my pulse begins to slow.

It's a simple, trusting gesture. I shouldn't think twice on it.

And yet, it soothes every dominant impulse.

She gives me a tired smile, and worry buries my fascination. Dark circles underscore her eyes, undoubtedly from little sleep on already sapped energy.

Did Jaykob not allow her *any* rest?

Jaykob spreads the maps out as the others join him in the sitting room, and delicately sketched structures of Bristlebrook and its surroundings quickly engulf the coffee table.

"I need a supply list," he mutters. "Someone—"

Eden pulls away, and a cold gust sweeps in. It takes every effort not to descend to Jaykob's level and snatch her back to me.

She pulls a folded piece of paper from the front pocket of her shirt.

Frowning, Jaykob stares at her chest.

Then at the paper.

"I got it from Kasey. I made some notes in the margins about rations. A few recipes." Her fingers knot together nervously. "But I think the weapons are listed on the back?"

Without a word, Jaykob plucks the list out of her hands and starts reading.

Ungrateful buffoon.

"*Thank you*, Eden," I murmur pointedly, and she glances up at me, spots of color appearing in her cheeks.

She tucks a strand of hair behind her ear. "Oh. Of course."

Jaykob's gaze snaps back and forth between us, and his eyes narrow on me.

He scowls. "Yeah. What he said." Then he looks at Eden and his shoulders roll uncomfortably as he mutters, "Thanks."

Her expression warms into an amused smile.

A moment later, Lucien's golden head pops up beside Jaykob, craning to see the paper in his hands. "So what *is* the deal with food? How soon before we need to go full cannibal?" Dominic rounds the table, looking at the maps, and Lucien nudges him. "'Cause I'm already looking at Dom. Thick flank piece off that bad boy with a nice wine? I'm ready."

Dominic gives him a dry look, and my lips twitch despite myself. Flashes flood me like light—Lucien's hot mouth on my abdomen, the roughness of his hair under my palms as I split his legs, his laughter against my chest.

He's here with me. The sun escapes the clouds, and I feel myself relaxing into his teasing.

"Too tough, I think," Eden offers with a small smile. "Surely we should pick someone softer."

"You volunteering, then, beautiful?" Lucien's grin turns wicked. "Well, all right. I'd be happy to eat your—"

"*No*," Jaykob snaps, and Beaumont runs a hand over his face.

The image stalls in my brain.

My brat winks at me, then nudges Jaykob. "So how long *will* the food last? A few months?" When Lucien doesn't receive a response, he frowns. "What, weeks?" Jaykob only grunts, and Lucien's hopeful expression becomes nervous. "*Days*? Holy shit, sorry, Dom. You were a real pal. Jasper, get the Chianti."

My attention sharpens.

I know our situation is dire, but surely we have longer than that.

"*Days*?" Beaumont's hand drops from his face. He turns away from the group. "God damn it. Can't we just catch one fucking break?"

A chill creeps up my spine at the hollow ring to his voice. He's spinning out. I study him, torn. Should I take him aside? The last time I tried, he refused to listen to a word.

Eden notices as well, her smile dying as she watches him.

Jaykob flips the paper, ignoring them all. "We have forty-four guns, only sixteen MKs. The rest are pistols. About 200 mags. Five pounds of C-4. The Gustaf, and a handful of rounds for that—"

Dominic braces both hands on the table, bending down over the maps. "You do want to attack."

His tone is mild, but Jaykob's back stiffens anyway. "I'm not a fucking idiot. They might look like target practice, but they came ready. They could have any kind of shit stashed."

Lucien looks between them. Blond hair twists around his jaw. "Hey, there's also the—"

"Right. We need an advantage." Dominic nods, examining the markings carefully and ignoring Lucien in a way that sets my teeth on edge.

Rubbing the back of his head, Lucien tries again. "You should really think about—"

Jaykob scowls, bending over the map too. "Yeah, no shit we need an advantage. You actually have an idea, or do you just feel like stating the obvious?"

Dominic's jaw flexes, and Lucien sighs.

Jaykob drops his soiled boxers onto my custom-made Mulberry silk sofa and hauls Eden onto his lap as he studies the maps. Dandling her on his knee the way he did when he sat atop his absurd throne.

It's a *statement*.

From our new king.

The air in the room snaps with tension as he wraps a possessive arm around her.

Lucien's eyes narrow, and Dominic stiffens, staring at them, before he forces his gaze back to the maps. Even Beaumont pauses, turning back to eye them, his lips flattening. Like a spreading shadow, the men's fury washes through the room, a quiet defiance of the morning's bright, sparkling sunshine.

My own ire simmers, and last night's resolve toward diplomacy begins to smoke.

Burning with restless irritation, I push off the wall and begin circling the room. Lucien squeezes my hand as I walk past, but this time, it does little to alleviate my displeasure.

This needs to end.

Why *did* I decide on civility? Jaykob has never listened to reason before. Why should I think he'll begin now? Why must *I* always take the high road?

As Lucien has so recently led me to discover, bending the rules is far more enjoyable.

Eden's gaze drifts between us, her worry draining into something careful. Something distinctly guarded.

Oblivious to the hostility, Jaykob tucks her against him to look over the maps. "We could use the Gustaf. That could give us some room, no matter what they're packing."

It's not quite a question, as though he can't even bring himself to ask for advice.

"What's a Gustaf?" Eden asks, twisting to look at him.

Dominic's brow kicks up. "The bazooka. You might remember it from your breaking-and-entering stint."

Delicate color kisses her cheekbones. "Ah."

"Aw, memories." Lucien sighs.

Moving around, he cups the side of Eden's jaw, leaning down for a kiss.

Jaykob's wide hand intercepts him, and, without looking up, he shoves Lucien back by his face.

"Hey. *Hey!*" Lucien bats him away, rolling his eyes. "Okay, okay, settle down, Dad. I won't kiss her in the house."

Under his humor, I hear the edge of irritation.

"We use the Gustaf," Jaykob snaps, and this time there's no hint of a question. "Send them running."

As he sits back in his chair, his hand begins to track up the inside of Eden's thigh, and her face floods with scarlet alarm.

Beaumont falls carefully still.

"Great, let's do it." Lucien drops down beside Jaykob and Eden on the too-petite sofa, his eyes glued on where Eden has trapped Jaykob's hand between her thighs. His humor fades, the mask they don't seem to realize is a mask is beginning to slip. "Hey, we're nice and within range, so we get to blow ourselves to smithereens while we're at it. Always loved me some murder-suicide action. Solves our starvation problem, too. Good plan. Solid. Dibs on being the one to fire."

He reaches for Eden but, in a single, smooth move, Jaykob moves her to his other knee.

And this time, Lucien's face hardens.

It's a look that reminds me, very vividly, that my sweet brat used to *switch*.

Muttering, Beaumont walks over to lean against the wall by the sliding doors like he wants to escape all of us, and Dominic's heavy arms fold over his chest.

The air is dark, electric, and the corner of Jaykob's lips lift smugly.

So. He's not oblivious.

He's waging war on multiple fronts.

I pause in my strolling to turn, studying him coldly. Studying each of the men around me.

Dominic pulls his eyes from Jaykob to look back at the map, but I don't miss the muscle ticking in his jaw. "Lucky's right. We can't use high explosives or area defense rounds. Maybe something with the smoke?"

The rug whispers under my loafers as I walk.

I stare at the vulnerable back of Jaykob's head, noting the raised hairs on the back of his neck with spiteful satisfaction.

Lucien tracks me across the room.

"Do we have to attack?" Those eyes of his prettily, silently implore me to stop. "That has to be our last option, right? They're not being aggressive. Why can't we just negotiate?"

Cold amusement touches my lips.

Eden's head cants to the side, listening for me as I pass behind their sofa. A deer twitching its ears as it senses danger.

Nefarious enjoyment licks down my spine. Jaykob may have taken hold of her, but he can't claim her attention. Not all of it.

She's attuned to all of us.

I wonder what she thinks about all of this.

I wonder if her *King* would ever bother to ask.

"A siege is a siege. I'm not letting Reapers pen us in here like fucking pigs," Jaykob growls. "If we can't get out, we can't hunt. We can't hunt, we die."

"They're worried about their people." Lucien meets his gaze, firm and serious. "They invited us to *breakfast*. Maybe we can leave the Gustaf behind this time. Listen to me. I think we should use the—"

"They're forcing our hand." Dominic frowns over the maps, and Lucien glares at him. "They've either got something to prove or they're as desperate as they say. If they really wanted to build trust, they'd move back—and it's hard to negotiate when we have no leverage. We need to turn the tables, get into a position of strength." He glances up, lifting his chin in question. "Beau? What do you think?"

A hollow fire burns in Beaumont—his eyes are locked on Jaykob's hand between Eden's legs. Then he swallows, shaking his head, and looks back out through the sliding doors.

His reflection is cracked and deformed in the injured glass.

Eden's gaze worries at him, and she moves to get off Jaykob's lap.

He yanks her back into place. "Let him sulk. If we hit *here*"— Jaykob indicates a green space on the map—"then we shouldn't get blowback."

"You can't guarantee that," Dominic disagrees.

"You don't know fucking everything, *Cap*."

Lucien slams his hand down on the map, finally bursting between Jaykob and Dominic. He jams his finger over a neat mark. "Shut the fuck up and listen. The side entrance is outside the moat. We have a way out."

Jaykob and Dominic frown at his finger, pointing out the hidden cave exit we use infrequently . . . and they whirl on Lucien.

"We can't evacuate ninety people without being noticed."

"We don't have anywhere to take them."

"They'd be dead in—"

"Did you even think—"

Eden sighs, deflating further as they bicker.

And just like that, my half-formed plans of stealing away damsels and humbling Jaykob vanish. With that single sorry sigh, I stop in my tracks.

My fingertips rest on the roughened stitching of an armchair as I stop studying the men.

I study Eden instead.

Hopeless, miserable despair flashes over Eden's face as she looks between them. She leans against Jaykob as though her weight is too much for her to bear, and my heart fissures.

Where does Eden find her peace among all the five of us? Between soothing egos and managing issues, does she ever have a chance to just ... *be*?

"Should we take the last bridge down?"

"The civs might want to cross. Just keep eyes on it. Blow it if they try—"

"Oh, sure, just leave them an opening. Why not?"

A displeased sound escapes me, and Eden's eyes crash against mine. Their shade of blue is so much softer than Lucien's. Dove feathers and silken ponds, rather than bright skies.

Caught and under watch, she hides her misery so quickly that I wouldn't have caught it had I not been fixated on her. Eden adjusts her glasses, forcing a smile. She glances at Beaumont, the worsening chaos of the others, and looks back at me as though it's nothing. But her throat is too taut when she nods at me.

I'm fine, her smile says.

I raise a brow in reply. *I think not.*

It's a far cry from our silent conversation earlier this morning.

A bittersweet heaviness settles in my chest. It's not *her own* weight Eden's struggling to carry at all ... it's ours. Our endless arguments and all the troubles beneath them. It's all the issues that have existed long before she ever arrived but that she's now forced to bear. Jaykob's defensive resentment, Dominic's guilty retreat, Beaumont's fury, and Lucky's reckless anxiety ...

My absence.

And our problems are not only affecting Eden, either.

My gaze drifts to Beaumont again, brooding by the window, looking smaller than usual. We've all been smaller than we should be —and lacking in direction.

Evidently coming to the same conclusion, Eden sets her shoulders like she's donning armor. I can see how much the transformation costs her.

"Bristlebrook."

The arguments cease in an instant, and every head turns toward her.

Eden pries Jaykob's hand from around her waist, and she shoves to her feet. "Stop arguing. Stop this. You're all so busy trying to talk you're not even listening to each other."

Jaykob frowns. "They're—"

"No." Eden stares him down. "*Listen*."

Guilt chases me wickedly as Eden strides into the battlefield sans backup. Not even thinking to look for it.

Then again, how often has she needed it, and only found more problems to solve?

I look at Beaumont's tense back, and something settles inside me. *This* is why I choose the high road.

Eden doesn't need more problems.

She needs *help*.

While she faces off with the others, I turn away from my irritation and my jealous plots . . . and find myself standing beside Beaumont.

Our shoulders brush as we watch the activity outside. In the sunshine, civilians line the defenses in neat rows, their weapons fixed on the Reapers with sharp attention. But there are a few breaks in ranks.

In the distance, I see Cole toss Kasey an apple across the moat, and Ida waves a colorful handkerchief in excitement.

I stay quiet, but I don't need to wait long for Beaumont to speak.

"Here to fix me?"

Beaumont's voice is raw, and too tentative. It's unlike him. In all my time knowing him, Beaumont has radiated confidence to an almost arrogant degree. He doesn't often slip from it. I've seen him through countless sessions—through losing friends in combat and lovers in his downtime. I've seen him make mistakes and pick himself up.

I saw him lose all the people he loved. I saw his resolve to die rather than face the world without them in it, and I was the one who took the gun from his shaking hands. Back then, it was me who pulled him back from the brink.

I wonder when I stopped pulling.

This is a different struggle. This time, Beaumont doesn't have anyone to mourn, or fight. This isn't a problem of the world and everything in it.

It's a problem inside him.

A lifetime of bad habits that need to be unspooled and examined.

My stubborn, stubborn friend. It will hurt him to change.

"I'm not here to fix you, Beaumont. I'm here *for* you," I reply softly.

"I know I'm fucking up." He doesn't look at me. "I'm just . . . I think you were right, that time we spoke. Maybe Dom was, too. I repress things. I don't know how to talk about it, and then it gets worse, and everything falls apart. And it wasn't him that always fucked everything. Or Eden. I did it too. And I think . . ." He chokes. "I think I'm kind of an asshole."

The sweltering heat leaks through the fractures in the glass, and a rogue beetle slips through a poorly taped hole.

"Ah, well. Admitting it is the first step."

My lips tilt, and Beaumont snorts, then his breath catches on a wild laugh. He glances at me, and then he laughs again, and I bump his shoulder.

I glance back at the sound of a gentle smack to see Eden shooing Lucien's hand away from her ass, and she turns to pat Jaykob's arm.

"Maybe you can find another use for the exit," she says placatingly, and Jaykob's attention narrows on her. His gaze turns inward, mulling that over. *Listening* to her, in a way he rarely does with us.

Jaykob's head tilts, and he glances between Dominic and Lucien. "Where were they storing their food?"

The air changes. From violent to electric. It's barely perceptible, but under the gravel, he almost sounds . . . excited.

Beside me, Beaumont nods.

"Can you help me?" he asks, more thoughtfully. "I need to figure this out. I need to be able to talk to them. It's hurting all of us now."

I press my tongue against my teeth as I resist the urge to point out how many times I've attempted to address this in the past.

It's different now. Now, he *wants* to change.

"Of course," I reply instead, and we turn back to the others. I give Beaumont a dry look. "It will save me needing to carve up your entrails for hurting our girlfriend."

The word slips off my tongue. It's not the right one. *Girlfriend* doesn't capture my obsession, or contain the ache of distance and longing between us. It doesn't hold the fascination I have with the wicked turns in her mind, or how I fall asleep tracing the fall of her hair.

But it seems to capture Beaumont's attention.

Startled, his gaze flies to mine, searching.

Finally, a grin spreads over his face, and he tips his head. "Ours."

Ours.

An answering grin forms on my lips.

Maybe that's a better word.

Leaning over the table, Dominic points out another spot on the map. The light shines over it like a halo. "There. Jayk, that's—"

"I see it."

Lucien laughs. "Holy shit. Eden, see that?"

She falls in beside them, until heads of onyx and gold, mahogany and rough bark are all bent together over the map, and the whipfire questions are returned with quick answers rather than arguments.

A strange string of hope twines itself around my chest.

"I do, I . . ."

Eden throws another glance over her shoulder at Beaumont, tired lines on her face and mahogany hair all out of place. Her gaze switches between him and myself, and I wonder what she sees in it. Us standing together like this. Suddenly, surprise and hope and gratitude flicker across her face so fast it's hard to track each expression.

Then she smiles at me.

It's a smile that could shatter heavens. A smile that could launch a thousand ships, or drive men to crash themselves against craggy rocks. It's the smile from this morning, wondering and awed and . . . *happy.*

Everything crystallizes—sharp and dazzlingly simple.

This is what she needs. This is what a family does, after all.

They show up for each other.

"You have a plan?" Beaumont calls, and there's a new lightness in his voice.

Lucien kisses Eden's cheek hard and smacks her ass. "*You* are brilliant. I love it when you scold us."

"It would be easier if you didn't *need* scolding."

But she laughs, blushing, and Dominic stares at her like his heart has been carved from his chest. It aches in his eyes.

Jaykob sweeps the map up off the table, and electric joy sparks through him. "Fuck yes we have a plan." A devilish smirk crosses his face. "We're going on a raid."

CHAPTER 26

JAYKOB

F uck me, I hope this goes to plan.

Light breathing ghosts around me as we move. It's past nightfall, and we're geared up and heading out for our raid. The damp, earthy smells of the forest creep down the tunnel—all leaves and bird shit and the Reapers smoking fires. The hidden exit out of Bristlebrook is carved from the rock, and it presses around us like a tomb as we creep forward. We're not about to give away our position, so the lamps are off and our flashlights are stowed.

We're the monsters in the dark.

The lights don't matter. Every one of us has taken this tunnel a hundred times. We know this forest. Bristlebrook has been a prison and a home for too many years now—and those years might not have been sunshine and daisies, but that doesn't mean shit when it comes to this.

I claimed her. She's mine.

These barnyard assholes don't get to shit on her doorstep without getting hit back.

"Slow," I mutter, and the echo whispers around us.

Eden's footsteps are pixie-light behind me as she slows down, not missing a step. She can't see worth a damn anyway, so I guess the dark don't matter much.

Of course, her ass is staying behind, but she was cute, wanting to see me off, so I'll let her tag along for the easy part. No one can say I ain't generous.

Dim light starts filtering through the end of the tunnel, and I gesture to Eden to hang back while I edge forward. Tension rides me as I bring my rifle around, and I quickly check the forest around us.

The trees are dark and thick, the scrub undisturbed. There's no one here, but I check it twice more anyway.

The tunnel entrance stays blackened and still.

I don't know why I'm so fucking nervous. It's a standard raid on a bunch of cow-kissing dicks who don't know their ass from their shotguns. We could do this in our sleep.

A bird streaks from a tree beside me in a bursting flutter of wings.

My heart scatters unsteadily, and I scowl as I head back to the tunnel.

It's this stupid King shit. This is the first op I've ever run, and I . . . damn it. I want it to go well. And if these fuckers don't hold together, if they don't listen to me, if I fucked this up, then it could go south really fucking fast.

Shit.

Why would they listen to me? They think I'm a moron.

You ruin everything.

I see their faces from this morning. Bitter and angry and dripping all their usual miserable contempt. If I could put it down to them being worked up over Eden, I wouldn't get my dick in a knot about it, but this shit has been going on for years.

Acid eats at my gut as I step back inside. I should call this off. I don't want to get anyone killed, and they don't trust me. Hell, they don't even like me. This is bound to go bad.

"Clear?" Dom asks, and I'm about to tell him to can it. To turn around and march his ass back home.

But then I see Eden.

She's pale in the dark, and her glasses manage to soak up the single hint of starlight leaking through the tunnel. If we were letting her outside, it'd be a dead giveaway. Those glasses shine a direct fucking spotlight on her pretty skull. She might as well beg for a headshot.

Jesus fuck, she's a hazard. And ain't we a matched pair.

She's going to get herself killed, and I'm going to do the rest of them in.

But she's not looking at me like I'm a fuck-up, or like she thinks I'm going to send her boy-toy crushes up the river. She's *smiling* at me, and her eyes are sparkling brighter than her damn kill-shot glasses. Like she's excited. Like this is *fun* to her.

She trusts me.

Fuck.

"Yeah, we're clear," I find myself muttering to the others clustered behind her.

Stupid fucking asshole. Ignore the girl. This is how you wound up thinking you could do this in the first place.

"Everyone clear on what they have to do?" I ask, even though we've been over it a dozen times, and it makes me look like a nervous asshole.

"Stay quiet and listen to Daddy." Lucky waggles his brows, and Jasper cuts him a dry look. "We got it, Pops."

Beau snorts. "Yeah, we're good here, Jayk."

Dom nods, still watching me in a way that makes my skin itch. All *understanding* and *supportive*. I scowl at him, and he rolls his eyes. I don't know where this shit is coming from, but I hate it.

I liked it better when he was taking swings at me.

Eden's hand slips into mine, squeezing lightly, and I look down at her.

"You know what you're doing?" I ask gruffly, conscious of the others' eyes on me.

It's different than earlier. Now's not the time to rub shit in, and I'm too nervous to make a point. This is real. I need her to be okay.

Fuck. All of them.

She nods. "Distraction. I've got it handled."

"Stay out of range." Her glasses blink at me again, and I glare at her to drive the point home. "You let Sloane handle it if they start shooting. You hide."

Rolling up on her tiptoes, she brushes a kiss over my lips. It's quick as wildfire, and then she's stepping back.

Her smile turns sweet enough to rot. "Yes, Jayk. I promise not to do something extreme—like walk into an enemy camp where the odds are over five to one."

Lucky laughs, and I scowl as her smile grows, turning back to the exit.

"Fine. Good. Whatever. Then everyone move. Don't get shot."

I'm already edging back out into the night when I realize they're not behind me.

I glance back to see Lucky *devouring* Eden. Up-against-the-rock, hands-on-her-ass, tongue-down-her-throat *devouring*.

"Sneaky little *shit*!" I snap, only remembering to keep my voice down at the last second. My heart thunders in my chest as she just lets him *eat* her fucking *face*, and for a hot moment, I debate whether to shoot him myself.

Instead, I sling my rifle, and I'm storming back down the tunnel when the springy bastard finally comes up for air. Patting her on the cheek, he says something that makes her giggle like a breathless cartoon idiot, and he steps into my path, stopping me short.

Lucky's eyes widen innocently. "We going or what?"

I glower at him, but he just grins, his dimple flashing at me like a challenge as he nods back the way I came. "Well, come on. What are you waiting for? Keep it moving."

Behind him, Beau smirks at us, then leans down to claim his own kiss.

Murder plays behind my eyes. Was I worried about getting them all killed? Fuck that.

Time for a new goal.

After Beau, Jasper presses a soft kiss to Eden's temple, and the way she ducks her head makes my blood howl. I glower at Dom as he pauses in front of her.

They look at each other, really fucking *look*, and the howl in my blood turns into a roar.

She's looking at him like she looks at me.

"Jayk, you know you're really holding us up here," Lucky remarks, examining his rifle. "As leader, I'd think you'd be a *little bit* more concerned with time management."

Dom unglues his eyes from her face and looks back down at us. He grimaces, then gives her one last look before stalking back after us.

Relief bites me.

No kiss.

Dom meets my eyes as he approaches, his jaw hard enough to break my fist against. "*What*, Jayk?"

I shrug one shoulder, glancing back at Eden . . . and for some reason, her crushed expression makes me want to punch him as much as the idea of him kissing her does.

"Nothing," I mutter, and he pushes past me to storm out of the rock.

We follow him out, and the birds fall silent. Quiet has settled over the forest like a blanket, and Eden's glasses wink from the mouth of the tunnel as she watches us go.

Beau eyes Dom like he wants to start some kind of open-dialogue, heart-to-heart bullshit, and Lucky shakes his head, tsking like my old school teacher whenever she thought I wasn't *living up to my potential*, but when I gesture at everyone to fan out . . . they do.

They actually fucking listen to me.

For about three fucking seconds.

We only make it half a dozen steps before Dom stops beside me in the thick underbrush.

I look at him, then around us, trying to spot what he's seen, but he only sighs, running a hand down his face.

"What's wrong?" Beau whispers, and Lucky pauses on his other side, gesturing to Jasper.

Suddenly, Dom's shoulders straighten, and his eyes are bright in the dim light.

"Fuck it."

Then he's turning, jogging back to the tunnel. I whip around watching, my rifle at the ready, only . . .

The captain isn't on the attack.

Dom sweeps Eden up out of the shadows, and even from here I can hear her breathy little gasp. He stares down at her again, in that punchable fucking way, before he tucks his hand behind her neck . . . and kisses her.

Lucky whoops under his breath, and Beau laughs, a low, *victorious* fucking chuckle, and I see red.

I take a step forward, but Jasper is abruptly in my path.

"Ah, my mistake," he murmurs.

I shove him to the side only to find Lucky stretching casually, right in my way.

He spreads his hands. "Dude, sorry. I'm all left feet, you know? It's a real problem."

I glower at him. "I will fucking shoot you."

"And give away our position?" he whispers. "Oof. Okay. You're the boss."

I look over his shoulder, and my chest feels too tight—too damn constricted and locked in to get air. They're still kissing. There's not even the illusion that she doesn't want it, either.

She's melted against him, her arms clinging around his neck, her feet dangling as she kisses and kisses him. He's holding her up, the way I fucking do. Kissing *her* like he wants to drown in it.

Lucky whistles low, and I scowl at him.

"Dominic, there *will* be time for this later," Jasper whispers, sounding amused. He's only just loud enough to be heard, and the cap flips him off with one hand.

But he doesn't stop kissing her.

She's smiling against his mouth, and the sight etches itself into my bones.

My fucking brain.

Every one of them with their mouths on her. Her wanting every one of their mouths on her. She told me. She keeps fucking saying it, but I don't want to hear it. I don't want to see it or hear it or know it. I want her for myself.

I'm fighting for it. For her. I've been fighting. I could fuck Dom up right now, but . . . she'll hurt over it.

Fucking *damn it*.

I back up, letting them have it. There's no point, not now.

I just need to do more to convince her. It's only been one night. I have weeks of them coming. She said this is a war, and she's fighting her side, so I'll just . . . I'll keep doing the same.

I'll leave her so wrecked, so god-damned dick drunk she won't be able to think about them without getting nauseous.

She won't need them. Neither of us do.

Only . . .

I look down at my rifle, thinking of the civs and our stores. The Reapers on our doorstep, and the Sinners waiting in the wings. My chest constricts a little tighter, and something else touches me.

Something miserable and cold that I've been running from for too many fucking years.

Something fucking . . . *lonely*.

I scowl. Damn it *all*. What the hell am I even supposed to do here? I don't think I *can* do this alone.

Beau falls in beside me as Dom finally sets Eden back on her feet. Whatever the shrink said to him earlier today seems to have pulled the stick out of his ass, because he's moving easier now. Looking less like he's going to try and take my head off for the hell of it.

"We still doing this?" he asks, and I scoff softly.

I don't know where all these doubts came from. Working in my barn, keeping to myself, I never had many of those. Now I can't seem to shake them.

Eden's hand presses against her mouth, then her chest, and she stumbles back. She turns back to the tunnel, only to walk into the rock, and I glower at her.

"You know, we can do this together. If you want."

Beau's careful drawl makes me stiffen, and I turn to stare hard at him. He shrugs, adjusting a strap on his kit, and moonshine makes splotches of his face.

He's bland as dry toast when he glances back over at me. "The raid, I mean."

My pulse is racing like we're mid-battle, not mid-conversation in the middle of the woods at just past dark.

"What happened to you 'not following me anywhere?'" I snark, unable to help myself.

His words have tunneled under my skin, and I can't get them out.

Beau rubs his jaw, watching Dom stride back over to us. He can't hide the self-satisfied fucking curl of his mouth, and I have to look away from it.

"Did you taste me on her?" Lucky asks him. "What does that make us?"

"I'll write you a poem later. Go get into position," Dom replies without missing a beat, scanning the still forest.

"Like . . . missionary, or . . .?"

Jasper grips the back of Lucky's neck and murmurs something into his ear that makes him shiver, then move out without another word.

They all glance at me, and I gesture to move forward, feeling like a fraud.

Beau was right earlier.

I don't deserve this.

But he moves forward through the bushes, keeping pace with me. Matching my steps. And like he's reading my fucking mind, he sighs.

"I'm sorry, Jayk. I shouldn't have said that."

Gritting my teeth, I signal for them to swing wide. It only takes them a moment to obey. We all know where we're going. We have a target—we just need to find our moment.

I don't need this surface-level Hallmark shit.

Beau doesn't know when to stop though.

"Don't get me wrong, I still think you have your head wedged up your asshole, and you need some kind of reality check about Eden, and we're *going* to have a talk about where you put all my underwear, but . . . this is a good plan. You did good. With tonight, I mean. The civs, too."

I press my tongue against my teeth at the condescension, but I keep my trap shut. He's being honest at least, and that's better than the touchy-feely crap.

And I don't think the doc knows how to stop being condescending.

The edge of the Reapers' camp flickers through the trees, and as soon as I hang back, so do the others. In their camo and kits, I can barely see them tucked between low bushes. Jasper is calm and confident, Dom nods at me, and even Lucky's quit it with the jokes. He's tense and focused, covering both of the others.

Adrenaline kicks in, hot and heady, and my nerves start to settle.

Patronizing or not, the doc is right—it *is* a good fucking plan.

Beau's voice lowers further, and I wonder how we're still talking about this now. "Anyhow, I figure I can give this a shot. I'll put my ego aside. I think . . . you know, I really do think we could do this if we stop trying to rip each other apart. We can make it work."

I stop. Leaves prickle against my neck as I stare at him.

"We still talking about the raid?" I bite out, and his teeth flash at me in the dark.

Beau picks up his rifle, rolling onto the balls of his feet as he chuckles.

"Ah, Jayk. Come on, now. You know as well as I do—it's *always* about the girl."

CHAPTER 27

EDEN

Exhilaration sparkles through every inch of me, bubbly and carbonated, and I giggle as I jog back through the tunnel. My lips are tingling, roughed from Dom's stubble. The taste of him still lingers on them, spicy and hungry and . . .

I laugh again.

He kissed me.

He really, *really* kissed me.

From dawn until dark, today has been a rollercoaster. It's like for weeks, months even, all five of us have been slowly ticking closer and closer to a precipice, and now we're starting to *drop*. It's rough and painful and swift, and all of us are crashing into one another, but it's moving.

I push into the house, my fingers still pressed against my smiling lips.

We're moving forward.

I walk into the gym, where the tunnel opens out, and it's where most of the civilians have set up their sleeping arrangements. A dozen of them are there to greet me, and they jump to their feet as soon as the door swings open.

"Was it all okay?" Ava asks, and she worries at her lip piercing.

I blink, confused, thinking of the way Lucky's cock pressed against me. Jayk's nervousness, and Jasper's sweet goodbye, and Beau's wink—how he looked so much brighter than he has been in weeks.

Dom's long, mind-shattering, darn-near-close-to-orgasm-inducing kiss.

"They're . . . Oh, Ava. They are incredible. You have no idea, I—"

Sloane snorts, shaking her head as she holsters her pistol.

"Eden." Ava massages her forehead. "I already know way too much about your sex life. I was asking about the raid."

Oh.

I look around at the group. Their guns and bows and the feather arrow fletchings in the basket by Jennifer's cushioned, elevated foot.

Of course she's talking about the raid.

Fighting my blush, I clear my throat. "Oh, yes. Well. That was fine, too."

It *was* fine.

It's a good idea, if they can pull it off. We need the food and if we can secure it without doing anything that would be seen as a betrayal of Alastair, then we should do it.

Of course, there's always the chance that the Reapers will attack us when they discover what we've done, but our defenses are as strong as they can be, and they're not trained fighters.

It's worth the risk.

Besides, if the Reapers truly want us as allies, then they should *want* us to keep up our strength . . . right?

I could see Jayk fretting—not that he'd ever admit it—but all five of them went over the plan for hours. Locked together, and after actually working as a team, that plan is as solid as it can be, given the circumstances.

Well, I was there too, but raids are decidedly *not* my expertise.

Instead, I spent most of the day poring over books from Jasper's library—even finding an oddly placed history section that had a delightful tome filled with old war recipes I know I can make good use of.

But while the details of their maneuvers were something I left to them, there was one thing they asked me to assist with.

I look around at the women. No two of them look the same, but they're all strong. All so, so beautiful.

I think I know just how to handle my little task.

I smile warmly at Ava—maybe too warmly, judging by the way her friendly expression retreats.

"What?" she asks suspiciously. "No, Eden. Congrats on your dick bouquet, really, but if they gave you warts or something, you need to go to the med bay. We're not that close."

My smile dies. "They do not have warts!" I huff and wonder if it's wrong to be vaguely offended that she wouldn't assist me with my hypothetical STI. "Look, there is one small favor I have to ask—and it *is* to help with the raid."

Sloane shrugs one shoulder, grimacing at the chipped head of an arrow. "Sure. As long as it doesn't involve taking our clothes off."

I take a deep breath, and steel my resolve.

"Well, actually . . ."

Twelve heads turn my way, and Sloane's eyes widen.

Right as my shirt hits the floor.

CHAPTER 28

BEAU

SURVIVAL TIP #29
Good friends watch each other's backs.
Best friends bust each other's balls.

I n the distance, Cole strips his shirt off, tossing it down, and he looks more like some kind of GQ city boy than anyone who works a farm. Crouched in the bushes beside Jayk, I scowl at the man standing right in front of our target. It's not right for him to look like that. Those right there are pretty muscles, not working muscles.

I should know, because I have the same ones.

Which is also how I know that Eden likes them. She likes them a whole damn lot.

I scan over Bristlebrook's lawn, but I can't see her anywhere. Can't see half the civilians, for that matter. The defenses are manned, and they've got people on watch all right. But I don't see Sloane or Ava, or Ethel or Ida—none of the usual suspects who usually ride at the front of the pack.

I also don't see our distraction.

The Reapers are everywhere.

Now, I don't know if it's because they're away from the natural tugs of their land—from the early morning drag to the fields, and the exhausted press toward an early night—but they don't seem to be readying to get their beauty sleep any time soon.

They're swarming over their camp, chattering and laughing, occasionally calling out friendly jibes at the women standing armed at their posts. A few of the civilians have ventured closer. Mila is all but tipping into the moat, chattering away with a pair of younger Reapers who can't seem to throw her bread fast enough.

In the forest ahead of us, I catch flashes of Lucky's blond hair, Jasper's back, and Dom's shoulders as they move into position. They'll be doing the ole snatch-and-grab of the supplies while Jayk and I cover them.

The targeted supplies lie right on the edge of the Reapers' camp, right at the head of it beside Sawyer and Cole's tents.

Our delicious, delicious target.

Even from this distance, even awkwardly through the trees, I can see it all. Bag upon bag of hardy bread and sweet apples spill open. Dried meat and jarred preserves. Flour and honey and hard, packaged cheese. Feasts' worth of food. *Lives'* worth of food.

My stomach rumbles, clawing at me to get it. To take it all. It's one of three stockpiles the Reapers seem to have brought with them, and the only real question we have is: how much can we carry?

Jayk yanks me back by my collar, and I choke as I fall back.

"Cool your jets, doc," he mutters.

A Reaper passes right by us, focused on his fidget spinner, and I touch my throat, glancing at Jayk. He's rougher than usual, unshaven and painted down in camo.

Well, I'll be.

He does care.

Which only serves to make me feel even more guilty for the shots I got in on him this morning. They were below the belt.

Well, some of them—some of them were entirely fair—but I was still the worst kind of asshole to him. I'll make it up to him, and not just for Eden's sake. I'll do it for mine, too.

Admitting it is the first step.

Jayk flashes me a glance, then rolls his eyes. "We need to get closer."

I nod as he starts moving around. "Sure thing. Got your six, King."

Jayk pauses, looking back, and I pause. "What? You drop something?"

Slowly, he shakes his head, looking at me all *strange*.

I raise my brows in question. "Is this about Eden? Really, I am happy to talk but now is *hardly* the best time."

He scowls, shaking his head, then pushes through the trees behind me without a word, and I sigh.

That man can be downright mercurial.

Still, I follow quickly. It's a good night. Clear and bright, and the damp air is finally cooling enough to enjoy. Small branches whip my face and twigs crack under my boots as we move, and my pulse starts to thrum as the action catches up to me.

This kind of op is delicate. Charged. It relies so much on timing, always just a hair-trigger away from going deadly wrong. With dozens of active combatants awake and at the ready, and us outnumbered, we've got to be more than careful.

We've got to be a team.

Jayk slinks from cover to cover, behind trees and boulders and creeping low under branches that would disturb the forest's stillness enough to catch attention. For his size, he's light on his feet, and that comes as much from his hunting kinks as it does from Ranger training.

He's rounding out behind a heavy boulder, where we're supposed to be positioned. That boulder will give us cover, and a clear line on the food so we can cover the others as they move in.

I'm a half dozen steps behind him when I see it.

A Reaper shakes himself off, zipping up as he steps out from behind a bush, a shotgun leaning against a tree next to him. He's a little ways away, but . . .

If he turns, he's going to see Jayk.

Blood rushes to my head, and I slam into action. Bolting forward, I crash against Jayk's back a moment later, throwing us behind a willow tree. Our legs tangle up, and we go down hard. Dried leaves scatter as we roll. My knee chops upward, trying to find purchase, and it crashes against his balls.

"Is someone there?" a wavery voice calls as we land under a dense, prickly bush.

I slap a hand over Jayk's mouth as he groans into me.

His eyes bulge, and I wince, mouthing an apology. My own balls ache in pure empathy.

"Scott?" someone else calls on the other side of our bush.

"Oh, Jerry. You scared the bejeezus outta me." The Reaper laughs, relieved. "I was taking a leak."

Jayk twitches, the muffled sound under my hand almost a whimper.

Yep. That, ah, that came down *hard*.

Which . . . makes me wonder, briefly, if Eden ever wants kids.

"A leak?" Jerry scoffs, and their footsteps join up. "Sounded more like you were evacuating a badger."

"Me? You're the one that's been bakin' up keister casseroles all day! I *told* you not to eat them purple berries. You ain't gonna impress none of them ladies like that."

"They're something, ain't they? Tough. We're going to keep 'em safe, right?"

My brows lift.

"Sawyer said we could. The Sinners ain't going to get their hands on them, even if we . . ."

It's almost . . . sweet.

Slowly, their voices fade. Watching for any movement through the forest, I take my hand off Jayk's mouth. Rising up to a crouch, I hover over him to peer out farther.

"Okay. Okay, I think we're in the clear."

"Yeah?"

"Yeah."

"Good."

Jayk's knee slams up hard between my legs, and I choke. Clutching my balls, I fall to the side in wordless, *mindless* pain.

He gets up, then hauls me out of the bushes and to my feet. My knees are wobbly, weak, and I bend over, gasping for air.

Jayk pats my back, panting. "Nice save. Thanks."

I think . . . this means we're actually *bonding*.

Wheezing, I force a watery-eyed smile at him, waving it off like it's nothing.

"Oh, sure." I'm going to throw up. "Don't mention it."

CHAPTER 29

LUCKY

"C an you see them?" Dom frowns, peering at the rock where Beau and Jayk were supposed to be waiting, his voice low. We're crouched in the middle of a dense copse of trees, well back from the camp, waiting on them to get into position to cover us before we move in.

Silently, Jasper places his hand over mine, and I realize I'm gripping a branch so hard it's cutting into my fingers. My grip loosens under his touch.

"No."

I can't find any more quips right now. Damn it, I thought I'd worked this out—that I was wound up and on edge over the whole Eden-getting-kidnapped-and-then-all-of-us-nearly-getting-executed-a-few-weeks-later thing, and I just needed to blow off some steam.

Jasper spent a good portion of last night blowing me thoroughly, so really, I should be fixed. I *felt* fixed this morning. I now know that Jasper does actually get morning breath, and he's prettiest when he's sleeping and his hair gets all tousled, and that he's happy to spend a stupid amount of time letting me kiss him awake.

Now, all I can think about is what happens if he catches a stray bullet.

Absently, I rub my shoulder over where my scar's still healing.

Thank fuck Eden is safe at least.

"Eden should have run her distraction by now, too." Letting a wide-leafed bush fall back into place, Jasper glances at Dom. We've moved back away from the camp, so we should be out of earshot, but he's still hushed. "At what point do we call this off?"

"Not my call," Dom mutters, still watching the rock on the other side of the pile of food.

We fall quiet as two Reapers walk past it, yapping loudly to each other.

I swallow hard when nothing moves, and my leg starts bouncing.

Jayk and Beau.

They're okay. They have to be. Of course they are. If the Reapers had found them, they'd be yee-hawing it from the rooftops, right? They're just slow, that's all. Just taking their sweet time.

Except Jayk is never slow.

I feel Jasper's eyes on me, but I don't look at him.

This is so *stupid*. I felt good earlier. We had a plan. A good plan. Everyone was on board, and we were acting like a team again. But then I kissed Eden, which was probably dumb fucking timing because I'm a natural trendsetter and the others have no impulse control, so of course they kissed her too, and then Jayk got all twisted up, and he's supposed to be running this and, damn it, if his head's not in it, then—

Jasper leans in, his knee pressing into the mud. "Lucien, do you need a moment?"

Nope. I need to know my friends are okay.

Not stopping to think about it, I unhitch my radio. "This is Steel Rain to King Kong. Confirming you're still on the approach? Over."

Whipping around, Dom rips the short comms out of my hand, and we all pause, waiting.

Nothing around us shifts.

Dom's brows come down, hard and merciless. "What part of *covert* do you have a problem with? You know better. You might have just given away their positio—"

The radio flares to life.

"Steel Rain is never gonna happen, Lucky," Beau drawls, and Dom's face relaxes.

My breath gushes out of me, relief kicking in hard.

Oh, thank fuck. Thank fuck, thank fuck, thank *fuck*.

Beau adds, "We had a minor ball ache on our end, but we're heading your way. Any sign of Eden? Over."

Dom lifts my radio to his mouth. "Nothing yet, but we don't have a visual. We'll get closer when we have eyes on your position. Stay off the comms. Over."

"Any of you call me King Kong again, and I'm feeding your guts to the pigs." There's a pause. "We're good. Eden will pull through. Watch each other. Just come back with something so I don't have to explain to eighty-five hangry fucking women that they're going to starve to death. Over and out."

The silence after the radio cuts off is painfully loud, and Jasper squeezes my hand once before withdrawing. He gets to his feet, brushing off his knees like we're still not mid-op.

"Happy?" Dom asks me tightly, and I grimace, my racing heart finally starting to slow.

"Sorry, Cap."

His jaw flexes, and he stands. "I'm not your captain, Lucky."

I snort, waving him off. "My bad, the ass-chewing just threw me right back to base camp."

Dom stops, frowning.

Still on my knees, I take a breath, watching Jasper peer through the dense leaves, waiting for Beau and Jayk to hit their mark. Which they will.

They're *good*, he said. Eden will pull through. The plan is still on track. Weird, but Jayk's pep talk actually is making me feel better. He has this. He's watching out for Beau, and we're watching out for them.

It's happening, we're doing this, and . . . and we're a team.

All this fighting and not talking or trusting each other has been killing me. Even worse, it's dangerous. It's why we keep making stupid mistakes. It's why every time I step out with them these days, I keep wondering what the next one will be. We haven't been a real team for too damn long.

I know because when we *do* pull our shit together, there's not a damn thing to be anxious about.

When we're a team, we're fucking invincible.

"I see them. They're in position," Jasper says suddenly, and I nod, hyping myself up as I stand.

Trying to believe it.

I start to stand, only for Dom to reach down. For a moment, I stare at his hand quizzically. Both of us know I don't need it, and I don't really get where the gesture is coming from, but I take it anyway, and he hauls me to my feet.

"Thanks?" I tell him, puzzled, but when I go to move, he doesn't let go.

"I'm not your captain anymore, Lucky," Dom says again, and I roll my eyes, forcing a smile.

"Yeah, I know, I know. I got the memo, the billboard, and the ass tattoo. We're good. I'm more of a vampire guy, but I can jump on Team Jaykob. You want a T-shirt?" I nod to myself. "I'll get you a T-shirt."

"No, I mean, I might not be your captain, but I can be your damn friend. You can talk to me. And out there, I have your back." His eyes flick to Jasper meaningfully before coming back to mine. "Both of you."

I let my smile fade, my pulse thrumming in my throat.

"I've got yours. Everyone's. I promise," I tell him, stilted, and he just nods once.

We haven't talked about yesterday—about me not following his orders. I couldn't leave Jasper and Eden, I just couldn't, and Beau was out there exposed because of it. Dom stepped down all of thirty minutes after that, and it's hard not to believe that wasn't at least kind of my fault, too.

Instead of blaming me for it, he saw why.

"Friendship application accepted. We can share our star charts later."

"Can't wait. Now move—" Dom cuts himself off, grimacing, and he starts again. "Are you two good to move out?"

I eye him, the sudden collegial tone weirding me out, but I nod, and he's peeling out of the copse before I can tease him about it.

Over logs, quickly through open ground, low under branches, we make our way to the edge of camp. I turn, watching our backs as I edge back, but we're clear.

It's all clear.

Through the forest, I catch glimpses of Beau and Jayk creeping in around the rock, their weapons drawn.

They're clear too.

But . . .

Dom raises his hand, and we stop on the edge of the Reapers' camp, just inside the tree line. We're right on the other side of Sawyer and Cole's tents. Jayk and Beau should have a clear line to cover us, and from this angle, we've got a clear visual of the food. All of that would be getting big old gold stars from me, if it wasn't for the dozens of Reapers swarming in front of us.

And Cole lightly snoozing on his pink lawn chair—*right* next to our damn food.

I could take five steps and I'd be sitting on his lap.

Jasper glances at me, grave and grim, and I don't bother to work up a smile for him. He sees through them anyway.

"Just wait for Eden."

"Where *is* she?" I run a hand down my face, trying to hold the panic down.

"She'll show up." Dom is quiet and certain, as still and calm as I am jittery. His eyes find me. "You know she will."

"You saw her walk into the rock, right? We melted her brain. She can't take all of us at once, it's too much," I whisper-shout.

A Reaper walks toward us, and we tense.

We're hunkered down behind a thicket, but if he clears the trees, he's going to see us—and it'll only take him a second to raise an alarm.

Jasper's chin lifts, his expression iced over. Confident. Ready. Nothing like the man who stroked my cheek until I fell asleep last night.

Cold fear for him queases through my stomach, and I move my hand over my rifle.

The Reaper pauses, turning back right before where Cole is now snoring loudly. "Naw, I'm just taking a leak. Don't you drink all of it! I know how much was there."

Suddenly, Dom grips my wrist, holding it against my gun.

He shakes his head at me in a clear but silent *don't*.

I stare at him hard, my hand still tensed.

I *really* don't want to shoot any of these guys. I get it, where the Reapers are coming from. They're in a tough spot, and they're doing what they have to.

But if it comes down to a stranger or either of the men next to me, I know what I'm going to choose.

I do what I have to, too.

The man pushes past the tent, toward the tree line, and Dom stares back at me just as fiercely. His grip tightens, just for an instant . . . right before he lets me go. My pulse throbs, beating in time with each of the Reaper's slow, crunching steps.

Damn it, he can't even help himself. The boss man will always take control, right?

Crunch.

Except he's not taking it. He's letting me choose.

Crunch.

Can I let him handle it?

Crunch.

Jasper needs to be safe.

Crunch.

Damn it, we're a team.

I pull my hand away from my gun right as Dom snaps up, ready to launch—only to pause . . . as *music* spills through the forest.

The Reaper stops, turning back again. The volume lifts and punchy rock music flows over the grass. It vibrates through the trees.

"What *is* that?" He scratches the back of his neck, then steps back toward the camp. "I know that song. Hey! Hey, Mark! What's that song called again? Wait . . . *waiiiit*. What are they *doing*?"

The man bolts back into their camp so fast that I swear his outline lingers in the air behind him.

Dom meets my eyes, panting, and my hand shakes as I press it to the ground.

*Ooo*kay. Okay. We're okay.

"Did you know there would be music?" Jasper asks me, his eyes wide, a stressed hand buried in his hair, and it's only then that I finally catch the tune smashing through the forest.

(Don't Fear) The Reaper.

I snort, then a shaking, impossible laugh leaves me, and I lean into Jasper as it hits me.

Holy shit, she did it.

Eden came through.

Everyone's coming through.

"A little on the nose," Jasper says wryly, but he kisses my hair before he stands.

Dom snorts, shaking his head as he cranes to look out at the Reapers' camp, but he's grinning too. "It's fucking perfect."

It is. The music is *deafening*. It'll hide any sounds we need to make like a dream. She promised a show—nothing dangerous, and all out of range of the Reapers—and that's what she's delivering. God damn, I don't know why I didn't think she'd use the speakers.

Gorgeous, genius, diabolical woman.

I can't wait to sexy-melt her brain again.

I move up beside Dom, and see Cole is somehow still sleeping on his fold out, bare chested and curled up under a blanket. He's kicked off his boots and one of his grubby socks is worn through on one toe.

Around him, Reaper after Reaper is peeling away, flocking toward the moat, and I shift sideways, lifting up to try to see.

"Thanks," Dom mutters, not quite looking at me. "For trusting me."

I drop back onto my heels, glancing over at him as the Reapers roar in approval at whatever Eden and the civs are doing.

My chest pangs. He hasn't been the same since Cyanide.

I frown, thinking that through.

Maybe even before that.

It's kind of shitty, but I've been so wound up in my own stuff, I haven't been paying that much attention.

It sucks, it really sucks that he's going through it right now. And I know Beau and Eden have him—they'll drag him out of the dark and sticky places, one way or another—but . . . I have some tricks up my sleeve, too. Maybe I can help.

If the bossman really *is* down to pull the stick out of his ass, then I'm just the guy to show him how to twirl it.

"I'm a Leo, for the record," I tell him seriously. "I know you're a Capricorn, but it could be worse. I really think we can make it work."

The deadpan look he gives me makes me laugh again, but when Sawyer tucks two fingers into his mouth and wolf-whistles, I can't do it anymore.

"Seriously, what is happening over there?" I mutter.

I edge forward, trying to see.

"Easy, Lucky."

"I know, I know. I just want to . . ."

The crowd parts, and suddenly . . . well, I see her.

Ho-*ly* hell, do I see her.

My jaw drops. "Oh. My. God."

I slap Dom's shoulder. "What? I can't—"

Wordlessly, I drag him a foot sideways, and he chokes.

"Oh, fuck."

Reapers are dropping their things. They're turning toward Bristle-brook, staring. Heads peek out of tents, and Pete is so mesmerized that he overpours his boiling kettle onto Buck's hand, sending Buck howling.

And you know what, I don't blame them.

Because right on Bristlebrook's lawn, under a river of string lights that look like stars, a hypnotic horde of barely clothed women . . . are *wrestling*.

Clare and Deanna spin and crash against each other hard, and Katherine flips someone I can't make out over her shoulder. Sloane has Mary Beth on the ground already, and her back tattoos ripple as she keeps her there.

In the cooling night, they're fierce and fast and pretty fucking hot.

But I'm not looking at any of them.

"Is that . . .?" Jasper breathes on my other side. "Is that *Eden*?"

"Yeah . . . that's her." Dom sounds hoarse.

Under the lit-up apple tree, in a sports bra and underwear that shows half her ass, Eden is facing off against Ava. She's moving back and forth in a way that makes her *jiggle*, and Jasper sucks in a hissed breath.

God *damn*, I love women.

The Reapers have flocked to the edge of the moat, hooting and hollering and whistling in a way that suddenly has my pulse thundering somewhere between pride and horror.

I strangle a laugh, my eyes glued on her in growing fascination. "Dom? You, ah, you know about this one?"

Ava gets a good hit in, and I wince, shadow boxing.

Left, Eden. Come on.

"I didn't know it would involve *booty shorts*."

"Where did she even *get* those?" Jasper asks dubiously.

Dom's eyes are glued to her ass. "It was a moment of weakness."

I snort a laugh, and Dom's lips twitch—then he makes a sound of approval, edging forward.

"Go. Yes. Go. *Go*, pet."

The song changes to "Barracuda," and the Reapers scream like they're pimple-faced teenagers seeing their first pop concert.

Eden jumps on Ava's back, and Ava whirls around, and it's like a mesmerizing ass mobile, glistening under the glowing lights.

Biting my knuckle, I groan. "Oh, fuck. Is she *oiled*?"

"I wonder where they got that idea," Jasper murmurs.

The three of us stand together, staring as Ava throws her off. Lean and strong, she swings forward a second later with a rangy punch, and Eden rushes her with a scream.

Dom grimaces, and I shake my head. "No, no. Points for enthusiasm. She might—"

It takes about three seconds for Ava to slam her shoulder into Eden's stomach, knocking her ass to the ground.

"Ooh." I wince, and Jasper frowns.

"Give her a moment. I'm sure she'll—"

Ava crashes into her, crushing her knee into Eden's ribs, and I instinctively lift my hands in defense, my whole body cringing into itself.

"Nope. Can't do it." I turn into Jasper's shoulder. "Just tell me she wins."

Jasper's next flinch isn't promising.

Dom sighs. "She tried."

"Let's just . . . keep her indoors," Jasper says, patting me reassuringly.

The Reapers cheer again, and I wrinkle my nose.

Right as my eyes light back on the food.

"You know, after all this, Eden's really going to need a pick-me-up," I muse as I pull off him, stepping closer to the tree line.

The coast is almost definitely clear.

They're all too busy staring at my girl's perfect ass.

Jasper stiffens. "*Lucky.*"

Dom's gold eyes light on me, more interested than scolding—and that right there? Well, that just makes me a proud lil troublemaker.

Winking at him, I tilt my head for him to join me, and a dry smile tilts his lips.

He's ready. He's got my back.

We've all got each other.

Without a care in the world, I step out from behind the tree line and start making my way toward the food.

This time, as I spring into action, my anxiety doesn't find me. My pulse is steady, and I'm still grinning, because Jayk was right—we're *good*. We're moving like we were trained. We know what the fuck we're doing and we're all doing our part. There aren't going to be any mistakes tonight.

We're not just a team. We're *the* team.

Tonight, we're invincible.

CHAPTER 30

DOMINIC

SURVIVAL TIP #147
Shut your mouth and wash your socks.

There's something in the air tonight. It's the kind of night where things just go right.

It's not the kind of thing I would admit if I were still captain, not even to myself. Soldiers can be superstitious little shits, and I'm not exempt from it. But I'm *not* their captain tonight. I'm just a guy on the team—and one who's done enough ops to see when one is pulling together in a way that's pretty damn close to perfect.

Or maybe I'm just still on a damn kiss high.

My tongue finds my lower lip again.

I fucking kissed her.

I smile.

She fucking kissed me back.

For maybe the first time ever, I don't have a plan, and it's as freeing as it is fucking terrifying.

All I know is I just couldn't *not* kiss her for one more second.

Now Lucky's laughing—with me, for once—and I kind of want to follow along and see where this goes. If anyone knows how to freefall, it's him. And I'm all on board with trying it myself, right up until he suddenly glides out from behind the tree line, his arms up like this is a trust fall exercise.

"Oh, for fuck's sake."

This is why you don't talk about perfect nights, idiot.

Sighing, I snap my rifle up. Beau and Jayk should be in place to cover us by now, but it's not the damn point.

"I am going to tie that reckless brat in a harness so tight, he'll have to *beg* me to walk anywhere," Jasper hisses, and I snort.

"Oh, yeah, that'll show him."

I step out more slowly, scanning for any stray Reapers, and Jasper steps out with me.

I'm not about to get sloppy now, but it's easy enough to move between Cole and Sawyer's tents to get closer, so we have some cover —it also doesn't hurt that most of the Reapers have dropped their weapons and are watching Eden shake her ass like they're ten beers deep at the UFC.

I don't love the viewers, but that view was . . .

Eden's round, perfect ass in those shorts is like a live wire to my cock. It almost makes up for the smug fucking smirk Beau sent me all those weeks ago when I picked them out.

It's a good night.

Lucky stops next to Cole's sleeping body right by the pile of food.

They're far enough away that between the cloudy sky and their shitty camp, they'd be hard pressed to get a clear visual of us in the dark, but he's still exposed. He doesn't even have hands on his rifle. It's slung over his shoulder as he tilts his head to peer down at the snoring Reaper, his hand tapping against his thigh to the music.

Jasper shakes his head, but the look in Lucky's eyes is all bazookas and bad ideas.

Slowly, he touches the toe of his boot to Cole's sweaty sock.

Jasper lunges forward right as the song changes to "Can't Take My Eyes Off You," and it doesn't matter that the leaves are dry under my boots, or that Cole flails awake with a panicked shout.

No one can hear a damn thing.

Frankie Vallie croons as Lucky cuts Cole back down onto the neon fold-out, then jumps on top of him, wrestling him into submission.

Lucky fares better than poor Eden, rolling Cole behind one of the tents.

Jasper hurries over, pulling a length of rope out of his bag as he kneels beside them. The French horn kicks in too loudly for me make out what he's saying, but from his face—and Lucky's grin—he's got plenty to say.

A reluctant smile tugs at my mouth as I creep closer.

Eden.

I don't know what I expected. That she'd set off a flare, maybe? Fake an emergency? Something that might buy us a few seconds or draw a few of the Reapers away, if we got lucky.

But this?

Pete and Buck grab at each other, bouncing, and pride burns in my chest.

She's got these Reapers losing their god-damned minds.

It makes sense. She's got me losing mine, too.

Jasper twines the rope around his elbow as Lucky snaps Cole's decoratively muscled arms behind his back, and I'm finally close enough to make out what he's saying.

" . . . while I'm pleased *you've* had this epiphany, I would appreciate at least some consideration to *my nervous system* before you go randomly waking up enemy combatants!"

"Help! *Help*! We're under—" Cole shouts hoarsely, and Lucky absently shoves his face back down into the dirt.

"Aw, come on, babe. Enemy *combatant* is a bit of a stretch. I swear I'm being safe. Look, he can't even break out of a basic hold." Lucky cinches Cole's wrists an inch higher as if to prove a point, and Cole thrashes under him, his boot slapping against the tent. Lucky pats his shoulder soothingly, then winks at Jasper. "Even you could restrain him."

Jasper stops, gripping his rope. Dangerous, elusive things slip in and out of his eyes, and my smile becomes a grin as I breathe in.

The area is still clear, the air is rich, the food is right there, and for once, I'm not hyper-focused on every part of this op going right.

I'm actually *enjoying* this.

"Weren't you just looking for some shibari practice?" I ask, not bothering to hide my amusement, and Jasper lifts his sour gaze to me.

"This wasn't exactly the image I had in mind."

I snort, my hands loose on my rifle.

Despite the sass, Jasper quickly starts restraining Cole, tying his hands in tight, artful loops before reaching down to secure his legs— and as soon as Lucky climbs off his back, Jasper speeds up, bending his calves back toward his thighs, knotting and looping in fast, efficient movements.

My adrenaline is singing, pumping and hot as Lucky pulls his empty pack around, then yanks out the second bag. He starts loading them up with every bit of food he can get his hands on.

Tucked into the shadows like this, we're invisible.

Jasper finishes his final tie one-handed, his other hand pressing Cole's squirming face into the dirt.

With a casual eye on our surroundings, I admire his handiwork. "What is that? Futomomo?"

"Mm. The spiral."

I nod. "Pretty."

A thick hunk of cheese in one hand, Lucky looks back. His gaze darts between the ties and the half-naked man in the dirt, Jasper's knee in his back, and a blond brow kicks up.

"You know, I suddenly don't know how I feel about this."

Jasper slips two fingers under the rope, running them under the knots. He's nodding, seemingly satisfied, when Cole suddenly wrenches his body to the side. He flops like a trout, then groans when it stresses the ropes.

"Stop wriggling," Jasper scolds him mildly. "Put too much pressure on these ties and you won't enjoy it."

Cole spits out a mouthful of leaves and dirt, glaring up at him. "Oh, now I do apologize. I'll try to be more relaxed while you rope me like *cattle*."

"Ooh, ooh! Put me in, coach!" Lucky laughs, then snaps the buckles closed on his second, bulging bag.

Jasper looks over his shoulder, then pulls another bag from his pack.

It hits Lucky in the face.

"The sooner you fill that up, the sooner we get home. We'll discuss."

Lucky's dimple turns sly. "I fill this up, you fill me—"

My bag hits him in the face a second later.

"Rough, guys. Really rough."

I snort, grinning, as the music bleeds into another song. It takes me a second before the tune hits.

We've Gotta Get Out of this Place.

Lucky tilts his head.

I glance up just in time to see Sawyer turn back from the crowd of Reapers, heading our way.

"Shit. Move your asses," I bark. "*Now.*"

Jasper looks up sharply, and I skid in beside Lucky and start throwing food into the last bag. There's still so much here, so much we can't carry, but it's something. It's a lot of something. I grab flour and oats, and Lucky tosses me a tub of honey that I catch neatly and shove in.

Sawyer swings down to pick up a canteen as he walks toward his tent—toward *us*—and adrenaline courses through me. The chorus rages over the speakers.

My clever fucking girl.

Cursing softly, Jasper throws one of the packs over his back and hauls Lucky to his feet as I wheel around.

Cole twists his head around, panicking. "Wait. *Wait.* You can't just leave me here. I—"

"We'll ensure you're found, as soon as we return safely," Jasper assures Cole politely, quickly taking up a bag from Lucky. "Thank you for being so generous with your supplies. Bristlebrook appreciates the gift, and now—"

"Now we have a girl to get to," Lucky finishes with a dimple, shrugging on his pack. He picks up the last bag, and we're all beating ass to the tree line when Cole calls after us.

"No! No! They're too tight, you . . . *assholes*! You tell your girl I said hello. You know those glasses are cute as hell."

The three of us stop, shoulder to shoulder.

I grit my teeth, and Lucky's head tips back as he blows out a long, hard breath.

"We don't have much time," Jasper begins, but his voice simmers with rage.

Lucky's shoulder lifts. "So, we'll be quick."

"Quick it is," I agree.

I sling my rifle so I'm not tempted to use it, and I'm kneeling over Cole in the next heartbeat. Jayk was clear—no lethal force—but the guy's an asshole, and hell, if I'm being a team player, then maybe I can take some inspiration.

What would Lucky do?

I rip Cole's sock off his foot, and his eyes bulge. "No. No, wait, I didn't mean—"

Grabbing his face, I stuff the filthy, sweaty sock into his mouth with two fingers. I rip a line of tape off with my teeth and slap it over his mouth. His nostrils flare, blowing over the tape, and he shakes his head, gagging.

I slap his cheek, and he looks up at me.

"Eden's *ours*." I raise a brow. "Nod if you understand."

Cole nods hurriedly, and I stand, then kick him onto his back.

"Good. Talk about her ever again, and this silencing will get a lot more permanent."

Cole shudders, and I smile, grimly satisfied.

Jasper nods his head for me to go, and Lucky is grinning.

The night is getting brighter, we have what we came for, and my . . . not my men, my *friends* are waiting for me.

I glance back, checking I'm in the clear, only to stop.

Sawyer is just a few feet away, yawning tiredly. I pause, my heart pounding, fast and ready. We're too close. If he looks up even once . . .

My rifle is right there, but I don't reach for it. This isn't how I want this to go. I'm not messing up this op. Not this time.

But Sawyer doesn't look up.

With one hand, he parts his tent . . . and ducks inside.

I'm clear. I was right.

It's a perfect night.

Victory pumps through me in a way it hasn't in too many damn years, and when I rub my hand over my jaw, I realize I'm smiling.

It seems to freak Cole out even more.

"Thanks for the food." I bring my rifle back around and let my smile turn dry.

"I'm sure we'll be great friends."

Feeling his glare at my back, I jog over to the others, and we take

off for home. Beau and Jayk join us in minutes, and it's a straight shot.
The Reapers are still hooting over the civs.

It's only as we're running through the woods, bags of contraband
in hand, that the last song hits me.

Invincible.

My chest squeezes, and it isn't from the light cardio. The five of us
are moving together, high on the win. Beau is slapping my shoulder,
even Jayk is grinning like we just scored the last touchdown.

We were a team today.

We can be a team.

We hit the tunnel, careful to cover our tracks, and my tongue finds
my lip again. Eden's waiting. *Our* Eden.

Fuck me.

The concept of *anything* with her had seemed so damn out of
reach, I hadn't given much thought to the fact that she's involved with
all of them except for how it affects the team. Too caught up
drowning in my responsibility to even imagine it. But now . . .

I glance at the others, at Lucky laughing as he rips open a roll with
his teeth, and I can't help it. I imagine it.

Sharing with Lucky. Being as close with Jasper as I am with Beau.

Jesus, *Jaykob.*

It's a bigger family than I've ever had. Bigger than I ever hoped of
having.

And Eden . . .

I bite down on the ghost of her kiss. I can still feel the press of her
breasts against my chest. Still taste how she smiled against my mouth
like she'd been waiting for me to kiss her for her whole damn life.

I still see her on her knees this morning, daring me to doubt her.

Fuck, I love her. I'm done pretending I don't. Whatever we need
to figure out, we'll do it together. Not as friends. Not apart. Together.

She's at the heart of this, and I'm greedy for all of it—her and
them and a loud fucking life.

Jasper raises an eyebrow at me, and I realize I've fallen behind,
watching them all laugh and push ahead. My throat feels crammed full
of rocks again, but this time, it's not a bad kind of pain.

So much for empty rooms.

CHAPTER 31

EDEN

Oof."

The air bursts out of my lungs as Ava flattens me again. Grass prickles my nose, and the glowing lights draped over the apple tree are dazzling.

Beside us, Mary Beth giggles under Sloane, and Sloane shakes her head, resigned.

At least it's not just me.

"We're going to need to do something about this. I'm embarrassed for you at this point," Ava tells the back of my head casually.

I groan, slapping the ground, and I shove myself up. "Again."

Our skin slips together as she eases back. "Come on, Eden, I heard something crack. I don't think—"

The wolf whistles and shouts make me grit my teeth, determined.

"They're not *back* yet. Again, Ava."

My arms shake, but I shove against her hard, and she sighs. She doesn't get it. This is what I can do right now. Every enthusiastic, enamored cheer from the sidelines is one more Reaper not looking for my brutes.

I'll let Ava throw my slippery, inept body down all night if I have to.

Sweat drips down my neck. *Please don't let it take all night.* The temperature might have cooled off, but *I* have not.

"Keep your arms *up*. Brace your core. God damn it, Eden. Brace it more than *that*."

Ava's leg twists behind mine, flipping my leg out from under me, and the music cuts out right as my back slams against the ground again.

Ouch.

Bristlebrook's door crashes open, and women around us stop sparring.

Sloane takes a step toward Bristlebrook. "Do you have it?"

My fingers twitch. Our bags lie within reach, filled with guns and our handful of grenades—to defend ourselves and Bristlebrook, if it comes to it. To blow the sole remaining bridge and our last hope of a truce.

To fight back with everything if this goes south.

"We got it!" Jayk shouts, loudly enough to be heard everywhere, and the answering cheer is deafening.

I sit up, gasping. Ava throws her arms around me, then women are streaming forward, abandoning their sparring, running toward my brutes.

Sloane leaps over the porch steps, snatching up a bag as she hollers. Kasey's hugging another to her chest, running forward to meet the half-naked horde. Food spills out onto the grass.

Grinning, Ava helps me to my feet, and I lean against her. My ribs ache, and I can't catch a breath, but . . . is Jayk *laughing*?

Lucky is hugging people as they run up, and Jasper is frantically telling just as many that they need to wait and ration everything. Dom's clapping Jayk on the back—and Beau is running toward me.

In seconds, he has me swept up in an impossibly perfect hug, swinging me around.

"Eden, you are *brilliant*!" He kisses my neck, my hair, anywhere he can reach. My body is screaming in pain, but I ignore it, throwing my arms around his neck. "You're so fucking smart. I'm so proud of you, darlin'!" More kisses, and his hug tightens. "I love you so much."

Tears prick my eyes as he sets me on my feet, and my hands slip down to his chest. His jaw is squared, his face full of fierce love.

I smile, trembling—in relief, in joy? I'm not sure.

"I love you, too," I whisper, and my heart soars.

Then someone is pressing a hunk of cheese into my hand, and I splutter a laugh, spinning to see Lucky's wink.

"Just for you, beautiful. It's Gouda for you."

He's kissing my forehead when suddenly all the hairs on the back of my neck lift . . . and I realize how densely, uncomfortably quiet it's grown on the other side of the moat.

Lucky's hand falls away, dropping to his rifle as we turn to the Reapers. He and Beau shift casually until I'm tucked, shielded, between them.

Sawyer is back, standing right in front of the sole remaining bridge leading to Bristlebrook, his face shadowed and impossible to read. The rest of the Reapers are muttering uneasily among themselves, hushed and uncertain, their earlier glee subdued.

I tense, holding my breath, and my heart beats in my ears.

How they react now could change everything.

Cole stumbles up beside Sawyer, rubbing his wrists. He only has one sock on. Glaring, he points at me, and I blink.

No, not at me. I glance over my shoulder to see Dom, Jasper, and Jayk grouped around me too—the five of them an armed, protective ring. Dom meets my eyes with a slight, reassuring nod, and it shivers over my skin.

Behind them, the women have stopped, watching the Reapers warily.

"That was rude and . . . and downright unhospitable," Cole growls, glowering. Then he grimaces. "And *disgusting*."

Dom shrugs heavy shoulders. "You should wash your socks more often."

Lucky snorts, and Jasper's lips twitch, but I frown, not getting it. Not caring to, right at this moment, because my eyes are locked on Sawyer as he tilts his head back, considering. His gaze drifts over the women behind us, and his fingers tap against his shotgun.

The Reapers tense up, watching him.

The women tense up, watching them.

Mistrust pours through every inch of me. Every instinct tells me something is off, this isn't right, these men are too much, they can't be safe.

And then Sawyer smiles, shaking his head. He looks up through his lashes, his lips a wry curve.

"Well, hell. Enjoy, I guess."

Surprise breaks me apart—and the women roar their approval.

CHAPTER 32

EDEN

SURVIVAL TIP #210
It's okay to dream.

Beau ushers me inside quickly as Jayk delivers instructions to keep a close watch on the Reapers, and Dom starts coordinating plates. Lucky's on the porch, jotting down item after item of our haul. Kasey lifts them up like an auctioneer, and the crowd *ooh*s and *ahh*s appropriately.

"No! Half of *one* bag," Jayk shouts, pulling away from Sloane when Kasey starts tossing food into the crowd. "Fuck it. Yeah, yeah, whatever, kid. Just give me the cookies. Pack the rest of the shit away."

Lucky laughs, springing to his feet and flinging open the taped-up sliding door as Jasper suddenly appears with a rolling cart of wine and spirits. Cups are handed out, and the music springs back to life, and the chattering and laughter settles somewhere deep inside my chest.

Beau squeezes my hand, and I realize I'm gripping him with bone-breaking intensity.

"You doing okay, darlin'?" he asks me softly.

We watch Dom pour Jayk a bourbon, and Lucky line up a string of shots that has Jasper backing up fast and grasping his canteen. We have food, and they're all together, and the Reapers aren't eviscerating us for daring to raid them.

I huff a rueful laugh, though it comes out too shaky. I have to swallow before I can reply.

"One day I'll understand why I get so terrified whenever good things happen." I bite my lip, and Jasper catches sight of us through the broken glass, his dark eyes warm. I smile back at him, strangely achy, then look up at Beau. "It just seems like too much to hope for. Do you ever feel that?"

Beautiful, wooded eyes drift over my face. "No, Eden. I don't. But I could see how you do." Something sore and tender works its way into his face as he watches me, and he hesitates before he says seriously, "I'm sorry if I ever made you feel like this was going to get taken away. We need to talk, and I need to get myself set right on some things, but . . ." He sighs, but when he meets my eyes, it's sure and steady, like he's pressing the words over me like a pressure dressing. "I'm not going anywhere, darlin'. Not while you still want me."

It pushes right up against something inside me, something soft and sick, something that has deep, aged roots . . . but that has less and less to feed it anymore.

I blink as I tear my eyes away, but he turns my face back to him. "No, I need you to hear it, Eden, because I don't think I've been clear. I love you . . . and *nothing* is changing that. Even if I have to remake every part of myself that ever had the power to hurt you."

"Beau . . ." His name sticks in my throat, and I shake my head. "It's not you. I'm just . . . I'm still learning. How to be happy, I'm . . ."

"Ah, pet." He draws me in for a deep, lingering hug, until finally, into my hair, he whispers, "It's okay to dream, darlin'. It really is."

My throat fills, sparks of panic and hope twisting together inside me like a whirlwind. Like maybe it *is* something I can get swept away by.

There he goes again.

Beau might not know how to be angry—but by God, he knows how to love.

Lucky sticks his head through the door, grinning. "What are you guys doing? We're mixing up some masterpieces. Get your asses out here so we can celebrate."

Turning in Beau's arms, I splutter a damp laugh. "I'm still

hungover from the *last* night I spent drinking with you. I'll stick to water."

He makes a face. "You can't celebrate with water, beautiful."

The idea of drinking while armed men are so close makes my stomach turn, good humored or not, but I don't want to spoil their fun.

"*I* am celebrating with cheese," I tell him primly, lifting my prize.

Beau snorts, nudging me forward, but his eyes are still gentle. "Booty shorts and cheese. That sounds like something to celebrate to me."

I join them outside, and the civilians are cheering Jennifer as, limping on her injured leg, she approaches the bridge where Sawyer is waiting. She's holding a bottle of rum.

Sloane edges forward on her tall defensive platform, quietly bringing her rifle around. She subtly flicks the safety off. Beside the platform, Jayk is shifting uneasily as he watches Jennifer, his drink in one hand and bag of cookies in the other. *His* rifle is still over his back.

But no one else reaches for their gun.

Sawyer just runs his hand through his hair, ducking his head as Jennifer steps up onto the bridge.

The cheering intensifies as she lifts the bottle—and goes wild when, obediently, Sawyer opens his mouth. The Reapers whistle, hollering, as Jennifer pours rum down his throat, and Sawyer drinks until he coughs, laughing, and she hands the bottle over with a tart farewell salute.

He watches her go for a long, regretful moment, but when she limps back under the glowing lights, I can see her bright eyes and red cheeks, and I chew my lip thoughtfully.

Sawyer turns back to his men, holding up his prize, and they shout, rushing in to get a drink—the offering accepted.

I relax as Jennifer makes it past the apple tree without trouble, but I'm not the only one hesitating. Ava is leaning against the porch wall, her arms crossed over her chest as she watches them. Glancing over the crowd of civilians, I finally take in the mix of emotions. For every civilian who cheered Jennifer on, there is another anxiously gripping their weapon or watching the Reapers with dark, apprehensive frowns.

Beau was right. This isn't something that can happen overnight. Trust needs to be earned.

Shaking his head irritably, Jayk turns around, but Kasey snatches the bag of cookies out of his hand, grinning, and his expression softens. He shoves her, playfully, I think, but she staggers anyway, and he rolls his eyes, saying something that makes her flip him off.

Beau tugs me over to the porch with the others. Jasper leans back against a post, watching me quietly, and I feel myself grow warm as I sit. My legs dangle over the edge comfortably, and Lucky sits on the grass in front of me, his cup full to the brim with booze. Beau drops down beside him a moment later, drawling something to Lucky under his breath, and Dom drifts over, drink in hand, to lean against the porch next to me. His heated body is just inches away.

He meets my eyes for a long, lingering moment—and I'm kissed senseless by the memory burning in them.

Jayk looks up from Kasey, and something flickers over his face as he takes us all in.

"Hey, Jayk!" Lucky twists, calling out to him before he has a chance to speak. "Get over here. Eden wants a cookie."

I slide a confused look at the back of Lucky's head, but don't say anything as Jayk relaxes a little. Jayk jumps up on the porch, coming to sit behind me. He tucks his body against my back like a looming shadow.

One by one, I watch the others take it in, and I wonder if this will devolve into another fight. But they stay loose and relaxed, even if their eyes linger a little too long, and Dom starts up a low, casual conversation with Jasper.

Thank God.

Settling his untouched drink beside us, Jayk shoves the paper bag in my face. Half the cookies inside are crumbling and broken, but they look delicious.

"Just one," he cautions, and my lips twitch.

At least I'm not the only thing he gets possessive about.

Patiently, I take a cookie out, and Lucky leans forward immediately. "Hey, Eden, can I have a cookie?"

"No! Fuck off, you rat. Get your own."

But I laugh, already tossing it down, and Lucky's dimples are as bright as Jayk's scowl is dark as he catches it.

"I'm not giving you another one," Jayk mutters balefully to me, and I shrug fatalistically, picking up my cheese.

I peel back the edges of the filmy wrap, and the scent hits me hard. Sharp. Pungent. *Perfect*.

Oh, God.

Saliva pools in my mouth as I take a delicate bite, and I'm already doing advanced algebra to work out how to make this small chunk last as long as physically possible.

"Are we interrupting, Eden?" Jasper asks, and I blush.

The biting, rich flavors are flooding me, and at this point, yes. They are.

"It's so good," I murmur, dragging the cheese through my mouth before I swallow. Reluctantly—so, so reluctantly—I lift my chunk, determined to be a better sport than Jayk. "Would anyone like some?"

Beau laughs, rolling onto one elbow as he gets comfortable. "We wouldn't do that to you, pet."

He drains the rest of his drink, and Lucky immediately refills it. They cheers silently.

"It's more fun watching you eat it, anyway," Lucky says, and his eyes track over my outfit. "A *lot* more fun than watching you eat dirt a dozen times in a row."

Dom grimaces, waving Lucky off as he gets up to refill his drink. "That hurt to watch."

They begin teasing me, laughing, trading jibes back and forth, and I settle back, watching them. Now I'm not moving, my sweat has cooled on my skin, and I'm a little cold. I press back into Jayk's chest.

He's quiet, watching them too, but with a slight wrinkle between his brows that I want to soothe away. Around us, the civilians are laughing and eating, caught up in their lives the same way we are.

Lucky's hair lifts in the light breeze, brushing over his lips. I ache to touch it—to touch *him*. Dom is right beside me, his forearm flexing on the porch, and I want to ask him what the kiss meant, and why there's a new intensity in his eyes that he isn't trying to couch. I want to talk to Beau and clear the air.

But I can't.

Any one of those things would set Jayk off, and right now, he's *here*. They're talking, making jokes around him, even including him occasionally, and I feel the same confusion and fear in him when it happens. Just for *being* here.

The tension in him winds tighter as they weave him in effortlessly —as they avoid pet names for me and keep the flirting to a minimum. As they wait for his gruff, cautious responses and move on when he doesn't offer more.

As they're being kind.

Thank you. Thank you, thank you, thank you.

I don't know if it's for them, or him, or me, but I'm not sure if it matters. They're including him.

Quietly, I touch Jayk's hand where he's gripping my hip as Dom snorts at something Lucky is saying—and he squeezes me back, almost too hard.

"I would like to make a toast."

Startled, I look over at Jasper . . . only to find him already watching me. He smiles, just for a moment, before lifting his eyes to look behind me.

He raises his cup sharply. "To Jaykob."

Every thick, heavy muscle against my back springs to life as Jayk tenses, and the others go quiet, waiting. Worry clutches my throat. Jasper is cool and impenetrable as he stares down Jayk, but the vicious argument between all of them this morning is still too fresh, and I can't help the dread seeping into me.

Please don't take this from him.

Then Jasper's face softens, and he inclines his head to the man behind me. "Thank you—for keeping us all alive today. It was a good plan, and you led us well."

Jayk's grip on my waist becomes punishing, but Beau doesn't wait for Jayk to run. He lifts his cup too. "To Jayk."

Silently, Dom lifts his cup, then Lucky, their eyes all on Jayk.

My throat thick, I lift mine, too.

"To you, Jayk," I whisper, looking up at him. "You deserve it."

Jayk is frozen, staring between them like they have their rifles raised and him in their sights. His chest is rising too fast, and he stares at them like he doesn't believe it—like he's just waiting for the punch-line so he can punch back already.

I feel for him, badly.

He's wanted their respect desperately, whether he would admit it or not. He just has no idea what to do with it now that they're offering it.

It's *not* a joke—but he doesn't get it anyway.

The others clink their glasses, Dom's finding mine, and we drink.

Suddenly, Jayk punches to his feet, dragging me up so fast my water sloshes over my lap.

"We're going to bed," he snaps.

"Cool. See ya." Lucky nods at Sloane and Mary Beth, who are sitting atop one of the defensive platforms. "I'll switch out a watch with the civs so they can have some fun."

"Are you going to be able to?" Dom asks dryly, and Lucky gives him a quizzical look over the rim of his drink.

Jasper matches Dom's tone. "I'll join him."

"Twenty-four seven. Do not take eyes off them. That bridge is blown the second they so much as fart in our direction," Jayk growls. "And get someone on the side tunnel, just in case."

Beau nods. "Agreed. We'll take care of it."

Jayk glowers at them, tensed like he's spoiling for a fight. Beau's mouth kicks up, and he eyes my legs with a regretful sigh.

"Have a good night, you two," he says softly, and Dom finally looks over at me again, his eyes burning like all the stars have settled inside him.

"Good night."

Jayk scowls at them all, hesitating and confused, and I take his hand to tug him away. Because there's no malice in it. There's nothing for him to fight right now.

They gave us this.

They gave *him* this.

They let us go with a smile and a wave, and I leave them wistful . . . and happier than I've been in a very long time.

The Reapers are singing across the moat, and Kasey giggles with Ida in the sitting room as we pass. Jayk's frown digs trenches into his forehead, and I wrap his hand in mine as I lead him through all the pretty possibilities.

All the *hope*.

It tugs at me, and I feel myself wanting to do it—wanting to indulge in it, wanting to believe in all the pretty things, too. In allies and honesty and a future where we're all together and not apart. I want to believe that I'm just too jaded—and so many of us are now—and so I'd forgotten that those things are real and not phantasms. I want to believe in a world without fear of Sinners or starvation and hostages. One where we won't need to live with one eye on the shadows.

Jayk is lost in himself, and it's not until we're showered and dressed and I'm slipping between the sheets and tucking myself against him that he seems to register I'm there.

Stroking his face, I watch him from the other pillow, and he silently draws me into a crushing, clinging hug.

And as he drifts to sleep, still locked around me, I whisper into his hair.

"It's okay, Jayk. I think it really is okay for us to dream."

CHAPTER 33

LUCKY

When Jayk and Eden leave, we all breathe out, the cautious tension deflating like slow-release balloons, and I laugh softly. Beau smiles ruefully at me while Kasey runs past with a bar of chocolate in her hand, shouting excitedly for Ava. Dom has to swerve back to avoid her running right through him as she leaps onto the porch.

Some civilians are up, chattering, and others have started turning in. A few more climb up onto the defensive platforms, watching the Reapers, who don't seem to be doing much of anything. Which is good, since I really don't feel like getting up any time soon.

Jasper is lounging on the porch, and his careful expression finally falls away as he looks up at Jayk and Eden's window. His lips tighten in displeasure.

Called it. Self-sacrificing sadist at it again, setting himself to a nice, slow simmer.

"How bad did that one hurt?" I ask, only half-teasing, and he blinks, tearing his gaze away to give me a wry look.

"Less than it could have, I suppose." He sighs, stretching out one leg, then shoots one last dour look at their window. "But ask me again tomorrow. He might have done well with us tonight, but he's still on my last nerve with her—and my patience isn't unlimited."

The new, stinging welts on my back tighten as I roll up onto my side. "Beg to differ."

A smile ghosts his face. "Beg all you like."

Beau groans, running a hand down his face. A rogue flower pokes up behind his elbow. "Jayk is killing me, too. I still owe him one for kicking me out."

Dom snorts. "The nads hit wasn't enough?"

"That was an *accident*," Beau argues hotly, then grins. "Almost entirely, bless his heart."

I laugh, but my gaze slips back to Jasper. After the fight this morning, I wasn't sure if he'd be able to let up on Jayk—even if he was twisting his notebook over Jayk's soft and squishy parts last night. I know how cold he can be.

Jasper wasn't cold tonight, though.

I smile, watching him laugh softly at Beau.

Jasper is warmer every day.

"Well, whether it hurt or not . . . it was very gentlemanly," I tell him softly, and his eyes flick up, sharp and surprised.

He searches my face, like he doesn't know what to make of me.

"Are you proud of me then, my Lucien?" he murmurs.

I toy with my cup on the grass, enjoying how he's looking at me. Enjoying his *my*s and the night and how his skin always looks like pearls under moonlight.

"Yeah, I'm proud of you," I tell him, and the clear amusement rising in him is equal parts indulgent and gently emotional.

I might even enjoy that the most.

But even while he's making me want to kick my feet like a love-struck schoolgirl, I find my eyes drifting up to the window.

I just wish Eden were still here. I kind of even wish Jayk stayed, too.

We all did this. We should be celebrating together.

In fact, if I had my way, I'd pull out the damn grappling hooks right now—fine ass gentleman I am or not. Because honestly, while I know Jasper *is* patient, and honorable, and *dignified*, and I really am super glad he's taking the high road and all . . . Jayk is *not* any of those things, and he'll take a dump on a high road before using it. Love is a battlefield, baby, and you've got to be in the war to win it.

Jasper's gaze flicks back up to the window again, irritation simmering across his expression, and I smirk.

It's probably fine—he'll boil over sooner or later. And in the meantime, I guess I'll just have to bravely bear the burden of helping him work out his frustrations.

Check. Mate.

Who the hell said I don't know how to play chess?

Dom settles back against the porch, looking between us then exchanging a silent amused look with Beau that I don't miss. I roll my eyes.

"Okay, it's fine. Don't worry. I'm proud of you both as well. That was some best behavior *magic* tonight from everyone. Did you see Jayksey's lil face?"

"That pure and total panic at the most basic human kindness?" Beau mutters caustically. "Yeah, caught it."

I grimace. I'm so *nice* to Jayk. Why is he always so surprised when I'm nice?

"Did you see Eden's face?" Dom counters, absorbed by the contents of his cup. "It meant something. We should be patient with him."

"I vote that we have fun with him," I remark.

Jayk could use a bit of fun.

And what's more fun than a little friendly competition?

"You'll do it at your own risk, Lucien. I won't have Eden mad at me because you want to beat Jaykob at his own game," Jasper tells me tartly.

Beau rolls onto his back, staring up at the thick clouds. "He's like her, isn't he?"

There's a pause as we all look at him.

"In what way?" Jasper asks.

"I always knew Jayk had a chip on his shoulder, and that he was kind of an asshole who just wanted to be alone." Beau tucks his arm under his head. "I guess . . . I never thought maybe he just didn't know how not to be."

That sits between us for a while, long enough for the chattering to get quieter around us, and for the Reapers' campfires to begin to go out. Mosquitos buzz around, but I still have knots of lavender in my hair, and I tuck some into Beau's pockets when he starts slapping himself.

He mutters under his breath, and I lay back beside him to look up at the clouds too. The stars peek out between them as they shift and swirl into Santa hats and misshapen dogs. The breeze smells like trees and woodsmoke, and something about it feels like being a kid, when everything was grass and friends and sky and stealing as much time as I could before my parents would come and chase me home.

And I just . . . I want to keep it.

So, I ask the question I've been wondering since the Reapers showed up on our doorstep.

"Do you think we could do it? If we had the Reapers with us, do you think we could get the Sinners off our ass?"

Beau scoffs next to me, his head turning in the grass. "Two days and you're already jumping into bed with them?"

"Hey, don't ally-shame me," I complain, and Dom snorts, kicking one foot back against the porch to steady himself. "Come on, you have to see it—these aren't bad guys. Alastair would have tried to rip our lungs out for that raid, not started body shots."

From farther down the porch, there's a burst of laughter, then a surge of hushed conversation I only catch snippets of.

" . . . *No*. I mean . . . I don't know!" Jennifer begs off.

" . . . oh, *please* . . ."

Jasper's voice drifts over their distant chatter. "If we don't give in to their demands, we could very well starve, and they would let us. Does that make them good? To put a price on another human's safety? Particularly when it's a price these women aren't comfortable paying? Is it good to leverage their strength over people who need their help, too?"

"Aw, now, who doesn't?" Rubbing his eyes tiredly, Beau sits up. "It's end of days. Safety *is* a commodity—clearly, or the Reapers wouldn't be begging for our help. Safety, food, resources. Everything is tradable. Or steal-able, like we proved today. They're not running a charity." Beau shrugs. "They made us an offer, same as we did with Eden."

Dom shoots him a look. "They have us under siege." His mouth tightens. "And our offer was . . ."

Beau leans forward. "It's barely a siege. They're not getting their panties in a twist about our little side quest tonight, so it doesn't seem like they're *really* intending on letting us starve. They're desperate, Dom. I think I'm with Lucky here. They don't seem like bad people to me." Beau's mouth lifts sadly on one side. "Maybe we're all just too cautious now. It's hard to trust that anyone has good intentions. Or as good as intentions get these days, anyway."

Dom stares at Beau, his face grim and unreadable, and I sit up, too, feeling weirdly trapped by this line of conversation.

"Yes, our intentions . . ." Jasper's head tips back, and his quiet voice is heavy. "I don't know, Beaumont. I'm not so sure the measure of a person should be taken by their intentions. And I'm not *at all* sure that the similarity between our actions and the Reapers' means they're good." He's looking up at the stars, his face troubled. A rogue lock of hair blows loose over his forehead as he sighs. "Perhaps it only means that we haven't been."

An uneasy jittery energy flicks through me as I try to work out what he means by that, because . . . I mean, he can't think that *we're* bad. We did our best to help people, from Day Death and on—and it usually ended up with us getting fucked over. We tried.

I think of Eden the first time I saw her, her feet bloody to the ankles.

Needing help.

We might have taken care of the men on her tail, but . . . yeah. Not exactly Prince Charming behavior.

I duck my head, guilt squeezing me in every pore.

Beau is clearly fighting with the same feeling. "It's a different world. I'm not saying we haven't made mistakes. We have. But . . . we learned from them."

"Did we?" Dom asks, his mouth tilted bitterly. Night wind lifts his hair. "Then why are we making excuses for the next people doing it? Jasper's right, intentions mean shit. There's a right and wrong, and it's the same before Day Death and after."

"Dom—"

"No, Beau. Innocent people—good people—get fucked by that new world bullshit logic. They shouldn't have to trade, or kill, or steal to be safe. That used to be our whole job, to make it so that they didn't fucking need to do any of that." A muscle in his jaw tics, and he looks away. "I forgot that. I got . . . it just got too hard to keep playing the hero. People can be so disappointing." His voice roughens. "And it's so hard to win when you're the only one playing by the rules."

Slowly, I lift my head to look at him.

These aren't questions I've ever even *thought* to ask before, and I feel like a fucking idiot for it. I've never wanted to be in charge. Following orders suits me just fine, and I've always been pretty damn happy to leave the moral grappling and hard calls in someone else's hands.

Only . . . only, if I'm honest, it's not like I never had doubts about calls. I've had questions. Worries. Over Eden and the deal, over lying to her about the hunters hanging around Bristlebrook before that all blew up, over letting civilians go, over Sam, over . . . a lot of things. I always just told myself it wasn't my place. That's being a soldier, right? I *let* it not be my place.

No, I benefited from it all on the sidelines even when I disagreed. I just let Dom take the actual responsibility for it.

The burden.

I swallow hard, a sick feeling spreading through my gut.

We took in the civilians, but only when Eden asked. She was the one who pushed us to help the captives. She was the one who did something about the torture happening in front of her.

She broke the shitty-ass deal and stood up for herself.

Shit. Maybe we *are* the bad guys.

And I've been a fucking coward.

Beau sits forward, staring at the cap. "Dom—"

"Maybe it was only too hard because you were doing it by yourself. We were all kind of just . . . existing apart, for a while there." The words spill out of me, and Dom looks down at me, stone-jawed.

Something flickers behind his eyes, though, and I try to work up a smile for him. "But we were good tonight, right? We made a good plan, and we did it together. We didn't even murder anyone."

I feel Jasper's eyes on me, but I can't look at him right now. I'm not used to feeling uncomfortable in my own skin, but right now, it's all I'm feeling.

Avoiding his gaze, I add in a rush, "And I mean, for the bigger picture stuff, I don't know what Red Zone does to get their food and whatever else they need, but they have to have worked something out, you know? They have tons of people there, a bunch since they were *kids*—it wasn't like they've been contributing more than acne and BO. Maybe we can get some tips from them? And being short on medicine sucks, but there have to be scientists and people who know how to make that shit still around somewhere, right? We could find someone."

Jasper gives me an amused look. "I'll place an ad in a newspaper, shall I?"

"Okay, sarcasm. That's nice. First, bite me. Second, point taken."

Dom's lips finally twitch, and he smiles into his cup as I redirect.

"So, we go old school for medicine, Eden-style. Hit the basics." I shrug, looking down at the grass to find I've shredded the patch in front of me to the dirt. "I don't know. We could spitball."

The moonlight shifts with the clouds, and a burst of laughter goes up from Jennifer's group, but it dies down after a moment.

Nodding slowly, Jasper ventures, "We need more allies. We've kept to ourselves a lot. With some trade, we'd have more options."

Dom lifts a brow. "We need something to trade for that."

Jasper matches his tart expression. "You all have skills, do you not? You can rig up defenses, create explosives, assist with surveillance cameras. Beaumont, I'm sure you could train people in basic first aid. Clare was a labor and delivery nurse. Jada is an electrician. Sloane was in carpentry. The civilians have an enormous amount of collective experience. Just some initial thoughts, but we do have things to offer."

My excitement sparks as he waves a hand. He's right. We've kept pretty close to Bristlebrook, not wanting the risk, but we could go farther out. There will be other communities *somewhere*, even if they're in hiding.

Hell, we have the Sinners, Reapers, Red Zone, and ourselves all within a week's walk. How many more are out there? Sure, we need to get past the maybe-not-a-siege siege first, but . . .

But Beau is looking between us like we're suggesting using his balls as a golf tee.

"This all sounds well and good for peace time, but I think you're all forgetting that we have the Sinners on our ass," Beau points out.

"They're going to come knocking. What's to stop them from taking anything we manage to barter, same as they're doing with the Reapers? They have an army. I don't know that we could stop them."

Dream squasher.

I get to my feet, looking out toward the Reapers. All the campfires, one after the other, burning against the dark. The civs are watching over them too, but they're all tucked away. Quiet.

They don't want to attack us.

I just *know* it.

"Depends how many new friends we can make, doesn't it?" I grin down at Beau.

I always said I could use more friends.

Friends make for a *great* army.

He rolls his eyes, throwing his cup at me, and I bat it away.

"Those *friends* sound great in theory, but when exactly do you see us having time to go door knocking? We're locked in here. Right now, we've got exactly three options for allies: Red Zone, the Reapers, and the Sinners, and they ain't exactly playing nice together, Lucky."

Dom rubs a hand over his head. It's weird to see his hair longer than a quarter inch. I can't tell if it's a finally-loosening-up thing or a please-help-I'm-letting-myself-go thing.

He drops down onto the grass, his back against the porch, like his brief shot of optimism was too much for his body to handle.

"Those options are shit. If we defend the Reapers against the Sinners, it'll be war," Dom finally says. His eyes turn to cold, chipped metal. "And Alastair still has Heather and Bentley. We go against him, they're as good as dead."

Across the grass, Beau grimaces at Dom. "Right. And if we don't join the Reapers—"

"They starve us out," Dom finishes. "Or we have a fight on our hands anyway to get them off our doorstep. We pick either side, we're in for one."

This time it's my turn to stare at them.

Man, these guys are *pessimists*.

I scratch my head. "Can we go back to the whole everything-will-be-okay, teamwork-makes-the-dream-work, make-peace-not-war conversation, or . . . ?"

Dom and Beau exchange a silent, bemused look, and it takes me so off guard, I smile.

They're back to their married-couple conversations.

But then Beau shakes his head with a soft snort, and humor shadows Dom's face before they both turn too-patient expressions toward me.

"Sure thing, Lucky." Beau pats the grass soothingly. "We'll just hug it out with them. It'll all be fine."

Dom nods, straight-faced. "Hugs not war."

Oh, no, no, no. They don't get to use their bestie powers on *me*.

"I— You . . ." I splutter. "You're both being so dramatic. It is *not* that bad!" I gesture up at the porch, where two bags of food still haven't been packed away. "Things are looking up!"

Indignant, I catch Jasper's eye, sending him my own disbelieving couplepathy look . . .

And he raises a puzzled brow.

Damn.

That one was a total soft ball, too.

Rubbing my forehead, I sigh. "I can't believe Dom and Beau are a better couple than us."

Jasper still looks like he has no idea what I'm talking about, but amusement touches his features. "They do have several years on us, darling boy."

Dom gives Jasper a dry look. "Nineteen next year."

Beau tilts his head. "Bronze? I'm thinking cufflinks."

Dom snorts, draining his drink.

Smiling, Jasper curls a finger at me, beckoning me to come to him, and my stomach leaps.

I jump up on the porch, and he tilts his leg to the side, making room for me. Mollified, I move closer until I can settle back against his chest.

"You need to back me up, babe. Tell them it's not all bad." I yawn, his heat surrounding me, and Jasper strokes my hair.

"It isn't." He sets his cup to the side. "I think we're all getting ahead of ourselves. Maybe it will be war, but we're not there yet." He's patient and calm when he looks over us, and it steadies me, too. "Lucien's right. We've had a win tonight, and that buys us time. We can radio Red Zone in the morning. We can afford to wait until they arrive before we make any major decisions. Who knows? They might open up options for all of us." His heart beats sure and constant against my back. "And we can use the time before they arrive to watch the Reapers. Learn. Decide whether we can trust them."

Dominic glances up at Jasper, his gaze surprised and considering.

After a long moment, he nods to himself.

"We're still likely in for a war, one way or another," Beau says. "We need to prepare for it."

"See?" I tilt my head to give Jasper an exasperated look. "Glass is always half empty with him."

He gives me one back that I do understand.

Please stop.

Aw, it's working.

His gaze flicks back over the others. "If it's war, then we need to make sure we're on the right side of it."

Dom is still looking inward, and I sober.

"We can play by the rules, Dom—the important ones anyway. Even if it is war." I meet his eyes. "We just need to start playing on the same team again."

To my surprise, his throat cords, and he looks away. His jaw is still stone, and my earlier guilt pings me again.

Damn, we've all been fucking dicks, haven't we?

Finally, he nods, still not looking at us, and Beau lets out a long, pensive breath, watching him too.

When Dom finally looks up, he nods.

"And Jayk?" he asks dryly. "We thinking he's going to be getting on board with all this?"

At that, Dom scoffs, and the look he gives Beau back is just as dry. "I don't think this is the part he's going to fight us on."

This time, we all look up at their window. They've cracked it open now, and the curtains flicker in the breeze.

"Well." I sigh. "At least we're allies in that, too."

CHAPTER 34

EDEN

SURVIVAL TIP #167
A truce is just the moment before things turn very good.
Or very, very bad.

We radioed the Reapers' home base the day after the raid, but it was already in flames. Alastair and a horde of Sinners had come in the night, stolen a huge chunk of their stores, and torched their livestock barn. The reedy-voiced Reaper on the radio was in a state over losing so much of their supply . . . and over the violence.

Two dozen dead at Alastair's hand.

It's time for the Sinners to reign, Alastair told us, and apparently . . . this is what it looks like.

When we handed Sawyer the list of names, every Reaper was silent. He read them out, and from the safety of our defenses, we watched them break, one by one. We watched them lean on each other, and rage, and Cole storm off into the woods and not reappear for two days.

"But why would Alastair do that?" I'd raged to my brutes, crippled with choking, miserable guilt as they looked on with shadowed eyes.

"He's claiming their land, Eden. Taking ownership. He's made it clear what he wants," Jasper gently replied.

An empire.

"But why would they kill the people working it?" I whispered back.

Dom stood beside me. "Not all of them. Only enough to make them scared. Enough that they'll remember the next time the Sinners show up. Enough that the Reapers won't want to fight back again."

But the Reapers didn't retreat.

If anything, the news seems to make them more determined to win our aid. From their side of the moat, they strike up conversation with every civilian who wonders close enough to talk. They throw over apples and overripe peaches. They turn a blind eye to Kasey slipping out every day to snitch food from their stores, no matter what Jayk does to keep her away. Akira floats around their camp, attending to chores but doing little to bother us.

And every day, Jennifer has breakfast with Sawyer on the bridge between us.

On the first day, they sat on opposite ends, a feast tucked in the middle, and we all held our breaths and our rifles as they shared it, all shy smiles and slow bites, and not a single word to send Jennifer limping back to safety.

The next day, they sat inches closer, and the smiles got a little less shy. The breaths a little less held. The rifles a little less tense.

Day by day, the civilians, on the whole, have begun to relax.

Except for a few.

Sloane, Ava, Ida. Deanna and Aniyah and a dozen others keep their rifles in hand. They haven't once loosened their grips.

After the Reapers, we radioed Red Zone. Jayk hadn't quibbled once over the others' plan, and Red Zone seemed as good a place as any to start building our allies.

They were already on their way, as promised.

They're as much in need of help as we are, as expected.

By day, Jayk has us on defense, on expanding the garden, on extending rations. He has us working on our shooting and our archery. He has us making arrows, and Katherine shows us how to make bows. He has me sparring, since he was apparently unimpressed with my attempt during the raid, booty shorts or no.

There's an uneasy truce at Bristlebrook—and we're all holding our breath until it breaks.

Unless we're talking about my brutes. Because that? That's been war.

CHAPTER 35

EDEN

I s Ava in . . ." Aniyah stops short. "Oh, Eden. It's you."
I drop my pen over my notepad, fighting another yawn.
Jayk isn't much for sleep.

"Aniyah!" Sweeping up a mug, I try not to look like I'm chasing
her down as I move around the breakfast bar. "You must be hungry!
Would you like some slop? It's a new recipe."

But Aniyah's already backing out of the kitchen as fast as she
entered it, a nervous hand clutching the pale blue hijab at her throat.
"Oh, no. I'm full."

"*Full*? Then why were you coming to the kitch—"

"Busy," she cuts me off, nodding. Her hand scrambles for the door
handle behind her. "I'm so busy. With surveillance. Cameras. And I'm
looking for Ava, too, so I should really . . ."

Flabbergasted, I stare at her. "But we turned off the cameras."

"Right. Sure. That's . . ." Her gaze drops to my mug just as the
handle turns, and the door opens behind her. Relief crashes over her
face as she flees. "Sorry, Eden! Do a girl a favor and stay away from
Dom for a bit, okay? I have two bread rolls on him winning zero face
time this week. Okay, thanks! See you, bye!"

The door swings shut, and I sigh, slumping into a chair by the breakfast bar. In the corner of the room, on the floor, Kasey is working on something with wires that sparks far too often for comfort, but that Jayk told me "not to get my panties in a wad" about. That was right before he forced me to eat, stuck me with today's friend-slash-humiliatingly-transparent watchdog, and ran off with more anxious mutters about checking on the farm animals.

Jayk has been stressed.

And stressed Jayk is a lot.

I suppose Kasey's better off here than thieving from the Reapers again, at least. She's had everyone anxiously fretting over that—to the point that the guys have been trading off watches of the side tunnel to try and keep her in here.

Through the window, Jennifer is still on the bridge, talking with Sawyer. They're a good foot closer than they were the other day.

At least *someone* is getting romanced.

The mug in my hand tilts, and I stare at the green liquid glumly. This is the third variation of my slop in the three days since the raid, and I'm still struggling to get anyone to drink more than a mouthful of it—which is becoming pathetic since, slowed by raid-rations or not, they're quite literally starving. All the urgency seems to have gone out of them to stretch those rations properly.

And that bothers me more than I care to examine.

"Why is it *gooey*?"

I scowl at Lucky over my shoulder as he eyes my mug, and I hug it to me, like it might hear the aspersions. "It's not! I mean, it's *slightly* viscous because of the aloe gel—I couldn't reduce it any more than that —but it's perfectly drinkable. The moss helped give it some texture."

"Oh, I bet." He nods solemnly. "I finished my pile of rocks for breakfast, and I was wondering what was for lunch." I open my mouth to protest when his dimple turns into a grin. "Have you actually tried your devil brew? Not to be dramatic, but I think I'd rather walk through Bentley's snake pit."

Miffed, I roll my eyes. "*I've* had two cups. *I've* eaten more of it than anyone the last few days."

Partially in an attempt to prove to everyone that my concoctions are edible. Partially because Jaykob and Lucky keep force-feeding me at every opportunity.

Jaykob and Lucky—because while we watch the Reapers and wait for Red Zone to arrive, my brutes have been going head-to-head. They might be supporting Jayk with anything he needs for Bristlebrook, but when it comes to me, it's been non-stop. No matter how Jasper cautions them all to find restraint.

Between their tasks, Dom and Beau have been laying distractions for Jayk. Overwhelming him as he leaves his room. Lying in wait around corners and dragging him away—and with far more child-like delight than the whole frustrating endeavor really calls for.

And if the two of them weren't so enormously outnumbered by the civilians—who seem to have their own strange, personal stakes in who gets time with me—I'm sure their plots would have worked.

As it stands, all their efforts still haven't bought them more than a few minutes with me.

Lucky has had a better run.

It isn't that he's been allowed special privileges exactly, but Lucky is creative. He's been bargaining and bribing and weaseling his way through the spies since the first day. It's only got him so far, but at least we've been able to talk and, for now, that's enough.

Jasper alone I haven't talked to at all, unless Jayk was also present, and he's been . . . very polite. So polite, it seems to be giving him a stomach ache.

I've been trying not to take it personally that he hasn't pressed for anything more.

While the men seem to be finding their private battles entertaining, I've found it more frustrating. I'm not sure how I'm ever supposed to work through anything with the others if we can't get within three feet of one another for more than five minutes.

Jayk and I have been having our own nightly disagreements about his behavior.

Unfortunately for me, I have no self-restraint and it usually ends with me stripping off his clothes and working out my frustration in other ways.

Lucky laughs at me, then wanders over to my pot on the stove. He begins to chatter about his day, examining the slop like it's a science experiment and not the result of two hours of cooking.

Kasey gives him a quick look, then—satisfied at his distance—goes back to work.

He's been especially sweet and attentive since the raid, sneaking me contraband cheese in uniquely creative ways. Wedged into a remarkably sturdy paper airplane he flew over Jaykob's head. Magically tucked into my pocket with some impressive sleight of hand. Somehow, inside my locked bedroom, horrifically squashed underneath the paperback on my bedside table.

We had words about that one.

" . . . *Twelve*, Eden! Twelve books. Do you know how long it took me to find twelve books in his stupid library? And then I had to find the passages he wanted. Skim through and Post-it them and—I feel like I need to repeat, it was *twelve* books."

I perk up. "Textbooks? What kind? Psychology, I'm assuming, but which . . ." Lucky straightens, staring at me with imploring, outraged eyes, and I stop, changing direction. "Sounds really boring, yeah. Must be horrible." I clear my throat. "Books. Research. Awful."

His dimple springs back to life, and he rolls his eyes. "It might be for a good cause, but at some point, he really should think of *my* mental health. I should be outside. Teaching people how to fight and stuff."

I lean over the counter, raising my brows. "*Or* you could conserve your energy and be a good person, all at the same time. Especially since you won't have any slop."

Lucky looks back into the pot, then picks up the ladle. Or he tries to.

It sticks a little.

"Have you made any progress with Dom and Beau?" he asks, shaking the spoon to try and free it.

I sigh, my mood dimming. "Jo let Beau smile at me from the other side of the porch yesterday morning. Does that count?"

The slop peels away from the ladle with a sticky squelch, then plops back into the pot. Lucky grimaces, and I rest my chin in my hand.

"Then no, nothing."

Kasey's equipment sizzles behind me, but I ignore her, too caught up in my own self-pity. "Oh, I just don't even know what I'd do if I *did* have them in front of me. They say we don't trust each other. What am I even supposed to do about that? Trusting people isn't exactly my strength."

Lucky gives me a commiserating look, then turns the burner on under the pot. I'm not sure why. It doesn't change the consistency much.

He nods, adjusting the heat. "I don't know. Why not just do the usual things? Keep your promises. Set expectations and then meet them. Talk about your feelings, even the annoying secret ones you don't really want to. Be consistent. You know, all that good stuff. It's not rocket science." The pot starts to smoke, and he squints into it. "Though maybe you're good with that. I feel like you had to do some advanced chem here to make food turn this color."

I frown, thinking about that. It makes sense, and it's not dissimilar to what I've already thought of, but when he puts it like that . . .

"Maybe I could make it a kind of habit? Show up every day to spend time with them?" I muse.

Though I don't know how I'll manage that, when I can't even get close to them.

I'm going to have to get creative, too.

"Oh, sure, well rituals are a thing. Not *my* thing, but you know." He winks, looking up from the pot. "You're a better sub than me."

"I very clearly am not," I tell him tartly.

I can barely get it through Jayk's head that I'm not leaving him for anyone else. Lucky, on the other hand, is here, romancing me, still proudly decorated in all the devilish marks Jasper has left on his shoulders and back. There's one pink, shiny mark peeking from his chest over the low collar of his tank. It looks suspiciously like a brand.

"A more obedient sub, then." He laughs.

The pot makes a loud cracking sound, and Lucky flinches, flicking the heat off and moving the pot to another burner.

He gives it a dark look before he considers me, nodding slowly. "But you could set something up like that. A ritual. You could base it around whatever you guys are struggling with. If it's trust and honesty, I don't know, maybe you tell them something every day.

Something about how you're feeling or what you're thinking? Something you're comfortable sharing, until you know you'll be heard?"

Ritual.

The word settles in me. It's a word of stained glass and reverence. Careful repetition and promises old as parchment.

A ritual appeals to me endlessly.

I straighten off the counter, thinking about that. What it might look like. How I want it to feel. In some ways, the idea reminds me of my coffee dates with Dom. Granted, he'd done most of the sharing then, but Lucky's right. That honesty and consistency was what started changing things between us.

And Beau, well, I had told him things when we were curled between our sheets, but then, I mostly shared the good. The little moments that made me smile and how he made me feel. At the time, I was so caught in my own head, those sweet hours with him felt precious. A balm against all my raw feelings.

And if I'm honest, there was a part of me that was so terrified of being cut out the way he'd done to Dom, I'd kept the worst to myself.

I take a deep breath. The worst of that wound is lanced now, and it's time to heal from it.

Beau isn't an escape. If I want him to be a partner, I need to treat him like one.

I want our promises to grow as old as parchment.

Lucky raps on the counter, and I look up.

"If you do this, it can't just be for them, beautiful." His blue eyes are serious. Unusually firm. "You have to get whatever you need, too. You can't just make yourself uncomfortable because you want to make them happy, or because you feel like you have to." He drags his lower lip into his mouth, his expression grim. "That's the last thing any of us want."

"I know. I've almost finished my essay for Jasper on safety dynamics. It was very enlightening." I smile dryly at him but hold his gaze so he knows I'm hearing him. "For me, I want them both to know I do trust them with the . . ." Quickly, I look at Kasey. Her head is bent over her project, but I lower my voice anyway. "I want them to know I trust them with the kink stuff too. Dom especially doesn't think he can . . . or should . . . I don't know. I want him to lead."

Lucky's eyes twinkle. "I bet."

Huskily, I laugh, because Lucky always makes me laugh, but my chest aches sweetly.

He's so painfully beautiful right now, with his hair twisted in awfully messy Viking braids he's piled on his head. With the loose silky strands around his face that should look feminine, but only ever make me notice how comfortably masculine he is.

Mostly he's beautiful because of who he is, and how he's always on my side.

He strolls back around the breakfast bar, and Kasey's clangs and hisses stop until he pauses a foot away from me, leaning against the counter.

After a moment, they resume.

Snitch.

Lucky grins at how I glower at her, but he nods his chin at me. "Look. You have to respect the cap's boundaries too—but if he's especially worried about . . . the child-unfriendly activities . . ." he says cautiously, side-eyeing Kasey " . . . then maybe you can keep those off the table? Offer to help them get ready for the day, or to just take care of them in other ways. Maybe he'll be okay with that, and you can all test the waters first before you dive into the filthy stuff."

All very sensible. Almost shockingly so, considering who I'm talking to.

I smile softly. He smells like Jasper's sheets and something bright and spicy. I hate that I can't touch him right now.

"How did you learn about all this?" I tease.

Lucky laughs, and after checking on Kasey, he shifts closer. "I have a very good therapist." Another inch closer, and I can feel the heat of him. "*And* I actually like listening to him, which is why I'm the best adjusted."

My laugh spills over, low and intimate, and Lucky bites his lip, his gaze zeroing in on my mouth. I'm just about to reach out to him when I realize Kasey's fallen silent. I look up.

She's stopped working, she's holding a wire in each hand, watching us suspiciously.

"Back it up, punk," she warns.

I give her a withering look, and Lucky laughs, letting me go.

"All right, all right. Chill out, 007." He glances back down at my gruel. "God, that reeks. How is it that we scored you flour and honey and all these delicious things, and end up with . . ." Lucky tips my abandoned cup toward him, and his nose wrinkles. "The Grinch's spunk?"

Oh. Back to the sass.

"Spunk?" I repeat flatly, and he shrugs.

"Honestly, it might be better than 'slop.' Your branding needs work."

Kasey rolls her eyes and turns her back on us, apparently uninterested in slop, too.

"Have *you* actually tried it, Lucky?" I ask with poisonous sweetness.

When I hold up the mug, he takes a step back, raising his arm defensively—then he coughs, changing the motion to run a hand through his hair, like that was his plan all along. His shirt lifts and his colorful biceps flash carnivals at me.

Tingles chase over my skin, and—sensing an opportunity—I spare a quick glance at Kasey's back before I shift closer to him, slipping into his personal space.

"Please?" Feeling brave, I slip my hand under the hem of his shirt, and he sucks in a sharp breath. His muscles lock up under my fingertips, and I look up at him through my glasses. "You need to eat, too. You need your energy."

The dimple disappears into his beard, and his eyes lock on my mouth. "Energy?" He clears his throat, and his hand drops from his hair to the counter beside my waist. "What do I need energy for?"

His voice has turned husky, and I hide a smile. I am getting *so* much better at this whole flirting thing.

I shrug one shoulder, tracing the ridges of his abs, and he shudders. Lucky never had much body fat to begin with, but they're unhealthily prominent now, and it won't be long before his muscles start breaking down in earnest as his body searches for new sources of energy.

Everyone is really overestimating what three bags of food and a few apples can do for ninety people.

My fingers dip. "I'll tell you exactly what for if you drink it."

Lucky catches my wrist. He drags in an unsteady breath, his pretty blue eyes accusing—and still caught on my mouth.

"I didn't sign up for two sadists," he mutters, but he grabs the mug out of my hand.

Pinching his nose with one hand, he downs it in three gulps, then slams it onto the counter with a full-body shudder.

"Delicious," he croaks.

In the next instant, Lucky's lifted me up onto the porcelain counter, and he steps between my legs. Heat stirs low in my gut. It's everywhere, really. With all the damaged windows, it's impossible to escape, leaking in from outside.

We're both damp with humidity. It just happens to look better glowing over his pretty, painted skin, and I trace the column of his throat with a soft smile.

Recipe-mocking aside, I've missed him.

He looks at me balefully. "I drank your poison, beautiful. Please tell me you have something sweet for me after that."

Laughing, I twine my arms around his neck and lean up to kiss him, but he pulls back. "It's still on my lips, so you probably shouldn't—"

I cut him off, kissing him thoroughly, with almost clumsy eagerness. He grips the back of my neck, laughing too, tempering the kiss. I fold my legs over his hips instead, drawing him closer, and his laughter turns into a muffled, helpless groan as he bends me backward over the counter.

The heat licks up my spine. Pools between my legs. His clever, clever mouth is waking me up, clearing out the fuzzy tiredness like a wildfire scorching through a forest.

"Whoa, hey! Nope! *Warning*! None of that," Kasey suddenly hollers from the corner. "I'll get the spray bottle! I'll get Jayk!"

I rip my mouth away. "Don't you *dare*!"

She glares at me, and I glare back. I like Kasey. I like her a lot, even. Most of the time, she likes me too, I think. Until Lucky or Jasper comes within two feet of me, that is, and I get the galling reminder that she is *Jayk's* through and through.

She takes a step backward, toward the door.

"No! Damn it, Kasey, we had a deal!" Lucky points at her. "You took the chocolate. I get twenty free minutes!" She takes another step back, and he lifts a panicked hand. "Don't! Don't. Come on, Freckles. All a person has is their word. You don't want to break yours, right?"

My heart squeezes happily. Lucky gave up chocolate for twenty minutes with me? *Supervised* ones?

Kasey shrugs, smirking. "All *you* have is your word. *I* have chocolate, and another whole bar of it on Jayk winning this dating show." She looks between us, wrinkling her nose. "Which makes you way too far inside the body bubble right now."

I tap Lucky's shoulder, narrowing my eyes on her. "Lucky. Lucky get her. Now, she's—"

She bolts for the door, and Lucky darts away from me, but he has to twist between the chairs. Kasey's sly body is twisting through the door, bolting into freedom before he can grab her.

"Shit!" He grins, then turns back to me, gesturing me to follow. "*Run*, Eden. Come on!"

With a screech, I jump off the counter and he grabs my hand as we race, laughing, through the house.

Not this time, Jayk.

Lucky's hand is callused and perfect in mine.

Today, Lucky's belongs to me.

CHAPTER 36

JAYKOB

"J ust figure it out! I don't fucking know," I bark, then immediately feel like an ass when Beau gives me that too-patient, flower-power bullshit look.

Ever since the raid three days ago, they've all been *nice*, and it's freaking me out. And yeah, nice for them also means avoiding trip-wires and dodging sneak attacks while they try to steal my girl from me, but at least that part is almost . . . fun.

I'm down for a fight.

I duck my head, looking away from those eyes and mutter, "I'll figure it out."

He settles his arms over his chest, still waiting, and I scowl, fighting the urge to scuff my boots on the floor. I glance around the med bay, but there's no one here to see me turning back into a scolded five-year-old, so I mumble through my teeth, "Sorry."

See?

I can be nice too.

He shrugs, rolling his eyes. "There's only so much we can do about it, Jayk. Their nutrition is poor, and has been for a long time. We're already getting reports of fatigue, depression, fluid retention, weakness, dizziness—bad breath." Beau eyes me briefly, and I glare at him. "We've also had a few fainters. I have a list of names. Keep an eye on them? If there's any way for them to get extra food . . . well, they're most at risk. Age. Heart problems."

Mary Beth was one of those *fainters*, right in the middle of sparring, and it's put me in a weird, panicky place all day.

Beau shakes his head, leaning back in his chair. A pile of loose cloths and random pieces of equipment sits on the desk in front of him. "It might be best to lay off the sparring until the Reapers actually give up something substantial. We might need to make a deal with them sooner rather than later. It'll only get worse from here."

"We're waiting for Red Zone. Any deal we make has to work for everyone," I mutter. "*If* we make one."

I've done war. I'm not looking for another one.

Don't know how the fuck we're going to avoid it, though.

I swipe the list from him, and there's a dozen names. The lead fucking weight on my shoulders gets twelve times heavier. I know these people. I even like some of them.

And they're starving.

God damn it. Why *did* I make this my problem? The thought of anyone dying because I decided to measure my dick against Dom's as captain is like a hot pit in my gut.

My eyes drop to the bottom of the page.

Kasey's name is on the fucking list, right under Ethel's.

Sweat pools under my pits. Is it really getting that bad? The kid needs to be okay. I can't . . . I can't take losing another Ryan.

Even if it does mean war.

Beau is still eyeing me, and I shrug, crumpling the list. "Whatever. The plan stands. We'll make a call after we talk to Red Zone. Either we fuck the Reapers off and take the shit they have here, or we join them. Ethel will be back to knitting throw blankets and being a nosey shit again soon."

"Right."

I glower at him. "You think I don't have this? No one's fucking dying."

He gives me a dry look, then turns back to sorting through supplies. "If you want an ego stroke, Jayk, you've got our girl in your bed, and she's probably more than willing. But this isn't dire yet, just something we ought to keep an eye on."

"Mine. *My* girl," I remind him.

It's been a fucking nightmare keeping them away from each other. Between the five of them, they have too many damn hands.

And Eden is sneaky.

Beau examines a strip of cloth, grimacing over a stain. "There are more than a few smart heads here. I'm sure it'll get sorted out. Eden's slop won't hurt anyone—I did check—and I'm taking care of everyone who needs medical help, I promise. We've got your back." He glances up, then smirks. "About this, anyway."

I grunt in sour acknowledgement.

Yeah. They're a real dream.

The assholes were like frags set to blow today after I rerouted the hot water away from their room. The memory makes me want to smirk. They might have their dicks in a knot over Eden, but they haven't been completely useless about everything else, thank fuck. We have a plan—and no one's shooting at each other, so it's looking up.

I tuck the list into my pocket. "I'll deal with it."

"You will." Beau looks up from the mess in front of him to level me with a serious stare. "And get some sleep? You spend all night throwing Eden against every loose surface you can find and both of you are going to end up on that list, soon enough."

Eden's pale face today slams into my head, and I stiffen. "The shit does that mean?"

His eyes look up to the ceiling, then back to me. "You need small words, asshole? Food good. Rest good. Use too much energy—bad. No energy for smart, sexy librarians and smart, sexy librarians end up here. In the med bay. With me."

His teeth flash in a smile.

"Funny," I grit out, and he snorts softly.

I examine his face, trying to tell if this is his latest ploy to keep me away from Eden, but . . . even I can admit, the doc doesn't usually fuck around with the medical stuff.

Then again, he was really fucking pissed about his shit getting dumped.

"Whatever. I'm taking care of her now." I smirk. "In fact, I'm thinking she ain't going to even be thinking about shitty, forgettable doctors anytime soon."

Beau's eyes flash dark. Smug, I rap my knuckles on his desk and turn to leave. I'm two steps from the door when a throaty, husky voice I recognize too fucking well crackles behind me.

"Jayk made me fight him again, poking at me until I did . . ." There's a brief buzz, then, *"He—he dragged me up his body until I was kneeling over his face."*

I whip around, spotting the tape recorder Beau has in one hand. He fast-forwards again, and Eden is panting—moaning like she does when she's fucking lost for it.

Beau's voice crackles from the recorder. *"Now Miss Anderson, do you really expect me to believe this cunt is all torn up because you rode a man's face and soaked him in your cum?"* He tsks. *"It is not advised that you lie to your doctor, my girl."*

Eden's raw, needy voice begs, *"Please, Doctor Bennett, there's more. I'll tell you. Don't stop . . . helping me. Please."*

Raw, furious horror floods me. "The fucking shit is that?"

Is she talking about fucking *me*?

Beau smirks back at me, crossing his arms behind his head and leaning back in his chair. His thumb presses the play button again.

"Please, Doctor Bennett, help me. It hurts."

Then again.

"I trust you, Doctor Bennett."

That one hits me like a gut punch . . . the shaky, vulnerable way she says it.

In front of me, Beau's grin becomes taunting. "Sounds to me like she enjoys her doctor visits just fine, don't you think?"

Rage punches through me, horrified and blinding. "You *son of a*—"

"Nah, not my mama, Jayk. Don't worry. I'll make you a copy. Lucky already has one, though the little shit edited me out." His expression turns condescending as fuck. "Eden's fine with it. In case you missed it, she did make it clear—she's *good* with sharing."

In seconds, I'm on him, hauling him over his desk, deciding whether I'm going to smash his face or the recorder first.

"Jayk! There . . ." Kasey skids to a stop in the doorway, breathing hard, and I stop, my fist raised to punch Beau in his stupid square jaw. "There you are."

Beau scrambles to turn the recorder off, just as Eden starts breaking apart.

I drop Beau and move toward the door, looking over Kasey's shoulder, fear disrupting my rage. "What—?"

"Eden. Lucky. Took off. Ten minutes ago."

Relief crashes into me hard.

It takes me a full ten seconds to shrug it off.

Okay, so Eden being with him isn't as bad as an attack, so what? It's still not *good*.

"Nice. Where?" I grill her.

"Aw, come on now, Jayk. Leave 'em be," Beau bitches.

Kasey shrugs her narrow shoulders. "I didn't see. I went outside, and I don't think they were there. Maybe inside somewhere?"

"Jayk. You're doing too much," Beau tries again, but I smirk at him.

"Weren't you just saying how no one should be touching her? Just doing my part." I point at the recorder. "Delete that fucking shit."

He grins. "Not going to happen. You take care of our girl."

I flip him off as I leave, trying to ignore the way the crush in my chest increases.

I fucked Eden a lot last night. A *lot*. There are rabbits high on pheromones that got railed less than she did, and shit. *Is* that why she's been so sleepy? I burned her out, bouncing on my dick?

I haven't seen her since this morning. Every fucking person had a question, and I had ten thousand things to do today. Kasey had eyes on her, though, she would have said if she looked bad. Even the fucking circus rat can't break her in ten minutes.

My stomach growls at me as I duck my head into the gym, looking for her—then back out when someone swears and throws a bra in my face.

Whatever. Not in there.

I head toward the kitchen.

My gut has been bitching at me all day over the missed rations, but I've ignored it. That shit doesn't matter. Used to do it all the time for Ryan, too.

She's not in the kitchen.

I glare at the empty space, then pivot.

I know Eden had shit to do today—and thank fuck she knows what to do with the weird ass collection of ingredients we have left—but this is stupid. I don't care if she's with Lucky, doesn't she know I need to see her?

Damn slippery woman.

My skin starts to itch, and I take the stairs in twos. My temper is starting to get testy when I slam open the library doors . . . only to see Eden's skirt around her waist and Lucky's hands on her ass as he presses her into a heavy bookcase.

Ten minutes is too fucking long.

"Lucky!" She *giggles*—like he's pitching stand-up and not trying to sink his dick in her. "Lucky, the shelves! Ah! Oh, *careful*!"

Several books crash to the floor, and I storm over as he kisses her again.

"Beautiful, you're really making me question your priorities here. Now, tell me I'm being too loud. Oh! And my library fees are overdue!"

"Wait, why wouldn't you pay your library fees?"

The blond rat starts cackling into her neck, and I see red.

"They help sustain our programs! Pay your fees, Lucky!"

"How about I work it out in trade?"

"How about you don't?" Shoving him back, I scoop Eden over my shoulder, then turn and storm back out.

She's fine. She's mine, and she's fine.

"Son of a— *Again*?" Lucky shouts after me.

This time, she doesn't struggle. Hanging over my back, Eden sighs. "Really?"

"You seemed upset." I shrug, and she bounces as I cross the interior balcony to our room.

She seems better than this morning—steadier—and my resolve strengthens. Sweet cheeks over here needs to *rest*.

To my ass, she mutters, "Scene of questionable sexiness aside, you know I wasn't."

I slam the door shut beside us and dump her on the bed, and she raises one finger, crawling up onto her knees.

"Oh no, if you think we are doing *anything* after you dragged me away from Lucky, you are *dead wrong*."

Crossing my arms, I lean back against the door, and her eyes dip to my chest. She dampens her lips with the tip of her tongue, and I roll my eyes.

Maybe Beau is fucking with me.

But maybe he's not.

It ain't a risk I'm taking, not until I have a deal in hand and our pantry fully restocked.

"Unwet your panties, sugar. You and me?" I smirk at her. "We're going platonic."

CHAPTER 37

DOMINIC

B eau leans over the floorplan of Bristlebrook. "What if we lock most of the civilians in the gym so they can't—"

"Too far." Jasper turns a page in his book, dimly lit by the orange glow of his lamp. His reading glasses are perched on his nose.

"Not *permanently*," Beau grumbles.

Lucky clicks his fingers. "I still have a few frags I could—"

"No!" we all say in unison.

"There. That's our opportunity." My pointer slaps over the floorplan. "Lucky, you go in. Take out the wires—that's just for the AC. It's fucked anyway with all the windows, but Jayk has been running it anyway. He hates the heat."

"I don't know. How do we know he won't just send Jada in? She's better with electrics than him," Beau argues, his head beside mine as we lean over the dimly lit table in Jasper's room.

Shit. Jada. She could fuck this up. The civilians have been more skilled in wrecking our ops than I anticipated. Only, losing to them— even losing to Jayk—hasn't felt like failure. For the first time since I can remember, planning and running these attacks with the guys has actually made for a good time.

The possessive asshole is hard to beat.

Lucky shakes his head. "Nah, Jada's fixing the kitchen wiring. He won't pull her off that. I'll take care of it, Cap."

I stiffen, the fun of it fading. "I told you to can it with that. I'm not your captain."

Lucky and Beau lift their heads from the battle map to look at me, and I grit my teeth, staring them down. Jasper raises an eyebrow from his chair—the same one he sits in during the sessions we've started back up this week.

He's had plenty to say about my relationship with authority.

Most of it has been ruthless.

While we've been deep in the trenches of our war against Jayk, he's been waging his own against me and Beau in this damn room.

But now, all he says is, "Once again, I feel the need to advise everyone to stop indulging Jaykob with this behavior. No, it isn't half as satisfying to be polite and *negotiate*, but I do think that my more measured approach with him is starting to yield results—and without placing any added stress on Eden. I do believe he'll grant her an audience with me soon. Patience wins out, I guarantee it."

We all stare at him for a moment, thoughtfully.

"Yeah, I'm not doing that," Lucky says.

"Jayk isn't conceding you shit," I tell him dryly.

"Did I tell you I told him that fucking her would put her in a medical coma?" Beau asks smugly, and I snort.

Jasper sighs, returning to reading his textbook under the lamp.

"You got him to stop fucking her?" Lucky asks, a laugh in his voice. When Beau grins, shrugging, he snorts, then bursts into laughter. "I can't believe he *did* it. That's . . ." He stops, then turns back with wide eyes. "Oh man, Eden's going to *kill* you."

Beau points at him. "You cut those wires, I'll make it up to her."

I give him a dark look. He *knows* we're taking things slow with her. We've still got things to work through.

Beau gives me an innocent smile back. It's the same one he used to give his mama after he stole her fresh-baked pies out of the oven.

I look back down at the map. This could work.

"What about Eden? It all hinges on her. If she doesn't take the opening . . ."

"You'll be fine." Lucky slings an arm over my shoulder. "Eden has war plans, too."

CHAPTER 38

EDEN

I 'm almost at breaking point.

It's been five days since the raid. Five days since the Reapers set up camp. The Red Zone representatives still aren't here . . . and Jayk hasn't given an *inch* of ground to the others.

Or to me.

If I have to spend one more night with his cock drilling a hole into my spine and not be able to do anything about it, I'm going to scream.

Platonic, he says. Asshole. If I get my hands on whoever put that ridiculous, absurd idea into Jayk's overprotective head, they're *dust*.

Simmering with frustration, I pick up my tray. The full pitcher of ice-cold water and the softly scented, rolled towelettes are prettily displayed. It was the kind of thing I used to arrange for Henry's parties, in a different life, but on a much smaller scale.

I just hope it does the trick.

Ava looks me up and down, not budging from in front of the door.

"Left pocket," I mutter.

She raises a brow, then reaches in, tugging free a small, wrapped parcel. She sniffs it and shivers. "So worth it." She steps out of the way, holding the kitchen door open for me. She tilts her head consideringly.

"Hey, so if you feel like losing your shit at Jayk for being unreasonable, kicking him out, and choosing yourself over the dick bouquet, I'll split my winnings with you."

Winnings? Are they . . . *betting* on me?

Again?

"Possibly to the first part, no to the second, and I'd like to choose myself *and* the dick bouquet, thank you very much," I tell her politely, and she sighs.

"Yeah. It was long odds."

I blow out a laugh as we head outside, and she helps me down the stairs. The humidity is as bad outside as it was inside; it's like wading through a warm pond. Sweat beads in the small of my back, and it *pools* under my heavy hair, which I've left loose and flowing.

Right at this moment, I'm regretting it.

We pass Ethel, looking thinner and frailer than usual, scolding a stubborn-faced Kasey—again.

"I was being *safe*! It didn't matter anyway," Kasey sulks. "They moved the food. I couldn't get you anything."

"That's not the point, my girl. You can't just take risks like . . ."

In the distance, I see Pete and Buck across the moat, chatting to Mila. Buck throws her something, and her laugh carries over the lawn.

A part of me had hoped that the Reapers would have given in by now and offered more food, particularly as things have become more dire, but it's a part I try not to let get out of hand. They're holding their advantage. We can hold our defenses.

They've still been very sweet, on the whole. Last night, they even put on an impromptu concert. Cole, as it turns out, has quite a passable singing voice—though since the news from their farmlands, the songs were far from happy.

Softly, I smile at Ava. "There's lots of potential bouquets out there now. Why don't you go give everyone something more interesting to bet on?"

Ava grimaces, glancing at the Reapers. It's twilight, but Jennifer and Sawyer have met back up for dinner today, as well as breakfast this morning.

They're sitting almost in the middle of the bridge, their feet dangling over the pikes.

The two other heavy, unused bridges for the moat lie stacked nearby, gathering dust, and I wonder, a little wistfully, if they'll ever be used. If we'll ever have enough trust to allow that kind of open access to Bristlebrook again.

Maybe with enough new friends or lovers.

More people kicking their feet over dangerous ground.

"Yeah, I'm good."

At my amused nod, she snorts. "Look, don't get me wrong, I love the *idea* of men—it's just the reality I have a problem with." She shivers. "They just have so many *opinions*. I like them better on that side of the moat. Or, you know, in my head."

I press my lips together to hide my smile, looking at her sideways. "Mhm."

She doesn't smile back. "Eden . . . are we joining up with them?"

My smile fades. "I don't know." My stomach is in knots just thinking of what's to come. "I don't know, Ava."

It won't be long before we need to make a decision and, selfishly, I wish I could drag it out as long as possible. Right now, my brutes are safe.

I'm not ready for that to change.

She nods, but her hands are impatient, settling over her pistol, then her belt. "Look, Jennifer, Clare, Sara—a lot of them, they have no problem with it." Something dark flickers over her features. "But, for me, even before Day Death, there were things that . . . I just can't. . ."

My throat thickens. "I know."

Ava's shoulders relax when I don't argue. "It was one thing going to Red Zone, you know? Heather supported the op, and they'd been giving us information for weeks. They had women and kids there— maybe not thriving, but they were content enough. And Bentley helped get Heather back . . . They stepped up."

The grass crunches underneath our feet.

"You came back here," I venture.

"Because Heather vouched for them." Ava's lips curve in a dangerous smile. "We also had your men more than a little outnumbered. It was different. It was always our choice." Her gaze flicks back to the Reapers boxing us in. "I don't like being pressured."

My hollow stomach clenches.

We're already almost through the raided supplies, and I'm almost entirely back on a slop-only diet. Yesterday, Ethel was put on official bed rest in the med bay, right along with Shelby, whose blood pressure keeps dropping.

I don't like being pressured, either—whether I understand their desperation or not.

Ava touches my arm, slowing me, careful not to disrupt my tray.

"We'll do it, you know? We'll go with them. If you think it's a good idea."

Hesitating, I shift my tray. "You mean if Jayk does?"

"No." Ava meets my eyes. "Not the men. Not for this."

But . . . why me?

As if she can see the question, she gives me a stiff smile. "Jasper was right, Eden. You got us out of Cyanide."

"Not all of us," I reply, and the quick surge of guilt makes my voice sharp.

Every day, I think about Heather and Bentley.

Ava nods, her face as grim as mine, and I sigh. Over by the dry moat, Mila is so close, she's almost pressed against the barbed wire. She wolf-whistles at Buck as he buckles a heavy bag onto Cherub the mule's back.

"I don't know if I trust them," I say to Ava. "But I know that if we do join up with them . . . it will be because it's the best option we have."

She exhales heavily. "I was really hoping this would be a more reassuring conversation."

I give her a rueful smile. "Sorry." I watch Buck turn red to his receding hairline as he stammers something back to Mila. "They do seem okay."

Ava looks over to watch the Reapers too, her eyes on Jennifer's feet kicking happily over the bridge.

"Yeah. They do." Her voice is heavy as she adds, "But men lie."

My throat fills, and I don't know if it's with fear or wistfulness.

But my gaze drifts, finding the two men grinning like five-year-olds over their matching bows, and it begins to ease.

"Some don't," I whisper, and Ava follows my gaze.

After a moment, she nods softly. "Some don't."

When Jennifer—pierced, tattooed, took-out-five-Sinners-without-flinching-at-Cyanide, tough-as-nails Jennifer—starts giggling helplessly, Ava rolls her eyes.

"Come on."

CHAPTER 39

EDEN

SURVIVAL TIP #286
Consider your cheese vs man ratio carefully.

We approach the makeshift archery range the civilians set up beside the apple tree to practice.

Only Dom and Beau are still out here, fumbling with their bows under the searing, final light of day.

And Jayk, wonderfully, is buried in a crawlspace somewhere, fixing something or other that I hope is really, really broken.

I'm taking my opportunities where I can get them.

"No. No, why are you gripping it there?" Sloane shouts down at Dom and Beau. Her rifle is still on her lap, and there are a few others scattered on the defensive platforms, but their attention to the Reapers is inattentive at best. "Dom, get him to lift his . . . *No*! Keep your feet planted. Jesus, Beau. You think you can hop your way to a bullseye? No, I said lift your *chest*."

She sighs, massaging her eyes with tattooed fingers as Dom snorts a laugh.

"Please don't make me come down there again; I really can't be fucked." Sloane sighs.

My palms grow sweaty—well, sweat*ier*—on the tray.

I feel like I haven't seen them properly in days, and it's days too long.

I pause on the sidelines as Beau finally lets an arrow fly toward the target. Despite Sloane's scathing commentary, it does actually arc up quite nicely.

Right before it thuds into one of the stacked bridges, about eighty yards toward the moat, and far to the left of the archery area. Nowhere near his own target—but close enough to where Jennifer and Sawyer are sitting that they both startle, swiveling to look.

"What the fuck, Beau?" Jennifer calls, and Beau winces.

"Sorry!" He lowers the bow, and his bare, slick chest glistens as he twists to look at the arrow. "Huh. Didn't realize they could shoot that far."

"Gets pretty fucking hard to be accurate after about fifty or sixty yards. Thirty for most people here," Sloane tells him lazily, then she eyes the arrow. "Ten for you."

He examines his bow, a grin edging his mouth as he draws back again. "Give me three days, and I bet I outshoot you."

Sloane snorts. "Put meds on it and deal."

After Beau's next shot goes just as wide in the opposite direction, Dom claps him on the back, muttering something amused and caustic that I can't make out.

My gaze is stuck to Beau's abs. I don't care where the arrow went. Right at this moment, I'm fairly sure he's the best bow-person I've ever seen. A drop of sweat drips down the ridges of his abs, and my brain fuzzes out.

Archer, that's the word.

Sure, it's only been a few days, but it's been a few days of Jayk wrapping his naked body around me and being none too careful about where he rests his hands.

Plus, I'm fairly sure I'm ovulating.

This is not my fault, is my point.

"Well, hi there, darlin'."

Dom turns sharply, his smirk falling away as he takes me in—and just as quickly searches behind me.

Looking for a barging, possessive caveman on my heels, I assume.

"You know," Sloane says lazily, looking down at me like a warrior queen. Or a Domme. "I'm under orders to let Jayk know when you try to talk to them." Her gaze flicks over to Ava. "So are you."

Ava grins. "She made it worth my while. She had *cheese.*"

"Well, well, well."

Panicked, I stare between them. "It's everything I have!"

Sitting back appreciatively, Sloane grins too. Waiting.

I look at Dom and Beau, watching me curiously, bows in hand. Dom tugs something off his fingers, and his gaze trails over my tray. I look back over my shoulder at Bristlebrook, but there's still no sign of Jayk. This could be my only shot.

Oh, damn it. *Fine.*

"Right pocket," I grit out between clenched teeth, and Ava laughs, yanking it out.

Mournfully, I watch her hand over the last of the precious, precious contraband that Lucky had smuggled me, and I question all my choices.

I have five men and no cheese.

She has no men but lots of cheese.

I have regrets.

"Satisfied?" I ask as Sloane flips open the wrapping to check it.

She bites her full lip hard with a dark, satisfied sound, then looks down at me dubiously. "Are *you*?" Shaking her head, she doesn't wait for an answer as she stands and stretches. "I'm heading to platform three. I bet my rations on these two getting past Jayk anyway."

Outraged, I wheel around. "Then give me back my cheese!"

Sloane snorts. She climbs down from the platform, then joins Ava as they leave me, finally, alone with Dom and Beau.

"For the record, I'm the one getting past Jayk, not them," I call after Sloane.

"Well, we helped. Those wires didn't cut themselves," Dom says dryly from very close behind me, and I jump, jostling the tray.

God, he's sneaky!

Beau comes up beside him, wiping his forehead with a laugh. "Lucky pulled through. Here's hoping Jayk didn't kill him for it."

And they're off cutting *wires* now? I bite my tongue in exasperation.

That's not why I'm here.

As if sensing my nervousness, Dom's gaze drops to everything I've brought. Unlike Beau, he's in a loose shirt, but the column of his throat is still damp with sweat.

"You brought this for us?"

His tone is unreadable, but there's something taut in his expression—like the bow he has in his hand. Nerves quiver in my stomach as I try to remember what I rehearsed.

"Y-yes, I . . ." I make the mistake of looking up into Beau's intent multi-hued eyes, and I dampen my lips. "I know you were . . . hesitant . . . about me submitting to you, Dom." His name feels uncomfortable in my mouth, but I force myself to use it. "But I prepared just a few small things. I'd really like to share them with you while I . . . I have a few things to say. If that's okay," I add hastily.

Beau's brows twitch up, and they exchange a slow look I can't parse out.

Sweat drips down my neck.

"Of course, darlin'. Whatever you want," Beau says.

Blowing out a breath, I work up a smile and gesture toward the apple tree for them to sit. The lights strung through it are off, but the day is glowing gently, like a candle sinking low at the end of its wick.

They lean their bows up against the trunk, which is finally starting to show signs of new growth, and they stretch out on the ground between its roots. I'm not sure they even notice how they arrange their long limbs in precisely the same way.

I place the tray on the ground and carefully pour out two cups of icy cold water.

I try to hide how much my hands are shaking.

"The first thing I wanted to share is that . . . I miss you both. This game is starting to frustrate me. A lot." I hand off their cups, and duck their surprised expressions. "I do really appreciate you all supporting Jayk with everything else though. It's made a difference in him." I shake my head. "I don't know, maybe even this silly game has made a difference. I don't think he's hurting quite so much, and . . . well, that means everything." I try to remember my notes. "I have more, just . . . give me a moment?"

I pick up one of the cool, scented towels and unroll it. I look between them. "May I?"

Dom doesn't look at the towel. His eyes don't leave my face. "What are you doing, pet?"

Color stings my cheeks, though I knew this was coming.

"I— Lucky and I thought, maybe this could be one way for us to start. If I could come to you every day, maybe I could help you get ready, or take a moment to relax. It doesn't have to be long. But I would promise to always show up, and to always share something." I bite my lip. "And I'd like you to listen without judgment."

Beau drags in a breath through his nose, nodding like that one stung a little, and my heart tugs. I don't want to hurt him—it's not meant as a slight. It's just what I need.

"A ritual," he says. "Just for us."

It's not a question, but I nod anyway. Whether Jasper intended for me to find it so or not, the research for my outstanding essay has been fascinating. Jasper's books had a wealth of interesting concepts. This was one I enjoyed. The structure of it, but also the reverence. The grace. It has an orderliness I could find romantic.

"Is that all you want from this?" Dom asks.

He's potent in front of me. Large and powerful . . . and *contained*. Cool water squeezes between my fingers, and I realize I'm gripping the damp towel too tightly.

"If . . . if you're comfortable, I'd like you both to lead this. Tell me what you want." Before they can say anything, I add in a rush, "It doesn't have to be anything sexual, Dom. And of course, if you don't want to do this at all, that is *fine*, I swear."

Beau's lips quirk up. His eyes travel over my face with so much banked heat that I'm left in no doubt about how *he* feels.

"You can call me *sir*, Eden," Dom says softly, and I bend my head over the tray, my lids fluttering closed.

Relief slides into me like a knife.

"Thank you." I look up at him through my lashes, my heart pounding. "Sir."

I realize Dom is holding himself very still.

When he doesn't say anything else, Beau instructs in a lazy, pleased drawl, "Cool us down, darlin'."

I shiver at the order, the easy bite of firmness to it. I love everything Jayk does to me, with me, but he's not as big on ordering me around. He tends to just put me where he wants me.

I've missed this, even as small as it is. Even if I shouldn't.

The more independence I get at Bristlebrook—Jayk's war notwithstanding—the more desperately I've craved to give it up elsewhere.

I walk around to Dom, and I hesitate, remembering their words the other day. Awkwardly, I crouch beside him.

His voice is low and rough when he says, "Get on your knees, pet."

A throb starts up low in my abdomen, my breathing shallowing. I glance around, suddenly feeling vulnerable, wondering if it's inappropriate to have done this outside where anyone can see. Civilians are scattered over the defenses, their rifles loosely in hand. The Reapers are wandering around, going about their business.

"What are you feeling?" Beau leans back on one hand, watching me.

The *seen* feeling increases, and I look at his face. He's patient and waiting, as soft with understanding as Dom is stern and unreadable. Beau has always made room for my feelings. For my thoughts.

"Nervous," I admit. "Exposed."

"Well, that's fair," he murmurs, and I wait—for the reasons why it's okay. Why I should continue anyway. Maybe an order. Possibly even an assurance that I could stop.

But he doesn't say anything else.

He just lets my feelings be okay.

Warm, liquid sunshine springs to life in my chest, and I smile at him, relaxing. The corner of his mouth lifts further, cozy and kind.

I slip smoothly from my awkward crouch into a kneel, and it's comfortable in ways that go so much deeper than the way my muscles flow. It makes me fall very close to Dom. Intimately close. I lift the washcloth to his face, and he turns it toward me. Watching me.

His eyes burn hot.

Not a single thing searing behind them is contained.

Slowly, I press the damp cloth to his sweaty temple, letting the cool water well up against his skin before I drag it away. With gentle care, I tend his face, wiping the dirt from the heavy ridges of his cheekbones and around the swell of his lips. I'm close enough that I can see every fleck of stubble on his jaw. I can count every blunt, black eyelash and feel every breath whisper over my skin. I drag the cloth down his neck, cooling the damp space at the base of his hair that I want to dig my fingers into. I ache as he shudders.

My skin isn't even in contact with his, but it feels deeply intimate. With his eyes locked on my face for every stroke, the dangerous weight of him beside me, I really could be tending to a weary warrior after a long battle.

The breeze stirs, balmy and thick, and it fans strands of my hair over my face. They stick on my lips, over my glasses, and Dom lifts a dirt-stained hand to tuck the strands behind my ear.

I'm shaking by the time I dip the cloth into the shallow bowl of cleaning water and take his hand from my face.

"Tell me more," he orders softly as I clean it. "Tell me a secret."

I turn his hand over, and he shivers as I slide the towel over his palm. "I don't trust the Reapers," I tell them. "I don't, and I've been thinking a lot about why—why, when they've done almost nothing to deserve it, I struggle with it. Why I still sometimes struggle with all of you." I sigh. "And the more I thought about it, I think I can't figure it out because there is no reason. I just think it might be me. I've never trusted anyone easily—especially men . . . and especially over the last few years. I did everything for myself, and that was it. It's become an instinct."

I stop moving the cloth, realizing his hands are more than clean. They're large and strong and steady under mine. I squeeze his hand lightly and look up.

Our gazes crash together.

"I want to create new instincts."

A deep, rumbling sound erupts from Dom's chest, his face inching closer. His eyes are intent, intense, and the tiny hairs lift on the back of my neck.

By now, I know the feeling of being hunted.

"What are your instincts saying now?" Beau teases gently, but his eyes as heated and heavy-lidded as Dom's. His accent is sinfully thick, and this time, I don't think it's on purpose.

Dom's mouth hovers over mine, and he watches me as our breaths twist together, our lips barely brushing. I can feel the hot, demanding heat of him like a waiting avalanche, just a brutal, bone-jarring millimeter away.

But he's not Jayk.

I'm his to claim, not the other way around. Not unless he commands it.

There's a sharp, punishing whistle from the music room window, and Dom looks up.

Away.

I shudder, heat pounding through me with ferocious force.

"Incoming," Sloane shouts down, throwing a thumb back behind her, and disappointment throbs—so acutely in this moment that frustration burns in my throat, and the usual humor I can find in it is missing.

Maybe this *is* how they bond, but I'm ready for it to be over now.

Dom seems to be thinking along similar lines. "Motherfucker," he curses, reaching for his bag. "I'll take care of it. You two stay here." His expression is intent, grim—more certain than I've seen it since Cyanide. "I'll buy you a few hours."

I want a few hours with *both* of them. I want a lifetime.

But for now, I'll take what Dom can buy me . . . and I'll continue making sure Jayk knows he'll always be a priority. That I'm not leaving him, no matter what.

Because *that's* where this comes from. Jayk has been left behind too many times.

And him needing to know that I won't is the only reason I haven't castrated him in his sleep.

So I nod to Dom, accepting it, and he stops, looking at my face.

"Is that okay?" he asks.

A question from Dom always sounds like it borders on a command, but there's something in him right now that feels like he's waiting on an answer. That if I told him right now it wasn't okay, he'd string up that bow and hold Jayk back by whatever means necessary.

He's listening.

Some of the tension eases from me, and my next nod is easier. "Yes, sir. It's okay. Thank you."

My gaze slips to his mouth, and I bite down on the miserable, regretful whimper that wants to escape me.

"Anything else you feel like sharing, little librarian?" he asks, and this time, his deep voice is dryer than dust.

I look up from his mouth, and his eyes are still molten. The things behind them are still scalding enough to make me flush.

"I want you. I want you so badly I think I would strip naked right here if you asked."

The husky words are out of me before I've thought them through, and Dom's eyes flare. Behind him, Beau groans. Distantly, there's a commotion in the house, but none of us pay it any attention.

Dom's gaze runs over my body, hot and impatient. "Then kiss me, pet. Make it count."

His order takes me by the throat.

I press up onto my knees, my hands tangling around his jaw and neck until my fingers press into that perfect hollow at his nape. My mouth collides against his, a desperate moan escaping me as I suck his heavy lower lip. He tastes like fire and dynamite, and like the other day by the cave, he takes control with fierce, uncompromising dominance.

He owns my mouth, overwhelming me easily until I'm squirming against him, riveted by need and trying to crawl up onto his lap.

He's never finished inside me. I've never seen him come.

God, all the *ways* I need to be fucked by this man.

Suddenly, his mouth is gone, and he wrenches to his feet. I fall back to my knees, back to the dirt, shaking. Throbbing and dazed.

Dom drags his hand over his mouth, looking down at me.

"Every day, pet. We find time every day for this."

I gasp for air. "Jaykob—"

"Jayk can keep his nights for now, but your mornings are for us. I had fun with his game, but I'm done playing." Dom's jaw firms, and his eyes blaze as his shoulders—finally—straighten. "Come to us at dawn. No one will stop you. You have my word, Eden."

My lips part, as pure, filthy lust shudders through me.

Just like that, I believe him.

I don't know what he's about to do, or say, but this is our commander, and he's taking control.

"Yes, sir. I'll be there."

He nods once, then storms toward the house. Civilians part around him like water, and I'm not sure they even realize they're doing it.

"About time. I was wondering how long it would take before he stopped playing nice," Beau drawls.

I duck my head, trying to steady my breathing. "The tripwires? The sucker punch on the porch? That was *nice*?"

Beau just smiles at me. "Not as nice as we plan on being to you."

Wicked, sinful things are alive in that smile, and I become aware of how he's stretched out over the grass. Of all that bare, naked flesh I can do very little with out here.

Silently, I pick up the other cloth without looking at it.

"That's right, darlin'." His eyes twinkle in the fading light. "Don't you forget about me."

In my mind, Dom's hand is on my ass and Beau's cock is in my mouth as he demands that very attention. Wetting my lips, I kneel closer to him and press the cloth over his chest. Over his heart.

"I'd sooner forget to breathe," I tell him fiercely.

His face softens, and slowly, I slide the cloth over his skin. Suddenly, he catches my wrist.

"I have something to share, too."

Apprehensively, I pause. I hadn't really anticipated that, but it is only fair.

Beau's tongue slides over his lower lip, but his expression is serious now and a little hesitant. His thumb coasts over my wrist.

"I'm sorry for how I treated you after Cyanide. I was unkind and unproductive and ... I shouldn't have cut you out. I was so caught up in being hurt that you didn't talk to me, I didn't stop to think about why. I made it worse than it had to be, and I'm sorry I hurt you. I never meant to make you feel like I didn't still care."

He sighs, and something in me eases at the ring of sincerity in his voice.

I knew he was sorry. Sorry enough that he's been meeting with Jasper often.

I'm still glad he said it.

"It won't happen again, Eden. I'll talk to you if I have a problem, I promise." He grimaces uncomfortably. "If I'm mad."

"When."

He looks up, and I smile softly.

"When you get mad," I correct him. "It will happen, Beau. Just like I was mad at you for being a wretched, miserable, uncommunicative plague on my days."

His lips part incredulously, and he huffs a laugh. His thumb stops tracing patterns on my wrist, and he grasps it, yanking me, and I collapse over him.

The green in his eyes becomes wooded, the gold sparkling. "More honesty." His lips tilt. "Keep it coming, pet. I can take it."

Wrapping a hand around my cheek, he kisses me deeply.

When he finally stops, I'm breathless and filled with the same elated giggles I hear whispering from the bridge, and my whole body is shivering as I pick up the cloth again.

I clean him, and we flirt.

We flirt until the flirting turns to talking, and we talk until it flows like air. We talk long past sunset, and for once, no one comes to bother us. Beau tucks me against the new sprouts in the tree and sinks me between its roots with kisses that feel like home. We talk about serious things and inane things, and his therapy with Jasper. We touch on my worries and hopes and I give up pieces of secrets like I'm baring my throat, and he takes them carefully, *gratefully*, like he's seeing now how much they cost me to reveal. We talk about my past and my herbs and he asks questions about tinctures and teas with rapt attention.

We talk and flirt, and he holds me until we fall asleep against the tree the way we used to in our bed.

We fall asleep to I love yous.

I fall asleep with hope.

CHAPTER 40

BEAU

SURVIVAL TIP #345
Catch yourself a friend.
Use a net.

I wake to a rustling. Hard roots digging into my back. A tugging. The warm, soft body draped over me being ripped away.

My eyes fly open.

Eden is wriggling in Jayk's arms, her eyes wide over the hand he has slapped over her mouth. In the pitch dark of the night, he spares one stupid, unholy smirk for me—then bolts.

"You asshole!"

I lurch to my feet, my muscles stiff and aching from where they were wedged into the tree and hard earth.

I only make it two steps before something cracks, then whistles, and my feet are whipping out from under me, and I'm launched up into the sky. The tight-woven camo net snaps into place around me, bound tight at the top, and I flail, pushing at it, kicking and ripping and doing everything in my God-given power to tear free, but it's professional grade and professionally rigged.

I reach for my hunting knife—the only thing I might be able to use to cut myself free . . . but he's taken that too.

Son of a goat-breeding pissbucket.

I'm guessing that Jayk's not taking too kindly to Dom's new Eden schedule.

I slump inside my net as it bobs under the heaviest branch of the apple tree.

"Anyone!" I call out. My sorry, flaunting ass decided today was a good day to go shirtless, so I don't even have the whistle on my kit, but the civilians *had* to have seen that. "Anyone? Get me down?"

No footsteps approach. In fact, I can hear almost nothing at all, until . . .

"Anyone have a bet on that?"

Sighing, I settle in for a long, uncomfortable night.

CHAPTER 41

EDEN

SURVIVAL TIP #76
*A problem shared
is a problem lessened.*

I clutch my notepad to my stomach, staring at the door looming larger and larger. It's getting closer. *I'm* getting closer to *it*, more precisely, and maybe this is a mistake.

Closer still, and now I can make out the detail on the door handle.

Nope, no, okay. This is definitely a mistake. I shouldn't even be thinking about this. I should find something more useful to do.

I turn on my heel and walk three steps in the opposite direction before I stop. As it has every day this week, sweat beads under my arms. Under my hair. At this point, it could be the heat or the nerves.

Coward, I berate myself.

It's been a week since our raid, and the sad truth is there *isn't* anything else to do. I have enough slop for days already made, and it's too hot to work in the garden. I can't help more with the Reapers, or do anything else for the civilians—not unless they actually start doing more than sipping at my food. And this is the first moment I've had where Jayk or any of the civilians he's set to spy on me aren't on my tail.

So I should do this now.

I turn back around, just as Jennifer limps out of Jasper's room, her eyes red-rimmed and unseeing. I touch her arm as she passes me, and she startles like I slapped her.

"Are you okay?"

It takes her a moment, but she forces a smile. "I'm fine, it's just . . ." She adjusts the journal under her arm, and understanding fills me.

I nod, squeezing her arm. "Me too."

Her eyes gloss, and she nods at me in silent understanding before she shuffles on. My chest aches as she leaves.

There's been more than a few tears and silent stares recently. The Reapers are bringing up a lot for everyone—even Dom and Beau have been in here frequently, together and separate. Whether it's for friendship or sessions I'm not sure, but I'm happy for them either way.

I wish I could be spending half as much time with any of them, but at least Dom's word held true.

When I'd slipped out of bed at dawn after Jayk's kidnapping, Jayk didn't say a word—just stared at the ceiling as I left. Admittedly, I hadn't thought our next "getting ready" ritual would involve Dom and me cutting poor Beau out of an apple tree, but it was a unique kind of bonding experience. Better yet, the civilians didn't try to stop us, on behalf of Jayk or their own bets, and that was another plus.

It's progress.

Now, if there's a chance of making even half that progress with Jasper . . .

He's the next piece on my board to take.

His door is still ajar, and I step toward it more quickly now, needing to see him. I inch it open . . . and then pause at the sight.

Jasper is discomposed. His silken hair is mussed, like he's been running his hands through it. His buttons are loose, his shirt crumpled, and he's massaging his forehead as he writes in the book on his lap, his reading glasses low on his nose and tension bracketing his mouth. He looks exhausted, and vulnerable, and much, much older than he did even a week ago.

My nerves liquefy into an aching, worried puddle.

"Oh, Jasper."

At my voice, he looks up sharply. "Eden."

His book claps shut as he stands hurriedly, staring at me like I'm a ghost made flesh and not the same woman he kissed senseless just weeks ago.

"May I . . .?" I ask, flustered, and he just nods, still staring.

Nodding, I tentatively step inside, remembering chess and the first time I joined him in here, and all my apprehensive worries about who and what he was.

I shut the door firmly behind me, and his brows twitch up, an assessing question.

"Jaykob," I explain in a single word, and his expression darkens.

"Ah."

Hopefully, this slows him down at least. I gave Kasey the slip ten minutes ago.

I feel him watching me as I wander through the room, lingering over paintings and pictures that I was too nervous to look at my first time in here. Or the drunken time after that, which I barely remember, since I spent most of it with my head in a toilet. Similar nerves to my first visit still flutter through my stomach, but they're edged with something softer now. Sweeter.

When I finally look back at him, I take in the empty teacups beside him. The reference books sprawled on his side table.

He follows my gaze down to the disarray, and color singes his high cheekbones. "Apologies for the mess." He touches his hair, then grimaces, sighing, and his tiredness peeks through again. "It's been . . . a long week in here."

He begins collecting the teacups, and I walk over, laying a staying hand on his bare forearm, right under where he's folded his silk sleeves back. He pauses, studying the touch.

"It's okay, Jasper," I tell him softly. "Please. Don't worry on my account."

Starless, unfathomable eyes lift to examine my face.

My stomach does a low, hard flip, and my nerves catch in my throat again. Am I overstepping? I'm never sure of the line with him. Yes, we had one of the most beautiful moments of my life in the woods together, where he laid all my fears to rest. But then Jaykob laid his challenge, and I've only seen Jasper in passing since.

There have been moments, but . . . they've been polite. Reserved.

He's been polite with Jaykob too—kind and generous, letting him sweep me away without a word of complaint. So kind, I just can't help but wonder . . . does he even want this anymore? Or *is* he giving way to Jayk?

I remove my hand, and a tiny line appears between his brows.

Stepping back, I clutch my notepad closer and glance at the door. "I just saw Jennifer leaving."

Tension threads between us, taut and invisible as he keeps staring at me, and I circle around the armchair, needing to get some distance.

It wasn't a question, but he replies anyway. "I've had an influx of patients these last few days." He sighs softly. "It's good that they're seeking help."

I nod, my lips pursing politely around my opinions, but he seems to see through my silence.

Jasper's brow lifts in cool demand, and I color at how quickly he reads me. Still, I stop on the other side of the chair, debating how to phrase my concern.

"Are *you* okay?" When he stiffens in surprise, I quaver but hold my ground. "It's a lot to take on."

Jasper takes in my expression—the careful distance between us—and his tone softens. "I'm used to it, Eden. You don't need to worry about me."

I do, though.

But I don't say it.

Instead, I let the silence stretch, and his eyes narrow, before the tension line of his lips softens too. He shakes his head ruefully, then he begins moving around the room as well—only this time, he's not chasing me. He pauses by the chessboard, and it takes me a moment to realize it's our game, still in its final freeze frame.

"It is different," he finally concedes. "I'm used to soldiers. They experienced heavy things, of course, but I was used to the kinds of problems they faced." A long, elegant fingertip lingers over a defeated pawn. "These women have so much trauma, in so many forms. You're right. It is difficult to hear." But then his finger lifts off the pawn, and he looks at me directly. "It's not as difficult as knowing they've been bearing their burdens alone. I might not be able to build a throne or scale a building, but I believe in my work. In my way, I can help. That's worth any number of nightmares."

He's softly hazed by the low, warm lights, sincere and sure, and I need to draw in a long breath. My heart was lost somewhere in his quiet speech. I need a moment to work out how to function without it.

"What you do takes just as much courage," I whisper, then flush at how foolish I sound, but to my surprise, Jasper flushes too, shaking his head in an immediate denial that I wonder at. Swallowing my nerves, I offer, "Do you need to talk? Is there something . . . How do you decompress?"

"I have Lucien." His affectionate reply is instant and shockingly warm, and I feel like a fool as soon as he answers it. Of course he has Lucky, and of course Lucky helps ease his burdens. He eases mine, too.

I bite my lip, tucking my notepad behind my back.

Who am I to worry about Jasper? What could I possibly offer him that Lucky doesn't already?

"I'm glad," I murmur, meaning it, and his return smile is just a bare brush over his lips.

This time, he doesn't reply, just traces my face with his eyes. My body. He lingers on my hidden hands and the fringe of his lashes dusts his cheeks. His full mouth is soft and inviting, such a stern contrast to the bladed angles of his face, and I realize the tension between us is curling tighter, stretching beyond politeness.

I need to stop staring at him. I need to leave. If he wanted to work around Jaykob, he would have done it—or said *something*, surely, beyond all this civility. Even his kiss before the raid was only sweetly affectionate.

And on my forehead.

We've been managing so many silent conversations. I know he understands me in so many ways. But I fear, in this, we're forever walking backward.

I clear my throat, backing up. "Well, I'll just . . ."

Jasper's breath leaves him in a gust of pent-up frustration, and for a moment, his manners slip.

"What do you have in your hands?" he demands, so impatiently that I stop, startled.

"My hands?"

My grip tightens, and the paper crunches between my fingers.

A dark, precarious light flares in his eyes, and he steps forward. "Yes, sweet girl, your hands. The appendages currently burrowing into your spine?"

Nervously, I laugh and the golden lamps find all the highlights and hollows of his face as he advances on me. The dip of his throat. The pale gleam of his chest.

He doesn't approach like Jaykob, like a hunter stalking through the underbrush—he approaches like a gentleman, or a lord from another time, one set on ruining me between his bedsheets so he can take me for his own.

I blink when he stops a foot away.

And holds out his hand.

I reluctantly draw my essay on dominant-submissive safety around, holding it to my hammering chest. His head tilts, and some of the heat ebbs from his features.

"More journaling?" he asks gently. "Forgive me, Eden. I didn't mean to push."

Oh, damn it.

Trying not to cringe, I tuck my hair behind my ear. "I— It's not . . . I brought you something, actually. Something not . . . feelings related." I shake my head. "Okay, it could be considered feelings-related, I suppose. I did obviously consider feelings, when I wrote it. But also custom, and the benefits of structure and setting expectations. I had several citations, though I'd have loved more sources. I used the APA style for them. I hope that's okay—we hadn't discussed it. But I figured . . . I figured it would be fine. You would . . . you'd be familiar, with the references. There's another thing, too. *The* other thing. Lucky helped me with that, between kidnappings."

Jasper watches me with close, amused patience. "Consider me curious."

His finger curls, beckoning me to hand it over, but still, I hesitate.

"I'm just . . . not sure if you still want it." My voice comes out a nervous hush, and I don't know how to raise it.

His head tilts, but he doesn't move, polite and expectant, so I sigh and place the notepad into his hand. He's pulled it to him in the next second, greedily scanning the neat lines with swift, confident speed—and as he reads, his face relaxes. He lifts the next page to read, and a laugh whispers out of him.

I crane to see what part he's reading, but he lifts a finger, signaling for me to wait. I pull my hair over my shoulder, my fingers knotting in the ends. "You don't have much in your library on non-monogamy, or how that intersects with kink, so I drew some of my own conclusions."

He hums in acknowledgement, turning the next page, and I dance onto my toes, watching him.

"Ah, wonderful point," he murmurs, and my heels drop back to the floor in relief.

My eyes flick between his face and my essay, my pride kindling at the silent delight tucked into his features. I'm not sure if it's the submissive or the academic in me, but I *really* didn't want to disappoint Jasper with this.

He finally lets the pages drop, and his fingers rest thoughtfully over the sloping script.

"Incredibly thorough. You have a gift for nuance. I'm not sure I've ever had a submissive articulate the need for safety so clearly—or dedicate themselves to a punishment so sincerely."

I duck my chin, trying to hide my happy—borderline smug—smile. The praise glows through me like a crackling fire, relaxing all the nerves and worries I had before turning my paper over.

Would it be in poor form to ask him to grade me?

"But do tell me, Eden . . ."

It's only then I see the dangerous slash of his mouth, and my smugness vanishes in an instant as he shifts closer. Now in front of the lamps, his shadows are thrown over me with dark, nightmarish claws.

"What did you mean—*if I still want it*?" he asks, and there's a treacherous edge to the question.

My mouth goes dry. "I . . ." I glance at the door, but it's closed—and so very far away. "Well . . . it's been a little while since we spoke, and you've been with Lucky, and Jayk had his whole—" I wave my hand, and he tracks the motion with poorly concealed frustration.

"His whole *thing*. I wasn't sure if . . . I just thought that maybe you had decided . . ."

I trail off, not wanting to finish that sentence under the hot, aggrieved look in his eye, but he's not about to let it go.

"Decided *what*?" The question is blistering, and I wince.

This close I can smell chamomile on him, and the lingering hints of my slop that he, at least, has had the grace to pretend to like.

I look up at him helplessly, not finding any good answers here. Though since at least a third of my essay centered on honest communication, I suppose I should just . . .

"I thought you might have decided it was all too much trouble?"

His lips part, aghast.

Which is . . . good?

"Oh, Jasper, you're just so distant, and I—"

"*Distant*?" The word bursts from him, strangled and inelegant and *mortified*. He opens his mouth, then closes it, then stares at me. "I've been negotiating with *terrorists* for you. I've been placating your boyfriend. I've— I've been *trying* not to put you in an impossible situation."

"Oh. Oh, well, that's very swee—"

He lifts a sharp finger, halting my words as he grimaces like he's in pain. Turning away, Jasper tosses down my essay, then massages the bridge of his nose.

"I take it back. Your grasp of nuance is on life-support."

My eyes widen, and a scoffed, offended sound gets caught in the back of my throat.

Sometimes I wonder at Jasper and Lucky, and how their private conversations might go after the sweat has cooled on their skin and their chemistry cools to a simmer. Now I wonder if they don't just bat insults back and forth until they're ready to go again.

Still . . . he's an excellent sadist. He might make a wicked slice, but it's tempered by what lies under it—by the nuance he's berating me for missing, I think sourly.

Jasper *does* want me.

He's just not always very clear in how he shows it.

It's not entirely my fault. All my other brutes, for better or worse, have led most of our interactions—I know what they expect from me. In fact, the only other one of them who gave me this many mixed messages just so happened to be the only one I knew instinctively how to read.

But I'm not sure that Jasper wants to be compared to—

The door slams open, and my shoulders slump.

I'm so tired of this.

At least when there was sex at the end, I was actually able to work out my aggravation.

But Jasper surprises me, whirling around with surprising vitriol. "Get *out*, Jaykob."

"Sure. Just collecting my things."

I wait to be scooped up—again—when Jasper strides forward, snapping with rage. He's *not* choosing politeness today. "You of all people know how intensely private these sessions are. Or would you feel comfortable revealing the most intimate details of your sessions, even to her?"

Like this, Jasper is . . . chilling. I lift my head, glancing back at Jayk, who pauses, scowling, like even *he* is rethinking here.

His eyes flick to me. "You're having a session?"

Screw the essay, you can't fight clean with Jaykob.

"Yep. Ah, yes. I am," I confirm, and the corner of Jasper's mouth twitches.

Jayk looks between us suspiciously, and his scowl deepens. "I'm waiting outside. Keep your clothes on."

"Actually, I'm getting a little tired of clothes," I murmur sweetly, and Jayk flips me off as he leaves.

There's a heavy thud as he rests against the door, and Jasper and I both stare at it as I realize I'm on yet another timer. Despair spirals through me.

How on earth am I ever going to get him to see sense?

"I'm sorry, Jasper," I say softly.

For Jayk, for *me* and the insecurities I still struggle to shake.

Jasper snicks his tongue hard against his teeth, then sighs. His hand touches mine, squeezing it gently.

"I have something for you, too, Eden."

He lifts an ornate hardcover book off his bedside table and walks it back to me, and my stomach swoops. More notes. More thoughts and feelings and quips, just for me.

He has been thinking of me.

Jasper stops in front of me, and he hesitates a moment before handing it over. When he does, I turn it in my hands, running my fingers over the foiled cover.

Othello.

My brows shoot up, and I scan Jasper's face. He's looking at me intently, his eyes still full of *things*, and as though the play was a codex, I begin to understand him.

Othello, driven mad by jealousy.

I wonder how many nights he spent agonizing over this. I wonder how many secrets he's poured into the margins.

I step into him, wetting my lips. "I'm assuming the subtext isn't that you're planning to murder me?"

Jasper's intensity doesn't fade. He just dips his chin to the side in a soft negative.

I look back down at the hardcover, my heart thudding.

This is a language I understand.

"There was something else in the notepad." My hands shake on the book, and I can't quite meet his eyes. "I think you missed it."

I can tell I've intrigued him. He picks up the notepad, flicking through the pages until he finds several printed sheaves of paper, these a cold, crisp white, poking from between the yellowed pages. He tugs them free . . . and his expression becomes intent.

Eden Anderson's Limits List sprawls across the top of the first page.

The first of *seven*.

He lifts the second page, and my stomach flips, as I try to remember everything I marked down. I catch sight of a word here and there.

What on earth is *bastinado* again?

Was it a food thing? Being basted with something? I catch sight of the heading.

No. It's under "Impact Play."

Impact. I had to strongly consider whether I wanted impact

anything. But I mean, as Lucky pointed out, *spanking* counts as impact, so I'd ticked yes to that. Paddles also sounded do-able. Maybe. That got an "Unsure but willing to try."

Oh, what if it's not enough for—

"Eden?" Jasper prompts carefully, cutting off my thoughts.

"Hm?" It comes out like a squeak, and I tear my eyes from the pages.

"This isn't a test. You can change these at any time. Before, during, after. I only need you to be honest." He's kind, assessing, but there's still an edge to him that makes me hesitate. One that breaks only a little with the caustic lift of his brow. "If *you* still want this."

Ooh, of course he's throwing that in my face.

I lift my chin. "I believe I made it quite clear that I do— Ah!"

Jasper pins me to the door by my throat, enveloping me against it. "Your essay was reassuring enough that I believe you know how to stop me if you wish it, is that correct?"

I blink, drawing in a sharp breath that mostly belongs to him. Light choking was *definitely* approved on my list.

"Yes?"

"Excellent."

Jasper kisses me—hot and barbed and sharp-edged, he doesn't bother to be gentle. This isn't a woodland dream or a coaxing test. I feel every inch of his frustration and jealousy and pent-up lust. I feel the manners being stripped away.

When his teeth cut my lip, I moan, shocking myself.

Shocking myself more when he sucks it, claiming the wound.

A fist pounds against the door, and Jasper snicks the lock *shut*, glowering at me.

"So we're clear—I am *interested*, Eden." His eyes are stygian, simmering and otherworldly. "I loved Lucien for seven years before we were together. I am patient. I am risk-averse, and I didn't want you to be hurt while the rest of us resolved our differences. Do *not* mistake that for indifference. I promise you, I am the furthest thing. What you do to me, pretty girl . . ." I pant against his mouth, trying to capture it again, but his hand flexes against my throat with mind-fuzzing control. "It *breaks* me."

Jaykob pounds at the door again. "I heard that, motherfucker. Unless you switched up your techniques, that's not fucking *therapy*!"

I ignore him.

At this point, he probably deserves this.

"Maybe I don't want to wait seven years. I don't want to wait at all." I'm proud that it sounds like a challenge, and not the whine I almost let out.

Jasper seems to hear it anyway, and his irritation melts into something deliciously condescending. He tsks.

"Poor, sweet submissive. One man fucking you into the mattress every night isn't enough?" His lips brush over mine again, a cruel tease. "You need more?"

"He's not," I mutter, irritated and flustered and aching.

That seems to take him aback. "He's not?"

"I thought Lucky would have mentioned. Jayk is keeping things nonsexual, something about preserving my energy and staying healthy. And that reminds me, I have a bone to pick with Beau."

Jasper stares at me for a long moment, like I've shocked him. It's a lot like the way Lucky looked at me when he found out the same thing.

His eyes lift to the door, suddenly suspiciously silent, and a frown creases his brows.

I suck my aching lower lip into my mouth, my tongue toying with the cut, and I feel the throb everywhere. It makes me brave.

"Jasper, please," I whisper throatily. "I need more."

His eyes snap back to mine, scanning my face. Whatever he finds there brings an infernally satisfied flare to his eyes.

"No," he says.

Still with that thoughtful expression, he unlocks the door, and before I can register any hurt, Jasper tilts my chin back up toward his mouth. His finger rubs over my cut. "I won't do anything before I review your list."

He opens the door, and ushers me out, and Jaykob pauses, lowering his axe.

Jasper sighs, pressing a thumb between his brows. "I'll work out what to do with him."

Jaykob glares at him, but when Jasper drops his hand, he looks only at me.

Banked, carnal heat curls in his eyes.

"You just be a good girl and think of me tonight. Don't fuck him. You need to stop letting him take everything too."

I step in front of Jayk before he can charge and nod, my heart fluttering wildly.

"I promise."

CHAPTER 42

LUCKY

SURVIVAL TIP #90
*There's a time to shut your mouth
and a time to open wide.*

H ey, Eden."

"Hey, Lucky," she replies, resigned, bent over Jayk's shoulder as he carts her down the hall, and I send her a sympathetic wave goodbye when he doesn't slow.

Her breasts are perched on his shoulder, pushed dizzyingly high, and I briefly consider going after them before I catch sight of the axe in his hand.

You know what, Jayk with an axe is not a fight I need right now.

Maybe tomorrow.

With back up.

The door to Jasper's room—*our* room—is ajar, so I push inside.

"Hey, do you know why Jayk had an—"

Jasper slams the door closed behind me and grips my shoulder, then slams me back against the door.

"Get down. I need your mouth."

He unbuttons his pants, unzipping himself, and he doesn't need to say another fucking word. I get to my knees, need and heat and shock all crashing in on me.

Jasper's never impatient, but he's dragging his stiff cock out of his slacks and pressing it against my lips in seconds, and I let him in with a needy groan as he gasps.

Eden.

He was with Eden.

Jasper buries himself deep in my mouth, his head tipping back as I enclose him in wet heat. His cock throbs against my tongue, and his taste, his smell is sudden and scorching and everywhere. He presses something on his wrist—his watch?—then fists his hand in my hair brutally hard.

"You have five minutes. Get me off."

I shudder around his cock, the hoarseness of his voice and the degradation of it hitting me in filthy places. My balls ache, brought to hot fucking misery in seconds as he looks down at me, his eyes glittering.

But God damn, I'm pretty sure I've been training my whole life for this.

I push forward, into that punishing grip, until he's buried in my throat, and I have all of him in my mouth and my face is pressed against the silk shirt falling loose and parted around his cock. I swallow hard around the heavy head of him, rubbing my tongue where his dick lies flat against it, coating myself in his perfect fucking taste, breathing him in—and Jasper's curses punch out of him as his hand slams up to brace against the door.

"*Fuck*, Lucien."

I pull back a little, releasing him from my throat, and as I drag air in, moisture rushes into my mouth. Bringing my hand up, I fist the base of his cock hard, sucking and fucking his dick between my hand and my mouth.

He starts leaking onto my tongue, and I groan again, needing it badly. Wanting him to spill in my mouth so fucking bad, I think I might actually come in my pants if he does.

He never lets me touch him like this, and I can't handle it.

"Three minutes," Jasper snaps, strained, and the thrill bites into me.

I drag my free hand up to his balls, cupping them, squeezing, greedy for everything. Tearing my mouth from his cock for a second, I let my mouth follow my hand, running my tongue down the seam of his balls, sucking them into my mouth.

"Holy shit, Jasper," I curse against him as he widens his stance, and I spit against his cock, stroking him hard.

I'm dizzy and on a timer, and I'm spoiled for everything I need to do right now. I suck my fingers into my mouth, then drag them from his balls to rub against his ass. The slick puckered press makes me whimper, my dick straining and painfully strapped against my zipper.

Jasper's thighs lock up, and he growls a second before he snatches my wrist, stopping me.

Dazed, I look up at him. My lips are still pressed against his balls. "You don't like it?"

His dick throbs in my hand, and I stroke him more absently.

Jasper shudders, his angular cheeks flushed. His hand flexes around my wrist. "I like it."

The timer on his watch shows two minutes.

"You— That's just fucking cheating, babe," I splutter, and his eyes are hot coals.

"It's my game. I say I'm not."

He throws my hand back away from his ass, and I suck in a shaky breath, looking up at him from my knees. By my hair, he drags my mouth back to his cock, and the corner of his mouth lifts. If there wasn't so much restrained violence in him, that smile would be pretty.

"You have thirty seconds. Surely you can put that whining mouth to better use."

Fuck me, he's still pretty.

"Fuck it, then. Take my mouth." Licking his taste off my lip, I give him the dimple I know he gets off on. "You can even pretend it's Eden's if you want."

Jasper's eyes flare.

Burning at the injustice of his damn rule break, turned on beyond belief by it, I take him in my mouth again and grip his ass hard under his shirt. My tongue trails along every hot ridge of his cock, but I can't take any of the time I want, so I suck him deep, groaning.

Jasper's ass clenches under my hand. "Suck me, Lucien. Fuck."

He fucks into my mouth, not waiting for me to move, and I don't care. I don't care if it's for Eden or for me, or both, or neither. I was made for Jasper to use. He can do whatever he wants with me, for whatever reason, and I'll only say *yes, please*.

He hits my throat, groaning, and his dick swells against my tongue. Gripping my hair, braced against the door, he fucks into me over and over until my mouth is soaked. My beard, my neck. Until his silk shirt is damp, and he bends my head back to look me in my wet eyes.

"If I'm fucking you, I'm only ever fucking *you*, Lucien."

His timer goes off, and he pinches my nose as he steps in, pinning my head against the door and pressing deep into my throat. He holds my head still, viciously cutting off my air from my nose, my throat, and I gag, strangling and choking around his cock as he fucks me. He pulses against my tongue as he unloads down my throat, staring me in my eyes as tears stream down my face, his expression rapturous.

My dick is throbbing, chafing in my pants, my heart slamming against my chest, but I can't get enough friction to come, and I sob as my vision darkens.

Jasper smiles at the sound with a soft, final shudder, then he releases my nose. He eases back as I cough, gasping, but he keeps one trembling hand against the door.

My thoughts come in stop-starts, but I'm so dick drunk I can't follow any of them through. Instead, I rest my forehead against his stomach, shaking, and his cruel grip turns just as painfully gentle, stroking my hair.

"I love you, my Lucien."

He says it simply, but with so much raw honesty that my throat thickens.

I roll my forehead against him, then look up.

"I love you, too."

His eyes kindle.

He studies me with indulgent, heated affection, and his hand slips down to play in the wet mess of my beard. "Are you okay? I didn't use you too hard?"

I huff a laugh, and it has more than a hint of desperation. My body is so desperate for release, there isn't much I wouldn't do to come right now.

"You can use me harder than that."

And yeah . . . that came out way more like a plea than I meant it to.

Jasper's lips curve, and he steps back to look down at me on my knees, his eyes trailing over my erection that's about as fucking obvious at this point as the tower at Pisa, lean and all.

Then he looks down at his watch, pressing a button on the side.

That fucking *watch*.

Giving me one last amused look, he turns and walks toward the bathroom.

"Come clean off, Lucien."

"Jasper?" I call, worry and horror starting to crash in. Jumping to my feet, I follow after him on shaky legs.

He knows if I said I'm okay, then I'm okay. I really only need him to check in after a scene like this—though the I love yous are nice—but . . . but we aren't *at* the after.

We're not at the after, right?

The shower flicks on, and I perk up. A sexy shower together could be promising. That's not an *after*, if that's what's on offer. That's sex. That's him fucking me into a shower wall. *That*, I can get behind—or he can. *If* that's what he means.

That may be a big if.

Because I'm having a big fear right now that he only wants to get clean so we can talk for hours and fall asleep together. *That* would be an after. That's the after-iest of aftercare.

Damn it, he's been raging about Jayk all week—and since he's not taking all that rage out on *him*, *I've* been getting an extra sadisty sadist with too much pent-up need on his hands.

At this point, I *need* Eden for backup.

"Are we showering together?" I ask, poking my head in to see him stripping off his clothes.

Greedily, I stare at every inch of uncovered flesh, and my balls *throb*, heat pounding through my abdomen.

"We would have been." He steps into the shower. "Had you shown a little more initiative and succeeded at your task within the timeframe, you'd be receiving much more than a shower right now."

My mouth drops open, and my cock bobs, like he's as worried

about this as I am. I adjust myself through my pants, and Jasper cuts me a warning look in the shower mirror.

Heart racing, I take my hand away.

"Are you *performance managing* me?" I ask incredulously.

Slick, soapy suds slide down Jasper's back, slipping over his ass. He rolls his shoulders languorously, and just as his obvious pleasure thrills me everywhere ... it's also a *fucking* turn on.

I grip the shower frame, staring in unholy desperation.

Jasper runs a hand through his hair as he turns to regard me. There's only sated, cat-like satisfaction in his face as he looks at my cheeks and my shaking hands.

"Perhaps, Lucien, if you spent less time sassing me at inappropriate moments and more time *applying* yourself, things would go ... easier ... for you."

"It was rigged!" I burst out, and his amusement deepens. Damn it, if he'd let me *really* apply myself like I was *trying* to, I would have had *minutes* on the fucking clock.

See how long he would really last with my tongue up his ass.

Fucking sadist. He gets off on this even more than me blowing him.

Frustrated, on edge, I run a hand into my hair. "I should get an A for effort, babe, come on. *Please*."

"More whining. Someone hasn't learned their lesson." His eyes gleam. "I'm not in the habit of giving out participation awards, Lucien. You'll just have to do better next time."

My eyes narrow on him.

First the spray paint, now this. I think I'm a bad influence on him —and Jasper's idea of mischief is just cruel.

Smiling at my outrage, he turns off the water. "Now, shower and meet me in the inner room for bed."

I know it's only pitiful to ask at this point, but we're desperate. I shift again, trying to ease the pressure in my cock.

"For bed?" I ask hopefully, handing him a towel, and he snorts as he steps out.

"For sleep," he clarifies with way too much enjoyment, and I sigh. *Sadists*.

"Look, do you maybe think that *I'm* not the one you're really—"

Wrapping his towel around his waist, Jasper gives me a forbidding, frosty look that warns of icebergs ahead, and I bite down on my protest.

He leaves to get dressed, and in rough, unhappy yanks, I pull my clothes off.

My stiff cock begs for attention, but even I'm not game to see what he'd do to me if I got myself off right now. If Jasper wanted me to come, I'd be turning the bedroom into a creamery by now.

"Yeah, I know, buddy," I mutter to my dick.

I get clean as quickly as possible—and as thoroughly, since I'm a natural optimist—and hurry into his secret lair. He's already in bed, his chest bare, and his long pajama bottoms sweep around his ankles. He's reading under the amber lamplight, making notes in the margins of another book.

I stop inside the room, just looking at him, my chest aching.

Not just my chest.

My skin is still too hot—the cold shower barely did anything to cool me off—and seeing him like this, casual and in his reading glasses and waiting for me . . . it's not helping.

Suppressing a tortured sigh, I throw my sleep shorts on the spanking bench and finish toweling myself off, tender around my rigid dick. I've been hard for too long, and it's sensitive as fuck right now.

"Another book for Eden?" I ask, smiling at his intense focus despite my discomfort. "What'd you choose this time?"

Jasper doesn't look up. "*Planet of the Apes*. I'm hoping she might draw some parallels with her current roommate."

I grin. "You do know how that ends, don't you?"

His expression sours, and he abandons the book to his bedside table. Thoughtfully, he picks up a sheaf of papers, thumbing through them.

"The man is impossible," he finally mutters.

"Yup," I say agreeably, toweling myself off.

He flicks to another page, his expression darkening. "It's just ridiculous. I've done everything I can with him," he hisses, his eyes scanning the page. "At this point, I don't care what he's done for Bristlebrook, Lucien—Jaykob is a toddler, and the adults in the room have indulged his tantrums long enough."

I nod, my dick still aching. "Totally. Big jerk. No reasoning with him. Shouldn't indulge it."

Maybe if he gets mad enough, Jasper will join Dom, Beau, and me. Though those two are on my shit list, since they somehow scored uncontested mornings with Eden and didn't throw *me* a single bone.

Alliance breakers.

As casually as I can, I shrug. "Shame you're on the high road, though, right? Something about gentlemen and being the better person? Not being *foolish*?"

Jasper's lip curls. "She called me *sweet*."

Oof.

No wonder I'm getting tortured.

Amused, I reach for my shorts.

"Don't," he tells me mildly, finally glancing up. He sets down the sheaf of papers, then removes his reading glasses. He nods at the sheets beside him. "Like that. You don't put clothes on in this room unless I give you permission."

My mouth goes dry, but I drop the pants, and Jasper's gaze runs over me. The way he looks at me is a cock stroke in and of itself, and I suppress a groan as new heat shivers over my skin.

I walk over to the bed slowly, letting him look.

He loves my body, I know he does. Maybe I can make him break. Maybe the glory of my cock will convince him to take mercy on me. I am *so* not above a seduction.

Hell, I'm not above anything. Begging doesn't seem to be cutting it.

When I slip onto the bed, I stretch out, as casually as I can, and the corner of his mouth lifts.

"Is this how you want me, then?" I ask thickly, pretending to scratch my chest, only to trail my hand down my abs. "You really should give me another chance, you know. Don't hold me back. You should see what I can do with ten minutes and a squeeze of lube."

He leans over me, and I shudder in shock as I stare at his mouth, full and pretty and inching closer . . . and closer . . . and closer. My dick strains toward him, my heartbeat scattering.

It worked? How the hell did that work?

He flicks off the bedside light next to me. "Get under the sheets, Lucien."

The darkness is deep and enveloping, and I scowl.

I know this is what I get for falling in love with a sadist, but fuck me with a pool cue if I wouldn't take his worst whip over *this* any day of the week. This is *deprivation*. Is this how poor Dom feels? No wonder he's miserable. In fact, I'm going to talk to Eden about it. The building trust thing is cute, but my guy is going to blow—in one way or another—and *then* where will she be?

I climb between the sheets, rolling over onto my side. My cock bobs despondently, and I'm glad it's dark because Jasper doesn't *deserve* to get off on this. There should be an appeals process for this— and damn it, a petition to rewire my own stupid, masochistic brain too, because there shouldn't be any part of me that finds *this* a turn on, and yet here I am with a hard on that could punch a new hole in the wall at the idea of him smirking in the bed next to me.

Stupid sadist.

Stupider masochist.

He wraps himself around my back a moment later, and I grit my teeth. His skin is hot against mine, and his breath stirs the hairs at the back of my neck in a way that makes gooseflesh ripple down my spine. He's half-hard, lazily hard, because *he's* fucking come already, but he presses his cock against my ass anyway.

Casually greedy, Jasper runs his hand up my thigh, his palm brushing over the coarse hairs, and I shiver again. He traces my abs lazily, the back of his hand brushing against my dick like it doesn't make my teeth punch together every fucking time.

Toying with me.

Torturing me.

Damn it, I've been *good*!

"My Lucien," he murmurs. "Is there anything you would like to say to me?

I bite down on every groan and whimper that wants to rise, refusing to give him the satisfaction, but there's no hiding how ragged my breathing turns.

Then he chuckles sleepily and wraps his hand around my cock. Hard.

"Goodnight, darling boy."

Blood roars in my ears. Or something does. At this point I'm pretty sure everything has rushed south. But *he* isn't moving. His hand just rests, still and punishingly tight around my swollen cock. Just rests for long enough that his peaceful breaths start to slow.

And for me to go silently mad.

He doesn't understand; I *need* to move. Not to fuck into his hand, exactly. If he asks, that's not what I'm doing. I *can't* even shift in his grip because of how tightly he's wrapped around me.

It's just snuggling.

Filthy, delicious snuggling.

"Stop squirming."

"I can't sleep like this, Jasper."

Against my neck, he hums. "Unfortunate. I'd advise against making that my problem."

My head tips back into him. I can feel the pulse of my cock in his palm.

Ah, fuck it.

"Okay, okay, I do have something to say."

"Oh, do you?" he taunts sleepily. His hand pumps my cock once, and my hands fist in the sheets as pleasure nearly makes me black out. "Is that what you want? Me to play with this silly little cock I own?"

"Well yes, and, not to play an Uno reverse on you or anything, but don't you think we should really get to the bottom of *why* you feel the need to leave me miserable and sleepless tonight?" Jasper's grip tightens in warning, and I gasp, squirming. "I think you're really mad at Jayk, and the noble thing was great and all, but maybe it's time you call it quits and stop torturing the poor, desperate love of your life and maybe take your frustration out on the person who deserves it."

There's a cold, terrifying beat of silence.

But in for a penny . . .

"And you should give me lots of orgasms. For being honest. And because I love you," I add.

"Hmm," he hums, and there's something dark and dangerous in the sound.

Oh, shit.

"Are you feeling shafted, my darling?" he asks.

"Funny," I mutter.

He pulls my hair free of its tie and kisses the curve between my neck and shoulder. I shudder, gasping at the gentle, heated press.

"Remember how Jayk's a toddler?" I say desperately, panicking. "Remember she called you sweet?"

Suddenly, Jasper bites my shoulder hard enough to break skin, and I cry out as scorching, liquid pain lashes through me. He shoves me onto my stomach and begins kissing his way down my spine. His hand slips out from around my cock, and he grasps my ass in both hands, squeezing. The bite on my shoulder pulses through me.

He licks the small of my back. "Do you not think I'm sweet?"

My brain has short circuited.

He parts my ass with his hands, holding me apart, and his mouth kisses squirmingly close. I leak onto the sheets, but he has me pinned, and I don't move, too afraid he'll stop.

He bites my ass cheek, hard. Then slaps it sharply enough that I flinch, and I can't help the way I fuck into his silk this time.

The little pains make me dizzy. Desperate.

When I've come back from the edge just enough, he strokes his thumb over the side of my cock, and I shudder.

"Am I *sweet*, Lucien?" he snaps.

Danger, *danger*!

There's no right answer here. He's setting me up to fail—*again*.

"You . . . you *can* be . . ."

His mouth presses into the cleft of my ass. With his fingers holding me open, his tongue slicks along my tight hole. Brutal pleasure punches through me, and I spill more precum into his sheets. He lavishes me with scorching, sucking kisses. With wet, laving licks and fingers that force their way into me with squeezing, brutal insistence.

"Am I sweet right now, my Lucien?" he taunts, his voice hoarse. "Is this what you wanted to do to me earlier? Do you want to fuck me?"

There's a high, urgent ringing in my ears, like the sing of a bell, demanding that I come.

He kisses over the bite he left on my ass, toying with my balls, his finger slowly pumping my hole with small, slick movements.

"Why stop there? Don't you want my mouth on your cock, too? Do you want me to let you come on my tongue?" he croons.

I arch my back, begging, choking out gasps into his mattress.

"I don't appreciate the attempted manipulations, Lucien." His voice turns wry. "Or you fibbing to me—white lie or not."

With one last, filthy kiss where he sinks his tongue deep into my ass, he pulls back completely, abandoning me to the stained sheets.

My frantic, panicked heart beats against the mattress, my brain scorched to ash.

I didn't think my need could get any more painful, but I've had whipping sessions that have ravaged me less.

I flip over to see Jasper in the bathroom, washing his hands and picking up a toothbrush.

Right then, my panic snaps, and I slap the bedsheets.

"You're sweet as the pit of a fucking peach, Jasper. You're not a gentleman. It's time you just admitted you're an asshole like the rest of us. You're—" Jasper raises a brow in the mirror at me over his toothbrush, and I glower at him. "You're a fucking *sadist*, babe. My sadist. You take what you want, even if it hurts." I shove a hand into my hair, my whole body trembling. "No wonder Eden was worried. You're treating her like glass when she *wants* you to treat her like a—"

"A prize? Something to be fought over and passed around?" His voice is terse. "She deserves more. She dislikes the infighting, Lucien. She wants peace between us."

"Like a *woman*. She wants to be fucked, Jasper. She wants *you* to fuck her." My body aches—for him, for her. I'm so done. Done and desperate. "If you want peace, you need to speak a language Jayk is going to understand. And if you want Eden, it's about time you damn well prove it."

Jasper's toothbrush hits the counter with a cold clatter, and he turns, his face frigid and intent. For a marrow-freezing moment, I'm sure I've gone too far, that I've actually said something that might hurt him.

Then his eyes drift to his bedside table, lingering on the sheaf of papers.

For a long, long time, he stares at them, lost in himself.

Finally, he smiles, and it's nothing short of terrifying.

"Lucien, it's time to fetch the grappling hooks."

CHAPTER 43

EDEN

SURVIVAL TIP #323
*Two on one
makes for wonderful odds.*

The night is deliciously warm, and moonlight trails over my skin like slow fingertips. I stretch, feeling Jayk pressed all around me, my head on his arm, his thigh between my legs. His hard chest firm against my breasts and all along my back.

I frown.

Wait.

I lift my head and squint against the hazy starlight. Jayk is snoozing in front of me. His lashes are dark against his cheek, his stubble rough and pronounced.

Someone shifts behind me.

Panic floods my nervous system. Blood pounds in my ears. I flinch back, swiveling, ready to pummel, to scream and fight and—

I stop an inch from battering the lean body wedged against my back.

It's *Lucky*.

He's cuddling me from behind, his blond hair fanning over Jayk's arm, his fingers tracing the dappled silver on my skin. My stunned, stuttering brain won't catch up, and I meet his bright blue eyes.

He winks.

I *squeak*.

At my voice, Jayk grumbles, his other arm shifting over my hip, and Lucky raps one finger over my lips to shush me.

A crinkle of paper makes me jump again. Snapping upright, I see Jasper perched in an armchair beside the bed, a single lamp casting him in harsh shadows. *Nineteen Eighty-Four* lies open across his lap as he surveils me from his seat. His dark eyes dip, and I realize I've dislodged the sheets, exposing my bare breasts.

I choke on my scream.

Just Jasper. It's just Jasper.

But the *door* is still locked.

"How . . . ?" My frantic breath catches before I realize that the window is now firmly closed, though those pitiable curtains are still wide open—and there's a large leather bag and neatly coiled rope on the floor that weren't there last night.

A wickedly sharp grappling hook rests atop them.

I stare.

The silver claws gleam.

No.

No.

Astonished, my eyes snap back to the window. To the grappling hook. To Jasper.

"You *didn't*," I breathe.

Oh my God. My brain trips over itself, trying to catch up to the fact that they just *broke in through my window*.

They've all gone mad.

There are *madmen* in my bed.

Jasper raises one whiplike brow, but he doesn't answer me.

Instead, he looks back down at his book, casually turning another page. "Jaykob, kindly remove your hand from my boyfriend's ass."

Jayk lifts his head, frowning sleepily.

Whiplash.

Confused, my gaze drops, and I follow the thick line of Jayk's arm, dusted in dark hair, to the narrower slope of his wrist, all the way to where his wide, rough hand rests comfortably against gray sweatpants.

Oh.

As if by reflex, Jayk squeezes a full palmful of Lucky's firm butt cheek.

He freezes, then pats around Lucky's hip more frantically.

Lucky snorts into my side, and Jayk shoots upright, his bleary gaze swinging wildly between Lucky and Jasper.

Casually, Lucky stretches, drawing every sleek muscle taut, then sits up. Brushing my hair off my shoulder, he kisses the sensitive curve of my neck, his beard tickling over my skin. I shiver, trying to take control of my still-hiccupping pulse, and turn for a kiss . . .

Only to get a mouthful of hair.

Lucky's not even *looking* at me.

His dancing eyes are on Jayk.

"Hiya, handsome," he quips. "Want to cuddle?"

Jayk looks wildly at the still-locked door, and his expression switches from bewildered to murderous in zero point two seconds.

Uh-oh.

They're not here for *me*.

"How the fuck did you get in here?" he bellows.

They're here for *him*.

Squealing, I press one hand against Jayk's thick chest and another against Lucky's, holding them apart like a referee. "Ah, maybe we should—"

"You left the window open," Lucky replies casually. "Felt like an invitation."

Jasper returns to his book. "If you intend to keep Eden safe, you really should be more aware of how exposed you are."

"So, so exposed." Lucky winces, his eyes dipping. "Need some pants, bud?"

Jayk's dark tattoos twist manically as he points at Lucky over my shoulder. "Okay, that's it. You came through the window, you can go the fuck back out that way."

"Eden, you should move," Jasper advises, lazily turning another page.

Oh, God.

Jayk looks down at me, eyes blazing, and in the next moment I'm flying through the air. Shrieking, I bounce against the pillows as

Lucky takes advantage of Jayk's momentary distraction and tackles him off the bed. They land hard, skidding across the floor.

I grab my glasses, then scramble to the edge of the bed to watch.

Jayk recovers quickly, flipping Lucky onto his back and crushing his pretty face sideways into the carpet. He's almost twice Lucky's size, and in that spare second, I realize just how much strength Jayk has been holding back from me.

Because he's certainly not bothering with Lucky.

"Jayk, get off him!" I yelp, gripping the mattress like it's a stress ball. "He's littler than you!"

Lucky's "*Hey!*" is muffled by Jayk's fist.

Jasper's book snaps shut, and he sighs as he stands.

"Fuck. That." Jayk grinds Lucky's cheek under his palm. "It's war. You agreed. And he's . . ." He grunts as Lucky twists under him, his grip slipping. "He's losing. Again. Monkey brains here doesn't deserve you."

"This is not what I meant!" I whack him with a pillow, my voice hitting an unfortunate pitch. "This is so *toxic!*"

"Not. *Losing.*" Lucky's fingers dig into Jayk's windpipe. "You took her. You keep doing it! You don't get to just *take* her."

Jasper strolls around the bed. With one swift snap, he untethers the rope tieback from one of the posts on the four-poster bed, wrapping either end around his palms. The draped satin falls like a curtain close.

He walks up behind Jayk, still preoccupied with the violent, twisting soldier beneath him, and Jasper tosses the rope around his chest like he's wrangling a bull.

Then he yanks hard.

Jayk flies backward. Freed, Lucky dives back on top of him without missing a beat, his cheeks pressure-pink. Together, he and Jasper wrestle Jayk over to the foot of the bed in a mess of flailing limbs, whipping heads, grunts, sighs, and curses.

Dear God.

We really *can't* last a day without a fistfight.

I flop back onto the bed. How is it that three of my brutes are in my room, and they're all focused on each other?

No one's even kissing.

"Eden, would you fetch me some more rope, please?" Jasper asks, his voice strained. Dark hair falls over his forehead as he fights for control. "I brought a bag. It's beside the chair."

I lift my head, incredulous.

He was supposed to be the sensible one.

"Perhaps you'd prefer some measuring tape instead," I suggest sweetly.

Jasper shoots me a sharp-eyed look over Jayk's shoulder, but with him so messy and discomposed, dodging limbs and wrangling rope, it doesn't have quite its usual effect.

He and Lucky drag Jayk onto the bed and against one of the posts and the ferocious red lines decorating Lucky's lean back pull taut. I wince. Oh God, *whips*. I ticked "Unsure" to whips on my limits list, but those lashes are a violent canvas over his flesh, punctured with bite marks. Vivid. Glowing.

Sadistic.

Skirting back to avoid a heavy kick, Jasper grimaces. "I have him, Lucien. Just hold him a moment while I secure—"

As they try to tie him down, Jayk roars, slamming his elbow back into Jasper's chest.

Jasper lets out a low, pained gasp.

"*Hey.*" Ice flashes over Lucky's face, and he shoves Jayk back hard, wedging a brutal knee against his balls.

Jayk falls utterly still.

Lucky tilts his head, and he glances up at Jasper. "Huh. That really is effective."

He winks down at his captive. "It's okay to be scared, but a little CBT can be fun, you know?"

Jayk growls.

Humor touches my sadist's lips, but he doesn't waste time tying off the rope around Jayk's chest and biceps, locking him against the post at the end of the bed.

Still pinning Jayk, Lucky suddenly shoots me a reproachful glower. His hair is tangled, half-loose over his bare shoulders.

"And you, you're no help. *Littler*," he mutters, and despite my intention to keep pouting, a smile slips out of me at his affront.

Jayk snorts scornfully. He may be forced still, but he vibrates with suppressed violence. "You are littler. I can crush you in my fist, rat."

Lucky ruffles Jayk's hair. "*You* are not crushing anyone, because *you* are outnumbered. It's all about teamwork, my cranky giant buddy, and you're going to keep losing until you work that one out."

Gently, he *boops* Jayk's nose, and Jayk's brows slam down.

After eyeing that murderous expression for a moment, Jasper retrieves another length of rope from his compartmented bag and ties Jayk's wrists behind the post as well.

"I'm going to beat you until you can't walk straight," Jayk grinds out as Lucky eases his knee away, laughing breathlessly.

"Hey now, don't you threaten me with a good time."

He bounces back onto the pillows, and Jasper drops a crimson throw blanket over Jayk's crotch with a finishing flourish.

I watch as Jasper rakes his disheveled hair back, exchanging a dark, satisfied look with Lucky. Dumbfounded, I look over at Jayk. Color rides his cheekbones, and the hot, challenging spark in his eyes reminds me of woodland hunts and firefights.

Oh my God, they're *enjoying* this.

These ridiculous men are still having *fun*.

Jayk's mammoth body pulls against his bonds, testing them, but he hardly moves at all.

"*Fuckers*," he curses explosively.

Jasper circles him, studying every inch of his handiwork. "Use 'Red' if you would like to leave, Jaykob. We'll remove the ropes. But to be clear, you'll be placed in the hall with your clothes—Lucien and I will be staying here. With Eden."

Ah, so it's still about me, but it's not *really* about me. This is part of their pissing contest, and apparently, I'm just the bonus prize.

Lovely.

Jasper stops beside the bed, giving Jayk a genial smile when he doesn't respond. "Grunt if you understand."

Jayk's eyes narrow with predatory rage, but he doesn't test the ropes again.

His short hair is mussed with sleep, and ropes crisscross his massive body, squeezing his tattoos. Naked and pinned down, he looks like a caged bear, ready to rip and rend as soon as he tears his way free.

Guilty, salacious heat ripples over me. I'm so used to Jayk chasing me. Trapping and taking me. To him agreeing to deals about my body and throwing me over his shoulder and ignoring how I feel for the others. But unless he uses his safeword, he's going to experience how that feels firsthand, because like this? He's helpless.

Like this, he's at *my* mercy.

I bite my lip, and Jayk catches the move. His midnight eyes narrow on my heated face. Stubborn. Considering.

Finally, he looks back at Jasper, relaxing against the post.

"I'm not going anywhere, asshole. Do your worst." His shoulders shift against his ropes in a slow, scathing shrug. "She's still going to be thinking about me." He smirks. "In the end, she's always going to pick me."

Everything. Jayk ignored *everything* I told him last week. It's almost impressive.

Jasper's amusement stiffens. Calcifies. A cold, hard challenge glitters in his eyes, and he's the vengeful angel again. The dark prince. Haughty and condescending and entirely untouchable.

But I see more now.

The way his eyes tick over to me for just a hint too long. The barely perceptible, worried lines between his brows. My new book on my bedside table, with his need and jealousies spilling out in ink through the margins. The fact that he's here at all, in my room before dawn, fired like Othello himself—*wrestling* of all things. Jasper isn't an angel, or some otherworldly being. His lethal beauty isn't fathomless and terrifying.

He's just a man . . . and he's clearly feeling as threatened as Jaykob ever has.

The two of them stare one another down, bitter dislike staining the air between them, and I fight a tired sigh, the shocked adrenaline draining out of me into a soft, helpless ache.

How on earth can I do this with all of them? Particularly when they're all so damn intent on tearing one another apart?

Lucky, at least, seems unconcerned by their standoff.

He grins lazily at Jasper. "Don't worry about it, babe. Eden doesn't have favorites. Especially when my mouth is on her—"

"Okay, all of you need to stop talking about me as though I'm not here," I break in, exasperated, and Lucky pouts. Praying for sense out of any of them, I settle my gaze on Jasper, softening and quote, "The robb'd that smiles, steals something from the thief; He robs himself that spends a bootless grief."

Oh God, is this going to make everything worse between all of them? I'm not sure I can handle it.

Jasper grimaces, avoiding my gaze. Color pinches his cheeks.

Lucky glances between the two of us, then rolls over the pillows until he's lying snug beside me. I glance back at him right as he trails his fingers up and over my navel.

My *bare* navel.

"Okay, I don't know anything about the boot situation," Lucky says blithely. His fingers are tanned, sun-dark against my pale skin, and he traces the line of the sheets pooled around my waist. He glances up at me with wicked humor. "But you shouldn't scold poor Jasper. He's had a hard week—lots of grief, bootless or not."

My brain stalls on his smile.

Moonlight halos his hair, and his every sinful, perfect muscle glows like a map for my mouth. His fingers toy over my skin.

"Lucky, I— I'm not *scolding*, I just . . ."

He shifts around and settles in behind me. His naked chest presses against my back, and my tongue sticks to the roof of my mouth.

I can feel every inch of his cock against my ass.

He's hard and scorching hot, even through his sweatpants. The pads of his fingers stroke over my bellybutton, then up my sternum.

"Lucky," I warn, but it sounds like a sigh.

He teases the underside of my bare breasts with his thumb, and my head tips back against his shoulder. My nipples furl in the balmy night air, tight and exposed to all of them.

Jasper exhales harshly, and my heavy lids crack open.

His dark gaze is guilty, but so caught on me, so intense as he catalogues every curve and dip of my skin that I'm tempted to drag the sheets down, just to have that gaze caress every intimate inch of me.

But he looks . . . torn.

Ashamed.

My head is fogged with Lucky, but the sight of Jasper's stiff discomfort is enough to spark my own. I've only been with him once. Sort of. Twice? But we haven't talked about . . . this. All of us. I don't know if this is what Jasper wants from me. If *this* is what any of them want from me.

"I'm sorry, I—"

Jasper shakes his head, glancing at me, then up at the ceiling. "No, *I* am sorry. We thought . . . *I* thought, perhaps, that after our misunderstanding this week . . . a grand gesture might be called for." Jayk snorts, and Jasper flushes deeply, grimacing. "But you're quite right, Eden. I've overstepped. This was foolish. Saying it aloud like this, I'm not quite sure what came over me. If I've made you uncomfortable, please say so. We'll release Jaykob and leave."

He really is so very, very human.

His lashes brush low for a long, bashful moment before his shoulders firm, and he looks back down at me. His gaze doesn't dip again; it stays steady on mine, apologetic and kind.

My heart melts.

Puddle, splash, gone.

"This is *romantic*," Lucky assures me in a whisper. "He scaled a building for you. He risked his *life*. That's way hotter than throwing you over his shoulder."

The flush deepens over Jasper's dangerous cheekbones, and he mutters under his breath.

My heart squirms in my chest. I didn't know Jasper could be adorable.

Or so foolish.

Flustered, I mutter, "I'm starting to think that out of all of you, Beau is the only one with any idea of how to romance a woman."

Lucky's answering kiss is deep and sighing. "Beautiful, I'll be so romantic your heart falls out of your chest."

I smile against his mouth. When he pulls back, he rests his forehead against mine. His hand comes around my waist, tugging at the soft sheets covering my hips, a question in his eyes.

Nervous excitement shivers down my spine.

This is happening. Just like my first night at Bristlebrook, exposed to a room full of men. Only it's different now—I know them. I know *myself*.

Minutely, I nod.

"Fucking stupid," Jayk mutters.

Lucky keeps me locked in his gaze as the sheet slowly falls away, baring me inch by inch. Chills race over my skin, and my breathing deepens, feeling their eyes everywhere. Knowing that they're looking at my body, tracking Lucky's hands as they dip down, down . . .

Quivering, I press another kiss against his mouth, and his hand brushes over my pussy in a silent, coaxing request. I'm spilling over his fingers, easing his way without even trying.

Jayk makes a rough, rumbling sound deep in his chest, and I feel the vibrations of it everywhere, hyperaware of him. I want to soothe and protect him from this, I do—but there's something about the threatening sound that hits me differently.

Jayk can't do anything about this.

His friends are going to fuck me, and he's going to watch me love it.

I part my legs, and Jasper's breath hisses out as his lover's quick, callused fingers part me, dipping inside. I'm slippery, *hot*, and Lucky's eyes darken.

"Oh, fuck."

Click.

Click.

Jasper walks around us, circling, his heels snicking against the floor with each step. "Lucien?"

His voice is a sharp, expectant demand, and I strain, trying to track where it's coming from.

Click.

Click.

Click.

Lucky has to swallow twice before he can answer hoarsely. "She's wet. She's . . . really fucking wet."

As if proving my point, he slips his finger over my slippery clit, and I let out a soft, squirming pant that makes his rhythm quicken, circling me until my thighs shake and my lips part on a breathless moan.

But then he retreats.

Playfully, lightly, he pulls away, his fingers leaving a wet trail over my abdomen. I arch, distressed at the loss of him, and cool air ripples over the damp path, clinging to it in obscene, perfect patterns.

Click.

Click.

Click.

"Lucien," Jasper warns, but Lucky's too focused on me now. His lips are ripe and kissed, his eyes a foggy, fascinated blue.

"You have no idea how much I need you," he tells me.

"*Lucky*," I whisper, somewhere between a scold and a plea— because I'm already shaking . . . and they're all *watching*.

But Lucky's dimples turn impish.

It's a challenge, but a different kind than Jayk's. He isn't inviting me to fight—Lucky wants me to play.

Unfortunately for Lucky, the only way I know how to play against him is to cheat.

I catch his wrist, dragging his hand back down to my clit, and he grins, obliging, touching in a way that's somehow everything and nothing at all. Impatient, I spread my legs wider, and he sinks an obedient finger inside me. Then another, filling me. Stroking me. *Stretching* me.

Click.

Click.

Click.

I still can't see Jasper, but I know he's there—the silent, careful predator, watching and waiting to act. Lucky knows it too.

His eyes press shut for a moment as he gathers himself.

When they open, they fix on my face, more intent than before. "You want more?"

Jayk snorts derisively as I whimper. "Set me free any time, sugar. I'll give you more. You know I won't waste your time with this shit."

Lucky's dexterous fingers are curving, slicked in me, slowly coaxing a response, and I roll my hips, holding him in place and grinding myself needily on his hand.

Waste? My melting brain can't make sense of the word.

On a groan, Lucky laughs.

"You know, that's not the flex you think it is, buddy." He slides Jayk a disparaging wince. "This *shit* is called *foreplay*." His thumb flicks over my clit, and I arch as a moan escapes me, heat twisting low in my stomach. Sweet vicious sparks of pleasure chase everywhere he touches. Lucky tilts his head toward me, then watches my face as I gasp. "See? She *likes* it."

A growl rumbles in Jayk's chest, but Jasper steps into view, his eyes glowing with unholy appreciation. They linger on Lucky's fingers making a mess of me. They flick greedily over my spilling breasts. My damp lips.

It gives me a strange, thrilling kind of courage.

I lean up to brush my mouth over Lucky's neck. To nip at him until he groans. The salt on his skin hits my tongue, and his pulse throbs through me as he sucks a stinging bite mark on the curve of my breast. I feel myself pulse around his fingers, hear the slick push as he rubs them inside me.

Jasper starts circling the bed again, and his heels *click, click, click* with every step.

The sharp pressure of his gaze prickles over my skin, and Lucky chuckles against my breast. "He's scary, right? Isn't it great."

"You. You're . . . the problem." I gasp, arching, as he teases me mercilessly.

He laughs, looking down at me, and tilts my face up toward his. "Why am *I* a problem? We just came for a friendly visit." His brows lift in challenge, and he pulls me closer. "Or is Jayk the only one allowed to drag you away?"

He drops a searing kiss to my lips, like a punctuation mark, and aroused amusement spikes beside my frustration.

"He's in trouble for that, too, you know." I kiss him back the same way, but he cups my jaw before I can retreat, his grip strong. Taunting.

"Well, I like trouble. Just for the record." He's so close, his eyelashes almost brush mine as he winks. "Let's make trouble together from now on."

Jayk makes a gagged, disgusted sound. "This shit can't fucking work on you, Eden. It's pathetic."

Lucky's dimple flashes as he kisses me deeply, his tongue questing, mischievous.

Um.

It . . . *might* work on me.

I give up, laughing, and he drops us backward onto the bed, curling himself over me. My fingers twine into his hair. It's soft and freshly washed, and when his muscular thigh presses between mine, my thoughts wink out.

Arching up, I feel his cock press along my stomach and my humor wavers too.

He rubs himself into me, and I shudder. I know exactly how his cock feels inside me—I remember exactly how he works his crown over my clit, and how he curves just right when he's buried deep. The sinful, destructive way he moves his hips. Swiveling. Touching me everywhere.

I grow hotter, slicker.

Jasper's heels *click*.

Click.

Click.

Gripping Lucky's colorful arms, I grind myself on his thigh, panting. I wonder how we look, mostly naked and starved. I wonder if Jasper likes seeing me touching him. If it makes him as messy as it makes me.

Lucky pulls my hair back, getting a better angle on my mouth. My body clenches around nothing, and I whimper, drawing him deeper, the others falling away as it all becomes him.

Lucky's mouth.

Lucky's hands.

Lucky's cock.

The wooden bedpost suddenly creaks loudly as Jayk thrashes forward. "Okay, this is fucking bullshit. That's my bed, dickwad."

Swiveling around to look at Jayk, Lucky quirks a brow. "Huh. I thought it was Beau's bed."

I blink in confusion at the loss of him. My lips still feel the burn of his beard, and I can't quite catch my breath. I can see him over me, but all points of contact are broken.

No mouth.

No hands.

No cock.

My stormy, infuriated glare returns in full force. Lucky stopped kissing me. He stopped kissing me to talk to *Jayk*.

No. I've had *enough*!

I pinch Lucky's beard and yank his face to look at me. "It's *my* bed."

My grip is fierce, painful, and the dark red over Lucky's cheekbones deepens.

His eyes glitter as he murmurs, "Ouch."

Jasper's boots stop clicking, and his breath hisses out.

I'm not sure how to deal with him—with any of them, really—but they started this, and I'm slick and aching and unbearably turned on, and annoyance is flavoring my arousal the way only Jayk usually musters, and I need *more*.

It's not enough to let them have their way with me.

I need to be more than half their attention and all of their frustration. I don't want to be the rope in their tug of war. They're big personalities. If I don't make myself clear, they're going to tear me apart.

I pull Lucky back to me until our lips are almost touching again. Slowly, I drag my hand down his body, panting and annoyed.

"I am naked. *Under* you." Through his sweatpants, I rub his cock, squeezing and deliberate, and he gasps.

"Jesus . . . *Fuck*, Eden."

I can't stop myself, so I kiss him again as he shudders. And again, and again. Against his mouth, I ask, "Please tell me if I'm in the way here." I lick the seam of his lips as he groans. "If you and Jasper would rather play with Jayk, I can leave."

Actually, I'm not sure that's true, given how badly I'm aching right now, but Lucky doesn't seem too concerned with details.

He thrusts into my imperfect grip, throbbing and hot through the fabric, shaking like he's falling apart.

The armchair beside us creaks as Jasper sits down.

His silence makes me jittery, but Lucky kisses me hard, almost clumsy in his urgency.

"*Eden*," Jayk growls, but it's not *Red*, so I just let the possessive sound do awful, delicious things to me.

Releasing Lucky's cock, I wrap my legs around his waist, and he immediately thrusts between them. The burst of pleasure is hard, shocking, but he makes a rough, displeased sound, then reaches back to shove his sweats down past his hips. His lips are hot on mine, his tongue in my mouth. He's not even trying for finesse, and I don't want him to. I want him undone. I want them all to see the undoing.

All of them need to remember that *they* are not in charge here.

I'm only letting them pretend.

Lucky frees his cock, and just as I feel him run the flared head down my soaking clit, down to notch himself at my entrance, Jasper speaks.

"Stop, Lucien."

"Seconded," Jayk grinds out.

No.

I whimper, and Lucky's grip tightens on me, almost painful as he locks up. As he *stops*. I can feel myself dripping along his cock, and I squirm against him, my body begging him for more.

He lets out a harsh, hungry breath. Beside my head, his forearms are corded as he braces himself. "Oh, fuck, Eden, beautiful, stop. Stop, stop, stop. I'm going to . . . stop."

Blue eyes blaze down at me, and I bite my lip against an infuriated sob. Then I kiss him, lightly, urgently, a dozen hummingbird kisses.

"Don't. Don't stop," I order. "Please, Lucky, please. I need you."

His cock twitches against my pussy, and he shudders.

My hands find his cheeks and I kiss him harder as he hovers over me. "Ignore him. Them. I'm here. *Please*."

Jasper makes a small, disbelieving sound.

Lucky's face is flushed and strained, and his hands are knots in the bedsheets. He looks almost panicked at my request. Pained as I rock against him.

He darts a desperate, pleading look back at Jasper. "Jasper, *please*."

I turn my head to see Jasper cast in shadowy light, sitting back in the armchair. Still rumpled from the fight, he looks artfully tousled now.

Raising a chill brow, he murmurs, "Now, isn't this amusing. Our librarian is giving orders."

He . . . doesn't sound amused.

Throbbing and breathless, I don't feel particularly amused, either.

Lucky is frozen, not moving a single, merciful inch. His throat is corded with tension, his hair snaring us both with blond ties.

Jayk's ropes press against his chest, and he gives me a snide look. "This shit really get you hot, sugar? Them doing it for each other first?"

"Oh, fuck you, asshole," Lucky snaps, hard and humorless.

Jayk smirks. "Me? You can't even fuck her without permission."

A lethal expression flashes over Lucky's face as he twists, lifting off me. My grip loosens as I let him go, my fingers curling in, the insistent beat in my body dropping into hopelessness as they fight.

Again.

Jasper shifts, his dark gaze clocking my reaction.

Lucky's eyes are chips of ice on Jayk. "You should watch your mouth while you're all tied—"

"That's quite enough," Jasper breaks in mildly, his eyes still on me. He pauses a moment, the pads of his fingers pressed in thought against his full lips. "Eden, I'm afraid you're under a misconception about how this is going to work."

Sitting up, I bring the sheet with me, covering myself, still trembling with my thwarted orgasm. I lift my chin, waiting, watching Jasper cautiously.

Ignoring me, he reaches back into the bag beside his chair. He pulls out a pair of glasses and a sheaf of papers.

My limits list.

My rage pauses, withers a little under a sudden, bright onslaught of nerves.

Why does he need my limits list right now?

He puts on the glasses and squints, examining the pages. "What is your safeword, dear girl?"

My lips part as I frown. I didn't even know he wore glasses.

I hate that he looks so good in them.

Out of habit, I adjust mine. "It's Bristlebrook. My safeword. It's . . . my safeword is Bristlebrook."

Jasper flicks over one page, checking something, and I try frantically to remember what was on page two.

"Lucien?"

"Houston." Lucky tears his glare away from Jayk, glancing at

Jasper and me. They linger on my irritated pout, and he touches my hand on the bed in silent reassurance.

But I don't want him to touch my hand. He's still glassy-eyed and breathing as unevenly as I am. I want his hands back on me.

I *want* to come.

Jasper nods complacently, like we aren't both squirming on the bed, then looks at me over the delicate rim of his glasses. "Eden, do you wish to adjust or remove any of your responses to this list?"

My stomach flips as I zero in on the papers, running through every single thing I checked *no* to. Worse, everything I said *yes* to.

Faint amusement finally lights Jasper's dark eyes.

"I— No?" I stammer, staring at the list like it's grown teeth.

By the post, Jayk yawns loudly, and his ropes creak. "Wake me when he's through with the paperwork."

"You're still comfortable obeying my orders?" Jasper prompts, ignoring him, and I have the abrupt feeling of being back in school, receiving a polite scolding in front of the class. "Because it seems to me, you're quite eager to circumvent them."

Ignore him, I told Lucky.

"Ah crap," Lucky mutters beside me, and his reassuring touch becomes a reassuring squeeze. "Sorry, beautiful. I already put him in a mood."

I don't know what Jasper's upset about. Lucky jumped to *his* command, not mine. I shoot Lucky a tight-lipped, sideways glare, trying not to look as jealous as I feel. I'm not even quite sure what I'm jealous *of*.

"Respectfully . . ." I say to Jasper, then stop. I adjust the sheet, then force myself still. Trying to shove down my prickling jealousy, I purse my lips and work up an equally polite look back at him. "Respectfully, you didn't give me any orders, Jasper. You rarely do."

He orders Lucky. He takes Lucky.

He *asks* me.

And he doesn't ask me for much.

A low, longing ache joins the empty throb through my body.

Jasper's head tilts, dangerous, calculating interest prowling over his face. He's hardly moved, but I feel under threat. In check.

"Hm." The sound is thoughtful. A breath of knowing that somehow only ratchets my nerves higher. "I think I understand now."

The shadows gather around him as he lifts one pale, slender hand off the leather armchair . . . and his finger beckons me in a single chilling curl.

"Come here, Eden. And *crawl*."

CHAPTER 44

JASPER

E den's mouth parts.
In precious, naïve surprise.
In a breathy, appalled rush of need.

In transparent *lust*, those pretty, puffy lips open . . . and it takes an inordinate amount of self-control to stop myself from joining her on the bed and tasting it for myself. Her bedsheets are tangled over her perfect breasts, and her glasses are knocked askew. The jealous ire slips out of her eyes and, abruptly, *she* looks knocked askew—hesitant and heavy-lidded and flushed with uncertainty.

Vicious relish licks through me at her reaction. At finally giving her a command—*that* command. Lust squeezes my cock with a tugging, sucking pressure at the thought of her obeying it. Of her *choosing* it.

And it's chased by the rampant, nervous anticipation that she won't.

I lift one brow at her, waiting.

Hiding my own thundering pulse.

Lucien's hand rests protectively on her thigh. His sweats are still halfway off, and his cock curves painfully upwards, full and rosy and glistening with want.

My possessiveness is almost enough to lock logic from my brain.

Eden meets my eyes, searching them, and I let my gaze travel over her body. I don't soften it, not this time. I let her see all the filthy things I want to do to her. I let her see the bite they'll carry, and all the reasons I need to be so, so restrained.

Delicately, she shivers, and satisfaction purrs through me.

But still, I wait.

I wait as color sweeps from her cheeks down to her chest. I wait as tension snaps in the air. I wait as her mind ticks through her choices—the abundance she has and can always make.

But I'm not *asking* any more.

If she wants my orders—if she wants *me*—then she needs to prove it to us both.

Lucien's breath is suspended as he looks between us, but it's not his turn now. He's painted with my marks. Despite his shower, my scent is on his skin. My fingerprints bruise his hips, purpling to indigo between older, scarlet lashes, each set an exact inch apart. I've made art with him.

Eden, on the other hand, looks like she's tangled with a bear and narrowly escaped with her life.

And still, her grip doesn't ease from her sheets.

I swallow, watching the steely curl of her fingers. They might as well be strangling my nerves. My *throat*.

It's a choking, fearful grip.

Because, whatever choice she makes, I *do* want her to crawl. I want it *wretchedly*.

But most of all, I want her to want that.

Jayk shifts back against the bed post, the crimson blanket slipping precariously over his obnoxious thighs. "Now, ain't that funny. *I've* never had any trouble getting her on her knees."

I'm going to kill him.

I shoot him a sharp, frosted look before I can stop myself—my writhing, murderous envy finally snapping free.

Along with an odd flickering of hurt.

It shouldn't *be* so easy for them and so fraught between us. I *hate* it. I hate that she's always trusted him like she's trusted her next breath while I've given her so much cause to hesitate.

Her limits list burns against my palm.

I hate that I spent so long focused on whether we'd work as sadist and masochist that I neglected all the ways we're flawlessly matched as submissive and dominant. As *people*.

Fuck Jaykob.

He assumes the worst of me every day, and I have been *polite*. I have been *patient*. I have given the beast every grace I can, but I've had *enough*.

Fuck civility.

If he wants to lay down a challenge, then I will answer it in a language this animal will understand. Tonight, Eden will be desperate for *me*.

I want more than her peace—more than silent, shared admiration. I want her to bring herself low for me, to drag herself to me on her hands and knees, just in the hopes I'll touch her. I want to see her beg. I want her to abandon her reserve. I want her to show me what a needy, wanton slut she is, for *me*. I want her maddened. To prove that she wants me beyond reason. Beyond self-respect.

I want to see her *crawl*.

And how she responds now will tell me everything.

Does she want this? Does she trust me to give it to her?

Does she know I don't want to make her less, no matter how low I drag her?

That white flag is still clutched around her, deliciously unsur-rendered. Her fingers twitch, and the way the delicate line of her throat works makes me want to bite into it. She's a fawn in the woods. An angel begging to be defiled. With those piercing, lumi-nous eyes, she examines me with as much anxious anticipation as I feel.

The others fade away as it all comes down to Eden . . . and that sheet.

Until, finally, she drops it.

It pools around her legs—it must—but all I can see is miles of soft, perfect skin. Bare and blushed, she's kissed with bruises and bites I want to replace with my own. Her nipples are budded dark and tight, and the shadow of her wet cunt is a cruel tease. I need to taste it—to bury my face in it. I need to feel it sucking at my cock.

My grip tightens on the chair as pride and lust and satisfaction and fierce, unholy relief slam into me, warring for dominance.

"Brave, beautiful girl," I murmur, dizzied.

Over the falling of a sheet.

It's such a small, simple movement, but the heady rush of her choosing this, choosing *me*, is raw. Intense.

Humbling.

I'm humbled as her eyes catch alight at the praise, and as a small, pleased smile replaces her solemn nerves. I'm humbled as she leans forward, her palms sinking into the soft mattress. I'm humbled by the hypnotic sway of her breasts. By the way her thighs shift together, and her lips part as she watches me. As she crawls to me.

I'm humbled by her trust.

Chained to his post, Jaykob is dark and turbulent as she moves toward me, caught in that too-familiar space between jealousy and lust. I can hardly blame him. She's lovely like this.

I absorb her every micromovement—the flutter of her lashes and the determined curl of her fingers in the sheets. How her pulse flickers at her throat, and the strands of hair tease her fragile cheekbones and the crooked tilt of her glasses. I study her like I want to make art of her, too. I lean back onto my elbow and touch my lips to stop myself from flooding her with every foolish compliment trying to escape me.

Instead, I let her see it.

My open lust and my hard desire. Without words, I coax her forward, telling her she's good, she's perfect, that I *want* her. Her pupils are blown, and she stares at my mouth, my painfully confined cock, and I want her to see it. That she's beautiful. Powerful.

She might be the one on her knees right now, but Eden has me entirely at her mercy.

Her back begins to arch prettily as she gains confidence—a graceful, proud curve that makes an obscene display of her dripping cunt for the men behind her.

Jaykob lets out a rough grunt.

"O-okay," Lucky breathes hoarsely, his fingers digging into his thigh like he's trying to find safe harbor. His eyes are fixed on her bare ass, empty of a plug. On her wet, greedy pussy, still throbbing for a cock.

And Eden knows it.

Her cheeks are lust dark, and her open, trembling lips catch me like a snare. The subtle, excited scent of her drugs the air, and the way she moves . . . It's old. Primeval. The way she moves is a thing of sirens and succubi and men lured to hopeless ends.

She has us in thrall.

By the time she's reached the end of the bed, she's in chaos. Flushed and shaking with need, she stops in front of me, her hair a riverine torrent all around her, her breasts still swaying.

Suddenly, Lucien groans, his face tortured. The mattress slopes as he moves closer to her, and his swollen cock bobs.

"God, beautiful. I can . . . You need help with that? I can—"

One hand grasps her ass, pulling her open. His head dips in, and vicious need clamps my balls.

But my irritation also spikes.

His mouth is a breath from her when I cut in. "Don't even try it, Lucien."

Eden's toes curl in frustration, her pained eyes pressing closed. But just like earlier, there's a moment of hesitation before he stops.

Unhappiness bites at me.

Lucien's rough hand tightens on her ass, his mouth still an inch from her pussy. He breathes on her, over her sensitive flesh, and she shudders.

"It's a waste," he begs. "Jasper, please. Please. Let me taste her."

Eden lets out her breath in a slow, trembling gush. Lucien's shaking, too, as he pleads with me. His voice is a husky wreck as Eden makes a mess of herself an inch from his tongue.

My cock presses painfully against my zipper, jealous and enthralled and possessive of them both. The begging is sweet, and Eden is no longer sassing me, but . . . my pique at them lingers.

It's my turn.

I rest Eden's limits list on the arm of the chair, then pat my lap kindly, like I'm not throbbing with the perverted desire to have her naked, dripping body in my hands.

"Come here, sweet girl," is all I say.

With a plaintive groan, Lucien releases her slowly, and Eden blinks multiple times, dazed and doe-eyed, trying to come back to herself as she slips off the bed. Her thighs are glistening, and I see the wet trails Lucien wanted to trace with his tongue.

Eden pads over to me, and I watch her, saying nothing as she stops in front of me and falls into a loose, natural Attention. She has perfect form. It almost hurts to look at her. Between the proud arch of her shoulders and the fevered color in her cheeks, her lust is painfully transparent, and it's so much more obvious when she's like this—that she's too young. Too eager. An old sadist like me has no business entertaining fantasies of a woman like this.

And yet.

She's standing there like an expectant student, naked, with every desire to please in her eyes, and I can't find any sense of decency at all. I *want* to take advantage of her. I want to make her please me in every filthy way I can think of. I want to wreck myself on her young, beautiful body.

I want to leave her shattered and soaked in my cum.

"Should . . ." Eden clears her husky throat. "Should I sit?"

My balls throb. I can almost taste her arousal, feel her heat. The thought of having her dutiful little ass nestled against my cock makes my vision haze.

I'm not pretending to be a good man anymore.

If she's offering, I'm indulging every desire I have for her until she begs me to stop.

I lean forward and, ever so lightly, I cup the sides of her legs as she stands in front of me. Her whole body tenses, and I almost groan at the instant response. I wasn't supposed to touch her yet, but I can't help myself. There's too much of her I haven't discovered yet, and I need it now like I need oxygen, or sleep.

I deserve it.

So, I allow my fingertips to trail up the outside of her silky thighs, luxuriating in the shivery softness of her skin. I trace the gooseflesh that rises over her hips. I curve my hands around her round ass until her breaths come in shaky little pants, and she trembles in my grip.

The trembles do it for me.

My sweet, obedient girl.

Drunk on her submission, I draw her in and press my mouth against her abdomen, tasting the salt on her delicate, tearable skin.

Eden's sharp, indrawn breath is startled, caught off guard by the sudden contact, and I can hardly blame her. There's nothing artful in this. I'm just taking what is on offer.

Her cunt is inches away, drugging me, and I roll my head against her stomach, fighting for control. My nose trails down, and I drag in a deep, hungry breath.

I could part her now, split her with my tongue and taste all the slick, warm desperation she's made for me. I could make her squirm, just like Lucien did. It's been so long since I've had a woman like this, but I recall enough. It's no matter if I can't, in any case. I'll simply pin her beneath me and fuck her with my tongue until it all comes back to me.

She's already quaking, my poor little doll. Her soft curves and secret nooks and her wet, wet heat beg to be explored with tongue and teeth and—

"*Fuck*, Jasper."

Lucien's rough, explosive curse cuts through my fog.

My fingers are buried in her soft ass, my tongue on her skin, and she's shaking like a leaf.

Ah.

I'm . . . *mauling* her.

"Jesus, sugar." Jaykob rolls his shoulders as he rakes his eyes over us, leaning back on his post. "Just get yourself a dog. Less mess."

My cheeks flood with heat, and I roll my forehead against her stomach.

Where on earth is my self-control? If there's any benefit at all to being with a man fifteen years her senior, surely it's that I can keep myself in check.

Breathing hard, embarrassment choking me, I lift my eyes to Eden's . . . but she doesn't look disappointed.

She looks *debauched*.

Her pupils are dilated, dark, and her bottom lip is drawn punishingly between her teeth like her needy little mouth just needed something to suck on. Her breasts are trembling above me, limned in sweat, and her scent is everywhere.

Suddenly, I don't care what Jaykob is sneering from his perch.

Eden's need is violent.

I don't believe in a god, but something divine must be gracing me, that she still wants me like this, because I don't know how I could have stopped myself from touching her tonight.

I've stepped outside of my rules now. I'm far from my safe paths, and I'm deep in the woods.

I'm lost in Eden.

Her hair falls from behind her ear, curtaining us both.

"Jasper," she whispers.

It's a question. A plea. Her desperation soothes my own, shaping it, forging it into something sharp and cruel and endlessly delighted.

In this unprivate place, we're finally together, and not galaxies apart.

"I know, darling girl."

I bring a curled finger up between her thighs, and very gently, I brush it along the hot seam of her cunt. She quivers, spilling over my finger, and I gather up her dripping need, captivated by her texture and heat and how very much in agony she is right now.

When I lift my hand to my mouth, her breath catches on a frustrated sob that strokes my cock. Her taste taunts me, bright and tart with a secret, pleasant lewdness.

I need to spend hours with my face between her legs.

I'll make Lucien hold them apart for me and hurt her every time she comes, make her scream until she learns just how exquisite the pain can feel.

I bite her stomach hard enough to bruise, and she squeaks like a chew toy.

I raise an amused brow at her as I sit back, drunk on the taste of her, on her awful, aching need, on how good she's being in spite of it —far better behaved than my Lucien.

He is still panting almost as hard as Eden, and Jaykob is still sneering, but with an audience or without, it hardly matters.

My librarian is in pain.

And I happen to know just what to do about that.

"My dear girl." I pick up her list again, tapping it on the edge of the armchair. Her foggy gaze follows it like it's fanged. "Is there anything you're concerned about? Anything you'd like to add?"

"No, Jasper." Her voice is barely audible. A sweet, scratchy whisper.

"Then bend over my lap," I order hoarsely, and watch as her throat cords.

"Thank you, Jasper."

Thank you.

No bratting from my librarian anymore. Just sweet, artless submission. My name, over and over, falling from her lips like bombfire.

She steps around my legs, studying my thighs like she's not sure how to splay herself, or the right way to bend. There's no delicate way to do it, so I watch her indecision with throbbing, indulgent amusement.

But as she steps in close, she absently reaches out a hand, like she's a princess stepping into a carriage—and I change my mind in an instant. She *is* delicate as she grasps my fingertips. Graceful as she lies over my lap. The elegant line of her arched back makes her into an instrument ready to be played. Orpheus's lyre, bewitching us all.

Her breasts press against one thigh, heavy and full, and her legs split over the other. Her pussy is hot and wet against the tailored fabric, soaking my thigh. My teeth lock together as she shifts to get comfortable, her stomach rubbing against my stiff cock.

She's everywhere, draped over me in erotic swells and carnal, feminine softness. I've never felt her like this—so close, so injuriously everywhere. There's no distance now, no manners.

Fuck my control.

I've never felt her cunt before.

Want pounds through my cock, and her heart is stuttering against me. As I watch, her ass twitches, flinching in agonized anticipation of a blow, and I want to purr like a lion over a kill.

"Eden, stop. He's a fucking—"

"You're making a mess of me already," I murmur, breaking over Jaykob's protest as if he weren't here, ignoring the sudden slam against his restraints. It's not his safeword, so I don't particularly care.

Her face, pink cheeked and lost, is pressed deep into the armchair, but I see her embarrassment at the remark. The way her eyes squeeze shut, and her hips shift as if that will stop the way she's leaking over me.

I bring my hand soothingly up the back of Eden's trembling thigh, and my fingers brush through her dampness. I trail over the cleft of her ass and watch her shiver before I repeat the deceptive strokes.

So charmingly nervous.

"Eden, remind me what you told Lucien earlier, while he had his disobedient cock fucking all over your cunt?"

She jerks on my lap, and like a cat pouncing on escaping prey, I slap her ass on instinct, right where the curve meets her thigh. The *smack* is snappy, vibrant, and her ass jiggles hypnotically. Supple and bouncy and pliable, my palm sinks into her lush softness. It's a warming slap, it barely stings, but she yelps like I've whipped her.

My fingers sink into her pinkening skin, calming her, then hungrily, I pull her open so I can see her bare little asshole and the wet sheen of her pussy, only to squeeze her cheeks together again. I'm spiraling, imagining every filthy thing I could bury inside those tight holes. Imagining how those cheeks would squeeze my cock, and how she'd let me fuck every inch of myself into her while she lay there like the good, amiable girl she is.

I give her another warming slap for good measure, and my lips curve at her nervy gasp.

I could spank this ass for hours.

"Did you forget, sweet girl?" I purr, tracing the dusty pink stains. She marks so effortlessly. "You gave him such *insistent* orders. I would enjoy learning, since you find me so deficient in the giving of them."

Eden must hear the danger, because her indrawn breath is slow and tremulous against the armchair. "I— I told him to ignore you. I begged him to . . . to make me come and—" I move my hand, and her bare foot flinches up in preemptive protection and she bursts out, "Please, I didn't want him to stop. I wanted to come. I want to come. Please. Jasper, I . . ."

I press my thumb into the slick mess between her legs, pushing it against her until I have her clit pinched and pinned against my thigh. Her pretty begging is cut off with a pained moan, her breathing becoming ragged again.

It brightens every nerve ending. It fills me with vicious, biting hunger as she fights her instincts to squirm. Her pussy is pink and silken and wet. It's spread for me to toy with, to hurt.

All my base instincts want to come out and play with her.

"Item one on your limits list, Eden—are you a dominant? Remind me what you selected." I pluck at her clit, like it truly is a string on a lyre, and I'm rewarded with a high whimper.

I glance up to see Jaykob roll his eyes at the question.

Joyless oaf.

"I don't . . . You already know what I—"

Smack.

The lively, sharp sting bursts over her open pussy, over my fingers, and she jerks back into me again with a shocked gasp. She sobs, and I pulse with pitiless, biting delight. She's too easy. That twitching little clit is right there—so very sensitive, so very mine.

I want to smack it again.

It's dangerous, how drunk on her I am. How greedy I am for every squirm, every gasp. I've had Lucien every night strung up and whipped raw, had him spread and fuckable beneath me just hours ago, and I feel the same kind of feral thrill now. I'm ready to come in my pants.

Over a *spanking*.

It's . . . unprecedented.

"Answer the question," I generously advise. I hope that she doesn't, though. More than anything, I want her to give me an excuse to watch her flinch. My fingers toy with her pussy, ruthlessly avoiding her clit. "Are you a dominant?"

Lucien's breathing roughens further as I taunt her, and Eden's head snaps around to give him a panicked look. Catching it, he chokes out a laugh, and I need to suppress my own amusement.

"*Promptly*, Eden."

At my silken warning, she yelps, "No! I marked no. I'm not a dominant. Or a switch. I don't want . . . That's not me."

She looks up at me over her shoulder, her hair falling over the armchair to the floor, and I look down at her patiently through my glasses. Satisfaction purrs through my chest. "No. You're a needy little submissive, aren't you?"

Her eyes glaze at the question. Or at me, perhaps, from the way she stares. Her hips shift restlessly over my lap, and my balls squeeze at the rush of moisture that escapes her, spilling over my fingers and onto my slacks.

She's as drunk on this as I am.

Her tongue darts out to dampen her lips. "Yes, Jasper."

I drag in a sharp breath through my nose, my pulse throbbing in my temple, my cock trying to punch through my slacks.

"Hm, that's what I thought," I murmur, then I *tsk*, scolding. "Now, now, clever girl, if you're going to play with dominants, then you really should remember the fundamentals."

She's new. Don't break her.

Don't break her.

Don't break her.

Don't break her.

With one fist, I grasp the back of her hair and drag her head back. She follows me, her expression a precious tangle of trust and nerves and pleading. I bend her until she's deeply arched over my lap, and her breasts bounce over my thigh.

I won't break her.

I'll only . . . bend her a little.

Her breath stalls, her eyes flicking up to mine as she waits.

"Submissives don't give orders," I croon.

The image of Lucien's cock running down her clit, seeking purchase, desperate to fuck into her is scalded into my brain. Their boldness with one another is so vastly different to how they are with me. Precious. It made me want to fuck them both.

Hard.

My fingers tighten in that dark, glorious hair until her breath catches, and I let my pique from earlier show in my face. Her nipples tighten, teasing my thigh, and my lip curls back at the sight. I could hurt her for that too.

It's cruel, how she makes me want her. Merciless, how her body tempts me.

She's a spiteful thing, to have kept it from me for so long.

My fingers between her thighs sink in deep, invading her hot, clutching walls, and she groans as I explain.

"If you want to come, you ask my permission. If you want to touch yourself, you ask my permission. And if you want Lucien to fuck you, then you'd both better beg me for it."

Outrage and acquiescence war on her flushed face, and I shudder with want as I kiss her cheek. She smells like wildflowers. Wildflowers and sex.

"I own you both now," I whisper against her skin. "Do you understand?"

Eden sighs, and for a moment, as her body sinks into me again, I'm sure her acquiescence will win out.

But then . . . Jaykob.

CHAPTER 45

JASPER

SURVIVAL TIP #142
Listening takes more than ears.

I fucking told you," Jaykob sneers. His heavy, tattooed shoulders strain against my knots. "You really want to keep spending your life begging for scraps, Eden? You really want to waste yourself on fucking assholes who never put you first?"

Livid rage snaps through me as he interrupts, taunting Eden again with ideas that could hurt her—*truly* hurt her. Making her believe there is any kind of competition here, or that there is *any* world in which she isn't as much a priority to me as Lucien.

I suddenly don't know why I let him stay for this. I'm not sure what I wanted to achieve. To school him, perhaps. To prove to him, and myself, that Eden wants me as much as she ever wanted him. Maybe even to find some sort of middle ground, a truce from which we could both accept this strange position we've found ourselves in with her.

But looking at him now, I only feel the same contempt for him that he's always shown me.

How dare he throw her past in her face?

How dare he question something he knows *nothing* about?

Worse, his comments appear to land.

Eden's eyes are suddenly blazing, uncertain and glossed with the wrong kind of tears. Her cheeks still glow with lusty color as she hesitates, then stammers, "Lucky's not just yours, Jasper. He's not yours *first*, not always. He's allowed to touch me. We were . . . you can't just stop things between us like—"

Enough.

I shove two wet fingers into her mouth, cutting her off as I press the taste of her own pleasure over her tongue. She stares up at me with wide, cock-throbbingly innocent eyes. Stunned silent, she licks up the tartness on instinct, and I feel the heated graze of her tongue. I watch with aching, scholarly approval as flashes of pink twist through my fingers, lapping up every last drop.

Lucky makes a raw, deprived sound, and I cut a sharp look his way. His muscles are taut, veined with strain. My lips curl against my teeth as I fight the need to taste him, too.

He looks driven to the brink.

"Do *not* come, Lucien."

"Uh-huh, sure thing. No problem." A glossy drop of precum squeezes from his crown, and he half-strangles a groan as he grasps the base of his dick. "Just get her to stop talking like that. Maybe stop fingering her mouth?" Tearing his eyes away, his head tips back, and he pulls his glorious length down hard. "The glasses. Oh, fuck. Why are you both wearing glasses?"

"What do you last, two seconds?" Jayk bursts out incredulously. "Take a cold shower, asshole. You're pathetic."

Lucky falls back on the bed, still strangling his dick in a severe grip. "Yep. You keep talking. That helps."

An impatient sound escapes me, and I look down at Eden with mild rebuke.

My thoughts are ravaged—in uncharacteristic anarchy. They're fucked by her body and obedience and her eager little rubs against me. Even the embers of hurt starting up in her eyes aren't enough to douse it.

My gaze drops to the indecent join of her pliant lips around me, and a growl rumbles in my chest. Lucien is carnal, filthy, and his tastes run as violent as mine . . . but I don't think I've ever met anyone so unpretentiously erotic as she is. Eden's glasses are tilted, her hair teasing against me in a thousand coquettish snarls, and the devoted licks of her tongue are making me spiral.

I have a point. We need to talk, to fix this, but I just . . . I *need* . . .

I adjust my hold, grasping her chin and pressing down on her tongue until saliva drips around my fingers. Gratification curls through me as she squirms.

"In your own time, of course you and Lucien may do whatever you please." I slip my fingers from her mouth and bring my face close to hers. "But when you're in my presence, dear girl, you're mine."

Smack.

Eden squeals, flinching, but I have her trussed tight. I'm an inch from her mouth. I can see every agonized expression flickering over her face as my hand claps hard against her ass.

"Your body is mine."

Smack.

"Your pleasure."

Smack.

"Everything you are . . ."

Smack.

"*Mine.*"

"Fuck. *Off,*" Jaykob roars, and the bedframe groans, but it only adds to the chaotic cacophony. Just like Lucien's cursing, and Eden's relentless, hitching gasps.

I'm so greedy for her body. For the way she wriggles and how she molds against me. She's little. Her squirming won't get her anywhere. I could hold her in place and just . . .

Smack.

Smack.

Smack.

Her mouth falls open on a soundless moan, and I see the moment it comes over her, when the bright, sharp edges begin licking away into sweet, throbbing heat. When adrenaline starts shooting through her in surprised little spurts.

My heart has lost all dignity, pounding in my chest in fervent infatuation, and I groan at the sight of the livid red prints all over her pale flesh. Marks of brutality, and passion.

My love language is written in scarlet.

"Jasper," she whispers, and it has wondering, teary edges. Her breath is hot on my cheek.

Wrathful affection crushes me. It makes me want to crush her, too, so she can feel it, but instead, I brush my lips against hers—as tender as I want to be violent. I shake with the twin desires, ruthlessly torn, and I'm rewarded with her wet sob against my mouth.

"You're losing it," Jaykob bites out.

"Do you want to leave?" I murmur, staring at her lips.

I'm not entirely sure who I'm asking, but there's something in Jaykob's voice, an undercurrent that pulls me back just a little.

"Hard pass," Lucien groans.

My lips purse in heady amusement as I glance at him, still lying on the bed, his cock in hand. To his credit, he has been unusually patient. My darling brat.

His hand flexes around his cock when he catches me watching, and my eyes narrow, but then Eden is tugging at my shirt—a heavy-lidded, throaty distraction. "I don't want to go anywhere."

Base, animal pleasure curls through me at her response.

I glance at Jaykob, raising one brow in caustic, taunting question.

Just say it. Safe out.

Let me have her.

His eyes spit vitriol. "Like hell I'm leaving you alone with her."

Despite myself, offense curls deep in my chest.

I know what I am. Sadists hardly have a glowing reputation, even in the community, but . . . he knows me. He knows my reputation and the respect I earned. We saw out Day Death, fought side by side to get dozens of civilians to safety. We took on the Reapers together, and I supported him then. I've even seen him cry in my chair—moments before he stormed out of our session, but still. Jaykob *knows* me.

I understand his jealousy.

But does he truly not trust me?

I glower at him, anger and hurt chilling some of my thrill.

"Jasper?" Eden asks, uncertainty threading her tone as she glances between us.

I drag in a steadying breath and look down at her, loathing the hesitation growing in her eyes. I reach up and smooth the line in her brow. When it eases, I cup the side of her face.

"So beautiful," I murmur, my thumb whispering over her cheekbone. "So filthy."

Her lips part.

I capture her mouth in a kiss, and she moans into my mouth like it was dragged out of her unwilling. My kiss is a punishment. I punish her for how much Jaykob's distrust hurts. I kiss her knowing that he'll detest every second. I kiss her and plan every single way I can fuck her in front of him.

She whimpers as I pull back. Her mouth is wet, and her eyes glow with pretty desperation.

For *me*.

Without shifting my fascinated gaze, I murmur, "Lucien, make yourself useful. I've brought some presents for our girl. How about we give them to her, hm?"

"Forget the stupid games, Eden. You need to rest," Jaykob snaps, but Lucien snorts from the bed.

"Beau was totally fucking with you, Jayk. She's fine."

Jaykob glares at him, then lashes against his ropes.

"Get off his lap and you can ride my cock right fucking now," Jaykob roars, and my heart jerks in my chest in sudden panic.

I give Eden a sharp look.

Her breasts are swollen, and her cunt is squeezing uselessly around nothing. I can hear Jaykob's frustration, as tangibly as I can see hers. Jaykob would fuck her in an instant. She could end this scene—this embarrassing, indulgent display, this *mess* of a scene that has been entirely railroaded by how much I want her. She could drop me with a single word and get everything she needs right now.

From *him*.

"Don't," I bite out, watching her, my own jealous need thrumming through my cock.

If she goes to him now, it might break me.

Something shifts in the fog of her eyes, and without asking permission, she turns on my lap, her arms sliding around my neck until her naked breasts press against my silk shirt and her pussy rides the furious line of my cock.

Her hand cups my cheek, and her thumb brushes my lower lip.

Eden's gaze twines with mine, and the whole world falls away.

"Make me hurt, Jasper."

Victory roars in my ears. Pure need hazes my vision as she kisses me tenderly, the way I kissed her earlier, and she's shaking like I did then. I grip her hip and grind her against my cock, just for a moment, because we're both too close to the edge for more than one, but I need to give her something—the world, maybe—and for now, all I have is the seconds I can give her.

My cock.

My heart.

My soul.

My Lucien is slipping off the bed, toned and beautiful, his cock aching like mine aches, when Jaykob slams against his ropes again.

"Stay the fuck there," he snarls, glaring at Lucien. "Touch that bag and I swear to fuck, I'll tear this whole bed down and you after it."

"Jayk—" Eden starts, her brow crumpling, but I squeeze her to stop.

This isn't about her, or even about Lucien.

My hurt ices over.

"Turn around, Eden. Now."

After a quick, searching look, she turns over in my lap, shifting until her ass is seated over my cock, and her head falls into the crook of my shoulder. With deliberate care, I spread her legs wide, and they fall on either side of mine.

Her cunt glistens in the silver moonlight, on full display.

Jaykob's curses split the air.

"Eden clearly enjoys her time with you, Jaykob, but it's not all she needs." My hand curves over her pussy, my fingertips brushing over her exposed clit, and she shudders everywhere. Rage bunches Jaykob's chest, and dark, spiteful enjoyment licks through me. "She loves this—even you have to see that. Perhaps she doesn't crave extreme pain, not like Lucien, but in her own way . . . she wants to hurt."

He won't admit it, but he *does* know it, as well as I do.

Because no matter how much he scowls—he's still hard for her under that pretty red throw blanket.

Eden's arousal demands a response.

I tap her clit, and she flinches, right on the brink. I breathe her in, listening to her ragged breaths, feeling her fight for control—and I fight for my own. My poor girl needs to come.

"Tell him, my dear Eden. Tell him how much you want it."

She sinks back against me, her breasts wobbling. Her disobedient hips tilt toward my hand. "I— I want it. I want them. I need— Please. God, I need it so much, Jayk. Please let me . . . let *them* . . ."

"*Fuck*." Jayk's head snaps back against the post as furious air punches out of him. His breathing quickens, the ropes straining, and when he looks at her again, his expression is wild. Frantic. "You *want* him to hurt you? He's going to do it, Eden. You know that, right? Not swat your fucking pussy. Have you seen the things he does to people? You *don't* want it."

Eden begins to shake, in need or in fear, I'm not sure, but something in his voice snags me again. I blink, fighting my lust, and I study him more closely.

There's a harsh downturn to his mouth.

A frenetic energy under his snarling rage.

"I *have* seen it, and I do . . . I *do* want it," Eden whispers, and Lucien makes a coarse sound. Kneeling beside us now, his pupils are blown dark.

Jaykob's head tips back against the post again, confused resignation in every line of his shoulders.

He's worried for her.

"Would you like to use your safeword?" I ask him, more carefully this time. My thoughts are a dizzy mess, but I'm watching him now . . . and I don't like what I see.

Jaykob's jaw flexes, and my throat turns dry.

He's worried about Eden.

He's worried about Eden because he *loves* her.

He's *worried*, and under my care, and rather than hearing his concerns . . . I'm showing him I'm exactly what he fears. Callous and cruel to a fault.

"Jasper?"

At Eden's tentative question, I draw a deep, defeated breath in through my nose. Suddenly, Lucien's words from earlier are ringing in my ears—*you're a sadist . . . you know where not to hit.*

I'm . . . every kind of fool.

Jaykob's throat works, and Eden shifts uncomfortably, and I want to slap myself. I've approached this wrong. Calamitously so.

Because I've spent far too much time on hate.

I came here out of spite and anger. I came here, telling myself every reason why Jaykob is my enemy. Every reason I have to loathe him, and to think he's wrong for Eden.

But he's not.

If I'm truthful, if I can truly set my own insecurities aside . . . then I can admit it.

I love him for her.

I *love* that Eden's shoulders stand straighter after seeing him. I love that she's no longer afraid to bite at me. I love that he protects her with bared teeth, with all the skills at his disposal, skills that I don't have . . . even if it means he also considers me an enemy.

I love how he softens for her, too.

Jaykob isn't the same man he was when I met him, avoiding connection and responsibility like a wild animal. He's grown. With her, with the civilians, he's a different man, one I glimpsed in our sessions but was rarely able to reach.

I run a hand over my jaw, my eyes locked on him, as serious and sincere as I'm able.

"You don't trust me, Jaykob, but you can. You always could."

Jaykob swallows, his face tightening as he stares at the ceiling . . . but he's listening.

Slowly, his rage drains away too. The sneering, crude bravado he likes to stab out with is gone. Anger is his defense, and he's lowered it.

We're both peeled back.

When Jaykob doesn't respond, I soften. "I have her, I promise you. I have you all."

Finally, he looks at me, and his gaze holds me to that promise. More serious than I think I've ever seen him.

Just once, he nods.

Something new, fragile and unexpected, lightens the space between us.

Hm. Perhaps we'll get our truce after all.

"Lucien, open the bag."

CHAPTER 46

EDEN

My clit is throbbing as Lucky bends down, and Jayk's eyes snap with furious heat, locked on my cunt. Jasper is scorching, sheathed in silk and pressed all along the line of my back, and I'm spread so open over his lap that my thighs ache. His breath feathers over my hair, and needlepoint chills chase down my spine.

I'm glad for Jayk and Jasper and their little heart to heart—truly, I am—but this isn't funny anymore.

I *need* to come.

Jasper's malicious hand whispering over my inner thighs, his flushed, college-professor face, his slacks against my sore ass . . . it's too much. I've never seen him undone like this, so clearly, obviously wrecked by need.

I shift again, rubbing the back of my head against him, and he exhales hard against my ear.

"Be *still*, Eden."

I bite down on my wobbling lip.

Lucky is taking too long.

My fingers twitch on Jasper's forearm. It wouldn't take much to get myself off. A quick rub would do it.

But, even as I quiver with the urge, I force myself still.

I want to be good.

Jasper envelops me in parchment and ink. It's the scent of all the pages he reads through, the thousands of lives he's lived between them, of clever quips and margin notes . . . and under it, there's something else. A sharp, supple leather that speaks of crops and polished toys—and raw lust. It's safety and danger, everything thrilling and terrifying.

I want whatever he has planned more than a quick climax.

Just.

My indrawn breath stutters out as his fingers grip my thighs. With greedy strokes and squeezes over my exposed skin, the ragged-rough pull of his breaths, it's like he can't get enough of touching me.

My heart sputters like an erratic flame. I shift my ass against the hard ridge, where he's throbbing like I'm throbbing, but the pressure in me only rises. There's no relief from it. Not like this. Not while I'm perched on his lap like a pornographic student begging for extra credit. Not while I'm soaking his cock through his professional slacks.

"Jasper . . ." I choke out.

It's a warning. A plea.

But he only presses his mouth to the corner of my lips, and I realize he's trembling, too.

"Shh, shh," he hushes me, squeezing my thigh viciously as he presses me wider. "You don't get to say *enough* to me. Not like that."

He drags one knee up over the arm of the chair, and he stares down my body as my pussy opens wide. His long fingers part me further, possessively, and with such delicate, restrained violence that I leak over his hand.

A deep, darkly satisfied sound escapes him.

Cool air hits my clit, and I clench around nothing. I'm aching. I *need* him inside me. I need to feel him spear through all that pressure. I need a cock to squeeze against. I need to be full, and to feel that too-much pinch of pain.

I need to feel him come.

"It's not enough. Nowhere near enough." Jasper's lips are at my ear. His breathing is heavy and rough, snarling with arousal, and I whimper, trying not to squirm. "Let me play with all your parts, pretty girl."

My thoughts liquefy, and I can't help my needy jerk against him.

Instead of scolding me, Jasper only growls a heated, "Lucien, hurry *up*."

"Yeah . . . uh. Yep. I'm just . . ." Lucky drags his dazed eyes away from me and Jasper, staring down at the unopened bag. "I think I blacked out for a second there, but I'm back."

He quickly tugs open the bag beside us, and when he finally pulls the mysterious items free, I . . . don't recognize either of them.

The first is a set of delicate silver chains that twinkle in the starlight—and three elegant, sharp-toothed pinching heads dangle off the ends.

The other item is a longer, thicker, wickedly curved hook with a round silver end . . . and the hook is attached by a chain to a beautiful leather collar.

"Fuck's sake," Jayk mutters.

I eye him, then squint again at the items, trying to figure out how they work. My thigh twitches restlessly under Jasper's hand.

I'm not sure I care what they do, so long as they do it fast.

"Choose one for her. Whatever pleases you most."

Lucky looks up at Jasper's voice, and Jasper settles back against the chair languorously.

"Aw, come on. Jasper, please don't put me in the middle of—"

"Choose, or she'll wear both."

Lucky's lips part, worry furrowing his brow as he looks between them, then glances guiltily up at me. His eyes linger on my breasts, his thumb rubbing over the delicate bundle of chains, and he grimaces. Tentatively, he lifts the collar.

"The hook," he says reluctantly, and Jasper's low laugh is frayed at the edges.

"Playing the hero, Lucien? Your loyalty is as adorable as it is misguided." Jasper is too knowing, even as he grips my throat with his free hand. "You should know better than to lie to me by now."

His fingers trail down my chest, and my gasping breaths nearly dislodge him.

Lucky's gaze tracks the motion.

"Do you think that by protecting her from what you truly want, she will love you better?" Jasper continues. When his other hand cups my pussy possessively, I moan. Sweat slicks my hairline as I fight the need to grind against his palm, and Jasper's voice whispers in my ear. "Do you think she's afraid of the dark?"

Jasper is playing chess with me again, but his hand on my pussy is almost all I can focus on.

"Whatever pleases you, Jasper," I murmur.

"Not Lucien?" he asks, jealously edged, his gaze a snare.

I brave a shift against his hand, and he squeezes me hard.

"Lucien who?" I moan, and Lucky splutters.

Jasper's eyes gleam with scorching amusement. "The clamps it is."

There's so much relish in the way he says it that a prick of nervousness shivers through my need. His hand curls under one of my breasts, and I gasp, arching as he tests the weight in his cool, elegant hand.

"Such pretty breasts." His thumb brushes over my nipple, and I shudder. "So sweet. So soft."

His thumb flicks over me again, watching me with visceral hunger. His eyes are flame-licked coals, intense and approving.

Suddenly, he stops his tiny flicks over my nipple, and he pinches it hard between two fingers, then tugs it roughly.

I yelp, twisting, as vibrant, spurting pain explodes in my nipple. I arch, trying to ease it, but Jasper only tugs me higher, watching me obsessively, *curiously*. Bright spots of color ride high along his cheek-bones, and his lean jaw flexes in an almost-snarl as he takes in my expression.

I whimper as the pain spreads, aching through my breast. This pain isn't hot and bright, it's cold and biting, with a throb that reaches somewhere deep and low inside me. I can't tell if I like it, if I want it, but the more he tugs, the lower the pain reaches, until it feels as though he's tugging at my clit with rough, icy plucks of his fingers.

Tears spring back to my eyes as I grip him around his neck, my fingers digging into his silky hair, and Jasper's expression becomes humiliatingly knowing.

"Poor girl," he croons.

Then he lets me go, and I curl up, pressing my arms protectively over my breasts.

"Ow. Ow, ow, ow."

Jasper tugs my hair back so he can keep watching my face, and his eyes glitter with feral delight. He strokes the back of a finger down my cheek.

My mind short-circuits, caught between the blistering, icy pain and his intoxicating tenderness.

"I know," he murmurs. "I know, darling girl. It's awful, isn't it?" He grasps both my wrists where they're still crossed protectively over my chest. "Open up for me now. Let me make it better."

Instinctually, I fight against him, but despite his lean build, Jasper is strong, and his forearms barely cord as he slowly forces my arms wide, exposing me again.

My breasts lift in rapid, panicked breaths, and he kisses my temple sweetly.

"That's a good girl. Ease it for her, Lucien—and stop pouting at me. She asked for this." His nose runs along my cheekbone. "Didn't you, sweet one?"

Still shocky, I'm stammering a response when a scorching mouth closes over my aching breast.

"Oh!"

My mouth parts, hanging open as Lucky sucks my sore nipple into his mouth, laving it with his tongue. The tugging suction, the heat, the wet—it floods over the pain, relieving it with shocking, brutal pleasure.

Lucky groans against me as I squirm. On his knees between Jasper's legs, he shifts his weight forward until I'm pinned between them.

"Color?" Jasper asks thickly, stroking my hair off my forehead.

Shuddering, I try to grind my hips up against Lucky, but the two of them have me pressed too close to move. I tunnel my fingers into Lucky's long hair to hold him to me instead, and my other hand flexes against Jasper's neck.

I'm leaking everywhere.

I thought I was sensitive before, but that was nothing—*nothing*—compared to how Lucky's mouth feels after Jasper's abuse.

Exquisite torture.

I watch Jayk's rough face twist, guiltily loving how the rope stands out against his tattoos, and how—no matter how much he scowls—he's still hard for me under the pretty red throw blanket.

Tearily, I choke out, "Green. I'm . . . green, ah."

Jayk's tense jaw works, but he drags in a deep breath through his nose, keeping quiet.

Lucky presses soothing kisses against my skin as Jasper greedily grasps my other breast, then plucks that nipple up with the same cruel, rough treatment.

Pain explodes again, followed by Lucky's scorching mouth. It's cold and hot, rough then wet, cruel then all delicious, silky suction. The confusing clash of sensations is too much. My tears begin to spill over, and Jasper shudders. He tilts my head back to claim them, his lips running over my cheeks with biting, needy kisses.

He twists my nipple, and I cry out, shocked as his cock rocks against my ass.

It's a different pain to being spanked.

It's more livid. More vulnerable and raw. There's no cushion here, no deep thud. And just when I think it can't get worse, I hear the jingle of chains and I twist.

The silver dangles from Jasper's fingertips like droplets, and his eyes glow with unholy light over mine.

"Ease back, Lucien. You've done well." Jasper grasps my inner thigh again, his fingers digging in, and roughly, deliberately, he tilts me open even wider. "Make yourself useful and lick up some of the mess she's making of me."

"Thank God," he groans huskily.

Jasper reaches around me to loosen a small, delicate screw. The attached clamp has vicious teeth like an alligator's, and even though it's tipped in protective rubber, I freeze, clutching at Lucky's shoulder as his mouth begins to descend down my body.

"Lucky . . ."

I try to hold him in place—to help me—because, as pretty as it is, that clamp looks *mean*.

Lucky's heavy-lidded eyes dart between the clamps and me with a sympathetic wince. "Sorry, sweetheart." His nips my navel, and he hardly sounds sorry at all. "Duty calls. Can't ignore the boss." He licks the crease between my thigh and my pussy, and his voice is muffled when he adds, "Important job here."

"Lucien," Jasper says warningly, and Lucky pauses with a curse. His breath is hot and flushed over my clit, and I can't help my squirm. "If you make her come, I will be extremely displeased."

"Mhmm." Lucky's tongue dips into my wetness, circling the rim of my hole with hedonistic enjoyment. His nose is pressed into me, and his beard is getting soaked, but he's still somehow *nowhere* I need him to be. "Got it. World's worst kitty-eating coming right up. Hey, Jayk, got any tips?"

"I hope you fucking drown down there," Jayk snaps back.

Lucky sighs. "Me too."

His head dips again, his tongue delicious and taunting and utterly lawless over every slippery inch of me, and I can't stop the shivers racking me now. Over and over.

I feel like a broken wind-up doll, one caught on the highest coil, left ticking there hopelessly and bound to break at any moment.

"I love you like this," Jasper murmurs, touching my cheek as Lucky's tongue slowly slips by my clit.

His eyes are dark as the spaces between stars—a dark made softer and deeper by the bonfire lights around it. I can't help but wonder if the stars know that they burn so brightly only because he's there to bank them.

My beautiful, selfless sadist.

"I love you every way." Trembling, the words tumble out of me softly. "Every day. Every moment. Every piece."

Jayk's sharp breath is harsh denial, and Lucky's head lifts, but these are background motions.

Surprise. Fear. Awe. Hope.

Tears fill my eyes at every micro-expression that flashes across Jasper's face.

Before it settles on fierce, unfiltered possessiveness.

Jasper grasps my chin and captures my mouth in a kiss, and it's so unexpected, I moan into it before I can stop the sound. I'm too needy to be composed. My kiss is chaotic and hungry, delighting over the taste of him, every warning nip of teeth and every luxuriant, claiming lick. Usually, Jasper controls himself carefully—how much of himself he gives, how much he allows me to take.

But not this time.

Jasper locks my mouth to his as he kisses me thoroughly, desperately, and this time, he lets me feel all of it. His gratitude and vulnerability, his tenderness and passion and all the banked, envious hurt I only tonight even suspected of him.

Suddenly, Lucky's delighted tongue slides through my pussy again with renewed enthusiasm, and I cry out into Jasper's mouth. He coaxes the sound into his, and I can *feel* his dark, selfish amusement as I strain for more.

Finally, he pulls back an inch, and our mouths are drenched in each other.

It's uncivilized, for us.

It's a kiss from the margins. His real self between the pretty stories he brings me.

"I love you too, dear girl," he tells me, and after a moment, his lips curve privately, his eyes glassy with lust. "Most ardently."

My grin breaks free, remembering his notes, and he kisses my temple with tender, restrained need. Unruly strands of his hair fall over his forehead, and he pants against my skin.

"I do hope you still love me after this."

Sharp, cold rubber-sheathed teeth bite down on my nipple, and I cry out, jerking. Lucky's hands flatten on my thighs, holding me wide. He sucks me, missing my clit again, and his beard is coarse against my inflamed, sensitive skin.

My toes curl.

"Shh, shh, shh." Jasper's face is flushed, strained with the cruelest brand of affection. He's lost in lust. In love. In all the pain and pleasure he's giving me. He begins tightening the screw, watching as my face distorts. "I know, it's nasty. I know it hurts. It'll settle, sweet girl. You can take it— A little more. For me, my Eden. Be brave. Hold on to me if you need to."

My tears spill salt over my lips, slipping out more freely as he releases my heavy, aching breast, and Jasper stares at the wet tracks like they're suggestive. Libidinous. Like I'm making him hurt by hurting for him.

Flinching, my nails dig into Jasper's neck as he cups my other breast. The silver jaws gleam as he opens the clamp, and I'm unable to help my sob of anticipation.

"Eden?" Jayk growls, and I gasp for words.

"Green! I'm still . . . *Ah*!" Jasper locks the teeth around my nipple, and my words skew on a squeal. "I'm okay. I'm okay. I'm okay."

The promises come between hitching, sobbing pants that don't sound okay at all, but it's the best I have, especially as Jasper starts tightening the second clamp to match the first.

It's agony.

Pure, ungodly, vicious pain that starts angry and sharply stabbing, only to seep into a deep, fanning ache.

It's like the pretty chain strung between my nipples is a live wire, sparking cold electricity between my breasts. It's delicate and thin, but my breasts feel heavy and full, hypersensitive to the slightest swing.

Jasper's chest rumbles as I cry, arching helplessly, uselessly, to ease the hurt. He drapes the silver so it spills like glitter over my body. A tiny third clamp brushes my pussy, but I'm too caught by the ache in my breasts to pay it much mind.

Maybe I can't do this.

I grit my teeth, my head falling back as tears leak around my nose and into my mouth.

I tremble against Jasper's silk shirt, and his racing heart hammers against me.

No, they're too tight. My breasts suddenly too full.

I need them off.

Only I'm not sure I *can* rip these things off me without taking my nipples with them.

My nails curl into silk. "Hurts."

Jasper tenderly kisses my quivering lips again, sweetly patronizing, but I'm too blinded by tears.

"*Hurts*," I whimper again, dizzily. My thoughts are turning airy and wispish at the edges.

Jasper groans, then kisses me again.

"Breathe through it, beautiful," Lucky whispers against my pussy, looking up at me between my thighs, his eyes heavy-lidded and hopeless.

"I *am* breathing."

I think. I'm breathing a lot, but I can't seem to find much air.

"Focus on Lucien, sweet girl. He has a clever tongue, hm?" Jasper bites my jaw, breathing hard. "Do you like me letting him taste you? How generous I am with my little submissives, letting you enjoy each other. How kind I am to you."

He jingles the chain with a low laugh, and I squeal as black dots spark in front of my eyes. My skin tightens, and everything in me begins to lift, rising with the giddy, painful tension.

"Yeah, this seems like a real hoot," Jayk mutters, his head knocked back against the post in bemused resignation.

Jasper's hot tongue slides against mine, and I moan, trying to keep up. Lucky's beard brushes my clit, and I flinch as I almost go over the edge.

Jasper makes a hot, hungry sound into my mouth at my shudder.

The pain is settling deep and low, throbbing in me everywhere, deep and aching and mixing with the vicious, empty ache inside me. It pushes me harder, higher, and my thoughts are edged out by need.

"Place the last one, Lucien," Jasper purrs hungrily against my lips. "You know where."

Last one?

"Fuck. Sorry." Lips press against my thigh. "Sorry."

My thought, Lucky's voice—it all comes from far away.

I force my dazed eyes to open as Lucky's fingers spread me wide, and he groans.

Blue eyes flash at me. "Sorry, sweetheart. Sorry, sorry, sorry."

Then my vision whites out.

I screech, my hips slamming back into Jasper's cock as white-hot pain explodes in my clit. Jasper's arm locks around my waist, holding me to him and grinding against me as I arch back against him. It's staggering—a pulsating, cold-fire bite, and for a moment I'm not sure I can even breathe for the shock of it.

"Fuck," Jasper curses, a gasp to his voice. His hands squeeze my thighs. My hips.

My throat.

My pulse throbs in my temple, my nipples, my *clit*, and my teeth grit as I whimper, teetering on a terrifying, too-intense edge. My mind is flying free, pulling out of my body.

Jasper's greedy hands finally settle on gripping my jaw and kissing my mouth again with fervent, plundering kisses. "Just like that, brave girl. I'm so proud of you. You're hurting so well, my Eden. So good to let me use you like this." His lips press over my wet cheeks. "You poor, helpless thing. You're so pretty when you cry. Do you know how fucking hard you make me?"

I turn into Jasper's neck, sobbing, but I'm not sure if it's from pain or just from need alone. His words heal me everywhere I'm torn apart, and I kiss his neck desperately, even though the movement tugs at all my chains.

Pleasure cramps through me in dark, hot spurts.

"God damn." Lucky's voice is drunk. Ragged. "Is this what I look like when you . . ."

"Kiss her better, Lucien. Cheer her up. She's trying so hard for us," Jasper interrupts gently.

Lucky shudders.

His tongue hits my pussy again in diligent, greedy laps, and I feel him lose himself to selfish need. No matter how I squirm, though, he barely touches my clamped clit—and my shocked, airy thoughts can't decide if that's a blessing or a curse anymore.

But then his head dips lower, his hands tunneling under me, and I hear a rough metallic *zip*.

Jasper stiffens. "*Lucien.*"

Lucky meets my teary eyes again, and this time it's with mischief, bright and dancing between the lust. It takes me too long to realize what he's trying to do.

A strangled, dazed laugh escapes me, and I use my grip on Jasper's neck to edge myself up, giving Lucky room to quickly free Jasper's cock from his slacks. When I shift back down again, Lucky helps Jasper's hot, bare cock to slide through my folds.

It presses against the clamp, and I freeze, gasping against the need to come.

"Lucien!" Jasper barks, a note of panic in his voice that makes Lucky grin, and me sob out a giddy giggle.

It makes everything scream and throb, and Jasper's cock rubs new, perfect waves of pain over my clit. I'm light-headed now, and the silver ripples over my skin with my every jagged breath. It's pretty, really. It's pretty, and it's all shivering together—all the burning and hurting and wanting, and I'm suddenly sure that when I come, it's going to tear me apart at my seams.

Adrenaline bubbles up, twisting through the pain.

"Oh, yeah, sure. This seems smart," Jayk mutters, kicking a knee up as he eyes my face in disgust.

I throw him a wild smile, my veins fizzing. I'm weightless. Vivid.

"What? You said to cheer her up." Lucky laughs, cupping Jasper's balls. "She looks pretty cheery to me."

Jasper's fingers dig into my thigh as he curses, and I laugh too.

My heart is beating panic-fast, like I'm at the top of a rollercoaster and the danger is about to drop. But Lucky's hot, intoxicated grin turns it thrilling.

Fun.

Jasper's heart thunders against me, shudders racking him and, soothingly, I stroke the back of his neck, then turn my head to kiss his angled jaw. My breasts scream as the chain jingles, the flare of pain fanning from my nipples, but I focus on the agonizing, luscious slide of his cock against my clamp.

Lucky leans forward, sucking the flared, glossy crown of Jasper's dick into his mouth, and Jasper's hips punch up, his head slamming back. A pained groan slips from his lips, his face tortured.

"It's okay," I murmur, choked and shaky. I press another soft kiss against Jasper's lips. "It's okay, love. Just focus on Lucky. He—" Lucky's damp beard bristles against my clit as he takes Jasper's cock deep into his throat, and molten pleasure sears through the pain. "He has such a clever tongue."

"Have you lost your fucking mind?" Jayk snaps from his post, nonplussed. "Even I would have your ass for this shit."

There's a wet slide, and then Lucky's beard is pressing against my clit again. Again and again, and I catch my breath as my climax edges closer, blacking out the edges of my vision.

Jasper's chastising grip suddenly moves from my hip and steals into Lucky's hair, yanking his mouth off his cock.

And away from my clit.

"No!" I shout. "Jasper, *please.*"

"Get on the bed, Lucien." Jasper shoves Lucky toward the bed by his hair, and Lucky staggers back.

In the next instant, Jasper's standing, hauling me up into his arms and storming to the bed, his face aflame.

He drops me onto the mattress, sending my breasts bouncing into blazing, vision-darkening agony, then captures my squeal in a fierce, rebuking kiss. He bites my lips, sharply enough to sting, then groans against my mouth. When he pulls back to stand, it's to step out of his shoes. His hair hangs around his cheekbones, unbridled.

My climax catches inside me, desperate to snap free, and I fall back onto the bed, curling into myself hopelessly as Jayk watches hot-eyed from the foot of the bed. My tears soak the sheets. I think they're sheets. The room is blurring away, and at this point, they might be clouds.

Only my brutes are carved in sharp relief against my fuzzy, desperate thoughts.

"And here I was, being so kind and gentle with you." Jasper's chest lifts in rough, choppy breaths. His hands curl around my thighs, dragging me to the edge of the bed. "Look at what you're forcing me into."

Lucky hesitates, running a hand through his hair, hanging loose and wild over his shoulders. His expression is as broken as mine, his eyes too bright.

"Next to her, brat," Jasper snaps, and his delicious cock bobs lewdly over his zipper. His voice is thick with lust. "I'll deal with you tomorrow."

Jasper's gaze drops to lovingly run over my reddened nipples, squeezed between silver, and he grasps his cock as he stares.

Lucky crawls onto the bed, color buoyant in his cheeks, and with a fierce squeeze, Jasper releases his cock. His dick glistens with need.

Dragging a slow, ravenous tongue over his lips, Jasper begins loosening his cufflinks.

"Spread your legs."

At the sharp order, I spread them wide, and his satisfaction glows. I shoot a panicked look at Jayk, who rolls his eyes at me.

"Play stupid games, sugar."

Jasper snorts, running a hand over his jaw in apparent disbelief.

Jayk's eyes are midnight stars as he looks me over, but he doesn't hold the same kind of tension that he did earlier. "Remember that safeword?"

Miserably, I nod, but then Jasper's finger is hooked under my chin, turning my face to his.

"In this house, we don't play our dominants against one another, you understand?" Jasper kisses me again, panting, and it feels like a warning. "In that game, you will *always* lose."

All the small hairs on the back of my neck lift.

Jasper drops to his knees between my legs, and a groan escapes him as he looks at my bared, soaking cunt. I'm a mess of me, and Lucky's mouth, and that bright, sparkling silver. My ass is hanging off the edge like an offering, and his hands tremble as he leans in.

Suddenly, a finger presses inside of me, then two, spearing against my hot, clenching walls. I squirm, bucking against the perfect pressure until a sharp, warning hand finds my clamp.

I freeze.

Resting his forehead on my mound, Jasper breathes in deeply, and his exhale quivers over my swollen, oversensitive clit.

Fogged, faint, my breathing starts to hitch, and the rollercoaster in me begins to tilt.

"Don't fret, darling girl. It'll only hurt for a moment," Jasper tells me. "Lucien?"

"Shit." Lucky kisses my damp forehead, my mouth, my cheeks.

But his hands move to the clamps at my nipples, and nervousness swoops through my stomach.

"*Wait!* No. No, wait." Fear and exhilaration spark wildly in me, and they both pause. "I don't know if I . . . "

Every tremble makes violent heat fan from my pussy, my nipples, but I can't make them stop. Panic and desperation and sharp, hot emotion fill the back of my throat.

I'm spinning out until my eyes hit Jaykob, still chained to the post.

Still silent.

Still watching.

He's turbulent, flushed, and there's an expression on his face I can't place. Something vulnerable and raw. And even when I look at him, while I'm overwhelmed and shaking, he doesn't close it down.

Instead, he just gives me a gruff, stormy-eyed shrug. "Come on, sugar. You got this far. If you want it, you take it."

Take it.

Bright, beautiful relief shatters inside me. At the concession. At what it means.

Jasper's watching me closely, and tears fill my eyes again as the throbbing pressure in my clit turns hot. Livid.

Take it.

Glancing between him and Lucky, I nod. "Okay. Okay, I—"

Jasper smiles.

The clamps release all at once, and blood rushes back in with a screaming rush. Then there are mouths—on my breasts, licking at my clit. Fingers fuck my cunt as sucking, scorching waves of pleasure engulf the pain, turning it into something sharply, breathtakingly beautiful.

My orgasm slams into me with ruthless brutality, and I spasm, curling into the pinning hands and wet mouths as they tear me apart. My mind rips away into the clouds, and sparkling, carbonated joy kisses away the pain and the fear, until it becomes something exhilarated and pantingly proud.

When I come to, it's hazed, and to the fingers slipping out of my pussy, followed by a thicker, heated, more insistent press inside, and a long string of desperate curses behind me.

Liquid hot pleasure-pain has me in thrall, and I don't resist as the cock works its way inside, inch by inch, before it bottoms out deep inside me. The cock is bare and raw in my pulsing cunt. My sore nipples press against the bed, and I rub into it.

"Fucking fuck of all motherfucking fucks," someone—Lucky?— groans. The cock in me rocks gently, *deliciously*, and pleasure ripples everywhere. "Oh *fuck*."

"Contain yourself, Lucien." A warm hand tilts my chin up, and my fogged gaze barely makes out a set of dark eyes. "Color? Both of you."

Lucky's laugh is strangled. "Neon. *Neon* green."

"Grn." I try again. "*Green*."

Bright, pretty green.

The hand strokes my jaw obsessively. "Good. That's good." The voice is rough raw. "Roll, Lucien. Please. On your back, bring her on top of you."

A colorful, muscular forearm tucks between my breasts as I'm squirming on the bed and pulls me backward. "Come have fun with me here, sweetheart."

His cock presses breathlessly deep as we switch positions, and I moan, giddy at the choking, frantic fullness.

God, I love *fun*.

I can feel myself sweating, but right now nothing is too much, or off limits. Right now, I'm sparkling, and everything is perfect.

I fall back against Lucky's chest, and I realize he's propped his shoulders up onto a pillow so we're not tilted back awkwardly. I squeeze my cunt around him, and he starts cursing again.

Dark, sleet-gray slacks edge between my thighs.

I look up at my sadist—my hungry college professor, still in his silk and suit, but beyond any professionalism now. His angelic lips are parted and wet, his eyes full of shattered, uncontrolled need. His pulse hammers in his throat, and his chest heaves with relentless need.

With one hand pumping his swollen, florid cock between the part in his slacks, Jasper reaches down and rubs my clit.

Pleasure bursts behind my eyes, and I cry out, but he talks over me. "I'm going to fuck you now, Eden. It will be a lot for you—a stretch—but I need to fuck you both, do you understand? I finally . . . I need . . ."

Jasper leans over us, capturing my mouth in a filthy, hot kiss that curls my toes. Then he leans over to Lucky and does the same.

Looking down, he grasps his cock and rubs the head of himself over my clit until I squirm. His jaw cords with tension, his lids sinking.

"Jasper—" Lucky starts, then cuts off, panting into my hair. From under me, Lucky punches his hips up, fucking into me, and I shudder, gasping. "Enough. Please. *Fuck*."

"Stay still," Jasper scolds, but he squeezes out some lube, then slides his cold, slippery thumb up against the base of Lucky's cock, pushing it inside me. Creating impossible, tight space for himself in the heat.

"Ah, what a pretty hole." His jaw is ruthlessly sharp, as he fights for control. "Let me in, loves."

Then he fits himself against my entrance, rubbing his cock up beside Lucien's. In the space he's created, he notches his head inside, and all three of us catch our breath as the pressure becomes dizzying. Almost painful.

Lucky quivers against my back, stirring my hair. "Lube. More. We need more."

The cold, liquid rush between the blinding heat makes me yelp, my toes curling at the violent contrast. But it doesn't matter, not now, because Jasper is *shaking*, breathing hard, and he grasps my hip with one hand as he begins to squeeze his cock alongside Lucky's. Into *me*.

My mouth parts in shock.

Breathing hard in my ear, Lucky reaches around to stroke my clit, and carnal, hedonistic ripples lift me higher. It does hurt, in all the brutal, opposite ways to the clamps. It's an aching, stretching pain— and it's the best kind, I decide. The absolute agony of every slow, slow shift.

I whimper, lost in Lucky's gasping breaths, and Jasper's cruel, controlling grip on my hip as he pushes past all resistance. Our legs are all in a tangle.

Pressure, *pleasure*, inches inside me. It's unholy to be this full. If I weren't so sinfully slippery and already humming in every nerve, I'm not sure I could have taken him, too.

As it is, I feel every inch of Lucky buried in my pussy, and as Jasper presses in, I can feel them notch against one another. I feel every ridge, every flex of both of them. I feel their cocks rub against each other, against the devastatingly sensitive walls inside me that shouldn't be able to fit them both but somehow do anyway.

The strain almost burns, but I'm too ready—too slippery wet and primed, and Jasper's too careful about the pain he delivers to cause a tear. It's only that *pressure* filling my cunt. My temples. My whole body. I feel it all the way to my throat, and Lucky's fingers working my clit make me choke on the shocking new rise.

"*Damn* it." Jasper groans as he pauses. He's strained, and his face darkens as he looks down at us.

"I have you both." I could float away on the broken, possessive look in his eyes as he tests a short, rough thrust. "I have you both."

Shuddering, he fucks into me again, and both hands fall to my waist. Jasper groans, leaning back, then punches in hard and deep— with a wet, rough slap, he pushes through all resistance. I cry out, and Lucky groans, too.

I can't get higher than I am. I'm already flying. In the clouds.

But I *am* rising.

"More," I gasp out, squeezing them both, and Lucky lets out a ruined laugh.

Jasper fucks into me again, then again, punching fast through all the burning pressure and I arch, *wanting* it. I want the decadent, lecherous slap. I want the rub of their cocks inside me and—

"My Eden. My Lucien. You—" Jasper shudders, his fingers biting into my hips as he slams into me again. "*You . . .*"

Jasper's face is flushed, strained as he breaks off, his cock rocking against Lucky's inside me as he presses himself deep. "*Ah.*"

"Jasper?" Lucky's husky voice is suddenly wickedly amused.

"Shut *up.*" He groans.

But it's too late.

Jasper's eyes widen in shocked, mortified panic.

And in a series of long, involuntary spurts . . . he floods me with hot, sticky cum.

CHAPTER 47

EDEN

"Did you just—?" Lucky stops, then snorts with laughter that makes his cock rock inside me.

"Don't," Jasper snaps. "Not a word."

"Oh." My arousal is too bright, too floaty, my throaty voice too raw, so I clear it and try to focus. "It's okay, I . . ."

I cut off as Jayk's shoulders start shaking hard enough to rock the whole bed.

"Jayk," I scold, panting, my pussy still pulsing needily around their cocks. "Be nice."

Jasper's eyes sink closed, and Jayk's choked, breathless laughter breaks loose.

"Aw what *happened*, Mr. In Control? Miss Manners make you lose yours?"

Dizzy, I glare at him, and the grin that crosses Jayk's face is possibly the brightest I've ever seen on him.

And the most malevolent.

"Untie me. I'll finish what he started." Jayk kicks out a leg so the red blanket falls around the clear outline of his cock. "You know *I'm* good for it at least."

Asshole.

But I can't help staring at the raw, beautiful lines of his muscles. The contained, flexing power that right now could really . . .

Jayk's grin becomes a smirk, but before I can fix my dazed expression or say *anything* comforting, Jasper slips out of me, and cum spills out with him, slipping down my thighs. He falls back on the bed, an arm thrown over his eyes.

Jaykob snorts, his breath almost wheezing, and when Lucky starts laughing silently behind me again, I slap his leg, only for him to suddenly push up and flip me over onto my hands and knees. It jostles his cock inside me, and my nerve endings spring back to life.

I'm still so floaty, so bright and breathless, and it's hard to focus on anything except how Lucky feels inside me.

"How's it going, beautiful? You got some more for me?" He spreads my pussy around his cock, pressing in deep, and I moan sharply. "I'm going to take that as a yes." Then he laughs again, tossing a heated look at Jasper. "Don't worry, pookie. I've got this. You rest."

"You're very smug for a brat who will be cleaning my bathroom with a toothbrush tomorrow," Jasper bites out.

Lucky laughs. Tangling a hand in the back of my hair, he starts to thrust roughly, and dizzy, desperate heat floods back into me. I feel every pump of his cock. Every brush of the coarse hair on his thighs against mine. Shuddering, I reach under myself and rub my aching clit. It's slippery, slick as Jasper's cum leaks out around Lucky's dick as he fucks me, and my breathing catches.

I did that.

I did that.

To *Jasper*.

Whose arm is still over his eyes for reasons I can't understand, since he's the reason I'm feeling so wonderful right now.

Lucky slaps my ass playfully when I start to shiver.

"Don't feel bad, babe. She feels like a wet dream. It could happen to anyone." Lucky's husky voice is bright with mirth, and not half as soothing as he's trying for, then he adds, "Not me, of course. But anyone."

A single middle finger lifts, and Jayk snickers.

"*Lucky*." I push back against him, squeezing my walls around his cock, and his laughter cuts off with a strangled groan.

A dark eye peeks out from under Jasper's arm.

"Mmm." Lucky's hips grind into me slowly, and his voice becomes strained. "*Mmhm?*"

Restlessly, clumsily, I work my hips back against him again in silent demand, my fingers working deliciously over my clit, and his breath gutters into a moan as he starts slapping into me faster.

"Look at that, sugar, you might get them two for nothing here," Jayk drawls.

Suddenly, Jasper sits up, then moves over beside us. With my head buried in the mattress, I can't see, but I feel Jasper's hand run soothingly over my back before it disappears.

Lucky's breathing turns ragged.

"Look at me," Jasper murmurs.

"Ah, nope. Busy. Focused. I—"

"Now, Lucien."

Lucky's cock swells inside me, and my fingers frantically slip over my cum-soaked clit.

No, no, no. Not again.

"There. Now I can see your eyes. You're so beautiful, do you know that, my Lucien?" Jasper's fingers drop, and I feel them dip through the lube and cum that have slipped around my ass, then down to circle the root of Lucky's dick where it's squeezing into me. "And *so* overconfident."

"Stop it. Fuck. Damn it. Think about Eden, she needs—"

"Kiss me, darling brat. I love you."

Lucky's groan is muffled, helpless, and his rough thrusts stagger, his hands clenching on my waist.

And he whimpers as he comes long and hard inside me.

"*No!*" I cry out, as Jayk starts snorting with new rounds of helpless, brutal laughter.

Lucky pulls out a moment later, bracing on my hips and breathing fast. "Son of a bitch."

A low, silky laugh rings through the room, joining Jayk's.

"Don't pout. I hear it can happen to anyone." Then Jasper adds dryly, "*Pookie.*"

Rolling over on the bed, I whimper, caught somewhere between giggles and burning, agonized frustration. Jasper's finger strokes down my cheek, then lingers over my lips. "You've done so well, Eden."

"Better than you," Jayk manages between snorts, and I shoot him another glare.

His amusement is starting to grate.

Lucky bends down over me, kissing me heatedly, and his breathless mouth works down my neck as Jasper settles back to watch.

"Ah, shit. *Sorry*, gorgeous, but I've got you," Lucky assures me. "It's okay."

Jayk cocks a disbelieving brow, and my eyes narrow.

"Wait," I murmur, and Lucky pauses at my breasts, swooping back to kiss my mouth hard. I kiss him and kiss him, then pull back. "Wait, wait, wait."

He looks at me with glassy-eyed confusion, and I roll him off me, my own sense of daring sparking to life between the giddiness and the need.

I kiss Lucky one more time, just because I can. Because he's beside me. Because his lips are sin, and because his dimples make my stomach twirl. When I finally, reluctantly pull away, he searches my eyes and understanding slowly filters in.

Then he grins.

Scooching back, he takes Jasper with him and settles in to lie against Jasper's chest at the head of the bed. Jasper's brows lift in puzzlement, glancing between us, but I'm already turning.

And my sights are set on Jaykob.

Ropes crisscross his tattooed chest. They bind his waist and lock his wrists behind him. It must ache, but if it does, he doesn't show it.

I crawl to him, dripping and filthy and shaking with the need for another release and Jayk's eyes lock on my body.

I feel like I did earlier, with Jasper—powerful, *sexual*. Even with two men's cum dripping from me and sliding down my thighs. Even with sweat catching strands of hair to my cheeks and my nipples red raw from clamps, I don't feel degraded.

I finally feel like the queen Jaykob told me I was.

When I reach the space between his parted legs, I kneel back on my heels and tangle the red blanket in my fingers.

Watching me, Jayk's eyes rake me in a challenge. "Ready to untie me now, sugar?"

Ooh, he's so *arrogant*.

My gaze travels over his caught, helpless body, and I bite my lip . . . then tug the blanket off his lap. His cock is thick, urgent and demanding, and I crawl forward.

"Eden?"

Grasping his jaw, enjoying the little pricks of his stubble, I kiss him lightly, then settle over his lap.

My knees press down beside his hips, and midnight blue stares down at me. "What are you doing?"

I lower myself down, until his cock presses against my cunt, and I need to look down, use my hand to guide him to my core. His heavy crown nudges into my sopping entrance, and he lets out a guttural growl as I begin to drip and leak over his cock.

"Problem?" I ask throatily, my head tilting back as my pussy sinks down another swollen, oversensitive inch. "*Red*?"

Jaykob slams against his ropes, trying to thrust up, but he's held so tight, he can barely move. "I'm going to fuck you raw, Eden."

"Mkay." My hands run greedily over his chest, teasing at the ropes and his muscles as I inch down further. He's charged and powerful and he can't do anything but let me explore. "'sgood."

I wriggle my way down his heavy cock, feeling the full burn build. When I'm finally seated, I lean forward and kiss the hollow at the base of his throat, panting against his damp skin.

But he's panting, too.

For all his talk, he's as close as I am.

It *has* been days, and I know he's been aching for me, too.

"You said *take it*, right? I think I'm going to take you, too, Jayk," I whisper into him. "I think I can have all three, don't you? All three to start?"

His Adam's apple bobs, and his chest rumbles a warning he can't follow through on.

I roll my hips, testing rhythms, and it's different like this—harder, when he's not directing, and I realize I'm too used to them angling me, putting me exactly where it works best.

"Lean back," Lucky offers lazily. "Hold onto his shoulders."

I glance over my shoulder, at where Lucky and Jasper are lying back against the pillows, watching me with avid, fascinated attention.

"Oh?"

"Undo the ropes, Eden," Jayk grits out, but I ignore him, trying to work this out.

Hesitantly, I slip my hand up around his neck and shift backward. "Like this?"

"More."

Hm. I arch my back, pushing down, and . . .

"*Oh*."

My lips part, and I feel the moment the angle becomes perfect, where I find enough leverage to move and feel good all at once. The way he's sitting up, if I push my hips forward just . . . *there*, my clit can grind against him too.

Moaning, I rock into him, and Jasper's cum, Lucky's, squeezes around Jaykob's cock.

Jayk grunts, and I do it again and again, faster and faster, watching the color rise sharply in his cheeks. My pussy grips his throbbing dick tight, and every grind and punch down is messy. I'm soaked in the others, and now I need him to fill me, too.

"Thank you," I whisper as he tries to move, cursing, his lips parting. "Thank you for tonight."

Midnight stars glitter at me.

I bite my lip hard as pleasure squeezes and shudders inside me, now fighting hard not to come. My mind fogs, zeroing in on the feel of his cock, the furious, helpless pleasure on his face, and I begin to lose my rhythm, just rubbing and grinding against him. I loop my other hand under the rope across his chest to help me hold on as I use him, as I ride him. As I claim him.

Frissons of pleasure are shooting down my spine, over every inch of my skin, and Jayk is breathing hard through his nose, his jaw locked tight as his eyes blaze down at me, working to hold himself back.

My warrior, at my mercy.

"Please, Jayk." My walls are quivering, clutching at him. My breasts ache and my clit is too sensitive grinding against his pubic bone. Pleasure and pain have me in thrall, and I teeter on the edge of something breathless and cataclysmic. "Please give it to me. Let me take it."

The blaze in his eyes flares hotter, his breath punching out.

My rhythm stutters, and I lean in and kiss him hard, rubbing over him feverishly. His stubble is rough, and it bites into my soft skin, and I sob into his mouth. Someone slips off the bed, but I'm lost in his lips and stubble and the fuck of his cock that's going to wreck me first.

Then Jayk's head hits the post, and he shivers.

My face is pressed into his neck as I rock desperately, and I feel his muscles cord . . . but he stops straining against the ropes to look down at me.

"Take it then. Take me."

It's enough—it's *everything*—and I bite down hard as I grind over his dick. We're stuck so tightly together that I can feel the thunder of his heart and every hot, pulsing jerk of his cock.

Then suddenly his arms are free. His waist. The ropes are falling down his chest, and he's slamming me onto my back, grinding his pelvis against my clit, and I shatter. On an ear-splitting scream, I curl into him as shocks throb through me in perfect, agonizing waves.

They go on and on until I realize Jayk's mouth is pressing against me, over every mark and bruise and red-raw swell. Softly, tenderly, checking my wounds as I twist and shiver my way through an orgasm that feels endless.

It takes a long, long time before the room starts to take shape again.

My fingers stroke through his short, springy hair as I pant, my emotions crashing everywhere, and tears flood my eyes before I can stop them.

I'm not sure why, because right now my chest is aching with simple, flawless happiness.

The mattress dips, and I look up to see Jasper settling in beside me, his expression soft. Lucky's behind him, and he gives me a warm, tired smile as he hands Jasper the arnica cream, which Jayk snatches from him without asking, and I huff a laugh as the tears spill over.

Together, with a few jostles and eye rolls, they wipe the tears from my cheeks. They rub the cream into my muscles, kiss me softly, and clean me up as they bicker about who is in whose personal space.

When I can walk, I slip into the bathroom, and when I come out loose and relaxed after a hot shower, I brace for more teasing . . . only to find all three in the bed.

And Jaykob and Lucky are sound asleep.

Jasper looks up from the center of the bed as I close the bathroom door, and he looks me over. Seemingly satisfied, he glances down at Lucky, curled around him—then at Jaykob, teetering on the opposite edge of the mattress.

"There was some discussion about whether or not we'd be thrown from the window, but after a counter offer of a hook in his ass, Jaykob opted for sleep," Jasper advises with a dry curl to his mouth.

Suppressing a smile, I walk over to the window to draw the curtains shut. Two figures are sitting at the center of the bridge—too far for me to make out more than the fact that they're locked very tightly together under the moonlight.

Softly, my smile escapes.

It looks like tonight is a night for crossing bridges.

Heart-warm, I leave them to it and climb into my bed.

But as I settle between Jasper and Jayk, I realize Jasper is holding himself tense, and I look up at him questioningly. Those dark eyes ease, quiet and watchful.

"Is this okay, Eden? Are you okay?"

I smile back at him, just as softly.

Hesitantly, I reach out and twine our fingers together. He lets me —just like he lets me tug him down until he faces me. Like he lets me wrap his arm over my waist as I snuggle close.

"I'm happy, Jasper. I'm so . . ." My breath catches when his throat bobs, and I have to bite my lip before I can whisper, "I'm so happy. Thank you."

I reach up, brushing my fingertips over his lovely, silken jaw. "You were right, you know. All those months ago. Our pieces fit." My throat is hot, but I swallow. "This is a family."

"Your family." His eyes run over my face. "Yours, Eden."

I press my lips together, smiling, caught on the tide of that *feeling*. We're so close to it—to having all of it.

"Beaumont and Dominic, too," he murmurs. "It will be all of us. It was always supposed to be."

I shake my head, laughing softly as he reads my mind again. Then I nod.

"All of us."

Jasper nods too.

Then he rolls onto his back, clearing his throat, and delicate color rises in his cheeks.

"And . . . about earlier, I can assure you, that . . ."

The next peal of laughter that escapes me is loud enough to make Jaykob scowl and roll over with a sleepy huff. I press the back of my hand to my mouth to stop the giggles, realizing that Jasper's ears are now glowing hotly.

Twisting, I lean over Jasper's chest. Lucky starts to snore, but I ignore it to kiss Jasper's mortified lips. His jaw. Up to his ear.

"I loved it," I breathe. "Every second."

Jasper's eyes crack open, and he looks at me wryly.

But I keep my expression warm.

Because I *mean* it.

I loved everything about how he touched me. I loved the hurt and the tenderness. I loved his mouth and the teasing and the unbearable squeeze of his cock inside of me. But I especially loved that I drove him to that.

I made Jasper—*Jasper*—lose control.

A thrilled, wondering sense of awe threads through me at the thought. How good must I have felt to him? In that one moment, every single fear and insecurity I ever had about not being able to satisfy him was banished, because I *made him lose control*.

Not with whips or blood or anything more than I can handle.

Just by being *me*.

Something of the dizzy, proud happiness I'm feeling must show, because his expression softens and he kisses me gently.

"How lucky we are to have you."

My chest fills, and he tucks me in, wrapping me in his arms for sleep.

And as I drift off, snug in a bed, safe with three men I adore, all I can think is, *I'm the lucky one.*

CHAPTER 48

EDEN

"J ayk?" Jasper mumbles. There's a knock on the door. "Jayk, get up. We have company."

Sleepily, I lift my head, but Jasper sighs and gives me a reassuring squeeze, already slipping over Lucky's sprawled legs. He ties his silk robe tighter around him and pads to the door, looking deliciously untidy.

Jayk flops over grumpily, burying his head in his pillow.

My eyes are gritty. Soft light filters around the edges of the curtain, so it must be dawn or later, but it feels like I only just put my head down.

Jasper cracks open the door. "What is it?"

"Jasper?" Ava's voice lifts in surprise. "Uh . . . is Jayk there?"

Groaning, I roll out of bed, ignoring Lucky's sleepy hands trying to snatch at me. I pull on Lucky's discarded shirt and come up beside Jasper.

"Jayk's sleeping, Ava. Do you need something?" I ask, rubbing my eyes.

Her mouth opens, then closes, then opens again. She shakes her head.

"You know what? None of my business." She flicks her tongue

piercing against her teeth. "Get him up. We've been scouting Red Zone's approach. They're here now—and they've run into the Reapers. No one's shooting, but . . ."

On the bed, the blankets are tossed to the side.

"I'm up," Jayk grumbles. "Get Dom and Beau."

"Hey!" Lucky complains. "No— Don't *shove* me. Hey! I'm moving!"

Ava blinks, then lifts onto her toes, trying to peer over Jasper's shoulder and into the room. "How many of you are in here?"

I blush to the roots of my hair, but Jasper only smiles politely. "We'll be down momentarily. Thank you, Ava."

He closes the door, and the four of us look at one another, disheveled and scarcely dressed—right as my alarm goes off to meet Dom and Beau. Silently, Lucky turns it off.

It wasn't exactly the date I'd intended, but . . .

What's one more group adventure?

DARK, roiling clouds cast an ominous shroud over the dawning light, and the morning's wet heat makes my clothes cling to my skin.

Dom's eyebrows twitch up as the four of us come out together, only passably put together, but he doesn't say anything. Beau squeezes my hand, taking it as we pass them, and we all head across the lawn together.

As a group.

Jayk's gaze only flickers over us for a moment before he refocuses on Arthur and his small group standing uneasily between the Reapers. The four from Red Zone all have short, heavy-looking bows that are much more complex than the simple ones the civilians hold, and a dangerous mix of other weapons strapped around their bodies.

I'm only marginally surprised to see Jennifer tucked beside Sawyer . . . on the Reapers' side of the moat.

"I didn't forget about our date," I whisper to Beau as he matches his long stride to my shorter one.

"I know, darlin'." His lips tilt up, and he slants a look down at me.

"I'm pretty curious about what you're going to share with the class later, though."

On his other side, Lucky seems to catch that, and he grins. "It's really more about what she shared with the class last night."

My cheeks flame, and Beau's eyes twinkle in amusement.

We slow as we get closer, and Jayk catches Dom's arm.

"I don't know them," he mutters.

They stop a few feet from the moat, and Dom stays silent, watching him. The cloud that crosses his face is as dark as the ones above us.

"It's yours, King," Dom says evenly.

Jayk's jaw flexes, and he scowls. "Shut up. Can you just talk to them? They know you."

I hold my breath, and Beau's hand tightens on mine.

I couldn't say exactly why but watching these two men like this feels like watching the Discovery channel. A David Attenborough documentary, where two pack leaders circle one another. Only this isn't a challenge.

It's an offering.

I just don't know if Dom will accept it.

"Can we cross?" Arthur calls from the other side of the moat, tension brittle in his voice.

Still, Dom hesitates, and Jayk's face turns grim.

It's too soon. Dom isn't ready.

Releasing Beau's hand, I walk between the two men, touching them absently, reassuringly. This much, I can do.

I'm getting rather good at speaking up.

"Welcome, all of you. We've been waiting for you," I call back to Arthur, glancing at the four people with him—two women and two men.

They're all in light armor, equipped with daggers and swords and bows that look far more impressive than the ones the civs have carved. Some look handmade, others are metal and I can only assume more modern.

The five of them stand bunched at the foot of the bridge. They haven't reached for their weapons, but they seem uneasy as they watch the large group of men surrounding them.

The Reapers watch them back with open curiosity, but most haven't even rolled out of their tents or bothered to stand up from their breakfast cookfires.

Pete waves, nodding his sweaty head to Arthur, and Buck is back in his "part-time farmer, full-time charmer" cap, frying up some more bacon with whole-hearted intensity. Beside them, Akira turns a page in her paperback, seeming to ignore all of us.

Sawyer and Cole stand next to Arthur with careful expressions.

I clear my throat. "Yes, please. Come across. I hope you don't mind camping on the lawn; we're a little cramped inside. We're happy to let you use our showers, though, and the kitchen. Anything you need."

With someone keeping an eye on them, yes, but we had all agreed that we owed them the same hospitality that they offered us, at the very least. They'd offered us a lot of trust, with arguably more to lose.

Sawyer's brows fly up as Red Zone begins filtering over the bridge, his gaze flicking between us and them. A kind of angry panic steals over him, and I hide my sigh.

I've worried about this.

Trying for soothing, I smile, then nod to Sawyer as Arthur steps off the bridge. "Arthur, this is Sawyer. He leads the Reapers, and they hold the farmlands a few hours south of you and Cyanide. Sawyer, Arthur is currently in charge of—"

"We've met." Arthur turns, patting a tissue against his round, kindly face. Now that he's beside us, with all his people on this side of the moat, he seems to have regained some of his confidence. "In passing. We've traded with them, once or twice. Bentley handled most of it."

Sawyer's tension hasn't subsided. He watches Arthur guardedly, his moustache twitching, and Jennifer runs a soothing hand up his back.

She catches me watching her and gives me a sheepish look.

But that look is free of the shadows that had haunted her as she left Jasper's session. Despite her bandaged foot and being on the other side of our moat, Jennifer looks . . . happy.

And so, I smile reassuringly back at her.

Sawyer's gaze snaps over us, and he shifts restlessly until Cole mutters to him.

Grimacing, Sawyer looks away, like he's struggling with himself, then he sighs. "Yeah, we were friendly. Red Zone makes good glassware. Knives, too, though I have to say, the beer was my favorite. You make it better than any of our sorry selves have managed to." Sawyer's lips twist, and he mutters, "We were real sorry when you cut contact."

Arthur stiffens, and Jasper frowns, watching his face.

"Ah. Well," Arthur starts uncomfortably. He pats his dusty forehead again, sweating profusely. "We saw the trucks of food coming through Cyanide. We understood. Business is business, and it's your right to find . . . more substantial . . . trading partners." Arthur's kindly face turns startlingly severe. "But the Sinners have given us a lot of trouble. We thought it was better to steer clear of any friends of theirs." But then he hesitates. He looks out over the Reapers, frowning, then looks at Dom. His frown deepens. "It does make me wonder why you're *here*, though."

This time, Sawyer can't contain his bitterness. "Friends? Oh, I see. Now we're the bad guys again, is that it? You all just going to team up and go on your merry way and leave us behind again? Leave us to be *killed*?" His voice lifts. "The Sinners came to *us*. We didn't want *nothing* to do with—"

"Cool it, Sawyer." Beside him, Cole catches his arm and gives him a warning look, but Sawyer throws him off.

Rubbing a frustrated hand down his face, Cole looks over at Arthur, his jaw tense. "The Sinners had our food, so you assumed, what, that we're allies? *Friends*?"

He laughs, and it's dark enough, edged wildly enough, that Sawyer looks back at him sharply. Despite Cole's call for calm, it doesn't look like either of them are managing to keep their cool, and Dom shifts almost imperceptibly closer to me.

"We're not their *friends*! We don't *have* friends." Cole points to his own chest as he looks between us and Red Zone, and I start to see this for what it is.

Desperation.

But Jennifer's lips turn down sadly as she watches him. "The Sinners have been raiding them for years. Threatening them. Killing them. Taking their food, their things . . . their people." She links her fingers with Sawyer's, and he swallows hard as she adds, "Just last week they lost a lot of people they cared about. It was a massacre."

At that, Cole's face closes down.

Arthur is tense, and his frown eases into something apologetic— and deeply uncomfortable. He glances at the others from Red Zone, and they shrug and shift with similar discomfort.

"Ah. Ah, well, I apologize, we might have been a little over-cautious, I—"

But Sawyer is shaking his head, and his eyes burn bitterly over us. *Hurt.* "Y'all are really doing this? You're just gonna let them go right on through? Let them use your showers. Trust them with *everything*?" He huffs a raw, incredulous breath. "What more do we have to do? We've been here for over a *week*, playin' nice and sharin'. Our people are *dying* out there!"

The last is a shout, and it has Jayk scowling in the dim morning light. He's still messy and unshaven, but he cuts an intimidating figure.

"You haven't been sharing shit, Sawyer. Scraps—we took the rest. Words mean jack. We're still starving in here."

Beau sighs. He's much more put together, particularly considering the pre-dawn hour, looking rested and showered. I wonder if Dom has him on his schedule now. Beau was always a lazy riser when he was living with me.

His look over the Reapers is more sympathetic, but no less grim. "Jayk's right. I've got two in our med bay right now with dizzy spells so bad they're fighting to see straight."

A cynical laugh punches out of Cole as he turns, linking his hands behind his head, and I soften my expression as I step forward, ensuring I appear as carefully open as they are closed. As relaxed as they are charged.

This needs de-escalating.

"Sawyer, we want more allies. More friends. But you have to understand our caution—the risks we're taking by even talking with you. If Alastair found out . . ." I trail off, letting that sit for a moment, until his gaze finally flicks up to mine.

He looks like a cornered animal.

"If you want friendship from us, you need to give us something," I murmur. "You *need* to meet us halfway."

Meaningfully, I look down at Jennifer, and Sawyer's eyes close as he unconsciously draws her close—in front of him, like she's his protection. Cole stays quiet, slumping into his chair by their fire, his handsome face still as he stares too blindly into the flames.

Anxious tension billows off the Red Zone newcomers.

Finally, Sawyer's eyes open, and they have a bright, suspicious shine.

"It must be nice," he whispers, and there's jealousy and bitterness and longing throbbing in his voice as he looks over Red Zone and the civilians behind us, "that you had each other. It must be nice . . . We've been surviving, we have, but it's been . . . low. You can't know how low we've fallen, out there by ourselves."

The hairs on the back of my neck prickle to life.

The darkness etched in him is something etched in me, too. It's still there, that cold, lawless place I clawed my way out of.

"We've never had anyone helping us," he says, and his expression is quietly imploring. "We're trying to be patient, but this food is all we have to offer. If we give it away, we lose all our leverage. We have nothing to bargain with. You could just . . . leave us to it." Sawyer swallows, then rubs a hand across his mustache. His voice is broken when he whispers, "And we *need* things to change."

My throat aches at the tone—at the sound that is far too close to begging.

Jennifer's breathing snags, and she wraps her arms around his neck. After a moment, his arms come around her, too, squeezing hard.

I glance at my brutes around me, seeing their caution and sympathy, their kindness and determination.

When she finally pulls back, she cups his face and shakes her head at him, tears in her eyes. "Then maybe you need to change, too."

He gives her a long, pained look, then glances over at Cole.

Slowly, Cole looks up from his fire. His pretty face is made infernal in the light of the flames. It's deprived. Hungry. Like he'd make any devil deal he needed to keep his people safe.

"We just want it to stop. We *all* want that." He swallows, his bitter gaze dark with need. "Don't we? We ain't alone there?"

Jayk doesn't answer, and neither does Dom. Sawyer and Cole both look over at us, at *me*, and I pause, caught. My heart rate picks up.

This is dangerous.

That *question* is dangerous.

Alastair holds all the cards. The captives. Our leaders.

But we're starving, the Reapers are being attacked, and Red Zone is desperate.

The Sinners need to be stopped.

Slowly, I nod, and choose my words carefully, "We do want an end to the attacks, yes."

At my words, Arthur's frown eases into something different—something vaguely befuddled, but . . . hopeful. He exchanges a look with his people, who give him edged, nervous nods back.

Finally, Arthur nods too, this time toward Sawyer. "The Sinners have pushed all of us too far, and for far too long. We can't commit to anything, but . . . maybe it's something we can all discuss."

In slow, tentative increments, Sawyer's shoulders unknot, until finally, he looks down at Jennifer.

"Is this what you think we should do? Give it all up?" he asks softly. "We just . . . surrender?"

"Surrender is just a word," she replies, just as soft. "A word that only means you're not choosing war."

Sawyer's head tilts as he considers that, and finally, his mustache pulls up on one side. "Well, far be it from me to ignore the wisdom of a pretty lady." He looks over his shoulder, his voice lifting, though it's etched with nerves. "Pete? Buck? Grab a few of them bags over there and hand 'em over."

My stomach swoops, then soars.

He's doing it.

The Reapers are actually sharing their food.

"No way." Lucky's groan sounds a little too like the sounds that escaped him last night, but I'm not sure I can blame him, and I toss him a sideways grin.

Pete and Buck get to it quickly, fetching the bags and walking them over the bridge. Beau meets them part way across it, checking the bags briefly before he hands them off to Jasper, Dom, and Lucky.

Oh, what are we doing? What does this mean? My mind starts to race. By accepting this, are we agreeing to an alliance?

Is this a resistance?

God, we need to be *so* incredibly careful.

As if sensing my thoughts, Sawyer nods at the food. "Consider it a show of good faith." He clears his throat. "Now y'all have a kitchen in that big ole house of yours, I hear. How about you whip up a few things in there and we'll cook up a few things out here, maybe get that music kicking on again, and we have ourselves a good old-fashioned barbecue. We can all talk shop over a hot meal." He shrugs, and a tentative smile spreads across his face. "Nothing makes for new friends and fair deals like good food, don't you think?"

His eyes plead for that to be true.

The civs come forward, taking bag after bag—at first tentative, and then with laughter, and a few teasing catcalls at Jennifer, who rolls her eyes and blows them a kiss. My empty stomach squeezes at the idea of so much food. We'll test it of course, check that it's still good, but . . . for the first time since Cyanide, it feels like we're not at a loss. Like this is the change we've been waiting for.

There is *something* here.

My heart beats fast, panicked and hopeful all at once.

Cole laughs again, this time a soft little chuckle that still has edges of darkness to it.

"To new allies, then." His eyes glow as he looks back into his fire. "May they not sell us out."

Arthur and his friends, dirty and clearly tired from their travels, take it all in with a hesitant kind of bemusement—like it's too much to hope for. A not insubstantial part of me agrees.

Allies.

It's a dangerous, thrilling concept.

Jayk's hand comes up around the back of my neck, squeezing hard, and I smile up at him too as the idea settles in me. Good things come in all kinds of rough packages, after all.

Finally, I nod to Cole, to Sawyer and Jennifer, and I settle on a word that feels less dangerous, but no less important.

"To new friends."

CHAPTER 49

EDEN

SURVIVAL TIP #181
Wars are won and lost,
for the dignity of choice.

My silk nightdress swishes around my legs as I walk my tray up the stairs, not terribly worried about being seen. The house is finally winding down after a long day, with everyone seeming to need time to think.

Today, things are changing.

My stomach is still in nervous knots of fear and anticipation. We talked all day—with Arthur and his people, and with Sawyer and Cole. It's still too new, far too early to make decisions, and things still feel tense between Red Zone and the Reapers, but . . . there are options. Thrilling, terrifying possibilities.

And today, while we were cautiously feeling one another out . . . the civilians were making strides of their own.

Bolstered by Jennifer, dozens of civilians finally crossed the bridge.

To bright, infectious music, they snacked on whatever the Reapers cooked, or brought their own meals from our finally bustling kitchen. They talked and laughed under the churning clouds—and for their part, the Reapers flocked to the conversation as though they were starved and the attention of the women were a special sort of food.

Whether out of respect or caution, not one of the Reapers

attempted to cross to our side of the bridge . . . and when the meeting broke up and most of the civilians turned in for bed, the Reapers let them go, with food still warm in their hands.

The music outside has fallen silent now, dropping off with the day, but I can still feel the beat of it in me, rippling with joyous energy. *Bristlebrook* is full of joyous energy . . . and it makes me as nervous as I am grateful.

I'm glad everyone's been fed.

I just worry what those meals will cost us.

It's late now, but I'm too wired to sleep, and my room was too silent for my restless thoughts. And given that the last time I saw Jayk he was organizing the night's watch, and Jasper and Lucky are nowhere to be found . . . I've decided to make up for my missed date.

After shifting the tray to one hand, I knock on the door, and Dom appears a moment later. He's only in his black boxers, his hair damp, and my tongue sticks to the roof of my mouth. His chest is wide and dusted in dark hair that trails down into places I can't let myself look right now, because I have a very precariously balanced tray, and the sight of him is a dizzy spell waiting to happen.

Shirtless Dom . . . may throw my plans awry.

When he sees me, Dom leans against the doorframe to take me in.

His eyes lift to mine, but he doesn't say anything, and I bite down against the immediate urge to stammer. My hair is clean and loose, and I smell *so* much better than I did at the end of today's meeting, and he and Beau picked this nightdress out for me all those months ago, so he must think it's pretty, right?

Which are all simply *ridiculous* things to be thinking about right now.

After all the serious things we discussed today, thinking about how I might look to him is silly and unimportant and . . . and it's so *awfully* vain.

But he *is* looking at me, quiet and heatedly intense.

"We . . ." I clear my throat, steeling myself. *Brave, Eden. You're brave.* "I missed you this morning."

And he still doesn't say anything. He just keeps looming. Considering me.

His eyes are *burning* over my body.

My inward breath is shaky. "I'm here now, if you have time?"

There's a shuffling and a loud *oof* from the room behind him, and his attention breaks.

Briefly, Dom glances at the clock on the wall—and his dark brow lifts in painfully slow increments. "At ten at night?"

The question is dry, pointed, and my cheeks heat in indignance.

"That . . . that is *not* why I'm here," I splutter.

Which is true.

But him being mostly naked isn't helping my resolve.

And it's true that my sore nipples are chafing against my dress and my inner muscles ache deliciously. I'm not sure I would turn *down* an interlude with Dom.

It's also true that I woke up with three of my brutes in my bed this morning, and while I'm delighted at how they were getting along today—awkward and warm—it does feel wrong that Dom and Beau weren't a part of it.

I have something I want to feel out—and regretfully, it's not Dom's body.

"Is that Eden? Tell her to come back. We're not ready yet."

I blink. "Lucky?"

Dom looks me over, his gaze lingering on where my nipples press against my cool dress. He shakes his head, offensively skeptical of my pure-ish intentions, but he steps back and holds the door open for me.

So I walk in.

His room is neat and tidy, though not so tidy as it was the last time I was in here, robbing him of a bazooka with Lucky cheering me on from the doorway. Now, there are pillows and disheveled blankets tumbling over his large couch, and a haphazard pile of Beau's clothes teeters beside a TV that is far too large for the space.

And Jayk, Jasper, and Lucky are all lounging around his room, while Beau fiddles with something that may or not be an ancient DVD player. Lucky winks at me, and Jayk's jaw sets as he takes in my outfit. He looks up at the ceiling with a sigh, right as Jasper gives me a small smile.

What on earth . . .?

"I'd apologize for the mess, but it's not mine," Dom says behind me, closing the door.

Unsure what to make of this, I give him a tentatively amused smile over my shoulder. "I know. I lived with him too, remember?"

The TV flickers on, and Beau gets to his feet, giving us both a filthy scowl.

"It's not mess, it's *lived in*. And if *someone* would give me a few drawers, I wouldn't have to pile everything on the floor."

Dom slides him a sardonic look as he opens up one said drawer. He hesitates over his clothes, then snags up a red T-shirt—perfectly folded—and tugs it on, to my crushing disappointment.

Jayk snorts from the armchair, kicking his boots up onto the coffee table, and Beau zeroes in on him, adding, "And if *someone* hadn't thrown me out of *my* room, my things wouldn't be here at all."

"Passive aggression, Beaumont," Jasper murmurs chidingly, and he gets up to lead me around Beau's discarded clothes with a gentle hand on my back.

Lounging on the floor, Lucky kicks Jayk's boots off the table, making room for me to place the tray down, and Jayk kicks Lucky back.

Beau huffs at Jasper, muttering under his breath, "And *someone* should leave our sessions in our sessions."

"You did ask me to point it out," Jasper replies tartly.

After dusting a sock off the corner of the coffee table with my foot, I unload the tray, fretting over the three teacups when there's now six of us here. I should get more. I might not be able to follow through on my usual ritual with Dom and Beau, or bring up everything I'd planned to with Dom, but we could all have a nice moment together, possibly. A debrief.

Straightening, I run my hands down my nightdress. "I'll go back down and pick up some more—"

Jasper kisses me as I turn, with such sharp-edged suddenness that my hands lift in startlement . . . before I sink against him, my fingers curling in his shirt. The silk-on-silk press of us is reprehensibly erotic. The heat of him seeps into me, and I can't reconcile how gently he holds my jaw with the swift cruelty of his mouth.

"Watch it, sugar. Few more seconds and he might blow," Jayk drawls, and Lucky lets out a surprised, strangled snort as Jasper breaks the kiss, his head whipping around.

I hold myself still as his nostrils flare—absolutely *refusing* to let my amusement slip free, because I do have *some* self-preservation skills.

"What's that supposed to mean?" Beau asks, his gaze flicking between us, and Lucky lies back on the floor, dragging a cushion over his face while his shoulders shake ruthlessly.

It doesn't do an awful lot to muffle his laughter.

Jayk smirks, and there's an impish sparkle in his eye I've only seen a few times. "Well, that *is* a funny story. Did you know that Jasper here—"

"Jaykob, I *will* fetch that hook and I *will* fit it inside your asshole. There should be plenty of room in there, considering it's usually where you keep your *head*," Jasper snaps, but his cheeks are flooded with endearing color.

"Can you fetch your dignity with it?" Jayk's smirk turns into a grin, and my breath catches at the almost boyish laughter in it.

He's *teasing*—and he's not doing it to be unkind.

Jasper's eyes narrow, but before he can issue another insult, I touch his arm, and he looks down at me. He kissed me . . . and he wants to do it again. His expression softens, and he sighs, letting it go with one last disgruntled look at Jayk as he sits down on the couch.

"Why *is* everyone here?" I ask.

It's become almost strange to see them all in one place, particularly with my feet on the ground and not dangling over Jayk's shoulder.

Lucky finally removes the pillow from his face, though he's still bright with mirth. "We were just hanging out for a bit, going over some things. You were invited, but you were in the shower." He sits up, winking at me. "I suggested holding it in there with you, but *I* was overruled. We were going to get you in a minute. Beau had an idea, but we need to talk to you first."

They were spending time with each other? *Voluntarily*?

Dom leans against the wall beside Jasper, who nods to me.

"We were just saying that today went well . . ." He pauses, briefly, sobering. "We wanted your thoughts on accepting the Reapers' deal. It would mean moving to their farmlands, potentially for quite a while, and—"

"War," Dom finishes heavily, his face unreadable.

My amusement vanishes.

Oh. Okay. So soon.

I'd hoped for more time.

The implications I've been pondering for the last week begin to crash in on me. The easy humor in the group subdues further the longer I stare at him.

"Why me?" I ask tentatively. "You all know much better than me whether it's a fight we can or should take on. I don't know anything about war."

Lucky slings colorful arms over his knees, unusually grim. It's not the same restless anxiety that lurked in him after Cyanide. This fear is weighted and quiet, matured by experience.

Lucky knows war.

And he doesn't offer jokes now. He looks at me like he knows the exact cost of it.

"You know Alastair," he offers. "You know better than we do how he might react."

Right.

Badly.

"He has Heather." Dom's voice is carefully controlled, which tells me more than anything how deeply that guilt cuts him.

Maybe even as much as it does me.

He's a solid presence against the wall, like an Old Testament angel, brutal and forged for war.

"Bentley too," he adds. His jaw tightens. "If we go against Alastair, they'll bear the brunt of it."

My stomach sinks, and I duck my head. I've spent countless hours thinking about them and the captives the Sinners still have trapped.

Into the quiet, Jasper sighs.

"Your perspective is important, too, Eden. It appears as though many of the civs have had a change of heart regarding the Reapers, but I know how complicated those feelings might be." Jasper's dark eyes are too knowing and shadowed with the exhaustion of the last week. From sessions and sessions with civilians that make me believe he does understand. His voice is as soft as his gaze. "We might offer our own services, but we can't make a decision like this for everyone. Not when it risks their safety . . . not unless you and they are comfortable with it."

"If we're doing this, we're doing it the right way," Lucky says, glancing at Dom and Dom gives him a long look before, finally, he nods to himself.

Around the room, my brutes are all as serious as one another. None look surprised.

This is something they've discussed before.

Together.

Emotion sits heavily in my chest. They really do understand, I think. We all know the stakes—how desperately we need a stable food supply, and how dire our future looks with the Sinners ruling our lives and the lives of everyone around us. We all know we need the Reapers to survive.

But they know that surviving means nothing without the dignity of choice.

God, how is it possible to be equal parts grateful and furious that they're giving this choice to me?

Beau comes around and sits on the couch, too, on the opposite end to Jasper.

"All of that is important, but . . . it also affects you, darlin'." Beau meets my eyes. "You know it will mean every one of us will be in danger. We haven't talked much about what it means to be with someone who leaves every day and might not come home. We haven't talked much about what that means for you . . . but it won't be easy."

Dread swamps me, and my teeth come down hard on my cheek as apprehensive tears prick my eyes. We might not have talked about it, but I haven't been able to stop thinking about what this fight could mean.

I remember when I believed they were dead.

I remember the dark.

Trying to buy myself time to think, I wipe my trembling hands on my nightdress . . . and frown as they stick sweatily against the silk.

"I need to . . ."

Be busy. Do something.

I need to think.

Haltingly, I walk over to Jaykob and kneel at his feet, absently, I reach for his boots, my mind racing.

He stiffens, then his legs flinch up as he recoils in his chair like I've launched myself at him. I blink in surprise, re-focusing on him.

He's on the chair by himself, and his thick, tattooed arms are almost bursting from his sleeves. His rifle leans against the couch behind him, and he's still entirely dressed. *Uncomfortably* dressed, for someone who's supposed to be relaxing among friends.

"The fuck are you doing down there?" Jayk shifts, then eyes everyone else suspiciously. He scoffs. "No. *No.* It ain't happening. Four of us was already two too many, sugar. Things might be getting cute in here, but if you're planning on running a train right now, then I'm jumping in front of the fucking tracks."

Affronted, I open my mouth, but Dom beats me to it. "You crashed our date. Just let her work. She talks more when she doesn't have to make eye contact."

The last is droll enough that I sneak a tart look at him over my shoulder.

He's sassy—but he's not wrong.

Already, between their banter and the task, I feel my panicked heartbeat beginning to settle. They're all here.

We're all here together and we'll figure it out.

"Can't she just face the wall or something?" Jayk grumbles, but slowly, he eases his legs back on either side of me, still flinchingly suspicious, and I suppress an eye roll as I start loosening the laces on his boots.

He is *not* used to people doing anything for him, and it shows.

It's a miracle he hasn't kicked me away, too.

"No need to be frightened of her, Jaykob. We're all here to protect you," Jasper soothes with droll amusement, and Lucky's serious expression flickers for a moment as Jasper wins a smile.

Jayk flips Jasper off, but he does look down at me, hesitating as I untie the last of his laces.

"You don't have to, you know," he finally mutters.

How can one man be so sweet and so infuriating all at once?

"If I didn't want to, I wouldn't, Jayk." Sweetly, I add, "And just for the record, it's actually far more comfortable down here than it is to be tossed over your shoulder every thirty minutes."

I yank off one of his boots, and he snorts, relaxing more as I tease him. I smile as I start tugging off his other boot more gently, but it quickly fades. I feel their eyes on me from all sides.

"I don't think Alastair will kill Heather. He might make her life miserable, but he's . . ." I shake my head. "He's fixated on her. Obsessed, maybe."

Dom stiffens, and his voice is thick with anger when he says. "What about—"

I stop him short. "He doesn't agree with rape, sir. I don't think it was a line, or that he was pandering—I sensed genuine contempt from him when there was any suggestion of . . ." I falter. "Of anything like that. I think that's one thing Heather doesn't have to worry about."

Memories threaten. Owen's narrow, lascivious smile and the eyes crawling over my skin, and my hands pause. Alastair might not have that particular vice, but there are hundreds of Sinners . . . and a clear majority of them had no issue with kidnapping women and worse. Sam attracted thugs and rapists in droves.

This world is too lawless, and those men are too bloodthirsty to agree to peace. There's no way Alastair could control them all, even if he wanted to.

And given the state of the Reapers' butchered friends, I'm not at all sure he does.

If he wants to keep his power, he'll need to sate his men's appetites one way or another.

It just isn't a threat we can afford to live under.

Jaykob nudges me with his foot, and I startle, catching his ankle. I realize the men are dead silent, watching me with dark, livid concern.

I squeeze him and offer them all a soothing smile. I tuck Jaykob's boots neatly beside the armchair, then get up.

"Heather might be safe, and I think the women are considered too valuable among the Sinners to murder out of spite. Alastair did say he'd keep them safe, but . . ." I purse my lips. "Winning against the Sinners is the only way I can see them walking free."

"And Bentley?" Beau grimaces. "I don't suppose you can see any reason why Alastair would save his hide, do you?"

My chest aches as I think of Soren.

I press a soft kiss to Jayk's bristled cheek, then move toward Jasper, needing his calm.

To my surprise, Jayk lets me go.

Jasper accepts me onto his lap easily, pressing his lips against my temple as I settle against him. Old books and sharp leather wrap around me. Easing me. Turning his wrist, I begin loosening his cufflinks.

Quietly, I say, "If they know Red Zone is involved . . . I can't see why Alastair wouldn't press hard on that leverage if he could. He doesn't make empty threats." I look at Jayk. "Can we keep them out of it?"

There's a beat before Jayk blinks and looks up, realizing the question is aimed at him. A hunted, troubled look falls over his rough features.

Absently, Jayk flicks open his pocketknife, toying with it for a long moment before he finally mutters, "Well, we could use the hands. Right?"

The question isn't directed at anyone, and Jasper, Lucky, and Beau sit back, pensive and frowning.

But Dom is already shaking his head, deep in thought as he stands over us.

"Red Zone doesn't have big numbers—and they have a lot of teenagers to protect. They're useful where they are. They're close enough to track Alastair's movements." Dom's brow knots, but he nods. "That counts for a lot. They can get us supplies to rig defenses. Intel. Maybe some of their weapons. They've got their base locked up tighter than a duck's ass, so they should stay safe enough. As long as we can establish supply drops. Secure a communication channel . . . Maybe the satellite phone, if we can track another one down for them. National Park might have one. Not too far out, if the Sinners haven't already cleared that out, too." He tilts his head, sighing heavily. "It's possible."

Jayk's pocketknife falls still.

Slowly, he lifts his head . . . and Jayk gives Dom a serious, contemplative look.

Jasper murmurs, "In any case, Red Zone needs to understand the risk. Their freedom might cost Bentley his life."

Another brick settles heavily in my stomach.

Heather and Bentley are fierce protectors. If it came down to saving themselves or the people they love, I know what they'd choose.

Only, the choice *won't* be theirs.

How can we make that decision on their behalf?

Then again, how many Reapers might die if we don't? How long will Red Zone be able to hold out under Alastair's nose? How will Soren get the medicine he needs? How many Ethels and Kaseys and Avas will die of hunger?

God, Heather would kill me if I let that happen.

Jasper strokes my hair, and quietly, I fold back his sleeve until it settles loose and comfortable around his forearms. It's casual, so much more casual than I'm used to, and there's something in this. A vulnerability in his exposed wrists and Jaykob's bare feet. In nightclothes and late hours and shared fears. The fact that they're seeking one another out to do that sharing.

They can do this.

These aren't men divided anymore. *We* aren't divided.

They'll keep each other safe.

My hand slides from Jasper's cufflink, and I fold that one back, too, as I take a deep breath.

"We need to do it."

Lucky's answering exhale is swift, soft and defeated. When I look over, tension is incised on every muscle, but he nods to himself like he knew it was coming.

He doesn't even try for a smile.

"Lucky," I call softly.

I reach out to him, and he stares at my hand before crawling over to me. I slip off Jasper's lap, settling between his legs and Beau's, and when Lucky reaches me, he kisses me hard, and I stroke his face until he softens. When I finally pull back, he sighs, and his head drops against my chest.

"I know," I murmur. "I know, Lucky."

He lets me lead him into lying down, and I settle his head into my lap, drawing his long, golden hair over my legs. Gently, I start working through the tangles.

No one else says a word. They all watch us, waiting.

Jayk's gaze is still turned inward, and the pocketknife turns slowly in his hand.

Jasper's leg is warm and firm beside me, and I lean into it, feeling steadier. "I have caveats." The thoughts I've been toying with all week come at me in a rush. "I agree this is the best choice we have, possibly the only choice, but that doesn't mean giving anyone blanket trust. I've spoken with the civilians—with Ava and Ida and several others. They'll all come with us. It makes sense to be together rather than dividing our efforts."

Lucky's hair twists and turns easily between my fingers as I start a small braid just above his ear. He has such beautiful hair, dark honey and amber and pale, buttery gold in turn. It slips through my fingers like satin.

Beau turns on the couch so he can see my face, and I glance up at him.

"We would all feel better if we approach any living situation there cautiously. We need to all be together, or within hearing distance, even if it means camping. We don't let up watches, and no one goes anywhere alone. Even if we're deciding to trust them as a whole, they said they had . . . was it just over two hundred men, they said?" My lips tighten. "Numbers alone say that we'll likely have some trouble, even if it's not the majority. We need Sawyer and Cole to take a clear, hard line on acceptable behavior. It needs to be enforced."

"*Ah*!" Lucky's hand comes up and catches my wrist. "Beautiful, the masochism thing only really works when you get me going first."

I blink, realizing I'm a moment from tearing a decent chunk of hair from his scalp.

I loosen my grip. "Sorry."

Blue eyes twinkle at me, and despite the brutal edge to my care, I can feel him relaxing into me. I smile at him softly before I look up.

"Jayk? Do you think we can manage that?"

Jayk rubs a hand over his jaw, glancing at Dom . . . who just raises his brows, batting the question back to him.

It's been happening all day, and I'm not sure what to make of it.

"Yeah," Jayk mutters. Then he sighs, running a hand over the top of his head. "Yeah, Sawyer will agree to that."

Relief flickers in me at one thing solved.

"I'll talk to the civilians tomorrow, see if they have anything else to add."

I tie off Lucky's braid, tucking it behind his ear.

"And the last thing, darlin'?" Beau asks from the couch. It's long enough that his long legs are sprawled behind my head, but his feet don't quite hit Jasper. Warmth is tucked into his eyes and slight smile as he looks over me and Lucky.

My Beau, who has always fought for me to have it all.

I see the worry in him, too. "You know what this could cost?"

A hot, hard lump lodges in my throat, and Lucky sits up, pressing a kiss to my cheek.

It could cost me one of my brutes.

It could cost me all of them.

Sure, there are things I can do to help. Ways I can, and will, work on the sidelines in charged preparation and in the awful aftermath, but in the thick of it, I can't be there. I have skills and strengths—ones I'm proud of—but . . . my books can't stop an army.

My brutes can.

They'll keep each other safe.

I don't know if they'd admit it yet, but I've been watching them this week. I don't think any of them have ever had so much fun.

They love each other as much as I do.

Shakily, I stand, and Beau takes my hand. Tears prick my eyes as I settle on top of him. His hand runs over my hair, then settles at my waist.

"I know the risk, Beau," I whisper. "I've lived every day knowing I might die—that I might drink water I didn't boil properly or food that I shouldn't. The whole world is trying to kill us, and that's bad enough, but living under the Sinners . . . we'd be in danger for the rest of our lives."

Aching with fear, I give Beau a tremulous smile.

I look at Jayk, gruff and unsure in his armchair.

Lucky leaning into Jasper, my braid in his hair.

Jasper, watching over me with quiet understanding, as he always does.

And Dom, dark and brooding against the wall, his eyes burning gold on me and Beau.

My chest throbs.

"I know what kind of men I fell for," I tell them, and the tears spill over as I huff a laugh that hurts everywhere. "I can't love you for all the ways you're brave and good, but never let you be those things." I swallow hard, and my smile becomes pained, too. "Those things will wither and die under the Sinners. It would kill you to watch people die knowing you could have done something. That we *should* have. You're all . . . you're so much braver than me."

Beau frowns, his eyes shining, but I sniff and shake my head before he can talk.

I know he'll protest, but he doesn't know the worst of my thoughts. How desperately I want to take these men and run far away from Sinners and civilians and Reapers and teenagers wearing chain mail. That I would leave the world to rot and burn if it kept them safe. If I thought they could do it and not loathe themselves, I would.

They're miserable thoughts, but I'll share them another time. Another day.

That selfishness belongs to another version of me.

For now, I need to let the best of them inspire the best in me.

Even if it kills us.

"We need a chance to make a better world than one the Sinners want to make," I tell them.

Beneath me, Beau lets out a long, shaky breath.

When I glance around, the others are all looking at me with the same tight, barely contained emotion.

God, the way these men love me.

It's enough to crack the last tenuous hold I have on my emotions.

I try desperately to rein them in anyway. "If we act now, we have an edge. Maybe a head start on Alastair." I wipe uselessly at my cheeks. "I'll help wherever I can, of course. I'll organize the packing, for a start. I'm quite good . . . good at th-things like—"

Dom's arms come around me, lifting me off Beau, and I bury my silent tears in his neck.

He holds me fiercely. "No one is dying," he swears, harsh and rough and just for me. "No one, Eden. I'm not letting that happen. You're not burying a single one of us."

My fingers curl in his hair like I can hold the promise to me. Like I can drag in his strength and his whirlwind, spicy scent.

"We'll watch out for each other."

Jayk's jagged voice across the room strikes me like lightning. That promise from him, of all of them.

Over Dom's shoulder, somber and lethally serious, he watches me —me with Dom—and he doesn't move from his chair. Ryan's pocketknife is still in his white-knuckled hand.

The others murmur their assent, and finally, my tears slow, as much from their sweetness as from my bitter fear. Dom sets my feet back on the floor, his eyes intense as they run over my face.

As they settle on my lips.

Suddenly, an obnoxious stream of music blares to life behind me, so loud I yelp, jolting back against Dom like his vote of protection extends to the Star Wars theme song.

Beau curses, twisting for the remote, and Lucky snorts a laugh. "That would have been so much funnier in the middle of the let's-save-the-world speech."

"Oh my God," I stutter, not computing.

I turn to the TV screen to see words begin to scroll up and over a galaxy far, far away.

Beau manages to yank the remote out from under his ass, kicking Jasper in the ribs in the process, and he jams down on the pause button.

"What . . ." I cut off, then try again. "I'm sorry, *what* is this?"

Beau gives me a sheepish look as Dom's hands settle on my waist.

"Uh, movie night?" Beau asks.

Like it's a *question*.

Dom rolls his eyes, looking down at me before he moves over to the couch, shoving Beau into the middle so he can sit beside him. "We were too wired to sleep, so we were going to stay up. Then the rest of the idiot brigade showed up."

Lucky winks at me as he gets up, dumping himself in Jasper's lap. "Honestly, we spent more time arguing over the movie than the whole war thing, so props to you for being the responsible one."

"They have shitty fucking options," Jayk mutters darkly, and he gives me a grumpy look. "We're not changing it."

Jasper sighs, shifting to get comfortable, and I look between them all in bewilderment.

The ache in my chest shifts into something softer, warmer as they all settle in.

"We can change it if you object." Jasper plucks a folded blanket from the side table and drapes it over him and Lucky. "We were supposed to wait until you arrived before we made a final decision."

Jayk kicks his legs up over the arm of his chair. "Hm. That's true. Might have been a bit . . . premature." He tilts his head to look at Jasper, smirking. "Don't you think?"

Jasper picks up a pillow and throws it at him, and it smacks the back of his head.

Beau whistles low, nodding like he's impressed. "Nice shot."

Jayk is still laughing as he tucks the pillow under him, and I narrow my eyes at him.

"Jayk, you lasted about thirty seconds longer than he did and with *none* of the foreplay." When he stiffens, shooting me an affronted glower, I smile. "Unless you consider watching Lucky and Jasper touching me foreplay, of course."

His brows slam down.

Lucky chokes on a laugh, then gives Jayk a serious look. "Have you always had a thing for cuckolding, Jayk, or was that a new discovery?"

Jasper hides a smile. "Don't kink shame, Lucien."

"Who's shaming? Good for him, I say. Super happy to tie him up again."

"Ha ha ha," Jayk grumbles, and Beau nudges Dom, a sneaky smile on his face.

"Aw, look. Their first sharing experience together. They got too excited, huh?" He gives Jasper and Lucky, who's sitting on his other side, a sympathetic look. "Don't worry, you'll improve."

Dom snorts softly. "Maybe. I don't think we've ever lost it before we got the job done—have we, Beau?"

But it comes out distracted. His attention is all on me.

He nods for me to join him on the couch, and I'm moving before I've registered the silent order. I take his hand, and he draws me onto his lap.

Beau watches me settle in, softly amused. "Legend says you're still waiting."

I shoot Beau a look under my lashes, and he winks at me, dragging my legs onto his lap. Jasper hands us another blanket, and they tuck me in, tossing insults and laughter back and forth until Jayk grumbles at them to start the damn movie already. Until, ignored, he finally snaps and storms over to snatch the remote out of Beau's hand so he can start it himself, only to resettle on the floor by our feet.

I rest my head against Dom's chest, taking them all in.

Thinking that there's nothing in the world more worth waging a war for.

PART THREE

WAR

CHAPTER 50

EDEN

Screams wake me. Bloodcurdling, raw male fear. Banging on doors. Women shouting.

By the time I sit up, panic punching through my fatigue, Dom has already rolled out of bed beside me, and Jayk is storming across the room to wrench the bedroom door open, his rifle in hand, and his makeshift bed of blankets abandoned on the floor.

By the couch, Jasper quickly tosses Lucky his shirt.

A bleary Beau starts pushing me out of bed, and I barely have time to register the fact that I'm somehow in Dom's bed—that I was sleeping *between* Dom and Beau and I didn't even get to appreciate it —when Jayk's face turns rigid.

"Get up. We're under attack." Jayk's eyes find me briefly, dark with exhaustion. "You stay here."

He disappears into the shadows.

Footsteps thunder through the halls. There's some kind of pattering, fast and distant like rainfall . . . only we're too deep in the rock for rain.

Jasper pulls on his loafers hurriedly, his brow in knots. "Reapers? I don't understand. Why on earth would they attack now?"

Heart hammering, I swing my legs out of bed and pull my hair back, only to realize I don't have a hair band.

Lucky whistles, and I look up to see him holding one, then rush over.

Beau curses, tugging on his pants, right as Dom pushes open the door behind Jayk, snagging up a rifle.

Gun. Guns are by the door.

"*Attack!*" someone shouts.

"Does it matter?" Lucky grabs up a rifle, too, and tosses it to Jasper.

By the time he's grabbed the next one, I'm there, and he passes it off. I've only used a rifle once, but having a weapon—any weapon—in my hand steadies me.

At the next distant scream, Lucky bolts, and I dart into the hall behind him, fear throbbing in my throat. There are women everywhere, armed and running down the stairs. Bristlebrook is noxiously dark, but as we head down the stairs, sounds come into focus, sharpening like knives against the stony night.

There's shouting. Bullets. Someone's calling something, but I just can't make it out, and—

The man's scream cuts off, and pure dread blanks my mind. It throws me violently back into the Sinners' camp, the bleak emptiness that swallowed me when I thought my brutes were dead.

Lucky. Jaykob. Dom. Bea—

No.

We're not there. It's not one of mine. I can see my brutes, all of them. Dom and Jayk disappear outside, identically armed, and Jasper, Beau, and Lucky are storming down the stairs beside me.

They're here. They're alive.

Deanna catches Beau's arm as he reaches the bottom of the stairs. She's still wearing her bonnet, but she has Beau's medic bag in hand, and he takes it with a hurried thanks. Leanne and Clare are behind her, their clothes sleepy and slapped together.

"Send any injured in to us." Deanna pauses at the next scream, then adds, "Any that can be saved."

Grim, Beau nods as he catches back up to Lucky, Jasper, and me in the doorway, and his arrival is heralded by a chorus of agonized screams from outside. Worry flashes through Lucky's eyes, and all three of them check their rifles.

My mouth turns dry as I look down at mine.

I'm not even sure what to check.

Silently, Beau reaches over and flicks off my safety.

Lucky nudges me, offering a weak smile. "Don't shoot the good guys, okay?"

Fear freezes my throat.

My glasses slip as I follow them outside, narrowly avoiding being taken out by Ida as she rushes past me. It's all too fast. Too chaotic. I can't even hear myself think. If it's not *my* men dying, then it has to be the Reapers. Are the civilians attacking *them*? Did something happen?

This makes no *sense*.

We spill out onto the lawn, though Jasper's cautioning hand on my back warns me not to go too far into the suffocating darkness. There's no bonfire tonight. No moon or stars escaping from the threatening clouds. The light from the house is pushed back by the night's oppressive weight, and I stand in the tiny crescent of defiant gold.

Still, I can't see.

There are flashes of light from firing gun muzzles. They flare through the trees like fireflies.

"Bridge is *down*! Moat secure," Sloane shouts.

Tearfully, Mary Beth begs, "Sloane, what is *happening*?"

"It's the fucking Reapers. Bethy, get down!" Ava snaps back.

"Keep to the platforms," Jayk roars from somewhere ahead of me. "Hold your fire!"

"Stay back!" Dom is farther to the left, by the apple tree. "We hold!"

"No, please!"

"Help! *Help*!"

More and more men's voices rise, and I realize it's not us. *We're* not doing this.

"Someone's attacking the Reapers," Jasper says, grave and cold.

"Let us cross, *please*!"

That one sounded like Pete, but the voice is lost to the black. To the deafening roar of bullets and bloody screams.

The civilians removed the bridge to protect Bristlebrook.

The Reapers have nowhere to go.

"We have to help them, right? Should we take the side tunnel? Pincer?" Lucky shifts between his feet, his eyes searching as sightlessly as mine. "Shit, they're pinned."

Beau gives him a grim look. "Are we sure the Reapers aren't the ones doing this?"

But he pauses as another scream cuts off, and Lucky lifts his brows skeptically.

"Why would the Reapers attack after today?" Jasper's lips are a thin, unhappy line. "No. This doesn't feel right. It has to be someone else."

Nausea swirls in my gut. My tired brain can't reconcile those screams with bodies. With *death*. They're night terrors, leftovers from my restless dreams, because the Reapers were laughing just hours ago. Sawyer was tossing apples to Kasey with a moustached grin.

He could be splattered in the grass right now.

"It could be a hundred things. Even if they are being attacked, we can't risk the civilians until we know what we're up against," Beau grinds out, but he sounds uncertain. He glances down at me, his eyes lingering on my face. "We have too much to lose here."

Jasper's brow creases. "Could it be marauders? Strangers making their way through the woods?"

Marauders, like the hunters who chased me. Only my hunters weren't any strange, rogue group, they were . . .

"I . . . I don't think it's marauders." My lips are numb, and goosebumps ripple down my spine with frigid, fateful dread.

Please.

Please don't be them.

Another Reaper screams, and my stomach dips.

"This is wrong. We have to help them," I whisper, clutching at Jasper's arm, but my throat closes around the words—so tightly I'm not sure they were audible at all.

But we . . . we *do* have to help the Reapers . . .

Don't we?

Jasper rests a hand on top of mine, silently reassuring.

Cold wind whips us, cutting through my sheer nightdress. Overhead, the churning clouds rumble, choking out every star.

I'm not stupid. I know the risk of stepping out of safety to save someone else. But there aren't enough people left in the world to be casual about death.

I am not a selfless person, nor a brave one. When I need to choose between my own skin or helping someone else, I know what I *should* do—and yet, it's still a choice I've failed so, so often in the past.

But . . . we already *made* this choice.

Last night, as we made ourselves a family, we chose to defend the Reapers.

And right now, we're letting them die.

Mary Beth's anxious face hovers a few paces away, searching the dark. I can't hear Jayk or Dom anymore, and it sends frissons of fear through me. Those men are far too reckless to be out of sight.

The gunfire stops.

My fingers dig into Jasper's arm, and I'm suspended, breathless. Waiting.

A fiery plume lights up in the forest to my left. Then another. On and on, in a half circle surrounding Bristlebrook, fiery torches spring to life in the deep, ravenous darkness of the distant trees.

The civilians fall quiet around us. Only whimpers and dying gurgles break the expectant silence.

In unison, the flaming torches move forward.

Inexorable, portentous, the firelight begins to extend its claws, illuminating the carnage on Bristlebrook's doorstep. It's a horrific, frozen tableau. Shredded tents and exploded earth, Reapers' bodies rent open and glistening wetly in the orange glow.

"Oh my God," I breathe.

Over a dozen Reapers lie dead. The remainder are huddled at the edge of the dry moat that is too wide and lethally piked for them to leap across, even if barbed wire weren't gating in the majority of our side. Some are hunkered down behind trees at the forest's edge, or worse, beside the paper-thin tents that will only cast their silhouettes into deadly relief. Some are firing back from whatever meagre cover they've been able to find. Some groan, wounded, where they lie, tangled in their sleeping bags or where they were gunned down as they ran.

Our people are motionless, guarded and armed as they line our defensive platforms. These are built up high enough to have an overhead angle on anyone encroaching, and the thick metal mantlets give them some protection against any weapons that can make the distance. The men and women from Red Zone stand beside ours, white-faced and grim.

Dom is atop one towering platform, looking over the battlefield, Arthur beside him, and Jayk is on the ground in front of all of them.

Waiting.

Everyone waiting, watching, as the torches close in.

I step forward, squinting through my glasses, trying to make out the shadowy figures, but either it's far too dark, or I'm far too blind.

"Stop, Eden," Beau mutters, snagging the back of my nightdress.

The blazing torches stop at the edge of the trees.

All except one.

From the center of the tree line, a man strides out of the smoky haze, dressed all in black, and an icy finger touches my spine.

His cobwebbed, cavernous voice carries over Bristlebrook. "You've all disappointed me."

My heart seizes.

Alastair.

Damn it. I was right.

Behind him, around him, gunmen step out from the trees on all sides. Three or four for every torch bearer, some with shotguns, some pistols . . . and a handful with heavy, military-grade assault rifles.

No. Stunned, confused betrayal cuts through my chest. This isn't what we agreed.

He lifts his hand.

"Stop!" I shout, panicked. "No, Alastair, don't—"

"You shouldn't make promises you can't keep," he says softly, and it feels like the words are meant just for me.

His hand drops.

Gunfire explodes around him.

It's thunderous, and Jasper yanks me back into his arms as Reaper flesh rips apart. The earth bursts in a dozen places around their camp.

It sprays the hazy smoke with dirt and bullets and blood until I can't tell them apart.

The screams follow.

Reapers try to flee back toward Bristlebrook, but without the bridge in place, they're pinned to the moat, helpless and terrified as faces beside them split apart like burst fruit.

I see Buck stand from behind his tent and turn, heaving himself toward the moat with white-eyed panic. There's nowhere for him to go.

This is a massacre.

"Stay back." Alastair's voice carries, resonant, despite his calm as he strides in front of the forest. "Hold the tree line. Fire from cover."

"They're stuck!" a large, bald Sinner shouts over the top of him as he runs forward. "Forward!"

"Back! *Mierda*! You're in the line of fire, idiot!"

I could swear it's Mateo, but I can't see him anywhere.

Men peel from the ranks of Sinners, leaving the trees as they begin to surge forward, firing on any Reaper they see. The bald Sinner clips a round-faced man through the throat, and I flinch.

The Reapers scatter, panicked—trapped. One man teeters on the edge of the moat, the ground crumbling under his heel as he backs up.

"Jasper . . ." I breathe, the cold air cutting me through.

I swear I can hear a woman's voice screaming among the men's, and Jasper tenses.

Akira? *Oh God.* My pulse squeezes panic into my chest.

Jennifer! Where's Jennifer?

The mule, Cherub, screams in panic, pulling back on its rope ties, causing bags of food to spill out at its feet.

If the Reapers die, it's not just their lives we'll lose.

I storm forward.

"Jayk!" I scream. "The bridge!"

Jayk's head whips back at me, then toward the Reapers. Buck fires back at the Sinners, and he howls in despair as he rings on empty.

Jayk hesitates for half a second, staring at them.

"Fuck!" he curses.

Then he runs.

"Ooh shit. He's doing it," Lucky groans. "We're going to die. This is stupid."

"Together, then?" Jasper asks, releasing me, and Lucky throws him a startled look, then lets out a choked laugh.

He dashes past me, running at full speed to help Jayk and, with a slightly flustered curse, Jasper follows. Katherine hits Ava on the arm, and Shelby looks up as Lucky bolts past them, and they all start running too.

But on the other side of the moat, the Sinners are getting closer.

Panic flutters through me, and Beau squeezes my arm.

Dom shouts from atop his platform.

"Bristlebrook, hold fire until my call!" He lines up his own shot. "I said *hold*! Snipers. Sloane, Sara, Valerie, June! Clear shots only! Do *not* risk friendly fire!"

The muzzle of Dom's rifle pokes through the rectangular hole in his shielding wall, and in seconds, he clips off half a dozen shots. Beyond the bridge, several Sinners drop mid-run.

It sets off a new round of terrified shouts, and my heart pounds.

Bullets start flying toward Jayk, then the civilians on the ground, too, as they near the firefight. A lot of them fling wide, and I glance around. Jayk and Dom have kept all our lights off.

We're entirely in the dark.

Jayk reaches the bridge first, and he kneels, trying to shift it, but it's too heavy for one person to carry.

We are in the dark, but if they get close to that moat, the torches will reveal their approach, too.

"Reapers, get the fuck down!" Jayk shouts, and they scatter back, away from the bridge. Half a dozen drop to hands and knees.

Jayk swings his rifle around and fires at the Sinners, buying time as, one by one, the others join him. Katherine, Shelby, Ava. Jayk jumps up and they fall along the sides of the bridge, hefting it up off the ground with obvious strain. When they begin to shift forward, it's slow. Shuffling.

Too slow.

A horde of Sinners winds through the woods after the first wave, torch light after torch light shining like funeral pyres behind Alastair.

Move, I silently urge, watching the bridge.

But then Jasper and Lucky join Jayk, ducking under the bridge and lifting it higher, until they can heft it up and the wood bites into their shoulders.

And then the group starts to move.

I step forward, and Beau yanks me back again with a glower.

"I can—"

"You can get yourself killed. Eden, I'm sorry. I need you to stay. Get the wounded inside as they come through, I don't know, but stay back," he urges before I can protest, shifting his medic bag over his shoulders. His rifle is steady in his grip.

He can do both—heal and kill and lift and fight. He can do it all. This is what they do.

My rifle sweats in my hands. I don't know how to use it, not really, and my strength isn't much to add to a team carrying a bridge. Out there, in this situation, I'm a liability.

But how can I stay here?

I watch as a man's knee explodes while he tries to run. He collapses into the dirt as another runs past Buck and jumps, trying to make the leap across the moat. For a moment, he's suspended, floating —but then he hits the sharpened pikes hard, skewered through from groin to throat.

I flinch.

Here, I can only watch.

I can only help the wounded if they live.

Buck skids to a stop, staring at the impaled Reaper, but a bullet kisses the dirt beside his feet, and he lets out a hoarse cry before taking off again.

"We're too late," I whisper.

We cut off the bridge. We saved ourselves.

They didn't have a chance.

"Maybe not."

I glance up at Beau, and he nods up and to the right, where a group of Reapers are firing furiously, carving out a small pocket as they push the Sinners near them back into the trees. Cole and Sawyer fight at their head, Pete and Jennifer behind them, and slowly, so slowly, they gain ground. As I watch, two more Reapers abandon their hiding places to join them. Then another. Then three more.

"Sinners, hold back! Fire from cover!" Mateo shouts again, and I finally make him out, standing beside a torchbearer, his dark hair dancing with reflected flames.

One torch bearer takes a bullet through his skull, and his light drops between gnarled tree roots, right as a Reaper beside Cole dies on a scream, his throat spurting blood.

It's horrific, twisted music.

All the while, Alastair looms by the trees, knighted by black.

"Bristlebrook, fire for effect!" Dom barks. "Suppressive fire. Clear shots only."

Arthur steps forward. "Elena, Theo, Amir! Fire in rounds!"

Like a sudden beat shift, bullets rise from our side—a synchronized counterpoint that adds roars of "incoming!" and shrieks of "back!" to the tune.

On the outermost defensive platform, the three from Red Zone step up too, letting loose a wicked barrage of dark arrows. One slams through a Sinner's thigh, and the man topples into the moat.

Beside me, Beau's jaw flexes, and my fear sticks in my throat.

Our bullets thud into the tents just beyond the bridge, several striking Sinners down. In response, more guns turn our way, and there's a sharp, metallic patter as some of their return fire slams into the protective steel mantlets guarding the defensive platforms.

All the while, the bridge moves closer to the moat.

"Please," I whisper. "Please, please, please."

As they begin to close in, Alastair's attention sharpens like throwing daggers.

"Stop the bridge," he says, and his voice is something that creeps out of the night.

My last, flickering flare of hope withers into dull horror. My brutes' safety was supposed to be guaranteed. We were supposed to be safe. The women and children were supposed to be safe. He . . . played me. About *everything*.

It was always going to be war.

In unison, the Sinners turn toward the bridge—toward *my men*—and there's no air left in my lungs. I can't negotiate here. There's no soup, no poison, no clever scheme to turn on its head. Only the

Sinners' guns and my unarmed Brutes and me, helpless on the sidelines.

I sent them out there, and now Alastair is going to make me watch them die . . . because I was wrong.

Because I was wrong, I might have killed everyone I love.

"Son of a bitch!" Beau swears, cold murder flashing across his face.

Beau explodes forward as I stand frozen. Numb.

Useless.

In his group, Sawyer turns with wild, desperate eyes, taking in the bridge, the guns, Buck running with everything he has.

"Reapers, to the bridge!" he roars.

Nearby, a man shouts. A woman screams. More bullets hit our defenses.

"Eden! What do we do?" Mary Beth asks, edging back, but I'm caught by the nightmare in front of me.

More Sinners step forward, dozens, directing their fire toward the bridge.

Toward Jayk.

Jasper.

Lucky.

I sink to my knees.

A bullet shatters the wood by Lucky's hand, but he doesn't flinch. None of them do.

"Eden!" Mary Beth shakes me, and I finally look up, glaring at her, only to see greying, kindly Valerie gripping one of the wooden struts on the nearest defensive platform.

Blood is pouring from her shoulder, and she sways as she stands.

Her husband tucks one arm under her good arm, shuffling forward. Behind them, I see two more civilians carrying Jessica, who looks to be unconscious.

This is only the start.

And the med bay only has three beds.

"Caleb! Help!" I shout, and Caleb looks down from the platform, spotting Patrick and Valerie. The younger man passes off his rifle to hurry down.

Urgency pounds me, and I get up, grabbing Mary Beth. I'm not sure which of us is shaking harder, but I shove my fear down as Caleb rushes over to help Patrick.

I'm not useless. Damn it, I *won't* be useless.

"Start clearing the furniture in the sitting room," I tell Mary Beth quickly. "Then go to the linen closet, and get as many sheets, blankets, and pillows as you can. We need more beds. Get Kasey to see if Deanna needs anything, then she can help you."

She nods, then bolts, and I turn to Caleb.

Beside him, Patrick is trembling, watching his wife.

"Get her to the med bay and then come back. Both of you," I clarify when Patrick's jaw sets stubbornly. Thick fear aches in my throat. "We're going to have more."

They go, and I edge forward and hold onto the platform's wooden strut, looking for more wounded.

Only to lock back in on the bridge.

"Again!" Dom yells from his platform, and another round of shots blisters out.

Sinners go down with staggering swiftness, and several others shy back from the moat, and Jayk takes advantage of the reprieve, pushing everyone faster, laden by the enormous weight.

They're almost there.

They're *all* almost there.

Buck's face is dark red and sweaty, only feet away from the moat— from the death that lies behind and ahead, unless they get that bridge in place.

Please.

My nails crack as I dig them into the wood, thinking of Buck shyly pulling his cap off when we met. Of him blushing, scandalized by Mila's flirting.

I don't want him to die, either.

How many people have I killed because I set Alastair free? How many people have I killed, because I was so, so sure I was right?

"Fucking pussies! Forward!" the bald Sinner shouts, firing hot and fast, and Mateo storms over to him, disarming him in seconds.

"Stay *back*!" Mateo backs up as a shot nearly takes him out.

But a bold Sinner steps out from behind the trees and lines up a shot toward the bridge—toward my brutes. The first one glances off the bridge, and the Sinner walks forward, lining up again. Zeroing in.

My breathing stalls—only for the man to slam backward, caught in the chest.

"Nice one, Beau, baby!" Ida hollers, and my heart squeezes as Beau slides behind the other brutes, firing on anyone approaching the bridge. Defending them. Protecting them fiercely.

Beau will always come out swinging for his family.

Tears sting my eyes, and damp earth presses between my toes. They're going to make it.

The civilians pass me with Jessica, and I check on her quickly before directing them to the med bay.

The bridge slams into place, and Buck's foot comes down on the bullet-scarred wood a moment later. The women let out a wild cheer, and a choked, relieved sob escapes me as a grin finally finds his exhausted face.

Then he stops.

For a moment, I don't understand what happened. Why he's just stopped in the center of the bridge with bullets still flying from all angles.

Then I see the blood trickle between his eyes.

Buck collapses gracefully, still smiling, into the moat.

I slam a hand over my mouth to trap my scream.

By the trees, Alastair pulls back his rifle. In the hazy, orange glow, I could almost swear it smokes.

CHAPTER 51

JASPER

W e fall back from the bridge, bullets slamming in around us. Caught by the darkness and the dizzying speed, I lift my rifle up to fire back at them.

Only to see Buck fall hard off the bridge and onto the pikes.

The group of Reapers tears through several Sinners, pushing toward the bridge, and Pete staggers out, staring at the moat.

"Buck!"

It's a broken, plaintive cry.

"Fuck," Lucien breathes, then shouts. "Jasper, up!"

Reacting like his instincts are mine—his instincts are far better than mine will ever be—I snap my rifle around and shoot. Two Sinners collapse in front of the bridge, and I shudder at the clunky, unanimated way they fall.

Sawyer jumps over their bodies, his men right behind him.

"Fall back!" Beaumont barks behind us. "To me! Fall back."

"Bristlebrook, hold!" Dominic roars as they approach the bridge. "Hold fire! Do *not* shoot our guys!"

Katherine shoots twice, then grabs Shelby's arm, forcing her into a run as our group falls back to Beaumont. Jaykob walks backward quickly, his rifle up as he covers us all, and Ava hurries him along.

Lucien is still firing off fast, neat shots beside me, and a bullet slashes flinchingly close to his ear. I grab the back of his collar, yanking him.

"Jasper, stop! They're almost there," he snaps.

"Beaumont and Dominic are covering us and them. Fall back, Lucien," I snap back, and he curses as he obeys.

Beaumont and two civilians have flipped one of the other heavy bridges, and we slide in beside Jaykob seconds later, helping him lift the final bridge onto its side for some cover, breathing hard.

"Jayk, get up on the defenses. You can't call the fight from here," Beaumont argues with him.

When I get my rifle back up, I see Sawyer's group rounding the edge of the bridge. He and Cole stand on either side of it, holding back the Sinners, as Reaper after Reaper pounds boots over the bridge to safety.

Three, five, until more than a dozen have crossed. Pete and Akira and more faces I know but don't have names for.

Not nearly enough.

"Dom can call the fight," Jaykob argues, sniping a crawling Sinner between the eyes. "I'm better down here."

"Argue with him about it, fucker." Beaumont lets off another shot, then stops, panting. "Jayk, these people might have been in some tussles, but this is something else. They need to see you. They trust you."

Jaykob stops, looking at him, then he curses and peels back.

Reapers stream past us, wild-eyed and frightened, and Jaykob directs them toward Bristlebrook before he falls back with them.

"Go. To the house, go!"

Over my shoulder, I see Eden on the porch, pointing men inside, shouting something I can't make out through the noise.

Lucien shoots again. Then again and again. Each shot shudders through me.

Bang.

Bang.

Bang.

I loathe this. I loathe the unhinged storm of my pulse, and the flinch of bullets by my face. I loathe the spurting death, and the glassy, staring eyes. I loathe the fear.

Most of all, I loathe that I'm not better at it. For all I've been prac- ticing—sparring and shooting and re-honing the skills these men have taught me—I don't have Jaykob's ferocity or Lucien's pinpoint accu- racy. I'm a psychologist. I dissect minds, not brains.

Damn it, I'm not *made* for this.

I know he was just trying to land a blow, but Jaykob was right. I might be the man who comforts Eden, but I'm not the man to protect her.

I release another shot anyway, right as Cole takes a hit to his thigh that immediately buckles his leg, and his pained cry splits the air. Lucien takes out the gangly Sinner who shot him, and Sawyer collects his friend in the next instant, dragging him over the narrow bridge with wide, terrified eyes.

"Shit," Beau curses, and he slings his rifle, pulling around his med bag. "Lucky, you—"

"Yep. Got you. Go," Lucien says distractedly.

"What are we? Decoration?" Katherine mutters tartly, and Ava snorts beside her, sending off a blistering round of shots that wipes out four Sinners just as they tear out of the trees.

Beau helps lift Cole, and he and Sawyer drag him behind us. Moving fast, Beau pulls out a tourniquet. Bandages. Pain relief. Antiseptic.

More Reapers storm past us.

"Shit! No, no, no! *Help!*"

The shriek comes from across the moat, sharp and distinctly feminine.

My gut wrenches sideways.

"*Jen?*" Ava snaps, panicked.

It takes a moment to spot her, limping toward the bridge as a small group of Reapers stream past her, her gunshot wound slowing her badly. A blunt-featured Sinner takes out a fleeing Reaper in the back, and Jennifer's sob rips the air as she drops down to crawl over the body.

The Reapers are on the run now. There's less than a dozen left alive on that side of the moat, and every one of them is making a break for the bridge.

And so, the Sinners grow bolder. More and more start encroaching from the trees.

Jennifer is fodder.

She's going to die without help.

Jaykob is back with Dominic, Beaumont is busy saving Cole, and Lucien . . .

"I'm going for her." I sling my rifle, and Lucien catches my arm.

"The hell you are!" he protests, alarmed, paling under his tan. He shoots a look at Jennifer, and the anxiety deepens on his face. "Shit, okay. I'll go."

I soften, looking at his fierce, beautiful face. "You're the better shot, love." I smile, though every impulse in me tells me to stop and think. To step back. To stay safe. "Just a quick trip. It will take two moments."

I might not be as skilled, but I can be as brave as my Lucien. I won't forgive myself if she dies.

Recognition sparks in his eyes—swiftly followed by panic. He said something similar to me, many years ago, on the night our world changed forever.

He said it right before he did something very, very stupid.

Indecision wars on his face for a moment as impatience wars within me—and I try not to be offended at how much of an argument he's putting up. I know he's been fighting with this.

Then Lucien releases me. "Go. Fuck. Go fast."

Katherine's face is set as she lines up her next shot. "These assholes won't touch you."

I nod, then jump over the shelter of our bridge, ignoring how much my body dislikes that particular motion.

"Jasper?" I hear Beaumont say behind me, alarmed, but I don't stop.

It's still so dark, but the hellish conflagrations puncturing the night cast it all in infernal shades. A Reaper slams into my shoulder as he flees past me.

Sinners are *swarming* from the trees now, and another stocky

Reaper sobs as he backs away from Mateo, who shoots him clean through the eye.

Okay. I swallow dryly. Okay.

Perhaps I won't look. I'll . . . I'll just focus on myself.

The others will cover me.

I don't stop to look down at the pikes spearing Buck's body in a half-dozen places. I don't stop when my loafers rattle the bridge or their unfit soles slip in blood as I hit the grass on the other side.

"Down, Jasper!" Jayk shouts in the distance, and I duck low, throwing myself to the side.

I land beside a body . . . and its face is largely missing a cheek. The body smells like released feces, and I press my lips together.

Repulsive.

"Now!" Dom calls, and another deafening round of gunfire fells more than a dozen Sinners.

Jennifer looks up from perhaps ten yards away, tears streaking her filthy cheeks. She has a pistol in her hand as she crawls. I get up, keeping low, and hurry over to her.

To my left, a Sinner I didn't even see drops hard.

"Come, Jennifer. I have you," I murmur, reaching out a shaking hand.

Determination crushes the fear in her face, and her hand slaps into mine.

As I drag her up, she chokes, "Is this covered by your session fee?"

"I'm afraid this will be extra," I tell her, and she huffs a laugh that's full of the same barely contained panic I'm feeling.

A bullet whistles through the air in front of us, then another behind, and I try not to imagine myself skewered by the pikes beside us as I drag her forward, taking most of her weight. The bandage on her leg is soaked in bright, fresh blood.

Glancing back at Bristlebrook, I realize that from this angle, it's completely cast in depthless, black night. Only the bare glow of the porch and windows to say there's a house there at all. I have to squint to make out the towering platforms.

The torch light has decimated my night vision.

Shouts and screams, gunshots and pleas for help crash in on me from all sides, but I can't do anything for them right now. We're still getting *shot* at.

A bullet skids by my foot, and I flinch to the side, only to slip on the edge of the moat.

My stomach flies into my throat. I take in the drop, the sharpened pikes as they stare up at me in lethal promise—only for Jennifer to slam her weight to the other side, onto her injured leg, dragging us back with a piercing, agonized scream. We collapse onto the grass, and she sobs again, her eyes flick behind my shoulder, then sink closed.

I look up, and a large, tattooed Sinner licks his teeth, his gun already at my temple.

Then his face explodes.

Hot, thick blood sprays me, and he teeters forward, but I shove him into the moat.

As he falls away, I see Heather run forward, shooting another Sinner through the throat, then spinning to catch another behind her between the eyes. She has a large military pack over her shoulders, but it doesn't seem to be slowing her down.

What on earth is the she-dragon doing here?

My mind is glitching, caught by the flickering firelight and the storm of death around me.

Heather dispatches another Sinner behind us, and a fierce, unholy gratitude strikes me with stunning force as I pant, my lungs on fire.

I think the she-dragon just saved my life.

Her gaze flicks to Jennifer, then she meets my eyes and nods.

Humbled, I nod back.

"Who let the whore out?" the large bald Sinner from earlier sneers, zeroing in on Heather.

I could have sworn Mateo had disarmed him, but he's sporting a shotgun and a pistol now. He's creeping between the torn, tattered tents, but a small man with cold, beady eyes darts forward from behind him.

They're everywhere.

And they're getting closer to the bridge.

"Up," I demand of Jennifer, new urgency crashing in on me.

We need to get to that bridge *now*.

But Jennifer is lying frozen, racked with shudders.

Heather drops another Sinner three feet from us.

I purse my lips, then bend down to Jennifer. "Jennifer, move now. You've done a lot, I know, but you need to keep going. Get *up*."

She squeezes her eyes closed, shaking her head, and I swallow hard, scanning the Sinners as they close in. They collapse, but more fill their spots. Heather backs toward the bridge, firing pistols from both hands to keep it clear.

"Fuck, what's taking so long?" she snaps, not looking back at us. "I know you're out of shape, but move your god-damned ass, Jasper."

Curse it.

Jaykob had better not give me grief over this too.

Kneeling down, I reach under Jennifer's arms to pull her up.

"Help me, Jennifer. Now," I say more sharply, and she shifts her weight.

Awkwardly, painfully, I drag her over my shoulder.

Even more painfully, I stand, and my thigh muscles scream their protest as I turn toward the bridge. I feel all the blood rushing into my neck, my face, as I strain to carry her to the bridge.

How on earth does Jaykob *do* this?

The man is three parts *mule*.

Still, I do it, my pulse pounds in my temples, and I keep behind Heather as she clears the way. As Lucien, and Jaykob, and Dominic all clear our way.

And Beaumont runs up, waiting on the other side of the moat for me.

My loafer finally hits the bridge, and as Heather suddenly pivots, turning to shoot, I see the small, beady-eyed Sinner creep up on her other side. I can't tell if he's focused on her or me. A torch flares right behind him, dazzling me.

"Heather, look ou—!"

But the man drops before I can finish the warning, and in the hazy glow, a tall, slender Sinner stands behind him.

Heather doesn't even turn.

"The fuck are you waiting for? Get her safe!" Heather drops one pistol, then rips another out of the grip of a dead Reaper.

"Stay safe, witch," I mutter to her, then take the bridge in long, ground-eating strides.

I crash into Beaumont on the other side, and he drags Jennifer off my shoulder.

"I've got her," he assures me.

"Cole?" I ask sharply.

"Eden got him back to Deanna. She's got a system set up." Jennifer is stuck in my arms, and Beaumont tugs her free. "It's okay, Jas. You got her clear."

Finally, I let her go.

And as Beaumont turns back to Bristlebrook, there's a thunderous, crashing roar.

It takes me a full moment to realize it's cheering. Facing the dark of Bristlebrook, I can see it, but the sound is enough to rattle my bones.

Rifles on wood, loud, raucous, irreverent *cheering* from every platform. From the porch. The house.

"What is that?" I call to Beaumont, bewildered, and he throws me a grin over his shoulder.

"I think that's for you."

For . . .

My eyes widen, and my adrenaline crashes into my throat, hot and swift as I listen to the roar.

I did it. I saved her. I didn't fail.

Maybe their cheers can battle the sounds of death in the nightmares that will come.

A bullet slices over my forearm, close enough to cut through the neat folds Eden made in my shirt and open a hot, pooling stream of blood along my arm, and I hiss in pain.

I stagger forward, remembering too late that being on this side of the moat isn't enough to keep me safe. The darkness isn't enough. With enough bullets, we can all be hit unless we fall back.

Except we can't.

The bridge is still in place.

The Sinners can cross as well as I can.

"Jasper!"

I turn at Heather's shout, and she runs up to the other side of the moat, unslinging the heavy pack from her shoulders.

And behind her, I see another volley of bullets take down a row of Sinners. They shy back from the bodies, hesitating to push forward.

I can still see most of them hugging the trees, illuminated by the torches.

"Now, how did you get that?" Alastair's boot crunches over a dead Sinner's hand as he walks in behind her, paying no mind to the death falling around him or the corpses beneath his feet. "Drop it, Deathwish."

He's abandoned his spot by the trees, and he's wholly focused on her.

And that pack.

Heather pauses, and a slow smirk curls up one side of her mouth as she hefts it into her hands, swinging it roughly. Her arms are corded with the weight of it.

"I told you once, baby." She looks over her shoulder at him. "I don't take orders like a nice girl."

He lunges forward, but she turns back and launches the pack over the moat.

It just barely clears the channel, clipping the barbed wire and slamming into my hands right as Alastair kicks her legs out from under her. With a brutal twist, she grabs him as she falls, taking him down with her.

Straining under the weight of the pack, I back up as they fight viciously, the two battling with a skill that makes me envious, until Heather punches Alastair in his tattooed throat, and he drops his whole weight on her. Mateo runs up to help, and he and Alastair both wrestle her back.

Across the moat, Heather looks me in the eye as they drag her away.

"Blow the fucking bridge."

CHAPTER 52

JAYKOB

SURVIVAL TIP #313
Don't steal things you don't really want.

They're clear," Dom tells me, standing like a stone wall beside me, and I nod, relaxing as I see the same thing.

Jasper backs away from the moat, a heavy pack in his hands, as Heather's dragged away and more Sinners start peeking their heads out of the trees.

The air smells like sweat and smoke and incoming rain, and something bitter and metallic, like new pennies. It's like every other shit fight we've seen.

But fuck, I hate being penned in.

"Reload!" Dom shouts. "Line up, they're going to storm the bridge."

I don't know what the fuck I'm doing up here. Dom has this. He's always had this. I should be down there in the action, sniping the fuck out of any dick-for-brains trying to take a shit on our welcome mat.

"No! Sawyer, you can wait. Wait, Sawyer—"

Eden's frustration rings from the porch, and I look over as Sawyer pushes through the crowd of injured and the few Reapers who just got themselves safe.

Below us, Sawyer pulls Jennifer right out of Beau's arms, gripping her tight against his chest.

"Oh, thank God. Oh, thank God, thank God." He's choked up and shaking, but Jennifer grips his arms, pulling back.

"I . . . You . . . you left me," she stammers in a small voice.

Sawyer shakes his head, gripping her so tight I shift my grip on my rifle.

"No," he says fiercely. "No, I didn't. It was all chaos. You were *right there*, I saw you *right there*, and then you just *weren't*, and I . . . I would *never* . . ." His voice breaks. "I'm so sorry, Jennifer. I'm so, so sorry. You're safe, I promise."

This time, hesitantly, she lets him pull her into his arms, and I wrinkle my nose.

Who the fuck leaves their girl behind?

"Beau, Deanna needs extra hands!" Eden yells through the dark, and Beau takes off toward the porch. "And can somebody please get Kasey, she had the supply list!"

My eyes lift to Eden as she rushes over to Mary Beth, who nods at whatever she tells her. Then Eden points up the stairs, her expression firming. As Mary Beth runs off, Eden enlists two Reapers to go fetch boiling water, and two more for this, and one for that—and not one of them stops to give her shit about it. She's got her snippy, bossy-as-fuck face on.

My lips kick up on one side.

She's tough as hell.

Dom slams his hand on top of the mantlet. "Bristlebrook, fire for effect."

I turn back to see Sinners drop as they head for the bridge, and the next line pauses warily, hugging the tree line.

Thunder rumbles overhead.

"We've got to blow the bridge," I say, and Dom nods, just as grim, as a thought hits me. "Shit, have we secured the side tunnel?"

Dom looks up sharply. "No. They shouldn't know where it is, but . . ."

I sling my rifle, heading for the ladder. "I've got it. You handle the bridge."

Distractedly, Dom shouts again for Bristlebrook to fire, and another round of shots rings out as he comes up behind me, grabbing my shoulder.

"Jayk, stop." Dom searches my face. "What the hell are you doing? You handle the bridge. Call it."

For fuck's *sake*.

"I don't need to call it. I don't want to call it. You're doing this better than I ever fucking could," I tell him, trying to pitch my voice low but not sure I'm succeeding.

Dom starts shaking his head. "No. This? This training, where everyone's at right now. You did it. Finish it, Jayk. Fuck your cold feet."

I give him a hard look through the shadows, trying to make him get it.

"It's not cold feet."

It really isn't.

I *could* do this. The idea doesn't panic me. I'm not being modest or losing my shit. I'm not wallowing in guilt that the bacon guy turned into a kebab. We lost Reapers tonight, sure, and that's rough, but in this kind of surprise attack, that shit is inevitable.

I'm *good*. The only thing ripping through me right now is impatience. I know enough to know where I should be.

And to know where *he* should be.

It's fucked that he doesn't.

From the ground, Beau shouts, "We've got creepers!"

"Hold!" I shout, distracted, and the battlements fall quiet, waiting.

Across the moat, it's quiet as Sinners start to edge out from behind the trees. A few bolder Sinners are darting forward, slipping in behind whatever shitty cover they can find.

Dom searches my face, his eyes hard and stupid stubborn. "See it out, asshole." He pauses, his jaw flexing. "We'll talk after."

Then he shoves me back, slinging his own rifle and making for the ladder. "I've got the side tunnel. You have the bridge and the call. Grenades are by Platform Three." He looks up at me, and he almost smiles. "Have fun."

Every part of me wants to strangle him for being a stubborn dick, but I snort anyway and turn, lifting my voice over the uneasy quiet.

Everyone is watching the Sinners skulk amid the trees.

"Okay, everyone. Hold on to your fucking bloomers, it's about to get hot." Grimly, I watch the Sinners creep forward again, emboldened by the reprieve of gunfire. "Hold fire. You hold until I call or every fucking one of you is going to lose all rations except Eden's slop!"

There's a ripple of chuckles over the platforms, and I smirk as I slide down the ladder.

This part *is* fun. The dangerous shit always is.

And as king, I guess I can choose to do that dangerous shit myself if I want.

"Love you too, Jayk," Eden calls tartly, and I snort, glancing back at her silhouette.

"Keep your tight ass on the porch," I order.

Back beyond the moat, I hear Alastair.

"Bane, secure the bridge. Sullivan, suppressive fire—hold cover."

Shit. Got to move.

"Sloane, get the heat and get it down now!" I shout, my adrenaline revving as I bolt for Platform Three.

"Jayk?" Ida calls as I pass, like she's got her panties in a knot. "Are we still holding? They're getting close."

"Still holding!" I shout as I run.

I pass another platform. Ahead, I can see the torches streaming forward, the twisted faces as the Sinners make a run on the moat, and I push harder.

Ida only pauses for a second. "Did you hit your head? They're going to take it!"

"Do not fire, you old goat!"

Jasper and Lucky are just staggering to a halt at the base of Platform Three as I get there, and they start loading up on as many frags as Sloane can hand over. Jasper's arm is bleeding like a bitch, but he's moving it fine, so it's probably only a surface wound. Breathing hard, I snatch a few frags for myself.

"More," I say impatiently, but she shakes her head.

"That's it."

Fuck.

"Fine, Jasper, drop the pack. The fuck is that . . ."

"Oh, shit!" Lucky says, startled, staring at the military pack Heather tossed over. "That's one of ours."

In seconds, he's pulled it off Jasper's shoulder and has ripped the zipper open.

It's carefully loaded with boxes of C-4, more frags, dozens of magazines.

Lucky whistles low. "Oooh, they made a danger pack."

"They'll kill her for this," Jasper breathes, and discomfort crawls over my skin.

Heather just evened the playing field.

There's a burst of shots from our side, and I snap my head up.

"I said *hold*, assholes!"

A few more shots cut through the dark.

"We'll be holding our intestines in a minute, you dick! Whatever you're planning, hurry the fuck up! They're here," Ava shouts from up ahead.

"Shit," I curse, and snatch several grenades out of their pockets, then look up at Jasper and Lucky. "Either of you ever throw a baseball?"

Lucky snorts, tossing one of the frags up and catching it as he edges back toward the moat. "Three-time Little League champ, baby."

Jasper gives me a disdainful look and snatches a frag from my hand. "I can handle a light toss, Jaykob."

I grin, slapping his back hard enough that he winces, as more of our people start shooting.

"Just remember: this ain't the time to set one off early."

Jasper's face turns wickedly dark, but I'm already bolting for the moat. Lucky veers off to the left, and the posh prince takes the right. The bitter wind whips my face. The temperature's dropped from ball-frying to ball-freezing in just two days, but my blood is on fire now and pounding through my veins.

We pass Ava, Shelby, and Katherine. The crowd of men surging toward the moat is like a horde of ants swarming to devour a corpse. The flaming torches are still in the trees, backlighting the writhing horde, and another crack of thunder crashes from overhead.

The first drops start to fall around us.

One man is shot halfway over the bridge, and falls with a twist, but another makes it to our side right as I skid in beside him, and I need to pull my pocketknife out to take him through the throat.

As he drops, I watch the Sinners approach, panting.

Almost. A bit closer. Fucking come *on*.

In seconds, they're close enough that I can see their faces. I can smell their rank, sour sweat.

Now.

Squeezing the safety lever, I wrench the pin from my first grenade.

"Bristlebrook, fire for effect," I roar. "Pins out. Frags. Go!"

Behind me, a hurricane of bullets thunders through the Sinners, and I throw the grenade up onto the bridge. It bounces once, and my heart stutters as I glare at it.

Don't you fucking *dare*.

It bounces back, teetering on the heavy wood.

A bullet grazes my cheek, and I flinch to the side, but I'm already backing up, pulling the next grenade out of my pocket and hurling it into the crowd of Sinners. Then the next. One more.

Two Sinners slam down onto the bridge, and I stare at the wobbling grenade in front of them.

Damn it! Just make like Jasper and—

The bridge explodes.

The force of it sends me reeling backward, landing me on my ass as burst splinters and chunks of wood splatter the air where I was just standing.

Then the next explosion hits, then the next, and the next—mine, and Lucky's, and Jasper's, hitting the throng of Sinners from all sides, over and over in brutal, obliterating bursts. And it's not wood that's reduced to splinters this time. Bodies are ripped apart in chunks and splashes. They're thrown in all directions as different explosions hit, and sprayed dirt and grass and body matter cloud the air in noxious fucking clouds.

It takes a while before the last explosion hits.

Before the last shot is fired.

Rain patters all around us like miserable fucking tears—but this time, when the thunder roars, nothing answers.

Everything is graveyard quiet as the dust, finally, settles.

All the torches have been extinguished, and I can't see shit as my eyes try to adjust.

A single pair of boots crunches out of the dark.

Slowly, painfully, I get to my feet. I need to squint to make out the lone figure walking out from the trees, but I shouldn't have bothered. I've only known the tall, tatted fucker as our captive, but between fucking with my girl at Cyanide and this, he's made it to the top of my To Kill list.

Alastair.

"We realize you've acquired one pack from us today," he says. "Know we have three more just like it here. Unless you'd like to discover just how creative we can be in making use of our supplies, I suggest you cease your fire on us for tonight. We can reconvene in the morning."

Alastair takes one final look over the moat, at the remnants of the bridge—the catastrophic amount of death that lies at his feet—and his mild expression doesn't shift.

Except for the smallest cold smile as he nods to us.

"Until tomorrow."

Loathing burns through my gut as I watch his back, and I reach for another frag I know I don't have and probably shouldn't throw even if I did.

Three more packs of heat.

Fucker. Absolute *fucker*.

The rain starts coming down hard, and the sky flashes with a blinding shot of lightning.

"Fall back to the platforms," I shout as I storm back toward Bristlebrook, thunder chasing me. "We keep watch all fucking night, do you hear? Thirty up at a time, the whole up if they so much as piss our way. Sloane?"

"Got it! First and second of our usual watch pull in now, we're up first. Can we get some umbrellas?" she calls back.

"Yeah, I'll get Eden on it."

Lucky and Jasper come up beside me, and Ava, Katherine, and Shelby aren't far behind as we hurry up to Bristlebrook, rain pounding us. It soaks my shirt, my socks—by the time I hit the porch, I'm wet to the bone.

"Visibility sucks. Is the watch going to be okay?" Lucky shivers.

"You got your helmet? Goggles?" I ask.

He nods. "Upstairs. Two sets."

We make it through the front door, and the cries and moans of wounded hit me hard. Harder than I expected. I slow. The furniture in the sitting room has been cleared to the side, and rows of people are lying on blankets and pillows—mostly Reapers, but a few civs, too, who look like they've caught ricochets.

More cries come from down the hall past the kitchen, where the med bay is, and Deanna strides past me. She's calm, her microlocs secured under a cap and her hands clean to the wrist—the rest of her clothes are splattered with blood.

Reapers and civilians mill around, pouring through the door, damp and dirty.

"Hold him *down*, Pete," Beau snaps as he tries to suture a flailing Reaper's arm. Pete hovers his hands over the Reaper's shoulders. "Use your weight, damn it. *Hold* him. I can't spare the pain meds."

I can't see Eden.

I feel blood trickle down my cheek from my graze, but I wipe it away, annoyed.

"Get the helmets," I tell Lucky distractedly, only to see he's scanning the room the same way I am. "Mine's in my closet, get Dom and Beau's, too—and any spares they have. Spread them out. You up to join first watch?"

"Yeah . . . yeah, that's fine."

"Where's Eden?" Jasper asks.

He's favoring his wounded arm, but he steps around me to look in the kitchen. Mary Beth shoves past him with a bucket of steaming water.

Anxiety springs up in my chest. There's more panic hitting me now than at any point under fucking fire.

She was on the porch, for fuck's sake. Dozens of people had eyes on her.

Jasper glances back at me, his throat corded. He's paler and more haggard than usual.

"And Dom?"

"Side tunnel."

My fists clench.

No.

I'm not doing this again.

"Someone tell me where the fuck Eden is—right fucking now!" I roar.

The busy chaos of the room stills, dozens of faces turning my way.

Dozens of clueless-as-shit, sheep-for-brains, stupid, fucking—

"Jayk?"

"Oh, thank fuck."

Lucky's voice is shaky, and we all look up to the top of the stairs. Eden is hurrying down them, still in her flimsy ass nightdress, though she's found a shirt from somewhere to throw over the top of it. Her eyes flick between us, relief as pungent as mine pouring off her.

But I only have a second to enjoy the relief because as soon as she hits the ground, she clutches my arm.

And her eyes are full of tears.

"Jayk, I've looked everywhere, but she isn't here," she tells me.

I look into her eyes, and in the reflection of her glasses, I see the casualty notification officer walking into my barracks, asking for a private word.

"Who isn't?" I whisper.

Ryan is dead.

Eden bites her lip, looking at my face like she's being torn to shreds.

"Kasey is missing." Her tears hit her cheeks. "Jayk, I think she was trying to raid the Reapers again. I think she's outside."

CHAPTER 53

KASEY

SURVIVAL TIP #225
There are more ghosts than people now.
Avoid people. They're worse to be haunted by.

D amn it, they've moved their food *again*.

After dumping the rest of the nearly empty food barrel in with the farm animals, I was supposed to be securing another bag of jerky by now, but instead . . .

I stare at the cleared spot beside Akira, where Reapers had moved their food pile to last time. It's in the center of their camp, but honestly, at this time of night, ninety-five percent of them are asleep, and I can usually walk right in. Their "watch" on the forest usually consists of two or three sleepy-as-hell dudes sitting against a tree and trying not to doze off, and their watch on Bristlebrook is even more pathetic.

Meaning nonexistent.

But they've *moved* the pile, and damn it, I can't see where they put it.

They better not have rigged it up a tree again, because that was just a disaster for everyone involved. I look up, but the stretching boughs are empty, groaning ominously in the wind. The clouds are rolling past thick and black, and it reminds me of That Day—how they blocked out the sky. How unnatural it felt.

How it smelled like fire and death.

The night suddenly seems full of shadows, and goosebumps race over my arms.

Scowling, I back up from the Reapers' camp, twirling my knife between my fingers. Whatever. It's not like we *need* food anymore, I guess. My gut churns. Ethel was sitting up today, so at least she's not going to die on me, too.

Not today, anyway. But it's only a matter of time.

First my dad, then my mom. Most of my friends. Even my dog ran in front of a car mid-playdate when I was five.

I'm cursed as shit.

From now on, I'm only making sturdy friends.

Hurrying back toward home, I tuck my knife into my pocket, then adjust the pistol in my belt. Jayk would flip if he knew I took it from the supply, but I'm not stupid. I'm not coming out here unarmed.

I'm a decent shot now, too.

Something prickles over my hair, and I jump, then slap down the twig catching in it, my heart hammering.

Ugh. Stupid.

It's the forest, Kasey, the hell do you expect?

But the forest is creepy as hell without any moonlight, and the swaying bushes are making me flinch. Everything is creaking and crunchy—except the quiet around the sounds is too deep for them to be anything but a horror flick's back-track.

Something snaps deep in the woods, and I freeze, eyeing the shadows.

It's followed by a thick, dragging gasp.

It comes from a dark tree, with long, drooping branches that slither over the ground—a weeping willow.

I back up.

Nah, I'm out.

I don't fuck with the spooky shit.

" . . . it was good. I'm glad we got to do this. It's better this way. Nicer, you know? Gosh, they're sweet as peaches, ain't they?"

My head snaps around.

Oh, come *on*. Bull *shit* this is the one night their watch has actually decided to do more than scratch their balls every five minutes.

I don't know what exactly a Reaper would do if they found me, but best case, I get dragged back to Jayk, and I get my ass handed to me on a fucking platter.

The answering voice is even closer. "Sweeter. We should've done it sooner. Imagine if we'd come years ago."

There's a thoughtful quiet as they stomp through the forest to my left.

Exactly where I need to go. Whoopie for me.

I throw a look at the shadowed willow, where I'm ninety percent sure the Grudge is waiting for me.

It whispers at me through the dark.

"Might've saved a lot of people if we had."

Damn it, ghost bitch it is.

Before the Reapers can round the massive boulder and see me, I skid over the underbrush and slip in between the crying, whispering branches. I back up toward the trunk as they enclose me like a curtain.

The back of my boot hits something.

And the next thick, dragging gasp comes from right beside me.

My scream traps in my throat as I stagger backward, tripping against the trunk, and I come down hard and clawing for purchase.

Beside me, a white, ghostly face jackknifes up. Its lips are blue, and long, thin fingers clutch at its throat. Its mouth is devouringly open.

Fear melts every brain cell I have as I scramble back, fumbling for my knife. My pistol. I don't fucking care what, just so long as I kill the motherbleeping ghoul ghost that's going to fucking end me and my cursed freaking *life*.

"He . . . *help*."

My shaking hands stop on my belt, and I look up.

Do ghosts speak? Aside from, you know, like *kill-die-kill* kind of stuff?

There are long, jean-clad legs underneath mine, and a bulging pack against the trunk—complete with a rolled-up swag—and I frown.

Pretty sure ghosts don't need to have packs. Or stuff to sleep in.

On account of being dead.

Boots crunch by our tree, the Reapers chattering, and the ghost tries to drag in another breath. Its head turns toward the passing men, and I leap forward, turning it back and shaking my head, gesturing for quiet.

It shakes its head back, its eyes just as desperate—and I should really stop thinking of it as an *it*, because with all my incredible powers of deduction, I'm becoming more and more sure that it's just a boy. A teenager. One maybe only a little older than me.

His hand catches my wrist, and his fingers are surprisingly strong.

I catch flashes of color—their clothes, glimpses of their faces. Then the boots walk past us, deeper into the woods.

"*Help*," he says again, this time more clearly, and I snort, staring wide-eyed at his face.

"Yeah, no shit you need help."

But there's no help here.

There's only me. And I'm *way* too cursed to help the nearly dead.

He shakes his head again. "Help . . . *them*. Hel—"

God damn it.

I grab his pack, ripping open the zipper. "Dude, take a hint. Preserve your oxygen. Do you have an inhaler or something in here?"

I pull out clothes. Maps. A compass. Rations. Why does he have like three freaking books in here?

No inhaler.

Oh, sure, bring books. Why *would* he bring something practical? Like maybe some *life-saving medicine*!

Idiot.

He slumps back into the dirt, and I glance at his face—it's all haunted hollows. Deep, dark hair, and sallow eyes, and skin I can almost see through. He doesn't have a single weapon on him.

He looks . . . fragile.

Not sturdy at *all*.

"Who the hell left you outside alone?" I mutter, but panic is making me frantic, and I dig deeper into his bag.

My fingers hit a container, and it rattles as I drag it out. I can barely make out the jumbled words on the label, and I have no idea what they'd mean anyway, but it looks vaguely medical. I hold it up.

"This? Will this help?"

The boy closes his eyes, shaking his head. "Only . . . for emergencies. You need . . . to stop. They . . . they need *help*."

Only for—

"My man, I hate to break it to you, but *this is an emergency*!" I hiss, opening the container.

As if in defiance of me threatening him with medicine, his breathing steadies a little.

It still sounds like he's breathing through a sieve.

I shove two pills into his mouth and hope it's not too much or too little, then unscrew my water and jam it into his face.

"I'll force it down your throat, I swear to all the undead I thought you were."

The boy's gaze flickers to me in the first spark of irritation—or life —that I've seen from him, and he takes the water and sips it, swallowing the pills.

He hands me back the bottle. "Not fast-acting." He drags in another breath and shudders. "Enough. We need to go."

His wrists are delicate, smaller than mine, and his hand shakes as he grasps his pack, pulling it toward him.

"You sound like a boat that won't start. How about you chill the hell out here for a bit? I can get help." I eye him.

This kid wouldn't die before I got Beau out here, would he? And yeah, he might be around my age, maybe even older, but out here, he's *not*. Ethel, Ida, and I were living out in the forest and around the towns nearby for two years before we hooked up with Madison. I know how to start a fire out of dry wood and wishes. I can carve up a fish or a rabbit without ever nicking the stomach. I know which way north is by how the moss grows on a tree.

Out here, it's dog years, and I'm racking them up.

This kid looks cold. His jacket is made for school excursions—it's not lined or waterproof or anything. He's in jeans and crappy, showy boots that have zero grip. His black hair is falling over his haunted face, he's so slender that his whole fragile body jangles with every breath, and damn it, his lips are *still* blue.

He's softer than me. Hell, he's *prettier* than me.

He shouldn't *be* out here.

He looks like a sad ending to a book.

I freaking hate sad endings.

But he's already tugging his pack on. "They're . . . going to attack. We need . . ." He coughs into his elbow, then drags another breath through his nose as he pulls himself up. "We need to warn them."

That gets my attention.

"The Reapers? How the hell do you know that? Did you hear something?"

Alarm spears me. Shit, I know we have people on watch, but like, five to one of them is Team Reaper after today. They're not expecting a fight.

But my ghost just stands, giving me only a brief look as he makes to go. "Not them."

I jump to my feet and grab his arm. "Don't just storm out there, idiot! You need to tell me what's—"

Somewhere behind us, there's the beginning of a sharp, male cry . . . and it cuts off just a second later.

My heart stalls, and a pulse flutters under my fingertips.

I look at him. His eyes meet mine, dark enough to swallow the night, and I realize we're about the same size.

Don't do it, I silently warn my ghost before he can disappear. *I can take you.*

My curse isn't getting you today.

But he slips out of my grip like a wraith, trying to make a run out of the willow's creepy ass branches. I grab the back of his pack with both hands and yank him back hard, throwing him against the trunk.

Through the night's whispers and groans, past the usual creaks and crunches, I start to hear more. The slithering of bodies over loose leaves. The punctures of brief, low mutters.

The boy wheezes in pain as he staggers, then drops to one knee, his laboured breathing growing louder again, and my panic increases.

Damn it, he's so *breakable*!

And *loud*.

I slap a hand over his mouth as a boot lands heavily beside our tree, and I bite down hard on my lip.

Please don't suffocate.

The silent plea wars with another—one maybe even louder.

Please don't make a sound.

But the boot doesn't stop. Neither does the one to my left, or the ones that come after. Men stream through the night, more than I can count.

More than I can shoot.

My ghost's hot breaths stutter over my palm, and I look down at him. His long lashes are sinking, but he's staring at my face, and my stomach does an odd, hard flip.

I wonder if my curse can catch a ghost.

I can't kill him if he's already dead.

"Well, I'm sorry you feel that way, but it's your own fault that you were gagged." The voice is like thunder. "They're being stealthy. This is just like the night attack at Târgoviște back in 1462. Do you think old Vlad was out there shouting about cutting people's balls off?" He chuckles. "No, he was *not*."

I frown. Why does that voice sound so *familiar*?

The boy stiffens under me, slapping my hand away so he can lean forward, peering through the gaps in the branches.

I can only see flashes as they pass us, my night vision carving out shapes and impressions. Enormous broad shoulders. Ropes.

And a gagged woman that looks a whole lot like . . .

She thrashes her head, and I see her face less than two feet from where we're hiding.

Madison.

"Then again, old Vlad probably didn't take captives along for his secret, sneaky attack who are set on foiling the whole thing. That seems like a basic tactical error, if you don't mind me saying, Mateo." The big voice rumbles on, and I realize it must be Bentley.

"I'm gagging you next if you don't shut up," another man hisses.

Mateo.

Which means . . .

This time, long, cold fingers lock around my hand, squeezing a warning, and I cover my own panicked breathing.

The Sinners are here.

And it's too late to warn anyone.

It takes too long for the last Sinner to pass us, and me and my ghost are both bursting with impatience as we wait for them to move out of earshot. His hand is still wrapped around mine as torches bloom to life and the first shots explode, the first screams, and I need to bury my face in my shoulder to hide my shout.

Sloane was on watch. Sloane would get the bridge down. They're going to be okay. I don't care if I'm a bitch. The Reapers can die if it means Ida and Ethel live. My friends. Jayk.

They can't die. I can't lose anyone else.

Damn it, damn it, *damn it*!

There must have been a hundred Sinners coming through here.

My ghost's breathing is almost hitching now as he struggles to catch air, and my stomach knots. With the torch light up ahead, I can see him a little better. He's deathly pale and not looking like he's improving as he stares out at the last Sinner's back.

Weirdly, it slows my panic, and the anger taking its place is almost a relief.

Being scared is for losers and dead people.

His freezing hand trembles around mine, and my anger grows as I stare at his profile. Why is he *out* here anyway, putting himself in danger when he has no clue what he's doing? When he's *sick*. This guy isn't made for this.

No wonder my ghost is a ghost. He's too dumb to live.

I look at him anxiously. He needs Deanna. Beau. Someone better than me.

Which means my stupid ass needs to get *his* stupid ass from A to B without getting nailed.

Great. Super easy.

I move over to the other side of the tree, peeling back a branch cautiously to look out. The trees are close around us. There's lots of cover, but we're only like thirty feet back from the tree line where they're shooting from.

The screams from beyond chase chills down my spine.

Over by the boulder, I see the push and pull of three figures— Heather, Bentley, and Mateo. They're backlit by the nearby torches, but it's more than enough light to make out how tightly Mateo wrenches Heather against a tree, and my hot, helpless anger *burns*.

This is so *stupid*! Madison is so close, and I can't do anything to help her. She saved me—and Ethel and Ida. We were holed up in a small town, starving and stealing from anyone who'd wandered into it when she showed up.

But I'm stuck saving *him*.

I glare at the boy as he stands to peer out between the branches.

"I need to go. My uncle needs my help." His next breath sounds like a dying cat's, but his big eyes find mine in the dark. "Are you okay?"

"*Go*?" I snap, incredulous. "Your uncle doesn't need your help. No one needs your help. You're a walking casualty!"

His face firms. "I'm going. Bentley's *right there*. I can . . . I need to . . ."

He breaks off, coughing, and I rub both hands over my face.

Bentley. Bentley's his uncle. He's from Red Zone.

"Need to *what*? Even if you do manage to free him, where are you going to go, dude? You going to run back into the woods? Your little pincushion lungs will burst inside your stupid *chest*!" I rage, but when he flinches, looking away, I feel like an asshole.

It's his family. Of course he wants to save his family.

Even trying when he's so obviously useless, is pretty brave.

Shifting, I try again. "I can get you somewhere safe, okay? I can get you to a doctor."

Shit, I hope Bristlebrook is still safe.

Those big, haunted eyes meet mine again, and his whole face is locked in.

"If you can get me safe . . . you can get . . . him safe, too," he whispers.

Shit.

Ugh, this is so *bad*.

But also . . . what if we *could* do it?

I look through the branches again, and it's not three figures anymore. It's only two, and they're both pressed up against a tree.

Pressed up against a tree *ten feet* from the Sinners.

But if we could free Madison and Bentley, the Sinners lose all that leverage. It wouldn't just help them get safe, it would help Jayk and everyone at Bristlebrook.

I swallow. I guess my stupid ass and his stupid ass are going to do something extra stupid then.

"Okay. Okay, fine. But I swear to God, if you die on me while we do this, I—"

"I won't. I won't slow you down."

My ghost's lips curve up on one side in a relieved smile, and I blink. That face looks built for sadness. It doesn't look like it should be able to smile.

It creeps me out, so I shove out my hand, hoping he'll stop. "Kasey."

It takes a moment before he slips his into mine, and it's chill to the touch.

"Soren."

When he releases me, I yank my pistol out of my belt, and all I can hear is chorus after chorus of screaming, painful death.

"Let's save the day then, I guess."

He gives me a faint, dubious look that makes me blush, and I peel back the branches to hide it, gesturing for him to get behind me.

There's another crack of thunder overhead, and as I creep out of our hiding place, I silently pray for more. I don't *think* the Sinners will be able to make out his breathing or our boots on the leaves over all the gunfire and murder and stuff, but I'll take any added distractions.

I'm not taking any chances, so we slip from tree to tree, making sure the coast is clear before we move again. I keep one eye on Soren, worried by how shaky he is, how his feet slide over the leaves, but he keeps his word.

He keeps up, and he doesn't make a sound, his face stubborn and intent.

The blistering gunshots grow louder, the shouts more defined, calling to advance or hold or fire. I can hear Sinners swearing, see them pacing impatiently behind the tree line, their eyes on the battle.

We slow as we approach. Their torches obliterate most of the darkness we could have used for cover. The crowding trees help, but if they turn back at the wrong time . . .

"Ever tried yoga, Mads?" Bentley asks. "No? Maybe you should. Very calming."

Peeking around the trunk I'm hiding behind, I see his wrists are actually tied to the tree next to Madison. She's glaring up at the canopy, gagged and seeming to ignore him. They both look okay, everything considered. No obvious wounds, and they look fed enough. Bentley has a big, disgusting beard growing over his face but that could be intentional.

I tuck away my pistol and tug out my pocketknife instead. I gesture at Soren to stay back, but he ignores me, slipping forward.

The backs of Sinners shift and slide through the trees ahead of us, paying no mind to their captives behind them.

For now.

Bentley's booming voice softens to a rumble as he looks at Madison. "It will be okay, angel. This will all work out. It's not as bad as it all seems."

I push out from behind the tree, and they both snap upright.

Madison stares at me—then glares over the wide cloth gag around her face.

Nervously, I smile. "It's not bad at all." With my pocketknife, I salute. "Rescue party, coming atchya."

Bentley's eyes lock on my ghost. "*Soren*?" Raw panic fills his face, and he twists, trying to see the Sinners. His voice lowers further than I thought it could. "What are you—? You need to *go*. Leave now. Run and don't come back."

Ignoring him, I move up to Madison and carefully cut the gag from her face.

"You're a fucking idiot," she hisses as soon as she's free, and I grimace.

"Yeah, I know."

Soren stumbles up to us, but he catches himself on Bentley as he drops to his knees.

He is *white*.

"You're having an attack," Bentley says, staring at him, then he looks urgently at me. "He's having an attack. He needs medicine. Soren, what do you—?"

"He has the pills in his bag," I interrupt as I cut Madison's wrists free, but I'm watching Soren as he presses a hand to his rattling chest. Bentley's fear is beginning to bleed through my anger, and my hands shake as I move over to cut Bentley's ties. "They're not doing anything."

Oh, damn it, I should have taken him to Bristlebrook.

My stupid curse is going to kill my stupid ghost.

A tear slips from the corner of Soren's eye as he bows his head, struggling, and I swallow down the guilty lump in my throat.

I killed my stupid ghost.

Madison pulls herself free of the tree, massaging her wrists as she glances quickly over at the Sinners. The battle booms and crashes, and the agonized screams make me feel like an idiot for being creeped out by the little wood whispers before.

Madison tears her eyes from them to crouch beside Soren.

"What do I do, Bent?" Madison snaps.

"I . . . CPR . . ." Bentley stammers, all his rolling calm gone.

Madison lowers Soren to the ground as his back suddenly arches. The hand pressing to his chest begins to claw at his neck, and tears storm my eyes. Angrily, I wipe at them.

Madison tilts Soren's head back, starting CPR, and I look down at Bentley's ropes, only they're already more than half frayed through, and I frown.

"Bentley, your ropes—"

"Hurry up," Bentley begs. "Kasey. It's little Kasey, isn't it? Cut me free."

I'm distracted by Soren's clutching, curling hands for one more second before I quickly slice through the rest of Bentley's ropes. He lunges forward, stroking Soren's black hair off his forehead as Madison starts chest compressions.

Soren's eyes are slitted as he looks at me—dark and sunken—and I begin to shake. It's only now, in the reflected flames, that I can see how pretty they are.

I didn't think ghosts were supposed to have eyes the color of rust and riverbeds.

I can't do this.

I can't do hospitals or sick people or standing here and doing *nothing*.

I don't have enough dog years for this.

"There's a side tunnel," I burst out, then glance nervously over my shoulder at how loud it came out. The Sinners are clustered together, shouting from the tree line. "You can come. We can get him there. Beau and Deanna, they'll have something, I know it. We . . . we just need to get him there, right?"

Bentley and Madison exchange a look, and she curses, looking over at the fight. Her hands work Soren's chest, using so much force I have to stop myself from screaming at her to be careful.

"The explosives. Bent, they're so close . . . Dom needs them," she whispers urgently, and I realize she's not just looking at the fight. She's looking at a guy waving one of the torches.

There's a pack at his feet.

Bentley's shoulders are rising fast, and his hand is working frantically, soothingly over Soren's head. But then he shakes his head.

"Take him, Madison. I'll get the explosives." More hesitant, he grimaces, then adds, "I'll follow after—"

"*Follow*?" She snorts, incredulous, and strands of red hair have escaped her ponytail. "Fuck off, Bentley. You're either not going to be able to track us or you'll put them on our ass. We need to go *through*. It has to be a run."

She bends down to breathe for Soren.

Bentley's face flares in stubborn anger. "You'll get gunned down before you make it ten feet."

Madison's face flares too as she lifts up. "Weren't you *just* trying to tell me how the bastard overlord needs me alive?"

"That doesn't mean the rest of these assholes give a shit! Bane will plant one in the back of your head. It has to be me. I have a plan. Just let me—"

Soren's throat makes the most awful, pained sucking sound I've ever heard, and Bentley cuts off, staring down at him in a panic, and Madison curses.

My fingers curl in, watching Soren's face the same way he's watching mine.

"Take him, Bentley. You can take his weight. You can get him to help faster." Madison's voice is a whiplash before she lowers it. "He needs his uncle, Bent."

Bentley stares at her hard, terror and concern writhing in his eyes.

"Fuck," he grinds out, then he starts to stand, hauling Soren into his arms.

Madison stands too, and the distant sound of a long, dying gurgle makes me shudder.

"Forget the explosives," Bentley tries one last time, pleading. "Just come with us. Get inside the house, we can—"

"I still have a job to do. I'm not leaving before it's done," she claps back stubbornly, but her eyes flick to Soren. "Go, Bent. Now."

Miserable, terrified resignation falls over his features—and he scans her face like it's the last time he's going to see it.

It puts another pit in my stomach.

Madison nods, smiling at him briefly, but I grab her before she can run.

"Here, take this." I pull out my pistol and give it to her. Then my pocketknife. The spare ammo I brought, because I'm not pulling a Jayk and forgetting it at a key moment.

Finally, she looks down at me, and then Madison pulls me into a rough, quick hug.

"You did good, Kasey. You did really fucking good, no matter what happens, okay?" she says into my hair, and I hate her for it.

Because it means she's going to die, too.

Then she pulls away, taking off, and I hear Soren dying over Bentley's shoulder, and I start running.

As the first rain starts to fall, with tears blurring my eyes and Bentley on my heels, I take the most shrouded route I can.

And I *run*.

CHAPTER 54

DOMINIC

SURVIVAL TIP #177
*Think about the words you take to heart—
or they'll define who you are.*

"It's over here. To your left. Your *other* left, Bentley, what the fuck?"

The civs at my back tense up, and I gesture at them to hold, frowning. That doesn't sound like Sinners, that sounds like . . .

Kasey bursts into view, and Bentley barrels out of the forest behind her like an overgrown bear, a limp figure in his arms.

"Dom!" The girl has tears on her cheeks, and she keeps looking over at Bentley. "It's Soren, he's from Red Zone. He needs Deanna. *Now.*"

"I know who he is, Kasey."

Slinging my rifle, concern slams into me as I run up to meet Bentley. He looks more panicked than Kasey, and my stomach drops.

Is he about to hand over a corpse?

Bentley pours Soren into my arms, and I vaguely recognize the waifish, quiet teenager who stood in the back of my battle room before we hit the Den. He weighs nothing at all.

Shit, he's just a kid.

"He's having an asthma attack. Severe. Do you have a ventilator? Oxygen, or . . ."

No. We don't.

"Beau will handle it," I say grimly instead of answering, already turning back. Soren's lips are blue, his chest barely rising. "Come in, *now*. Emerson, take point here."

"I can't." The words boom behind me, raw and devastated, and impatient, I turn back.

"What do you mean, you can't?"

Bentley looks rough, as hulking and huge as I remember, except for the beard, but it's the gritty seriousness lining him. He's not playing the carefree history nerd today.

"I just can't. I'm going back. Things aren't . . . they're not as simple as they seem, okay? They need me. I can do more good there," he says in a rush, but his eyes don't leave Soren.

Foreboding sets up in my bones, and I look him over hard. "Come in and explain, Bentley. That doesn't make any—"

"Just get him to your fucking doctor!" Bentley roars, loud enough to shake the trees, and Emerson lets out a string of curses behind me.

For fuck's sake.

"Dom, please!" Kasey demands, her voice thick with tears, and I curse too, looking down at the kid.

They're right. He can't wait.

With a final grim glare at Bentley, I turn and tear through the tunnel.

"Move!" I shout, and civilians flatten themselves to the side to let me through.

Soren's limbs flop, kicking me with every pounding step. Kasey is right on my heels, her fast, fearful breaths just an exclamation mark over Soren's near silent flutters. Dread soaks me.

Fuck, I hate it when it's kids.

I punch through the door at the other end, falling out into the gym where there are too many civilians and Reapers and fuck knows who on the other end.

And they're already parting.

"I said, get the fuck out of my way!" Jayk snaps, and I see him punching forward in full fury, Eden anxious at his side, and Jasper and Lucky behind him, armed to their teeth.

Jayk stops when he sees me.

Not me, I realize a half second later.

Kasey.

His hard expression breaks.

He runs forward and sweeps her up, crushing her against his chest. "Fuck. Thank fuck."

Behind him, Lucky peels away, running a relieved hand down his face, and Jasper's head tips back.

Eden hovers beside them, her eyes bright.

Kasey starts squirming immediately, pummeling his shoulders. "Stop, stop! Jayk, you asshole! Let me down!"

He drops her, looking her over. "What? Are you hurt?" He roughly turns her around by her shoulders. "Answer me, you little shit, are you *hurt*?"

Not stopping, I stride past them, and Eden's gaze flicks to me—to the body in my arms—and she pales.

"Come on," she says, running ahead of me to get the door as Lucky and Jasper look over.

"I can't see. Who is it?" Jasper asks worriedly.

"Soren. Bentley's nephew," Lucky mutters back. "The one who needed our meds."

"We need to get out to the watch, Lucien . . ."

"*I'm* not hurt! It's Soren!" Kasey cries as I shove through the door and into the hall.

Med bay.

Soren drags in a breath, the loudest one so far, and I kick into another jog.

Door, door, door, the next one is already open, and as I bust inside, Beau looks up. The beds are all taken by Reapers sporting gunshot wounds, and fear hits me hard. We're going to be too late.

"What have we got?"

"Dom! My room. I've set it up," Eden calls from down the hall, already hurrying up the stairs.

"Asthma attack. Soren. What is he, fifteen? Weighs fuck all, Beau. He's barely breathing," I tell him, fighting to keep my voice even.

Kasey is hovering, watching me with wide, frightened eyes.

Jayk is watching her from several feet back, something shattered and openly vulnerable on his face. And I *get it*. It's always kids that fuck me up. It was the kid dying on our way to Bristlebrook after Day Death that nearly broke me.

Beau just nods, calm as he starts grabbing equipment, catching my fear and fixing it without a fucking word.

"Has he had any meds?" he asks, and I look at Kasey, who nods frantically.

She swipes at her cheeks. "Yeah, I made him have two pills. I don't know what they were. They were in a yellow container in his bag."

"Okay, that's good. You did a good job doing that, Kasey," Beau says soothingly as he picks up an IV stand from the corner. He nods for me to go, and I make for the stairs as he comes out after me.

Between his fucking accent and those words, he should sound patronizing, but Kasey's staring at him like she needed to hear that as much as Soren needs treatment.

We hit the stairs.

"Now, sometimes the medicine can take a minute to kick in, especially if he's been out there in all the cold and dust and battle mess. None of that is great for the lungs. Did anyone try anything else?" he asks, eyeing Soren's face as we pound up the steps.

Eden's waiting for us at the top.

Kasey's voice is a little surer this time. "Madison did CPR, but I don't think it helped."

That breaks Beau's calm, and he slices a surprised look at Kasey, who shrugs sheepishly. "I kind of freed her and Bentley." The shadow crosses back over her face. "Not that it mattered."

"It mattered," I tell her. "She saved Jasper and Jennifer."

Eden holds the door open to her room, and Kasey sucks in a harsh breath.

"Did . . . did she . . .?" she whispers.

Jayk rubs his jaw, coming up behind her, and his voice is gruff when he says, "Didn't see her get ganked. Alastair has her, though. She got us some serious heat, so I don't know, kid. We'll have to see."

Kasey falls silent, but she nods once.

Leaving them in the hall, I take Soren over to the bed. The room's empty at the moment, but Eden's cleared space on the floor too, setting it up for several others to sleep if they need it.

"Thanks, pet," I murmur to her as I pass, and she nods.

"There are still things I need to do. Are you okay if I . . ."

"Go on, darlin'. I have this," Beau says, coming up beside me and quickly pulling his stethoscope into place.

Eden moves to close the door, but Jayk slams it back open.

He and Kasey both hover in the doorway. Kasey watches Soren, and Jayk pulls back to sit by the door, staring at the ceiling.

Waiting.

Beau's face lightens as he listens. "Okay, good. Or, not catastrophic anyway. Get his jacket off. Shirt can stay."

I strip the kid's jacket off, hating how limp he is. Beau pulls an array of small bottles out of his bag. Clothes. He unrolls a set of needles over the side table. Several vials. The IV bag. He runs off to wash his hands and comes back with gloves on.

"Okay, bring the stand over." He lowers his voice as he works. "I don't have BiPAP. Inhalers have lost all damn efficacy. No oxygen. I'm going to try magnesium sulfate. If that doesn't work . . ." He grimaces, shaking his head as he wraps a tourniquet around Soren's upper arm. "If that doesn't work, he's in for intubation and a manual vent, and that's not going to be a good time for anyone."

He swipes an antiseptic swab over the back of Soren's hand.

We work together, me following his instructions, and then both of us waiting for what seems like a million damn years before Soren's face relaxes, color pinkening his cheeks again. When he's stable, Beau finally stands back and mutters something about checking on his other patients, squeezing my arm before he snaps his gloves off and leaves with a murmured reassurance to Kasey.

Kasey wraps her arms around herself, pacing, and Jayk gets to his feet, muttering to her. By Soren's bed, I rub the back of my neck, reluctant to leave the kid alone, stable or not. His IV bag is dripping steadily, and outside, the storm rages in fierce, violent force, buffeting the windows.

When I glance back down, Soren's tired eyes are open. He's quiet, his lips turned down as he looks around the room, and I wait.

He's so small, just this thin wraith, but I've seen kids of all ages in all kinds of places. Overconfident eighteen-year-olds joining the ranks. Hollow-cheeked ten-year-olds sitting on the side of the road, even tinier siblings tucked beside them. Thirteen-year-olds with rifles or bullet holes. Thirty-year-olds who've never had worse than a paper cut.

I sit on the end of the bed, watching the door. Watching Soren. I don't know exactly why he was out there tonight, but I could take a guess.

Soren has old, exhausted eyes. He wasn't out there because he had something to prove.

He was out there because he had something to lose.

"Bentley's gone, isn't he?" he whispers.

I nod, and he sighs, leaning back against the pillows.

"It was his choice," I tell him softly.

He stares down at his hand—the IV line taped to the back of it— and he doesn't answer.

From the doorway, Kasey's voice rises, tearful and stressed.

"I tried to keep him safe. It's not my fault he got sick! It's too dangerous for him. It's not my fault. He couldn't breathe. He's so weak, Jayk. He shouldn't have been out there." She chokes on her tears. "It's not my fault."

Ah, hell. Flinching a little, I cut a look at the bed, but Soren doesn't say anything.

He just takes the hit, turning his head to the side. He swallows hard.

Jayk drags Kasey into another rough hug, and this time, she takes it, crying into his chest.

"Is he really going to be okay?" she asks in a small voice.

"He's going to be fine," Jayk says gruffly. "The doc is good. He's the best there is. He's got this. You don't need to worry about this shit."

Slowly, Kasey begins to calm down, her adrenaline crash easing out, and I hear Ida calling out to her from the hall, her own terror sharp. Like it's a wake-up call, Kasey steps back, wiping her face and shaking her head.

"Don't go expecting this gushy shit again, okay?" she says darkly. "This was a one-off."

A beat too late, Jayk snorts, running a hand over his head. It's still shaking.

"Yeah, whatever, kid. It's like hugging a bag of twigs, anyway. Fucking eat something, would you?"

Ida runs up to Kasey, dragging her up into a bony, clutching hug. Over Kasey's shoulder, she glares at Jayk.

"You didn't even *think* to tell us where she was?" she snaps, her voice shrill, and Jayk backs up, muttering an apology that makes his voice crack.

He's too pale. Too damn shaken as he beats a fast, stilted retreat.

While Ida starts berating Kasey and hugging her in turn, I sigh, standing up off the bed, knowing what I need to do.

It's time.

Before I go, I look back down at Soren one last time. He's still staring at the storm.

"Hey," I say, and it's a long sigh later before his head tilts slightly in my direction. "You know she's just—"

"Worried," he finishes softly. "I know . . . Everyone always is."

I study him; he's serious and somber, IV fluids leaking into him.

Weak, she said.

I've been lucky enough to be pretty healthy most of my life. It was never wounds or colds that made me the sickest.

My old man's voice rings in my ears.

"I always knew you were mediocre, Dominic, but today, you were a bad leader. And sometimes, the best thing a bad leader can do is walk away."

I let out a heavy breath, watching the quiet teenager as seriously as he's watching the window.

"You're not weak, Soren." His lips compress, and I soften my voice. "But you need to think about which words you take to heart—or it won't be long before they define who you are."

He doesn't look at me, but his throat works, so I nod to myself.

He's heard it, at least.

"I'll have someone check on you regularly. Water's on the side table."

I turn for the door to see Ida watching, and as I pass, she murmurs that she'll take care of it. She looks over at him in concern, and as Kasey yawns, Ida harries her toward the couch.

Turning down the hall, I leave them to it.
And decide to take my own advice.

CHAPTER 55

DOMINIC

SURVIVAL TIP #360
A good leader knows when to step back.
But also, when to step up.

I t takes me nearly thirty minutes to find him.

The house is a mess. There's mud all through the halls and more than a little blood. People are swarming everywhere, charging through the halls with medical supplies or blankets, or trying to find some food or a place to sleep.

Eden seems to be everywhere. Directing people to the gym or to sleep in certain rooms, dragging medical supplies under her arm one minute and a pot of foul-smelling slop the next. She tells me distractedly that I'm not on watch until tomorrow morning and orders me to sleep, then rushes off to kneel beside Beau before I can check if she's okay.

I watch her for a moment, the quiet determination set in her face as Beau snaps a dislocated shoulder back into place.

She has this.

But there's one thing I can take off her plate.

I find Jayk sitting in the surveillance room, staring up at the ceiling. With his boot against the wall, he rocks his chair absently, lost in himself. He doesn't flinch when I enter.

The wall of screens behind him is finally lit back up again. Over a dozen are blacked out, their feed cut. The rest display various shots of soaked, sad leaves, or branches being whipped by the wind. Several have shots of Sinners pitching a wall of tents between the trees, creating a perimeter around Bristlebrook.

Walking over to the HAM radio, I lean against the table.

The silence stretches for a long time before he grits out, "Just say whatever you came to say and fuck off, Dom."

It doesn't have the heat it might have had even a few weeks ago.

He's not the man he was even a few weeks ago.

Neither of us are.

"Do you remember the first time we met?" I ask.

A frown flickers over his face, as Jayk shrugs at the ceiling. "Base camp, assignation. What does—"

"It was before that."

Jayk's chair stops rocking.

"I went to as many as I could—the graduations," I continue. "The Colonel liked to make an appearance for the new recruits coming through. For morale. I'd tag along because . . ." I grimace, remembering dozens of days of uniforms and handshakes. Endless days off spent on base, chasing something I never found. Humorlessly, I laugh. "Because I thought that's what he wanted from me."

That day had been hot and dry, the sun beating down on our uniforms as they welcomed a new class of Rangers to our ranks. Beau was beside me, trying not to get caught muttering about how we should be down at the club with whichever sub he'd been flirting with at the time.

"They got to the tap outs. They were always my favorite part."

My small smile is more genuine for that, remembering the stern ranks of new recruits, not allowed to move—not allowed to *break*—until someone came to claim them.

Proud mamas hugging their boys.

Girlfriends pressing desperate kisses to their hard-missed men.

Small kids tangling chubby arms around uniformed legs.

"You see who people are at a tap out," I tell Jayk roughly, and finally, he turns to look at me, his face stiff.

It's when the bravado breaks and their loved ones crash in, and their careful ranks fall apart as they hug back their mamas and kiss their girls and sweep their kids into their arms. You see the tears.

"You see what they're fighting for," I say softly.

Jayk's boot drops off the wall.

His jaw works, tense, as he stares back.

That day, the families and the soldiers finally bled away, leaving the field. Beau left my side, groaning about finding a hot dog.

They all pulled to the side.

Until five men stood alone on the field.

I watched a fellow recruit jog back and tap out two of them. One of those tapped out the third, and they clapped each other on the back —more subdued, but still laughing. Another man slunk off the field by himself, not waiting for a tap, and I watched my father's mouth tighten, unimpressed.

The last man, the other recruits shied away from, and I remember the fucking rage that sparked in my gut as they left him behind.

I watched him stand at attention, too proud to walk away. I watched the crowd milling about on the sidelines, paying him no mind—the families too busy clinging to one another in a way that always felt so far away. I watched the Major overseeing the ceremony grimace and step forward to do it himself, muttering something about this always being awkward.

I remember striding onto the field, burning with an anger I've never been completely able to understand.

Anger at all these families and friends and the easy love they throw at each other. The kind that I'm not a part of, and this stranger isn't, either.

"Why did you go?" I ask.

The ceremonies aren't mandatory. The tap out is just a custom. He didn't have to put himself through it.

Jayk buries his face in his hands, rubbing his eyes before he looks up at me. "My mom was so fucking mad when Ryan and I went through Basic. Off her meds. She was . . . I don't know. She was fucking terrified, I guess. We didn't think she'd come." He gives me a rough smile that looks like it hurts. "She did, though."

Behind him, the screens flicker and change. Alastair strides past one camera with Heather in his grip, pushing past a big bald man.

Jayk grimaces, sitting up. He's slowly turning his pocketknife through his fingers, and his gaze turns inward. "Ryan always wanted to be a Ranger. He never qualified. Too fucking sloppy." He shakes his head once, and I realize he's not bitter now. He just looks like his heart has been ripped out. "After the accident . . . I don't know, I signed up. Did it. I wanted to be there. It's fucking stupid, but . . . I knew he'd want me there. He'd have been proud." His voice is raw. "If he didn't go and get himself killed, Ryan would have tapped me out."

But his brother wasn't there.

That day, I walked up to the big, rough, tatted soldier instead, just the two of us alone on the field.

Jayk stared straight ahead, over my shoulder, while the sun all around us seared us both.

"Congratulations, Ranger," I told him.

He didn't shift, didn't move, not until I clapped a hand to his shoulder, releasing him.

Then, his eyes moved to my face, bitter and full of an anger I recognized.

I nodded, but didn't step back as I met the look. "Hope you're ready for it." I smiled dryly. "You're one of ours now."

He didn't say a word to me as he looked me over. Not as he turned away and stalked off the field. Not in the weeks after when I had him moved to my unit, for reasons I could never quite put my finger on.

Just like I didn't say a word to the Colonel when he came up beside me with a brief nod, telling me that was "well handled." When I should have felt the usual kick of relief at his approval, but all I felt was a slightly sour unhappiness.

Across the room, Jayk and I look at each other, the memory sitting between us, and I swallow roughly.

"I can tap you out again, Jayk," I tell him. "You don't have to lead them anymore."

Jayk's eyes sink closed, and his head drops. I hear the long, slow release of his breath.

The brutal fucking relief.

I feel my own shoulders take the weight, but . . . that's a relief, too. A different kind. This isn't a weight I want anyone else to have to bear. Not for me.

My throat thick, I add seriously, "It has to be for the right reasons. You've led them well, Jayk. You've led me well. If you wanted it, I'd follow you to the end."

When Jayk's eyes open, they're glassy.

It takes him a long minute to nod. "I know."

He swallows, and I blink, looking to the side, my jaw clenching.

When he continues, it's rough. "I don't want it, Dom. I don't . . . *need* it. Not anymore." He lifts one shoulder, but it's more thoughtful than dismissive. "I took it for the wrong reasons. It's not where I want to be. I'm glad I didn't fuck it up, but . . ." He laughs then, but it's raw. Finally, he looks at me. "This job is fucked. The responsibility. The lives. Kasey, just . . ."

He clicks his pocketknife closed.

Kasey. Eden. Soren. All the lives crammed into Bristlebrook. The army on our doorstep, which streams past on the displays in the background, and the weight of it all increases on me. It's a weight I'm used to, one I'm willing to take back, but . . .

Between Jasper's sessions lately and our quiet talks after, between Eden and Beau's rituals, Jayk stepping up, and even Lucky coaxing me into this stupid, ridiculous battle for time with Eden, I've been feeling . . . good.

Less like a heavy chess piece at the top of a board and more like a person. More like a person than I've ever felt before.

Loss pricks me, sharp with regret.

So "yeah," is all I say, and Jayk's gaze narrows on me as he sits back.

The room is close and quiet, but Jayk's never been one afraid to break things.

"You don't want it, either," he says, and I shake my head.

I can put my fears to the side. I have enough other voices sitting with me now that I can put my father's to the side. Voices I value far more than I ever did his.

My own, most of all.

I can do this. I have the skills—and the best team anyone could want.

"It's not that. It's just . . ." My lips kick up ruefully. "It's lonely at the top. I'll miss this."

Jayk snorts, so rough and rude against the somber moment that my teeth click shut.

"Fuck you, too, then," I mutter, pushing off the table. "Forget it. I'll see you tomorr—"

"You're not ascending to the heavens, asshole. It's just a job."

I stop at the door, turning back, and Jayk scoffs.

He rubs his jaw as he stands, awkwardly gruff as he tries again. "Look, your old man might have been hot shit, but I sure as fuck don't plan on kissing your ass." He meets my eyes. "You don't have to do it his way. I didn't. You don't have to keep your distance to be the boss." He smirks, strolling up to the door. "Matter of fact, you're a dick when you try."

Despite myself, I snort, and Jayk's next smile is almost genuine.

We leave the surveillance room together, heading back toward the chaos and the gamut of responsibility. Both of us pause when we reach the inner balcony, looking over the ordered frenzy downstairs. Jayk leans on the balustrade.

There are rows and rows of wounded laid out on the floor. Filtering between them are the nurses, Deanna, and Beau, checking on the patients laid out in their makeshift beds.

Eden is standing to the side, pouring out cups of water and passing them off for delivery to groaning Reapers. Her hair is escaping the bun she's pulled it into, and she's moving too quickly. Her pace hasn't dipped since I last saw her.

Beside me, Jayk sobers, watching her too.

Outside, all I can hear is the falling of rain.

"I'm too wired to sleep," he finally mutters, straightening.

I don't comment on the fact that he looks like a warmed-up corpse.

He hesitates, then turns to me, abruptly reminding me of how we stood on that field all those years ago.

"I have Bristlebrook for the rest of the night. You should go to bed." Jayk glances back down at Eden, then he sighs and mutters, "Bentley's brat is in my room. Eden needs somewhere to sleep, too."

Surprise hits me like a lightning strike.

I fight to dismiss the implications. This is Jayk, after all.

But Jayk's eyes lift to mine, and he presses a rough, awkward hand to my shoulder . . . then he walks away.

Tapping me out.

CHAPTER 56

EDEN

SURVIVAL TIP #49
If you move fast enough,
your feelings can't catch you.

Sawyer hasn't had any water. A cup is in my hand, and I'm passing it over before I've finished the thought.

Soft, male sobs echo through the sitting room, like razors scraping down my spine.

"Has anyone seen the second set of scalpels?" Deanna calls from the other side of the sitting room, where she's bent over a thick-set Reaper.

I speak up before anyone can give her the wrong answer, banishing the sobs with guilty, vicious force.

"Beau had to use them. They were in the autoclave." I glance up at the clock on the wall. "They should be ready now. Jada, can you get them for Deanna? Clare's covering the med bay. She'll show you where they are."

Jada startles out of her dazed staring at the wounded and nods at me. She pushes off the doorway and rushes toward the hall.

When I turn back, I see a Reaper trying to stand up from his bed and stride over to him. It takes several minutes of arguing to convince him that he, in fact, cannot walk on a shattered ankle by himself, no matter how much he needs to use the little boy's room. David, a reed thin but surprisingly strong Reaper, comes over when I call and helps the injured man to the downstairs toilet.

David has been helpful with the heavy lifting over the last few hours.

I direct two more Reapers upstairs to the games room for sleep, then drag out a warmed towel for Anaiyah, who has trailed in from the storm outside, her teeth chattering.

On and on it goes.

My feet ache, and I haven't had enough sleep the last few nights, but the little discomforts are far away as I work.

And every time I pause, those sobs chase me back into action.

I turn again, looking for the next task. It's getting quieter, but there has to be more to do. Someone else will need a bed or food or medicine or supplies or—

The sound of weeping invades my space again.

Somehow, it's louder than the groans of the injured, or the muttered conversation. It's more violent than the rain outside as it lashes the windows.

The rain that even now is leaking through the poorly taped holes.

Holes that I need to patch.

Leaks can turn into deluges if they're not patched.

The thoughts come hard and disjointed, turning rapidly from observation to action with no room for detours.

Pivoting, I try to think what I can use to fix the glass—anything to shore it up for just a few hours more—when I see Pete, curled up in the corner of the sitting room. His head is bent, his cap in his hand, and his shoulders shake as he cries with his whole body.

I stop hard when I see him.

His sounds engulf me.

Alastair's rifle fills my mind. His cold, brutal calm as Buck tipped onto the pikes.

I grip my nightdress, shoring myself up everywhere I'm leaking. I don't get to keep running away. Not from this.

I lined up the shot.

I deserve to face the damage.

With shaking hands, I move to one of the tables I set up earlier and pour a cup of tea. It's not steaming anymore, and there are too many dregs muddying the lukewarm water, but it gives me something to do with my hands. I can offer Pete something, even if it isn't much.

Quietly, I walk over to Pete and sink down. I shift back against the wall until I'm sitting beside him in silent, inadequate comfort. He sobs harder, his dirty, wiry body turning into my side like he's desperate for the warmth.

Or maybe just desperate not to be alone.

As he weeps, I take in the wounded on the floor. The bullet wounds and bandages. The streaks on the floorboards where I mopped up blood. Beau and Deanna with their heads bent together over gaping flesh that closes, stitch by stitch. So many pained, sleeping faces—the dirt cleaned off them at least, because I could do that much.

So much for our resistance.

Alastair blew it to pieces in just one night.

Awful, thick feelings fill my throat as I let Pete cry into my shoulder like he's a child, until he's finally able to sit up, wiping his tears on a filthy sleeve. He chokes out his gratitude and takes the teacup and saucer from my numb fingers.

The porcelain clatters in his shaky grip.

After he takes a gulp, he stares down at the sludgy dregs like they might tell his fortune.

"Buck and me, we were a team, you know?" Pete's face is red raw, and I can't look at him directly.

I just stare ahead, listening to the words.

Like listening is its own form of self-flagellation.

"Me and him, it was always us. We weren't good at much of anything, you know, but we were together. Came in together, too, from two towns over, and Sawyer knew. He knew. He never once split us up." He drags a sleeve across his wet nose, and his smile is full of tears. "Buck . . . we kept mucking up the planting. But Sawyer, he thought . . . he liked to bring us up to meet new folks passin' through. Said we were good. Friendly-like. Made it so maybe they didn't want to fight none. We . . . we were good at makin' friends." His lip trembles. "It was a good job for us."

I squeeze my eyes shut, my gut writhing.

Pete's voice cracks. "What am I gonna do now? I can't bring anyone in without Buck. No one's gonna trust my ugly mug. *No one.* What if Sawyer doesn't need me anymore?"

The cup rattles in his hands as a new round of sobs shakes him.

I think I'm going to throw up.

I stand up. "I . . . let me get you some tissues."

Pete lifts his face, and it's bloated. Swollen with tears.

I back up. Hit the wall. I turn, feeling for the doorway.

Another crack of thunder hits, and the lightning flashes outside, briefly illuminating the room.

The kitchen. If I can just get to the kitchen, then I can get tissues, and then find something for those damn *holes*, and . . .

"Stop, pet."

Dom's wide, heavy hand catches my shoulder, steadying me before I crash into him.

I stare at his chest—at the crimson shirt that looks so much like the blood I mopped earlier. Breathing hard, I don't look up. I can *feel* his assessing gaze.

Dom always sees too much.

So I keep my voice calm. "No. Sorry, sir. I need to get tissues. Actually, you could help. Do you know where there might be anything I could use to patch the doors? There's water getting in."

Dom loosens his grip on my arm, but his words might as well be a vise.

"Forget the doors." He releases my arm, and his fingers wrap around my wrist. "Come with me, pet. You need bed."

The abrupt feeling of his skin on mine trips my mental rush, sending me staggering for a brief, dizzying moment.

I look down at his rough hand—the nicks and scars, the dark hair dusting the back of it, the strong fingers encasing my wrist. Not holding my hand, where our fingers might twine together. He took my *wrist*.

To take.

To lead.

I flex my fingers, and his grip tightens, almost imperceptibly.

My next shiver is delicate, chasing over my scalp.

Oddly, my miserable thoughts begin to slow.

They slow enough for me to remember I'm in a room full of people with a house full of tasks, besieged by a forest full of Sinners.

Sinners like Alastair.

Who I might as well have invited to this bloodbath.

"I'm sorry, Dom. I have too much to do," I say again, more firmly —using his name for good measure, since he doesn't seem to be getting the point.

Surreptitiously, I tug my wrist.

His grip doesn't loosen.

Dom's dark brow lifts, and he doesn't even have the grace to put a *challenge* in it.

There's only silent expectation.

"Alastair is *outside*," I try again, fighting to keep from raising my voice. "Attacking us. *Firing* on us. I need to—"

"He's not firing right now," Dom breaks in, calm. He looks at me with weighty consideration. "It's raining. Jayk has it covered. Lucky and Jasper are on watch. You can stop, Eden. Take a break."

The order brooks no argument, and mine suddenly sticks in my throat. His hand burns against my wrist.

Then I hear Pete sniffle, and I flinch.

"Eden." Beau's call across the room turns my head. He's holding a light for Deanna while she sutures the Reaper in front of them, but his eyes are on me. "Darlin', Dom's right. We've got everything under control here now. Most everyone is either on watch outside or they're getting some rest before their turn. You got us all organized, so we're doing okay. Take some time." His soft, coaxing voice turns grim, and he sighs as Deanna finishes up. "We're going to need you tomorrow."

My guilt pulses in my throat.

But, looking around, I see he's right. Most of the wounded are sleeping. Civilians have turned in for bed. A chill seeps through the doors—through my shirt and silk nightdress, right into my bones. It's quiet.

But even the thought of sleep right now is impossible.

Lightning flashes again, and it shines over every patient golden hue in Dom's eyes.

My voice comes out too small when I whisper, "I don't have a bed."

Dom's face softens, and his grip on my wrist grows tight.

It's the only point of heat in this bitterly cold room.

"Come with me, pet. I have you."

CHAPTER 57

EDEN

SURVIVAL TIP #182
*When hot men want you to slake
your troubles on their cock,
let them.*

Dom's door clicks shut behind me, pushing out the sobs and the groans, all the chatter and the rain. It all becomes muted, almost silent, as we're enclosed together.

My back whispers against his door, but he doesn't move back. Dom looms in my space, quiet and dauntingly large.

His heavy hand is still around my wrist, and my pulse frantically batters his fingers.

My breathing shallows.

His room is still a mess of blankets and empty cups, the remote control tossed carelessly on the floor beside last night's DVD case. It looks lived in, its military edges blunted. Softened.

"Give me a truth, pet," Dom says finally, and I close my eyes, wishing I'd never started this ritual.

Furious that he feels he has the right to turn it against me.

I tug at my wrist again, but this time, he slams it above my head, pinning it against the door, and I gasp, heat snapping through me. In seconds, he's lifted his other hand, and his fingers bite into my cheeks as he forces me to look up at him. My glasses slip down, and I'm dazed as I stare.

He holds me with careless, casual force, like my struggles don't mean anything against his size and intimidating strength. Like I'm not even strong enough to be worth fighting.

I hate the slow, slipping lust that rolls over me as his fingers tighten.

Rule three: Stay where I put you.

He's infuriatingly calm, those brows still raised in dry expectation. "Speak, Eden."

I pant, looking up at him, my brain short-circuiting. Dom is . . . *handling* me. I can only remember two occasions he's handled me like this, and both ended in me getting obliterated with orgasms.

The last few times we've talked, he's kissed me. He's even ordered me around, like he was testing our comfort with it, but this . . .

Dom is taking full control.

"You . . ." I try to swallow down the huskiness in my throat, but it's hard with his blunt fingertips indenting my cheeks. "You smell like gunshots."

It is *a* truth. His smoky metal scent is mixing with his usual dark spice, filling my head, my nose. He sits on the back of my tongue. Maybe that truth will be enough for him.

Right now, I think sex with Dom could patch every hole I have. Right now, him *handling me* might be enough.

I can feel myself melting into his touch. I want to turn myself over to him, like he did by the river when my world was crashing out.

I want him to handle it.

But Dom's brows finally lower, in stinging disappointment.

"Is this it?" he asks quietly. "This is you talking to me?"

My anger flares again. Fuck him for pushing this. If he wants the truth, then he can have it, for all the good it does either of us.

"You *know* why I'm upset, sir. Alastair is *out there*, and he's out there because of *me*."

I yank away from him, but he just flattens me against the door, dragging my wrist up the wood until I need to slide up onto my toes. Until I can't move at all.

His jaw is heavy, the stubble rough and dark over the tight planes.

His grip loosens slightly on my cheeks so I can talk.

"There are so many dead. So, so many. Fifty-three Reapers came here, sir. Do you know how many are left?" My throat is hot and choked, my guilt a miserable, sticky thing I can never fully seem to escape. Like it's something that needs to be managed, rather than eliminated.

Dom is silent, watching. Waiting.

"Nineteen. Only nineteen lived." My lips tremble, and I feel the way Pete looked. Raw and swollen and stripped to the bone. "I trusted him when I shouldn't have. I was only looking at one way a person can be evil. I didn't know . . . I didn't *see it*. Now we've lost before we've even started."

Dom sighs heavily, and he moves my wrist back down to a comfortable height. His thumb tracks shivering strokes along the sensitive flesh.

But his gaze is battered armor, used to this kind of battle. "I could have killed him when we had him captive."

I blink, frowning, but he doesn't stop.

"We could go back further? I could have killed Sam before he ever recruited his first Sinner. We could have moved. We could have made a deal with the Reapers sooner, been back at their farmlands with two hundred more men at our back. The Reapers could have grown a spine and asked for our help a year ago. My point is . . ." Dom's voice is rough, impatient, and he rolls over my silent objections as he steps into me. "Eden, we've argued about this already. We're both taking a hit on this, and neither one of us is going to agree on who should be taking it. We could go back and forth all night about whose responsibility this was, or who could have done what differently, but the truth is that it doesn't matter."

I want to argue, bitterly, because I can *feel* it in my chest—this responsibility and guilt that is crushing my lungs, but Dom is hot and hard and so *certain* in front of me.

And the closer he gets, the less he smells of gunshots and the more he smells like spicy, hungry man. But he's still keeping too much space between us.

"It doesn't matter," Dom repeats, limned in determination. "Alastair's here now, and we're all dealing with it together. Don't count us out yet. This is just one battle. Whatever mess of decisions brought the Sinners here also brought all of us together to fight them. And we're ready to tear Alastair and his whole fucking empire to the ground."

My pulse batters against his palm, and I can feel every callus on my skin.

For the first time since those torches sprung to life in the forest, hope ignites inside of me.

It's just one battle.

One battle with . . . God, with so many casualties.

"Sir, I don't know how to just . . . switch it off. I know what you're saying. I do, and I . . . God, we'll deal with Alastair. I'll help, however I can. I'll help you beat him, somehow." My wrist strains against his hand, just to feel his steely grip. His inexorable control. "But my mind is *racing*. Jasper gave me things, exercises, and usually they help, but all I can see is Buck's face, and—"

"Give it to me."

Dom's voice is thick and dark. This time, when he steps closer, I can feel him through my nightdress. My nipples tighten painfully, budding against the fabric.

I lift my free hand to touch him, and he pins it beside the other one in seconds.

I feel the slickness welling between my legs, spilling out over the panties I shoved on quickly while I was in my room. The fabric presses wetly against my thighs as he nudges me back against the door.

Give it to him?

He can take it all. I've wanted him to, with biting, humiliating desperation, since the moment we met.

But he's slowed me down every time. He wants it to be right. He wants me to trust him, and to trust myself, before he ever fucks me. Before he ever takes control.

Is he really saying . . .

Dom is fierce—forceful as he advances. "Give me your guilt, pet. Give me the stress. Give me all that fucking responsibility you're carrying. Give it all to me."

His shoulders block out the light, and finally, he presses against me. His cock is hard and shockingly thick, demanding and insistent against my stomach. Instinctually, my body yields to him, softening. Giving way to his strength and control.

Handing myself over.

I can feel the relentless pulse in his cock, see the locked strain in his muscles as he contains himself, but he's steady when he meets my eyes.

He's potent and powerful and kingly confident . . . and finally as sure about it as I am.

"I can take it, Eden. I want it all."

Chapter 58

Dominic

Survival tip #305
*Bottle anything up for too long,
it's going to blow.*

S ubmission slides over her, fuck-fogging her eyes and turning her pliable and soft under me. It slams my need to dominate into overdrive, and I don't even think she knows what the fuck she's doing. How every single way she moves provokes me.

Her needy little squirms.

How she pulls against my grip, then shudders when she can't escape.

The way her body begs me to fuck.

Every time I get close, her body responds. She parts her fucking legs, and her pulse goes fucking haywire. Her damn nipples are always tight and begging for teeth. She ripens with color and stares at my mouth and my hands and my cock, and the worst fucking part of it is, she isn't doing a single part of it on *purpose*.

My balls are cramping with the need to fill her up. Demand drills through my cock with so much goddamned force my head feels light.

There's only so many times I can fuck my fist to thoughts of her. I can't spray the shower walls with the image of her presenting her cunt to me over battle maps again.

"Please, sir." Her hot, shaky breaths pant over my face. "Take it."

Take me.

"Safeword?"

"Bristlebrook," she answers immediately, *eagerly*, and my need rides me.

I have her limits list from Jasper. I have her safeword.

I'm going to soak her in all the months of pent-up need I didn't get to use her for.

"Rule number five, Eden," I snap.

Rule five: When I ask for a hole to use, you better present one to me. Fast.

My impatience lends more heat to the order than I usually aim for, but my librarian doesn't seem to mind. Her lids flutter and her breath catches on a moan, and as soon as I release her wrists, she's stripping off her shirt, then hiking up her nightdress. Her breasts sway heavily under the silk, barely contained, and I grit my teeth.

That fucking nightdress she *innocently* turned up at my door in.

The other guys there or not, she's lucky she didn't get fucked over the couch.

I brace my hands against the door, leaning over her as she drags down her underwear, and my cock nearly punches through my jeans when I see the wet little cling before she tugs them away.

The small victories roar through me—clean shots, every one. She memorized my rules.

And they're turning her into a helpless mess.

When her underwear is gone, she hesitates, glancing up at me, her silky nightdress still fluffed up around her waist. I can see her pussy like this.

But that isn't what I asked to see.

I raise my brows again, wondering how far she'll take this.

Another husky, whimpered sound escapes her as she looks up at me over those crooked, cute fucking glasses. The next sound is half a gasp, but she turns around in front of me and presses her cheek against the door, spreading her legs.

I look down as she arches her back, and her slender fingers slide over her ass . . . as she peels herself open. I step back so I can see it—her presenting herself to me. Her tight little ass and that sopping wet, lust-fucked cunt.

Two holes.

My little submissive likes to go beyond the call of duty.

No wonder she fits in with the rest of the guys.

I unzip my pants, tugging them down around my ass until I can pull my stiff cock free. It's wet already, scorching and beading over and over with my desperate fucking precum. As I give myself a rough stroke, Eden's fingers play nervously around the curve of her ass, slipping around in her mess, and I nearly come in my fist.

I'm not even going to be able to think until I fuck her at least twice.

"Rule three, pet," I growl, and she tries to look at me over her shoulder, but I'm already kicking her legs wider with my booted foot, lining myself up with her pussy.

When my crown finds her hole, I punch inside an inch, and the blinding, wet heat clenches around me so tightly, I lose all rational thought. Wrapping an arm around her, I grasp Eden's neck, yanking her upright so I can push her against the door as I bury my dick to the hilt inside her.

I groan into her prim little bun, feeling the shocked spasms of her cunt around me, and Eden cries out sharply. Her cheek, her breasts are trapped where I have her flattened against the door. The pulse at her throat begs for mercy against my hand. Her whole sweet, delicate body is shaking under mine as I drive my hard cock between her wet legs again and again. Her cries have desperate, moaning edges, and I squeeze the hand at her throat as I drag hot, grunting kisses over the side of her face. When her glasses fall off her face, I bite her shoulder.

There's nowhere for her to move. Nowhere for her to run.

It's just her body begging me to fuck it again.

"Sir!" she gasps, sharp and high, and I feel her walls tightening, gripping me with dragging pressure that I punch through without a care, fucking her deep.

Deep enough that her wetness drips over my balls and soaks my pants.

I grunt a laugh in her ear, flexing the hand on her throat. "Come, little librarian. Come because I told you to." I kiss the side of her mouth, licking into that wet too. "Give it to me."

Tears fall from her eyes, and she comes with shuddering fucking recklessness, with my name on her screaming, perfect lips. I control her squirming, pulsing body with easily caught hands, and the pressure of my dick fucking her up into the door. My body is wider, heavier, and as I pin her where I want her, Eden begins to sob through her orgasm—a broken mix of "sir" and "Dom" and "please."

Her spasms are a hot, milking drag, and I groan against her, my hips slapping against hers as my cock swells, encased in the best fucking thing I've ever felt. My librarian's perfect satin pussy that's taking my dick like it was made for me.

She was made for me.

The hot fist of pleasure at the base of my spine explodes through my system, and my orgasm rips through me with annihilating force, punching out of me in thick, violent spurts. I feel myself flood her pretty cunt with my cum. I feel her pussy fluttering around me like a thank you. I feel pleasure drip through my veins with each pulse, spreading everywhere—through my gut and chest and down the backs of my legs and into the tips of my fingers still clamped around her neck.

Our shuddery pants mix, and Eden strokes my wrist with sweet, silent gratitude, and we stay there, enjoying the feeling until our cum begins to leak out around me.

Eden wasn't made for me.

I thought I was made for battlerooms and barracks. For cold nights creeping through woods and hot days stalking over sand. I thought I was made for the Creed.

I wasn't.

I was made for her.

"You're perfect, Eden. You're the most perfect fucking thing," I say against her ear.

The way she melts back into me tangles thorns around my chest, and the pain that pierces me is better than any I've felt coming off an op. It's heavy and sweet, puncturing something cold that's been sitting in there for a long damn time.

"I love you, Dom," she whispers . . . and it feels like she's holding her breath.

Wanting to see her face, I pull back enough that I slip out of her, then turn her to face me. Color is high in her cheeks, and her eyes are a glowing, unholy blue.

And they're filled with trepidation.

Those words have been sitting between us for a long time . . . but she finally said it.

"I love you too, Eden," I tell her, just as softly, and her eyes get suddenly shiny.

She smiles, blinking. Then she blinks again, ducking her head. She banishes the tears, but that shy smile stays.

I stare at it, memorizing the curve and how the strands of her hair play around her face. Memorizing this perfect, quiet moment.

When she glances up, she hesitates, and I can see the moment she remembers my rules. She's already broken rule four—*don't speak unless you're moaning my fucking name, answering a question, or safeing out.*

But I might make an exception for 'I love you.'

"Spit it out, pet—but be respectful," I advise her, and she shivers, nodding once.

Her nipples are still pushing against that damn nightdress, and my cock stirs lazily. It's been too long. I need her too much.

"I just . . . wanted to say that I appreciate you helping me, sir." Her voice is breathy, a little tentative, but in a way that I can tell is getting her the hell off. She looks up at me between her lashes, and I need to bite down on my amusement.

The little shit is trying to seduce me.

It's going to work, too.

"I know that you take on so much, sir. I know how much weight you carry, and I . . ." The color deepens in her cheeks. It swirls over her delicate collarbone. "I want to help you with it, too. I want to make it better. If there's any way I can . . . serve you, sir, I . . . I want to. Please let me."

My hindbrain kicks back in hard, and I barely trap the raw fucking growl from escaping me at her words. My body reacts in rapid, deprived demand.

Of course my sweet little librarian wants to serve me. She's been begging for it for months. She wants to make me feel good.

Her chest is lifting quickly, but I don't think it's out of nervousness at offering me another service fuck—like we didn't both just come like an unpinned grenade. Like my cum isn't staining her pretty dress and leaking down her thighs.

She wants to be my prize, my fuck doll, my medicine. She wants me to use her body in every way I want to use her.

I lean down and grip her mouth so I can deliver her a filthy fucking kiss.

She doesn't move, taking it like a good, obedient girl.

"Then you better fucking serve me well, pet."

CHAPTER 59

EDEN

He flicks on the water in the shower, and I stagger against the bathroom counter on shaky legs, still thrumming with pleasure and arousal and the throb of being well used.

God, how do they all wreck me so differently?

Dom doesn't throw me around so that I'll fight him, not like Jayk. He throws me around because he can, just so he can use me how he wants.

He made me come without even touching my clit.

In front of me, Dom pulls his shirt over his head in one smooth move, and his chest is a wide expanse of thick muscle and a dark dusting of hair that I want to bury my fingers in.

There are no apologies in his body. There's no compromise or softening. He's big and rawly masculine, slicked in sweat and rain from the fight and our fucking. My body is still aching from the uncompromising force of his pounding into me.

I'm not afraid of aches anymore.

I'm only afraid that he'll stop touching me.

He kicks off his pants, and his thick thighs and his stirring cock are too vivid for the respectable beiges and pastels of the bathroom. My tongue sticks to the roof of my mouth, my body vividly awake.

I've been having enough sex with the others enough to *know* how long it takes a man to recover—but whether out of deprivation or sheer force of will, my commander seems to be defying the rules tonight.

"Strip," he demands, his eyes hot on my body.

"I—"

"Rule four, pet. You want to serve me? Shut your mouth and show me what color your nipples are. I need a reminder."

He orders me with all the confidence of his military rank, but with enough filthy intent that I need to rub my cum-slick thighs together.

I can be quiet. I can remember his rules.

And if Dom wants to look at me, then I'll show him anything he wants.

Five men are desperate for my body. My old insecurities don't really have a place here anymore.

My hands trail up to the straps of my nightdress, and I slip them over my shoulders, my breaths embarrassingly loud in the silence.

It's different, being so quiet.

Beau's filthy roleplays beg for a partner. Lucky's games mean laughter and teasing. Jayk usually has me shouting something at him between his snarks. Even Jasper delighted in teasing out humiliating replies and whispered confessions.

But I like this, too. Dom sharing my quiet.

His silent expectation wells between us.

While he watches, I catch my lower lip with my teeth, and as I slowly peel the silk dress from my body, I move my fingers through the cum between my legs.

I've been learning to talk in different ways, anyway.

Dom locks on my mouth, my thighs, then on my budded pink nipples.

His eyes darken. "Get in the shower, Eden."

It's not a question, so I don't say anything, just slip over to the monolithic shower that takes up half the room. It's a relief, really. I desperately need to get clean after the last few hours.

As I open the door to step inside, Dom watches me, his eyes lingering over my ass and the mess he made of me.

And his hand jerks along his stiff, swollen cock.

It distracts me enough that it's not until I'm under the water that I realize it's as cold as a hailstorm.

"Ah!" I yelp sharply, slamming myself against the tiled wall farthest from the spray.

No. *No*! I am a trooper. I'm on board with quite a lot. At least one whole third of my limits list was dotted with big eager ticks, and a good many more *willing to try*s.

Not *once* did *anyone* say *anything* about needing to *drown* myself in a glacial *waterfall*!

Dom steps inside the shower, right under the icy stream, and the miserable man's lips are tilted in glinting amusement.

"Suck it up, pet. It's just water."

Also not a question.

My fingers curl against the tile that isn't much warmer than the water, and I war between wanting to continue and the fierce desire not to be cryopreserved before I get another orgasm.

Dom's smile becomes dry, though his eyes are still trailing over my body. "Blame your boyfriend. This was his handiwork."

I have multiple boyfriends, but funnily enough, I don't need to ask who he means.

God *damn* it, Jayk. He'll be the death of me.

Hesitantly, I step forward. Every drop is like the sting of an ice pellet.

Water sluices over Dom's body, spraying off his wide shoulders and soaking through his hair. He soaps himself up with a netted sponge, and the suds drip down his body. Despite the cold, his cock demands attention.

Dom reaches out a hand.

Resigning myself, I take it.

A second later, he has me yanked against his body, and he's dragging my face up to his. He kisses me hard. It's hot and deep, as much of an invasion as the way he fucked me.

I stay still, though it's a fight not to rub myself against him. I let him take my mouth the way he wants me. Press my stomach into his cock the way he wants me. He licks and sucks and takes from me until I'm shuddering.

He's sizzling hot, and the frigid water bites everywhere he isn't touching me. My nipples are hard and achingly sensitive, buried in his coarse chest hair, and he holds my face firmly in place as he sucks on my tongue.

Finally, he drops me, and I fall back against the glass wall, blinking against the spray, shivering fiercely from the cold and my desperate need for him to fuck me again. I want him to add to my aches.

I quake in the cold, but Dom's golden, molten eyes pin me in place. "Hold still and let me touch you. You're too dirty to be a good fuck toy for me yet."

My head falls back against the glass as he pulls down another sponge, lathering it in soap before he skates it over my neck. It's a little coarse, enough to scrape along my skin as he works it over my chest and down my arms. Over my thighs and ass. It makes me squirm when he drags it over my wrists and between my fingers, but he doesn't stop, moving in ruthless efficiency . . . until he makes it to my breasts.

There, he makes a crude, hungry sound in the back of his throat, and his heavy cock bobs between us in silent demand. Dom's hands are rough over my breasts. Blocking most of the spray with his back, he lathers them until they're slick and soapy, gripping them and pressing them together and scraping the sponge over my nipples over and over until my clit is throbbing and I'm choking back my pleas for him to just fuck me already.

But I stay quiet and leave my hands by my side, letting him ravage my breasts as he likes.

He finally shifts to the side, dropping the sponge, and the punishing cold spray against my skin rinses the soap away. A moment later, he's bending his head and biting over one breast, sucking it into his searing mouth. His tongue laves against the tight, freezing nipple, before he sucks harder, his teeth digging into the tender flesh.

I sob, and my hands curl into fists against the glass behind me.

He ignores me, delivering the same treatment to my other breast with undisguised masculine relish. Feasting on me as I'm battered by the cold.

Bent over me, he spanks a hand under one nipple and water glances off it. "You have perfect breasts for fucking, pet. I like a slutty little librarian giving them up for me."

The slap hurts, but I swallow the cry, aching at his words.

A flush slashes across Dom's tight jaw as he watches it jiggle, and he fucks his hand with delicious purpose.

Desperately panting, I watch the head of his cock disappear into his heavy fist. I watch how he pumps himself and the milky drop that appears at the seam and then is wasted, washed away by the shower.

"Open your legs. You're still too filthy for my cock."

Swallowing hard, I spread my legs on the shower floor and cold water leaks between my toes. Between my legs, I'm scorching hot, dripping wet for reasons that have nothing to do with the shower.

The backs of his fingers touch my stomach, and I flinch as he drags them down to my pussy. They slip into me, holding me open, and I clench as he exposes my clit to the cold rain.

He grunts as cum squeezes out.

"So fucking filthy."

He doesn't even pretend to make it sound disapproving this time.

Dom drops to one knee, and all I can see is his dark, wet hair as his breath puffs over my clit. The shock of heat makes me flinch, and he brings an arm up between my legs, tipping my lower body into him until he has me pinned to the glass by my shoulders.

"Stay like that," he orders.

It's not a comfortable angle, and it makes freezing water pool along my body, trailing down to drip into my pussy, but he doesn't pay it any mind. He brings his thumb up to press against my entrance, until more cum leaks out—and then he rubs it against my clit with a hard, punishing finger.

Pleasure slices through me, and I can't strangle my cry this time. At the last moment, I only just turn it into a sobbing, breathless, "*Dom.*"

He ignores me, and his thumb begins stroking all through my pussy, pushing the cold water through every fold and crevice. He works two wet fingers inside me, and it's only then, as I fight not to squirm and fuck his hand that I realize he's still *cleaning* me.

"*Dom. Sir,*" I moan again, the only words I'm allowed. The only words that are in my head except for *please* and some broken, hopeless prayers.

"Stop whimpering. I'll use this fuck hole when I feel like putting my dick somewhere nice and wet. You squirming about it isn't going to make any difference." His voice has hints of its usual dryness, but it's edged in a careless indifference that wrecks me.

His choice. His body. His hole.

I'm only here for him to play with.

His thumb moves to my clit, teasing the bud with the same ruthless efficiency. Cold water spills over my clit in a searing splash, and I jerk hard, sobbing as I come hard to his careless, cleaning rubs and his even more careless words.

I'm shaking, shuddering in reckless pleasure, and I can't tell if it's a reward for staying still or if he just doesn't care so long as he can take what he wants from me.

He slaps my pulsing pussy as he stands, shaking his head. "You're getting it dirty again."

I'm still gasping when he slaps my cheek lightly next, then grips me around my jaw to give me another drugging, invasive kiss. His tongue pierces me, his mouth hot and insatiable against my quivering lips. I drink him in, taking him in with the sprayed water that dribbles between our mouths.

Pulling me back, he turns the water off. He's still holding my cheeks, and as he looks at me shivering, he digs two fingers into my mouth, holding them against my tongue.

His eyes flare.

"Out of the shower."

He backs me out of the shower, and my eyes dart to the towel, but he ignores that too, dragging both of us out dripping wet.

In the bedroom, he releases me. With casual assurance, he pulls a bottle of lube out of the side table and turns to sit on the very edge of his low bed.

He leans back, spreading his legs, and his cock curves up, swollen and insistent. His balls sit heavy and water-damp under him, and every inch of him is primed, glistening potency. Even leaning back like he is, he seems too big to handle.

I ache with eagerness.

My lips are roughed raw from his stubble and kisses, and my breasts glow with red bite marks, but all I want is to take him inside me again. I want to fight to stretch around his cock. I want to hear him grunt with pleasure again.

God, I want to milk his cock into my mouth and take his cum down my throat.

"Get down."

Dom nods for me to kneel between his legs, and I move into place with embarrassing speed. A rough amusement glances over his hard, kingly features before he snags up the lube. He squirts it into his palms, working it between his hard, veined hands, his eyes hot on my wet body as I kneel for him.

His bed is low enough, and I'm close enough, that if I were to lean up, I could kiss his mouth. I could dip my head and take him to the back of my throat with his hand on my head.

"I'm fucking your tits, pet," he informs me.

I could also do that.

He palms my breasts between his slippery hands, working them over with the lube. Then he gives them a final, coarse squeeze before he pinches my nipples hard enough for me to arch into him.

"Ah!" The sound escapes me before I can stop it, and Dom's jaw flexes.

I can see the vein throbbing in his dick just inches away.

Be good. It's all for him. He's allowed to wreck his toys if it makes him hard.

Helpless, liquid heat floods me, and I feel my need dripping down my legs.

I can't even blame Dom's cum this time.

I just need him to keep using me. I'm lost in it.

Dom tugs me up by my nipples until I push off my heels, dutifully kneeling up as high as I can go. Sweet-hot pain lances through me, but Dom keeps directing me until *I'm* leaning over *him*, and the fat, gleaming crown of his cock slips heavily against the underside of my slick breasts, seeking something to fuck.

Dom lets me go, and I gasp at the release of pressure-pain as they fall into place.

His eyes are on my face, overbright and heated, assessing and brutally intense.

"Offer them to me, little librarian. Hold them up."

I gather my breasts into my hands, pressing them together like the offering he wants. They're swollen, too, oversensitive and zinging with electric hurt. My nipples have darkened to a deeper rose, poking needily between my fingers like they're begging for our commander to pay them more attention.

He squirts a long, debauched stream of lube over my breasts, painting them until they glisten luminously and it trickles wetly down my body. With rough, deliberate hands, he rubs the lube over my chest, then works it between them with slick, pumping fingers.

Lust and miserable pleasure chase over my skin in hot little bursts as he preps me.

Dom leans back again, and his eyes are heavy-lidded now.

"Now work for it, pet. Pump my cock between your tits." His cock is trailing a wet, sticky mess along my breasts. I whimper, and his eyes darken over my face. "Show me why the good little service slut is worth my time."

Heat flushes through me as I spread my knees.

I haven't done this before, but as I take him between my breasts, the *how* doesn't worry me. He's throbbing and hot, and there's so much lube that even as snug and tight as I can press myself around him, he slips between my breasts with relentless ease.

I want to make this worth Dom's time. The need to make him feel good is as fundamental to my own pleasure as my heartbeat is to living. I want to see the pleasure crashing over his face. I want to take away every trouble he's ever felt, if only for a short time.

And I can do it. He needs this as much as I do. He needs to take as viscerally as I need to give.

And he trusts me to know what I need to hold back.

And I trust him to respect it.

Testing my rhythm, I squeeze my breasts down his cock, and I win a choppy, dragged-in breath. An answering moan slips out of me as I do it again. It's all so erotic I don't know where to look or what to focus on.

His cock is steel and satin, crude and magnificent and impossibly hot as I engulf him and rub him toward climax. I can see the twitch of his abdomen under the curling hair, the tip of him flooding over with needy precum and pooling over my breasts. I can smell the spice of him and feel him shake and hear his breath turning choppy. I can hear the edges of snapping growls slip in when I find the perfect rhythm.

I see the rampant strain on his face.

My mouth waters with the need to close over the tip of him, to suck him deep and lick every drop out of his hole, but that wasn't what he asked me to do. This isn't my decision. It isn't for me.

If he wants to fuck my mouth, he'll grab my head and bury himself there.

As if hearing the thought, Dom's heavy hand digs into my hair. "Stop. Drop your hands."

His voice is throaty. Gritty with lust and pleasure, and I start to pant helplessly. My thighs are slick again, as slick as my breasts, and my body is pounding with silent demand.

But I stop as soon as he speaks, letting my hands fall away.

His cock stays resting against my chest, and I wonder if he can feel my thumping heart.

Another fat drop wells at its head, just inches away.

Dom roughly tugs my head down. "Give it a kiss."

Thank God.

His hand dragging me by my hair, I press my lips against the drop, and it spills, spreading into the seam. I kiss him again, this time with a suck. Then again so my tongue can slick over his glossy crown, and when I see his balls tighten, I open my mouth to suck him in, but he yanks my head back with a curse.

His eyes are incinerating as they linger on my mouth, and he's breathing hard.

"I should have had your cunt wrapped around my cock from the first day we met." His gaze lifts to mine. "You're a fantasy fuck, Eden. You better know how incredible you are."

My head is beginning to feel floaty again, giddily light, and happiness bursts under my chest in smug, delighted little spurts.

A fantasy fuck.

I can't stop the thrilled smile that splashes across my face, and Dom's fierce expression softens.

"So fucking beautiful."

Then he stands, shoving me onto the bed by my hair.

"Now lie on your back. I'm not through using that fuckable little body yet."

I draw myself back, lying flat, and he's shoving my legs into the air a second later, resting them both over one shoulder. With his hand, he shoves his cock between my soaking thighs, right over my aching, hollow pussy, and he grunts at how wet they are.

I close my eyes, holding down every whimper, every bubbling plea for him to shove lower. To take my cunt again.

Squeezing my legs together around his cock, he fucks my thighs.

When he tires of that, he slaps my legs back down and then positions them wide, ordering me to stay there and let him taste his new toy. His fingers and tongue find every curve and hollow along my legs and thighs. He licks into the crease between my pussy and my thigh and sucks too briefly over my sopping clit. He tunnels his tongue into my cunt until my legs start to shake, then nips over the crest of my hipbone. He laves the hollow there with wet heat and continues up.

Dom slaps me around and drags me into place—tucking my legs up around his thighs while he fucks over my stomach, and extending my hands up above my head so I'm stretched out and arching for him. Offering him my body to torment and use.

His hands and his mouth travel over the dip of my waist and kiss every rib. He devotes more time to my breasts and sucks on my fingers and licks into the crease of my elbow. He takes my mouth with his tongue or cock as it pleases him.

He ignores my broken cries and moans and the erratic sounds of my breaths, and my toes curl mindlessly into the sheets as I desperately try to stay still. I'm dizzy and gone and airy as Dom shoves me into different positions. He moves me like I really am a doll, and he wants to know every button and hole and feature that might make me more fuckable.

Finally, he straddles my chest and grasps his cock in his hand.

He's impossibly large on top of me, looming and powerful as he pins me underneath him. His thick, coarse thighs trap my arms to my side, and he begins to jack himself off.

"Open your mouth. I want to see your tongue."

Obediently, I open my mouth, panting, and his golden eyes lock on my tongue as he pumps himself. His balls are a heavy, shifting weight between my breasts as he moves, and his hand is making slick, sucking noises with every stroke.

His cock is ruddy, and I watch it with unrestrained, licentious fascination.

Dom's eyes are glassy as he shakes his head at me. "You're the perfect little fuck toy, Eden. Your smell . . ." He grunts, his hand working faster. "Your taste . . ." His head tips back, but his eyes are still open, staring at my open mouth and my nipples. "Your *cunt*."

With a brutal groan, he starts coming in hot, jetting bursts. They splash over my breasts and pool in the hollows of my throat and stomach, and he lifts up, slapping his cock over my tongue so he spills into my waiting mouth and all over my chin. He grips my hair and holds my head in place as he works his crown over my lips and into my mouth, his squeezing fist eking out each drop for me.

I'm squirming under him, my body frantic and disconnected and throbbing with a needy viciousness that brings tears to my eyes, but I moan as I lick him up, entirely focused on his dick. His cum. The pleasure crashing over his face.

He curses roughly, shuddering.

Finally, he edges forward a few inches, slipping over his own cum, so I have better access to his cock.

"Clean me up, pet," he orders, sounding drunk, but I'm already floating on the pleasure of it.

My arms are still pinned, trapped by his heavy legs, so I just use my mouth, licking and sucking over his shaft that is barely softening. I drag my tongue over the vein until it pulses against me, and Dom hisses as I lap against the oversensitive flesh.

He lifts his cock and drags his balls over my mouth so I can suck those in too, as gently and thoroughly as I can. I kiss at the soft skin under them until he shoves his cock back in my mouth, and I keep suckling on him eagerly, intoxicated by all of it.

My own need spills out between my legs, staining the sheets, and his cum starts growing sticky on my chest, but I don't stop until a rumbling hum of pleasure starts up deep in his chest.

I don't need to be fucked again.

I could live and die with his cock in my mouth.

Finally, he gets off me.

"That eager fucking mouth, Eden. You could rouse the dead," he grits out.

Then he grasps my hips and drags me down the bed until my ass hangs off the edge. He's staring at my pussy, and my fuzzy mind explodes into overdrive.

I sit up, stunned. "*Again*?"

The question comes out high and shocked, and Dom's face flares into heated life.

In one second, he has me flipped onto my stomach, and his hand claps down on my ass with brutal, bruising force. When I flinch, crying out, he presses a pitiless hand to the center of my back, shoving me down, then spanks me three more times, each one harder than the last.

I yelp in surprise and at the stinging, delicious pain, but halt my squirms just in time.

I'm too far gone for anything he does to me to feel anything but good.

"That was rule three *and* rule four," he bites out. "Give me one reason why I shouldn't spank your ass raw and leave you like this."

"Thank you, sir," I choke out, remembering his request by the river. My face is buried in the sheets, and I feel his cum everywhere. "I . . . I don't have a reason." Miserably, I add, "I'm yours to leave however you want to leave me."

I breathe shakily into the sheets. My clit pulses, my empty pussy aching as the sting melts into heavy, throbbing heat.

I can take some more spanks. If I end this night with a burning ass and an aching pussy, wrapped around Dom, it's still one of the best nights of my life.

I catch my breath, waiting for the next stinging blow.

But this time, when Dom's hand comes down on my ass, it's to soothe over the sting, and my suspended breath trembles out.

"You're not even trying to weasel your way out of it, are you?" he mutters, and tenderness throbs in his voice as he flips me over onto my back.

His flushed face is stern as he looks down at me, but he can't hide the softness in his eyes as he runs them down my body.

"Don't talk, pet. Don't make me remind you again." He dips a finger into my pussy, fucking me with it slowly. He doesn't touch my clit, just rubs inside me. "I'll fuck you as many times as I want, Eden."

His next smile is dry. "I'll be nice and put your shock down to the other assholes' performances and not mine."

I melt, shuddering, into the bed, and my pussy takes another finger from him, then another, and he watches my face as he pumps them into me, his gaze growing hot.

Then Dom hauls me back up the bed, crawling over my body until his cock settles between my thighs. He reaches down, running the crown briefly over my clit before he notches himself at my entrance, then he kisses me again, his mouth hard and drugging.

Grasping my hand, he brings it down to his chest, and I sigh my gratitude against his lips. My fingers rub through his rough hair, tingling at his heat and texture and at all the touch I've been deprived of.

Dom tilts my chin up so I arch against his body. "Touch where you can reach, but don't get in my way," he warns. "Understood?"

"Yes, sir," I agree in a husky rush, greedily running my hands over his arms and pausing to grip the back of his corded neck. "Thank you, sir. Thank you."

The *sir*s and *thank you*s put a light in his eyes, and he snorts softly as I rub my hands over his chest.

Dom begins to press into my pussy with slow, inexorable force. I arch into the thrust, not completely able to hold myself still—not for this. My body is humiliatingly ready, and he's still a strain to take as he pushes past my panicky walls.

My mouth falls open as he fucks into me once, rocking lazily.

His elbows settle beside my shoulders, and he begins to toy with my hair, teasing the loose strands against my face and stroking my cheekbones. All the while, he watches my expressions with the same hot, tender severity.

Dom fucks into me slowly, leisurely, like he's luxuriating in every inch of the obscene drag of his brutal cock through my cunt. His cum slips and sticks between us until I feel both cherished and degraded, used and fucked and adored.

Dom fucks me like that for a ruthlessly long time, making me ride the crest sobbing and squirming under his pinning cock while he strokes my face, murmuring sweet filth.

"This hole might be my favorite."

"You're so good to take me like this."

"I'm going to fill you up, pet."

"Do you want to come, too?"

That last one is a question, and I sob in tortured relief.

"Yes, sir, please. Please let me."

My cunt clutches at him, but Dom only kisses me on the nose with a hot, dry smile, then draws back. He flattens one of my knees to the bed.

His next thrust slams in hard and deep and to the hilt, and I scream in desperate need. My pussy is so wet, we slap wetly together, my pleasure coating and spilling around his cock. He does it again, then again, fucking into me faster and deeper until I'm straining around him and struggling to take him so far into me, but he only holds me in place, making me take every thrust.

Dom groans, watching my face. "This cock is for you, little librarian. Take it."

He leans back down over me, kissing me deep, then reaches down to stroke my clit, not letting up the brutal speed, and I grip the back of his neck desperately. My nipples drag against his chest hair, and he's everywhere, all around me as I squeeze around his cock. He claps another hard hand against my ass, and suddenly, sharply, the strain transforms, avalanching into an orgasm so violent, I white out.

When I come to, it's sobbing into his shoulder and with his hand in my hair, my pussy still spasming helplessly around him.

His whispers in my ear.

"I'm never letting you go. Not even if it kills me."

CHAPTER 60

EDEN

SURVIVAL TIP #296
There's no such thing as a night that never ends.
For better or for worse.

Dom is militaristically exacting in his aftercare—he checks in with me like he's receiving an after-operation report, watches me finish my water and snack with rigorous attention, and he bundles me into the freezing shower to wash me down with thorough, deliberate meticulousness.

I'm flushed and still shaking, my emotions crashing and lifting everywhere, and when I reach up to kiss him, his returned affection is stilted and perfunctory, too—like he's checking a box. He's so precise, so determined, that it takes me over twenty trembling minutes to realize that's *exactly* what he's doing.

It's my limits list, the aftercare section, where I ticked and noted down everything I might like: check-ins, food and water, cleaning or wound tending (by myself or my dominant), affection, kindness, cuddles . . .

"Get into bed, pet. I'll hold you until you fall asleep," Dom orders from the bathroom door, and my lips tilt up.

Right on time.

The anxiousness that was building in me settles as I realize what's happening.

Bundled in a fluffy towel, I turn back to him. His towel is slung low on his waist, and I let myself enjoy the view before I glance up at his face. He frowns at me when I don't obey, but this isn't a scene, and this poor man is a mess.

"Sir . . . you don't do this very often, do you?" I ask.

I don't think I disguise my amusement well enough, because the dark brow that Dom kicks up is unimpressed.

"I didn't come to you a virgin if that's what you mean."

I roll my eyes, sitting on the bed. He's already replaced the sheets.

The last ones may need to be burned.

"I mean this part. The aftercare," I correct softly, a little tentative, and he stiffens, tensing—enough that I feel bad for him, and I rush to add, "Beau did it, didn't he? He took over that part?"

It's a guess, but an educated one. I've seen and talked to both of them enough to gather that Beau tended to take the lead on emotional intimacy.

The dominance and discipline side, Dom has pretty well covered.

It's not as though he *wasn't* intimate tonight. He was. Between the fierce control, I felt his tenderness. I saw the appreciation and thrill and gratitude. We've been getting closer to this for weeks.

He just needs a little practice.

And I'll just . . . not mention the fact that somehow, shockingly, even Jayk had better natural instincts for this.

Dom studies me from the doorway before, finally, he sighs.

"That obvious, huh?" he mutters. His jaw clenches, and he looks up, his golden eyes determined. "I'm sorry. What do you need, pet?"

I soften, smiling at him. My body is liquid and tingling, and now that I know his awkwardness isn't him trying to escape, I can actually enjoy it.

"I could use a shirt?" I ask, and he nods, immediate relief breaking over his stern features.

My sweet, task-oriented man.

I take my hair out of its bun, and the release of tension makes me sigh. He passes me one of his shirts, and I slip it on gratefully, then catch his hand before he retreats, tugging him onto the bed beside me.

Tentatively, I crawl onto his lap and rest my head on his chest. My fingers play absently in his chest hair, and slowly, his arms come around me. His thumb begins to track hesitant lines over my thigh.

"Cuddling," I explain.

Between his warmth and the sweet little touches, I begin to feel sleepy.

"It shouldn't be a chore, sir. I just like you holding me. I like your smell." I rub my cheek into him with a happy sigh. "I like to feel reminded that I'm more than just a toy when the scene is done. I love it during, but this . . . this is nice, too."

Dom's grip tightens. "Right."

In seconds, he has me lifted up, and he resettles us against the headboard, tucking the sheets around me. And he keeps me between his legs, locked against his chest.

He rests his chin against my head, and his breath fans my hair.

"You're not a toy, Eden. You never were. You're the smartest person I know. The kindest. You're braver than you should have ever had to be. That you're all those things and still want to put yourself in my hands, that you let me play with that perfect fucking body, that you trust me with it—I don't take it lightly." Dom's voice turns rough on the last, and he tilts my head back so he's looking at my face. He's as brutally intense as he was in the scene, but there's an ache behind it as he finishes. "You're not a toy, Eden. You're a formidable fucking woman . . . and you're the love of my life."

My lips part, my throat filling with stunned, pretty tears, and Dom's mouth hooks up.

He presses a kiss to my forehead, then pulls me up closer. Another sigh fans out of him as he settles his cheek against my hair.

"And I like holding you, too," he murmurs.

My fingers curl against his skin, and I smile into the curve of his neck.

After today, after the death and the misery and the guilt, I didn't think I'd be capable of smiling for a long while. But I'm not in the same place I was a few weeks ago. I didn't freeze tonight. Even when my feelings dipped and my fears rose, I was able to fight through it and do what I had to. I have tools to help myself now. Work I'm still doing on myself.

And when I'm feeling brittle, I have a whole family here who believe in me even more than I do.

There's too much good in my world to be swallowed by the bad.

They can live alongside one another, and I can let myself feel it all.

Eventually, Dom's breathing begins to slow, and sleep begins to slide over me, too.

"You know," I murmur against his chest, "for a dominant, you take direction *very* well."

And I fall asleep with a stinging ass and Dom's arms around me, with giggles still in my throat.

CHAPTER 61

JAYKOB

Rain batters the tarp we set up, but my clothes are already leaking water into my socks and every fucking body crevice I have. Jasper and Lucky just moved from Platform Two to mine, and they're soaked worse than me.

I nod to them as they settle in, the circus rat shaking himself off like a dog before he leans against the mantlet. Jasper smiles back at me briefly, like we're *friends* now, before he pulls down the night goggles to check on the Sinners again.

It's weird.

It's been weird since they broke in through my damn window two nights ago—but I know what they look like when they blow their loads now, so of course it's fucking weird. A lifetime of premature Jasper jokes might make it worth it, though.

The movie night didn't suck, either.

The guys having my back.

Eden.

I've had worse weeks, I guess, even with the shitfight tonight. The rain can fuck off, though.

"Dom's on tomorrow morning?" Lucky asks, fighting a yawn.

Another fat drop drips off my hair and slides under my collar, and I scowl, pulling my goggles up so I can see them better. "I can't believe I chose to sit out here and grow mold on my fucking junk instead of going to bed."

That'll teach me to do the gushy shit. Could have just shaken the fucker's hand. Saved the grand gesture bullshit for a dry night.

"I bet Eden's warm," I mutter sourly. "Motherfucker got the good end of the deal."

Jasper stiffens, and Lucky's head lifts fast.

"Uhh . . . come again?" Lucky asks.

I roll my eyes. "Yeah, I don't usually do that shit with a crowd. Don't hold your breath for a repeat."

The rat grins with full face pits, but Jasper's still making the shrink-face at me.

"Dominic is with Eden?" Jasper asks carefully. "And you . . . are fine with that?"

Why do they always need to talk this shit to death?

It makes it weird.

I give him an irritated look, then yank my goggles down to stare out into the rain. No movement. It smells like wet earth and damp sweat up here, but it could be worse. The ground is thick and soggy out past the moat, the bodies there getting a final shower.

Shit. Who's going to move those?

Jasper and Lucky exchange *another* look, and I scowl.

"Whatever. So we're doing the stupid everyone-in thing with her. Just stop riding my ass about it—and no more breaking into my bed," I mutter. "It's fucking creepy."

I remember the other thing.

"Also, the cap is the cap again starting tomorrow."

"He's *what*?" Lucky exclaims. "How did you get him to do that? Does he want to? Do *you* want him to? Is he happy? Did you hug about it?"

I yank down my goggles and glare at them under the tarp, daring them to say another word, and Lucky laughs, running a hand over his hair.

Jasper gives me a long, piercing look.

He's given me that look a lot over the years—the one where he picks over my insides with his fancy engraved fountain pen. But . . . I don't know. It feels different now. Less like he's checking to do damage control on all the fucked-up shit inside me, and more like . . . like he's checking *on me.*

Like he cares if I'm okay, too.

Finally, he smiles at me and squeezes my arm briefly before he turns back to the watch.

Thank fuck.

The rat doesn't let it go, of course.

" . . . more movie nights. Family dinners. I'm thinking Eden would have fun with a tea party, so let's do that. How do you feel about golf?"

Jasper glances at him. "I enjoy—"

But Lucky is already shaking his head. "Nope, scratch that. No one fun likes golf. Basketball? We could make a team. New plan—beat the Sinners, start a basketball league with RZ and Reapers. We'd wipe the *floor* with them. Collect prizes from everyone. Win glory."

Snorting, I decide it's not worth bruising my knuckles to shut him up. The ladder starts to creak behind us, and I look back to see Beau climb up onto the platform, looking wrecked.

He's had a shitty night. Nearly got his head blown off getting rid of one of the bodies.

Beau nods in greeting, wiping a tired hand over his wet face. "Night, guys. I'm hitting the hay. Deanna has the wounded for now. Need anything before I drop off?"

Lucky laughs, low and wicked. "Oh, man. You have a *good* night, okay?"

Beau's hand drops. "What's that supposed to mean?"

Jasper turns around, amusement in his face. "You have a surprise waiting for you, I believe."

It takes a long fucking time before realization dawns on his face.

The doc can be slow on the uptake.

"Eden went with Dom," he says, looking between us. He steps further under the tarp, ducking his head. "Eden is *with* Dom?"

I roll my eyes again. "What do you need, confetti?"

Beau laughs, relief and joy crackling over him. "Yes!" He laughs. "Get the confetti. Hell, I'll throw it."

The lightning flashes like a firework, and I eye it testily.

Yeah, yeah. I get it. It's a good thing. Whatever.

"He's also resumed his command. Jaykob relinquished it back to him," Jasper murmurs.

I didn't *say* that, mostly because I didn't want them to read more into it than there was. Dom is better there. I'm better here. No need to write to Hallmark, it's not a big fucking deal.

"He . . . *You* . . ." Beau's gaze swings to me, wide and searching, and the idiot needs to wipe his face again. Those had *better* be raindrops.

Beau grabs me into a big, rough . . . is this a *hug*?

Is Doctor Dickhead *hugging* me?

"Okay. Okay, fuck off. *Stop it*, asshole." I shove him back, rolling my shoulders.

Fuck. Do *all* of them have to make it weird?

Beau blinks hard, laughing, and he rubs a hand over his mouth. When he looks at me, it's skin-crawlingly soft.

"Thank you. *Thank you*, Jayk," he says.

"Yeah, just say *that*." I scowl, rubbing at my itchy skin. In a mutter, I add, "Hug me again, and I'll push you off the platform."

Lucky laughs, and Beau's grin is too amused.

I'm not joking. I'll do it.

"Well, on that fine note, I will turn in. Y'all have a good night. Jayk." He tips his head, then disappears into the rain.

I hope he gets drenched.

But there's a strange, warm ache in my chest that wasn't there before. Like how I feel when I'm with Eden—only less hard-on inducing. It's enough to battle the cold and the wet.

And it's enough to make the idea of standing out here for hours with these two not feel like the worst way to spend the night.

As the rain falls around us, we look out over the battlefield and . . . it's almost peaceful. Water leaking between my toes and all.

Into the pattering quiet, Lucky muses, "So . . . what are we calling ourselves? Pussy Posse? No? Clam Crew? Booty bros? What about . . ."

Jasper smiles at me, and I roll my eyes.

And Lucky doesn't shut up for the rest of the night.

CHAPTER 62

EDEN

SURVIVAL TIP #351
*Good dreams make
bad days go away.*

The sound of a shower running drifts in and out of my awareness. A door closing. Dom shifting to lean up on the bed beside me.

"This was a good surprise," Beau murmurs, like he's talking to himself.

"Everything okay?" Dom asks, his voice pitched low and gritty with sleep.

"It's quiet for now," Beau replies, and the sound of his tired voice begins to drag me out of my dreams. "Everyone's stable. Deanna slept for a while and she's monitoring now. She'll make sure no one else dies on me before I wake up."

No one *else*.

I sigh against my pillow, my heart hurting. Turning over sleepily, I take in his face in the low lamplight. Dom left it on for him. He's in a towel, holding another, and he looks exhausted, his frown lines as pronounced as his laugh lines, for once.

But Beau's lips tug up as he glances over me briefly, and he slides his towel up the back of his neck, half-heartedly drying his hair. My eyes begin to drift shut again, two nights of broken sleep chasing me.

"Smells like you two had a better night than I did," Beau says wickedly, and it halts the slide.

Smells?

I make a distressed sound, lifting my head, and Dom snorts, shoving me back down onto the pillow.

He's just lucky it's so, so soft.

As I snuggle back in, Dom lies down again. "She's an agreeable little pet. I decided we're keeping her."

"*You* decided," Beau repeats, sounding amused. He tosses his used towel carelessly to the floor against the wall, and my lips twitch. He *is* messy. "Huh. You know, I'm happy enough about this turn of events that I'm going to let that slide."

He strips the towel from around his waist carelessly, then walks over to the sitting area, snagging up some briefs.

My lids droop drowsily, but I watch him from my stomach, my cheek turned over my pillow.

Beau sighs as he glances toward the sofa, and I feel the fresh sheet being tugged off me. I shiver in the cool air. I'm only in Dom's T-shirt, and it's not enough to block the chill.

Beau pauses, briefs still in hand, watching.

"You should end a shitty night on a better note," Dom says, his voice thick with sleep. A rough, callused hand curls around the back of my knee, and he drags my limp leg up and to the side. My shirt is flipped back around my waist a moment later, revealing my ass to his friend. "Come spend some time in her cunt. That will cheer you up."

Sleepily, I suck in a surprised breath.

I am awake, just, and *somnophilia* and *dormaphilia* were big, approved *yeses* on my limits list, but it still startles me in the most delicious way. I've already been so, so used tonight—and that's after being so, so used last night, I should be desperate to rest and recover.

I don't know what it says about me that the idea of Beau fucking my sore, sleepy body only makes me wetter.

"Unless our tired toy has any objection," Dom adds dryly, apparently noticing the change in me, and I pout over how well he can read me.

Silently, I spread my legs further in invitation, and a soft groan leaves Beau, his gaze stuck on my pussy. His hand falls to his cock, stroking himself absently.

"You know, I could use a pick-me-up."

Dom snorts softly, rolling over like he's going back to sleep.

Blinking through my sleep fog, I watch Beau as he tentatively walks over and kneels onto the bed behind me, settling between my legs. His hands squeeze my ass, spreading me open, and I drowsily tilt my hips up toward him.

He's not Dom. He doesn't have rules.

He strangles another groan.

"Are you awake, darlin'?" he asks, his voice soft but needily edged. "Do you know who it is?"

"Mmhm," I mumble into my pillow. "Beau. My Beau."

Sleepily, I wriggle into his hands, and his fingers trail down to play with my clit. I feel his thumb pressing against my asshole, then he begins slowly rubbing against it.

His breathing grows rougher.

"It's 'Bristlebrook' to stop me, pet. Yellow if you need a second. Can you say yes for me, darlin'? Tell me you understand? I need to fuck you. I'll be gentle."

"Mmm, 'snice." I sigh, relaxing against the bed, letting him touch, and pleasure wells in me, heated and wet. I bury my face in my pillow contentedly.

He removes his hands, and an unhappy sound escapes me.

Words. He wants words.

"Fuck me, please," I murmur drowsily, and the words are interrupted by a yawn, and I begin to slur as warmth slides over me. "Bristlebrook stop . . . yellow . . . remember. I'm sorry . . . if I fall 'sleep. You can keep going. I don't . . ." Another yawn. "I don't mind."

I shiver at the understatement. The idea of Beau squeezing himself into my limp, sleepy body is unbearably hot to me.

From the way Beau's shaky grip returns, tight on my ass, it's not just hot to me, either.

"Told you. Agreeable," Dom mumbles from my other side, and Beau hums his agreement as his hold on me gentles.

His hands run over my skin, and I feel him lean over me, tugging my shirt up a little further so he can drop a reverent kiss to my lower back.

"I'll be quick, pet," he whispers to me. "You don't need to do anything. I just need to feel you for a little bit."

Beau lifts my hips, propping them so they hang over a pillow, and I close my eyes, enjoying the feel of him moving me. His fingers whisper between my legs, stroking up my thighs soothingly, then teasing at my clit and my entrance. I feel his face settle against my cunt, his mouth closing over me with wet, open-mouthed kisses that make me shudder. He licks through me lazily, then up to my ass, dragging my wetness everywhere.

He disappears for a moment, and I begin to drift off, aching.

I'm half-asleep when Beau grasps my hip lightly and starts pressing his cock into my pussy, inching in like he's trying not to wake me. My groan is muffled by my pillow when he bottoms out, and he runs his hands soothingly, greedily over my skin, rocking gently back and forth.

I feel my over-used pussy wince hotly around him.

I hear his uneven breaths. His whispered apologies. "I'm sorry, darlin'. I couldn't wait. Go back to sleep. I'm almost done."

His fingers run over my ass as he rubs his cock inside me, and his thumb fits against my hole. When he slowly presses it inside, playing with the wet suck, I let out a soft sigh, and he makes a rough, helpless sound behind me.

"That's it. Just relax."

Beau reaches around with his other hand, leaning over me and pressing down on the pillow until he can toy with my clit while he fucks me. Until he can take full advantage of me.

My sleepy body begins to tighten and contract around him, and I moan.

"Shh, shhh," he whispers as my body squirms back against his. He swirls his finger over my clit. "It's okay, pet, you can sleep. Just take my cock. You can come. It's just a good dream."

I whine against my pillow, caught somewhere between wakefulness and sleeping as pleasure overtakes me and I come, slick and stuttering over his cock. Beau groans, his grip gentle as he fucks into my spasms, and he holds my hips steady under him, burying himself inside my limp body as he takes his own pleasure.

"That's it, darlin'. Oh, that's it. Oh, you're a good girl letting me do this." He spills over, and he groans again as hot, liquid heat fills me. "Oh shit, oh damn. You're going to wake up all wet. I'll clean you up, sweetheart. Just rest."

He does clean me up, thoroughly and sweetly, with murmured praise and I love yous and a confidence that very much reconfirms my suspicions from earlier. I end up getting up to use the bathroom anyway, and when I come back to bed, both Dom and Beau are fast asleep, facing one another like kids at a sleepover who couldn't finish their horror stories.

I crawl in between them, and they both notch in against me until I'm surrounded, snug on all sides. I fall asleep stroking their arms and trying not to focus on tomorrow.

And all the horror stories yet to come.

CHAPTER 63

EDEN

SURVIVAL TIP #62
*The tightrope between despair and hope
can become a safety line
. . . or a noose.*

The next day, the Sinners are still suspiciously quiet.

As the rain continues to pour, I watch the trees from the porch outside, Lucky's arms around my waist, but I only catch glimpses of the Sinners.

Occasionally, Dom sends Jayk, Jasper, or Lucky up to the moat for a better look, but an immediate storm of bullets is always quick to warn them back.

Occasionally, a Sinner creeps forward—from the front, the sides, sometimes fast, sometimes slow, sometimes one after the other, and sometimes with long dragging waits in between. Each time, Dom sends his own bullet-storm back.

It keeps everyone tense and on their toes—and between that and the wounded groaning through the house, the rain soaking cold into our bones, and the awful moment we hit the last of the raided supplies from the Reapers . . .

Bristlebrook feels like a tomb.

TWO DAYS after the attack on Bristlebrook, we lock ourselves into the surveillance room, deciding to watch the Sinners through the few remaining cameras instead.

My brutes gather around to watch the screens, their shoulders and matching intensity feeling too large for the small room. Not even Lucky makes a quip when I slide onto Jasper's lap, and his arm slips around my waist with warm reassurance.

Leaning us forward, Jasper skips through footage from the attack, then slows it.

Through the blurry drops that mar the camera lenses, we see Alastair directing a strictly regimented camp into life that rolls with so many neatly ordered tents, we can only get a partial view. We see the heavy-set bald man from the fight shouting in the face of a distinguished-looking older man who cleans his glasses in disgust when he walks off. We see Mateo overseeing a dozen men as they chop down trees, and Dom curses.

When I glance back at him, his face is grim.

"To span the moat," he explains, and my stomach turns.

Jayk grimaces, crossing his arms over his chest as he leans against the wall. "It was never going to slow them long."

I went to bed with him last night in Dom's room, though at some point he traded out for Jasper, and I somehow woke up with neither —Lucky and Beau stirred me awake with kisses and small jokes before Dom stuck his head in and told us to get dressed.

Now, Lucky's eyes are cold on the screens. "We still have the C-4. Frags. I want to see them try."

Jasper taps through a few more images and the recording shifts to another angle.

And we see Heather.

My breath catches in shock.

"Oh, no. No, not that. Better to beat her." Beau's distress crashes into my own, and I slip off Jasper's lap to step in close to one of the screens.

"She's lucky they didn't kill her. Those explosives are invaluable," Jasper mutters, but he sounds equally unhappy.

Deliberately, through the muck and the mud and fighting every step, Heather is being hauled along behind Alastair by a leash.

A dog's leash.

Heather is shackled and collared like a dog.

Jayk mutters a curse as another Sinner spits on her face, and rows of the filthy men are lined up to do the same. They trip her and shove her back when she staggers, and I search her for any sign of injury. It's not much relief when I don't find any.

I'm not sure Heather has it in her to cry, but I might for her.

At one point, she rushes Alastair's back, crashing into him, and he twists the leash, dropping her to her knees under him. In the rain, they glare at each other as the Sinners shout from the sidelines, and my palms sweat as I touch the glass like I might be able to change the outcome.

Bentley tries to shove forward out of the crowd toward Heather, but he's shackled, if not leashed, and Mateo kicks the backs of his legs out from under him.

Behind Alastair, the bald man stalks up, his eyes on Heather, until the distinguished man from earlier intercepts him with a nervous expression.

Finally, Alastair drags Heather to her feet.

And she spits in his face.

THREE DAYS after the attack on Bristlebrook, a dreary sun begins to peek from the clouds—and the Sinners grow bolder. They run forward in random bursts to fire on us, and the sound of their bullets pattering against our makeshift metal defenses replaces the rain. Each time, the Sinners roar their approval.

And Alastair stands right on the tree line, watching with spine-chilling calm.

The Sinners are far enough away, and our defenses are thick enough, that the bullets rarely pierce through, but the fear of ricochets keep everyone's heads low and someone from the medical team on standby.

And it doesn't help anyone's nerves.

Not even when Dom manages to snipe several Sinners as they retreat.

More death just means more bodies, and with the new sun, our moat is beginning to reek.

"Mantlets," Arthur offers with a wan smile as I pour him out a cup of pale orange slop. "You made mantlets."

He's sitting on the porch amid dozens of other Reapers and civilians and his own people who are all mixed together. Despite the carnage and the fear, despite everyone keeping one eye on the trees, there's a low roll of friendly chatter over the group.

The good living alongside the bad.

I smile softly.

There's far too much banality in a siege to spend the entire time fretting.

"Jayk did it," I tell Arthur proudly, and he nods as he drinks my slop.

He doesn't even flinch, still staring, and I follow his gaze. He's looking out over the battlefield.

No, not the battlefield, I realize. He's looking at the moat.

"The rats will come here next," he tells me in a low, sure voice. "We need to talk to Alastair."

Rats.

I stare at him, stricken, then look back. There's a Sinner corpse half-hanging into the moat, and it takes a moment of watching before I see it . . . *move.*

The rats are *eating* him.

Arthur begins murmuring, describing deterrents for rats, but I can't look away from the twitching body in the distance.

There are two Reapers close to death in the med bay, and Cole is fighting a vicious infection from his leg wound. If they die . . . what are we going to do with the bodies?

I know now Beau almost lost his life dragging the man he lost into the moat.

It takes me another long moment before I can swallow and move on. We don't need to borrow trouble.

There's enough already here.

This time, as I move over the porch, people hold up their cups and take the ladled slop with tired smiles and quiet murmurs of "thanks, Eden" and "appreciate it, ma'am."

Sawyer pauses his debate with Jennifer when I approach, tipping his head like he's still wearing his hat, and when I move to Jennifer, curled against his chest, he absently gestures at me to give her more.

" . . . I just think it would make sense to see if the Sinners are willing to negotiate. I don't want my friends to die," Jennifer is saying. "Madison is still there, and—"

"They'll do much worse than kill you if they get their hands on you," Sawyer argues heatedly, and I feel the anxious desperation bleeding off him. "Forget Madison, sweet one. She's gone. Just . . . just trust me on this. You don't want to surrender yourself to the Sinners. There's no talking. We *need* to attack."

My hand shakes as I reluctantly pour a little more into Jennifer's cup, silently calculating every ounce we have left.

No one pours it out or makes quips about the taste. We're down to two scoops a day, so they only close their hands around it and drink it gratefully.

I hate that it makes me want to hoard it all for myself and my brutes.

I hate that it makes me afraid.

I'm as exhausted and hungry as they are. My brutes are exhausted and hungry. By unspoken agreement, no one is fucking anymore. Instead, we take our rest when we can get it. Where we can get it. I take it with whichever of my brutes I can when I'm not drowning in tasks.

When I finish feeding everyone, Jayk's waiting for me at the end of the porch, and he slugs a cup of slop back without a word, those midnight eyes on my face.

He's dirty and tired from the day, and he lets me lead him upstairs and strip him off. I wash him under Dom's cold shower just to see him smirk at his own asshole-ish handiwork.

And then we sleep.

FOUR DAYS after the attack on Bristlebrook, we gather in Jasper and Lucky's room at my request. It's the most comfortable place for all of us right now.

As we sip our slop, I tentatively broach the topic of the farm animals. Kasey had food dumped in their pen the night of the attack, but they haven't had anything since. There's nothing left *to* give them.

But they could feed us.

" . . . I think we need to try it," I finish, trying to ignore the way Beau is absently playing with my hair. "We only have a few more days of my slop left, and if Alastair is intent on waiting us out . . ."

Lucky walks away when I suggest it, running a hand down his face, and my heart tugs.

He's been fine with most of the farm animals being used as livestock, but I know he has a soft spot for a few of them. Henrietta the needy chicken. Billy and Baa-bara, his favorite goats.

My favorite goats.

They give me cheese.

"Too risky," Dom tells me grimly. "They're too loud. We try to get them through the side tunnel, there's a good chance we give it away. The chickens . . ."

"Likely wouldn't have survived this long. Maybe some, on insects and . . . and carrion." Jasper's eyes are sympathetic on Lucky's face, and Lucky grimaces as he sits on the arm of a chair.

But he nods.

"Their cave is all of about fifteen feet away from the side tunnel," Beau pipes up, his fingers tangled in my hair. "We've only seen a few patrols out that way, and there's no sign Alastair has any idea that we have another exit. We should do it. Ethel is . . ." He sighs. "We have a few that could use the food. It might give us enough that we can at least evacuate a few people. Small groups during the night. If they're careful and have enough rations to get them back to Red Zone . . ."

They might make it.

I finish his sentence in my head, and I lean back against him. He presses a kiss to my hair.

"Damn it, why *is* Alastair waiting us out?" Jayk growls, prowling the room. "If he has his fucking explosives, why not use them?"

"You think he's bluffing?" Lucky asks, his head lifting, and Dom stands, severe and grim.

"Is it a bluff you want to call?"

THEY GO for the animals that night, in the early hours just before dawn, coming back with just two pigs and three chickens. I close my eyes as I listen to the sounds of the subsequent slaughter. I'm not usually squeamish about death—not after several years in the forest. When I was lucky enough to catch a rabbit or fish, I did what I needed to. Hunger has a way of stripping away anything but the need to survive.

But this time it feels different, and it's not because these animals were cute and familiar.

It's because their deaths mean we truly have nothing left and no way of getting more.

Once that meat is gone . . . we're next.

They work for hours, stripping the meat, smoking it, preserving the blood and bones and organs. We'll use everything.

When it all becomes too much to bear, I turn inside, taking the stairs two at a time. Jasper has already turned in to rest before he needs to go back out on watch. I'll lie with him for a while.

No one is more calming than Jasper, awake or asleep.

But when I turn into the hall, I freeze.

Hearing me, Lucky and Jasper freeze, too.

Between them, a patchy brown goat bleats, backing into its friend.

My jaw drops as Lucky and Jasper exchange a look, and I realize Lucky has a silky black hen tucked under his jacket.

"You went *back* for them?" I hiss, my heart jabbing, panicky, against my ribcage.

The danger of it is *stupid*. Reckless. Besides, those animals are food, and we don't have anything to feed them, and oh God. No. He can't have gone back for them just *now*. Dom wouldn't have left them behind if they'd been with the others when my brutes did their trip.

Which means . . . they'd already been moved.

Lucky's guilty expression makes me narrow my eyes on him.

Exactly *how many times* did he risk his neck today to get his pets back here?

I look at Jasper and color floods his cheeks. He grimaces.

"He begged very nicely," he admits, and I press a finger between my brows.

Jasper *helped*.

I'm not sure if I'm more impressed by Lucky's ability to wheedle what he wants out of our supposedly terrifying sadist, or if I'm still mostly frightened for them risking so much . . . especially when I only see this ending one way.

I try to ignore a third feeling nudging its way to the surface.

"Eden! Move your ass. Food's almost ready," Jayk barks from downstairs, and I jump, my head whipping back toward the inner balcony.

"Eden," Lucky calls softly.

My name is a plea.

In his jacket, Henrietta squawks, her head bobbing up to peck at Lucky's beard. His fingers are buried in her feathers.

Giving him a final glance, I stride over to the balcony and look down at Jayk. He's leaning tiredly against the wall, waiting.

"I'm just helping someone. I'll be down in a few minutes," I call to him with as straight a face as I can muster, judiciously not lying.

He scowls, the beginnings of a stubborn glare kindling, and I brace my hands on the balustrade.

"Jayk, who gets to decide my priorities?" I ask with a dangerous smile, and the glare turns grumpy.

"You do," he mutters.

"And *whose* responsibility is it to feed me?"

He kicks off the wall, rolling his eyes. "Help them fix their shit, then get down here. We can fight about it while I stuff your face."

Can't wait.

When I'm sure he's gone, I rush back down the hall, and Lucky whispers a fervent, "Thank you, beautiful."

"Just open the door," I tell him, and we hustle Billy, Baa-bara, and Henrietta into Jasper's room.

I close the door behind us, and when I turn, Billy is already nibbling on Jasper's bedspread, and Jasper chases after her with a panicked admonition.

Lucky sets Henrietta down, and she pecks thankfully at his feet before strutting off. He straightens, giving me a nervous smile.

I lean back against the door while Jasper enters into a tug of war with a goat, his expression narrow-eyed and livid.

"How did you get them past the civilians?" I ask evenly, and Lucky gives me a sheepish look.

"I didn't. I bribed a few of them with hair care products and they let us through."

"Of course you did," I mutter to myself. "The others didn't notice they were missing?"

Lucky rubs the back of his head, and it dislodges his hair tie. The golden strands bunch and fall around his shoulders in a way that I'm not entirely sure was an accident, no matter how innocent he looks.

"Nah, they just wanted to get in and get out. There was already . . . a lot of death." Something darker flickers over his expression, and my stomach turns.

In the background, Jasper succeeds in wrenching the bedspread out of the goat's mouth—only for the other one to start urinating on his rug.

Jasper's head tips back, defeated.

But I'm focused on Lucky.

"Why didn't you just set them free?" I glance at Henrietta, and my heart tugs as I remember my first night here and the way she snuggled against Lucky's chest.

I've been sharing him even before I realized it.

"It might have been kinder," I add more softly.

Lucky's expression firms up, his dimples nowhere to be found. "I'm not having civilians die because I'm sentimental, Eden. I just . . ." He looks down at Henrietta, too, and his lashes brush his cheekbones as he sighs. "I just don't think we're there yet. There's still hope."

Hope.

My eyes grow hot as I watch him. He's so beautiful, I ache.

He still has hope. Despite everything.

And he believes in it enough to *fight* for it.

I've never had that kind of optimism, but with him . . . I'm starting to.

I look away, swallowing hard before I burst into tears, and I hear Jasper murmur.

"You see? He's wicked, isn't he?"

I choke on a laugh, nodding my agreement, then fix Lucky with a stern stare as I walk over to him. Grasping his shirt in both hands, I shake him lightly.

"Next time, *come to me*," I tell him, and his startled blue eyes have all the quick-running currents of rivers and waterfalls.

I dampen my lips as the prick of hurt and jealousy comes to the surface. "I'll *be* your distraction, Lucky. I'll be your partner in crime. I'll . . . drive the getaway car or steal the bazooka or cover for you, even from the others. I'll help you with the stupid plans, okay?" I sniff as my voice wobbles. "And, okay, I might try to make the plans a little less stupid, but my point is . . . you don't need to keep secrets from me." Tears well in my eyes, and I soothe my hands over his chest. "If it's important to you, then it's *everything* to me. I'm on *your* team."

His thumb finds my cheek, wiping away the tear, and the next thing I know, he's spinning me around, kissing me with the kind of reckless, joyful passion only Lucky lives and breathes.

When he finally sets me down, he laughs, and his eyes are glassy, too.

"That might be the most romantic thing anyone has ever said to me," he says, then adds absently, "Sorry, Jasper."

"Oh no, never mind me," Jasper mutters behind us.

But Lucky's still looking down at me with the brightest, softest glow, his dimples staggering my heart with their cruel happiness in the middle of this awful day.

"Partners in crime it is, beautiful."

I grin back at him, drinking in the joy, when there's a musical rap at the door.

"When you're all done being as sneaky as a cow in a bullpen," Beau drawls from the other side, "come down for some food."

Lucky freezes under my hand, and Jasper looks up from where he's scrubbing at his rug.

I hear Beau push off the door as his voice turns dry.

"And Dom says to take the goats outside. At least out there they can graze."

FIVE DAYS after the attack on Bristlebrook, the arguing gets heated and this time, we can't even contain it to a quiet room.

The clash between Arthur and Sawyer breaks out in the kitchen while I'm showing Soren how to make a bone broth, and it's loud enough to make Kasey stick her head in.

Her brows drop as she takes them in, and she disappears a moment later.

" . . . so, we need to attack," Sawyer snaps, his mustache bristling with anger.

Arthur throws his hands up, his cheeks red and splotchy. "They have us starved. Out-gunned. If they bring those trees across the moat, they can storm us—"

"Then we'll shoot them! Throw grenades before they get them down!" Sawyer slams his hand down on the counter, and Soren flinches, then hides it with a grimace. Sawyer's voice lifts. "There's no *talking* to Alastair, you old fool. We're not trying it!"

Behind them, in the distance through the cracked kitchen window, the apple tree sways, and Jayk's abandoned throne glints in the sun. Too close to the moat to be protected, it's peppered with bullet holes now.

"Don't you call me an old fool, you uneducated lout! I have three PhDs! I know what I'm talking about!" Arthur roars back.

"You don't know Alastair!" Sawyer claps back.

"Oh-ho. No, not like you do."

"What the hell is that supposed to mean?" Sawyer grits out.

There's sweat beading along his hairline, though the afternoon is cool, and I glance down at Soren, standing carefully still.

He only just got out of bed today.

Setting down the pot lid, I pat his hand, then take a few steps forward, enough to get Arthur to abandon whatever argument he was about to spit out. I keep the counter between me and the men as my lips firm.

"You two need to find somewhere else to have this discussion," I tell them politely, and Sawyer finally looks at me, anger and frustration snapping in his eyes.

My pulse leaps nervously, but Arthur's shamefaced expression bolsters me, and I find more steel as I add, "I suggest finding Dom. You'll need him for any decision-making, anyway."

I've barely finished the words before Dom and Beau are skidding through the door, Kasey cool on their heels. She nods at Soren to come, and with a sigh, he removes his apron and leaves the kitchen.

Dom waits for him to leave, then slams the door in Kasey's face before she can barge in.

His expression is hard and disapproving as he turns to look at Arthur and Sawyer. "What's going on?"

Too casually, Beau strolls over to the other side of the room, leaning against the wall.

Boxing them in.

Arthur sighs, relaxing as Dom appears. "Yes, well, I think we need to concede. Nothing is changing, except for the worse. Historically, sieges are effective unless there's something significant to change the status quo. After their raid on the Reapers, they have enough food, water, and resources to sustain them—far more than we do. We . . . I'm sorry to say it, but we need to surrender, or we're going to die."

Sawyer is shaking his head as Arthur talks—panicked little shakes.

"No, no, *no*. We can't surrender. There *is* no surrendering to Alastair. He's ruthless, he'll *kill* us." Sawyer looks over at Dom, desperate and imploring. "We can't talk to him. *You can't.* We need to kill him first. We *need* to attack! If we want *any* of us to survive, we need to attack." He points at me, and I stiffen. "Her. Eden. You want to keep her safe? If we hand ourselves over, Alastair will kill her too."

Tension snaps through the room.

"Stop pointing at her, friend," Beau drawls, but his pretty woodland eyes are deep, dark forests right now.

Sawyer drops his hand, but he shakes his head again. "We can use the side tunnel. Blow 'em up while they're sleeping, like how you ambushed us for the raid. We can—"

"Alastair was a SEAL, Sawyer. He knows how to keep a watch. It's different. We attack him, it won't be much of a surprise," Dom bites back, impatience simmering under his words. "They have explosives too, three times what we have. It could be worth trying to talk to him before we give away our side tunnel. If it doesn't work, we might be able to get some small groups out without them getting caught."

"*Do* they have explosives?" Sawyer bursts out. "I heard even your boys muttering about it. Why haven't they used them? Talking to Alastair is a *death warrant*."

His desperation crawls over my nerves.

"They don't need to waste their explosives!" Arthur interjects heatedly. "I'm sorry, I've tried to be polite, but you're being unreasonable. We should look at every avenue to survive before we do something we can't take back!"

Sawyer turns, storming toward him with blazing eyes, and Dom lunges forward to catch him with a curse.

"He killed *dozens* of us. Here, back home." His voice cracks. "You can't trust anything he says. He's bluffing. I bet you he doesn't have *any* expl—"

The air detonates in a deafening, blistering roar, and I've dived behind the counter, my heart hammering before I realize it was outside. Something exploded outside.

"Eden?" Beau calls sharply.

"I'm okay, I— What was . . .?"

"Grenade launcher. Single directed shot," Dom replies, and he storms out of the kitchen.

I stand as fast as I dove, my hands shaking . . . and it doesn't take long to see the damage.

Through the window, the apple tree is no longer swaying. Two of its branches have been blown off, and its trunk is newly blackened and peppered with debris.

Beside it, there's nothing.

Only a giant, flaming crater where Jayk's throne used to be.

Six days after the attack on Bristlebrook, we raise a white flag, and Alastair finally leaves the tree line to walk up to the moat.

And he agrees to parley.

Chapter 64

Eden

Walking across the bridge feels like walking to our gallows, but we were left with little choice. Alastair had very distinct instructions, and we had no grounds on which to negotiate.

Just beyond our moat, he's set up four seats in a half circle on the grass—for himself, Mateo, and one each for the cold-eyed bald man and the disapproving distinguished man we saw through our surveillance cameras.

The area was cleared by Sinners this afternoon. They kicked putrid corpses into the moat until their flesh split over the pikes and gaseous juices spewed out. The half-eaten faces of Sinners and Reapers alike stare up out of the moat, and I fight my rising gorge with every step over the bridge . . . because that *smell*. It's swamp-thick—sour and miasmic in the humidity. I've smelled death before. I've smelled rot and decayed flesh. But never so much. Not like this.

"Watch your step, Eden," Jasper murmurs behind me on the bridge, and I readjust the chair in my arms, determined not to look down.

Behind me, Jayk, Lucky, and Beau back away from the bridge with slow, pained reluctance, but I don't look back.

We argued for hours about who should be here for this meeting. It started three to one against my presence at all—Jayk, Lucky, and Beau all having very vocal opinions about me needing to be safely inside. Preferably bound and in Bubble Wrap.

In Beau's case, with a butt plug in place waiting for him to return.

Dom and Jasper were quieter, letting me speak for myself. And I did. Because I need to be here.

Alastair knows me. He's willing to deal with me. I'm the only one who has had conversations with him outside of beatings and interrogations, and I'm the one who got us free at Cyanide. I understand him. Worse . . . I *trusted* him.

Alastair is my mistake to fix.

My brutes might be better equipped for raids and razing buildings, but if I need to wait on the sidelines while they put themselves in danger to utilize those skills, then they need to do the same for me.

This is *my* battleground.

And we need cooler heads to prevail.

Which is why Dom and Jasper are with me, and Jayk, Beau, and Lucky are on sniper duty.

Dom steps off the bridge first, and he holds out a hand to me to help me down. I don't have it in me to smile right now, but I squeeze his fingers as I pass him.

The seated Sinners watch us approach with varying degrees of civility, their rifles all within casual reach.

Nodding to them with as much politeness as I can muster, I set up my own chair opposite Alastair. Jasper sits beside me, then Dom on my other side. Arthur and Sawyer trail over last, setting up on either side of Jasper and Dom respectively, until we're all sitting in a matching semi-circle opposite the Sinners.

I have reservations about what either Arthur or Sawyer might say or do to risk any negotiations—particularly Sawyer, given the emotional state he's in—but we had no right to keep them from this. This affects their people, too.

"Why'd you bring the female?" the bald man asks, throwing one muscled, sunburned arm over the back of his chair. His eyes are light and lecherous . . . far too much like the snake tattooed on his hand.

On his other side, the older white-haired man adjusts his glasses as he glances at the bald Sinner. It doesn't quite hide his moue of distaste, and relief flickers inside me. If we can rely on the Sinners for anything, it's chaos and division, and if Alastair is trying to balance battling factions, then there might be *something* we can use there.

The Sinners do love their coups.

"Be polite, Bane," Alastair replies softly, though from his voice or demeanor it hardly looks like he cares. "We all enjoy our toys."

Bane snorts, and Dom turns to stone beside me, and I silently pray for him to stop being so easy to read.

Being Dom's toy is galaxies apart from being a man like Bane's.

A galaxy of choice. A galaxy of respect.

Jasper remains far more impassive, only lifting a single, bored brow.

"Oh, that's not . . ." Arthur starts, shifting uncomfortably in his chair before he falters. His hands are visibly sweaty and shake in his lap as he adds in a mumble, "I don't think that's productive."

My heart warms at his defense, even as I wish he'd drop it. I don't need him to defend me.

Rage sparks under my ribcage as I look at Alastair, but I force a smile.

"Hello, Alastair. I believe you've met Dominic, our commander at Bristlebrook, and Jasper. Arthur here took over for Bentley in his absence at Red Zone, and this is—"

"Sawyer," the older man finishes for me with a brief glance at the Reaper. "Yes. We've . . . encountered one another."

His moue of distaste increases, and I begin to wonder if I'm mistaken.

Perhaps it's just his face.

Sawyer scoffs, slouched in his seat, and he presses the palms of his hands against his eyes.

"*Encountered*," he mutters. Dropping his hands, he looks at me and Dom bitterly, desperation raw in his eyes. "You hear that? They *encountered* our home. They encountered Buck right here! His body is still in the . . ."

He cuts himself off, shaking his head, and concern hits me hard.

He's sweating, far more than the late afternoon heat can account for.

"Interesting," Alastair murmurs, lifting his hand to quiet the men by his side. His pretty, pale green eyes are like shards of sharpened sea glass on Sawyer.

I don't need to look to know what he sees.

If Dom is transparent, Sawyer is holding up a billboard of anxious grief and rage.

Sawyer hasn't shaved in days, and his mustache is beginning to bleed into the beginnings of a beard. There are deep, stressed lines etched into his face, and he's spent as much time by Cole's fevered bedside as he has on watch against the Sinners. I don't think he's been sleeping.

He fought right up until the last moment against this meeting, and I'm deeply worried he shouldn't have come.

Some blood feuds run too deep, and he's lost too much.

Mateo catches my eye briefly, his glossy brown curls glinting in the sun, and he gives me a tense half-smile.

He *cannot* be serious.

My eyes narrow on him at the sheer audacity. I haven't forgotten how he threatened my brutes at Cyanide. I remember Beau's split cheek, and the rifle he pressed to the back of *my* head. I remember him shooting that Reaper in his face. God, they've been firing on us for days. It's a miracle no civilians have been seriously hurt.

And then there's Heather.

My lips flatten, remembering Mateo holding Bentley back from helping her. Doing *nothing* to stop it.

The oozy stench from the moat is thick enough to taste, and Arthur presses a patterned handkerchief to his bulbous nose.

"Very interesting," Alastair repeats, but then he sits forward, his forearms pressed to his thighs, and his gaze flicks to me . . . and then continues on.

To *Dom*.

The surprise of it has me studying him sharply.

What is he *doing*?

"Say what you came here to say, Ranger. You have our attention." Alastair's smile is like a cool, warning slip of ice before an avalanche. "You would like to petition me to spare your lives, I imagine?"

"Good luck," Bane mutters. He yanks a heavy dagger out of his waistband and begins picking thick muck out from under his blunt fingernails.

Dom pauses, glancing down at me in silent query, and I bury a frown.

We'd all assumed, after the way Alastair talked at Cyanide—after he insisted on dealing only with *me*, and the scathing way he insulted Dom—that it would be the same here, but . . . something is off.

Alastair is barely acknowledging my presence.

Insecure thoughts and gnawing worries surge to the surface. Have I overestimated myself? Alastair has already manipulated me soundly, after all. He secured his freedom from me, and maybe that was the only reason he ever dealt with me.

Maybe he's ignoring me because I've served my purpose . . . and now I can be disregarded like all the rest.

Like I have been most of my life.

My gaze tracks slowly from Alastair to Bane, lazy and crude—a Sam man through and through. I look at the older man, who offers me a bland, polite acknowledgement as he examines Dom with thick suspicion. I look at Mateo, silent and watchful.

And I banish my insecurities.

Alastair is always playing a game, and I don't need to trust him to trust my own instincts.

He's an intentional man. Ignoring me is intentional. Bringing both of these men out here is intentional. I don't know yet who he's performing for—and why—but I do know what he *wants*.

Power is a slippery thing, and Alastair is clutching at it with both hands.

And *that's* a game with possibilities.

It's a lot easier to take a throne than it is to keep it.

Surreptitiously, I nod to Dom. If Alastair wants him to take the lead as his first move, then I'll allow it. Dom can have this conversation as well as I can.

And it gives me a moment to understand the nature of what's on the board.

"We're not petitioning for anything," Dom says coldly. "You need to leave. Pack up your weapons and go back to your Den. Do that, release the captives you're holding there, and then we'll *consider* discussing other arrangements that could benefit you. Trade deals for food and the goods you need for your people. But this siege is done. Your harassment of Red Zone and your continued attacks against the Reapers are *done*. It's not the Sinners' reign anymore—and if you want to have any place in this new world, you'll do it by agreement and not by force."

This time, as Dom faces Alastair, his shoulders are straight, and there's nothing but contempt in the harsh set of his mouth. It's the most chilling expression I've ever seen on his face.

I never, *ever* want that look directed at me.

At Dom's words, Mateo's brows fly up, and a startled grin flashes over his angelic face. He shakes his head to himself, glancing at Alastair . . . who has only tilted his head curiously. It shows the shiny, slow-healing burns that crawl up his neck, mangling his tattoos.

Burns from *his* last loss, right here at Bristlebrook.

To *us*.

The reminder steadies me.

"You fucking *what*?" Bane drops his casual sprawl over the chair, and he starts to laugh. It's a harsh, chopping sound. "You hear this shit, Alastair? They've got some heavy fucking balls, I'll give them that."

Bane gets up off his chair, stalking around behind it, his dagger swinging up so he can rub his scalp with the hilt, and the sudden motion makes me flinch. With apparent boredom, Jasper crosses his legs. It shifts him slightly closer to me. Close enough that his leg brushes mine.

The light breeze makes my scalp tingle.

"You don't seem to get it, shit for brains." Bane snorts, then points his dagger at the trees. "*Army*."

Turning, he points it back at Bristlebrook. "A whole lot of dead bitches."

His blade glints in the fading sun.

Dropping his arm with a smirk, Bane turns back to Dom and grips himself through his jeans. "Unless you want to hand your whores over for a bit of fun. We can work out a good price . . . like your neck." He smirks, and he glances at me. "I'll even let you keep that one. Though she looks like she has a real fat pair of—"

"Ugh, Bane," the older man interrupts, waving a hand like he's fanning away a bad smell. "Can you think of nothing else?" He turns to Alastair, dipping his head confidingly. "Respectfully, I think we should at least hear out the suggestion here. It's certainly more sustainable than—"

"Yes, Sullivan. I'm aware of your position," Alastair murmurs with cavernous finality as Bane sneers at the back of the older man's white head.

My gaze flicks between them, then over to Mateo, who is glaring into the sky like the lone cloud has committed some personal offense against him.

Alastair sits back in his chair slowly, watching Dom, the hint of something dangerously humored in the cut of his face. "I am curious why you think we would agree to your demands. As my dear friend Bane here has . . . eloquently . . . pointed out, we do have you at a disadvantage."

Dom's face doesn't change. "We have ten pounds of C-4, two dozen frags, more than a hundred trained recruits, all armed and ready to fight, a Gustaf with dozens of rounds—you might remember it," he adds to Alastair, who dips his burned chin in polite acknowledgement. "And that's just what I'll tell you about. You know what Rangers can do, SEAL. I have no concerns at all about doing it to you."

Alastair's eyes gleam.

His body is lean and hard and dark-clad. He has a pistol at his hip, but no other weapons visible. Just his tattoos snagging their thorny branches and poisoned flowers into his skin.

Alastair doesn't need to throw himself around like Bane.

The more still he is, the more he makes me afraid.

Mateo's curls shake again. "These Rangers, Alastair. The egos. Always with the egos."

Alastair exchanges a brief, knowing look with him before glancing back at Dom.

"You have all that and you haven't used it yet," Alastair muses. "Why?"

"We want peace, Alastair. It's all we've ever wanted," Arthur interjects evenly. His damp hands haven't stopped anxiously knotting in his shirt since we sat down.

"They *haven't* used any weapons because they fucking can't! They're *afraid*," Bane mocks.

Whipping around, Bane stabs his knife into his chair, then yanks it out again . . . and he watches my face the entire time. A sick, expectant anticipation crawls behind his eyes.

And it twists into a hot, dark rage when I only glance back at Alastair.

I hide the clammy nervousness that courses through my stomach at Bane's look. I hate that I'm still so afraid of men like this, when they're so unworthy of it.

But his reaction tells me a lot.

Sullivan's tells me more.

The division among the Sinners clearly wasn't cured by hanging Sam and a few of his cronies. It's still thriving, and Alastair is still riding the chaos.

Only, this time, Alastair isn't playing the quiet hero.

Alastair is dismissing me to pander to Bane, and he's sidelining Sullivan for the same reason.

So, how much pull do Sam's men still have among the Sinners? Is this all just a show of strength for Bane's benefit? Are these attacks on the Reapers, on *us*, designed to appease the bloodthirst and resource-mongering of Bane and all the rest of Sam's disgruntled men? Is he here to put us in our place and be seen doing it?

If that's the case, if that's who Alastair is catering to—if that's who really controls the Sinners—then the captive women have no hope.

Alastair won't risk losing his position.

That, I can be sure of.

"You know why we haven't attacked," I say softly to Alastair, testing the waters.

I've never wanted to be wrong more in my life, but right or wrong, I'm tired of being his pawn.

Alastair doesn't turn his head, but his eyes flick to me, and I examine his face.

"A lot of our people will die if we need to fight, Alastair. We want to avoid that, if we can." My gaze hardens. "But if we can't, I will personally ensure that we wipe out as many of your men as we can while we do it. Starting with you."

"*Why* is *the bitch* talking?" Bane shouts, his cheeks flushed with anger.

Before I can flinch, Dom has me yanked onto his lap, and Bane's knife slams down again.

This time into the seat where I was sitting.

I stare at it as it vibrates—and I'm vibrating, too. The metal winks in the day's last sun, and my pulse roars in my ears as Dom shoves me behind him, his pistol drawn.

A bullet explodes in the grass between Bane's feet, and I scramble back.

Another comes from the trees, and it buckles one leg of Sawyer's chair.

This isn't a game.

Someone grabs me, taking me to the ground as the men start to surge together. Bullets mince the ground around me as my blood roars in my ears, adrenaline flooding me. I cringe, and damp dirt smears against my cheek.

It's not a game, it's not a game, it's not a game.

Damn it, I know it's not. It never was.

I watch Sawyer's back as he flees across the bridge. Arthur is sprawled over me, and his large, soft body shakes around mine in a protective shield.

" . . . weapons *down*," Jasper is saying sharply. "We have several sharpshooters with you in their sights. That was a warning shot, Bane. The next will be between your brows, even if your men take us all out in the next moment."

"Idiot!" Sullivan is shouting at Bane. "You'll kill us all with this!"

"Whores. Shouldn't. *Speak*," Bane shouts back.

"Eden?"

Alastair hasn't moved from his chair.

He's the only one still seated.

The chaos around us pauses at his soft, spidery voice, and it takes me a moment before I can lift my head. Two tries before I can speak, one wary eye on Bane.

"Yes?" I whisper.

"Go and fetch us all some ale and a pot of this morning's lunch." Once again, Alastair's gaze only glances over me as he nods toward the trees. "My dog will help you bring it out."

He gives Bane a slight, amused smile, and finally, Bane stops glaring at me long enough to snort.

His dog.

I remember the leash. Her collar.

He's talking about Heather.

I stare at Alastair, horrified, trying to find any hint of the man who told me harming women was not his vision for the future, but he doesn't so much as look at me.

He's so cold, I catch the chill.

"Mateo, show her the way?" Alastair asks dismissively, and Dom steps forward in warning as Mateo stands.

Mateo has his own wickedly sharp dagger in hand in the next instant—but he only palms it once, and then it disappears as fast as it came.

"She's not leaving the clearing," Dom says bluntly.

He looms over Alastair, and Jasper's hand falls to his pistol.

Alastair only smiles. "Then neither will you."

The air feels too thick to breathe—soupy with tension and testosterone.

Beyond the moat, I hear the creak of wood and Jayk's distant shouts to hold fire . . . so many friends who have my back. I can have theirs.

Defuse. I need to defuse this.

I need to go, like Alastair said.

It's not trust. Maybe I will die if I walk into those woods—out of range of my brutes' snipers and in among the snakes. Maybe I'll become their hostage. Maybe something awful will happen.

But something awful will certainly happen if I stay.

And there are worse things than getting a glimpse behind enemy lines right now.

Especially if I can see Heather.

"I'll do it," I whisper, and Mateo's shoulders loosen. I hide my frown and raise my voice. "I'd . . . I'd like to serve you all. It would be my pleasure."

Jasper's eyes press closed in defeat, his lashes a dark crescent against his cheekbones.

"Eden . . ." Dom starts tightly, but I turn to him, resting a hand on his arm.

"Please, sir, I want to do this," I whisper. "*Trust me.*"

He flinches, looking away, and his jaw clenches.

"Shit." Bane smirks, the angry color riding his gleaming scalp beginning to calm. "*Sir.* Now that's fun."

Dom's arm is trembling under mine, and I ache for his restraint.

I won't go if he refuses.

I won't undermine him again . . . even if it kills me.

"Go, Eden," Jasper says, his voice so sharp and clipped it slices me.

This hurts him too, but he knows better than most why I need to do this. And as his gaze lingers on Mateo, I know he sees it.

Because Jasper plays chess, too.

"Bring us back something good," he murmurs.

Finally, Dom nods, and I breathe out a sigh of relief.

As Mateo leads me into the woods.

CHAPTER 65

EDEN

SURVIVAL TIP #129
*You can't find the right answer,
if you only ask the wrong questions.*

The broody trees close in around us, hiding us from my brutes, and the small hairs on the back of my neck prickle to life. Mateo starts humming, and it takes a moment for me to recognize the tune.

If you go down in the woods today, you're sure of a big surprise . . .

"Stop that," I snap at him, hating the fear that bites at me.

Mateo slides a look at me. "Stop acting so afraid."

"Why would it be an act?"

Sinners stalk through the trees, some watching the meeting from the tree line, most lingering around their camps. I hate that they look organized. I hate the bulging bags of food I see near almost every tent. I hate the smells of things being cooked and how my stomach begs on its knees for a taste. I hate the weapons and ammunition that flash at me with my every step.

They're so prepared.

There are also so many more tents than we could see from the cameras, and silently, I begin counting them.

"Because you're supposed to be smart," Mateo breathes.

His hand is light on my back, he gestures for me to turn.

I swallow hard, eyeing him. He's beautiful and broody, and he still looks as sweet and unassuming as he did the first day I met him.

I know he isn't, though.

I step over a branch, and when I crane my head to keep counting tents, I accidentally bump into a rough-faced Sinner. He whirls around, his hands raised to grab me, but then he catches sight of Mateo.

His hands drop.

But his dark eyes follow me as I scurry past a line of tents, trying desperately not to be noticed.

Focus. You're okay. Don't pay attention to them. They're not here.

Ten tents to a row. Nine rows deep.

God. They still have ninety men. How many more times do I have to watch my brutes face death?

Sooner or later, the odds will catch up with them.

I slow, staring at the tents, at the *men*, and Mateo reaches out a hand to guide me.

I walk past it without glancing at him.

"Are you mad at me, *gatita*?" Mateo asks, and he sounds amused, though it's etched in something closer to . . . resignation?

"You killed friends of mine," I reply, my voice feeling tight and too hot. I hate that I still feel betrayed by them. "Yes, I'm *mad* at you, Mateo."

Mateo stops outside a sprawling clearing, and I catch glimpses of an enormous tent inside it, far bigger than the ones lined up outside. There's a sudden shout through the trees—and a violent crash of metal.

His eyes narrowing at the sound, Mateo nods at me to go ahead.

Tentatively, I lift a branch as I make my way in, his footsteps at my heels.

And his murmured reply chases me.

"You need better friends."

I step out into the clearing, taking in the smoking fire and the small cookpot Heather is standing next to. A metal ladle is sprawled in the dirt some feet away, and there's a metal bowl on its side beside it— the cause of the crashing, I assume. The enormous tent's unzipped opening flutters in the breeze, and I catch a glimpse of someone's long, crossed legs just inside.

Nausea hits me, and I stare at the collar around Heather's neck. The rope tying her to a tree near me makes her look like a dog given some extra leeway to roam the yard.

But I was prepared for that, at least.

It's the newly felled tree sprawled to one side of the clearing that sends fresh chills down my spine. We saw the Sinners chopping them down, but . . .

Its branches have been cut away, and they've flattened the thick trunk on two sides. It's more than long enough to span our moat. How many more of these do they have?

With a few of those, the Sinners could cross into Bristlebrook.

Into my *home*.

It's the first one I've ever had. My safe place. My sanctuary. I can already see them soiling my room—tearing pages from Othello and cutting down the curtains Jayk sewed for me so terribly. I can see them shattering Beau's hideous lamp and breaking Dom's TV. I can see their filthy hands on Jasper's toys.

Panic holds me in its silent, shuddering clutches.

They're planning to invade.

The civilians are inside . . . oh God, forget the house. They can't touch my friends.

There's a lean Sinner sitting, bored, on top of the felled tree. There's a rifle by his dangling foot.

"Pick it up, Madison," he says, not looking up from the knife in his hands. It takes me a distracted moment to look away from that knife and notice the small wooden figure between his fingers.

He's carving something.

I didn't know Sinners could create. I thought they only knew how to destroy.

Heather's brows flick up dangerously at his command. In the next instant, she's grabbed the small cookpot off the fire, swinging it back to haul at him—but as soon as she starts to throw it, her leash grows taut, and she's jerked viciously backward by the collar at her throat.

She lands hard on her back, and the cookpot drops, spilling out onto the dirt. Gagging, Heather curls onto her side, clutching at the tight, strangling collar.

Horrified, I shove Mateo hard . . . and his foot reluctantly comes off the leash as he steps back.

The tension eases, and Heather starts coughing, dragging in air.

"Oops," is all he says, and when I glower at him tearfully, he gives me a smile sweet enough to make the heavens weep.

My rage nearly engulfs me.

Stop acting so afraid, he said. He *makes* me afraid.

"Thank you for the reminder," I finally manage to whisper. My voice shakes with anger, and I wedge as much disappointment and disgust into my tone as it can hold. "You're right. I've made too many mistakes when choosing my friends."

Mateo's smile dips, and his eyes run over my face. The awful enjoyment drops out of it.

"Stop it. We saved you at Cyanide. We *told you* what we want for the future," he hisses.

A bitter, huffed laugh escapes me. "You also told me you don't hurt women." I watch Heather pull herself onto her knees, hurting for her, and my lips twist. "Men *lie*."

"Men—" Mateo's angry snarl cuts off with a frustrated, snapping growl.

When I glance at him warily, stepping back, he tracks the move— and he has the gall to look *offended*.

"Yes!" he shouts at me, imploring and hot with irritation. "Yes, Eden, they *do*. They do!" Bitterly, he laughs. "How can you not . . ."

Mateo stops again, gritting his teeth, and he points at Heather. "*She* is a stupid, reckless liability, and we should have killed her *weeks* ago. I'll treat her like any other dangerous prisoner." He looks at her, and something dark lurks behind his eyes. "Like she did to me."

My fear for Heather deepens at the undisguised loathing in him.

Even the Sinner on the log watches him warily.

"Well." My hands knot together nervously before I can make them stop, but I level him with a cool look anyway. "I imagine Alastair might have something to say about that."

Mateo stiffens, and his next glance at me is like the cut of a blade.

A cruel, petty part of me is satisfied when the jab lands, but Heather snorts a hostile laugh as she gets to her feet.

"Alastair would kill me in a heartbeat if he didn't need me," she says, and I blink.

What?

"Heather, he *doesn't* need you. We're in open rebellion. If Alastair wanted to kill you, or try to use you as leverage, he'd have done it already," I object, as mildly as I can.

Mateo's breath hisses out, and he mutters under his breath.

Whatever he says, his treatment of her isn't just caution or even revenge. Sour jealousy pours off him in waves.

I need her to pay attention to these things. Her hatred is blinding her to everything but her own rage.

Mateo's anger is something she can use.

Alastair's *obsession with her* is something she can use.

When Mateo doesn't make another move toward either of us, my racing heart begins to slow, and I examine Heather more closely. Aside from that collar, she looks good—fed, clean, healthy, and unhurt. It's something. Maybe more than something.

Those things count for a lot in this world.

Mateo walks past me, brushing so close I feel the threat and reminder . . . this conversation is being watched.

He settles beside the other Sinner on the tree, and they begin talking in low voices.

Heather rakes her eyes over me, but all she says is. "Why are you here, traitor?"

I suppress a sigh.

"Alastair sent me to fetch some food and water for the meeting . . ."

Turning her back on me, she swipes up the ladle and bowl from the dirt before she dumps them in a barrel of water, and I start edging closer. When she turns back, her gaze is a cold, grey tempest warning me away.

I stop, and her lip curls.

"Stop *flinching*. Did you just leap to do whatever he says? After everything? Looks like he doesn't even need to put you in a leash to make a dog out of you." There's a bite to her words that feels wounded and defensive—like she's hitting me before I can get one in.

It reminds me of Jayk—the Jayk I met when I first came to Bristlebrook, the Jayk who was drowning in his own hurt and needed to make everyone else feel it too. That Jayk, not the protective man he's grown into.

And it puts another lump in my throat.

Heather is hurting in ways that have nothing to do with her body.

My gaze drops to the collar, where it's chafing at her skin. It's made from a stiff, faded red fabric, and large, ugly block letters are splashed across it.

BEAST, it reads.

My eyes *burn*.

"I'm so sorry, Heather. I'm so . . . so sorry," I whisper, aching everywhere.

Her lips flatten. "Don't be *sorry*." She shoves past me, bending down to the overturned pot. She scrapes the stew back in, though it's thick with dirt and leaves. "You were supposed to protect them. You brought his fucking army down on my civilians. You let Kasey just wander the woods. What the fuck are you doing, Eden?"

I take the hit, but I push the throb away as soon as it lands.

I know she's angry. But we don't have time for her to take it out on me.

Striding forward, I yank the cookpot out of her hands, ignoring the filth swirled in with the stew. This might be my only chance to talk to her.

And more than that, I need to make sense of why I'm here. We could have fetched some water or food from any of the men along the way. They had plenty.

Does Alastair want me to see how he keeps and humiliates his captives? Is this another threat to cow us into a willing surrender?

But then I think of Mateo imploring me to trust him. Why would he bother? Is this a good cop, bad cop situation?

Or is this chance to talk to Heather supposed to be a kindness? So I can see that she's unhurt—physically, at least?

If that's their intention, they miscalculated badly.

Actions speak so much louder than words.

Heather glares at me as I take the cookpot from her, and my next smile for her is full of teeth.

"Would you have some bowls? I think Bane is hungry," I prompt, and she blinks, startled, looking down at the filthy stew.

Just for a moment, I see an edge of vicious humor tilt her mouth, and she nods. She heads toward a bag by the tent, and I follow.

As I bend down behind her, I ask softly, "I know you're angry with me, but you've been angry with me before, and we were still able to work together. Heather, we still want the same things—we both want the captives to be safe. We want the civilians here to be safe. Please, just . . . help me understand what it's like there. Is Alastair . . . is he really as bad as Sam? The captives—how are they doing? Is he hurting them? He said he'd keep them—"

Heather's dark, incredulous laugh smashes through my words, and she yanks the bowls out of the bag.

"Is Alastair *good*? Is that what you're asking me?"

Inside the tent, the man's giant legs uncross lazily, and Mateo briefly glances up from where he's sitting on the felled tree before he returns to his conversation.

Or seems to, at least.

"No! He's not *good*, Eden. He's not *sexy*, or *morally grey*, or able to be *saved*. He's not. He's done too much to ever . . ." Heather doesn't even try to lower her voice. It's breaking with anger and grief. The storm in her eyes grows darker, spitting with electric intensity. "Alastair and that sadistic freakshow over there are still handing out women to his men like they're *prizes*. And the captives who aren't locked in with his men? They're slaving away in the kitchen and scrubbing floors. None of them are *safe*, or *free*, or *happy*. Alastair *lied*, and any moment of decency he's ever shown is to *manipulate you*! He's the worst man who ever lived, Eden—and you were a fucking idiot to ever believe he was anything more." Her fingers curl into fists. "If I ever get the opportunity, I'm ripping his throat out."

Each word hits me with flinching finality.

He lied.

My last thread of hope spirals into the dirt. The world around me suddenly feels very distant . . . and very full of danger.

There's no silver bullet. No way out of this mess. By starvation or in our last stand . . . we're going to die.

"Do we find Alastair sexy?"

Bentley's musing voice from the tent is so loud, so incongruously humored, that it snaps me back to myself. Mateo is standing from the log, and his limpid eyes are glacial on Heather.

He heard every word.

And he doesn't take kindly to threats on Alastair.

"We'll be just a moment," I call to him, trying to keep my voice pleasant. "We . . . we still need water."

Like Heather wasn't just shouting about death and dismemberment.

I drag her over to the water bucket with the dirty dishes in it and pull her down to kneel beside me. The bowls in her arms clatter as she drops down. There are only three, but at this point, I don't care that there aren't enough. I don't care about anything but saying my piece and getting safely back to my brutes.

"Heather, please. I need you to use your brain. Be discreet, please. I believe you. I believe you that he's awful, but he *is* infatuated with you. You can use it, if you just—"

"Whore myself," she sneers, and I close my eyes.

Her pride is going to be the death of her.

I grab the empty canteens beside the wooden bucket and dunk them in the water. It bubbles and slips between my fingers, like all the emotions I can't catch right now.

How am I supposed to leave Heather behind again?

Fighting tears, I rush on in a whisper, "You need to find your moment, okay? Like we did back at the Sinners camp. Like with the soup. Please, Heather, I just need you to be safe. I won't be there to protect you this time." I press my lips together before my voice can break, then add, "No matter how much you hate me, you're my friend . . . and I need you to keep yourself safe. *Please.*"

I look at Heather, and I'm surprised to see the bright, angry shine in her eyes, too.

"I don't need your protection, Eden," she whispers back. "You're the reason I'm here."

She stands with the bowls and jerks her chin at Mateo and the other Sinner.

"She can't carry it all herself, so unless you're planning on lifting a finger, you need to let me off my leash," she snaps.

The woodcarver sighs, rolling his eyes. He tucks his carving away as he stands.

"I'll take her. You've got the other one," he mutters to Mateo, and Mateo nods.

I blink back my tears as they leave the camp, finishing up with the canteens. The scent of stew, richly seasoned and heady, is enough to make my stomach cramp, even despite my despair. Even knowing it's coated in dirt.

I'd eat it anyway.

God, I'm so hungry, I'd lick it off the ground, if Mateo weren't watching.

Misery cuts me sharply.

There's nothing here for me to use. Only enough numbers to ice my spine—more weapons, more Sinners, more ways into our home.

Maybe that's why I'm here, outside of defusing Bane . . . to see how hopeless it is.

Swallowing, I pull some twine from the pouch at my waist and thread it through the loops on the canteens so I can sling them over my shoulder. I take the mucky cookpot with me, but when I stand, I feel heavier than water or stew can account for.

"Is Soren okay?"

Caught off guard, I turn to see Bentley stepping out of the tent, stretching like a bear coming out from hibernation. His wrists are tied together, though they're far enough apart to maneuver a little. His ankles are also tied, but with some more give—allowing him enough room to walk, though not to run.

Unlike Heather, he's not anchored to anything.

Like Heather, he seems unhurt.

He desperately needs a shave, though.

When I take too long to answer, Bentley swirls one finger, gesturing for me to speak. "I'll take that to mean he *is* okay, or you wouldn't be looking me in the eye right now—but for the record, that's information you really shouldn't hold in suspense."

Pulling myself from my lingering dread, I give him a weak smile and nod.

"Soren is fine, Bentley. Beau took good care of him. He's up and walking around now."

Bentley grins, and there's so much relief in him as his head tips back that it lifts my mood, just slightly. For now, Soren is safe.

"Let me help you carry that," Bentley offers, taking in my heavy load, and Mateo stands from his seat.

I glance at him uncertainly, but he seems unconcerned as Bentley takes the string of canteens from me. They clatter together obnoxiously as he struggles to arrange it around his wrist ties with a puzzled frown. In the end, he gives up, holding the string of them together like an awkward bundle of caught fish.

"We should go," Mateo mutters as he walks past us, and I nod, following him silently.

As we walk back, Bentley glances down at me a few times, then at Mateo's back. I frown, letting my steps slow a little, and Bentley matches my pace.

It's not enough for us to fall behind, it just . . . creates a little distance.

Sinners swarm through the trees around us, busy with chores or weaving through the woods to peek out of the tree line and check on the meeting. Their lingering glances, their body odor as they deliberately pass close enough to brush my skin, is enough to keep me tense and watchful.

"You shouldn't take Madison's words too hard," Bentley finally says, keeping his voice low and his eyes on the Sinners. "That one has a lot of feelings fighting each other right now."

Even his whispers sound like a rumbling beehive, but I purse my lips.

"It sounded to me like her feelings were quite clear—and valid. Unless you know something I don't?"

Bentley bends to duck under a branch.

I don't.

But he considers my question like he's been given a ticking bomb. A Sinner strides forward, looking over me with too much heat, and

Bentley casually steps into his path, ushering me forward while he thinks.

I can't even tell if the seamless defense was intentional or not.

"Well," Bentley says slowly, none of his usual bravado in his voice. "There is *some* nuance. Shades of grey, you know? You can't . . . How do I . . .?" He eyes a passing Sinner, then mutters, "Nope, can't say that. *Okay.*"

He nods to himself, then leans down close to me as he walks.

Darting a worried glance around us, I listen intently as he begins to whisper.

"So, Alastair and Mateo's men pulled all the women and children out of the Sinners rooms the night we attacked. Hear that? They pulled them *out*. It was chaos inside. Fighting. They got them all free of Sam's men. Put them in one place so they'd all be together. The captives, they're not being beaten or . . . or bothered there, if you catch my drift."

Lifting the clanging canteens, Bentley scratches his beard, then nods to me to keep moving.

Reeling, I force my suddenly stalled feet to restart. Alastair *did* protect the captives? But . . . if that's true, then why would Heather be so upset about how they're being treated?

Mateo glances back over his shoulder, catching us whispering, but he turns back after a single searching look. If anything, his shoulders relax.

Does he want me to hear whatever Bentley is saying? Was this planned? Is Bentley being pressured to say all of this?

Or . . . is this the truth?

I frown as I walk, my eyes sightless on the mulchy leaves in front of me as I think. "So, Alastair *isn't* giving the captives away to his men? As *prizes*?"

Bentley winces, then tips his head thoughtfully. "Well, yes . . . *technically*, he's—"

"Bentley!"

My horror slams back into me in full force. Alastair is selling the women off. God, how could Bentley *still* defend him after that? Shades of grey, my ass. And he all but called Madison *emotional*.

Damn it.

He's supposed to be one of the good ones.

The tree line where Mateo and I entered comes into view, and Mateo turns toward it.

I dodge another Sinner, then lower my voice. I hate that it sounds like I'm begging. "So, Heather isn't lying or exaggerating? It's not that she has it wrong? Are the captives being treated like servants, too?"

Bentley gives me a torn, guilty look. "I mean, no, not like servants."

I breathe out in relief.

Okay. Okay, at least there's that.

"Servants, historically, get *paid* for that kind of . . ."

Catching my sick expression, he trails off.

They're everything I feared they were.

Mateo breaches the tree line, and we follow more slowly. Bentley's dragging feet don't seem to have anything to do with his ropes.

"Look, Eden, just . . . just forget that for a minute. I wouldn't take risks with this. I—"

Another Sinner comes up beside us, just a few feet away, heading for the tree line, and Bentley closes his mouth, eyeing the Sinner sideways.

The large man sighs, seeming frustrated.

"It's complicated, Eden," he says, his voice as close to a whisper as I think he can get. "With everyone here. With you. Just be careful. People aren't always what they seem to be."

Watching Mateo's back, bitterness clogs my throat. "I'm aware."

"Good."

Bentley tugs at my shirt, just before I step out from the trees, and reluctantly, I stop.

He slips a small, folded piece of paper into my pocket . . . and his eyes meet mine.

"Then make sure you're looking beyond the surface."

I look down at my pocket as Bentley pushes through the trees, and when the Sinner pauses to eye me, I follow Bentley with a quicker step.

My fingers touch the folded paper in my pocket like it might burn me.

I wouldn't take risks with this.

People aren't always what they seem to be.

Does Bentley mean himself . . . or Alastair?

Night has begun to fall over the group by the moat, and their chaos barely registers as I approach. Sullivan appears to be arguing with Bane for negotiation, Bane is making more threats. Arthur is quivering.

Heather is on her knees by Alastair's seat, her leash wrapped tight around his wrist.

Somehow, I doubt she approved that on any limits list.

But my brutes' desperate edginess as they catch sight of me squeezes my chest, and when Jasper draws me into his side, I lean into him with more relief than I should show.

But my thoughts are still thundering in my ears.

Bentley gave me a note.

Distantly, I hear Alastair decide that we're at an impasse and that there's much to think on. Distantly, I hear him order us to return at dawn tomorrow to convene another meeting.

Distantly, I notice everyone has risen from their seats.

And as I retreat back over the bridge with my brutes and Arthur, my stomach churns.

Because I suddenly have no idea what to believe.

Chapter 66

Eden

Survival tip #64
Some people aren't built to fight . . .
so they learn to protect themselves in other ways.

Jasper's cool hand is tense on the back of my neck as we stride toward Bristlebrook, but it reassures me anyway—just a silent anchor. A skin-on-skin reminder that he has me. That he's okay.

That *I'm* okay.

His thumb skates up the side, and I breathe out shakily. I have a note to read.

But first . . .

Jayk, Beau, and Lucky are waiting for us on the porch, and Jasper releases me with a squeeze. Before I can jog up to see them, however, Sawyer shuffles out in front of them, stepping down off the porch.

Shame and misery tangle in his eyes as he approaches us.

"I'm sorry," he whispers. "I'm sorry. After the attack the other night . . . I heard the bullets and I just . . ."

Ran.

My own remembered guilt stings through me.

"It happens," Dom says, clipped but not unsympathetic.

On my other side, Jasper nods, his gaze dark and assessing. "Come and see me, when you have some time. It might help."

Sawyer looks away, his throat working, and we continue on, more subdued.

"I guess you don't really get used to it," I whisper.

Jasper's assessing gaze slides to me. "The Sinners' attack was only recent. He has time to heal."

I force a smile—it comes out sad anyway. "I meant all the other raids on their home. He must be living with years of that fear. I don't think I could have stayed." I shake my head as we walk up the stairs. The dimming late-afternoon light is starting to feel uncomfortably dark. "I don't blame him for running."

"You shouldn't. Some people just aren't built for this. It's not their fault." When Dom stops at the top of the porch, he turns to look down at me, and he adds darkly, "They shouldn't have to be."

The others stride over, but Dom gestures at them to give him a minute.

Jayk rolls his eyes, muttering, and Lucky salutes with his middle finger. Beau snorts, but his anxious gaze runs over me.

I smile at them, and when I reach the top of the porch, Dom tilts my chin one way, then the other, checking me for . . . I'm not even sure. Bruises? There's still a grim worry living behind his golden eyes.

Maybe he's just checking on me because he needs to.

I was gone for more than long enough to worry them.

When I steady his wrist, leaning into his palm, he sighs, finally relaxing.

"You shouldn't have to be," he tells me softly.

Shouldn't have to be afraid. Shouldn't need to go to war. Shouldn't need to second guess the intentions of everyone around me.

Except for theirs.

It's been a long time since I've doubted my brutes.

Taking his hand from my face, I link my fingers with his, and I meet his eyes.

"*None of us* should."

That is what I'm fighting for. A world where my brutes don't have to stand as my shield.

They're so much more than that.

Lucky is on me in the next instant, and I hold up a halting finger toward Jayk before he can toss Lucky off me. He waits impatiently until Lucky is finished pressing frantic kisses against my mouth—and then crushes me against his chest until I squeak. Beau's cuddle afterward is as soft as pillows, as sleep and comfort, and it relaxes me enough that it's his side I anchor myself against.

Bentley's secret note is like a live wire in my pocket.

But this time, it doesn't even occur to me to keep it a secret.

"We need to talk."

WE HOLE up in Jasper's room again. The sheets are still tousled on his bed where I slept last night. We've all been gravitating to his rooms —not just because, between this and his secret room, he has two enormous beds as well as the couch . . . he also has hot water.

We've gathered around his sitting room, and Bentley's note lies in the center of the coffee table.

Only, it's not from Bentley at all.

> *If you want your Rangers to live,*
> *meet me by your "secret" tunnel at midnight.*
> *I have an offer to present.*
> *Consider this me calling in your tithe.*
> *P.S. Only bring one of the armed idiots,*
> *or none of you will survive the night.*

"No," Jayk growls, breaking the heavy silence.

He's in the leather armchair opposite my couch, and I lean forward, trying for delicacy. "Jayk, I really think we need to think about—"

"No."

His rough face is set and hard, and I glance up at Beau, who is pacing by the bed. Catching my look, he shakes his head silently.

I don't think it's in denial.

Beau looks worried.

"We could just kill him?" Lucky offers. "Can we do the murder thing?"

"Then we have Bane to deal with instead," Dom mutters. "No better. I say we go."

"No," Jayk snaps again.

Massaging his temple, Jasper shoots Jayk a look riddled with forced patience.

"I agree with Eden," he says in a repressive tone from his armchair. "Bane . . . is extremely concerning, and his opinions hold weight with Alastair. Sullivan can be disregarded for now, unfortunately. He appears to have little influence. But if we do nothing, given what we've seen today . . . I do think we'll be attacked in force in very short order. If we have any other options, I think we should explore them. Dominic and Eden should go."

"And if it's an ambush?" Jayk grits out.

Jasper's expression gentles. "I can't imagine what the point would be. They could have taken Eden today. Killed Dom and myself. No need for all the subterfuge."

Jayk glowers at him . . . but it doesn't take long before his expression cracks, and he looks back at me in silent, tight-jawed demand.

"It's outside the side tunnel. I'll bring a whistle," I tell him softly. "You'll be able to hear it on the other end . . . and I'll be with Dom."

After a long moment, Jayk nods, his shoulders dropping in defeat.

Straddling the arm of the couch beside me, Lucky's looking down at the note with a sour expression. It's the worst possible place he could sit.

His foot is half wedged into my ass.

"That dude really needs to learn the art of asking nicely," he mutters. His long hair sprawls around his shoulders, and he rakes it back irritably.

I pat his foot.

I've already filled them in on the important details, the numbers and supplies and the trees ready to span our moat. But the rest . . .

"When I spoke with them all today . . . Mateo, Bentley, and . . . and Heather," I begin hesitantly, then shake my head. "I don't know. I'm conflicted. Heather seemed so sure. She doesn't trust Alastair, or his intentions with the captives. With us. She has so much hate for him, and that could be clouding her judgment, but . . . with what we've seen, and what he and Mateo have done to us and the Reapers . . . I can't imagine trusting them."

Dom braces against the top of Jayk's chair as he leans over it, watching me.

"We shouldn't," Beau says, sitting heavily on the end of the rumpled bed. "You two need to be careful. I'm not losing any more of my family."

He and Dom exchange a silent, grief-edged look, and Jayk drops his head into his hands, his fingers knotting over the back of his neck.

"Agreed," I murmur, hurting for all of them. Praying that particular hurt is one I never have to feel myself. It takes me a moment to find my voice again. "I just . . . oh, I can't reconcile any of it. Bentley seemed so adamant, talking about them not being what they seem, and . . . I mean, he gave Alastair the location of the tunnel—which leads to *Soren*. He must trust them. Or he's being tortured in some unimaginable way that wasn't obvious to my admittedly inexperienced eye."

Princely and calm in his chair, Jasper nods to himself, smoothing down his pants absently.

Lucky glances down at me, and the ghost of his dimples appears in his cheeks. "Bentley, huh? Is he still flirting with Mateo? Hey, Jasper, how many points for Stockholm Syndrome?"

Silently, I yank out several dark golden hairs from behind his ankle.

"Ah! *No*. Those were aesthetic. Don't make me patchy!" he complains.

Beau talks over him in a slow, thoughtful drawl. "So we've heard what Heather thinks, and what Bentley thinks, but darlin' . . . what do you think?"

Across the room, his hands are buried in the bedsheets like he's got a stranglehold on them, but he's watching me intently, the way he does every time I speak. Every ritual, every day, he listens with his whole attention.

My opinions *matter* to these men.

I tuck my hand behind Lucky's knee, leaning into him.

"I think . . ." Frowning, I sigh. "I think that whether Alastair is trustworthy or not, we're in a bad position, and so is he with his men.

I think we should try to negotiate something—some route to resolving this without a fight."

Looking around this room, I imagine it destroyed and tarred by Sinners.

I look at my men.

"At midnight, we work out a solution with Alastair . . . because too many will die if we don't."

CHAPTER 67

BEAU

SURVIVAL TIP #276
Love means safety.

I t's almost dawn," Jasper mutters, checking his watch for the fifth time in the last two minutes. "The next parley with the Sinners is supposed to start at any moment. Eden and Dominic should be back by now."

He's pacing like a mare in labor outside the entrance to the side tunnel, like he's been doing all night. His hair's a mess, he's still in last night's clothes, and anxious lines bracket his mouth.

Not one of us looks any better.

Eden and Dom left for their secret meeting with Alastair at midnight. Since then, we've only seen Eden once, hours ago. She ducked her head in to reassure us she was alive and that they were still talking—and that was pretty much all we got before she hightailed her pretty little behind from whence she came.

In the gym, with dozens of civilians finally starting to stir for the day, we're sitting by the door, our rifles lined within reach against the wall.

Lucky is tossing a ball against the wall, over and over, his eyes blank. Jayk's been storming back and forth between here and the defenses outside for most of the night, but he's finally stopped.

I checked on my patients, nearly cried like a baby when I saw Ethel finally sitting up in bed, with apples in her cheeks, and Kasey snuggled in next to her like a blanket. Ida next to them both, looking like she was trying not to cry.

Every day I've had civilians slipping me their extra rations to give to her—all the little things they've been keeping back. Chocolate bars or jerky. Stale hunks of bread and dried fruit.

And I gave her everything I had, too—every bit I had greedily stashed away after the raid for the next time I needed to eat my feelings.

These days I'm working real hard to listen to my very clever girl-friend and talk those feelings through instead.

Besides, those old hippies are my grandmas now, too. These days, I have sisters and cousins and aunts flooding my halls . . . and my family always comes first.

The extra food was enough.

Kasey is up there, probably still chattering a mile a minute, and Ethel was feeling feisty enough to sass me about my lack of showering and apparent body odor, so it was more than enough.

It was everything.

Almost everything.

Eden and Dom still aren't back.

The back of my head falls against the wall, and I rub my tired eyes.

"Do we go out?" I ask, worry eating at my gut. "If it's taking this long, it has to be good news, right? They're working things out?"

Jayk suddenly snags Lucky's ball out of the air, and Lucky stiffens, blinking out of his mindless staring. Jayk is unshaven and looking rougher than usual, and I brace myself to break up a fight.

But then Jayk just bounces it back to Lucky, and they silently start tossing it back and forth instead.

It's cute.

But it's still not enough to stop me from staring at the heavy door to the side tunnel. Anxious worry claws at me. What could they be talking about for so long? I just need them to—

The door bursts open, and we all surge to our feet.

Eden rushes through first, Dom right on her heels.

Their expressions aren't encouraging.

Eden's pale and tense, and she pushes her glasses back up her nose, blinking at all of us as she hurries past. "Oh, hi. *Hi*. Have you been out here all night? I told you all to go to bed. What time is it?"

"Dawn," Jasper answers, dropping a brief kiss on her lips as she walks past, then catches her arm. "Are you—?"

Gently, she tugs herself free, and I see how deep the circles are under her eyes.

"Sorry. I'm sorry. I'm okay. We're just late for the meeting, and Alastair wants to feel everything out with the other groups there before he agrees to anything," she calls back, but she doesn't stop walking toward the hall.

The concern only deepens on Jasper's face as he follows close behind her.

"Nice to see you, too, sugar. Thanks for the rundown," Jayk mutters, tossing the ball back to Lucky with an eye roll, but at least he doesn't look like he's about to punch a wall anymore.

Lucky frowns, but jogs to catch up to Jasper and Eden.

Dom nods at us to move, and I fall into step beside him. The sudden burst of movement after hours of sitting on the floor isn't kind on the knees. Or the nerves.

"You really having us walk out there blind? Did you come to terms with Alastair? What took you so long?" I ask him, Jayk right behind us.

Dom is as grim as Eden. His heavy jacket widens his shoulders, and he brushes against me with every step.

"I—" His jaw tenses. "I think we got there. Alastair's a fuck to negotiate with. We made an agreement but . . . we had to make some concessions." He glances at me. "You're not going to like them. We were still arguing about it when we left. He wants to finish it out there. Needs to act like it's all his idea, of course."

We push out onto the porch, and Jayk jogs up beside Dom. "*Concessions*? The civs are staying here. The Sinners aren't fucking—"

"The civs won't be touched," Dom snaps . . . then he stops mid-stride on the grass and turns to Jayk. He runs a hand over his exhausted face. "Sorry. Long night."

Jayk's arms cross over his chest, his brows lowering as he looks at Dom. But he's not angry. He looks worried.

Just beyond him, Sawyer is hovering, looking pale, his mustache twitching nervously.

Ah, damn. We can't have him running again, but I feel for him. He's just a farmer.

Dom sees him the same time I do, and his jaw flexes. "You stay here this time, Sawyer. We have it covered."

Instant relief breaks out over his queasy expression, and he nods. "Sure, if you think it's best. Thanks."

Dom jumps off the porch, but he slows, his eyes on the distant field beyond the moat.

Bane and Sullivan are already setting up their chairs, and there's at least five more Sinners than there were at the last meeting—most of them talking to Bane.

Eden, Lucky, and Jasper are loitering near the bridge beside Arthur.

"Why the fuck are they bringing more men?" Jayk scowls. "I'll be up top. I have a fucking bullet for Bane if he tries that shit again."

Impatiently, he peels off, heading for Platform Three.

I squint against the rising sun as Alastair and Mateo stride out of the trees.

It's about to start.

Worry bites at me, and I shake my head.

"That's it, I'm going out there with you. You need me. I know your cues better than Jasper if things go south," I tell Dom in a rush, bracing for an argument.

Bracing for him to tell me there won't be a fight, and that he's sure they sorted it all out.

I'm ready for him to tell me it'll be fine.

Instead, Dom sighs, a silent war in his expression. "Fine, but no losing your temper and shooting this time, no matter what he says. Eden was right. Bane has too much fucking influence. Alastair is going to make this ugly for us so he can make himself look good, so just . . ."

Silently, I cringe at the memory of firing on the Reapers.

I cringe even more deeply as I remember how bad I let things get bottled up, but . . . I'm not there anymore. Just yesterday, I told Dom I was *mad* he hadn't cleared a drawer for me yet, and he spent five minutes making room for me.

Turns out talking about it really *is* just a lot easier.

And I've been a fucking idiot . . . one who has a whole damn mess to make up for.

My time with Jasper these last few weeks has cleared up a lot.

"I'll keep it together, Dom." I meet his eyes. "I'm with you. You and Eden. I'll follow her plan to the end."

That promise means different things to me now than it did most of my life.

The Plan that Dom and I always talked about was something two teenagers brewed up—it was a plan that was always about us not wanting to lose each other to time, or moves, or different lives. It was a plan that included a woman, any woman, because monkhood didn't suit us, and even pretty as Dom is, that kind of love bug never hit us.

All my ideas about loyalty and love and friendship were always swept up in the dramatics. Defending each other under fire and putting him before anything and everything, no matter what. Love was supposed to be flawless and our partnership unbreakable, and I imagined dying someday right by his side, doing something heroic.

My plan was built on quicksand.

But then I met Eden.

And she refused every pedestal I tried to put her on.

Eden has been saving *herself* her whole life. She's never lived in a flawless world or found limitless loyalty. To Eden, everything is break-able. She doesn't want heroism, or her problems to be kissed away, because heroism kills and those problems will still be there when the kisses are done. She doesn't want everything to be *fine*, because she knows it can't be, not always.

Eden's Plan is better than mine ever was.

It's a plan for grown-ups.

It's a plan built for love with flaws, and rage, and fears, and pain. It's a plan she custom built for our whole family, where one person isn't above anything and everything . . . but where everyone stabilizes each other. It's a plan where love means safety, and cracks are explored and tended carefully. It's a plan where it's okay not to be fine.

And it's a plan where no one has to die, not until we're all old and ready to go off easily into the night.

That's my plan now too—for today and all the ones after.

Dom stares at me, and he must see something of what I'm feeling in my face because his Adam's apple dips hard, his jaw flexing.

And I see his reply in his eyes.

I love you, too.

"It'll be okay," he mutters after a long moment. "With this deal, we'll be okay."

Around us, civilians are moving, switching out the watch, and Dom stiffens.

"I already told everyone I want all hands on deck for these meetings." His voice lifts. "Jennifer, get back on watch. Sloane, you too!"

They pause, exchanging a look. Jennifer's hair is flying away in a thousand messy strands, and Sloane is so fatigued she looks drunk.

Breathing out slowly, Dom adds, "Please?" He nods at the meeting. "They've brought backup."

His expression is tight, but it's a gentler order than I'm used to hearing from him.

Jennifer drags out a long sigh. "*Fine.* You can take my watch later as a thank you."

"Deal," Dom says dryly, rubbing his forehead.

Sloane just eyes him, then the men on the clearing, and heads back toward the platform.

He's stressed. We're all too tired.

"Come on, Dom. Let's get this done. The sooner we're through this, the sooner we get Eden all to ourselves again. I have plans." I clap my hand to his shoulder, and Dom's snort is mostly a heavy exhale.

"I'm not dressing up this time," he mutters, and I grin.

When we meet up with Eden and Arthur, the Sinners are already still and watching.

Waiting for us.

Lucky and Jasper head back to join up with Jayk, and my eyes fix on Eden's ghostly, worried face. As Dom takes to the bridge, I lean down to press a kiss to her forehead, letting my fingers twist through her hair for just a moment.

"You did so well, darlin'. Just a bit of ugliness and we're in the clear," I murmur.

I have to admit, the idea of playing bitch-boys to the Sinners for the foreseeable future doesn't sit right, but if it means peace and food and trade, I can live with it.

Eden softly touches her hand to my chest, and then she draws herself up.

Her expression is flint.

"One more bad day, then we'll be safe," she says.

I nod, and she turns to stride over the bridge.

Every inch our queen.

Smiling softly, I follow.

CHAPTER 68

BEAU

Bane yawns, scratching his crotch as we sit down. He has five men milling lazily around him, walking up to the moat to stare at the decaying bodies and then strolling back again. At least they've only got pistols on them, but it's still five more trigger-happy assholes than I want at this meeting.

They put me on edge. The rot-ripe smells put me on edge. Alastair's cold, smarmy little smile puts me on edge.

I want this done.

"No Sawyer today?" Sullivan asks brusquely.

"He wasn't well," is all Dom says, and Alastair's smile deepens. "I'm sure."

But Bane snorts, shaking his head. "What a fucking pussy."

"So what else is new?" a short, beady-eyed Sinner drawls, and Bane laughs.

I don't even bother to hide my disgust. I want these men away from my home, away from my people—away from Eden. Their world doesn't allow for softness, or kindness. It doesn't allow for fear, unless they're the ones to instill it.

The Reapers were right to come to us.

No one deserves to face men like this alone.

"Yesterday," Alastair begins, his eyes on Dom. "You were disrespectful. You made demands of us that my friends here and I found . . . unacceptable. I hope another night with empty stomachs has made you reconsider your approach."

Everything about him makes my skin crawl.

His pale eyes and bladed face. The scar through his eyebrow and the poisoned plants on his skin.

But mostly it's the deadness in him.

There's an absence of *something* behind his eyes that should be there. A conscience. A soul, maybe. He looks . . . empty.

Dom leans forward, his neck stiff as he bends his head, and my fingers curl into fists at my side. I hate this. To my *bones*, I hate this.

"We . . . have," he says, his voice as rigid as his neck.

Dom is no actor—his participation in my roleplays is nominal at best—but his obvious discomfort is enough to sell this. The gloating already splashed over Bane's face tells me it will work.

"We shouldn't have . . . demanded," Dom finishes through gritted teeth, and Arthur darts a surprised, nervous look at his face.

Eden is silent, her lips drawn and unhappy as she stares straight ahead.

It's a look she used to get sometimes while she journaled for Jasper —like she's gone someplace endless and bleak inside of herself. A place I'd have to come and coax her from, part of me terrified every time that she might not come back out.

Mateo is closest to the trees, and he's staring out into them as if he's bored of the conversation, but his corded neck betrays him. It takes me a moment to make out Bentley and Heather, tied to the edge of the tree line.

They're watching, too.

Alastair shakes his head, his eyes approving. "No. You shouldn't." That scarred brow lifts expectantly. "You should have *begged*."

Arthur's breath leaves him in a soft, wobbly *oof*.

Sour slime fills my stomach.

This reminds me too much of the Den. It's different, I know it is —we all decided to play this game together, and I know Dom and Eden wouldn't have agreed to anything if we wouldn't be better off, but . . . this feels like having shit served up to us and then being forced to eat it with a smile.

Dom stares at Alastair, a muscle ticking in his jaw, like he can't force the words out.

Alastair's brow lifts higher, waiting.

A sharp pin could burst the air.

"It's okay, Dom," I breathe, just above a whisper, and his chest expands slowly.

"*Please*," Dom says, low and rough. "*Please* consider trade arrangements. Stop this war, I . . ." He swallows hard, stalling, and Eden takes his hand, squeezing it hard.

"*We beg you*," she finishes in a husky, pleading rush.

I only just hide a flinch.

I know why this was Eden's solution. I know she thinks this costs her nothing—that being bendable means not breaking. It might be the right—or even the only—solution here.

But she's wrong about the cost.

Eden should only get on her knees for the people who make it a joy.

Bane laughs appreciatively, sitting forward with rampant eagerness. "Looks like you can bring all the bitches to heel, Alastair."

Rage roars through me with white-hot intensity. It fills my empty stomach, fires my veins, and I clamp my teeth together against the onslaught, breathing through my nose.

I know why Dom warned me now.

I want to kill them all.

Beside Alastair, Sullivan looks down and adjusts his glasses, like he's uncomfortable.

As he damn well should be.

Sitting in his chair like it's the throne he blew to shreds, Alastair considers Dom. Finally, still wearing that same slight, cold smile, he stands.

He begins to stroll, calm and thoughtful. Absently, he gestures the other Sinners back as he paces behind the chairs, and they move like obedient cattle dogs, clustering by the moat in a small pack.

"Trade arrangements," Alastair muses, his voice still so flat. So empty. "It's an interesting concept. Sullivan is in favor of it; we discussed it last night."

He gestures at Sullivan, who nods, a small measure of relief breaking over his features.

"Yes, I think—"

"That wasn't an invitation, Sullivan," Alastair speaks mildly over him, not pausing in his slow, hypnotic pacing.

Bane smirks at the correction, exchanging amused looks with his men by the moat. One of them nervously edges away from the pikes as dirt begins to slip beneath his heel.

"So, the Reapers would give us the food we need instead of us taking it from them, and they'd agree to cease any of their idiotic rebellions?" Alastair asks.

Bane leans back in his chair. "I *liked* taking it from them. It's better that way. We got to take the good stuff . . . and it was so *easy*." His eyes glitter as he grins. "Like slaughtering pigs. It's the screams that make it fun."

The rage churns through my gut, remembering the pigs we were forced to kill just days ago. I've got no squeamishness about doing it . . . but it's not fun. Ending a life is never *fun*.

Ending Bane's might be, though.

How do we make peace with this guy? I don't even want to sit through a meeting with him.

"It'll be less fun when there's no one left to farm it," I bite out, and Bane shrugs.

"There are more around."

More places for them to burn through.

"*Beau*," Dom mutters in warning, and I grimace, nodding.

Alastair lifts a cautioning hand to Bane, too, who rolls his eyes.

And I see Alastair's gaze sharpen on the disrespect.

Dread prickles over me.

Alastair stops pacing. Instead, he walks over to stand behind his chair.

The sunlight is weak and delicate, and his dark clothes seem to repel the light. Those clothes are made for midnight.

"And what would you offer?" he demands of Dom. "More

weapons? Tools? There are some things we're low on that are hard to find. Would you be my errand boys?"

Is that what we agreed? That's not too bad. Takes us away from home, but we could do some family trips out.

I shift in my ancient fold-out chair, hope battling the flare of dread.

Dom breathes in through his nose, but he says, "Yes."

Alastair looks at Arthur. "And you? Your Bentley said you have artisans who can make alcohol and candles. Even custom glasswork? Blacksmithing?"

My hope shines brighter.

Perfect. Things they can't make or get themselves. Things they need allies for.

Show Bane what Red Zone can offer, too.

Uncertainly, Arthur glances at Dom and Eden before he slowly looks back at Alastair. "Y-yes. We can do that." He attempts a smile. "I-I've measured up the windows for Bristlebrook already. We need some ingredients, but if we have those . . . yes. If we have free range to the buildings in the city too, then . . . we can even do complex work. We have an horologist there too—for timepieces. Clocks, I—"

"Fascinating," Alastair says, so blandly that Bane snorts again, his shoulders shaking.

A smile begins to edge Alastair's mouth.

It's a dangerous smile.

I don't trust it at all.

I don't let myself tense, but casual as I can, I move my hand to my pistol. Beside me, Dom tilts his head just slightly, his jaw locked.

Don't, he says without words.

My heart starts to pound.

I know they want this to work, that they have a deal, but Alastair . . .

No. I trust them.

Adrenaline is thrumming through me, as cold as my rage is hot . . . but I take my hand from my gun. I'm following Dom and Eden.

To the end.

"Sullivan?" Alastair asks, but his eyes are on Dom. "This is the deal you want?"

Sullivan's white head lifts, and he wipes his hands nervously over his thighs. "Yes." He nods, glancing at us. "Yes, I-I think that would be best for everyone. No casualties, more opportunities for goods that would make our lives better. *Yes*. We should take the deal."

Take it, Alastair, I silently urge.

Alastair nods, a quiet, thoughtful *hm* escaping him.

But Bane's smirk is dying, his gaze darting between Sullivan and Alastair. "You're not fucking considering this? We have them pinned! With those whores, there's enough holes for every fucking Sinner back home."

Alastair's pale eyes drift to Bane.

There's a rumble of dissatisfaction from the men by the moat, and Alastair's head tilts, listening.

Dom tenses beside me, sitting up in his chair. His eyes are sharp on Alastair.

Silently, Mateo gets up, stepping back from the group, and the prickle of dread in my gut turns into a flood.

Don't do it, Alastair. Stick to the plan.

"You object to the deal?" Alastair asks Bane, like he's curious.

Bane stands so he can look Alastair in the eye. His bald head gleams in the sun. "Yeah. I do."

"Alastair . . ." Eden begins carefully, and Bane's head whips her way.

"Stop *talking*, woman," Alastair snaps, with the most snarled heat I've ever heard in his voice.

Bane's men snort, laughing among themselves, but Bane is still tense. So is Alastair.

"Well, it is my decision whether I take the deal or not, isn't it?" Alastair asks Bane, his voice ice-frosted silk.

Bane smiles.

Smiles like he's considering that.

And Alastair nods softly. Carefully.

The dread pools in my throat.

"I do have one more question, Ranger," he murmurs.

Urgently, I glance at Dom, looking for a cue.

Dom shakes his head again, telling me to stay, but he's like a boulder beside me. "What's your question? Are we making a deal or not?"

With a whispered, terrifying finality, Alastair asks, "For all these goods you're willing to *trade* us, what exactly is it that you want in return?"

There's a tense, breathless silence.

As Dom stands to his full height, his shoulders seem to fill the space.

"Dom," Eden says nervously. Her eyes dart to Alastair, and she scrambles up too. "Dom . . ."

But it's too late.

"We want your captives, Alastair—every last fucking one. No matter the cost," Dom snaps.

And Alastair sighs, still face-to-face with Bane.

"Such a pity. It was almost a good deal."

And then he shoots my best friend in the chest.

CHAPTER 69

BEAU

SURVIVAL TIP #28
Plans can die in a heartbeat.

There's blood everywhere. Dom's bleeding. It's soaking his jacket. The grass. My hands. Eden's hands. Was it one shot or two? There's more now. I can't remember. Eden's crying. Running past me. I'm dragging him backward. I think. I don't remember moving, but the bridge is under my feet.

Dom suddenly gets easier to move, and I see Arthur has his legs. Lifting him. We're carrying him. Med bay, I need to get . . .

Eden. Where's Eden?

I look and she's there. Her mouth is moving but I can't hear.

Dom's bleeding. Dom's shot.

There are Sinners trying to run. Alastair's gone. Bane is shot in the shoulder. There are bodies on the ground. Bullets are tearing up the ground around our chairs. Civs are around me, running, shouting, but Dom's stubble has blood in it.

We hit the porch, and I can't breathe.

Deanna's face. I tell her something but I don't know what. Dom's bleeding. She has to help.

Lucky's there. Jasper. Eden. Eden's safe.

But not Dom.

Dom's bleeding.
Dom's *shot*.

CHAPTER 70

LUCKY

SURVIVAL TIP #132
Sometimes, getting blown by your girl?
Not that great.

N*o, no, no, no, no, no.*

Sawyer and another Reaper pass us, carrying an unconscious Cole toward the sitting room. Beau needs the bed.

Because Dom was *shot*.

"Beau? Why is he bleeding?" Eden shouts, her voice breaking. "Beau, he's hurt! Is he okay? Beau, answer me! Alastair wasn't supposed to—"

"Get her out. *Beau!* You, too. Out," Deanna barks.

"No!" Beau roars. "Scissors. Clare! Get me scissors!"

I can't see anything. In the hall outside the med bay, all I see is the trail of blood dripped along the floorboards.

"Just wait, sweet boy," Jasper breathes.

Right. Beau has him.

My boot smears through Dom's blood.

Fuck, how did this go so *wrong*?

I look up at Jasper, and I force a smile. "Was it like this when I got shot?"

Jasper's head falls back against the wall, his eyes closed, and it's only then that I see how pale he is. How strained his face.

Shit. Maybe not the thing to bring up.

"Hey," I say, swallowing down my own fear. I wait until his eyes open—and they're silent, horrified pools. "I'm okay. He will be too."

Jasper's eyes glisten.

"Jayk needs hands! Where are the Rangers?" Ava shouts from the front door.

I look back at the med bay. Damn it. I need to know. I need him to be okay before I—

"I'll go." Jasper grabs his rifle, his face closing off. He doesn't even see it—how natural he looks with it now . . . or how much I hate that it does. "I need to do something. I loathe waiting."

"Oh, holy fucking Jesus!"

Beau's shout has both of us stopping in our tracks, staring at the half-open door. Shadows shift inside. Deanna's shouting instructions and . . . was that Dom? Dom's making sounds? Dom's *able* to make sounds?

"Oh my God. Dom." Beau's relief finally has my heels touching back to the floorboards.

"Dom!" Eden's sobs are choked.

"Okay, enough. Out, Beau! I have him. Do you trust that I have him now?" Deanna snaps.

"Do you know how to—"

"It's not arterial. I can suture. Get *out*."

Jasper releases a relieved breath that trembles the whole way out.

Dom's okay. If Beau's leaving then he's really okay.

Beau and Eden burst out of the med bay a moment later, and there are tears on both of their faces. Beau turns to look at her, lifting a shaking, blood-stained hand to his forehead like he's trying to keep it together, but another tear spills over his cheek.

"*Eden* . . ." Beau's voice is thick. Raw. "*What . . .?*"

Staring up at Beau, Eden's eyes fill, too. "Alastair wasn't supposed to do that. He wasn't supposed to get hurt." She breaks, and her tears overflow. "I'm *sorry*. I'm sorry, Beau. I'm so sorry. Are you mad? I . . . I'm *sorry*."

Beau shakes his head, blinking. He wipes his tears with the back of his forearm, then drags her into his chest, wrapping her in a hug.

Dom's blood stains the back of her shirt. He gets it in her hair when he holds the back of her head, whispering to her shakily.

"I am mad, Eden, but not at you." A sharp sob escapes her, and he holds her close, soothing her quietly. "He's okay. Deanna has him. It's okay. We're all going to be okay. I'm with you, darlin'. All the way. To the end."

This wasn't part of the plan. My last bit of hope snuffs out.

We got played.

Again.

"Rangers! Hands! We have Sinners incoming *now*!" Ava shouts again, and Beau looks up.

"Shit," he curses, and Eden snatches her glasses off her face, cleaning them on her shirt as she talks.

"The trees. Beau, they're going to try to cross into Bristlebrook. Anyone coming across the moat, they need to die. Jasper, they need to—"

"We'll stop them." Jasper glances up at Beau. "Are you—"

"Nope. Not fine. I feel like a pile of dog shit." Beau sniffs as he laughs, but then his face firms. "You think it's okay to work some of my feelings out on these Sinners, Jas?"

I swing my rifle around as amusement flashes over Jasper's face.

"Consider it a recommended treatment," he says wryly.

From the hall, Ava begins shouting again—this time for *any* extra help—and Ethel's thin, dusty voice echoes from upstairs.

"I'm getting my rifle! Kasey, put your ass back in your bed. Ida's out there—don't you make it for nothing."

Oh, hell.

Exchanging a grim look, Beau and Jasper start running. I make it two steps after them before a soft hand tangles in the back of my shirt, pulling me back.

Eden's piercing eyes are still red-rimmed and luminous, but her face is set.

"Still my partner in crime?" she asks . . . and the fact that she's asking that *now*?

Yeah. Pretty sure it's the scariest question I've ever heard her ask.

"Yesss," I reply cautiously.

She takes my hand and starts dragging me toward the porch. "Wonderful. I need you to help me blow some people up."

I grin, and in the next instant, *I'm* dragging *her* to find our new danger pack.

"This is couple goals for me, I hope you know that," I tell her, and Eden's weak, snuffly laughter makes my steps begin to fly.

Murder by explosives might be couple goals—but making Eden laugh is my life's goal.

"What are we blowing up, anyway?" I ask as I push open the front door.

Her face darkens. "The side tunnel. Alastair knows where it is."

My stomach sinks.

But I'm glad one of us is thinking.

"Come on," I mutter.

Outside, the battle is raging. Under fire, dozens of Sinners are carrying three heavy, flattened tree trunks toward the moat. Makeshift bridges.

They're coming to us.

Between the trees, there's another swarm of men waiting impatiently for them to be placed, their weapons at the ready.

They'll blitz us as soon as those bridges are down.

"Take them *out*!" Jayk roars from the forward-most platform, storming down it. "Now! Fire for effect! We are *not* inviting them for a playdate!"

Beau runs toward the moat, lobbing a grenade, and it takes out several Sinners in a deafening burst. The remaining men stagger under the weight of the tree—but more Sinners race out of the forest to replace them.

Jasper kneels beside Beau, pounding out shot after shot. Covering him.

"How many Sinners did you say there were again?" I check with Eden, as casually as I can, tugging her toward Platform Two.

Billy and Baa-bara are straining against their ropes, tied to the porch, and my girl Henrietta's all in a panic as we pass her. I'll make it up to her.

If we live, I'll make it up to her.

Eden's wide eyes are on the encroaching Sinners. Another grenade goes off, and the blaze is reflected in her glasses.

"Ninety. Or . . . ninety tents? Do they sleep more than one to a tent?" she asks while we jog, like the idea only just occurred to her.

Almost definitely.

"Nope! Probably a bunch of decoy tents up, too. Inflating their numbers, you know? Nothing to worry about," I tell her in a rush, then shout up to the platform. "Hey, Katherine! Danger pack me!"

A heavy backpack drops from the high platform a second later, and I catch it with a yelp.

"Oh my God," Eden mutters, staring at it, her pulse pounding in her delicate neck.

Shouts and blasts crash through the background.

The tidy pocketed rows of C-4 are still secured, the frags still in their pouches, but . . .

My heart pounds as I laugh. Fuck me. "It . . . probably wouldn't have exploded."

Probably. C-4 is usually nice and stable.

They're pretty old, though.

Eden pivots toward the platform. "Do *not* throw the danger pack, idiots!"

Laughing, I grab several blocks and stick them into my pockets, and she scowls at me, too. I snag some clips. The shock tube initiator I slip into my jacket pocket.

She's so cute when she's bossy.

"Beau, get it loaded up. I want cover. On foot, push in! Target the left. Fire on three!" Jayk shouts. "One, two . . ."

Behind us, beyond the moat, there's an explosion so heavy that the ground rumbles under our feet, and the harsh smell of fumes stings the air. Smoke seeps out along the field beyond the moat, engulfing the Sinners, the bridges, the forest.

Eden's head whips back toward the moat.

"Three!" Jayk roars.

A ferocious, rhythmic crash of gunfire follows, and men begin screaming, lost and dying in the smoke. Pained shouts and confused panic roar from the Sinners, and one man runs shrieking from the billowing cloud, only to impale himself on the pikes.

Quickly, I grab the reel of detonating cord and some tape and spring to my feet. I take Eden's hand . . . but she holds me still.

Her eyes are scanning, searching for the screams in the smoke.

"Lucky? What is . . .? We can't see them." Her chest rises quickly. "What if they make it over here? What—"

"Back up!" Jayk shouts. "Back up before it settles!"

The civilians retreat, falling in behind the platforms.

And there's a beat as the cloud begins to fade, falling like a mist of snow.

When we can finally see, Eden presses a shocked hand to her mouth—and the civilians' weapons begin to thunder as they cheer.

The left bridge is down, over fifteen men shot down around it, underneath it, *running* from it. The other two lie abandoned in the grass, left in the Sinners' panicked confusion. Several more men lie dead around those.

"Oh my . . . *God*," Eden mutters, and I tug at her hand, laughing.

"Come on, beautiful. Jayk has this covered." When she stumbles after me, adorably incredulous, I can't help my grin. "He's letting Beau play with the *Gustaf*."

As the smoke dies, there's a shiver of movement by the tree line.

Alastair stands at their center, right where he stood the night of the first attack—only this time he's not cloaked in midnight and fire.

The sky is still streaked in orange and red with the sunrise.

A new dawn for all of us.

"Sinners!" he says simply. "*Attack*."

Shit.

Are we too late?

I take off.

Squeezing my hand hard, Eden races behind me back into the house. We dodge Ethel as she shouts back at Kasey and twist around Clare as she comes out of the med bay. I let go of Eden's hand so I can start tying the knots I need in the detonation cord before clipping it.

One block would probably be enough to cave the tunnel. Two to be safe.

I tug the first one from my pocket, backing through the door into the gym.

"Should you really be doing that while you're running?" Eden asks.

"According to our EOD training officers, or . . . ?" I ask, connecting the second charge to the first as we head over to the tunnel's entrance.

I almost drop the detonating cord, and Eden flinches.

"You're *really* making me second guess this, Lucky."

I snort.

I open the door and duck inside, taking a second to work out where to secure the charges. Annnd . . . maybe a bit farther in. The civs won't be happy if I blow out half their sleeping area.

When I glance back, checking the distance, Eden's tense face looks back at me from the doorway.

Does it look small enough?

Should I go deeper?

I take a few long strides backward.

Here?

"You're . . . you're joking again? Damn it, Lucky! Please don't blow yourself up! This *is* safe, right?"

Well.

No.

I'm eyeballing weights and guestimating how much rock is about to get blown into pixie dust—not to mention that I have no *idea* how this will affect the structural integrity of the house.

So, yeah. My officers really *would* have had my ass for attempting this one without clearance, but . . .

Muttered curses echo through the shadowed, rocky tunnel.

Gotta do what you gotta do, I guess.

My pulse kicks into fast, frantic action. Quickly, I secure the second charge to the rockface with as much tape as I can rip off with my teeth in one swipe.

Eden's eyes widen in sharp panic as she hears them too, and she gestures urgently for me to come back.

Fuck. If they rip through here before I can set up the initiator . . .

Eden is *right there*. Dom is in the med bay, and I doubt he's up for a gunfight. Clare. Deanna. *Kasey* is upstairs.

The footsteps echo louder, clattering close enough that—

Ice freezes my veins as the realization sinks in.

They're around the next corner, *maybe* the one after that.

"Go!" I shout soundlessly at Eden, but she shakes her head stubbornly, on the verge of tears.

Damn it, *no.*

I back toward Eden, unravelling the detonating cord with harsh, hurried tugs.

Almost, almost, almost.

"*Lucky*!" Eden whisper-shouts from the doorway, and I'm so close. I cut the cable with my pocketknife, and fumble for the initiator.

"Run!" I beg her,

"No! Not without you!" she snaps.

The men turn into the final bend, a crowd three-wide and I can't see how many deep. They stop dead as soon as they see me.

Then the one at the front steps forward, smiling.

Partners in crime.

I can't do this. I need her gone. Away from the men and the charge and—

Shit. Is there anywhere safe right now?

Where the *fuck* is my initiator?

The man at the front laughs, then surges forward.

Taking my own advice, I scramble backward, shoving my hand into my other pocket. I can't blow shit without my initiator, but I can't *find* it.

The men are running toward me, crashing against each other and the walls.

"Left side!" Eden urges me, tugging me back. "Lucky, your jacket!"

Shit.

I pull it out, connecting it to the cord, just as Eden drags me out and into the gym. I secure it in seconds—and she secures me.

We back up farther, and a few moments later, I see the Sinner's face in the doorway.

Eat dirt, motherfucker.

"You want the honors?" I ask Eden, passing the initiator to her, and she grins.

Then yanks the pump.

Damn it. This is going to hurt.

The force punches us back in the next instant, ripping us off our feet with bone-bruising force. I crash into Eden, grabbing her to me and twisting at the last second in a way my mom would have been proud of. It's not exactly what she had in mind for aerials, but . . .

I slam hard into the gym floor, and Eden comes down on top of me in a mass of knees and elbows I never appreciated for their sheer brutality until now. We skid through blankets and knock over water bottles and someone's lacy panties end up locked around my boots.

And then we stop.

Both of us roll onto our backs, gasping in shock.

Blackened plumes of thick, ashy smoke unfurl through the room, spreading out from where the side tunnel used to be. Small pebbles of rock and debris clatter onto the floor with shuddering little cracks.

I blink, then cough, my mouth full of dust—but it sends a thousand spurts of agony all through my body.

I think I finally did it.

I think I crushed every bone in my body.

"*Ow*," I groan.

Suddenly, the rock wall groans, and I shove myself up, dragging Eden farther backward as another chunk of wall crumbles in front of the side tunnel, burying the twitching hand of the Sinner in rubble.

"Next time . . ." Eden gasps. "Use *less*."

CHAPTER 71

LUCKY

I snort. Then laugh. Then laugh wildly enough that my ribs start to creak like the rock walls around us.

Next time.

"I fucking love you," I choke out, and she shakes her head, laughing too.

Until the rock stops grumbling.

And the shouts start to register.

"Come on, beautiful. Get up."

Every inch of my body aches, but I help Eden to her feet, and we run back toward the hall. Beyond it, I hear shouts and orders and feet —too many feet.

It takes us a minute to clear enough rubble to open the door to the hall, but when we do, there are civilians everywhere, blocking the hall.

"What's happening?" Eden asks Mary Beth, who's staring over our shoulders, horrified.

"What happened to our *room*?"

I start pushing through the hall, twisting between civilians and

Reapers and past Arthur, and I catch Deanna's worried face sticking out of the med bay.

"What in the *hell* was that?" she asks. "Do we need to move? Is there more? Should I—"

I don't stop moving, but I shout back. "All fine, just a teensy *tiny* bit of C-4 to murder our enemies! Shouldn't bother you anymore unless the room collapses." I tug Eden through the thick mass of bodies, and bounce up on my toes to shout, "Is Dom still okay?"

"He's stable. What—?"

"Tell him I said hi!"

I glance into the sitting room, seeing Sawyer sitting between the rows of wounded, next to an unconscious Cole. Sawyer's face is white and grim as he stares through the cracked sliding doors.

As he watches from inside.

Eden and I finally shove free of the crowd, coated in dust and joined by the hand.

"Back!" Jennifer is shouting on the porch. "Everyone inside, *now*! *Go!*"

Eden and I exchange a look.

We both push forward, moving against the surge until we make it outside.

Reapers and civilians are abandoning the defensive platforms at speed, racing back to the house. In the distance, I see the second Sinner log bridge has been taken out, lying burned and discarded on its side, but the third . . .

I start to run, and Eden is right beside me, the same fear on her face.

She's not armed, but it doesn't matter.

Ava, Katherine, Ida, Ethel, Sloane, and Jasper are too close to the moat, under the shitty cover we used the other day, firing on every Sinner approaching the bridge. A small horde lies dead on the other side, and more bodies dangle over pikes, but the Sinners are like a wave. Like the ocean. There's too many of them, and they're all headed for us.

And then I see them.

Beau is kneeling right in front of the bridge, holding the Gustaf over one shoulder.

Jayk is behind him, loading up a heavy round.

"Oh, fuck," I breathe.

Jayk has used our smoke round. We've only got high explosives or area defense rounds left.

"Fuck?" Eden asks, staggering to a halt beside me. "Why, oh fuck?"

The civs—the goddamned Valkyries out there protecting my guys —they stand, firing on the Sinners as they back up.

Henrietta squawks at my feet, her wings batting my legs in distress, and absently, I pick her up, tucking her against my chest. My heart's pounding as quickly as hers.

"Well, you know the C-4 we just used?" I tell Eden.

Jasper rises beside them, lobbing two grenades, and the explosions make pockets in the horde in front of them. It buys Jayk and Beau enough time to run in.

Eden goes still. "*Yes*?"

Beau finally stops, stepping one foot onto the bridge, and the bazooka over his shoulder winks in the sun.

For the first time, the Sinners hesitate.

"Well, Beau just whipped his out," I sigh.

A Sinner at the front lifts his pistol at Beau, and Jayk takes him between the eyes. Then another beside him. Jasper nails one in the thigh, then one in the gut—not as neat, but they're not firing on Beau either way.

The civs run toward us, just as the Sinners start scrambling back.

I look at Eden regretfully. "And his is bigger."

Beau fires.

In slow, mesmerizing motion, the blast lights up the trees in a violent, volcanic burst. It tears their roots out of the ground, ripping a hole in the forest, the fiery blast roaring outward with brutal, rushing force. It rushes through the Sinners from behind, a mass of trees and dirt, stone and rubble slamming into them in a vicious wall of debris. The earth churns up, splitting in a biblical fissure.

Men are thrown hard into the moat, skewered by pikes, or they land in the barbed wire, where it snags in their throats and cheeks. A flying branch crashes against the back of one man's head, and a Sinner runs from the trees, screaming and writhing in flames.

In a thunderous crash, the force pushes out farther, faster, and Beau flies back off the bridge, hurtling hard into the grass, debris peppering him too.

I grab Eden to me, and Henrietta is hugged between us as Jasper, Jayk, the civs, are slammed to the ground by the shockwave. Platform Three's wooden struts crack and then crash under force, until the whole thing crumples with a thud.

When the blast rushes past us, it only has enough strength to make us stumble back a step and the other platforms creak threateningly.

The field falls quiet.

Eden's breath is hot against my face.

"Are they okay?" she whispers.

Silently, tense, I watch the field. I'm sure Jayk and Jasper were clear, but . . . Beau was closer.

For a long, long moment, nothing moves at all.

Then Beau staggers to his feet.

"Yeah, beautiful. They're okay," I whisper, seeing the others shaking themselves off too. "We're okay."

A few lucky Sinners get up, dragging themselves toward the trees. A few scream and moan, too damaged to move. Most don't move at all.

And through the flashes of the blazing fire, I see the rest of their army . . . and they're running away.

Henrietta's soft, downy head rubs against my chest, and I pet her, smiling tiredly.

"I think we just won our first fight."

CHAPTER 72

EDEN

SURVIVAL TIP #113

Give a girl the right costume and she can conquer . . . well, maybe not the world, but definitely a few lovesick men.

My muscles are sore and aching, but the hot water beating down on my back is a steamy release. I'm covered in bruises from being tossed about by explosions like I'm a ping pong ball, but it could have been worse.

Dom is recovering well. The heavy bullet wound in his upper arm is stitched and clean, and he has comfortable access to our pain medicine. He has three cracked ribs, and the bruising is deep and swollen over most of his chest. It will take him a while to regain full mobility, but . . . he's alive.

Beau's stint in the med bay was quicker, cutely laid up in the bed next to Dom's. He had a slight concussion and various cuts and bruises, but he quickly decided he was fine and checked himself out.

But despite our win here yesterday morning, the last day and a half of recovery was intense, and the mood is heavy and somber.

After we'd confirmed that the remaining Sinners were truly gone from our woods and on their way back to Cyanide, the cleanup began swiftly. The bodies of the Sinners and the Reapers were gathered and burned—or burned still piked in the moat if they couldn't be recovered.

With the acrid scent of kerosene and roasted bodies in the air, we began collecting the discarded tools and tents the Sinners left behind in their panicked retreat. Grim and methodical, we took blankets and cookery and anything of value they didn't grab on their way out.

The food most of all.

We dragged their abandoned food in by the armful, load after load —until our stores grew fatter than they had been in months and there was nothing more to carry.

To secure the slipping rock around the side tunnel, Jayk and my brutes worked with Sara, a bright-eyed brunette who used to be a structural engineer—and who became decidedly less bright-eyed when she saw exactly how much damage Lucky and I caused.

Reluctantly, I turn the shower off and step out. The others will be in soon for their turns, and not just because we've given up all pretense that we're not all sleeping in Jasper and Lucky's rooms.

But also because Jennifer is currently crying her heart out in Dom's room, nestled between Ida and Ethel, and she needs some privacy.

There have been some . . . hard decisions made since the Sinners left.

Faced with the two options of going to farmlands alongside the Reapers and facing all the danger and all the risks of being *there* right now, or staying here at Bristlebrook, the civilians were heavily split on what they wanted to do. They talked for hours about it yesterday, long into the night, with all Reapers and Red Zone locked out of the conversation so they could discuss the pros and cons freely.

But in the end, about thirty-two civilians decided to go with me and my brutes—and tomorrow, we'll leave for the farmlands to prepare for the onslaught attacks we know will be coming from the Sinners.

The rest of the civilians will stay at Bristlebrook and re-fortify.

Despite the mixed reactions to *that* decision.

Many of the Reapers objected loudly, begging and arguing in turn about the dangers of staying here alone, but the civilians wouldn't be budged.

The Sinners have been defeated twice at Bristlebrook—and the women here have proven they can defend themselves.

Bristlebrook is where they feel safe.

Which, as far as my brutes were concerned, was all there was to it.

And quietly, I'm relieved about it. I don't want these women to have to face the same dangers we're up against.

They've been through more than enough.

Slowly, my stomach sick and heavy, I begin to towel myself off.

Everyone heard the break-up between Jennifer and Sawyer yesterday, just hours after the battle. They heard his confusion and heartbreak and how he begged her to *please* come with him. That he'd keep her safe.

That he loved her.

They heard *her* tell *him* that she wouldn't feel safe there anymore. That she doesn't feel safe anywhere right now. That she needs to be here with her people.

I listened by the door with my heart in my throat, ready to intervene if she needed it, unwell to my marrow.

Taking a steadying breath, I hang my towel and resecure my bun.

It's okay.

It's for the best.

Someone as fierce as Jennifer should never be with a man as weak as Sawyer.

Those of us who are leaving will set off for the farmlands first thing tomorrow morning. The Reapers' home base has been radioed, and they know to expect us. Arthur and his people will travel with us most of the way, until they can safely avoid the Sinners on their trip back into Red Zone. We've given Arthur our satellite phone so we can stay in close, more secure communication through the coming days.

The decisions all sit heavily on me.

We all know death is following us now, but at this point, we have little choice but to turn around and face it. We're committed to this war—and those Sinners need to die. It's the only way we can be safe . . . and it's the only chance their captives have, too.

I swallow hard.

God, I hope Heather's okay.

She saw Dom get shot, too.

Dismissing the thoughts I've already spiraled over too many times, I pick up my glasses. I need to get dressed and then check on Dom again. I don't think he's used to being on bedrest, and he's already testy and impatient to get up.

But right before I leave the bathroom, I see a note pinned to the door.

> *JUST TRUST ME ON THIS, BUT I'D TURN THAT*
> *INTO A DEEP CLEANING OPERATION*
> *XOXO LOVE YOU*
> *PS LEG SHAVING HAS NEVER LOOKED SO HOT*

Lucky.

I stare at the paper, torn between laughter and a vague incredulity. That is a *hell* of a note to receive cold after the last few days.

But . . .

I turn back into the bathroom and spend the next fifteen minutes judiciously cleaning, remembering the entire time how thoroughly Dom inspected me in the shower last week.

And that was only my pussy.

By the time I've slipped, naked, to the bathroom door, I'm tingling with the memory and anticipation is prickling over my skin.

If Lucky is leaving me a note, am I in for a night with him and Jasper?

My breathing quickens at the thought.

Then again, the others are all meant to be sleeping here tonight. I know it's only just dusk now, but how does that . . .

I hear footsteps in the next room.

Slowly, I crack the door open, peeking out.

"Hey, beautiful."

Edging closer, I open the door, craning my head to see him.

Lucky's eyes sparkle at me in amusement. He's standing not-so-casually in front of the bed—and on *top* of the bed is . . .

"Um. Lucky. What is *that*?" I ask, my voice too high.

I slip out of the bathroom, trying to get a better look at the familiar wooden box, the lingerie, and the utterly *absurd* red-and-white costume that—

"Hm?"

His gaze is traveling slowly, heatedly over my body.

My *naked* body.

My tripping pulse begins to thrum in my throat. It's been such a heavy few days, terrifying and sickening and disillusioning, full of so many betrayals.

There's something so simple and so . . . so *freeing* in seeing that kind of undisguised mischief ready to be unleashed.

Especially in *him*.

My Lucky, with his perfect, lickable dimples, and stupidly carnal sweatpants, and big, beautiful heart.

Slowly, I walk up to him and stretch my arms up over his shoulders. His hands immediately slide around my back, then cup my ass, dragging me against him with a low sigh.

His cock presses provocatively into my stomach through the soft fabric of his sweats, and his fingers begin to knead my ass, like he can't help himself.

My mouth an inch from his, I smile. "You making plans for us I should know about, sweetheart?"

Lucky's eyes brighten, and his soft laugh gusts over my lips. "Sweetheart, huh?" His mouth slips over mine. "I could get behind that."

I lean up to kiss him, and our lips slide sinfully against each other. It's a hot, slow, delicious tease, a game of anticipation and release, rushes and sinking, heated need. I pant into him, and he groans, stealing that too.

Whenever Lucky has his mouth on me, I cease to exist for anything else.

He lifts me up by my ass, moving me to the bed, his mouth still working over mine, and I cling to his neck as he leans down over me, my body waking up with vicious eagerness. I tunnel my fingers into his hair, tugging him down harder.

The next sound that leaves him is half a laugh and half a groan as he hikes my legs wide and crawls onto the bed, settling over me. His mouth hardly leaves mine, and by now we're just a tangle of tongues and hot breath and panted whimpers. He sucks on my lower lip, and my tongue and presses his fingers between mine until we're tangled everywhere.

Lucky kisses with his whole body, with unbridled eagerness and wicked cleverness. More than any of them, I think he enjoys it the most, just *kissing*.

His mouth moves briefly to my neck, and I gasp, my head spinning, my lips damp and desperate for more.

Although . . . I also know exactly what he can do elsewhere with that mouth.

"I love you," I whisper between pants.

It wasn't what I meant to say, but it spills out anyway. After the battle and the misery and . . . and *all of it* to come, I feel like I can't say it enough.

His golden hair is long and loose, and its silky strands tickle over my breasts as he sucks softly at my throat, nips at my collarbones. It's like being gilded in him.

But Lucky glances up from his kisses, his laughter settling into something soft and warm and quietly solemn. "I love you too, Eden."

"And I love you both," Jasper says from somewhere behind Lucky, then I hear a soft sound of exasperation. "I knew I shouldn't have left you here alone. Don't distract her, Lucien. They'll be up in less than half an hour."

They?

Don't *distract* me? Isn't this my surprise?

"It's Eden's fault. You know I have a weakness for . . . well, her, I guess." Lucky's head briefly dips, and he runs his tongue up the inside curve of one breast.

Gasping out a heated giggle, I tug up his head and bring him back to my mouth for another reckless, hungry kiss.

Technically Jasper ordered him and not me, so until he—

"Stop, my Eden."

Delight and pleasure thrills through me at the order, and I stop kissing Lucky, panting into his mouth. Obediently, I lift my hands off him and cross them at the wrist over my head.

Showing Jasper just how seriously *I* take his instructions.

Lucky lets out a long-suffering sigh, but his blue eyes are hot and amused he mutters, "Goody two-shoes."

I grin. "Brat."

He winks. "That's the beauty of the sub club, beautiful."

Sub club.

My heart squeezes happily.

"You two . . ." Jasper trails off, his voice husky. I hear the clip of his loafers pause, but I can't see him from here.

Lucky twists back to look at him, and it presses his lower body into mine. I bite down on a shudder as his cock presses against my pussy through his sweatpants.

"New plan," he says to Jasper. "Forget Dom and Beau. We lock the door, and *we* play in your room with her all night instead."

That startles me out of my battle not to squirm against him.

"Dom and Beau?"

Lucky turns back to look down at me, his brow slanted judgmentally. "Who'd you *think* the nurse's outfit was for? Come on, beautiful. Keep up."

My mouth drops open as I glare at him. "You threw me onto the bed and started ravishing me, Lucky. I didn't have the brain cells to think!"

"Huh. On second thought, you're right. Brain cells are overrated."

Lucky's dimples deepen, and his eyes drop back down to my breasts. His tongue teases his lower lip, and I can *see* him considering whether the punishment for continuing will be worth it.

"Get off her, Lucien," Jasper orders again, this time with so much silken warning rippling through it that we both shiver.

Sighing again, Lucky pushes back off the bed—off *me*—and I shiver again in the sudden cold.

Jasper steps into view a moment later, surveying me as I lie on the bed. I'm stretched obediently for him, naked and still, my breasts rising faster the longer he looks at me.

I know they said Dom and Beau were coming, something about *this* being for *them*, and it's not that I'm opposed to the idea at all, but it's truly hard to think about anyone else while Lucky's kisses are still dizzying my brain and with Jasper's eyes traveling down my body like slow-burning coals.

They linger on my pussy, and that devilish curl of hair slips over his forehead.

"So beautiful, darling girl." He steps closer, and with his knee, he slowly draws my leg wider, spreading me until I'm wide and glistening, and his jaw is like the cut of a blade as he takes me in. "I suppose it doesn't hurt that you're all warmed up for them."

Hurt? It hurts *me*. My nipples are achingly tight, and I'm already throbbing with the need to be filled.

But there's that *them* again.

"For . . . for Dom and Beau?" I ask huskily. "I thought . . . Dom's still in the med bay, isn't he?"

Jasper nods, but his head tilts as I clench my empty pussy, his eyes gleaming.

"Beaumont thought Dominic would be more comfortable recovering up here before we leave tomorrow—and I believe he wanted to see whether Dominic can, in fact, move comfortably enough to travel. They have a difference of opinion regarding that matter, I believe."

I'm sure they do.

I arch my back for Jasper, watching his face, and a hint of a smile touches his lips. Lucky groans as he walks around the bed.

Biting my lip to stop from begging, I ask, "So how . . . how do I fit in?"

Jasper's gaze finally lifts to mine.

"You've all had a difficult few days," he says softly.

"We all have," I murmur, and he nods.

"You three in particular, though." Jasper's severe angles soften. "Lucien and I thought we might arrange something for the three of you. Something that might make you all smile before we leave."

My chest squeezes fiercely, and I stare at him, at Lucky, caught and touched and suddenly tangled with emotions that have nothing to do with my need.

They planned something.

Not for themselves, or just to make me happy . . . but for Dom and Beau, too.

It's completely selfless—and entirely to help our little family when it's hurting.

My lip trembles, and Jasper shakes his head once, but the small smile on his face is unbearably warm and full of empathy.

"I'm sorry, dearest, but we don't have time for those. You need to get dressed. If you spoil my surprise by being late, I will be very unhappy with you," he advises, and I sniff, a reluctant smile returning to my face.

Lucky picks up the skimpy, deliciously slutty outfit from the bed. "It's going to take you at *least* that long to get into character. Just remember—the poor, rough, cranky soldier was wounded, the sexy doctor is overseeing his care, and *you*, little nurse, need to obey every instruction to tend to his recovery."

Twisting my head on the bed, I give Lucky an amused look. "The poor, rough, cranky soldier *was* wounded. The sexy doctor *is* overseeing his care. And I *am* obeying every instruction to help tend to his recovery."

"Sure, but you've got to make it dirty."

Jasper reaches out a hand, and I take it delicately. He pulls me up until I'm standing torturously close to him.

Lucky tears the tags from the outfit, tossing them on the bed, and I see it's in my size. It's a tiny little red-slashed white dress that will barely cover my ass. It has a red zipper at the front that promises plunging cleavage, and a cute red heart with a small white cross inside it that will sit right over my pussy.

There's a tiny little white-and-red hat sitting to the side, and Lucky has a matching, scandalously red set of lingerie to accompany the costume.

"Where on earth did you even *find* all of that?" I ask on a little laugh as Lucky hands Jasper the wooden box that I recognize too well.

"Not us," Jasper corrects, bemused. "I believe Beaumont—quite optimistically—picked that up for you himself when he and Dominic collected clothes for you after you arrived. Lucien noticed it in the pile of his things—which I would like removed from my hall, by the way. Now bend over the bed for me, Eden. Spread your legs."

The change in his tone makes my breath catch, but I obey quickly, my breasts pressing into the bedspread and my legs set wide apart. I quiver there, knowing what's coming.

"Safeword? Any concerns today, any amendments to your list?" Jasper checks in.

"Bristlebrook, and none, thank you. I'm . . . please don't hold back," I tell him as demurely as I can.

Lucky's grin tells me I failed.

I sound every inch like I'm desperate and begging.

"How long has it been since anyone used your ass, sweet girl?" Jasper walks up behind me.

I hear the latch on the box un-snick.

My breaths tremble against the sheets, and Lucky meets my eyes, raw need darkening his into restless, stormy skies.

"Not . . . not since Jayk. The bond-fire," I whisper.

"And the plug? Have you used that since?"

"No. Fingers and . . ." I blush, and Lucky's lips twitch with too much laughter. "And tongues."

I scowl at him, but his smile stutters with his ragged, tortured breath in.

Jasper makes a pensive sound behind me. "They might be a challenge for you today, then."

A bottlecap is popped, and then there's a soft, wet squirt, and I twitch in anticipation, waiting for the cold drizzle.

"Remind them to take it slow if you need to, please," Jasper murmurs.

There's a soft rustle, then a hot fan of breath against the sensitive join between my ass and thigh. He's *kneeling* behind me.

Lucky's grip on the nurse costume tightens as he watches us, his eyes slipping between Jasper spreading my ass and stopping to watch my face.

"Have you cleaned yourself?" he asks, and my blush deepens.

Lucky gives me a smug, knowing look, heated color high in his cheeks.

Right now, I'm feeling very grateful for his note.

"Yes, Jasper," I whisper.

I feel the first liquid touch of lube against my tight, puckered hole . . . but it's not cold. This time, it's warmed by Jasper's fingers as he smears it over me, slicking it up and down the forbidden cleft of my ass.

My breathing becomes frayed and fast, and Lucky crawls up onto the bed so he can get a better look. The outline of his cock curves hard and needy against his sweatpants, and I fight the urge to reach out and touch it.

Jasper had made himself clear—he's in control now.

The pad of Jasper's finger begins to press against my hole, teasing the lube into it, testing the give, until he finally begins to push inside, breaching the sensitive ring.

"Ah," I whimper as he adds a second finger almost immediately.

"Sorry, darling girl. We don't have time to take this slow. You'll just have to take it," Jasper tells me, his voice edged and tight.

Ohhh.

My brain melts between my ears, the polite demand in his voice turning me liquid.

"I'll take anything you give me. I . . . I want them to fit. Thank you, I—" My pant borders on a whine as he curses hoarsely under his breath.

Jasper lifts up over me, bracing one hand on my lower back as his fingers test the tight, tugging grip. There's a pause, a rush of more liquid, and then he begins pumping them into my ass with a deliberate stretching, massaging speed.

My mouth opens on a muffled cry against the bed as I feel his fingers everywhere, tunneling, rubbing deep, touching every sensitive, hidden part inside me. The initial, overwhelming strain quickly turns into a needy, uncomfortable pressure.

I moan as he pauses to push unbearably deep, my ass lifting off the bed to press into it.

Lucky's laugh is pained, and he has to tear his eyes from my ass to meet my gaze. "Look at him pretending he doesn't want to make you work for it."

Jasper lets out an amused breath, full of strain. Then he pinches my ass with his other hand and spreads the fingers inside me wide.

Stretching me until I cry out.

"This will be nothing to her when they both take her at once. Better a little pain now," he muses. "Lucien, pass me the plug. No— You know which one. Don't be soft on her. It won't be kind in the long run."

"Your age is showing, babe. Gentle parenting's the thing now," Lucky teases, his dimples wicked as he passes Jasper the largest plug.

Jasper pauses. "Lucien. Would you *like* to go back in the cage?"

The cage? Under Jasper's bed? My head is spinning, my body shuddering in pleasure but . . .

"You put Lucky in the cage? As punishment? For how long?" I choke out.

The tip of the cold, metal plug wedges into my ass.

As Jasper pushes it in, ignoring my gasps and the violent arch of my back, he mutters, "Long enough for me to finish my notes. He becomes a pestering little slut when he wants attention."

Lucky flops back onto the bed beside me, but Jasper is working the plug in slowly, pushing the fattest, heaviest part past the tight ring in my ass so I barely hear him as he complains.

"For *hours*! He left me in there for *hours*! No food, no water. Alone, and—"

Jasper snorts, and the plug pops in. I gasp, squeezing instinctively against the cold, intense pressure.

"You had food *and* water, and I was on the bed the entire time, you brat. The amount of grief you gave me, you should have been in there for days."

Lucky rolls onto his side, looking me in the eyes while I squirm to get comfortable, feeling desperately, painfully full.

"Do you see how he speaks to me? Cold. Cruel." He tuts, then he smiles, leaning in to kiss my panting mouth. "Not like you. So warm. So kind. Oh, beautiful, you're struggling, huh? They are going to *wreck* you."

Jasper tilts my hips, encouraging me to turn over, and I roll onto my back, flushed and full and aching.

"We have about ten minutes before they're up," he says. "Have you eaten yet?"

I nod breathlessly, distracted, still squeezing helplessly against the plug.

"Yes, I-I've had plenty."

Too much, possibly, and all through the day. I almost made myself sick from gorging on the Sinners' abandoned rations yesterday.

It was hard to resist once I knew there was enough for everyone for a long, long time.

His eyes scan my face, as though he's checking for half-truths, but not *wanting* to eat has never been the demon that haunts me. Fearing not being able to find a next meal . . . fearing hunger and wasting away? *That* haunts me.

Finally, he nods. "Okay. Sit up, then. Let's get you dressed."

Sit?

Gritting my teeth, I let him pull me up to sit on the bed—and the position buries the fat plug deep in my ass. The ball inside clatters, and I flinch.

Damn it. I'd forgotten about the ball.

"Hurry now. Lucien, pass me the garter belt."

The two work on me quickly. Jasper clips my garter belt into place and helps me step into the skimpy, lacy red underwear. Lucky's fingers trail over the nape of my neck and scoop my breasts into the dizzying scarlet push-up bra, clasping it at the front.

Ordering me to stand, Jasper's breath teases my thighs as he carefully rolls the thigh-high stockings into place, securing them with the clips while Lucky pulls the dress over my head and squeezes it over my breasts.

Lucky tidies my bun, and Jasper secures the tiny hat's small clips into my hair.

Their breaths and their touches are at once stirring and soothing, and I watch them work with quiet, adoring fascination. Their serious little frowns and the careful way they fix everything to me.

"Thank you," I say softly, and both of them pause.

Lucky tilts my chin to him and gives me a soft look before he kisses me, long and slow. The next breath I breathe in is Jasper's as he kisses me too.

"Anything, Eden. All of it. Whatever brings you joy," he murmurs.

I smile. "You do." I lean back against Lucky, heartsick and desiring no cure in this ridiculous nurse costume. "You all do."

There's a burst of voices at the door, and I freeze.

The door swings open.

CHAPTER 73

EDEN

Not even glancing our way, Dom grabs the front of Beau's shirt and slowly pushes him back a step, his face set with strained patience.

"Stop. Hovering."

"Stop acting like you weren't shot. Twice!"

"*Beaumont*," Dom says warningly.

"*Dominic*," Beau mimics in the same tone.

Despite my sudden, fluttering nerves, my smile widens, the warm ache in my chest deepening. It reminds me of the first day I met them.

They're finally back in rhythm again.

Dom looks better than he did this morning, with more color in his face. He has a heavy bandage around his upper arm on his left side, and bruises crawl out of the neck of his T-shirt, but he's moving on his own.

Beau has a few nicks and bruises on his face, but not many more than I have.

"A-*hem*." Lucky mock coughs behind me, and I whip a glare at him.

His grin is impossibly cheeky, his dimples shining like stars, but my sudden nerves are storming me. This outfit is *absurd!* Beau leading me through a role play is one thing, but me *volunteering* one?

"Oh, Jesus, Mary, and Joseph," Beau drawls from the door in pure shock, and I wince, feeling the heat racing into my cheeks.

Hesitantly, I look back.

Dom slowly steps into the room, making way for Beau, his dark brows climbing higher the longer he looks at me. A reluctantly impressed smile begins working its way across his face, already wider than I've ever seen from him. He shoots a sideways glance at Beau.

Who is staring at me like he might drop to his knees.

A rude hand at my back shoves me forward, and I stagger a step before I stop, blushing. The metal ball inside my plug clatters heavily inside of me a moment later, and my ass clenches hard.

Damn it, Lucky!

I don't know how to *do* this!

And to do it in front of Dom? And *Jasper*?

But . . . I'm pretty sure Beau's hands are shaking.

Oh, hell.

Okay.

I wipe my sweaty hands on the front of my dress—only I run out of dress before they're dry.

Nurse. I'm a nurse.

"Oh, um, hi . . . Doctor Bennett. It's so good to . . . to see you."

So natural. Perfect. Wonderful.

End me.

"I see you've brought our . . ." I gesture helplessly at Dom, who crosses his arms stiffly over his chest, his brow quirking in an amused question that makes me want to melt away, and I finish in a mumble, "Our . . . patient?"

Lucky turns away, muffling his laughter with zero success, and I cringe, my face flaming.

But I've come this far, I suppose . . .

I gesture behind me at Jasper and accidently whack him in the chest.

"Sorry," I mouth, and he gives me a wry, sympathetic look before I turn back.

Beau is approaching me slowly, his stunned mouth still hanging open.

I clear my throat. "I just finished up with these two. Mr. Douglas here was wonderful, but *that* one needs a brain biopsy," I growl, glancing at Lucky, who is rolling against the wall, choking on his giggles. "Given I'm concerned he was born *without* one."

Dom snorts.

"You know, she might be on to something there, doc," he says dryly. But then he looks at Jasper, searching. "You organized this?"

Jasper spreads his hands. "The brainless patient and I assisted. It was nothing. Your nurse is fed, thoroughly prepped, and comfortable with her current list and the prospect of the scene, her delightful embarrassment aside. You're welcome to use my room and my tools, though I'd ask that you clean them after. I believe you showed interest in my medical chair, Beaumont? Yes? Good. Eden, safeword?"

Beau sucks in a sharp breath, his eyes widening further, darting between me and Jasper and the hidden door to his private rooms.

"Bristlebrook," I say, though I'm reeling a little at the peremptory handover.

Like he's my babysitter and my parents just arrived home.

Jasper nods, and there's a twinkle in his eye too as he looks down at me. "Have fun, little nurse." He looks over at Lucky. "You. Shower. Now."

Lucky's snickers cut off, and he grins. "Bye . . . Nurse Anderson."

He bails for the shower, and Jasper gives us one last amused look before he follows him in.

When the door closes behind them, I look back at Beau nervously.

Only to find him very, very close.

My gaze travels from his chest all the way up to his face. His gaze is hot and appreciative and mostly lingering on my breasts, which are shoved so high out of the cleavage of this dress they ought to qualify for space training.

His fingers play with the straps on my garter, brushing against my thigh.

"Why, *hello*, there, nurse," he says slowly, those woodland eyes glowing with growing delight. His accent is thicker than usual. "You know, I had wondered where you'd run off to. I had to bring our patient upstairs all by myself, and he . . . well, he has not been very agreeable."

The heat in my cheeks changes, slipping into something delicious at the thick, rampant lust in his voice. I glance over at Dom in time to see him give Beau an overly patient look.

"Or your patient is perfectly fucking fine. I have painkillers. Nothing's broken—"

"Your arm was ripped open by a bullet—"

"Which hit nothing important—"

"Except your arm—"

"And it's sewed up all nice and pretty. I'll live, *doctor*."

Beau sighs, and his fingers slip higher up my thigh, under my dress.

His eyes caress me. "As you can see, nurse, we're in need of someone a little *sweeter* to help bring our patient around." His fingers brush against my panties. "You can be sweet, can't you?"

My breath catches, and I lean into him, staring at his mouth before I remember the game. His fingertips stroke lasciviously over the lace at my pussy.

I swallow. "I . . . I can try, Doctor Bennett." I catch his wrist, living for the feral gleam in his eyes when I call him that. It's enough to remember how much fun I had playing with him last time. "But we'll . . . we'll remain professional, won't we?"

His hand falls away from my panties to chuck me lightly under the chin.

"Of course, little nurse. This is a very professional environment." Beau's lips tuck up in a patronizing smile. "We do everything possible to make our patients comfortable. Speaking of . . . you should fetch him. Bring him to my office."

Unable to contain his eagerness, Beau hurries over to Jasper's hidden door, peering into the room curiously before he ducks inside.

Slowly, I turn to Dom, my fingers knotting together.

He's parked his ass against the back of Jasper's couch, leaning against it as he watches me patiently. Those hot, golden eyes are molten with interest—and curiosity.

He's waiting to see what I'll do.

Damn it, what *do* I do? Beau makes the role I take with him extremely easy.

In our scene the other night, Dom also made my role extremely easy—but that was predicated on my complete submission to him. His *rules*. How does this work when my role is to . . . *handle* him?

Well, I guess I'm breaking rule number four.

"I . . . will you come with me, sir?" I ask tentatively, begging with my eyes for him to help me here. It only makes the amusement in the heavy lines of his face grow, and I bite my lip. "Please? The . . . Doctor Bennett would really like to see you get well." Shifting, I add more seriously, "We both would."

Dom considers me softly for a long moment, and then he takes a deep breath, nodding to himself like he's having a moment, too.

When he looks back up at me, it's with a challenging, raised brow . . . and such a dry, self-deprecating smile that I find my own lips curving up, too.

"Come here, pe—" He rolls his eyes skyward. "*Nurse.*"

I bite my lip against a grin at his struggle.

It makes me feel better about my own . . . and I find myself more than a little charmed that he'd go along with this for Beau's sake.

Dom's eyes meet mine again, and the heat creeps back in. "This patient is going to need some incentive to go along with *Doctor Bennett* today."

I press a hand against the excited flutters in my stomach, ducking my head demurely to hide the smile I can't stop now.

"Yes, sir."

I walk up to him slowly, and when I get close enough, Dom sits on top of the couch, and parts his heavy legs, creating a deep nook for me to traverse into. He gestures sharply for me to step between his thighs.

I can see the heavy jut of his cock, demanding freedom.

Dampening my lips, I glance up at him through my lashes. "I'm not sure that's appropriate, sir."

"Your call, *nurse*," he replies dryly. "But I'm not going anywhere until you let me taste your fucking lips. Call it medicine."

My pulse leaps, shocked and thrilled.

So *this* is how he's playing it—how he controls me within the bounds of Beau's game. It reminds me, suddenly, of the riverbank, of his crude orders against Beau's gentle indulgence.

Good top, bad top.

A push and pull between all three of us until they box me in exactly how they want me.

I step between his legs, shivering at the size of him, shivering at the feeling of being enclosed in his heavy strength while I'm in this flimsy, cock-hungry outfit for him, trying to play the good girl.

Tentatively, I place my hands lightly on his thick shoulders, conscious of his injuries, and he watches me with heated interest.

The plug in my ass tugs and clatters as I move, the wide, flared base of it pressed against my tight hole, slowly stretching me. Preparing me.

I wonder if it'll be Dom's cock in my ass or Beau's.

Keeping a slight distance between us, I lift up on my toes and brush a soft kiss against his stubbled jaw. I'm about to pull away when he grabs me by my cheeks and turns my face to his.

He looks at me for a long, deliberate moment, like he's making me *feel* the correction, before he lowers his mouth to mine. He watches me as he licks inside, tasting me.

Taking his medicine.

Holding me immobile as I whimper, Dom deepens the kiss, still watching me as he claims my mouth.

Then he releases me, and I back up, panting hard.

Dom's intensity is brutal, delicious and demanding, and as he straightens up off the couch, still intent on me, I swallow.

Submitting to Dom entirely is easier in many ways. The clear rules. The structure.

But this little hunt is luscious in its own way.

One way or another, my sir will *take*.

Dom nods his roughened chin toward the secret room. "Go on then, little nurse. Don't tell your doctor what I made you do."

CHAPTER 74

EDEN

Show your medical professionals just how much you appreciate them.

I'm still trembling when I slip into Jasper's private room, my sensitive nipples needy and trapped and my panties too damp for decency.

The space is enormous, high-ceilinged, and I'm not sure how long it might take for it to feel commonplace, but I've been in here so few times that it still thrills me. The dark, heavy woods, the warm lights, and the sumptuous scent of well-kept leather are enveloping. Erotic.

Every item of Jasper's custom furniture is at once intriguing and alarming, and the wall of display cabinets with all their carefully arranged items makes my heart speed up. His four-poster bed sprawls along the far wall, obnoxiously large and swathed in luxuriant fabrics. There are hooks and tethers notched all along the frame . . . and the infamous cage is housed threateningly underneath it.

Between the bars, I can make out several pillows, a blanket, and a discarded pack of cards I imagine Lucky getting fed up with quickly.

Beau is standing beside a large, padded gynecologist's chair. It's wide and thick and reclinable, with far more straps and cuffs and attachments than any normal doctor would ever require. There's a rolling, completely stocked medical cart sitting to one side, alongside a wheeled office chair that has the word "DOCTOR" stitched across the backrest.

Beau is bent over, retracting the chair's stirrups to the side, but he looks up as I enter. And then his eyes lift higher behind me.

"Oh, now. See? That's good work, Nurse Anderson. I told you—every difficult patient can be brought around when you have the right attitude." Beau's innocent smile is more than a little wicked. "Did he give you any trouble?"

I glance up at Dom to see him giving Beau a sardonic look.

"I told you. I'm no trouble," he says, and I suppress a scoff.

I start walking over to Beau. "Well, *actually*, doctor, he—"

"Sure you aren't," Doctor Bennett agrees caustically, ignoring me. "Come sit."

Dom closes the door behind him with his back, but winces a little when it jolts his arm, and I purse my lips at the reminder.

It might be a game, but he *is* actually hurt.

But Dom just eyes the stirrups, his lips twitching again.

"I don't think I have the right equipment for that chair, *doc*," Dom says, like we both just missed his flinch.

And Beau straightens, scowling. "Just shut up and get in the chair, idiot."

Dom pushes off the door and comes over to sit down. Even his heavy frame sits comfortably in the padded monstrosity, and it's wide enough around his hips and head that if we reclined it, I could . . .

Stop.

I'm a professional.

I don't care *how* stupidly attractive my patient is.

"First I'm going to check his arm, and then we'll change his dressings," Beau tells me as he pulls the overhead surgical light around to shine on Dom's arm. "I want a good look at his chest—I'm fairly confident that he's not bleeding internally, but we'll keep monitoring for symptoms."

Beau sits in the doctor's chair, wheeling it close to Dom.

I blink, glancing at him as he sanitizes his hands then pulls a pair of gloves off the medical cart.

Mesmerized, I watch him tug them on, remembering his clever, gloved fingers pushing inside me all those weeks ago, back when *I* was his "patient."

One who got a decidedly different treatment from the one Dom is getting now.

"Wait, you're really treating him?" I ask, and Beau pauses, giving me a look of such forced, indulgent patience that I know it's Doctor Bennett looking at me right now.

"Well, of course. I told you he's been difficult. I need you, little nurse, to make sure he stays still while I work," he drawls. "Get in nice and close there. Why don't you cut that shirt off him? Help me get him ready for his examination."

Beau hands me a pair of scissors, and Dom's head drops back against the padded head of the chair, resigned. *I* need to handle *him*.

Eyeing him breathlessly, I inch closer.

It puts me right in Beau's path, too close to where he's shining the light on Dom's bandages, and I hesitate.

I'm about to move around the chair when Beau says, "Up you go, nurse. Climb on."

I pause, glancing at Dom's big, sprawled body, reclining in the chair. It's a wide chair, but not wide enough for us to sit two across.

I would need to straddle him. Straddle his *lap*. Ride all up over his . . .

Stop! Be professional, *Eden!*

"Doctor, I'm not sure I should be sitting on top of patients like that," I tell him throatily.

Dom snorts, amused, and secret delight tugs at me.

He's actually having *fun*.

So I lower my voice and add primly, "He might get the wrong idea."

Beau glances between us, his color high and hungry. I'm standing so close to him, and Beau's hand dips under my dress again, slipping up to my ass.

My breath catches. "Doctor Bennett—"

"If he gets the wrong idea, it's because you're not being professional enough." He cups my ass softly. "You do encourage the wrong sort of attention, Nurse Anderson."

Every ounce of my attention is hyper-fixated on his soft, seeking hand.

Until it pauses.

"Now, you're in my way here so go on up there and remove that shirt—and mind his ribs."

Beau gives my ass a squeeze before patting it dismissively, encouraging me to climb up.

And his fingertips brush the cool base of my plug.

The plug jiggles hard inside me as we both freeze.

My stockinged toes curl against the floorboards as it awakens the sensitive nerves inside me all over again.

Dom raises one brow, watching my face.

"My, my," Beau murmurs thickly. "It looks like our little nurse *did* come prepared."

I look over my shoulder at him, panting, my nerve endings scattered, and Beau gives me a dangerously heated look.

"Must you touch me like that, Doctor Bennett?" I ask huskily, and slowly, he bites his lip, watching me.

Finally, he says, "How *do* you want me to touch you, nurse?"

My breathing stalls.

A soft smirk on his lips, Beau gives my ass a final, slow squeeze before he rolls his chair back around to Dom's arm.

"Cut that shirt *off*, Nurse Anderson," he orders as he starts removing Dom's dressing.

Shirtless Dom.

On the lap of shirtless Dom.

Riding the cock of shirtless Dom.

Yes. Okay. *Yes.*

I can do that.

Professionally.

It takes me a moment to work out how to get up into the chair, but I'm finally able to dig my knee into the seat and pull myself up. Bracing against the wide, padded headrest on either side of Dom's head, I straddle him carefully.

And when I'm finally astride him, I realize just how close we are. How my breath is fanning over his face. The way my knees are nestled in beside his hips.

How close my breasts are to his mouth.

Dom's face is dangerous. Intense. He might be under me, might be letting me act this out . . . but there's no doubt who is in control.

Slowly, I push off the headrest and settle back, hovering modestly over his lap, despite the way I want to grind down against him.

"I'm . . . I'm going to take this shirt off you, sir. Please stay still while I cut it," I tell him politely as I bring the scissors carefully up to his sleeve.

They're shockingly sharp, and I have vague background concerns about why Jasper needs scissors that sharp. Or the set of scalpels. Or the wicked-looking needles.

Dom scans my face as I begin to cut through the fabric, then looks dismissively away to watch Beau unwind his bandages.

"They're fine as they are, you know. You don't need to waste supplies," Dom says under his breath.

"Well, when you get your medical license, you let me know," Beau replies tartly.

They begin to bicker lightly, *warmly*, about supplies and his health, and I manage to cut away one sleeve. The freed fabric folds back a little, and the awful, deeply purpled bruises on Dom's chest make my stomach clench. They spiderweb out from where he was shot, crawling over his abs and up to his collarbone—and while the swelling over his ribs on his left side has gone down, it still looks tender.

But, reluctantly, I *can* admit . . . that shot did do the job.

If Alastair wanted a war, he's certainly got one now.

Very lightly, I trace some of the bruising.

"My poor soldier," I murmur, half in the scene, half not as my heart aches, remembering my fear.

Bending down, I press a gentle kiss to his chest, and Dom stiffens, then relaxes on a sigh. Tentatively, his hand comes up to stroke over my hair.

"I'm okay, pet. I told you I'm not letting anyone die." He tugs my head up so I look at him, and his eyes are dark-fringed and soft as melted butter. "That includes me. I'm right here. Are we clear?"

He somehow makes even his doting demands sound stern.

I give him a small smile. "Yes, sir. No one dies."

Beau watches us both with tender, marveling eyes, and when I glance at him, his quick smile is emotional. He blinks twice, then clears his throat.

"You're kind, little nurse . . . to show your appreciation," he says huskily, and when I reach out for him, he shifts close enough that I can run a finger over a tiny cut on his face.

"I do appreciate you. I appreciate you both," I whisper.

Beau turns his head to kiss my palm, and I breathe in shakily as I pull it back, switching my scissors back to my dominant hand.

"I'm very grateful for this job, doctor," I tell him more decisively, and Dom huffs a laugh.

Beau's smile curves up, and he winks at me. "Well, you ought to get to it, then, nurse. You're taking your sweet time."

Unable to repress my smile, I roll my eyes at him, then lean back over Dom.

Ignoring his injuries for now, I start cutting through the collar on his other side, down through the sleeve, being careful not to get too close to Beau. I've just finished cutting and I'm pulling the scissors away . . . when a heavy hand cups my pussy under my dress.

The hand squeezes me possessively.

I flinch in surprise, pulling back, and the move jostles Beau. Dom's hand slips away like it was never there, and both of them turn to look at me.

Beau frowns, but there's an undercurrent of slow, provocative heat in his voice as he drawls, "Nurse Anderson, that was careless. I could have hurt our patient."

My pussy still throbs where Dom squeezed me.

Professional outrage pricks me. I *was* being careful.

Dom gives me a bored look, but there's a smug satisfaction in the tuck of his mouth. His lips are cruelly sensuous against the roughness of his dark stubble.

"But, doctor, he—"

"Don't blame the patient," Beau raises one chastising brow. Unlike Dom, he's clean-shaven, and as classically handsome as Dom is hard hewn and raw. "It's your job to manage him. Now, finish removing his shirt."

"*Carefully*, little nurse," Dom adds, his eyes raking over my breasts. "Or you'll need to make it up to me."

I narrow my eyes on him as he turns back to Beau, who is collecting a fresh dressing off the medical cart.

Both of them dismissing me.

The dominant dream team is apparently back in action. It's almost cute, how they're practically finishing each other's sentences.

Almost.

If they weren't teaming up against *me*, it would be cute.

Carefully, I lean in again, bringing the scissors around to cut through the shirt on Dom's other side. I eye the side of his face warily between snips, my breathing unsteady. He smells good, clean and spicy, and he doesn't seem to be paying me any attention, so I finish my cuts on that sleeve.

I pull back, deciding to make the next cut down the center of his shirt when his hand slips under my skirt again—only this time, his fingers tug my panties to one side, and he begins to explore greedily through my slickness.

I freeze as he strokes over my clit, then pinches it in slow, rolling squeezes.

Heat floods me, everything in me clenching, and I shudder, leaning over his chest with a little moan.

"Nurse, his shirt still isn't off," Doctor Bennett chides me. "Stop flirting and do your job." He looks up at Dom. "These silly nurses we get through here. She comes in here dressed like that, kissing soldiers and all but begging for cock, and then acts offended when we offer her one." Beau shakes his head. "If she wants to be a professional, she should stop moaning like a little slut."

"I—" I try to shift up, but two fingers sink into my pussy, chasing me, and my voice breaks on another moan. "If . . . if he could just . . ."

Dom's fingers rub deeper, pushing against the plug through the thin, sensitive strip of flesh between my pussy and my ass. The plug shifts, shooting white-hot pleasure through me.

I catch Dom's corded wrist, and he stops rubbing but doesn't move it away.

Instead, looking me in the eye, he slides his thumb through my pussy and starts circling my clit. My walls clench around his fingers, squeezing the plug into him, and my brain can't dislodge the image of his and Beau's cocks squeezing into me just like that.

My pants become high-pitched as his thumb tick, tick, *ticks* over my clit.

My thighs quake, and I look at Dom desperately. He's watching me with hot, undisguised lust, his fingers inside me, circling me, and I . . . have *orders*, damn it.

And I know better than to forget Beau.

"Please, sir. I need . . . I have to take your shirt off. The doctor . . . he ordered it . . . please, I-I can't . . ."

I tug at Dom's wrist and, sighing, he lets it fall away.

Beside me, still working on Dom's arm, Beau's smile deepens into a warm, undisguised approval that only sends another rush of hot, wet need to slick my core.

When he finally glances up, the greens and golds in his eyes are soft and pleased. "It's nice to see you recover your sense of decorum, little nurse."

"Speak for yourself," Dom mutters, before he sucks his wet fingers into his mouth.

O-okay. My thoughts are just as filthy and shuddery as my body as I watch those fingers sink between his lips, coating them lewdly. I feel his cock nudging against the inner curve of my thigh.

I am . . . so incredibly outmatched here.

They're not just working against me—they're competing with each other.

Working quickly—though I have to shake my hands out twice to stop them from trembling—I cut Dom's shirt clean up the center, then gently tug the fabric away.

He sits there like a king on his throne while Beau finishes on his arm.

His poor, brutalized chest comes into full view, and I run my fingertips lightly over him again with silent care . . . which turns into silent need as his rough hair brushes against my skin. His pec twitches as I slowly coast over his skin.

Suddenly, Beau is standing, plucking the scissors from my hand and placing them on the tray. I can see the outline of his cock through his pants, as hungry and as insistent as Dom's, and my whole body aches to be filled with it. He removes his gloves.

The plug shivers in my ass as I shift, and I stifle a helpless moan.

Both sides.

I want to be filled on *both* sides.

"Is this . . . is this what you wanted, Doctor Bennett?" I ask huskily.

Briefly, Beau looks Dom over. "Excellent."

He comes over to stand beside the large, reclined chair, just behind me, and his hand wraps around mine before I can lift it from Dom's chest. He begins dragging my fingers slowly, lightly, down Dom's body, over the coarse hair on his abdominals and ignoring Dom's soft, strained release of breath, until he rests my hand over the button on Dom's pants.

"Now open his pants, little nurse," Doctor Bennett instructs in my ear.

I shudder, desperate for it.

My fingers are between my legs as they linger over Dom's button, and his abs tense in anticipation. Beau squeezes my wrist in encouragement, but I look up at Dom from under my lashes, enjoying his impatience.

"Does she always take this long to obey?" Dom's mutter is hoarse, and he gives Beau a scorching look. "Get her hands on me, *doc*. Make her do her job, or I will."

Beau laughs huskily. "Well now, hold on. Maybe we should see what her concern is," Beau's voice is thick with a sympathy I don't believe—and apparently, neither does Dom.

His golden eyes narrow on his friend.

"Is everything all right, little nurse?" Beau asks me kindly, and he strokes my wrist. "Why aren't you helping our patient?"

My cunt, my breasts, my ass around my plug, everything aches, throbbing with the need for contact. Needing to be filled and fucked and taken.

But this is Beau's fantasy—and I want to make it a good one.

"Well . . . he wasn't shot there, Doctor Bennett," I protest innocently, and Dom narrows his eyes on me.

I can practically see him losing his patience for the game, but Beau laughs again in a soft huff, and his hot breath in my ear makes me squirm.

"Are you a doctor, Nurse Anderson?" he asks patronizingly, and he tugs my hand down until my palm rubs against Dom's stiff cock through the straining fabric. "There are many unexpected side effects to a gunshot wound. We need to be thorough in our care. I won't have you cutting corners. Our goal is to make our patient feel good, after all."

Beau squeezes my hand around Dom's dick, and my whimper mixes with Dom's grunt as his head tilts back against the chair.

"You do care about making our patient feel good, don't you?" Beau whispers in my ear, his voice shaking with want, and I feel my need begin to leak down my thigh.

"Yes, Doctor Bennett. Yes, I do."

Seeming satisfied he's made his point, Beau releases my hand and taps my wrist to continue. My mind is gone, a lusty mess of nurses and doctors and the raw desperation to feel Dom's cock again.

I open the button on Dom's pants with difficulty, and it takes two hands to slide the zipper down between my thighs.

"What do you see, little nurse?" Beau asks, watching me sharply.

Dom's cock is caught heavily in his briefs, pinned by the uncompromising fabric of his pants and wedged against my thigh.

My mouth is too dry. "There . . . there does appear to be some swelling."

"Just as I suspected." Beau nods, and he gives me a gently disapproving look. "And you would have had us ignore such an obvious source of discomfort. It appears you need a little more training, Nurse Anderson. Now, assist our patient."

He might be enjoying this a little too much.

"Why, you're right, doctor," I agree, sweet and saccharine. "You *do* know so much more than me. Why don't you show me how?"

But Beau doesn't bite.

He just kicks up one brow and slides a polite, professional look at Dom. "And you, Mr. Slade? Would you prefer to be treated by me or Nurse Anderson here?"

Dom's reply is dry as dust. "I want the nurse."

"Great. Pull out his cock."

"Doctor Bennett!" I exclaim, though it's an effort to stop my breathy laugh.

Beau's eyes dance as he shakes his head reprovingly. "No, I'm not going to do your job for you, nurse. You're a medical professional. Act like one."

He stares at me for a moment, heat slipping back into his features . . . and he strolls closer. We're almost at eye-level like this, and he watches me as he wraps a hand around my throat.

"Unless you're determined to act like a little slut? I would like to teach you how to care for our patient properly, but I could take you in the back and fuck you raw if you need a cock that badly?" he drawls against my lips.

My pulse throbs against his fingers, and when my breath hitches, he tightens them. His mouth is so close. I press into his grip, trying to reach him, but he holds me an inch from his lips.

"What a selfish little nurse you're turning out to be." Doctor Bennett *tuts* at me disapprovingly, and his other hand slips into my dress, palming my breast. He squeezes that too, and I arch into his touch. "What do you think, captain? We can't have her working on patients when she won't dedicate herself to their care."

"I can think of a few other uses for her." Dom's hands creep under my dress again. "Give her to me when you're done. I can fix selfish. I'm sure if we use our little nurse's holes a few times without letting her come, she'll start feeling real generous again."

Ohhh . . . oh no.

"Oh, I don't—"

Dom's calloused hand finds the plug and rolls it hard. I yelp at the sudden stretch, then moan, but I'm so caught between him and Beau's hand around my neck, I can't even squirm.

Beau's lids begin to dip heavily as he watches me whimper over his lips.

"Aw, now. It's not your fault, is it, darlin'? You're just built to be fucked." His mouth drifts hungrily over my cheek as he breathes, "You can't even help yourself, can you? You just can't think until you've got a cock in you. Women like you shouldn't be nurses. You get too distracted as soon as your patient has a thick one for you."

"*Beau.*"

He kisses my lips softly, as desperate, wet need slips through me.

I kiss him back clumsily, eagerly, but he teases my mouth.

And it's not fair. Because as lusciously crude as he is, he's also *right*. I *can't* think, and I *do* need their cocks, and right now, I *feel* like I was built for fucking.

But I also want to take care of Dom, and to play Beau's game, and the thought of leaving either of them unsatisfied—no matter how much I know they'll enjoy fucking me, too—is one that sits unhappily.

So even while I shudder as Beau drags his mouth over my skin, I reach into Dom's pants, tunneling under his briefs to grasp his scorching cock.

Dom's breath hisses out as my hand closes around him.

"I'll be a good nurse, Doctor Bennett. Teach me. Please, I'll be good," I beg him softly, and Beau pauses.

His grip loosens on my throat so he can watch me tug Dom's cock free of his pants.

Dom groans as he's released, and his grip on my ass tightens.

"Are you in pain, sir?" I whisper, and Dom looks at me from under heavy, heavy lids, with eyes like liquid gold.

"*Aching.*"

He says it like a demand, like an accusation, like I am indeed not doing my job in caring for him. The vein along his cock throbs against my palm.

Beau releases my throat.

"You surprise me. Good for you, putting your patient's needs first." He strokes the backs of his fingers over the lingering throb with soft approval. He glances at Dom. "You sure you're up for this? You're feeling okay?"

Dom gives Beau a direct look, hearing the same worried undertone as me. "I'm good, Beau. You got me out. You patched me up. I can take it."

The two of them look at each other, memories with feelings layered into them passing between them. Things I'm both a part of and not. Things I'm so glad they had one another to help them through those hard years.

Then Dom raises one dark brow. "You're the doctor. How about you use that fancy degree of yours to figure out what will make me feel better?"

Beau's lips curl up in a knowing, answering smile, and his voice turns clipped. "We need to relieve the swelling."

Beau looks down at me, but despite his tone, his eyes invite me in on the fun.

And I'm just so glad they're having fun.

That we all are.

I nod, breathless. "Is that okay? The medical board . . . ?"

"Are often afflicted with the same malady. Don't make me drag them all in here," Beau warns dryly, and his eyes dare me to push him. "You'll have your hands full all day."

Yes, please.

"Yes, doctor," I say instead.

All of them at once seems too ambitious.

Or too much to hope for, anyway.

I look back down at Dom's cock, dragging my hand up his length, and Dom shudders, his hips tilting up into my grip.

I bring my other hand to wrap around him, too.

"Doctor, could I have some lubrication? I think it might help me treat our soldier properly." I rub my hands over Dom again, enjoying the unfettered access, drunk on his twitches and the flex of his jaw, and Beau's approving gaze.

Suddenly, I'm dragged forward by his hands on my ass. I gasp, my hands flying up to brace on the headrest again as Dom grinds my hovering cunt down over his cock.

"Don't bother, doc. I found some," he grits out, and he yanks my lacy panties to one side.

His cock is hot and thick as it pushes between my folds, getting obscenely soaked by my swollen pussy. I moan, shuddering, trying not to collapse against his chest as the flared crown nudges my clit.

The plug in my hole shifts and clatters brutally as Dom's fingers dig into my ass.

As he grinds my pussy over his dick.

"Doctor! Is this . . . okay? The patient is—" I'm cut off by a moan as the motion makes my clit rub wetly over his cock.

As my sir uses my body.

"Hurting," Beau finishes for me, his voice soothing.

He swallows, and I hear the shake in his voice as he reaches under my outfit too. He tears my scarlet panties to shreds in two hard yanks.

My head tips back as Dom works my cunt over his cock, and Beau kisses the side of my face softly. "He's hurting, and you're doing a very good job at helping him, nurse. That little cunt is making him feel so good."

My mind begins to fog. I can't see it anymore, but under my dress, I can *feel* the messy wetness and his demanding cock and the rough hands that are reducing me to something hot for him to fuck against.

The slick sounds are filthy, carnal, and I begin to shake.

My breasts feel too trapped, my body too tight and sensitive, and I'm only wound tighter with every slick roll.

Beau snorts, watching me.

"Feeling generous?" he asks Dom dryly.

I try to squirm, but Dom keeps fucking against me, holding his rhythm as he slides a look at Beau. "Don't you keep telling me . . . to respect our healthcare professionals?"

Beau throws him an amused grin, but Dom's cock is rubbing so perfectly along my cunt that we both shudder.

His stubbled jaw sets, and his eyes blaze as he looks down between our bodies.

Beau eyes him for a moment, then comes up beside the chair. He presses a button, and the chair reclines further, until I'm tilted over Dom.

The new angle has him holding my hips still above him, and he starts fucking up quickly, each thrust rubbing his cock against my clit.

"Sir, I . . ." I gasp as the pressure builds brutally, squirming, but his hand claps down hard on my ass in a sharp spank before he grips me tight.

"No. Stay still, little nurse," he demands.

I cry out at the spank, as it shocks the plug in me and spreads heat over my skin. I'm soaking Dom's cock as he thrusts against me. His heavy balls. My stockings and thighs—until I'm wet everywhere, and we're both a slick mess.

Beau walks over, then kneels up onto the chair behind me. The weight sinks the padding near my knees, but I'm too lost, coiling too close to—

Beau yanks my hips back, out of Dom's grasp.

"Fuck! Beau!" Dom's shout is like a gunshot, and I sob at the sharp, desperate loss.

Beau runs a soothing hand over my back. "You've seen what he needs now, little nurse. How about you climb on and ease him yourself before our stupid, overconfident patient tears his stitches open."

"Then you can stitch me back up again!" Dom bites out through lost, ragged breaths, his powerful body shaking.

"Weren't you just getting on me for wasting supplies?" Beau counters, and his hand dips under me to absently toy with my oversensitive clit.

I moan, bending into his touch.

Under me, Dom's cock is heavy against his abs, glossy from my pussy, and flushed and aching with need.

My body squeezes uselessly in response, and Beau cups my pussy, using it to nudge me over his friend's lap again.

"Fuck the supplies," Dom mutters.

"Fuck the nurse," Beau offers soothingly instead, releasing me with a final squeeze as I crawl back over Dom.

Dom grasps his cock at the root, holding it up for me to sink down on, but he looks at Beau as he says, "Fuck her with me."

Oh, God. It's happening.

Beau's hand finds the plug in my ass, and he begins working it out of me in eviscerating, twisting little tugs. My mouth parts as it finally slips free, my body shaking, my ass clenching against the sudden loss.

The sudden, awful *emptiness.*

"Only if *you* promise not to hurt yourself, Dom. Let me and our nurse take care of you," Beau orders him, and I feel a chilly trickle of lube against my sensitive hole.

Hot, golden eyes travel between us both before, finally, Dom nods.

He taps his swollen cock against my cunt in a silent, impatient demand for me to get moving, and I hurry to shift into place.

I need to be filled. I need someone to ache against.

The wide head of Dom's cock slips in my mess briefly until I manage to press it against my entrance. My next shiver takes me from my scalp to my toes.

Dom's eyes are on my cunt, his hand holding his cock steady, and I'm a panting, squirming mess as I begin to work my way down his thick length. I bite down hard on my lower lip as my walls part around him, beginning to stretch as he spears me deeper and deeper, as I take him into me with slick, wriggling rocks.

Dom finally moves his hand from his cock to unclasp my bra, but every ounce of my attention is on the way his dick is spreading my cunt.

As Dom's hand starts greedily massaging my breast, Beau groans behind me.

"Fuck, darlin'. That's a sight. Look at that pretty pussy taking him like that . . . Oh, that's it. Look at that pretty stretch." Fingers start teasing at the lube around my ass, rubbing against the sensitive hole. "We're both going to stretch you out, little nurse. You're going to be so full. You're going to make both of us feel so much better."

With a last hard roll of my hips, I bottom out on Dom's cock, and I cry out. With him at an angle like this, my clit rubs against the coarse hair at his base, and I grind myself over his cock, rubbing into it. My pussy squeezes him hard, lost in the little shocks of pleasure and the fingers behind me that are teasing lube in and out of my ass.

"Look at that," Beau breathes. "All in. Doesn't that feel good? Now hold still, darlin'. Get used to how he feels. I want to get a bit more lube into you before I take your tight little ass, too."

Dom groans roughly. My nipple is pebbled needily against his palm, and he gives it a rough, self-indulgent tug before his hands drop back to rest lightly over my hips.

I can feel the restrained violence in him as I pant against his collarbone, like he's stopping himself from working me over his cock again.

"Fuck, that's . . . good. That's good, pet." Dom shudders, his hips tilting up just enough to press into me another quarter inch. His abdomen rubs against my clit. "You . . . Beau. This hot cunt is squeezing the ever-loving shit out of me."

Beau's chuckle is ragged behind me. "Careful now. We talked a big game during movie night. Don't you go making liars out of us."

Dom's molten eyes squeeze shut. "Get inside her. Then talk."

Beau snorts, but he leans in to kiss the curve of my neck, raking his nails up the back of my thighs. "Color, little nurse. Give me a color."

"Green," I say huskily, desperately, and Dom's hands shift around just slightly . . . and he pulls my ass cheeks apart for Beau.

He watches my face as another squeeze of lube is squirted through the cleft of my ass, and I shiver as it dribbles into me.

"He's going to line himself up, pet. He'll fuck into you nice and slow. It's going to feel like too much." Dom shakes his head, his jaw tight. "It's not. Your body wants it. It wants us both."

Beau's heat is incinerating behind me, and I feel the brush of his cock over my stockinged thighs and the curve of my ass.

Then, with Dom spreading me for him, Beau teases the head of his scorching, heavily lubed cock against my open, needy hole. His silky crown presses slickly into it, the tip only just spearing the sensitive ring.

Dom is breathing hard and heavily under me, his cock throbbing desperately against my walls, and I tense, anticipating the punishing strain I know is about to come.

But it *doesn't* come.

I expect Beau to fuck into me, but he just rests there, his cock head toying with my hole while his nails run soothingly over my heated skin.

It's not soothing, though. It's *torturous*. Everywhere he is, everywhere they are, reminds me of where Beau *isn't*, and urgency throbs through me. I start to wiggle, rubbing Dom's cock deliciously inside me.

I'm just about to start begging when Dom grips my face in a biting grip, then lifts my mouth up to his. His golden eyes watch me, like they did earlier, and he kisses me hungrily, filthily. It's wet and full of hot breaths and panted groans until my eyes begin to sink closed.

Beau stops stroking me, his hand coming up to replace Dom's on my ass to hold me open.

And I feel Beau begin to work his cock into my ass.

"Beau," I whine into Dom's mouth, and Dom kisses me harder, his tongue teasing the cry out of me, penetrating me in a way that's both like Beau's cock and not.

Beau's flared cock head pushes through the first, gripping ring of my ass, but unlike the plug, there's no dip—no deep, relieving curve to clutch him into me with. No reprieve from the thickness rocking into me.

Beau pauses, squeezing more lube around us both, slicking his dick and rubbing the wetness around my greedy hole before he rocks again, slipping in another inch.

"Ohhh, yes. That's it, little nurse. Take my cock in that pretty ass. Take us both. You can take it all, darlin'," he encourages me, his voice dark and throaty, lost in his own pleasure.

Beau rocks into me more roughly, claiming another brutal inch, and the pressure, the *fullness*, inside me becomes dizzying. Luscious and overwhelming.

I love it when Beau gets like this, when he has me in thrall and he's tortured himself to the point of desperation by what he's doing to me.

His cock begins fighting for space against Dom's, and every rock, every pump, rubs them together inside me. They tease along that slippery, sensitive strip inside me, and I can feel Beau's crown squeezing along the fat ridge of Dom's cock.

My rapid pants turn to sobs into Dom's mouth, and his fingers tighten on my face. His teeth close over my lower lip, and he drags it down in a dangerous, possessive bite before he kisses me punishingly.

"You were right, darlin'," Beau groans. "You're a good, sweet nurse, aren't you? Look at you, helping your patient. Isn't it better like this? Letting us use your little holes?"

He spreads my ass wider, and he lets out a little grunt as he fucks into me. It makes him rock against Dom's cock, and Dom fucks back up against him, like an answer.

Beau's voice becomes hoarse, almost broken. "Do you have any idea how good my cock feels right now? Do you feel us both inside you? You're gripping me like . . . Fuck, Eden. I'm going to come so hard in your hot little ass. We're going to make such a mess of you."

Dom breaks the kiss, his head tilting back, his face strained. "*Fuck*, Beau."

His heavy-lidded eyes find mine in urgent question a moment later.

"*Green*."

The word comes out as a groan, and Beau's fingers bite into my skin. It feels like I'm being taken everywhere.

I *am* being taken everywhere.

The need in me coils higher, as pressured as the squeezed space inside me.

Ducking my head, I begin to squirm over Dom's cock, and his hands find my breasts again as I lean over him. He tugs and pulls and roughs my nipples, but with Beau claiming the rhythm, I can't quite get friction against my clit.

Beau grunts again, and with a hard, final thrust, he shoves the rest of the way into my ass, until they're both buried deep inside me.

I cry out, arching my back, shudders overtaking me as my ass squeezes against him but finds no give, no relief. His slick cock is relentless, and Beau groans, rocking into me, stirring up every nerve, his crown obscenely battling Dom's inside me.

"Son of a—" Dom curses, and I desperately look back up at his face.

He's deeply flushed, his lips drawn back with the tension. His eyes glitter at me, his pupils blown dark . . . but he breathes through his nose.

"Take your time," he bites out, and it doesn't sound impatient, or snarky.

Despite all the feral need and desperate urgency on his face, he sounds like he means it.

"I don't need *time*, sir, I need . . . Beau," I beg softly. "Help me."

Beau shudders behind me.

"I know." Beau flips up my skirt and smooths his hands over my ass again. "Of course, darlin'. You tell me when, okay?"

His hands guiding me, his cock thick in my ass, he lets me squirm between them in tiny little shifts until my soaking clit grinds into Dom's abdomen, and I find that perfect, toe-curling angle again.

My breath hitches, and Dom's eyes darken as he pinches my nipple. "Like that, huh?"

"There," Beau breathes. Gripping my hip, he tests a short, sharp thrust against me, and I moan sharply, feeling it everywhere.

"You tell us if you need to stop," Beau whispers over my back, and I shake my head frantically in denial.

"Please . . . don't. Please don't stop."

"You lead, Beau," Dom instructs, reaching down to hold me apart, and Beau breathes in shakily, fucking my ass again.

It rubs my clit into Dom, and lights everything up inside me.

I begin to tremble all over. The dual press in my pussy and ass is overwhelming. Intense. Beautiful and painful and perfect and awful.

But that pressure against my clit transforms it all into something that eclipses every discomfort. The motion, the *friction*, turns the pressure into something urgent, needed, and I arch over Dom.

"Oh, my . . ." I moan, shuddering, and Beau begins to move, finding a rhythm.

His thrusts are short and pumping, a grind as much as a fuck. It makes a mess out of all of us, teasing over every nerve ending. Dom and Beau's cocks squeeze and slip against each other, and when Beau starts to use more force, his body slapping into mine roughly, Dom grunts under me.

Dom gives me a hot, knowing little smile, his eyes dangerous and dark. "Get ready, little nurse. You're about to be fucked apart."

Fucked ap—

Holding me tight against him, right where my clit gets maximum pressure, Dom fucks up into my pussy—then Beau fucks into my ass.

It's all sloppy wet and hopeless and overwhelmingly brutal.

They take me hard, their hands greedy and demanding, their grunts and groans hot and desperate and unselfconscious. Their cocks squeezing pleasure from each other as much as from me, only that one thin barrier holding them apart.

I cry out sharply, pinned and caught as their cocks work into me, around me, their short, relentless thrusts pumping my holes in hard, fucking beats, one burying deep, only for the other to wreck me on the other side. I can't catch the rhythm, can't move, only feel every pressured build.

My clit grinds and rubs into Dom, and my violent pleasure starts to prickle over me in a thousand hot pinpricks. The pressure is so intense I feel it throbbing in my temple, my throat. I can't breathe until it bursts, but their cocks are still relentless, fucking into my wetness, thrusting to the edge of pain.

"Beau. Sir, I'm going to—"

"You'd fucking better," Dom growls.

Beau laughs, but it's mostly a groan. "It's like she . . . doesn't know how this works."

Dom snorts, still fucking me, our bodies making lewd, wet sounds. "Should we show her?"

"That's the plan," Beau says. Thick satisfaction curls through his voice, but there's also something hotter, sweeter pinning it down.

The plan. The three of us.

No, *all* of us.

"It's a good plan," Dom says roughly, that same soft *something* in his tone.

My heart squeezes as his eyes meet mine, filling me up in every other way too.

Then Beau shoves me forward hard and starts hitting me in a deep, ruthless place. My moans become helpless, punished cries, and the pressure begins to push out, rolling over me.

Watching my face, Dom grunts, shuddering, and I feel his cock swell.

"*Fuck.*" The word bursts out of him, and he grips my ass tight as he comes hard, his hips punching up as he soaks me with wet, scalding heat.

"I love you," Beau whispers, and I'm not sure if it's to me or Dom or both.

He says it right as his hand claps against my ass, and the bitter sting is enough.

I shove back into their cocks as the pressure in me bursts. It comes hard, in devastating, mindless shockwaves, and my orgasm rips through me from my clit, and deep in my cunt. It hits again from my ass, where Beau's cock is jerking, filling me with cum. Pleasure rolls out from the base of my spine and down my legs and into the tips of my fingers.

I come so hard, I don't even realize I'm sobbing, or that I've been moved to the bed, or that I'm brokenly telling them how much I love them, or that they're murmuring it back . . . until I come to much, much later, with both of them wrapped around me.

And both of them tend, with that same, perfect synchronous rhythm, to my aftercare.

IN THE HOURS THAT FOLLOW, Jayk filters in for a shower, rolling his eyes over the slow, happy kisses I'm trading with Beau and muttering something about getting me tomorrow. Lucky and Jasper dip in, sitting on the end of the bed and making me blush all over again about the scene.

When Jayk reappears, he sits with his back to the wall, tossing out smirks and gruff, fangless jibes with surprising ease, and we all talk and tease until it grows late and the heavy anticipation of tomorrow begins to set in.

Tiredly, Jasper sighs. "Are we really ready for this?"

Lucky's dimples fade, and his face settles into something somber. "For war?" He shakes his head. "This one shouldn't be as bad as some we've fought, I guess, if we can keep the right things quiet, but . . . there's still a lot that could go wrong."

Jayk scoffs. "No shit. You're going to have to hold me the fuck back from—"

"We're ready," I say softly.

I let my gaze travel over our group. Our family.

Just a few months, that's all this should take, and then we'll be done with it all. The civilians will be safe, we'll have freed the captives —and every last person who ever put them in danger will be gone.

The pieces are already set, the game is in play, and it's finally our board.

There's no backing out now.

I know there will be others—others with sick and damaged souls who will crawl back into our world. But we'll deal with those when they come as well. Theirs is not the world we want to live in.

We're going to create our own.

"We're ready," I repeat. "We're going to make them pay for every nightmare, every fear, every lie. It's their turn to be afraid . . . because they're going to pay with their lives."

PART FOUR

DEATH

CHAPTER 75

JAYKOB

SURVIVAL TIP #115
No amount of flowers can cover up the stink of shit.

ONE WEEK AFTER LEAVING BRISTLEBROOK

I sneeze for the fifth fucking time in five fucking minutes. There are flowers everywhere, and pollen is choking out the air like mustard gas. The flowers crawl over the Reapers' farmlands, stalking us on both sides of the wide, winding road through the forest that leads to their main compound. They skulk over the pastures surrounding it and burst out of the road like land mines.

The Reapers' compound has one tall, corrugated tin gate "protecting" the entrance—a wall thin enough that a can opener could saw through it—and even the gate is being eaten away by vines and those shitty, throat-swelling little buds.

The gate swings open, and we pass the Reaper sentries standing up on their outposts. They stare at the civs like they're seeing Victoria's secret instead of thirty-plus tired, pissy soldiers walking right through their front door.

Sawyer's mustache twitches as he points. "The radio room is next to the machinery shed. We've got the henhouse there, greenhouses over to the left, pigsty around here. Slaughterhouse is over by the forest past the corn, next to the smokehouse. We usually keep a nice stock of meat right in there, so I'm thinking we should make a big ole welcome home feast tonight. Tower silo is over past the wheat fields—don't know if you can see it in the distance there, but over them hills, we've got . . ."

Sawyer keeps pointing shit out, but I don't know who he's talking to. The Reapers who came to Bristlebrook with us have mostly fucked off by now, and the civs are ignoring Sawyer, their rifles cautiously in hand as we get shown around.

Eden is walking next to him, but she pauses every few minutes to frown at a building like she's shooting for a building inspector license, not paying any attention to him, either. Dom and Lucky are right on her heels, so I pause to blow my nose.

Again.

I run to catch up, gripping my pistol at my hip as more men line up to watch Eden and the civs walk through the compound.

" . . . and there's the mess hall. We converted one of the old cowsheds so we could all have meals together. New ones are over there. We've got most of us sleeping in the big barn beside the henhouse, but me and Cole and a few of the others stay in the big house up front."

Sawyer can't shut the fuck up.

I sneeze, hacking at the shit coating my throat, and hang back. We've been traveling with the Reapers for a week to get here, and it's a week more than my patience is willing to handle.

My temper's already frayed, and I'm ready to shoot the fuckhead.

I don't want to be here. I want to be home. I want Eden and my guys and all the fucking civs back at Bristlebrook, and for none of us to have to deal with any of this shit. I don't care that the Reapers are all sleeping in a barn because they're *scared*. Boo fucking hoo.

They *should* be scared.

Alastair's coming for them.

We head toward the fields and pastures beyond the compound, and the flowers are choking out the buildings. The little shits are vomiting out of garden beds and window pots, colorful and reeking, on every corner.

I sneeze again.

Who the hell plants this many flowers? It's *creepy*. Get some fucking potatoes or something.

Beau tosses me a packet of pills as he walks beside me, and I almost miss it because my damn eyes are watering like a bitch.

Sniffing back my runny nose, I squint down at the packet.

Antihistamines.

"Thanks," I mutter, popping one.

Beau slides me a wry, sympathetic grimace, but his eyes don't leave Eden for long. We're *all* watching her, trailing after her like a pack of guard dogs, and these days, it feels like a relief.

It means it's not just me who'll rip shit apart to keep her trouble-attracting ass safe.

We finally finish the stupid two-dollar tour of the flower factory compound and reach the first fence. The civs spread out along the fence line, staring out at the view like they're about to film an infomercial.

The rolling pasture beyond the fence is milling with cows and sheep, but there are fields on all sides, stretching on and on into the distance—fields overflowing with wheat and corn and a bunch of other shit I couldn't pick out of a lineup. Dirt roads run between them and along the outer fences that hug the edges of the forest.

Other buildings sit on the outskirts. Stables and machine sheds and barns, and that smokehouse is practically sprawling into the woods.

The Reapers haven't done anything to secure their boundaries from attack.

It doesn't look like they have anyone watching the woods at all.

I can't help but track along the enormous, rolling expanse of fields and buildings again. From just looking at this shit now, I can see this place would be a fucking nightmare to defend.

In the far distance, there's a big, burned-out barn that reminds me too much of my old workshop, and thick, sludgy rage tightens my gut at the sight of it.

Alastair has a hard-on for fire.

There's a lot here to burn.

Dom's jaw sets, his eyes travelling over the fields, too.

Beside him, Eden turns, looking back at the buildings, then turns around again to scan the fences and the animals in the pasture, her face grim. Finally, her eyes linger on the burned barn, sitting like a skeleton on the edge of an empty pasture, and her lips tighten.

I wonder if she can even see it.

She's blind as shit. She needs new glasses.

" . . . we'll harvest the wheat come winter, if nothin' else slows us down. That'll get us—"

"That was your livestock barn?" Eden asks Sawyer softly, still looking at it.

He blinks at her, then slowly, reluctantly, he looks at the barn.

Sawyer grimaces. "It was. It's a shame to lose it. I . . . that's . . . that's where Clayton said Alastair killed them all. Easton and Miles and Tanner and . . . " He pales, looking all queasy again as he trails off. When he speaks again, his voice is low. "We have to stop him. They don't hear reason. Clayton tried everything, offered him all of it, like we did, but . . . Alastair just wants to *kill*." Sawyer looks at Dom, his face soft and guilty. "You know. As good as anyone, you know. When that shot went off . . . I'm sorry I wasn't there. I should have been."

I stare at Sawyer, and my rage settles deep. It burns hot enough to bite. The flowers everywhere are fucking sickly in my nose, and it makes me want to burn them away, too.

Sawyer's a fucking coward.

To his bones, he's a fucking *coward*.

Eden's eyes are blazing, too, glistening with filthy hot tears, and the sadist tugs her in for a hug, murmuring to her softly. It doesn't even piss me off.

She needs it, and right now, I ain't the one to handle the quiet cuddling shit.

I'm gritting my teeth, debating whether I can get away with slugging him at *least* when Dom steps in front of me, cutting me off.

"Get your men together, Sawyer. We need sentries as a bare minimum—two each, every fifty meters around the entire perimeter. Your guys take left, front, and back, our civs will take the right. Me and the Rangers will coordinate." Dom nods back at the civs. "On our kits, we have PTTs—our push-to-talks that connect into our radios—and we can use those to direct teams where they're needed. We need to get you—"

"Whoa. Whoa, Dom. Slow . . . slow down." Sawyer lets out a

short, panicky laugh that makes my eyes roll. He shoves a hand behind his neck, rubbing it awkwardly. "We can't do all that. We have work to do, on the farm, the fields, and we lost people . . . I thought . . . Look, maybe you and the women have this handled. They're so good with those rifles. We could hardly believe our eyes. We can be backup, maybe . . ."

I've just about decided on the punch when the circus rat links his arm with mine. Clenching my fists, I breathe out heavily through my nose, and Lucky pats my arm like he's keeping tabs on a toddler.

Dom just crosses his arms over his chest, looking down at Sawyer with cold judgment.

At least one of us can keep his fucking head.

Sawyer swallows, his gaze darting between all of us. "Please, we don't know how to . . . Maybe if all the women had come, we would have had enough help to—"

Dom stiffens, his eyes flashing as he bites out, "We're not doing everything for you, Sawyer."

Casually, Beau steps in on Sawyer's other side, boxing him in with a friendly smile that packs about as much punch as my fists.

Sawyer's mustache twitches like rat whiskers.

"You're sitting on a gold mine," Dom tells him, dangerously soft. "If you want to keep this place, then you need to learn to defend it— or you need to leave and stop hurting people trying to keep it."

Behind him, the rolling crops and fields full of livestock stretch out under the sunshine.

I remember killing one of the fucking rats in the moat, watching when it fell off the corpse it was getting fat on. I remember my stomach cramping, thinking of Kasey's stomach, and Eden's ribs, and Ethel in her bed, the old bat not able to get up.

I remember spending two hours of my watch trying to work out how I could get that rat without getting my brains blown out.

Those fields look like pure fucking gluttony.

Sawyer's hands shake as he stares back at Dom, but slowly, finally, he nods.

"Okay. We'll . . . we'll do that. You all . . . come back, and we'll get you set up in the barracks. I'll get the men out here, and . . ." He nods again. "We'll do it."

"Not the barracks." Eden finally steps out of Jasper's arms, clear and firm and bossy as fuck. "Our people will camp together in the empty pasture."

Shaking his head, Sawyer opens his mouth to argue when Dom's expression seems to change his mind.

Ignoring them, Eden looks back out toward the empty pasture. The barn's blackened corpse sits on its edge, and her face turns to ice.

"We'll camp in that one. That one right there."

CHAPTER 76

EDEN

SURVIVAL TIP #257
Choose books not war.

TWO WEEKS AFTER LEAVING BRISTLEBROOK

I t was molten oil. Bentley always wanted to try it," Arthur explains, his voice crisp and satisfied coming from the satellite phone on the table. "So when they came down that alley—oh, ho! They got a shock. That took out three, maybe four, if he doesn't survive the burns."

"Any casualties on your end?" Dom asks grimly, leaning over the table.

Beau is curled around me, and we're both sitting on the floor of Dom's enormous tent. Lucky, Jasper, and Jayk are all sprawled around us, listening, in their full Ranger kits. We arrived at the farmlands a week ago, and it's been one of the longest, most grueling weeks of my life, both physically and emotionally.

It's become woefully obvious that the Reapers are incompetent at everything besides sweet-talking and farming.

And the Sinners have already attacked Red Zone three times.

"None. One burned hand and another caught some shrapnel but nothing serious," Arthur replies. "The minefields took out more than ten of theirs. We're locked in here, don't you worry about us. We'll follow instructions."

Relief breaks over Dom's face, and he straightens, swiping up the phone. "Good work, Arthur. We'll touch base same time tomorrow. Anything unexpected comes up, you call ASAP. We can be there in three hours."

"It won't, Dom. It's a good system," Arthur soothes, his voice gentling, and I smile, the lump in my throat growing thicker.

Arthur is a kind, intelligent, unexpectedly brave man. I hate that he's caught up in all of this. He should be in my book club, arguing with me over historical inaccuracies in Regency novels, not pouring molten oil on ruthlessly violent men.

"We radioed Bristlebrook, Arthur," I speak up huskily, and Dom walks over to hand me the phone. "Soren is doing well there. I think you were right not to move him."

I pause, feeling my brutes' eyes on me. This is only the beginning. There's so much risk. Anything could happen to him, or to any of us.

"Please keep yourself safe," I murmur.

"You too, Eden," he tells me warmly, and we end the call a moment later.

The overpowering scent of flowers has soaked into the tent, and it's making my stomach permanently queasy.

Am I going to worry every time that each call will be the last?

Beau's stroking hands coax me to blink and, looking up, I realize they're all watching me as I stare at the phone.

"I'm sorry. I'm okay. I was just . . ." I look around at my brutes' kind, understanding faces, and I lift my chin. "I'm listening. What were you saying?"

"I was saying that we need to get ready," Dom says grimly, his eyes meeting mine. "I was saying that . . . we're next."

CHAPTER 77

JASPER

SURVIVAL TIP #356
It's a cold, cruel world.
Be a safe place for the people you love;
they need one as much as you do.

TWO WEEKS AND TWO DAYS AFTER LEAVING
BRISTLEBROOK

The distant sounds of bullets and battle echo through the rolling hills. They're too far away, too lost and layered to make out defining details—who might be winning or losing, or who might be hurt. The Sinners have finally tested their first attack.

The sun faded several hours ago, and I'm sitting in front of the fire, on one of the heavy logs we pulled over a few days ago to help make our camp more comfortable. A handful of the civilians who weren't called in for this fight are milling around, giving me and Eden tight smiles when they catch our eye, looking too edgy to settle in and rest the way they should.

This fight won't be the last.

We'll have our turn soon enough.

"I have my tent set up with blankets, water buckets, towels, and the extra medical supplies," Eden tells me as she paces around the fire. Her hair is back in a tight, exacting bun—the way she always styles it when she's feeling anxious. "Emerson has two pots of food ready to go as soon as they come back. I'm sure they'll be hungry. We have fresh water as well. Do you think that there's any benefit to—"

"Come here, sweet girl," I order her softly, and Eden stops.

She turns to me, and the firelight flickers over her face. Her fingers knot in front of her, but she doesn't hesitate as she walks over to me, and I part my legs to make room for her.

As she sinks into an easy, graceful kneel, she lets out a sweet little sigh. I touch her hair, directing her gently until she rests her warm cheek on my thigh, and I begin unwinding her rigid bun. Her hair is long and heavy, and as I ease it out of its confines, it spills over my hands like satin.

Her breathing grows steadier as I soothe her, and my chest constricts.

She's been so angry. So sad and hurt and betrayed. I would give my world to take it away, but it's outside my power. All I can do is sit with her and help her find her way through it. Here at my feet, I can carve out one safe place for her. One place where she's held and cared for and nothing bad can touch her.

A fierce patter of gunfire echoes through the night, and I slowly stroke her hair.

She's frightened for them.

"You know, for years I was forced to watch them leave," I murmur. The fire crackles, burning off the scent of cloying flowers. "I would hear about their operations, and I would be briefed. I'd wait, in my office, for word on how it had gone. If anyone was hurt. Who I needed to speak to. And occasionally, if there were any I'd never speak to again."

Eden draws in a long, deep breath, but I don't stop my quiet pace, the silky twists and turns of her hair through my fingers calming us both. I draw in warmth from the perfect heat of her cheek on my thigh.

Through the hills, the battle rages.

"It was an incredibly lonely fear," I confess, in this private place of ours. "The wait felt so many hours, weeks, and months longer than it ever was. I might have been their psychologist, but I came to know those Rangers well—all their fears and hopes, their kindnesses and their bravery. I cared for them, and some nights I would sit awake and simply wait on their return . . . because someone had to know. Someone had to care. And for some of them, very few others would."

Gently, I ease Eden to turn, until she faces me, and I can see those luminous, intelligent eyes. They pick me apart and pull me back together in moments.

Someone screams in pain, and her throat grows taut until the scream cuts off.

I lift a rogue strand of hair from her face, easing it from where it caught by her mouth, and I tuck it back over her ear.

"It isn't easy to be the vigil holder. It isn't easy to wait, no matter how much faith in them you have. It takes a special kind of strength." My thumb brushes over her lips, and she kisses it softly, her skin warmed by the firelight. "You're a brave woman, Eden. I hope you know how strong you are, in all the ways that have nothing to do with how hard you can hit. It's only because of you that this was possible."

The sounds of battle finally dim and stop, and I cup Eden's cheek, my heart aching at how she melts into my touch. My precious, beautiful, fierce Eden.

"It's because of you that we'll win."

CHAPTER 78

LUCKY

SURVIVAL TIP #190
People with cool call signs never die.
Pretty sure it's a law of the universe.

TWO MONTHS AFTER LEAVING BRISTLEBROOK

Dom's voice crackles over the radio on my kit. "Steel Rain, this is Boss Man, do you copy? Over."

No. Fucking. Way.

Beau looks up from his breakfast and grins, and the sunshine beats down on his tan.

Giddy laughter bursts out of me as I bounce to my feet. I press the button on my push to talk.

"Boss Man, this is Steel Rain. Hell *yes*, I fucking copy! Over."

He *does* like me! He really, really likes me!

Jayk rolls his eyes, but he gets to his feet. There's only one reason Dom calls these days. We left Bristlebrook just over two months ago, and the attacks are coming against the Reapers' farmlands multiple times a week now. Different places, different times. They burned our wheat fields just last week.

It's exhausting and dangerous, and eight Reapers have died, but Dom has finally accepted the order of the universe, so he's allowed to throw me into any damn fight he wants to.

The radio crackles back on, and Dom snorts. "Got the call. Red silo, thirty minutes. Whole team. Get your party shoes on. There's about twenty this time—so let's throw them a surprise, over."

Jayk starts pulling Jasper out of his tent, and the civs filter over, tired but ready as they pull on their gear. Sloane heads over to the truck, taking her time to warm it up because the Reapers have two whole barns full of gas that I don't even want to know what they did to secure. Beau ducks into my tent to grab my weapons for me.

They know the drill.

"Roger, wilco. We getting the tweedledumwits to join us this time? Over."

The Reapers are so useless that, no matter how carefully we orchestrate an op, they're still finding ways to fuck it up by sheer incompetence. I know we need them there, but at this point, it might be safer just to shoot them ourselves.

Beau brings me out my rifle, and I nod him a quick thanks as I take it from him. I'm still charged up over Steel Rain, and his eyes twinkle at me like he knows it.

"Sure. Bring five of them. Get me Quentin, Price, Jones, Lee, and Smitty. They're up next on rotation, and I've got somewhere to put them this time, over."

"Roger, Boss Man. Oscar Mike in five, over."

Jayk jogs back up from his tent, his rifle over his shoulder, and Jasper hesitates as he walks past me toward the truck, his eyes still tired with sleep.

"Why is he so happy?" Jasper mutters suspiciously.

Jayk shrugs, but Beau gives him a mischievous smile.

I grin at him as I sign out. "And thaaat's *Steel Rain*, over and out."

"No," Jasper says immediately. "*No*. I absolutely refuse to call you—"

I push past him, racing towards the truck. "Everyone! Guess what you get to call me from now until the end of time?"

Ava snorts a laugh as I climb into the wide tray beside her, and the guys walk over more slowly. Jasper looks like his head is about two minutes from exploding.

And I decide he needs a call sign, too.

MY MUSCLES ache as we head back to the truck, but I'm buzzing in all the right ways.

Dead Sinners, check.

No casualties or injuries among civs, check.

That Reaper, Price, took a Sinner bullet through the eye when he stepped out of cover, but he kind of had that one coming.

So far, so good in the reign of Steel Rain.

SITTING in the crappy makeshift bed beside me, Eden ends the call on the satellite phone and exchanges a look with me. Her hair is sex-kinked all around her face and naked breasts, her eyes glowing with the orgasm she just managed to claim before the phone rang.

It should be illegal to answer the phone during sex, whether we're getting news of an incoming attack or not. I'm proposing it at the next Apocalyptic Council.

First step: create Apocalyptic Council.

"Sorry! Sorry, sorry. I'll make it up to you, I promise," Eden whispers, already pulling on her clothes.

"We'll call it an incentive," I agree, watching her sexy-as-hell ass disappear into her pants.

Sighing, I flop back onto the bed, and Eden kisses me thoroughly, then hurries out to find Dom.

On the upside, the prospect of going out in the cold rather than spending a night alone with her *does* make me want to shoot someone.

I find my kit, several straps only half unsnapped where Eden was ripping them off me, and I decide that I'm okay with it.

The Sinners can just die extra painfully tonight.

I TWIST THROUGH THE TREES, reaching for an extra mag for my

rifle. Bullets slam into tree trunks near my head, and I roll behind a boulder. I pat on empty.

Ah, shit.

"Fuck. I'm out," I shout, hearing the rock I'm crouched behind take heat. "Boss Man, some support?"

"Copy! Jayk, Jasper, Ava, Katherine, put lead down range. Hit a wedge. Suppressive fire, then break! Mag dump!" Dom shouts back from somewhere to my right. "Everyone else, support by fire. Stay behind cover."

We were already half-fucked when the Sinners caught onto the ambush early. They redirected half their force around while they let the rest of them get nailed.

Ruthless, but smart as hell.

I really hate it when they can think on their feet.

Means I have to break a sweat.

The four of them push out from the trees near me, firing together and blanketing the forest in bullets. The barrage stops as the Sinners scramble for cover.

There's a whistle to my right. "Hey, baby. Heard you need someone to fill you up?"

I laugh under my breath as Beau skids in behind the boulder.

Neatly catching the mag he tosses me, I grin at him as I reload. "You always get me when I'm needy."

Beau grins back, tucking two more mags in the empty pouches of my kit. "Some more for later, too. Never say I don't get you anything nice."

I press my push to talk. "Steel Rain and Doctor Desirable here and clear, Boss Man. You ready for us to come round back? I've got a nice, big load for our new friends here, over."

Beau snorts a laugh as the radio bursts to life.

"For fuck's sake, Lucky," Dom mutters. "Yeah, circle round. Watch for squirters, over."

I open my mouth, and Beau smacks me, and I roll my eyes.

Fine. It was too easy, anyway.

"Roger. Over and out."

We start shifting around the firefight, watching for muzzle flashes

—or runners, like Dom asked us to. We take out two Sinners crawling from beneath some underbrush that made for pretty crappy cover.

I see Sloane between the trees, pushing forward beside a short, stocky Reaper who keeps stepping in front of her. Eventually, she kicks his legs out from under him and kneels on his back to take out a Sinner.

When she stands back up, she walks over the gasping Reaper with open impatience.

I chuckle softly. "She's great, isn't she?"

"Real sweetie pie," Beau agrees as we duck behind a thick tree.

We fall quiet as we creep into position. There are at least ten Sinners crouched behind various trees and rocks, firing on our guys. Beau and I slow, maintaining some distance, then lift our rifles.

Katherine and Ava have pulled back to the base of fire, but Jayk and Jasper need an opening before they can move out from where they're pinned.

Just before I fire on the Sinners, I hit my push to talk.

"Boss Man, this is Steel Rain confirming we have eyes on target. Give us two moments to clear out this mess here." I grin, then add, "King Kong and Early Bird are in safe hands, over and out."

"Lucien, you did not just name me—"

Beau chokes on his laughter just as the Sinners turn, and we start to spray bullets.

It might not be anywhere close to as good as spending a night with Eden, but it feels good that we're finally doing this. Our team is solid, and we're hitting the wins we need to.

It's worth it.

Because a few more months of wins like this, and we might even be able to go home.

CHAPTER 79

BEAU

THREE MONTHS AFTER LEAVING BRISTLEBROOK

I don't know how to—"

"Just get it in, for fuck's sake. Just shove it in the hole, don't pussyfoot."

"Well, forgive me for not wanting to break it."

"It can take it. It's used to doing it rough. Fuck, that part—"

"See, that's just 'cause your fingers are too thick. You shove, I'll finesse."

Jayk grunts, and I wince as my fingers slip. Damn, he's right. This isn't easy.

"How did you do this right next to me when I was sleeping?" I mutter dubiously.

"You sleep like the fucking dead, I could have done a lot worse," Jayk mutters back.

There's a rustle in the trees, and Jayk curses under his breath as we rush to finish with the trap. Through the branches, I can see the four Sinners stalking cautiously through the woods, their rifles raised, watching for any movement. The sounds of the fight to the north filter through, muffled by the trees and the leaves. It's just enough to deaden their footsteps.

The Sinners are trying to slip through with just a few guys—these hay-headed idiots have slipped away from their primary attack to the north and they're trying to sneak up on our camp in the field.

On Eden.

Of course, Dom knew all about that, and he sent us to give them a little welcome present.

The last three months of ops have been nothing short of a masterclass in exacting military strategy. Between Dom's planning, Eden coordinating calls and information, and our team's execution, we haven't lost a single civ or Ranger.

But if we can't get this done in time, then we might be the first to go.

Jayk and I finish the tie and step back just as a sharp, alarmed shout rings through the trees.

"There!"

Jayk slams me to the side right as they open fire, and we both scramble back.

Why did we go rogue? This was overconfident. We should have just done the usual ambush.

A bullet slices my jacket, but doesn't make contact with flesh, and I curse.

"Go! They're running!" one of them shouts.

"Bit more," Jayk breathes as he yanks me behind a tree.

They're close. Our camo is good, the coverage over-top was done quickly but thoroughly, but if they look too closely, then they'll spot the trap before they—

The trigger hits, and the military-grade net snaps up around them, flinging them off their feet and into the air.

Jayk and I open fire on them before they can get their bearings, taking them out before they can fire a single shot.

Before they can get anywhere close to our camp.

I re-sling my rifle, admiring the trap.

"It was a nice net," I concede to Jayk.

And as we turn back toward the sounds of the fight, Jayk slides me a smirk.

"It doesn't suck for catching fuckwits." His smirk turns into a grin. "Or friends."

Grinning over at him, I clap him on the shoulder.

And we head back into war together.

CHAPTER 80

DOMINIC

SURVIVAL TIP #298
If you don't keep your eyes open,
someone will take them out.

FOUR MONTHS AFTER LEAVING BRISTLEBROOK

I run up in time to see the flames.

The smokehouse is an inferno, and men are screaming in and around it. Over two dozen Reapers lie dead where they were either keeping watch or from where they'd come to help their friends—and that's only what I can see.

I fire off a dozen shots at fleeing Sinners, and catch one in the back, but it's too late. Most have disappeared into the forest, laden down with heavy bags.

Pete drops to his knees beside one of the bodies, tears streaming down his face.

From somewhere in the chaos, I hear Lucky yelling orders. Beau's demands for bandages. Jasper's clipped instructions. Jayk's long strings of curse words.

"No!" Cole shouts, limping up.

It's been four months since he was wounded at Bristlebrook, but it's been a slow recovery. Slow enough that Beau can't stop rolling his damn eyes every time his "wound" is mentioned now.

"That's all our stored meat. They can't . . ." Cole's voice breaks, then he turns to me, his handsome, punchable face twisting in anger. "*You*! You were supposed to stop this! This isn't supposed to happen, you need to—"

I shove him out of my face, and I don't bother to hide how much he's pissing me off. "Those were your men on watch, Cole. Blame them."

Cole rakes his eyes over my face, apparently disgusted by *me*.

What a fucking joke.

"They're *dead*," Cole snaps.

"Then they should have kept a better watch."

I leave him behind before he can bitch about it.

The flames are heavy, but a small horde of Reapers are working to contain it, so I edge around the building, my rifle up, checking to make sure no Sinners are hanging around where they shouldn't be.

And then I see him.

Lowering my rifle, I stare into the forest as my guys come up behind me.

Quietly, Eden slips in against my side to stare, too.

In the heated haze of the night air, Alastair stands between the trees—and despite the distance between us, I can feel him looking right at us.

He salutes.

And then he disappears into the dark.

CHAPTER 81

EDEN

SURVIVAL TIP #211
A pretty face isn't everything.

FIVE MONTHS AFTER LEAVING BRISTLEBROOK

I feel the earth-shaking boom first. I hear the screams next. This time, not just men, but women too. *My* women.

My brutes.

Katherine rushes past me, then past the rest of the civs who weren't in on this fight. I fumble to find the extra medical bag that was in Beau's tent, then break into a run, my terror turning me cold and numb.

This was just a normal fight. We've been doing this for five months. Dom has this down to an art. Why would there be explosions?

And why are my women screaming?

They don't scream. Not like this.

Not without a reason.

We race over the pastures, toward a tractor parked lazily on one of the dirt roads, and Katherine starts it with visceral urgency. My heart pounds as I watch her turn the key, and I feel the tires skid out while Emerson is still climbing in the back.

"No, no, no, no," Katherine prays under her breath as she speeds toward the violent sounds.

I stay perfectly still in my seat, staring into the distance like sheer will alone might improve my eyesight. But my hands shake in my lap.

It's my nightmare. The one I've been having since we agreed to all of this.

Something's gone wrong.

Something even Dom can't control.

And one of *us* is . . .

For all I'm feeling and hearing, it's still far too long before I *see* anything.

My brutes spill out of the forest, the civs right behind them just as our tractor stops hard. A few Reapers stagger out from the trees, but I don't pay them any mind as I jump out from the side door.

I'm too busy staring at the carnage.

"Area's clear!" Dom shouts, and he's the last to exit the woods.

I see Ava first. She's burned all up her left arm, and her hand is spurting so much blood, she's soaked in it. It floods Jayk's shirt, and he drops to his knees to settle her in the grass.

"Beau! We need you here!" he shouts.

"I need five!" Beau yells back, and Sloane shifts to the side enough for me to see him bending over Jasper, whose entire face seems ripped and is pouring blood.

A scream leaves me, and I stagger to a stop, staring as Beau snaps rapid instructions to Dom. Lucky is standing next to them, his bloody hands in his hair, silent, terrified tears coursing down his face.

"We don't fucking have five!" Jayk growls, and shockily, my head turns back toward him.

Ava's screams have stopped, and her eyes roll back in her head. From this close, I can see it's her ring finger and her pinky. They're *gone* above the first joint.

The burns along her arm are . . . they're not good, they're blistering but not blackened, a little more raw on her forearm, but that blood is still pumping.

Shaking, I drop down to my knees and pull the medical bag around. It takes me two tries to unzip it, but I find the gauze in moments, and I bite my trembling lip in relief when my hand closes around it. I pull it out.

"Could someone please bring me some water?" I ask huskily, though I'm not quite sure who's near enough to listen. "Only pre-boiled, as much as you can. Thank you."

I hear someone's footsteps move away.

I don't know why everything feels like it's moving so slowly.

A second ago, it was so fast.

"Hold her hand up, please. It needs to be elevated," I choke out, and it's too polite, but Jayk only gives me a sharp nod, holding up Ava's poor hand.

Someone sets down a canteen of water, then another, and I pour it over her bloody fingers.

Do I even try to clean them when there's this much blood flow-ing? I don't *know* . . . This is beyond my textbooks. Trying to stop my shaky jerks, I give up and press the gauze against the stubs where her fingers were. It soaks through in moments, so I grab more.

"Jayk, could you hold pressure there for me. The burns . . ."

Jayk's hand closes around the gauze, replacing mine.

Gently, I pull Ava onto her non-burned side, and Jayk moves with me. My hands hover over her skin, and I pick up one of the canteens.

Clean. I need to clean the burns.

"Eden? Darlin'? What do we have? Can you tell me?" Beau calls, his voice soothing despite the violence fogging the air.

"Is Jasper okay?" I yell back as I sluice water over the awful red-raw skin on her arm.

"I have Jasper. I need you to tell me about Ava." His voice is firmer now—in control, but not harsh—and it gives me enough room to breathe.

"She . . . she's lost her ring and pinky finger on her left hand above the first joint. They look like they were blown *off*, Beau."

What the *fuck* happened?

But I swallow. "There's blood, but Jayk is h-holding pressure. She's unconscious but breathing. Shallow but . . . but I don't think her airway is blocked? Some cuts. I— She's burned, Beau, all along her arm. It's blistering already. I th-think that's the only place. I'm trying to rinse it, but I— I need more *water*, please!"

Beau is still crouched over Jasper, but he's clear and calm as he calls back to me. "Okay. Okay, it's okay, darlin'. I'm going to talk you through it. Dom, we need to get them somewhere sterile. Lucky? Lucky! That's it. I have him, I promise. I need you to listen to me now, okay? Get my bag. I need you to bring Eden . . ."

The next thirty minutes are a blur of instructions and medical supplies and terror pounding in my veins. I can't see Jasper even when I glance over. All I see is Beau's back, flashes of the blood coating his gloves . . . and Jasper's still, limp legs.

We finally get a truck around, and they race Jasper and Ava back to the main compound, heavily guarded by Lucky and Jayk, and watched over by Beau.

I'm shuddering from head to toe as I watch them drive away.

Terror and hot, streaking rage have me in thrall.

I turn to Dom, and his gentle expression turns to sharp worry as he sees my face.

"What happened?" I snap.

"Jasper took a Sinner bullet over his cheekbone. Ava . . . Bane is dead. Frag or explosion, I didn't see it. There were a few of them that came out of nowhere. But I saw his body. What's left of it." Dom's face is grimly satisfied, but then it fades into something sombre. "Ava was too close to him. She got caught in the blast."

No.

No.

This is unacceptable. There's an order to these things. There's *meant* to be an *order*.

My stomach churns with fear and wretched anger for Ava.

For *Jasper*.

"This shouldn't have happened," I snap, and he tenses.

"This isn't the time. We can go over it when we're not—"

"No!" I snarl, and as I push past him, my fury is in full storm. "Now is exactly the time."

CHAPTER 82

JASPER

SURVIVAL TIP #52
*A woman with a grudge
is the most dangerous brute of them all.*

SIX MONTHS AFTER LEAVING BRISTLEBROOK

I turn out of the medical bay after checking on Ava, who will finally be able to move back to camp tomorrow. The burns up her side weren't bad enough to need grafts, thank God, but it's taken a long time for her to be well enough to move. Beaumont insisted on checking my cheek yet again, but it's healing as well as it can out here. The thick scar is, unfortunately, unavoidable.

I'm debating whether I should fetch myself some food here or wait until I'm back at camp when a roar of activity by the Reapers' mess hall stops me in my tracks.

"Yes! Hit her lower, yeah, that's it! Softer on your knuckles!"

I stiffen as I hear Lucien's wicked, gleeful shouts. Beside me, Jaykob's brows slam down, and we exchange a look.

We take off in the next instant. The shouts and the whistles are deafening. It's right after lunch, the sun is blistering, and it sounds as though most of the Reapers are converging.

My stomach tightens at what that could mean.

But Lucien sounds *thrilled*.

We turn the corner to see over a hundred Reapers gathered in a wide circle, their cheers a thunderous crash. It takes another minute for us to push through the crowd, and I flinch as I catch an elbow near my hideous, healing cheekbone. It's been a month since I was shot, and thanks to Beaumont's stitches, the flesh has been knitted back together, but the pink, new-forming scar is still taut and tender.

"*Yes*, Eden!" Lucien shouts, just as we burst into the center of the circle.

"Oh, shit." Jaykob snorts, his worry immediately changing to enjoyment. "That's it, sugar! Like I showed you."

My heart rate begins to slow, and I allow myself a single moment to enjoy the sight of Eden's fist connecting with Akira's stomach. She's kneeling on Akira's chest, wrestling the woman into the dirt, her face fierce and set, her glasses dangling around her neck by their chain.

I know Eden's temper has been riding her hard lately, particularly since the incident with Bane and Ava and me getting shot, but we're so close to the end now. It's unlike her to overplay her hand. What on earth did Akira start with her? Whatever it was . . . Eden appears to be ending it.

The Reapers are roaring in amusement, making no move to stop the fight.

Though it's less of a fight, and more of an evisceration.

"Lucien . . . what on earth . . .?"

But he's not paying me any attention.

He laughs, his hair golden and dazzling in the sun. "Creamed! Go, *go*, Eden!"

My lips twitch.

She *is* faring far better than she did in her delightful booty shorts when she sparred with Ava.

But someone should be the adult here.

I step into the circle, shifting around until I'm in Eden's line of sight. "Eden? Come on now, sweet girl, that's enough. She's down. You won."

Eden throws her head back, her hair a mess and her eyes hot as they find mine. Breathing hard, still kneeling on Akira's chest, she stares at me for a minute, then, finally, she nods.

I help Eden up off the cringing woman's chest, eyeing her in concern. Eden has been particularly solicitous toward me since I was wounded, but right now, she's almost lost in her anger.

Lucien moves in to hug her, and Jaykob lets out a low laugh.

"Nice moves, sugar." He smirks.

"Well, I'm hardly going to slap her." Eden's chin lifts, and her voice turns dark. "She didn't steal my lipliner."

Jaykob's lips curl up, and I begin ushering her towards the truck, leaving Akira on the ground.

We can cool down back at camp.

We've had six months of this, and it's felt far too long for all of us.

"We'll be done soon, my Eden," I murmur to her as the disappointed crowd disperses, and as she flexes out her bruised knuckles, she lets out a long, heavy sigh.

"Not soon enough."

CHAPTER 83

BEAU

SURVIVAL TIP #19
*The stars that shine brightest,
are the ones who guide you best.*

SEVEN MONTHS AFTER LEAVING BRISTLEBROOK

The six of us are lying under the stars. It's been seven months since we left home, and more than a week since the last attack, and after that last phone call . . . it's looking like we've just about done what we came here to do.

My chest aches in a soft, confusing mash of feelings.

It's a clear, cloudless night, and for some unknowable reason, all I can think about is the night I lost my family. Day Death. That night, the sky was choked by dark clouds and thick ash. I remember them snuffing out the stars the way those bombs snuffed out my sisters. My dad. My mama.

And I also remember Jasper and Dom, Lucky, Jayk, and even Thomas standing all around me when those stars finally reappeared.

My family.

Now, the skies are blanketed in stars, thousands and thousands of sparkling silver pins in a cushioned, never-ending night.

Always there, even if I lose sight of them every once in a while.

My throat burns as I send up a silent prayer to my family, wishing them well and thanking them for watching over me, even when I was being an ass. I know Bailey would have been up there wishing she could throttle me, and Brooke would be pulling out the popcorn because she always did like reality TV . . . and I think we've been putting on a damn good show. One I really pray has some strong parental controls in place.

I hope I've grown into someone that makes my mama proud, and that she smiles when she checks in.

Because I know I must have been stressing her out something terrible lately, but I really am happy, in spite of it all.

I send up one more prayer for all the other families up there, watching over the few of us that are left. I promise them quietly to take care of the ones that I can. There were too many we couldn't save, and too many we didn't step out of home long enough to try, but that ends now.

We need more stars down here, burning on the ground.

Stars like the five people who surround me now, who I love with an ache I don't think will ever go away.

The others are talking happily, making jokes and laughing, dragging Eden over for kisses and easy flirting, and I smile as I listen, staring up at those stars.

Finally, I feel Eden settle in beside me.

"Hey, stranger," she whispers, and I look at her as she leans over me.

Her long, pretty hair falls around us like a curtain, and her eyes are as soft and bright as the stars I was just admiring. She touches my cheek with the back of her fingers, gently soothing away the few tears I didn't realize had slipped free.

I reach up and brush my fingers over her hair, overwhelmed by this gorgeous, clever, flawed woman who let me into her life.

Who lets me love her.

"Thank you, darlin'. Thank you for everything." My voice catches. "For all of it."

Eden's face warms, and she bends down to give me the softest, sweetest kiss of my life. When she draws back, it's to rest against my chest, her eyes gentle on my face.

"I've been waiting my whole life to fall in love with you," she whispers. "With all of you." Eden smiles. "Just you wait, Beau . . . we're going home."

CHAPTER 84

DOMINIC

SURVIVAL TIP #261
*Sometimes stars align,
and sometimes they cross.*

But *that's* why your rising sun means you and Beau are basically soul-mates," Lucky finishes, scraping out the last oats from his bowl as he winks at me.

We all stayed up too late last night, talking under the stars, but no one's complaining this morning.

It feels good to celebrate.

Beau rolls his eyes as Eden laughs beside him, pink-cheeked and happy in the brisk morning air.

"Where does that leave me?"

"Oh, beautiful. Let me just tell you what *your* chart turned up," Lucky begins, and he tugs a notebook out of the bag by his feet. "First up, you and Jayk. It's a miracle you—"

Jayk snatches the notebook. "Let me see that."

"Hey! Jasper, he—"

"I've told you before, I am not getting involved in your bickering. You're a big, strong Ranger. You deal with him," Jasper says dryly, collecting up the empty bowls.

The scar on his cheek has faded a lot in the two months since he was shot, but it's still a jagged tight line. He looks like a real soldier now.

"Jayk, give Lucky his dream book back," Eden says soothingly, and Lucky shoots her a filthy look.

"It's not a—"

"Anything that says Jayk and I aren't an excellent couple counts as a dream," she says primly, getting to her feet. Then she pauses. "Possibly a nightmare."

I'm snorting at all of them when Sloane whistles, nodding behind me.

I get to my feet in time to see Sawyer pulling up in his truck, grinning ear to ear.

And it kills every bit of light inside me.

I don't want any part of something that makes this asshole smile.

"Dom!" He jogs up, panting lightly, his eyes overbright. "Guess who just radioed?"

Yeah. That's not happening.

Impatient, I cross my arms over my chest, and Sawyer's smile falters.

He looks around our campfire. "*Sullivan*. From the Sinners, you remember?" He looks back at me and laughs. "He's been working against Alastair this whole time! After Bane died, he finally managed to get enough support to take over."

Oh . . . *fuck*.

Eden draws in a harsh, shocked breath.

Sawyer's grin dims a little more, and he looks around at our suddenly tense group.

"He says he has Alastair and Mateo in custody, all their supporters too," Sawyer explains slowly, his eyes flicking between each of us. "He says he'll be here in three hours to offer us the peace deal we wanted, all them trade agreements we talked about . . . and Alastair's and Mateo's heads as an apology." He sucks in a breath, frowning up at me, confused. "I'm sorry, am I missin' somethin'? This *is* good news . . . ain't it?"

My mind ticks like a bomb. The six of us are frozen.

From the tents, the civs begin to filter over, whispering between themselves.

Until Jasper clears his throat, stepping forward smoothly. "Of course it is. It's more than any of us hoped for."

Jasper shoots me a warning look under his lashes as he passes me, and my heart pounds like a war drum.

"It's overwhelming, the idea that this might finally be over. We've been away from home for a long time," he explains gently, and Sawyer's expression eases.

"When will he be here?" I ask, and it comes out like a bark. I grimace, then try again. "So we can welcome him."

Sawyer's mustache twitches uncertainly, but he works up another tentative smile.

"A few hours from when he called, and that was, what? Thirty minutes ago?" He nods. "I think a welcome would be a great idea. We could make up a whole feast for 'em, really get these peace talks movin'. Can you believe it? No more fightin'." Sawyer rubs the back of his neck, and his eyes grow wet. "We've lost so many already."

"Yeah, yeah," Jayk says impatiently. "Feast sounds good. Glad it's all done. We should—"

"Set it up in the mess hall," I cut in, my mind racing.

Only two exits from that building. It holds all of them. If we can just contain this . . .

Jayk pauses, then nods slowly. "Sloane and the civs will help you get set up."

I nod, and Sawyer tips his hat to Sloane, who looks flatly back at him.

Fucking hell, what a clusterfuck.

"We'll meet Sullivan first," I tell Sawyer. "Make sure he's on the up and up."

Eden walks up to Sawyer and takes his arm, casually leading him back towards his truck. "Maybe everyone should leave their weapons at the door, including the Sinners, just in case tensions run high. I think it might be a lovely gesture of good faith, don't you?"

Urgency pounds through me, but her sweet, demure little suggestion almost makes me snort.

Dangerous little librarian.

She dismisses Sawyer back into his truck with easy promises that we'll come down soon, and our camp watches him leave in brittle, catastrophic silence.

As soon as he's gone, I turn to the civs.

"We need to fucking *move*," I order.

Jayk nods and turns to talk to Sloane, and they start arguing about who to take, how to handle them, and what they need to do.

"I need intel," I snap to Beau as he comes up beside me. "I need to call Arthur. What the *fuck* happened? Everything was fine last night."

"Well, I think we *know* what happened," Lucky mutters, grabbing up his kit and pulling it over his uniform.

Eden's face is rigid and hot as she storms back into camp. "I *told* him not to underestimate her. This could have been avoided. Maybe they are perfect for one another—in pure and total *stubbornness*!"

"I need the phone. Someone get me the—"

Jasper places the satellite phone neatly in my hand . . . just as it starts ringing.

It's Red Zone. Exchanging a look with Beau, I answer and put the phone on speaker.

Only it's not Arthur who speaks.

"Eden? Dom? Oh shit, it's bad. It's really bad." Bentley's heavy, booming voice is rough with raw panic. "Sullivan still thinks he's doing the right thing, but he took Alastair and Mateo. All of them. It was a clean sweep. Heather didn't even tell me until it was done, and she was supposed to take me, too, but she, fuck, I don't know. Had a crisis of conscience? She let me escape with the captives. I have them all safe here at Red Zone, but—"

"Bentley?" Eden breaks in gently, easing past Beau to squeeze in closer. "Bentley, take a breath. You said you have the captives? All of them? They're safe? Then we can sort this out. We'll handle things here. And once we explain—"

"No!" Bentley bursts out, his voice cracking with fear. "Sullivan wants to kill them, Eden, and your word won't be enough. Alastair . . . he's done too much there to play his part. I tried to talk to Heather but I . . . I don't know if she listened. If you don't do what I say, in a few hours, they're going to kill him."

"Them," I correct, and Bentley draws in a deep, shaky breath.

"Right," he says softly. "Them."

The day is bitter and cold enough to bite, but we've prepared for this. We're dressed warm and every single person in this team knows how to handle themselves.

We've survived seven months of death.

We can survive one more day.

Eden's face firms, and she lifts her chin neatly, battle plans in her eyes.

"Okay, Bentley. What do you want us to do?"

And he only says one word.

"*Stall.*"

CHAPTER 85

JAYKOB

I climb up the ladder of the wooden sentry post. It towers just behind the Reapers' shitty-ass front gate and is only wide enough to fit a handful of us, but any visuals are better than none. At least the stupid sneezeball flowers have died off—only withered, brown vines are rubbing up on the tin walls now.

When I reach the top of the post, I stand between my guys.

I stand next to Eden.

My skin prickles as I fall into place with my team. This shit will be interesting.

"The civs have them contained. They've got it covered, and they're ready to go." I glance down at Eden, and I snort. "They left their damn rifles at the door, too. Like it was a church fucking potluck."

Beau shakes his head, and Jasper rubs his forehead disbelievingly.

I eye Dom. "You sure this is worth the trouble? We could just let those two get ganked and take over here. It wouldn't even be that—"

"*No!*"

Eden, Jasper, Beau, and Dom snap the word with different flavors of annoyance, and Lucky laughs, shooting me a grin.

Rolling my eyes, I look out down the wide, long drive.

"Do you think we need any more of the civs up—"

"Any sign of 'em? They should be here any time now!" Sawyer calls from the ground.

I grind my teeth as he starts climbing up. Cole and Akira linger at the base of the post with forced little smiles on their faces.

Eden links her fingers with mine without saying a word, and I force a breath out my nose.

Fine. I won't punch him.

Yet.

Sawyer wedges himself between us, just as I hear tires approaching in the distance. It takes another minute before I see them—more than a dozen trucks and cars, all in a convoy, rolling on in.

I seriously hope they're not here to fight, because if they are, we're fucked.

The convoy stops a short distance away. Beside me, Dom's phone starts ringing, and he frowns, staring down at it.

"Here we go," Lucky mutters, pulling around his rifle.

I pull mine around, too, and brace myself as the tall, white-haired Sinner—Sullivan—gets out of the first no-guts little car right in the center.

In moments, more Sinners spill out around him, dragging two men who are tied up like Thanksgiving turkeys. They're kicked onto their knees a short distance from our gate.

Alastair and Mateo.

The sun winks off dozens of loaded-up rifles as the Sinners circle around them, wearing too many fucking accessories for this time of day. Frags. Gustafs. Grenade launchers. Rifles and pistols and too many freaking mags.

Sullivan lifts his hands up as he walks behind them, showing he's unarmed, and it takes everything in me not to shoot him on principle.

"Hello, Reapers! Hello, Bristlebrook!" he calls.

Right as Dom answers his phone.

"Who the hell is this?" he asks, staring at Alastair and Mateo.

And a woman's broken voice crackles over the line.

" . . . *Dom*?"

CHAPTER 86

EDEN

"Well, how are you doin', Sullivan?" Sawyer calls out expansively beside us. "You have no *idea* how happy we were to get your call."

"Oh, please," Jasper mutters.

Dom grimaces at Sawyer's back, then toward the Sinners, the satellite phone pressed tight to his ear as he listens to her. To *Heather*. Maybe she can stop this. We just need to . . .

"Stall," I breathe, and I turn urgently to my brutes. "I need to get down there. Can someone come . . .?"

"Two should go," Beau says worriedly, eyeing the deep circle of Sinners behind Alastair and Mateo's gagged, kneeling figures.

I'm not entirely sure what difference having two of my brutes there instead of one will make if they do decide to attack, but now's not the time to quibble.

"I'll go," Jayk says, straightening as he looks over at Dom, whose golden eyes are sharp and focused on a distant problem.

Of course he will.

He steps up every time Dom needs to step back now.

"Me too," Lucky offers. His hair is tied back, and his face is lethally focused.

I nod my thanks and glance between Beau and Jasper. "Handle things here?"

I drop a significant glance down to Cole and Akira, who are still loitering at the base of our sentry post, and my brutes nod once.

Turning back over the edge of the wall, I interrupt Sawyer's effusive explanation of the feast they've prepared.

"We're coming down now, so we can talk more easily," I call out as lightly as I can. The last thing we need is them shooting us. "Just give us two moments."

Sawyer grins at me. "Now, that *will* save us some shouting. Let's welcome them in."

As I turn to the ladder, Sawyer claps me on the back like we're the best of friends, and Lucky shoves between us a moment later, forcing him to drop his hand.

"Oops, sorry," he says, not sounding sorry at all.

Lucky reaches out to help me onto the ladder. We reach the bottom quickly, and Jayk bluntly tells Akira and Cole to "stay the fuck there," as we hurry over to unlatch the gate.

"Piss-poor fucking security," Jayk mutters as it swings open.

With the sun glaring in our eyes, we walk out to meet the Sinners. Jayk and Lucky are a step behind me, and Sawyer shuffles along beside us with almost lascivious eagerness.

We stop a short distance away from Sullivan, but my eyes find the kneeling figures first. Alastair and Mateo don't exactly look untouched, but I'm not seeing any bloody wounds or obviously cruel treatment. Alastair is sitting back casually on his heels, looking as though the thick gag was his idea and he's bored by the whole affair, while Mateo's eyes shout a demand at us to free them.

I don't know what to make of the lawyerly-looking Sinner standing over them, but whatever else Sullivan might be, it doesn't seem as though he's the type to mistreat his prisoners.

Eyeing my brutes behind me, Sullivan adjusts his glasses, and I drop my hands when I find myself doing the same.

"Hello, Sullivan. It's good to see you again, even under such . . . well, such interesting circumstances." My eyes drift over the men behind him—because he's brought a lot more than two.

Please, God, don't let this turn into a fight.

Sullivan grimaces as he glances back over his shoulder, like the armed men make him uncomfortable, too.

He spreads his hands nervously as he works up a smile for me. "I am sorry about that. I wasn't . . . completely *sure* how we'd be received."

I nod quietly, running through options about how to approach this.

Sullivan looks at Jayk and Lucky in tentative question. "And, forgive me, you are?"

Jayk just glowers at him, and I shoot him a quick scowl.

"This is Jayk," I say, "and this is—"

Lucky steps up beside me, nodding to Sullivan with a cautious but friendly smile. "Lucien, Lucky, Brat, Circus Rat, depending who you talk to. My preference is Steel Rain, though, if you really want to get on my good side. We're with Team Bristlebrook."

Team . . .

I slide Lucky a sideways look, which he ignores.

Sullivan's brows flick up like he doesn't quite know what to make of that, but he gives them a polite smile back.

The new winter wind is brisk and fresh, and I let it fill me. The bite calms me as much as Jayk and Lucky's presence behind me. Jasper, Beau, and Dom watching over me.

Sullivan is a thinker. A planner.

Sullivan is like me.

I can do this.

I glance down at Alastair and Mateo again, but before I can talk, Sawyer breaks in with a too-loud laugh.

Sullivan can't quite hide the derisive crinkle of his nose as he glances at the Reaper.

"As friends!" Sawyer tells Sullivan. "We're receiving you as *friends*, of course. Why don't you—"

"We came because we want to make you an offer—or rather, to accept yours, if it still stands." Sullivan interrupts Sawyer, but he's only looking at me and my brutes, and he's hesitant as he shifts forward.

I sigh. "Sullivan, there are some things we should discuss before we—"

Sullivan is already nodding before I finish, and he gently breaks in. "You have reservations. I have a few of my own, I'll admit." His glance at Sawyer is almost too quick to see, but I find it oddly reassuring as he frowns back at me. "I know this is a lot, but please let me explain."

He's somber, quietly serious, and I stifle another sigh, nodding for him to continue.

Sawyer eyes me, impatient irritation sparking behind his eyes, but I pretend not to see it as Sullivan gestures toward his bound, kneeling prisoners.

"Alastair's methods. Sam's methods. Men like Bane. I'm . . . I'm so tired of them. Many of us were tired of them. When we joined the Sinners, so many of us just wanted a safe place. Regular meals, if we were lucky." Sullivan's smile becomes bitterly self-deprecating. "Some company. It wasn't until after that we saw what Sam really was . . ."

He shakes his head, his lip curling in disgust.

Mateo jerks against his ropes. Sullivan doesn't look at him, but another Sinner presses a rifle against the back of his head, and I shoot him a quelling look.

He falls still against the gravel, his head tipping back impatiently.

Sullivan continues without pausing, "I saw people working against Sam, and most of them died as soon as they were discovered. I saw Alastair gathering influence, but he was just as cruel and terrible a leader in his own way, capricious and following the whims of his followers. Engaging in this useless, senseless war when we had so many more reasonable options. So I . . . "

Trailing off, Sullivan takes his glasses off, ducking my gaze. As he cleans them, I see his cheeks are turning bright pink, almost glowing beside his white hair.

He looks up at me ruefully as he replaces his glasses. "Forgive me, it sounds so ridiculous when I say it *out loud* like this, but I decided to try my hand at some politics. I've been working in the background for, well . . . for quite a long time. This absurd war between us was the catalyst, in the end. There's no benefit to it. And I was finally able to gather enough men on my side who don't want anything to do with Alastair's way of ruling. No brutality. No war." Sullivan meets my eyes across the road, and his shoulders firm. "And no more captives. Under my rule, the Sinners won't deal in humans, in *women*, as livestock. Never again. Every man supporting me voted and agreed."

The sun pierces between the trees, not enough to warm the frigid air, but it's oddly beautiful, and I look up, blinking the rays from my eyes.

Never again.

Slow, slippery relief slides through me.

I'm not sure I'll ever be able to completely trust the Sinners, but Sullivan's quiet, earnest sincerity feels real. This is something he fought hard for. Something he believes in enough that he's willing to bring us the heads of those he thinks fought differently.

Sawyer shifts uncomfortably, and he glances at me, then back at Sullivan with a disarming smile. "Well, of course. You know we have plenty of food to trade, and we'd be real interested in your medic—"

But Sullivan makes a small gesture, and suddenly the Sinners shift their weapons around in a swift, uniform move.

Mateo's head falls back in defeat.

Lucky and Jayk's weapons snap up in the next instant, and Sawyer staggers a fast step back. My pulse leaps in my throat, but I don't move.

Sullivan is still looking at me and my brutes, but his nervousness seems to have faded, and his expression is hard. That pretty sun shines over every Sinners' weapon behind him.

"Any agreement we make is contingent on one thing," Sullivan tells us. "We refuse to trade with any group who participates in any action relating to the capture, confinement, or trade of another human. It's a matter of principle. We intend for the Sinners to be at the forefront of a new rule of law, one that centers justice. We would like to start working toward a world that improves upon the mistakes of the past. We have no interest in repeating them."

Despite the rifles pointing at us, despite the coldness of his expression, I smile at Sullivan, my throat tight. Softly, I touch Jayk's tense arm, and he only glances at me once before lowering his gun.

I lift my chin and speak clearly enough that all the Sinners can hear me. "We have no interest in becoming, or associating with, anyone who would do those things. Your world is the one Bristlebrook wants as well. What we've been working towards."

Sullivan's head tilts, and he looks at me sharply.

But beside me, Sawyer seems to have had enough.

He's shaking his head, walking back from us, and his laugh sounds like greasy gears. "All of us want that. It's all we've ever wanted. Peace and quiet. It's them—" He looks at Alastair and Mateo. "They attacked us. The Sinners have always threatened us. Killed us. You come here and lecture *us* about *good* and *bad*? We were just surviving, the only way we could. The only way you *let* us! We *never* wanted this!"

Oh, *crap*. Sawyer getting emotional is the last thing we need right now.

The Sinners' grips tighten around their weapons, and Sullivan watches Sawyer warily.

"Well, as I said, that's over now, as you can see. If we can agree—"

"You have *no* right," Sawyer snaps. He stops his retreat, and rage makes his cheeks red and splotchy.

My stomach tightens in quick panic, my pulse racing as Lucky shifts in front of me, but he's not focused on us.

When Sawyer turns back to Sullivan, he's vibrating with anger.

"We were *welcoming* you here. We made a *feast*. You show some gratitude when you come begging. You said on the radio you wanted to make things right? Well, we lost over eighty men in this war that *they* set on us. Good, hardworking men whose hands grew the food that *you* got fat on," he spits, then points at Alastair and Mateo. "You want to make things right? Then they need to die. Them and everyone like them who attacked us. Maybe then we'll consider if *we'll* work with *you*."

Sullivan stiffens, his lips tightening, but he glances at Alastair and Mateo grimly.

This was what he came here for.

My anger smolders alongside growing panic as I watch Sawyer snarl at the Sinners, but I try to keep my voice firm.

"Sawyer, maybe we can take a moment . . ."

Sawyer doesn't even turn around, waving me off with a dismissive hand, as though even my voice is annoying him, and he wanders up closer to Alastair and Mateo.

"Should I shoot him?" Lucky asks me darkly, and I'm not at all sure it's a joke.

Sawyer pauses, looking down at the prisoners. Tucking a thumb into his belt, he sniffs.

"You know, no one ever treats us with the respect we deserve. I think it's about time y'all remember . . ." He points a finger at his chest. "We're the ones with the food." Slowly, he points up at Sullivan. "And you, you don't know how to plant it. You don't know how to harvest it. You *need* us."

Sullivan's hands twitch nervously, and dread soaks into me at the uncertainty in his face.

"We do . . . *appreciate* how much you do," Sullivan says carefully, and Sawyer scoffs.

The Reaper starts walking backward, his arms spread.

"Then we have no problem here! Kill *them* and come on inside. We'll be squared right up!" Sawyer shouts, and with a tight grimace, Sullivan nods to his men.

"No, Sawyer!" I snap.

"Shut *up*, woman," he snaps back, and I grab Jayk's gun before he can shoot him.

Mateo punches to his feet, but a Sinner kicks him back down, and Lucky trains his weapon on the Sinner. About two dozen rifles whip up to point back at us.

Beyond the convoy, I hear the shriek of tires.

Sullivan's hands lift, his eyes widening in alarm as fingers slip to triggers and tension crackles in the brisk air.

"Sullivan, don't do this," I urge in a hurried, demanding rush. He *needs* to keep his head right now. "There are things you don't understand, and that I can explain. Things about Alastair and Mateo that mean they absolutely must *not* be killed today."

Sullivan looks me over, but his white brows lower.

Somewhere, a car door slams.

"No," he says slowly. "I've seen what these two are capable of. Sawyer's right. Nothing can save them now."

No.

My chest squeezes in panic. No, not now. Not after all of it. We've worked so hard.

I'm not ready to lose them yet.

There's so much more good they're still capable of.

"What are we doing, beautiful?" Lucky asks under his breath, but I don't have an answer for him.

There's too much. It's too big to explain, and they don't want to listen, and . . .

Alastair meets my eyes. His are pale and pretty, and even now so, so cold, and he lifts one fatalistic shoulder as I stare at him.

Mateo is hauled into place beside him.

And rifles are pressed against the back of their heads.

"Stop! You son of fucking whore, Sullivan! Don't you kill him, *please*! I'm going to rip out your throat! *Stop*!"

Everyone turns as Heather rips through the line of Sinners.

"Is that Madison?" one of the Sinners mutters from behind Sullivan.

"I was wondering where the hell she got to," another says.

Heather's a mess. Her flaming hair is tangled around her face, and her eyes are swollen raw from crying, but she has a pistol in each grip —one pointing at Sullivan, and one at the Sinners.

A sob escapes Heather as she stares at Alastair, and for the first time, his calm snaps. He flinches forward, panic slipping into his features, but the Sinner behind him shoves the rifle hard into his head, and he stills.

I press a hand to my throat.

Okay. Well.

This should calm things down.

"Back the fuck away from them," Heather snarls. "That's an order, Sinners."

"Don't!" Sawyer snaps. "Who the hell is this? Shoot her."

No one moves, and Heather fires a shot into the air in one quick, blistering move, then points it back at the Sinners.

"*Now*! Move your *fucking* asses!"

The two Sinners holding rifles on Alastair and Mateo back up, and Sullivan grimaces.

I close my mouth. Apparently, there are some benefits to sheer belligerent courage after all.

Sullivan eyes her nervously, but he's edged with impatience as he shifts to face her. "Heather, enough. It's been a stressful few months, but this is what we've been working toward. I'm not sure what Bentley said to poison you against our cause, but I can assure you, the goal is still the same. Peace. Freedom. I don't know why you're so overwhelmed by—"

"Do *not* call her emotional," I bite out coldly. "Heather is intervening because you're making reckless decisions based on incomplete facts, and instead of dismissing her or Bentley, you should have been listening."

I nod to Lucky, flicking my gaze to Sawyer, and he shifts around seamlessly, falling casually in behind the Reaper.

It settles me marginally, and I draw in a steadying breath as I turn back to the Sinners.

This is it.

The space we need to stall.

"Heather's intervening because you don't have the full story," I tell them firmly, "And it's about time that you did, so please . . . settle in."

CHAPTER 87

EDEN

SURVIVAL TIP #370
We don't get to know who the villains are.
Not until it's too late.

SEVEN MONTHS EARLIER

My breathing feels too loud for the silent side tunnel as Dom and I make our way to our clandestine midnight meeting with Alastair. The susurrations of it echo around me until it feels like someone is breathing against my neck. It's grave-dark in here, and it smells like rotting leaves. The chill raises the small hairs on my arms, even under my jacket.

"Come on, pet. Let's make this quick."

Dom's rifle is slung, his pistol casual and ready in one hand, but he's steady as he indicates for me to move. Quietly confident.

He didn't bother with a jacket. Dom always runs to molten temperatures.

I muster a grim smile and nod, letting his confidence infect me as I pick up my pace.

This will work.

It'll work because it has to.

As we turn through a slight bend, I see a crescent of moonlight against the rock wall, and my pulse leaps. We edge closer to it, then Dom lifts a hand for me to stop.

He rolls off the wall and takes a few steps forward, keeping his pistol raised as he checks the next small bend. Seemingly satisfied, he nods, and I hurry over to him. We do it once more before we slow, and he disappears to check outside.

A moment later, he calls grimly, "Eden."

Here we go.

I slip out of my tunnel and join Dom under the stars. It's cloudless and bright tonight, the moon at full wattage, but it still takes me a moment to see Alastair's dark-clad figure between the trees. Behind him, there are at least two more.

Nothing else moves.

No rabbits scurry away from the flower blossoms and no birds twitch from the trees.

"Should we go back?" I whisper nervously, and Dom tilts his head, just slightly, in a negative.

"He has Mateo and Bentley with him. Let them come out," Dom mutters, his gaze not shifting.

Bentley?

I squint, but all I can make out are fuzzy shadows. Maybe one of them *is* bigger than the other one . . . but why is Alastair bringing a prisoner to the meeting? And *will* he come to us? It's as much of a risk for them as it is for us to make the first—

"Eden! Dom!" Bentley booms, striding forward with his arms open. "You came!"

I flinch, my nails digging into Dom's arm, already scrambling a half step back. Dom gives me a dry look, though he edges in front of me, his pistol loose but ready in his hand.

I examine the trees around us, where they almost seem to sprout from the cliff-face on one side all the way around to where they stop on my other side. There are shadows and hollows everywhere but . . . I can't see anyone else.

Would I see anyone?

Damn it. How good is Dom's eyesight? And how good is the Sinners' hearing? Because Bentley sounds like a blasted *train* blowing its horn.

Alastair and Mateo finally appear from the trees, and as Mateo steps into the starlight, his narrowed eyes are on Bentley.

Bentley claps Dom on the shoulder and winks down at me.

It's only then that I notice he's entirely unbound.

"Hey there, sweetheart. Ready for a little cloak and dagger? A little subter-*fuge*. It's fun, isn't it?" He turns, breathing in deeply, his chest expanding like a hot air balloon. "The best things happen after midnight. Right, Mateo?"

He gives Mateo a look scorching enough for my brows to skyrocket, but Mateo's return glare roils with frustration. If I didn't know better, I'd call it *sullen*.

"I'm finding you a matching leash," Mateo bites out.

Scratching his beard, Bentley gives him an amused look. "I told you how to make me behave, dollface."

Alastair's pale eyes track over them, his boots whispering over the grass. When he finally stops beside Mateo, his expression is unreadable. His gaze travels to us next, and with one glance, I know he has every weapon Dom has on him cataloged and assessed.

He nods to us in a polite hello.

In the moonlight, the scars from his burns are shiny on his neck, and his clean-cut face is a mix of shadows and light. He's armed as well, and he has a heavy pack on his back, but unlike Dom, his weapons are holstered.

Whatever I was expecting tonight—more bullying, possibly, or Alastair urging us to surrender and hand ourselves over—it wasn't this. It wasn't Bentley. And it *certainly* wasn't Bentley making sex eyes at Mateo.

Oh no, was Lucky right? Is he Stockholmed?

"What is this?"

My confused, whispered question makes Bentley turn back to me, and his expression softens. "You're safe. We're just here to talk."

"They're safe if they *listen* to us," Mateo corrects in a mutter. "It's a miracle they showed up at all, with you going on and *on* today about how we were handing women off to our men."

Bentley's suffering sigh is like the crash of an ocean wave. "But you *are* handing women off to your men."

Beside me, Dom stiffens.

Seeming to give into his frustration, Mateo pivots to glower at Bentley. "Why would you *say* it, *cabrón*? You know *why*. You know they're with people we trust, so why even bring it up? Stupid! It's so *stupid*! It's like you want us to fail!"

"You want me to *lie*?" Bentley booms.

"For the last time, *yes*!"

Bentley towers over Mateo as they continue bickering over what he should and shouldn't have said today, and the moon is bright enough that his shadow casts an eclipsing wall of black over the grass.

I wince at their volume, but if no one has come bursting through the trees by now, I can only assume we're out of earshot. It takes me a clammy moment before I register what they're really saying.

There's a *we*. There's an *us*.

I'm not sure what to make of the rest of it, but . . . *they're with people we trust*, Mateo says. The captives Alastair "gave away as prizes" are with people *Bentley* trusts.

So . . . they *are* safe.

I'm starting to feel tipped. Dizzy. It's like someone has taken me by the shoulders and spun and spun me and now they're asking me to know which way is right.

I have no idea what's right anymore.

"I don't know why we trust you with anything!" Mateo hisses at Bentley, and he might be shorter, more lithely muscled than the other man, but he moves forward with a dangerous confidence.

Which Bentley seems to ignore.

Bentley grins down at him. "Because you're a bitter little thing and you have no friends."

Alastair's eyes find mine across the grass, pale as grave markers.

What game are you playing? I silently ask back.

Ever so slightly, he smiles.

"I'm waging a war against the Reapers—and I want your help to do it."

Alastair's cobwebbed voice is soft, but Mateo's mouth snaps shut mid-sentence.

A thousand pricks of ice shiver over my skin. There's a gravitas to Alastair. A certainty that isn't sneering or spiteful. He's made a decision, one as careful as any I've ever seen him make. A decision to . . . to fight . . . to *kill . . . innocents*?

My pulse stutters unevenly, clattering over the audacity and the questions and the sudden dread that swamps me . . . because Alastair's words start shaking things free.

"You have some nerve," Dom says, cool and firm, but I press a staying hand to his arm.

So I can *think*.

I can't help the disbelieving breath that escapes me, and I back up, needing to get some air. The trees are towering, and they go on in waves, farther than I can see, and I stare out at them as my chest constricts.

Why? All this for . . . for *food*?

It's the *Reapers*. Sweet, terrified Reapers.

Our ally. Jennifer's people now, too. They've fought *so hard* to prove that they're trustworthy. Sympathetic. God, they're the *victims* here.

And they're so, so anxious for us to join them.

The Sinners have given us a lot of trouble. We thought it was better to steer clear of any friends of theirs, Arthur said.

A mistake, Arthur wasn't sure. It was explainable. The Reapers *weren't* friends with the Sinners . . . except Sullivan . . .

Sawyer. Yes. We've . . . encountered one another.

Alastair's amusement when Sawyer spluttered his sweaty, panicked defense.

Interesting. Very interesting.

Nausea crawls up my throat as the pieces start to fall together, and I look at Bentley, needing him to tell me I'm wrong. My pulse is battering frantically at my throat.

He smiles at me sadly.

"People aren't always what they seem to be," he echoes his earlier self. "I wanted to tell you then, but . . . well. There's a bit to it."

Bentley wasn't talking about Alastair earlier today. He was warning me about *Sawyer*.

Sawyer, who was so *desperate* for us not to talk to the Sinners.

"Eden?" Dom prompts, tense and watchful.

Mateo shifts back beside Alastair until the five of us stand in a small, clandestine circle under the stars.

Cloak and dagger indeed.

Finally, I turn back to Alastair, and my lips are numb.

"What did they do?" I whisper.

I don't want to know. We were careful with them. We were cautious. We're not *stupid*, we looked for signs.

We're supposed to *see it* when they're preying on us.

Alastair doesn't mince words. "The Reapers supplied Sam with a quarterly dividend of food—a generous one, in exchange for their safety from the Sinners and, occasionally, outside threats." Alastair only pauses briefly, scanning my face before he adds, "Sometimes the Reapers fell short of Sam's requirements, and to appease him, the Reapers would supply Sam with women. In some quarters, they provided only a few—in others, Sawyer would hand over more than a dozen."

My pulse pounds at my temple. In my ears.

His voice sounds far away.

Alastair meets my eyes. "More than half the captives at the Den are there because of the men currently inside your home."

I press a hand to my mouth, and it's shaking.

Oh, God.

"Breathe, pet," Dom mutters under his breath, and I suck in a breath, nodding.

Dom's throat is corded, tight, and his grip is white around his pistol. The thoughts are racing in him too.

I nod again, seeing it. His fears. I start shaking all over, and I think I'm still nodding.

I need to breathe.

Dom's right. I need . . . I have to . . .

"I'm sorry." I back up farther. "I just need a . . ."

My back hits the cliff face.

Buck's face flashes into my head. Alastair's gun. Jennifer and Sawyer sitting on the bridge. Sawyer holding up the drink to his men after the raid, and the civilian's cheers.

Pete's heartbroken sobs.

His story.

But Sawyer, he thought . . . he liked to bring us up to meet new folks passin' through. Said we were good. Friendly-like. Made it so maybe they didn't want to fight none. We . . . we were good at makin' friends . . . I can't bring anyone in without Buck. No one's gonna trust my ugly mug.

Silent, horrified tears spill out over my cheeks. Over the hand that is still the only thing holding me back from vomiting on the grass.

Making *friends*.

They were drawing them in with this . . . this *kindness*. They used it as a trap. They offered them food, and compassion, and . . .

I remember Lucky unwrapping the cheese when we first met.

Beau's slow drawl and how he tended my foot.

The call of a real bed.

What if I'd met the Reapers instead of my brutes that day?

"Oh my *God*," I moan, fear and nausea and some awful, shuddery despair crawls over me.

It's not fair.

It's not *fair!*

How are we supposed to know who's *good* when they *all act the same*?

"Fuck," Dom curses.

I feel him come up beside me, and he pulls me against his chest. He still has his pistol in his hand, watching them, but . . . I press my face into him, and I realize I'm crying.

"How were we supposed to *know*?" I beg, sobbing, and Dom grips me harder.

"I'm sorry, pet." He's shaking, too. "I'm so sorry."

"Jennifer. She's with him right now, Dom. She's—" My voice breaks, and I grip his shirt like he's a lifeline.

How am I supposed to tell her that the man she's falling for is a predator? How is she supposed to react to that? Knowing the man she finally allowed into her life trapped and sold women to save himself?

How would *I?*

I sob into Dom's chest, shaking. The heat of him almost hurts.

He would never. My brutes could *never*. I always had a choice. Always. They helped me find my voice. They protected me and anyone—*everyone*—who needed it. They heard me when I spoke. They *learned* from their mistakes.

But God, there *were* mistakes.

"I'm sorry," Dom whispers again.

I feel like I'm unravelling. I'm sick, and angry . . . and I don't want to *do* this anymore. I'm so *tired* of being afraid. I'm so *tired* of guessing who is going to hurt me. I'm so *tired* of needing to be smart and perceptive and *prepared* . . . only for it to not matter anyway.

I wish my brutes had been better then. I wish Alastair and Mateo and Bentley were better.

I wish none of them made this so damn *hard*.

Because I'm *tired*.

"Jennifer's on watch tonight," Dom tells me. "Sawyer's with Cole. We'll . . . we'll fix it, Eden."

I breathe out, slowly coming back to myself. Remembering where we are. Why we're here. Remembering the trees and the shadows and that this is just a footnote to what Alastair is here to talk about.

War.

Finally, I step back from Dom, and my throat is full of tears.

"We'll tell Jennifer the truth." I remember her stepping out of Jasper's office, her eyes red, holding a journal not so different than mine. "But it won't fix her." I swipe away the next fall of tears from my cheek, and my mouth twists. "It won't fix her at all."

Shoving my hands into my pockets, I walk back over to the Sinners. To Alastair and Mateo, and Bentley standing by their side.

My villains, who may not be the worst I need to face.

My villains who, strangely, after everything, might just be among the few who rise above my expectations instead of crushing them.

I don't apologize for my tears.

After everything, they're the least of our concern.

"I'm assuming you saw this?" I ask Bentley, my dull voice still a husky wreck.

The humor has been stripped away from his face, and I see the man underneath.

I see his sympathy.

And his anger.

The breeze buffets us softly, and the trees whisper through the forest. Ents and wild things sharing our rage.

Bentley runs a slow hand over his hair, but he nods once. "I freed nineteen women from a barn while Alastair attacked their main compound. Bane and Sullivan watch these guys and their men closely." He lifts a heavy shoulder. "But they assume I'm under watch, so no one's looking for me. It's easy enough for Mateo to slip me out without me being noticed."

"He can hide well enough when he wants to . . . for a giant," Mateo murmurs, but his Adam's apple bobs as he swallows, like all of this disturbs him too.

I feel Dom's heat again as he comes up behind me, but this time, I don't lean into it.

I'm glad he's here, but I feel too cold to be touched right now.

"It was bad," I whisper.

Bentley's face darkens, and he looks away. "It was bad. They were chained up in stalls. They had buckets. I heard . . . one of the Reapers was leaving when I got there. He apologized to them the whole way out." When he looks back at me, his eyes are hard. "He didn't make it."

Somewhere, there's a vague sense of satisfaction at that, at least. Of relief.

But it's drowned out by the dull, seeping horror.

Not the Sam kind that grabbed me out of the dark. Not the kind that lives in shadows or that throws knives at my chair.

It's a fear of sunlight and smiles and the men inside my home.

"I need them out of my house," I tell Alastair. "I need them out *now*."

Away from my friends. Away from Kasey. Away from *anyone* they could ever hurt again.

The air is so cold it burns my wet face. It scalds my tears into my cheeks and blisters the raw end of my nose.

It's so cold that even those burns become numb.

Alastair's lips are compressed as he studies me. "So they can go on doing what they've been doing? I won't buy from them . . . but there are others who will."

Of course there are.

An ember of something begins to burn, deep in my chest.

Giving me a knowing look, Alastair wanders over the grass. He glances curiously over our tunnel, then finally, his gaze returns to me.

"I want a war, Eden," Alastair repeats. "I want a war in which only the worst kind of people die."

"According to you, I suppose?" I ask.

Dom shifts into view beside me, glancing at my face far more often than he was doing earlier.

I'm numb to my fingertips. I look down at them, rubbing them together.

It reminds me of my first days in the Sinners' camp, when I thought my brutes were dead.

When my rage first truly woke up.

Alastair pauses in his strolling, and he crouches to examine the dirt, his forearms on his knees. When he lifts his hand, I see he's holding a fluffy black feather.

Henrietta's.

It makes the small ember in my chest flare, thinking of Lucky protecting her. Of all my brutes helping him keep her safe.

Trying so hard to keep all of us safe.

Twirling the feather between his fingers, Alastair ducks my question. "You saw the issues I'm having."

Studying him, I nod slowly. "You have people who want to take your herd."

He glances up, and the moonlight catches in his eyes. They gleam at the reminder of our conversation months ago, when he told me he wanted to take everything from Sam.

It was the conversation that saved his life that day.

"Bane is an issue," Alastair agrees, rising. "Or rather, who he represents. The Sinners, as a collective, were recruited to be henchmen and thugs, and if Sam managed anything, it was bringing in the hordes. We have two hundred and fifty Sinners remaining at last count—of those, there are at least one hundred who follow Bane's persuasion of thinking . . . but it could be as many as one hundred and eighty."

I close my eyes—against his words, and the night, and the deceptive, bright moon.

One hundred and eighty Sinners who need to die, at the very least, and so, so many Reapers. I don't have enough soup for that many men.

Alastair's right . . . I can't do it alone.

When I open my eyes again, all I see is Dom, grim and intent. My military man. I know he'll help me. My brutes are helping all of us—and they're not asking for anything in return.

Not anymore.

Dom meets my gaze, and I see the trust. The resolve.

He's in this.

If I ask, he'll go to war for me.

"Bane isn't a leader," Alastair tells us as he walks over. "He's a loud voice that starts louder echoes. In some ways, it makes it more difficult than if he led them outright. At least then he might have gathered them together so we could know who agrees with him." Frustration edges Alastair's whispery voice. "Mateo and I have been trying to work out who we can trust since the day we joined. We're working through our lists. Testing them. We're extremely cautious about who we bring in on our plan, so our numbers are . . . fewer than Bane's."

"Fewer? By how many?" Dom asks, his voice steel-edged, and Alastair's gaze chills.

"*Somewhat* fewer." Alastair's lips tighten, just slightly, when he looks at me. "And fewer than that after dear Eden here wiped out several of them."

"And Heather," Mateo breathes, not bothering to hide his sour tone.

But Alastair's cold smile is more appreciative. "Heather has also done some damage."

All I can see is her collar. All I can see is *BEAST*.

"I'm assuming she doesn't know about—"

"No," Alastair says. "We've tried to bring her around but she refuses to see anything redeemable about me. Keeping her alive is becoming a full-time job. You'll have to forgive my creative solutions. She doesn't leave me much choice."

"You could let her escape," I say coldly.

"You think she would? She's devoted to my demise." Hollow amusement crosses his face. "Heather is currently busying herself with

Sullivan, trying to whip up a rebellion under my feet. Bentley here is keeping it under control."

Bentley gives him a filthy look. "Sure, that's what I'm doing," he mutters. "Next, I can stop a volcano from erupting—or track down a crop of silphium. Simple!"

"Don't laugh about Heather's hate. She earned it," Dom tells Alastair quietly. His eyes are as cold as I feel. "You killed Thomas . . . and he was my friend, too."

Alastair's amusement dies hard.

"He was in the wrong place at the wrong time," is all he says.

His words linger on a white puff of air in the night, chilling in the cold.

A sound escapes Dom, like he's been hit, though his face doesn't change. Silently, I shift closer to him, and this time, he leans into *me*.

The anger in me flares hotter, burning away at my numbness.

These men have cost my brutes, too.

"Heather isn't wrong for her hate," Alastair murmurs, and his eyes glitter like blood diamonds. "But they were stupid to attack us that night."

Moonlight shifts over Alastair as he strolls past, and his boots rustle through the leaves. He steps on a purple flower, and its scent bursts, wasted under his heel.

"I need another way to eliminate the men like Bane—a way that won't have the rest of them turning on me while I sleep. I need to eliminate those men *before* the captives can be freed, or else they'll hunt them down . . . and myself and Mateo shortly after. The captives are protected for now, but they won't truly be safe until Bane and all the Sinners like him are dead," Alastair explains, brusque and unapologetic.

"You want to use us," I breathe, filling in the blanks. "You've already been using us."

The woods are musty with old secrets, and they hang thick and heavy in the air, whispering at me to understand.

And, finally, I do.

Alastair needs a *war*.

Dom's brows come down. The darkness gathers in his hair, deepening the slow-growing strands into inky midnight.

He's still watching Alastair with careful suspicion when I turn to him.

"In a battle, where would you send men if you wanted them to die?" I ask, and he tilts his head, listening even if he doesn't take his eyes off the threat.

I still see Thomas's death playing out behind them.

"To the front," Dom says slowly. "In a forward charge like that, to the front." But he shakes his head once. "Alastair didn't order the Sinners to break cover. He ordered them to stay in the trees."

Alastair inclines his head, and his next look at Dom is more assessing.

"Many of Sam's men—men of Bane's persuasion—they don't take well to my orders, and so they disobeyed a command that would have kept them safe. A pity." He smiles slightly, and it reminds me of a viper strike. "But not my fault. I did warn them."

Alastair's using their own stupidity against them to sidestep the blame. He disposes of a problem and walks away clean.

"You need us to be your villain," I finish.

Alastair needs us to kill Bane's men for him, so that he can escape the blame there too. Bane's men would love a war. We don't have enough to interest them here, not anymore, but the Reapers . . .

The promise of owning that rich land is more than enough.

The promise of blood would seal it.

Watching my face, Alastair nods. "The Reapers are cowards. They won't fight back if they're unsupported. The Sinners could run them through in a day—and they would do it with pleasure. Bane is not too happy that his Reaper friends were trying to get out of their deal. But if you were there running their defense, orchestrating it with me . . ." His shoulders lift fatalistically. "Well. I think there would be a lot of casualties in this war."

"We could make them take each other out," I murmur.

It's so, so cold.

Finally, after a long, searching minute, Dom holsters his pistol.

"How would it work?"

"I tell you where and when Bane's men will attack. You ensure they die there." Alastair's brow slides up, the one notched by a deep, old scar. "They will need to win on occasion, or else they'll balk. Secure food. Eliminate some Reapers."

"I'll give you a list of names, Ranger." Mateo's brown, beautiful eyes are fathomless—too dark for the moonlight to touch. His lip curls in disdain. "Some of the captives had a lot to say about their time in the farmlands."

Bentley is stone and steel beside him, offering no objection.

The vicious satisfaction in his expression reminds me of a barbarian king planning a raid.

Under the moonlight, discussing murder and mayhem, I see it all. The Reapers' farmlands will become a theater of war—and we're the directors. It's an orchestra we conduct, a puppet show where we pull the strings.

Alastair just needs to kill enough of Bane's men off to overpower them.

"When it's all over, the captives decide what happens to the Reapers," I quietly demand. "They choose their payment and their justice. It's the least they're owed."

"Agreed." Alastair, finally, seems pleased. "I'll delight in carrying it out for them. We both know what they'll choose."

The hot, deathly rage inside me is too tired to enjoy the thought. The men deserve to die, and I would poison them myself for what they did, but . . . it doesn't change any of it. It doesn't change the betrayal. It doesn't change the women's fear or how they were hurt.

It won't stop their nightmares.

And it won't change all the ways Jennifer's last trust in the world is going to shatter when I tell her the truth.

I'm going to protect my friends, in all the ways they trusted me to. The civilians can decide for themselves if they want to be part of this fight. They can choose if they can bear to live alongside the Reapers long enough to bring this war to fruition.

Dom's hand touches my waist lightly, in silent support. Neither of us need to lean on each other for this.

We stand side-by-side, instead.

Ready.

Glancing up at the sky, I see we still have a few hours until our dawn meeting begins. We have some time to discuss logistics.

"So how do we start this war?" I ask.

Alastair unslings his bag from his shoulder and empties it onto the grass at our feet.

A bulletproof vest, a satellite phone, and a man's large jacket spill out in soft, neat thuds.

Alastair smiles.

"With a bang."

WHY IS THERE SO much *blood*? There wasn't supposed to be blood. Alastair shot him in the chest, we *planned* for that, but why did he shoot him *again*?

And why is there *blood*?

"Beau? Why is he bleeding?" I shout, my voice breaking. "Beau, he's hurt! Is he okay? Beau, answer me! Alastair wasn't supposed to—"

"Get her out. *Beau!* You, too. Out," Deanna barks, moving around the bed, and I back away to give her space, my heart in my throat.

She just had Sawyer and another Reaper carry an unconscious Cole out of the med bay so that they could free up a bed for Dom. It took everything in me not to stab them with a scalpel.

I hope Cole dies out there.

"No!" Beau roars at Deanna, and his face is dead white as he settles Dom into the bed. "Scissors. Clare! Get me scissors!"

Clare immediately places a pair of scissors in his outstretched hand, and he begins cutting away at Dom's jacket, Deanna doing the same on Dom's other side, fast and efficient.

Beau's breathing is jerky, but his hands are careful. Smooth. He's working but, oh God, he's panicking. I can see his panic. I told him that this was part of the plan, *shouted* it at him, but I don't think he heard me—and I don't even know if it's true, because Dom was never supposed to *bleed*.

I can't help my sob, and I back up more, until I hit the wall and can't escape.

Did I choose wrong again?

Did I just kill Dom?

The jacket falls away, and there's a deep gunshot wound right through Dom's upper arm on his left side. The rent flesh is gaping, ugly and pouring blood, and Beau curses, taking gauze from Clare quickly to sop up the blood.

I stare at Dom's face. His stubble, the blood on it, the stillness of it, and tears coat my cheeks.

"Did it hit a nerve?" Deanna murmurs, looking up at Beau. "It's not in proximity to an artery."

Beau shakes his head as he works, but there's the beginnings of a confused frown starting on his forehead.

Under his breath, he replies, "No, it's ugly, but it's . . . I don't . . ."

I freeze.

Did Dom's eyelashes just twitch? Is he awake?

Beau's face sets in hard lines, and he grabs the scissors, cutting right through Dom's shirt in a long, swift swipe.

And the dark, thick bulletproof vest comes into view, a single bullet wedged over Dom's left pec.

"Oh, holy fucking Jesus!" Beau shouts, and he steps back from the bed, lifting his arms.

His expression breaks, and tears start slipping down his face as he looks at Dom.

Relief? My eyes dart between him and Dom. He's relieved, right?

"Clare, help!" Deanna snaps.

Deanna takes over, moving around the table so she can put pressure on Dom's wound, and Clare begins unsnapping the vest, until it falls away from his heavy chest.

Dom sucks in a hard, groaning breath, and this time his lids do fly open, his face a rictus of agony.

An awful, viciously swollen bruise mars his chest, right under where the bullet hit, and it spreads out from there.

Dom grunts, groaning again and Deanna pushes him firmly down against the bed.

"Painkillers, Clare," she instructs, and Clare nods, her stern face relieved as she pours some pills out of a mostly empty bottle.

She presses them between Dom's lips in the next second, then tilts a cup of water to them, kindly murmuring at him to swallow.

Deanna pushes Beau out of her way so she can wheel around the tray of needles and bottles, and God, too many things that I just need her to be able to use *now*.

Beau staggers back against the opposite wall to me, squeezing a hand over his swollen, red-rimmed eyes as he shakes helplessly.

"Oh my God. Dom," he chokes out, raw and relieved.

"Fuck," Dom groans, low and pained, pushing away the water.

"Dom!" I sob, and my relief is enough to make me sick.

The vest worked. It worked, and Deanna is already nodding over his shoulder wound, her face calm, her hands steady. It didn't hit a nerve, he's okay. Dom's okay.

My rage hits alongside my misery.

Alastair . . . *fuck* Alastair. He *wanted* the drama. He *wanted* the blood.

I was terrified I wouldn't be able to act my part well enough.

So he made sure I did.

"Okay, enough. Out, Beau! I have him. Do you trust that I have him now?" Deanna snaps, glaring at Beau over her shoulder when he shifts forward to watch what she's doing.

Dom's face is tight, set in harsh lines of pain. But beneath his lashes, his eyes are on me . . . and he nods.

We've done it now.

Our charade has started.

Only it's already more real than I want it to be.

Beau swallows, watching Deanna's hands. "Do you know how to—"

"It's not arterial. I can suture. Get *out*." Her face is kind, but firm, brooking no argument, and Beau nods, blinking.

Oh, Beau. My heart breaks for him—for the family he's already lost, and the brother he was terrified to lose today.

He didn't deserve this. It was supposed to be cleaner than this. I was supposed to be able to tell him about it right away, and he was supposed to be able to see that he wasn't hurt.

I didn't want Dom to be shot at *all*, but we ran out of time while we fought about it.

And Alastair needed it to be convincing.

Beau steps in, pressing a hard kiss to the top of Dom's head, and he storms out of the med bay. I touch Dom's ankle softly as I leave, following right behind Beau.

Dread and the shocky leftovers of fear spill through my veins.

There are other things I need to do. Alastair is sending men to the side tunnel for us to kill. Men who have done things that made me want to peel off my own skin, and Dom isn't here to take care of them, so *I* need to.

But *Beau*.

Lucky and Jasper are in the hall, hope and relief on their faces, but all I can see is Beau as he turns to me.

Tears glisten on his cheeks, and his lips are trembling like a child who's just learned to be afraid of the dark. I see the moment he puts it together, that he realizes this was the plan, and he turns to look at me.

He lifts a shaking, bloody hand to his forehead, struggling, but another tear spills out over his cheek.

Is he going to hate me again?

My own tears burn my throat, all my old fears welling up.

We've come so far, we've done so much work. I know he sent us out there, that he agreed we could make a plan for everyone, but this . . . this could break anyone's trust.

"Eden . . ." His voice is thick. Raw. His eyes are confused and pleading, "What . . .?"

My gaze blurs, hot and wet, and I burst out, "Alastair wasn't supposed to do that. Dom wasn't supposed to get hurt." Something in me shatters, and my tears spill out everywhere. "I'm sorry. I'm sorry, Beau. I'm so sorry. Are you mad? I . . . I'm sorry."

But I only have to wait for one vile, agonizing second before Beau shakes his head, blinking. He wipes his tears, then drags me into him, wrapping me against his chest. I drink it in helplessly, crying against his shirt, and his heart beats like a drum, heavy and restless in my ears.

"I am mad, Eden," he whispers against my hair, "but not at you."

The fear and relief and anger and *hope* all crash into me, a storm and a whirlwind that swallow me whole.

He doesn't hate me.

A sob breaks free, but he strokes my hair, whispering to me— soothing me . . . just like the first time we met.

"He's okay," he murmurs. "Deanna has him. It's okay. We're all going to be okay. I'm with you, darlin'. All the way. To the end."

All the way.

We're all going to do it together.

I hear Ava shout for help, and I take a breath.

I need to play my part.

Which means that we have a siege to break—and I have Sinners to kill.

EVERY BONE, joint, and muscle in my body aches . . . and I would take that pain a thousand times over if I could erase what Jennifer is feeling right now.

The battle only ended a few hours ago. Lucky, Jasper, and Jayk are out in the forest, ensuring that the Sinners are truly on the run and none are lingering among our trees. Beau is in a bed beside Dom's, being treated for a light concussion and a dozen cuts of various severity from the debris blow-back.

The civilians are waiting on the all-clear before they can begin the clean up—and start collecting from the trove of supplies the Sinners left behind as they fled.

And I'm not feeling any of it.

Not the relief nor the joy nor the fearful anticipation of the battles in our future.

All I can see is Jennifer's face as I told her what Sawyer was.

A coward.

A traitor.

A dreg of humanity who entraps and sells vulnerable people to save himself.

We've gone through disbelief and rage, and now she's only curled up on the couch in Dom's room, her head in Ida's lap. Silent, soul-breaking tears slide down her face, and Ida strokes her temples with wrinkled fingers and slow, soothing love.

Ida's crying, too.

We all are.

Sloane, Ava, Katherine, and Ethel are all dusty and hurting around the room after my brutal explanations about all of it. Alastair. The Sinners. The war we're planning to fake to kill every bad apple Alastair can find.

And of course . . . about the Reapers.

Ethel sits in the armchair, her brief flare of energy through the battle seemingly hard spent. Ava's back is to the wall, her eyes closed as she listens to Jennifer's soft, gasping sobs.

I gently wipe my own cheeks.

"I can't do it," Jennifer moans, tucking her face into Ida's lap. "I can't face him again. I can't pretend. Please don't make me . . ."

The agony in her voice scrapes over my nerves, and I swallow hard.

Katherine kicks Dom's side table, her dirty face a streaked, splotchy mess. "Fuckers! Absolute *fuckers*!"

Sloane gets up from where she's sitting on the bed, shaking her head as she paces. Her eyes are sightless, and a bruise lines her right cheekbone.

"It's your choice," I tell her, my voice thick. I glance up. "All of you, I . . . You had a right to know. Sloane, if you can tell the other women, they can choose what they want to do. It's always your choice."

The last thing they have.

Their choice . . . and each other.

I sniff. "Anyone, all of you, you're welcome to stay here. Between the food the Sinners left behind, and what I'll send you back from the farmlands, you'll be fed. Alastair won't attack Bristlebrook—after being defeated here twice, he has a good excuse to keep the Sinners away. He'll focus on the farmlands, taking them, using the food as a draw."

I look between the women, aching, and they take my words in grimly. Ethel sighs tiredly, her creased face heavy with sadness. They've already had to fight too much.

Jennifer stares at me numbly from Ida's lap.

A lone tear slips from the corner of her eye.

"It'll be safe here," I whisper. "You'll be safe. Jennifer, you can stay. We'll leave the day after tomorrow, as soon as we can get packed. Tell . . . *him* . . . tell him you can't leave your people, that you need to protect them here, and that they're too weak to leave. I can be there. I can be close when you speak to him, or . . . or I can do it for you."

Jennifer's eyes squeeze shut, and my heart feels like it's being ripped out of my chest.

I remember her giggles on the bridge.

She *believed* him.

We all did.

"Whatever you need," I tell her softly.

"And you?" Sloane asks, turning from the door to look at me. A slow-burning anger simmers behind her eyes. "You're going with the Rangers?"

"I am." I straighten as I nod, and my aching muscles scream. Ignoring them, I hold up a phone. "I have the sat phone from Alastair. Dom will give ours to Arthur as well, so we can all communicate more securely than the radios allow. I'm going to help Dom to coordinate it all. The fights, the deaths. My Rangers, Jasper . . . they'll make sure it all goes to plan and . . ." I breathe out heavily, the prospect of months of fights, of them risking their lives for this, already weighing on me. "Well, they'll put on a good show."

Simple enough, but dangerous.

All we need to do is convince the Reapers that we're defending them, and the Sinners that the war is worth it, and slowly let them whittle each other away.

Without my brutes getting hurt.

But God, even so, one miscalculation, and . . . I rub my arm over the gooseflesh.

Ava finally lifts her head off the wall, looking at me dully from her seat on the floor. "They didn't want to be here for this conversation?"

I meet her gaze across the room. "I thought it best if they weren't." I take a slow breath. "Not the men . . . not for this."

Her eyes glisten, recalling her own words to me.

Ida looks between us, sharp and thoughtful as she takes it all in.

But her fingers don't stop stroking Jennifer's temple.

Clearing my throat, I continue firmly, "We don't expect anyone to come with us—all of you can stay here. There's no reason to put yourselves in danger. From the Sinners . . . or from living beside the

Reapers." My skin crawls at the thought, but I hold their gazes, one by one. "This is not your problem to solve."

"Bullshit," Katherine snaps, crossing her arms over her chest. "The Reapers came here. They lied to us! They're in our home. They—"

She looks over at Jennifer, who is shattering silently in Ida's lap.

Katherine swallows, but the rage settles deep in her face.

Sloane nods to herself, and her tattooed hand rests on her pistol. "Are we *sure*, Eden? Sure beyond doubt that the Reapers did this?"

I nod. "Bentley confirmed it. He saw it himself. He . . . he freed some of them."

Sloane's face hardens. "Then these fuckers need to get nailed. I'm coming with you."

Ava looks at me. "Me too."

"Me as well," Katherine says, her voice holding a snap I know isn't for me.

In the sitting area, Ida and Ethel exchange a look that says a thousand words.

"We'll stay here," Ida says finally. "Here with Kasey. We'll stay."

No one looks at Jennifer, but with slow, agonized movements, she sits up.

"I . . . can't go," she says, her voice hoarse. "I need to stay. I can't lie when I'm like . . . I'm staying."

Then her face crumples. "How could I not *know*?"

My last hold on my emotions shatters, and I storm over to sit beside her, wrapping her in a hug. "You couldn't have. It's not your fault. He's a liar . . . this is what they *do*."

"It's what they *did*," Sloane snaps.

And my own rage burns.

She's right.

Every last one of them needs to die.

Hearing the soft voices inside, I tentatively touch the door to the med bay with the bouquet of flowers I'm holding, and it opens just a fraction. My heart is still aching hours after meeting with

Jennifer and the civilians, and I want to check on Dom before I turn in.

But it sounds like someone beat me to it.

I peek inside the room to see Beau sitting up on the bed next to Dom's. He checked himself out officially a few hours ago . . . but he's still barely left his best friend's side.

Slow tears slip over Beau's cheeks as he looks down at Dom. As I watch, he sniffs, blinking his tears back ruefully. "I'm just . . . I'm so sorry, Dom."

"Beau," Dom starts gruffly, grimacing as he sits up. "Come on, you don't have to—"

"I do, though," Beau interrupts, soft and serious. "I do. Just let me say it. I know I told you before, but I should never have cut you out. Not a few weeks ago, and not after you chose Heather. I didn't . . . I didn't know then, I didn't get it. I had these ideas about love and family, and when you sat me down . . ."

Beau trails off, swallowing, and he rubs his jaw as another tear slips out.

He shakes his head once. "I guess it felt like I was losing the last family I had left."

Dom looks back up at him, his brows low, eyes hurting. "You weren't, Beau . . . you wouldn't. I'm here for good."

Beau's hand tightens on his face, until his fingers turn white, and he doesn't look at Dom for a long minute. His throat is taut, and my heart bleeds for him as I lean against the door.

This isn't for me. I shouldn't watch.

But both of them have come so far, and I've never loved either of them more than I do in this moment.

Dom sighs. "I didn't make that clear. I handled the whole thing so fucking badly."

Beau scoffs a small laugh that sounds more than a little wet. "I think we both did a number on each other over that one, but . . . it was just a mistake. Shit happens. It's going to keep happening, and it's . . . I just need you to know it's okay if you don't get it right the first time, Dom. I'm not your dad. I don't need you to be perfect. I'm not walking away from any of you again."

This time, Dom's the one who looks away, and he clears his throat hard.

"You—" He stops, shifting uncomfortably on the bed.

His chest and arm are wrapped heavily, and Beau gets up to get him some painkillers.

"Beau . . ." Dom sighs as he pulls himself to sit up with his good arm. "I appreciate this, I do, but we're good. You got mad and you didn't know how to deal with it, and you figured it out. Fucking slowly, but . . ."

Beau snorts softly as he empties some pills into his hand, then pours out a cup of water, and Dom's mouth curves up in a smile at his back.

"I love you," Dom finishes, watching him, his voice soft and heavy with his seriousness. "*You're* my fucking family, Beau. Even when we were on the outs, I knew you were coming back because you're too damn loyal not to. Because you love with your whole damn chest. And . . . because that's what family does."

Beau turns back around, and his throat works hard.

He blinks back his tears again, looking at Dom. "Love you too, Dom."

Quietly, Dom nods, and it takes a minute for Beau to nod too, and he smiles wryly.

"It looks like our family got a whole lot bigger than we planned," he murmurs.

"I like it better this way," Dom replies, and Beau's smile warms as he pushes off the counter.

Beau hands Dom his painkillers and the cup of water with a small smile, then holds up his own canteen. "To the new plan, Dom."

"To a loud, flawed fucking life," Dom murmurs back.

And to that, they drink.

"SLOW DOWN, sugar. You're going to break your fucking neck."

"No."

It's well past dark. We're finally at the Reapers' farmlands. Our camp is set up, sentries are posted all around the perimeter, our stomachs are full of their filthily bought food . . . and I'm so angry I could choke on it.

I almost trip over another burned beam, and Jayk mutters a curse, then yanks me into his arms, carrying me bridal-style toward the Reapers' *livestock* barn. I glower at him, even as I settle against his chest—and I *only* glower because I wouldn't put it past Jayk to throw me over his shoulder again instead. This is at least marginally more comfortable.

Plus, I really am struggling to see anything in the dark.

And I do need to go there. We have flashlights to pull out once we're hidden by the building.

Because I need to see it for myself.

"Did you *hear* him today, Jayk?" I'm almost shaking again, just thinking of Sawyer's audacity, the sheer, repulsive *manipulation* dripping off every word.

Jayk's chest is the only warmth against the bitter night.

My lips twist. "The way he was *crying* about those men dying like *they* were the victims. Trying to get us to pay the price for all of *his* mess, and *his* failures, and his . . . his *evil*! God, he thinks we're so *stupid*! A *livestock* barn! With the henhouse and the pigsty and two cowsheds and the sheep milling around right in front of us. The whole place, every building except this one in *pristine* condition." A harsh scoff rips out of me. "Hardly evidence of years of raids and heartbreak and patching up. No gunshots. They're *flourishing*!"

Jayk rounds the back of the barn, and he nods once, slowly. Grimly. His eyes are locked on it. He hasn't stopped raging all week, no matter how many times I slip him far, far away from camp with me to try to help ease him.

Maybe it hasn't worked because I've not been easy either.

We've been a storm.

"I heard him," he says flatly.

He sets me down on my feet and pulls out his flashlight, shining it up at the barn. We're close now, and the building should block most light.

"It's pretty fucked, Eden. I don't think it's stable. We should stay out—"

I pull out my own flashlight and quickly push past him into the narrow opening.

"*Fuck*! You little . . ."

He's quick to follow me in, and I slow as I step inside. The stalls are hollow husks, and there are broken, charred beams splitting the room. Wood lies everywhere, and each step stirs eddies of ash into the air that glimmer in the light.

There's a strange feeling to the air in here.

My breathing becomes shallow, *careful*, like I'm in danger of disturbing ghosts.

I twitch my flashlight around as I walk in slowly. Something about the burned remains sends chills up my spine. A heavy melancholy seeps under my skin with every step, one that could have everything to do with what I know about this place . . . but that I can't help feeling goes deeper. It's like these blackened walls have seen so much sadness, so much fear and rage, that they've been stained.

"Eden . . ." Jayk's voice is grim, and softer than I'm used to. "I don't feel like I should be in here. I don't think I'm . . ."

Not we.

He.

Briefly, I look back at him, and he's eyeing the walls too, his mouth grim and sad. He shakes his head as he trails off, like he's not entirely sure what he's saying.

But I think I know.

Deep in the barn, the wood groans, and electric prickles lift up the small hairs on the back of my neck.

These stains were made by men—and here in the dark, with ash motes floating in the air, it makes a perfect kind of sense to me that men wouldn't be welcome between these walls.

Swallowing the lump in my throat, I nod once. "Okay. Okay, we can go. I'm sorry, I just needed to . . ."

I turn, and my flashlight catches on a metal reflection.

My breath shivers out. Slowly, I walk past Jayk, my flashlight fixed on the stall, and with each step, the fear and rage and grief sink into my bones. My blood. My emotions swirl like the disturbed ash beneath my feet.

If these walls rejected Jayk, I feel the opposite from them—like

I'm being drowned in their feeling, sharing in it, grieving for it with them. Like they needed it to be seen.

These stains needed a witness.

I kneel gently in the ash and char, and a tear slides down my face as I brush away the debris, my sorrow in my throat. My hand trembles as I pick it up, lifting it off the wall, and the heavy chain links jingle together like church bells. More tears follow the first, silent and sad.

Manacles.

Slowly, I turn my flashlight, seeing stall after stall, blackened chains after blackened chains.

There are manacles chained to the walls.

The walls groan again, and the feelings swamp me, fill me to the brim, fill me until I'm overflowing.

"We need to go, sugar. Now. Get up."

They penned them in. Their livestock. Their trade.

Their safety for all this *pain*.

I bury my face in my hands. "Jayk, they . . ."

There's a malicious *crack* somewhere deep in the chest of this place, and Jayk curses.

"Out. *Now*."

He grabs me up off the floor, hauling me out, and I find my feet, sobbing, just as one of the heavy beams crashes down from the ceiling. The earth shudders beneath us, and the whole barn begins to groan as we run for the opening. Jayk yanks me forward, tossing me out onto the grass, then runs out seconds before the whole left side of the building crashes in on itself, exploding ash into the night.

He pushes me away with rushing, urgent shoves.

"Stop!" I finally snap, pushing him back hard as the barn makes its last, furious groan.

Tears course down my face, dust is choking me, and all the fury I absorbed is bursting from beneath my skin.

"*Stop*," I sob, shoving him back again, though he isn't doing anything anymore. "Why didn't they . . ."

Then he sighs.

And gruffly, he says, "Come on. You can do better than that, sugar."

My nails dig into his arm and more hot tears spill out. "They kept them out in a *barn*, Jayk. It's so *cold* out here. They—"

The cold was probably the last of their worries.

I spin away from him, but Jayk yanks me back in, and the small scream that leaves me is animal pain. Pure fury. I shove him back again, then hit his chest with both fists.

"They *what*? Come on, Miss Manners, I saw you today. You wanted to gut him." Jayk grips my chin and looks me in the eye. "I would have fucking loved to have seen it."

Sawyer, and his wheedling, smarmy fucking cowardice.

I did want to kill him. I had my knife in my pocket, and he had the nerve to compare the scum that died here to my Dom. The nerve to try to manipulate us, manipulate the women here, our civs, Jennifer, *me*.

If Jasper hadn't held me back, I'd have buried that damn knife in Sawyer's throat.

More wrathful tears spill over my cheeks, and Jayk's expression is rough, *knowing*, and so full of its own rage.

"Hit me, Eden. Show me how you would have done it," he orders.

Sawyer.

I lift my hand to slap him, but he stops it, adjusting my hand into a fist.

"Don't fucking slap me. He didn't steal your lipliner. *Hit* me," Jayk snaps, and the fury snaps through me.

I throw the punch, and it connects with Jayk's stomach hard enough to bruise my knuckles. The pain of it thrills through me. The brutal relief of connecting, of having a target, pumps my veins.

And it's not enough.

I punch him again, and Jayk grunts at the contact.

Sawyer's face as he cringed away from the barn.

"He didn't even have the balls to *look* at it!" I snap, punching him again. This one he catches, tossing me back, then gestures at me to try again.

So I do.

"How *dare* he act ashamed," I growl as I make contact again, lost to my fury. "How dare he act like a guilty, sad fucking child when he's been doing this for *years*? Where does he get the *audacity*? To trap and use and sell people and act like *he's* the victim? How am I meant to act like I don't want to fucking *kill* him?"

Nodding once, Jayk adjusts my arm, then kicks my leg back for a different stance as I rage.

For the next hour, he lets me slake my rage on him. Until he's covered in bruises, and I'm trembling with exhaustion. Until we both curl up on the grass together in grim, understanding silence. Until air finally fills my lungs, and the ash has settled back to the earth, ready for the next wind to stir it.

And as I nurse my aching hand and gratefully kiss Jayk's bruises one by one, I decide the women don't only need a witness.

They deserve justice.

I STOP in the middle of the field, kneeling in the grass as I tug the map out of my pocket. Wedging the phone between my shoulder and my ear, I measure out the coordinates and make a mark on a small patch of green. A cow eyes me sideways from the next pasture, but I shoot it a frown then ignore it.

Even the cows have ears.

"Okay, so that's by the red silo. What time?" I ask as Dom crouches beside me.

He's sweaty and dirty from the last fight—he only got back from it an hour ago, but he decided to go for a walk with me instead of cleaning up. His eyes narrow on the map, and I put the phone on speaker.

"They're forty-five minutes out. Twenty-two of them. All are fair game. Mateo is with them. Don't shoot him," Alastair advises curtly.

Dom's jaw tightens, and he plucks up the phone as he stands. "We need more fucking notice than that. You're three hours out. The least you can do is tell us when they're leaving.

"You Rangers are rapid deployment, aren't you? *Rapidly deploy*," Alastair bites back.

Dom's brows flatten, and I take the phone back from him before he can rip into Alastair. I hold it against my chest.

"Do you have what you need?" I ask Dom calmly, and he stares at me for a long, hard moment.

"Yes."

I nod, softening my expression. "Be careful then, please."

Dom eyes my face, and a touch of wry humor spills into his irritation. He kisses my forehead.

"You're managing me," he mutters, and I try not to smile.

"No, sir. I wouldn't dare."

Dom's brow kicks up. "Right back to camp when you're done. No detours."

Camp is quite literally in the next pasture, far away from any Reapers or Sinners whatsoever, but I nod to him anyway.

He smacks my ass hard and leaves me smiling as he speaks into the little radio on his kit. "Steel Rain, this is Boss Man . . ."

I bring the phone back up to my ear, watching Dom head for camp.

"Dom is on his way. We'll take care of it," I tell Alastair, and I hear his testy exhale.

"Fine."

Before he can end the call, I quickly say, "Alastair?"

"What, Eden? I don't have much time here. I have more ammunition for you, by the way. I'm having Mateo leave it by the silo during this attack."

The small white flowers under me are crushed, and I stare at the bruised petals with a frown.

"Is everything okay on your end? Forgive me for saying so, but you sound . . ." *Snappish. Cold. Distracted.* "Tired."

There's a long, taut pause on the other end.

Then Alastair sighs briefly. "Heather and Sullivan are whipping up more trouble than expected. Their influence is growing, and it's becoming more . . . difficult . . . to contain. But we're managing it. It's been an effective distraction for Bane as well."

Heather? Is this about the rebellion Alastair mentioned?

I sit back against the fence, running through the worries and dangers and implications of that. The sun is dazzlingly hot for the time of day, but it's not the only reason I feel sweat beading on my skin.

"Don't underestimate her, Alastair," I tell him urgently. "I know Heather lets her emotions rule her, but she isn't stupid. I really, *really* think you need to let her in on what's happening. This could get out of hand so easily, and that's not to mention how much I loathe that she's being lied to—"

"What, exactly, do you want me to tell her?" Alastair snaps back. "I told her your captain is alive, that I didn't kill him, and she *refused* to believe me. I've told her, shown her in a dozen different ways that I'm protecting the captives here, that I'm keeping her safe. I've shown her the kind of future I want to build. Bentley has tried, Mateo has tried—the stubborn fucking woman won't believe a word. I am her *villain*, Eden, and she will never let me be anything else."

Slowly, I close my mouth, stunned.

Alastair isn't just obsessed with Heather.

The man is head over heels in love with her.

These days, I know very, very well what that sounds like.

The cow sidles over to me, nudging me with its heavy muzzle, and I absently rub it back.

Alastair draws in a deep, shaky breath, and I can practically hear him regretting his outburst. He's not the type of man who has them often.

But with enough pressure inside it, every bottle will burst at some point—and I somehow doubt he shares these feelings with Mateo.

"I'm sorry, Alastair," I tell him, meaning it.

And I am.

I know how deeply Heather loves . . . and her hate burns just as fiercely. There's no hope for them. He's fallen for the wrong woman.

"There's no truth I could give her that she'll accept . . . not when the one truth she cares about is the one that broke her heart." Alastair's hushed voice is almost too soft to hear, like this is a confessional, and I'm his priest. "That one truth will condemn me."

Thomas.

I stroke the cow's soft nose, trying to choose my next words carefully. If there's no chance of him or Bentley bringing Heather around, then her being there is only a liability to our plans. If she's insisting on working against him, she's also working against *us*.

"You need to free her, Alastair. Send her to us," I coax him softly.

"It's the kindest thing to do for everyone. Then she can see it for herself. She can—"

"She won't leave the captives," Alastair says bitterly. "She's had her opportunities to leave, and she won't take them."

"Then put her on the phone. Let me talk to her, or Dom. We could—"

"*No!*"

The word is loud, a break in his hush, and the sudden difference frightens me—it frightens me despite the warmth in the air and the soft nose under my fingers and the fact that he's hours away.

He's not a man I ever feel easy around, even though I believe in his code.

Because that code is still a cold, violent thing.

Alastair's wintry voice burns down the phone. "If Heather has a death wish, then she'll pursue it with *me*. If she wants a villain, then I'll be hers . . . because it means I *am* hers. She's safe, Eden, and she's made it clear this is where she wants to be. Don't bring this up with me again."

The call cuts off with brutal finality, and the phone trembles in my palm.

Their hate could kill us all.

"No!" Alastair snaps on the other end of the line, his usual control as frayed as ours. "We can't take any more losses right now! The small raids on the outbuildings aren't *enough*."

Dom's face darkens, and he bends over the maps strewn over the table. "You've killed over fifty Reapers. You burned the wheat fields. It's not like it's one-sided here."

We're all back in his tent. It's late, too late, but we need to get the next few battles ironed out, and Sawyer's been sticking annoyingly close to our camp lately.

When I sigh, Lucky kisses my cheek absently, like it's a habit, and I lean back into him.

"Bane's numbers are gutted, but there are still enough to cause trouble for me—if I don't deliver them a win, a *substantial* win, they'll refuse to continue this war," Alastair argues. "Sullivan is trying to use our losses to demonstrate my incompetence. He's gaining some traction. I don't think you understand how volatile—"

Alarmed, I sit back up. "Then you need to contain it, Alastair. You said you had this under control."

"This *is* me containing it," he snarls back, and Jayk stiffens, his eyes flashing at Alastair's tone.

"Fine!" Dom bites out, straightening. He rubs a hand over the back of his neck. "Fine. What do you want?"

"I want the smokehouse—everything inside it. These men want meat. And I want devastating losses on your side. A clear win for the Sinners," Alastair says immediately.

Jasper sighs, pressing a tense finger between his brows.

I know why.

Cole and Sawyer are getting surlier with every Reaper death. Particularly as we're not sustaining the same number of casualties. Luckily, the Reapers are incompetent enough that their losses are still relatively easy to explain away.

It takes more than a little patience to deal with them, though.

"Do you have more names?" Dom asks gruffly.

"I have a list. I stand by what I said, though, Ranger. The captives have been extremely clear. Every one of those Reapers was complicit," Alastair finishes softly.

They finalize the details and the call ends.

"I'm not having our people anywhere near this one," Dom says, and I nod tiredly.

I'm not sure how much more risk I can stomach.

"YOU SON OF A BITCH!" I shout into the phone. "You said it was under control. What the *fuck* was that?"

My hands are still sticky with Ava's blood, my mind still stuttering over images of the burns up her side and Jasper's ripped face. The grass scratches against my thighs as I walk farther away from the few straggling Reapers and the pools of blood in the dirt. I'm well out of earshot, but I can't be anywhere near that place. Not right now.

Dom jogs up behind me, watching me with a taut jaw and worried eyes.

"What happened?" Alastair asks, and I hear the scrape of chair legs being pushed back.

"What *happened*? You fucking asshole. You haven't contained *shit*. Your Sinners today had grenades. There were bombs going off. They weren't where they were meant to be, and our people got *hurt*!" I rage at him.

Hot, violent nausea bubbles in my gut. They need to be okay. Jasper and Ava, they both *need* to be okay.

"I'll look into—"

"No!" I cut him off. "You won't look into *anything*. *You* got Jasper shot. *You* got Ava blown up. Bane might be dead but—"

"Bane is dead?" he asks sharply. "You're sure? He's been difficult to handle quietly. He's a cockroach when it comes to survival. That's a huge win for us, Eden, I can't overstate it."

God, I want to reach through the phone and *stab* him!

Didn't he hear? My Jasper is *shot*.

I can feel the sun burning my skin but it's nothing next to the fury that's scalding me.

"He's *dead*, Alastair." I'm shaking from head to toe. "Jasper could die. Any one of them could have died today. What the *fuck* happened?"

There's a pause. "Perhaps you should put your Ranger on the phone so I can—"

Murder flashes through me.

Dom's brows lift in slow, cautious question as he watches me. I don't think he can hear Alastair, but my eyes stay on Dom's as I take a deep breath.

When I speak next, my voice is as chilling and calm as Alastair's usually is.

"You aren't speaking to anyone but me right now, Alastair. Now I don't know if this was your incompetence today. I don't know if this was you not handling Bane or his men the way they needed to be handled. I don't know if this happened because Sullivan and Heather are *still* working against you—because you are a controlling, untrusting bastard who is letting his obsession with her risk *everyone's* safety."

My bloodied hand tightens on the phone, and Dom shakes his head, like he doesn't know, either.

Alastair, finally, falls silent on the other end of the line.

My rage resettles into something cold and sharply purposeful. "I don't know why today went so wrong, but whatever it was, you'd better fix it. Because from here on out, anything you do to my people, I will be doing to you."

Dom is staring at me, his eyes a slow, rolling smolder, and he runs an absent thumb over his lips.

I end the call, and Dom is still staring.

"What?" I ask, trying to keep the testiness out of my voice.

It isn't for him.

He shakes his head once, but his heated gaze doesn't shift. "Just glad you're on our side, little librarian."

Softening, I give him a small smile and look back toward the main compound.

My smile withers fast.

"Now that's done . . . I need to go see Jasper." My voice breaks, and the adrenaline begins to crash in on me. "And I would really like you to hold my hand when I do."

LUCKY'S SHOULDER is heavy against mine as we sit in the cold, tiled hall together. The door in front of us looms large, and I try not to flinch at every sound that makes its way through it.

Behind that door, Beau is operating on Jasper.

Lucky's fingers are laced tightly through mine, and silent, matching tears run down both our faces. The heat of his calloused hand against mine is the only thing holding me together.

Ava is stable now and resting in the next room down the hall, but Jasper . . .

I can't lose him.

Silently, Dom sets down a cup of water for each of us, then sits beside the door, waiting with us. Jayk paces up the hall, his fingers laced anxiously behind his neck. His eyes settle on my face, and his brows lower.

"The doc has him," he says gruffly, for the fifth time in an hour.

It's beginning to sound like a promise.

Or a prayer.

Lucky's head turns to look at me, and his lashes are wet with tears.

"I can't . . ." he starts, and I nod, my own tears falling.

"I know."

"I know he had to go. I know we're all doing what we need to, and I'm okay with that, I swear, but if he—" Lucky's voice breaks.

"I know, sweetheart," I whisper, tasting the salt on my lips.

"We only just got him, Eden. We only just started. He can't . . . I can't . . ."

Pain squeezes me apart, and I crawl onto his lap until we're curled together.

We break together, our tears mixing like holy water, just the way Jasper likes.

And when the door opens, neither one of us looks up. Lucky only squeezes me tighter.

"He's okay, everyone. He's stable," Beau's gentle voice tells us kindly. "Jasper is going to live."

"Man, it smells like BO and peonies in here. We should have waited to eat back at camp," Lucky mutters to me, his rifle hanging casually over his shoulder as we get some food from the Reapers' mess hall.

We spent some time chatting with Ava, who is more than done with her room in the med bay, no matter how many of us visit or stay to keep her company.

Being this close to the Reapers has all of us shivering.

There's a new darkness in her eyes that doesn't look like it will shift any time soon, and she's quietly protective over her two missing fingers.

While we were in there, Jasper had lingered in the doorway, his beautiful face marred but no less beautiful for his own wounds. He's struggled in his own ways with the new, permanent addition to his face, and we're giving him space to work through his feelings about it.

By tacit agreement, I ushered Lucky out of Ava's room to give Jasper some privacy while Beau checked him over . . . and to give Jasper some time to talk to Ava.

But it did mean ending up here.

Among *them*.

"Ooh, let me get a bread roll. Don't move," Lucky says distractedly.

He shuffles down the buffet line to pluck up a bread roll, and I run into Akira. She turns, plate in hand, and her dark eyes are unfriendly.

My grip tightens on my own plate, but I try to force a smile.

It doesn't come.

This woman left us and came straight here. She was with the Sinners first. With Alastair and her Logan. She had to have known what the Reapers were, and she not only told them about all the civilians . . . she led them right to our doorstep.

To *Kasey's* doorstep.

And she did it while she still thought Sam was in charge.

It goes beyond a grudge. I don't know if it was solely to secure a position here. Maybe—considering the way she now seems to be living in a repulsive level of comfort. But it's not a decision I can understand, not even in the name of self-preservation.

She *is* like the Reapers she joined.

Cowardly to the point of evil.

"Move, Akira. I want some bacon."

My words are blunt, blatantly rude, but I am so far beyond caring what she makes of it. It's the politest thing I'm able to say.

What I want to say would ruin the last six months of planning.

Akira's lips twist in amusement, but she steps back with a mocking little bow, and I ignore her, piling crispy strips of bacon onto my plate. My mouth suddenly feels so sour, I'm not sure I can eat them.

Akira leans against the table, and I see Lucky look over at me, his eyes flicking between us cautiously. I give him a small, reassuring shake of my head.

"You know, you never did thank me, Eden," she muses, and I pause, staring down at my plate.

A fly lands on one strip of bacon, before crawling all over it.

"*Thank* you?" I bite out, and I drop my plate on the buffet table as I turn to her.

My rage has been burning ever since I learned about the Reapers, and it's quick to rise to the surface. Flashes of memories flick through my mind—Sawyer's smile, the Reapers cringing from a fight, Jennifer's tears, the manacles in the barn.

My eyes scream a warning at her to stop, but her smile only sweetens like the reeking flowers none of us can escape.

"Well, for bringing the Reapers to you. Now you're all here, and fed, and thriving. I just thought you must be—"

My fist connects with her jaw before she can finish her sentence.

"Oh, shit!" Lucky shouts, but I'm already dragging Akira by her hair out of the mess hall.

She tries to take me down, but it only makes me land on top of her, and I channel every single hunt, every single sparring session with Dom and Jayk, every single moment of unanswered rage I've needed to keep on lock.

I feel blood spurt and hear her cries and every hit is a joy and a relief.

This bitch could have put Kasey at Bane's mercy.

Vaguely, I hear the crowd. I hear Lucky and his shouts. I hear Jayk as he arrives.

And eventually, I see Jasper's gentle eyes and his elegant face. I see where he was hurt by all this violence.

It makes me loosen my fists.

I let him lead me away, curled into his side.

And I try to believe his promise that this will all be over soon.

MY BRUTES and I are all sitting out under the stars in the pasture a little way from our camp. It's a cool night, but we're bundled in blankets and heavy clothes, and the easy company is more than enough to keep me warm.

There hasn't been an attack in a week.

The satellite phone is on speaker, resting on a blanket, and I'm tucked against Dom. Happy, relieved tears are welling in my eyes, and Lucky dimples at me across the blankets, his eyes soft.

Most of the flowers have died off for winter, and the air is crisp. Almost fresh again.

"So it's done?" I ask wonderingly.

Alastair is apparently off doing something terribly important, so we have Mateo and Bentley on this call, and it's nice to hear their voices.

"There's only a dozen or so men here I don't trust now. They should be easy enough for us to round up. It's been so much easier since Bane died." Mateo sounds exhausted, but there's as much relief in his voice as there is in mine. "We'll have some work to do convincing Sullivan's group that we're not the spawn of Satan, but the captives will help us."

"Thanks to me," Bentley interjects. "They thought *you* skinned baby seals for breakfast until *I* brought them round."

"I *baked* for them," Mateo mutters sulkily, and Bentley's laugh booms.

"Oh, dollface, they definitely thought those cupcakes were poisoned. They got dumped so fast. You made it so much worse."

Mateo sighs, and Bentley comforts him quickly. "Don't worry. I stole one when you weren't looking. It was very nice." His deep, rumbling voice turns wicked. "In fact, it tasted almost as good as—"

"How have things been with Heather and Sullivan?" Jasper interrupts politely, and Beau rolls onto his back as he chuckles.

The stars twinkle down on us.

Smiling, I exchange a curious look with Lucky, who shrugs, his dimples deepening.

"They're almost definitely fucking," Dom mutters in my ear, and I splutter a laugh.

"They've been quiet. Since we stopped the attacks they haven't had much to complain about," Mateo says with the air of a shrug. "I think we're past the worst now. Once we break the news to them this week, we'll free the captives and let them choose where they would like to go. Then Alastair and I will bring our men to you to help you contain the Reapers—we might need Arthur's help to fill out our numbers. We still don't have as many as we'd like." He sighs grumpily. "Maybe after Sullivan comes around."

Then . . . that's it.

Bane and his men are taken care of.

The Reapers have taken heavy casualties, and between us, Red Zone, and Alastair's men, we can pin down the rest and let the captives decide on their justice.

We'll have to decide what to do with the farmlands to keep production going, but . . .

"It's done," Jayk says heavily, his voice rough, and I look at him with tears in my eyes.

"We did it," Bentley agrees, with much more cheer in his voice. "And better yet, *I* get to see the look on Heather's face when you and Alastair release the captives, dollface. Then she'll really have to admit that she's in love with—"

Mateo snorts, then lets out a tired sigh. "We're not there yet. Let's get through the next few days."

We say our goodbyes, and when the call ends, there's a full, beautiful ache in my chest.

It's finally over.

Very, very soon . . . we're going home.

CHAPTER 88

EDEN

Survival tip #233
Sometimes the good guys win.

By the time I've finished explaining, my voice is hoarse, and there isn't a single set of stunned eyes not turned on me. Sullivan's mouth is hanging open, and he blinks at me like his brain is short-circuiting.

A bird trills somewhere in the trees.

"Look, sugar, you even managed to shut the banshee up." Jayk smirks.

It's enough to break the silence.

Mutters spring up like rustling leaves among the Sinners. Heather whips a scowl at Jayk, and Sawyer takes a step back, only to run into Lucky's rifle. Behind us, I hear Dom barking orders for someone to move, and Beau's low, warning murmurs, but that doesn't matter now.

The danger's not over yet.

I clear my tired throat, my eyes still on Sullivan, who is staring down at Alastair and Mateo like he's never seen them before.

"I don't know what happened after our phone call with Mateo and Bentley." I glance at Lucky, who is disarming Sawyer in a few quick, rough moves, then back at Sullivan. "We assumed that they must have been wrong, of course, and you and Heather had just been waiting for the right time to strike. Bentley did call us, and he mentioned that he had the captives with him, though, so I'm not sure how that . . ."

There are still pieces I can't quite make sense of, but . . .

"No!" Sawyer snaps, pushing back on Lucky, his voice panicked. "Let me go, I—"

Lucky's face is cold as he brings his pistol down hard on Sawyer's face, kicking his legs out from under him until Sawyer staggers to his knees, and Jayk raises his rifle so it's pointing at Sawyer.

"Stay still, Sawyer, and maybe we don't shoot you." Lucky steps back with a humorless smile. "Then again, my buddy over here has been having the *worst* hay fever. Can't promise what'll happen if he sneezes."

"You've been murdering us!" Sawyer shouts, staring between us, his eyes wide and disbelieving. "We let you into our home. We fed you. We—"

"Don't you *dare*," I snarl, my cool finally breaking. I take two steps forward and slap him hard across the face. He's lucky I'm not the one with the gun. "How dare you throw that in our face? How many women, Sawyer? How many women did you let into your home? How many women did you feed? How many women felt *safe* here before you trapped them and bound them out in the cold and then shipped them off like *livestock* to be raped?"

I slap him again, and the Sinners around me grow louder.

The panic in Sawyer's eyes writhes as he looks at me. He jerks, but Lucky holds him still for me.

"Or did you do it yourself, too?" I whisper, searching his face, and my skin crawls at the desperation there. "Why hold yourself back, right? It's going to happen anyway."

"I never fucking *touched* them," he bites out, word by word, and I glower down at him, letting him see every ounce of contempt I hold for him.

God, the relief not to have to *hide* it anymore.

From this pathetic, loathsome coward.

I turn my back on him, and he shouts, "We didn't have a choice! We're not bad people. You're making it sound like . . . like we're predators."

I stop, my skin prickling with the need to hurt him.

A short distance away, Heather's face is darkening with each word, and the Sinners are moving restlessly, their mutters breaking into low arguments.

Sullivan's rubbing his forehead like he's trying to think, uncertainty spilling into his face.

"The Sinners attacked *us*," Sawyer pleads. "*Everyone* was attacking us. We didn't know how to make it stop. We weren't brave like you. It was . . . Sam wanted women. It was the only way to stop the killing. We didn't even go searching for them, it was only when they came to us and we . . . we made it gentle. We gave them blankets. Food. We . . . the Sinners wouldn't have done any of that! We didn't want to!"

There's another hard smack behind me, and Lucky snaps, "You really need to stop fucking talking."

Jayk cocks one brow at me, lifting his rifle in question, but I shake my head. He's hurt a lot of people. They have the right to choose how he's handled.

But Sawyer doesn't know when to quit. "When Akira came to us, told us about all you folks, we weren't going to trade you! We wanted out of this deal with the Sinners! Doesn't that count for anything? As soon as we saw *any* other way, we took it. We're *not* bad men!"

I only spare him one cold look. "You can ask the women you traded how much it counts for."

Behind me, Dom, Beau, and Jasper come up with Akira and Cole at gunpoint. They kick them down into the dirt beside Sawyer.

"The civs have secured the mess hall," Dom tells us in a low voice, standing tall over the Reapers. "There's not much the unarmed Reapers can do unless they want a face full of bullets."

"I'd love for them to give Sloane a reason," I mutter back.

"No, I'm sorry, I . . ." Sullivan breaks in, finally looking up. His face is creased in confusion and worry, and a touch of stubbornness. "Stop. Stop, Heather. Everyone, stop! There's . . . I'm sorry, there's no evidence of any of this. We need to investigate, or . . ."

Adjusting his shirt, he looks around, finally settling on Alastair and Mateo. Mateo is wriggling, like he's trying to escape his bonds without anyone noticing.

But it's Alastair who gentles some of my rage.

Alastair's intense, shadowed eyes are locked on Heather, not shifting, and she's staring back at him the same way.

I wonder if she knows how much of what she's feeling is in her face right now.

Sullivan's breath leaves him in a hard exhale.

"*No*. I have watched these men kill and torture and inspire fear. I've watched them . . . I *saw* . . ." He shakes his head. "*No*. It's not possible. They were handing women out to their men like they were desserts. They . . . they collared you!" He swings around to look at Heather. "They—"

There's another screech of tires behind the convoy.

Then another.

And another.

"Oh, for goodness' sake, what now?" Sullivan huffs, turning.

"Are we too late?" Bentley's frantic voice sounds like an earthquake as he comes running around. He's unshaven, heavy circles under his eyes, and his clothes are barely slapped together.

Arthur appears beside him, and a dozen more from Red Zone, in their chain mail and holding weapons that shine bright enough to reflect the sun.

And slowly, tentatively, women whisper up behind them.

Women of all ages, races, heights, and sizes. Some of them hang back, looking like they might bolt. Others have rage burning in their eyes.

The captives.

Tears burn my throat, finally seeing them. This . . . this is who I did all of this for.

And they're not captives any longer.

"Please! Someone tell me I'm not too fucking late right—" Bentley's voice breaks as he sees Alastair and Mateo on their knees, and he bends over at the waist, heaving in a breath. "Oh, thank fuck. Thank . . ."

He straightens, running his hands over his face, then he strides forward. A few Sinners lift their rifles, but he doesn't even glance at them.

Bentley hauls Mateo to his feet and yanks him against his chest in one smooth move. His wide hand presses against the back of

Mateo's head, his fingers tunneling into his soft curls as he holds him tight.

"Bentley, what . . .?" Sullivan mutters, his brow creasing again as he takes in the new arrivals.

Bentley ignores him too, and he turns to look at Heather, his eyes hot and bright.

"Thank you, angel," he says, his usual booming voice tremblingly soft. "*Thank—*"

"No. Stop. *No.*" Heather shakes her head, blinking hard as her lips twist, then she finally snorts, sniffling hard, and looks at Mateo.

She rolls her eyes. "Bent, you might want to . . ."

Bentley looks down at Mateo, who seems to be doing his best to pull himself free of Bentley's heavy arms, and Bentley releases him abruptly. Mateo glares over the gag, and Bentley laughs.

"Oh, yeah."

He tugs the gag down over Mateo's chin, and Mateo glowers at him, waiting patiently until Bentley works him free of his ties.

Struck silent, looking between the women gathering around and Sullivan and even Heather for direction, none of the Sinners say a word.

Sullivan meets my eyes, silently frantic and confused, and I give him a soft, sad smile. I can understand his panic. This is clearly something he's planned for a long, long time, and he's just lost all sight of who his enemy is.

I know what that feels like.

Arthur whispers to a tall blonde woman by his side, and after a moment she nods, and he leads her over to Sullivan. And as she speaks, Sullivan's eyes get wider and wider.

Slowly, Alastair gets to his feet, and he stands straight and proud as he waits, though not for the Sinners' judgement.

His eyes are still on Heather.

Tentatively, she holsters her pistols and walks forward.

My lips part, and I know I should be focused on what the captives are saying to Sullivan, but . . . Heather is looking *back*.

With her *eyes.*

Bentley tugs Mateo out of her way, and when she reaches Alastair, she leans up and pulls the cloth gag out of his mouth, letting it fall around his neck.

He looks down at her with that same silent intensity.

"I liked it better when you were on your knees," Heather finally says to Alastair. Her words are pitched with her usual cocky swagger, but there's a huskiness to her voice, an emotion I can't quite put my finger on.

But Alastair's expression doesn't shift.

With hushed, deliberate seriousness, he says, "If it means you like me at all, Deathwish, then I'll kneel."

A soft squeak escapes me, and I look over at Lucky, who turns his back on them so he can grin at me, his brows lifting in amusement.

Sawyer shifts at his feet, and Lucky absently kicks him back into place.

Someone touches my back softly, and I look up to see Jasper. I lean into his side, looking over the crowd.

Some of the Sinners have come around and they're talking to Dom, while Jayk walks over to Beau where he's monitoring Cole and Akira. Sullivan is starting to nod, his expression softening as he talks to the blonde woman, and Arthur sends me a small, friendly wave.

Several women peel away from their group and jog over to hug Heather and laugh with Mateo, whose face warms as they speak until his kindness really does make him look like the angel I always saw in him.

The sun is high in the sky now, finally warming up the day, and it almost looks like it's . . . over.

" . . . *him*! *He*—"

I turn, my grip tightening on Jasper as one of the women near Arthur breaks away from the group, running back to the cars. Several women follow her.

My stomach turns, and slowly, I walk up to their group.

A small, unassuming woman steps out to intercept me, her expression wary.

"I'm Eden," I tell her, and she nods, but her gaze drifts to Sawyer and Cole.

"Cassie," she murmurs after a moment.

"The Reapers are all being contained by our people. We . . ." I take a deep breath. "It's not enough, but it's your decision what you want to do with them. You can take as long or as little time as you want—and if you don't want it at all, then we can handle it ourselves. Either way . . . they're not doing this to anyone else."

She's silent for a long while after that, just watching everyone move about, and a small frown starts to form in her forehead.

"It's . . . it's really over?" she whispers.

My lip trembles at the raw, disbelieving confusion in her voice.

And my eyes find my brutes, all standing together under the sun.

"Yes," I finally whisper back. "It's really over."

CHAPTER 89

EDEN

I t takes a few months to make even the most initial agreements between all parties. Months of meetings and discussions. Months of building trust. Months of arguments.

But in spite of all that, they're also months of respite.

Months of relief.

Months where our healing finally has a chance to begin.

In the end, the most important things were the easiest to agree on. The Free Women, as they've called themselves, have claimed the farmlands for their own, as partial payment for their treatment.

There were a few weeks in the beginning when the tension between Alastair and Sullivan almost spilled over, but after a week back at the Den, they came back strangely calm, with Alastair in command of the Sinners and Sullivan appointed as the head of his new council.

After some discussion with Bentley, the Free Women agreed that the teenagers from Red Zone and a portion of their protectors could join them at the farmlands.

Including Bentley, who has resumed control of Red Zone . . . and Mateo, who can't take his eyes off him.

And, both for their own interests and to provide as much defense as needed for these people who have already been through too much . . . our civilians agreed to leave Bristlebrook and join the Free Women as well.

The Free Women had their own debates about how to handle the Reapers. In the end, nearly two thirds of the remaining Reapers were executed—every single man directly involved in the capture, captivity, or trafficking of the women.

Sawyer, Cole, and Pete were among them.

And not a single person questioned the Free Women's decision.

The remaining Reapers—those who turned willful blind eyes and who bore the guilt of doing nothing—are being kept as closely watched prisoners for now.

They'll be kept only for as long as the Free Women decide they're useful.

And currently, their only use is in sharing their knowledge of the land and livestock and how to keep the farmlands flourishing. Red Zone and the civilians will oversee their imprisonment until the new inhabitants of the farmlands can take over . . . and then the Free Women will decide what becomes of them.

More happily, all groups agreed that the farmlands, as the source of all food, and that the people now living inside the farmlands, as the source of our new hope for the future, must be kept safe at all costs.

The specifics of the trade agreements are part of ongoing discussion, but it was generally agreed that all parties are committed to a new era of exchange. A commitment to a free flow of ideas and training. A commitment to mutual defense and security. An openness of trade and ongoing communication.

It took weeks to arrange even that, with the promise of much more discussion to come.

And then, it was time for the brutes to return to Bristlebrook.

IT's mid-morning and spring is just starting to bloom when we finally say our goodbyes out in front of the main compound. Bentley wraps me in a hug that lifts me off the ground, making us promise to come back to visit the farmlands for the May Day festival he has planned—because of course, if he's going to become a farmer, then he'll bring back some old traditions while doing it.

Over the months, the heavy, long-overgrown road through the forest to Bristlebrook has been cleared, and now we're just a few hours' drive back home. We've been back and forth a few times now, to get supplies and oversee some of the Red Zone artisans, who, as promised, are installing new custom windows. Fuel is still too precious to make the trips more than occasional.

Still, I wouldn't miss Bentley's festival for the world.

Mateo kisses my cheek and squeezes my arm, gratitude soft in his eyes as he sends me off. He goes back over to Bentley with a grin and a glow he never once wore with Alastair . . . and Bentley makes no secret that Mateo is the new center of his world.

Soren waves to me from beside them, and I wave back to him warmly.

They'll be happy here, I think.

Alastair wanders over to talk to Mateo, and he gives me a polite nod, one marginally less arctic than they used to be. Maybe with a few more years of friendship, I'll be able to work my way up to lukewarm.

Ava, Sloane, and Mary Beth tackle me with fierce hugs and promises to visit. Sloane hasn't let Mary Beth out of her sight since she arrived—apparently long distance didn't work for either of them, and Mary Beth was ready to climb Sloane like a tree on arrival.

Ava is healing well, both inside and out, and I'm relieved to see the spark returning to her eyes the longer she spends here. Before they all back away, she winks at me . . . then tucks an enormous hunk of cheese into my pack. That alone was almost enough to make me stay. Billy, Baa-bara, and Henrietta are all being kept here now, since my brutes and I are planning to spend much more time out hunting for precious resources and medicine for the farmlands.

Which means I'm on a finite supply of cheese until we either get visitors or make our next trip back.

And I'm about eighty percent sure they were so pleased about the arrangement because it meant I *would* come back.

Ida and Ethel are saying goodbye to my brutes, winking at Lucky's flirting and patting Jasper's scarred cheek with tender smiles.

And Kasey and Jayk are standing awkwardly in front of each other, their hands tucked identically into their pockets.

"Well, bye, I guess," Kasey mutters, her jaw set and surly.

Watching her, Jayk scowls heavily. "Don't say bye to me like that, you little shit. I'm coming back. I saw how you mangled that fucking engine yesterday."

Her head snaps up. "It wasn't *mangled*. It was already broken. I wasn't done fixing it."

Jayk rolls his eyes. "Fix it like that and it'll never run again."

"Oh, and you're going to show me how to do it?" She crosses her arms, and the stubborn curve of her lips turns soft and shaky. "You're leaving."

Jayk stares at her, then he yanks her in for a hard hug—and her arms come around him fast.

"I told you, I'll be back so often you're going to be throwing that wrench at my head," he mutters to her fiercely.

Finally, Jayk drops her back on her feet, and they both step back, rolling their shoulders like it was nothing, and I bite my lip to contain my smile. Behind them, Ida rolls her eyes.

"Anyway, you're my apprentice or whatever, so I need to visit a lot. New agreement, all that," Jayk says gruffly, shrugging, and Kasey shrugs too, her eyes wet.

"Okay, sure. For the agreement or whatever."

She leaves with Ida and Ethel, and Jayk watches her go with a scowl, until Beau comes up and claps him on the shoulder, talking to him quietly.

My brutes start gathering up their bags, their goodbyes almost done.

"Ready to go home, pet?" Dom asks me softly, and I look up at him.

Home.

"Almost." I let out a heavy, bittersweet breath. "There's just one more person I need to talk to."

Heather's leaning against the tall gate to the compound, watching Alastair with that same, absorbed intensity.

For the last few months, she's been non-committal about where she's planning to settle. The civs and the Free Women have both begged her to join them here to lead their defense, and even Mateo sounded like he meant it when he told her to stay.

I also heard Sullivan and several of the Sinners talking to her over lunch the other day, proposing that she help them train and run a security force for the area—one that might also help any new groups they come across find safety.

But Heather has refused to agree to anything.

She's also hardly let herself within three feet of Alastair.

Smiling softly to myself, I walk over to her, and she looks up at me sharply.

"Eden," she says, pushing off the rusty tin gate. "You're going."

"I am," I say softly, watching her, and she avoids my eyes with a grimace.

"You going to make me do the big feelings apology stuff? Bent won't shut up about it." She rolls her eyes, but she says it with so much affection that I smile, too.

"No, we can skip it, but . . . does that mean we're good?" I ask.

Meeting my eyes, Heather smiles back at me. "Yeah, babe. We're good."

Her deep red hair lifts in the breeze, and she shoves it irritably out of her face, and I laugh softly as I help her tuck it back.

"Then, at the risk of overstepping, there's one last thing I want to talk to you about," I tell her, and her stormy eyes flash to Alastair.

Because she knows.

When I'm through, I worry for a long minute that she's going to punch me.

But instead, she wraps me in a brutal hug.

"Thank you," she whispers.

I turn around with tears in my eyes to see all five of my brutes waiting for me, standing together in front of our two new trucks, both loaded high with supplies. They're standing like a team.

A family.

My family.

My brutes are taking me home.

WE'RE quiet as we park in front of Bristlebrook, and I slip out of the passenger seat with too many feelings battling inside me.

Ten months ago, we left Bristlebrook scarred, burned, and deeply damaged. There were bodies and bullet holes, deep divots in the earth from grenades and explosions. Our windows were broken and taped, and Bristlebrook was overwhelmed by too many starving people doing their best to survive.

The civilians have tended our home carefully in the months since we left, and while we've been back for quick visits, this is the first time all of us have been home together.

It's the first time I've really paused to take it in.

My brutes gather behind me as we look out over Bristlebrook.

It's like returning to see a beloved friend.

The pikes have been cleared from the moat, and the defensive platforms and archery field have been pulled down. There's a new, beautifully constructed work shed out in front of where Jayk's barn used to be, and the large vegetable garden we worked so hard to grow is now lush and sprouting.

The grass is thick and flowing, the divots in the ground filled in. More than half the windowpanes have been replaced, and the fresh glass winks in the sun.

And out the front of all of it, our apple tree is starting to turn a new leaf.

I wipe away a happy tear from the corner of my eye, my heart aching at the sight.

It's really here. We're really *home*.

"You okay there, darlin'?" Beau asks me, and I look up at him with a wide, tremulous smile.

Dom's eyes melt over me, and Lucky's return smile is warm and dimpled with kindness.

"I've just . . ." I swallow down my husky voice. "I've never really had a home like this before, and I . . . it just means a lot. To be here, it means so much."

Beau's face softens, and he draws me in for a tight, enveloping hug.

I catch Jayk's eye over his shoulder, and he's staring at me hard, as many emotions in his face as I feel in my chest.

He knows.

When I finally pull back, I laugh huskily, and Lucky winks once before he takes off over the bridge, shouting something about a shower. Exchanging a look with Jayk, Dom and Beau follow him more slowly . . . until I'm left alone with Jasper.

Who I realize hasn't said a word as he looks over our home.

He stands tall and beautiful against the forest, the sun doing its best to coax sunshine into the depthless shadows of his hair.

"It's quiet," he says, and I nod.

There's no Kasey hollering at Ida and Ethel, no chatter flooding every hall.

Jasper draws in a deep breath, and it has notes of bittersweet nostalgia in it. "That will take some getting used to."

Smiling, I lace my fingers into his, and his thumb coasts over my skin.

"It looks different from when you first arrived," he finally says, his voice tentative and a little hushed. "I'm not sure it will ever return to how it was."

Oh, Jasper.

"It's been through a lot," I agree softly. "We all have."

My eyes hot with tears, I look up at him.

The scar on his cheek is still textured and raised, but the healing pink is almost faded now, and I'm becoming used to it, loving it for the fierce character mark it is. The roguish slash turns his beauty from something distant and refined into something devilish. The dangerous edges of him feel tantalizingly close to the surface now.

But the harshness also throws into relief all the ways he *is* soft. The full, gentle curve of his lips, and the dark, sooty crest of his lashes.

And he makes my chest ache.

I squeeze his hand hard until he looks at me.

"It's flawed and it was hurt—and *look* at it. It's your teapot. Those flaws have turned into something truly spectacular, Jasper," I whisper. "And you should be so, so proud."

Jasper searches my face for a long, tender moment, then he squeezes my hand back. "I love you, too, darling girl."

To the sound of our brutes calling for us to hurry up, he kisses my forehead.

"Welcome home, Eden."

EPILOGUE

EDEN

SURVIVAL TIP #77
Dedicate yourself to people who give you a choice.
Who listen when you speak.
Who care when you're scared, or lonely, or hurt.
Dedicate yourself to people who dedicate themselves
to being better people.

FOUR MONTHS LATER

I'm tucked, freshly showered, under Dom. He's tilting my head back on the bed, kissing me softly as Beau tries to find a way to edge onto the mattress.

"I'm not saying don't kiss her, I'm just saying move your ass over so I can get in too," Beau tells him, exasperated.

Dom smiles against my lips, and I cup my palm over his cheek, kissing him again.

We just got back from our first big trip out since we got home, after spending weeks investigating new towns and cities, even an abandoned military base, traveling much farther than any of us normally would have risked. We went deep, building by building, factory after factory, clinic by clinic for supplies.

And it was more profitable than we'd expected.

We traveled back to the farmlands with medicine, weapons, gas, and tools the brutes had been unable to find for far too long. We tracked down replacement parts for vehicles and some of Red Zone's machines, as well as copper wire, satellite phones, and several other items they were on the lookout for.

We also found two more small communities of survivors who have set themselves up in different towns, and those we put in contact with Alastair—he and the Sinners will decide whether or not they can be trusted.

And we found several hungry families in need of a home, who cried when they finally arrived at the farmlands.

The four days we spent celebrating with our friends there were wonderful.

But we were all glad to come back home.

And not only because there is much, much more privacy back at Bristlebrook.

Jasper has given all of us free use of his private room, and we've been taking full advantage.

Now, hours after a delicious scene with Dom and Beau, I'm warm and sated and tingling everywhere. In our home, everything's the way it should be.

In this room, I'm happy to the bottom of my soul.

"You two are adorable." Beau pushes Dom over another inch, then grunts. "And *heavy*."

Beau flops onto the bed, and I'm laughing as the door crashes open.

I stick my head up, already knowing who it is.

Jasper would *never* open a door like that, or let Lucky open his door like that, so it must be—

"Jayk!" I exclaim.

"Did you do it?" Jayk points at the bed as he stalks into the room.

His hair is wet, and he's bare-chested, but he's in soft sweats, looking deliciously cranky.

Oh, good. He's found our present, then.

"*Who?*" Jayk growls. "How the fuck did you even *get* that here? Who did you let into my barn? I just stepped out to check because someone left a light on. It better not actually need fixing, because I'm not fucking dealing with that shit again."

Grinning, I pull out of Dom's arms, bouncing off the bed to run to Jayk.

Jayk's eyes narrow on me, but he catches my naked body as I leap on him and squeeze him in a tight hug. I wrap my legs around his waist, and his arms naturally settle under my ass as he snatches me close to him.

I tuck my face into his neck, breathing him in. "It doesn't need fixing, I promise."

Jayk stiffens. "You?"

I pull back enough to grin mischievously up at him, and he scowls. "You and the—"

"The circus rat, yes." I laugh. "We thought, since you haven't taken your turn at laundry in about, oh, three months, that you could use some help."

His eyes roll.

Beau sits up on the bed, looking between us. "What's all this?"

"Lucky had Arthur send someone out with a washing machine for us while we were away," I say innocently, glancing over my shoulder, and Dom's brow kicks up.

But it *is* innocent. Mostly.

We really did need a washing machine.

Turning, Jayk parks my bare ass on the top of one of Jasper's glass display cabinets, and I gasp at the cold as Jayk scowls at Dom and Beau.

"It was in my workshop with the side panel dismantled and a set of rubber fucking tools on top."

"They were cute," I say primly, as I zero in on Jayk's chest.

"And a sign that said, 'Fix me, I need to take it like a good machine,'" Jayk finishes, accusation thick in his voice.

"Well, that part was Lucky," I say absently.

We probably shouldn't have left the light on, but Lucky was more than a little distracting at the time.

I run my hands down his bare chest, and my palms tingle over his muscles. It was *hard* to find comfortable places to really *savor* anything on the road. Just like the months camping at the farmlands, there were a lot of quick fucks and nights stolen away by one or two of them.

I've been walked in on mid-orgasm more times than I can count now, and everyone's become rather lax about their state of dress or how they might find the others tangled up with me.

Just last month, Jasper had a complete conversation with Beau about the state of the dishwasher while Beau fucked me over his pretty, upholstered sofa.

I suck my lower lip into my mouth as my hands grow greedier over Jayk's chest.

For all that they've been casual with each other, I haven't really had a proper scene involving all of them. Once upon a time, even the idea of it felt too wildly ambitious for reality. Once upon a time, taking *any* man into my bed felt wildly ambitious . . . but now? After the last year?

I don't think I've been ambitious *enough*.

Jayk looks down at me sharply, glancing between my hands and my face with thick suspicion, and I bite my lip.

At this point, I'm fairly confident I could convince my brutes to do just about anything I wanted.

"Have you assholes been in here all day?" Jayk finally mutters, the beginnings of a pout forming on his mouth. "It took me *four hours* to clean the gutters."

Beau stretches out lazily beside Dom. "Eden sassed us. It was out of our hands," he says fatalistically. "We had to—"

"Discipline her. Hard. For hours," Dom finishes. He lifts one brow at Jayk, and his lips curl up, drowsily satisfied. "She learned her lesson, didn't you, pet?"

"Yes, sir," I murmur, trying not to snort.

My *sass* was me asking Beau for a hug with his stethoscope around my neck.

My *discipline* was several orgasms and hours of cuddles from both of them.

"Yeah, she looks devastated," Jayk mutters under his breath, sounding more than a touch sulky.

I stifle another smile. Poor Jayk. It's been over a week for him. Which should be nothing compared to the *years* he spent without, but . . .

His abs are hot under my fingers, but it's his little pout that decides me.

My hands drift back up to his shoulders, and I lean in to press an open-mouthed kiss to the side of his heated neck. Hungrily, I suck on him hard enough to leave a mark, and he flinches, cursing, but he presses back into my mouth like he can't help himself.

Elation thrills through me. I can feel his pulse pounding against my tongue. His breathing is snagging as I touch him, and satisfaction makes me shiver.

I *know* I can break him.

Trailing my tongue down to the spot where his neck meets his collarbone, I nip hungrily at his skin, and he grips a handful of my hair, yanking my head back.

"The fuck, sugar," he growls, but he's panting, his eyes dropping to my mouth.

I lift my brows innocently. "You earned it."

Jayk considers me, scanning my face, then nods. "Fine. You can suck my dick for me then. You two, you can leave now."

"Jesus, Jayk," Beau says from the bed, sounding amused, and he leans his tanned face on one hand, watching us.

"Is it the romance that does it for you, pet?" Dom adds dryly.

I shoot him an incredulous look.

"You spent a good portion of our first time together calling me a fuck doll, so I'm not sure you're one to talk," I tell him in the same tone, and Beau snorts.

Dom shakes his head at my sass.

He's only in a pair of black briefs, and his broad shoulders manage to look intimidating against Jasper's monumental bedframe.

Jayk's scowl deepens, but I slip off the cabinet, letting my breasts rub over his chest on my way down.

I nudge him back against the cabinet . . . and then I keep going down.

Jayk's hand tugs in my hair. "Yeah, look, Miss Manners. I didn't bring my showgirl outfit today, I . . ."

I press a hot kiss to his thick abs, right over his dark, curling tattoos, and he trails off. I press another kiss to his stiffening cock through his sweats, and he leans back against the cabinet, cursing.

His chest lifts sharply, and I look up at him, a low ache starting up in me again. This ache feels different from my maddening lust from earlier, not edged in desperate eagerness after a week of nothing more than heated kisses. This one is rolling and lazy and slipping cheekily out of my luscious, giddy glow.

"Should I stop?" I ask Jayk, and I press my open mouth against his cock through the soft fabric, letting my hot breath soak through.

"*Fuck*, Eden."

Jayk's hand tugs at my hair again, but this time, it's to pin my mouth against him. His midnight eyes are dark and swirling with lust. Shifting his hips, he rubs his cock against my lips, and I meet his gaze.

And press my tongue against the fabric.

As soon as he sees the pink flash, he growls, "Okay, that's enough. Bozo, Bimbo, get *out*! Sugar, you'd better—"

"Get out? But we just got here," Lucky complains, strolling into the room. "Am I meant to be Bozo or Bimbo? I'm not hating the Bimbo vibes, but Jasper really doesn't scream Bozo to me."

"Thank you for that, at least," Jasper murmurs tartly, shutting the door behind him. Then his steps slow. "Ah. That's a pretty sight. Are you putting on a show for us, darling girl?"

"We're not putting on a—"

Kneeling up, I press another hot, sucking kiss to Jayk's abs, and he cuts off, his head dropping back. When my tongue trails to his waistband, he shudders, his hips tilting up.

"You're a little shit, sugar. You're killing me."

A show.

The idea lights me up.

Everyone's here.

Everyone's *watching*.

Just like the first day I arrived at Bristlebrook, only this time *all* my brutes are here.

I tuck my fingers into his waistband, and Jayk tenses, the knuckles on his bracing hand growing white over the edge of the cabinet.

Ambitious. I can be *ambitious*.

"Ooh, free mouth-fucking? I want in." Lucky comes up beside us, stroking my cheek in greeting, and I smile impishly up at him.

"Fuck off. It's my mouth to fuck. Get your own. And fuck you very much for the washing machine, by the way." Jayk shoves a snickering Lucky back and turns, dragging me possessively back down to his cock. His voice lowers, hot and gruff. "Slap my legs if you need to, sugar. You know the drill."

Lucky staggers back, then hops up onto the cabinet to watch us, unperturbed. "Did that this morning. Had a blast. Down to try that mouth again, though. And you're so very welcome, cutie. Have fun filling her up. I hear the spin cycle's a blast."

Before Jayk can argue, I start tugging down his sweats until his thick cock springs free. His hand tightens in my hair as I lean in, licking up his length in a long, hot swipe. He's satin and steel under my tongue, and I've missed his taste so much I feel greedy for it.

Jayk's breath leaves him in a hard exhale.

A lusty, *resigned* exhale.

Maybe if I'm quiet enough, I can just work my way through all of them.

"I think I was meant to be Bimbo," Beau drawls, fluffing up a pillow and dragging it under his head. "Pretty sure Dom is Bozo."

"Ah, and it all becomes clear," Jasper murmurs from somewhere behind me. "Did you enjoy your scene?"

Steadying myself on his thighs, I suck and kiss and lick Jayk's cock. He's hot and freshly showered, and he throbs in my mouth as I suck on him gently, enjoying the rare chance to explore.

He usually just takes my mouth and fucks it the way he wants.

"Our patient was a very dedicated little slut for us," Dom says gruffly, and I let out a happy, muffled sigh around Jayk's cock.

My body still feels deliciously used, and it's turning slippery for more.

Muttering irritably, Jayk tunnels two hands into my hair, yanks me close to his body, and starts fucking my mouth. My fingers dig into his hips, and I shudder at the sudden onslaught.

His cock slides between my lips, filling my mouth, tapping my throat roughly, and I moan as he grunts.

I love it when he takes.

"It doesn't look like she's done," Jasper muses.

"She *was*," Beau mutters, sounding somewhere between amused and miffed.

The lush, needy ache in me spreads to my breasts. It deepens, throbbing low in my abdomen while they talk about me.

As Jayk uses me in front of them.

I run my hands over Jayk's abs, his thighs, tonguing his cock as best I can as he drills my mouth with rough, greedy thrusts. He's gripping my face against him so I can't look at the others, but I can hear Jasper *is* behind me.

And he's right.

I'm not done.

Feeling bold, I spread my legs over the floorboards, arching my back deeply for him, and I hear a sharp inhale . . . followed by his low, silken chuckle.

"Hm. I think our little submissive is asking for something."

Dom lets out a hard, amused snort. "Trouble. She's asking for trouble."

"Why the fuck do you all have to make this so weird?" Jayk complains to the others, his voice thick and throaty. "Just fuck off and let a man come in peace!"

"*Is* it weird?" Lucky asks. "Hey, Beau, do you think it's weird?"

"I think it's weirder that he'd ask his poor, deprived comrades to miss out on the fun," Beau replies tartly.

"You spent *half the day* fucking her," Jayk bitches, but he's distracted, his breathing growing ragged.

Somewhere in the room, I hear the slide of a drawer opening.

Jayk's cock begins to leak against my tongue, and he groans softly. I look up, and his gaze snags mine. Slowly, some of the tension trickles out of him, and he thrusts deeper into my mouth.

I whimper around his cock as he fills my throat, and he curses.

There's a brief pause and Dom mutters, "Look at her cunt. She does like a rough fuck, doesn't she?"

Jasper makes a dark, delicate sound of agreement. "She's a cruel thing. She might not be as loud about it as my other brat, but she enjoys taunting us. She knows she's getting us hard."

Lucky's laugh has hot, husky edges, and he sinks down to sit against the cabinets beside me. I feel his gaze like teasing hands all over my body.

He lowers his voice. "Fuck, beautiful. You're so damn pretty when you're bare."

My fingers tighten on Jayk's abs, getting lost in the praise and crude taunts around me. Drunk and dizzied by their eyes on me, and the hungry scent of Jayk's spilling need, and the unbearably provocative feeling of his cock pumping against my sensitive lips.

"Eden, do you recall the challenge I set you in the woods after Cyanide?" Jasper's voice is as smooth and threatening as the richly fragrant leather paddles hanging above me, and the cool clip of his loafers punctuates his question.

Click.

Click.

"Miss Manners can't speak. Her mouth is full," Jayk snipes.

Suddenly, he yanks his dripping dick out of my mouth, and I suck in a harsh, ragged breath. Holding his cock up, he drags my mouth down to his balls. They're hot and heavy, and I lick over them with wet, hungry attention.

Click.

"Suck, sugar," he demands, and I shudder, then draw them into my mouth, one by one.

"What happened in the woods?" Lucky asks, his head swiveling up. "Was this back when you betrayed me and handed me off to Dom for babysitting?"

Watching him in my peripherals, my gaze snags on Lucky's tight chest. My tongue sliding over Jayk, I admire the colorful sprawl of Lucky's muscular arms and the golden mess of his hair, braided back off his face and falling loose around his shoulders.

Dom's voice is mordant. "And here I was, thinking we had a nice night together."

Click.

Holding his throbbing cock, Jayk drags my mouth wetly along it.

Click.

Click.

Jasper sounds nearer—dangerously so, and I shiver as I track his footsteps behind me.

"It was a curious matter. It seems Eden had some difficulty recognizing who was touching her the first night she arrived here at Bristlebrook. Who had their mouth on her. Who had their fingers in her pretty little cunt." Jasper's voice turns like a blade, the sharp edge tilted out, threatening to cut. "I told her I expected her to learn the difference, whether she could see us or not, and I must admit, I'm beginning to wonder . . ."

Click.

"Do you think she has?"

Jayk's cock cuts off my breathy moan. My knees are biting hard into the floorboards, and I'm covered in shivery little goosebumps.

The threat in Jasper is clear, but I'm *sure* this is a test I can win. I know them now. I know their tastes and their scents. I know their bodies. I know how they handle me.

More than anything, though, I'm thrilled at the idea of proving it.

Jayk scoffs. Without looking down at me, he buries his cock deep in my throat. Holding my face there, he strokes my cheekbone as my fingers dig into him again. I fight for air through my nose, my mouth leaking around him, and I moan helplessly.

My needy, neglected clit throbs, and I look up as he presses my face into him, begging desperately with my eyes for him to fuck me . . . but his heavy-lidded gaze is still fixed behind me.

"She sure as fuck knows me anywhere." Jayk smirks, rough and taunting, and he punctuates his claim with a dizzying thrust. "I'm the one who gets her off."

Lucky sighs. "My man, I had to explain foreplay to you. It's a miracle you're not going in dry."

"To be fair to Jayk," Dom begins darkly, and there's a soft creak as someone rolls off the bed, "sucking cock is foreplay for our little slut."

There's another creak, and then Beau mutters, "How is she this fucking wet *again*? She was legless for thirty minutes."

I rake my nails over Jayk in sharp demand, and he snorts, fucking into my throat again in answer. He leans back heavily against the cabinets, spreading his legs to give me more room. His sweats are pooled around his ankles, and my saliva drips over his balls as he begins to fuck my mouth with rough, delicious urgency.

Click.

Click.

I shift again, trying to keep a pretty posture for Jasper while Jaykob makes a mess of me.

"Eden, your safeword? Is there anything you'd like to . . . Jaykob. Jaykob, will you let her take your filthy cock out of her mouth for just a moment? *Please*?" Jasper's patience is forced, but it's present, and Jayk mutters a sigh.

He yanks my mouth off his dick, and I gasp for air, shivering at the loss.

In a hoarse, hurried rush, I tell the room, "Bristlebrook. No changes to my list. Please can I have Jayk's filthy cock back in my mouth?"

Jayk grunts his approval, his grip in my hair tensing to move me back when Jasper lifts a hand. "Just a moment."

I blink, realizing I can *see* Jasper's hand. I can see Jasper, standing tall and silken and lethally beautiful beside me.

I can see all of them.

Beau sitting on the edge of the bed, watching me as he leans his veined forearms over his knees. Dom walking around slowly, his eyes hot on my body. Lucky sprawled beside me, impish dimples teasing his cheeks. Jayk standing over me, his cock in hand . . . while he *doesn't* try to escape.

All of them, watching me.

A heavy, padded black blindfold drops, dangling from one of Jasper's cool, slender fingers.

"A test, Eden. Do you think you can tell us apart?"

My slow inhale is shaky with need, some of my giggly giddiness burning off as the idea of it sinks in. Jasper's serious. He wants me blindfolded as they touch me. Kiss me.

Fuck me.

He wants me to study them. He wants me to know who has me.

Staring at the blindfold, I whisper, "Yes, please."

"Good girl," Jasper murmurs.

He steps in close, batting Jayk's hand from my hair as he coaxes me around to face the room. Tenderly, he smooths the loose strands back from my face, and his dark eyes are soft, not feeling like galaxies at all anymore. Nothing so far away.

I lean into his delicate touch.

Jasper feels like home.

The home he promised me. The home he delivered.

He smiles as he slips the blindfold over my head, adjusting it carefully over my eyes. I've never had a blindfold engulf me so entirely in darkness before, and it catches me by surprise for a dizzying moment before I settle into it.

He adjusts me until I'm left kneeling up high on the floorboards, my knees spread almost painfully wide, and my folded arms tucked against my lower back. His fingers stroke up my throat in an approving caress, before his hand falls away.

"We're not going to speak, Eden, to give it away. You're going to be given hands, and cocks, and mouths, and whatever else they choose to give you. When they pause, I'll expect you to tell me who is handling you. Do you understand?"

"Yes." My voice is so husky it's barely audible, so I clear it, then whisper, "Yes, Jasper."

In front of me, I hear a soft slide of fabric, a little *thunk*, and then another.

I feel Jasper move away, but this time it's silent as a whisper.

I stiffen, disbelieving as I strain for the sound of his loafers on the floorboards, but I don't find it.

That *sneak*! He *knew* I was tracking him.

They're not going to make this easy.

In the eclipsing darkness, it takes me a moment to get my bearings, to breathe in enough air for the room's now-familiar scents to soothe me. I reach out again for where Jayk had been a moment earlier, but he's not there anymore.

My hand curls back in against my chest, and I feel my heart pound against my palm.

A moment later, someone kneels in front of me. A gentle, coaxing hand slips around my jaw to the back of my neck, and hot lips find mine. A tongue slips into my mouth, drawing out a soft moan as he takes my mouth.

The kiss is luxuriant, hedonistic, and it cajoles every response out of me, until I'm drawn back to a calming river and laugh lines— and the first man who ever kissed me in a way that shocked me awake.

His mouth draws back, pausing against mine, and I smile softly. "I love you, Beau."

He laughs, just as softly, then kisses my forehead. "I love you too, darlin'."

Beau leaves me aching, and it takes a moment before my next brute appears. My lips part as I wait for a kiss, but it doesn't come where I expected.

The kiss comes wetly sucking against my pussy. It comes from underneath me, and I flinch in surprise, gasping at the delighted, indecent rush of pleasure that crashes into me. Clever hands hold my thighs apart over his head, drawing me down, and the mouth opens hot and filthy over my cunt.

The mouth devours me with obscene, slippery eagerness, and I cry out, my orgasm threatening me with every wet suck. While I'm spread open, his tongue fucks into my hole until I shake so hard I almost lose my balance. He shifts to suckle at my clit with hard, perfect little pulls, and I'm just about to come when he . . . *stops*.

I sob, my breath coming brutally fast, and every inch of me is quaking.

My orgasm hovers as close as my pussy still hovers over his mouth.

I'd know that mouth anywhere. He spent his whole first night with me fucking me with it. That clever, hot, funny, *incredible* mouth that I want to taste for the rest of my life.

And I didn't even need to feel his beard to be sure enough to choke out, "*Lucky*! Lucky, *please*—"

"Aw, cute. Hey, Jayk, isn't it funny how she knew it wasn't you?"

Lucky presses one last cheeky kiss to my clit before he slides out from under me.

There's the soft padding of feet moving away, then a smack, a loud *oof*, and the next steps coming toward me aren't so soft.

A rough hand grips my hair, and a still-damp cock is pushed between my lips.

"Fuck," Jayk sighs in relief as he pushes in, and there's a loud round of curses and groans around the room.

I would grin if my mouth weren't currently full of cock.

"Seriously?" Dom says dryly.

"You could at least *pretend* to play," Lucky complains.

"Can you all just shut up and let a man come!"

Jayk starts fucking me roughly, with purpose, and I shudder. He's as close and edged as I am already, and I feel him swell against my tongue.

I relax for him, letting him take whatever he wants from me.

Making sure I'm nice and wet, like he ordered the very first time we slept together.

Because it doesn't matter if he spoke or not. I'd know it was Jayk. He loves my mouth just as much as I love his cock. I know how he takes me. I know the taste of him. I know that for however rough he is with me, he's twice as careful in making sure I'm safe.

Jayk fills my mouth in quick, hard shoves, until his rhythm stutters and slows. Until he groans, soaking my mouth with hot, jerking pumps of his hips, holding my forehead against him. When he's done, I try to swallow, but he drags his pulsing cock along my tongue until he drips out over my chin.

I kiss the flared crown as he pulls back.

"I really would know you anywhere, Jayk," I murmur, and he gives my cheek a rough, affectionate squeeze.

"I know, sugar," he tells me gruffly.

"Can I just say, you're all making this incredibly easy on her," Jasper says from somewhere far away, sounding wry.

A few laughs echo around me, then there's some shuffling around.

My sight cut off, I strain to hear every sound. Jayk's taste dances over my tongue, and I still feel the ghost of Lucky's mouth on my pussy. Goosebumps lift over my skin, the decadent anticipation of who and where and when starting to make me dizzy.

Suddenly, there's another hand in my hair, this one sharp and cruel.

It holds me tight, close to the roots, lifting me to my feet, and I catch my breath as the light pain prickles over me.

Is this . . . Jasper?

My scalp cries out as they drag me sharply through the room by their tight fist, holding me far enough from their body that I can't get any sense of their size or texture.

Suddenly the scent of rich, oiled leather floods me, and I'm guided carefully up until I'm kneeling over Jasper's low paddling bench, straddling the wide beam in its center.

It's not the first time I've been on it, and the padded leather under my chest and hips supports me well. My hard, hot breaths warm the cool padding under my cheek. There are straps against where my arms and calves are resting, but my brutes make no moves toward them.

Bondage is still a no on my limits list.

Damn it, who *is* this?

They're apparently taking Jasper's instruction to make it harder on me seriously.

Unless it *is* Jasper, and this is all a double fake.

I strain to hear anything, any sound that might give away who is behind me—or who isn't. But all I hear are a few soft breaths . . . and the gentle creak of someone taking something from the display cabinets.

Oh, God. Am I being whipped?

Jasper has tried a few different *tools* on me, with varying success. He's been filling out my limits list with the exacting detail of a scientist forever on the brink of a major discovery.

The sudden hand trailing down my back makes me twitch in surprise. It's slow and possessive, but light enough that I can't feel more than their heat and the hint of scraping calluses. And I wish that were more of a tell, but all my brutes have calluses—though Jasper's are by far the lightest, so maybe it's *not* him . . .?

The hand slips down over my hips, pressing covetously between my ass cheeks before carelessly nudging me wider, and I shiver as I move quickly for them. I tilt my hips up, presenting my ass as eagerly as I can.

The bench is low enough that I'm at the perfect height to spank *or* fuck. They could take my mouth, or my ass, or my cunt. With just a few shifts, they could take me any way they want me.

Or several of them could.

The air is cool on my overheated pussy, clinging to the slick mess they've already made of me, but it's not a cock I feel next.

A hard hand cracks down over my ass cheek, and sudden stinging heat blooms at the contact. I jerk, yelping, but another swat lights up my other cheek a bare moment later. It's bright and shocking, somehow even more so when I can't see where it's coming from. When there's no instruction, no way at all to gauge what's next.

The hand pauses on my ass, as if in question, and I say, "Green" before I realize that's probably not what they're asking.

They're asking *who*.

"I—" I stammer.

Dom likes to spank me, and he's bossy enough to drag me by my hair, but they've all spanked me before, and I just don't think it *feels* like Dom. But it doesn't feel at *all* like Beau, and . . . *could* it be Jasper?

Another sharp, demanding swat against the curve of my thigh sends heat sparkling over my skin.

"I don't know!" I wail, starting to panic, because I'm seeing where this is going now.

I feel a hard, thick drag of leather up the back of my thigh.

A paddle.

Jayk snickers from across the room. "Better figure it out quick, sugar."

There's another thump, then, "Oh fuck off, she knew it wasn't me!"

The paddle slides over my ass, and I shiver again. I know better than to tense by now, but I can't stop my toes from curling in anticipation before—

Swat.

Left cheek.

Swat.

Right cheek.

Swat.

Left cheek.

Swat.

Left cheek again, just because I waited for the right side again, I'm sure. Then there's a pause as I moan, squirming against the bench. The paddle drops, and rough, gripping hands callously knead my raw, burning skin, both soothing the skin and adding to the ache.

My breasts feel trapped by the leather, and my thighs are forced too wide by the paddling bench. I can't close or ease the throb in my clit or stop the trickle of my need from sliding over my clit and onto the leather under me.

"Please," I beg my mystery brute.

I'm too wound up by Beau's kiss and Lucky's tongue in my cunt and Jayk taking my mouth.

"Please fuck me. I don't care who you are, just fuck me, *please.*"

The sound of hot, panted breaths fill the room, and they don't only belong to me.

They're all watching my brute squeeze my bruised ass with greedy, pitiless self-indulgence. They're all watching me squirm into his hands. They're all watching me beg like the little slut Dom called me.

Then the hands pause.

And I still don't know who it is.

"I don't . . . wait. I'm sorry!" I squeal as I get another hot spank.

Then the hands spread me wide apart, and my brute fucks into my open, aching pussy in one, sharp thrust.

On a helpless moan, I shove back into him, and his fingers bite into my hips as he starts fucking into me in a fast, slapping onslaught. Shuddering, I clamp around his cock, savoring the ruthless invasion, lost in the drag of his dick against my desperate, oversensitive walls.

My breasts rub against the leather with every thrust, and when I arch, he shoves me back down, swiveling his hips. I feel my slickness spilling out over him, hear the wet slap as he takes me hard.

I need him to touch my clit. Just once. I squirm, trying to get friction, but his cruel grip doesn't let me go anywhere.

But those hands *don't* feel like Jasper's.

I let out a hoarse, tense whimper as I teeter on the brink of an orgasm, and he ignores it. I've already been fucked today, and I'm too sensitive for this, especially when his cock curves in the most perfect . . .

Oh, *shit*.

"*Lucky*?!" I cry out, and he snorts behind me.

"God damn, took you long enough, beautiful. I was starting to get offended," he teases, but his rough, punishing thrusts don't let up, and I shudder, stunned.

And hopelessly turned on.

He yanks me back again by my hips, and I feel every inch of his cock as he fucks me deep, not letting me move.

My Lucky, sweet Lucky . . . is fucking me like . . . like a *dom*.

One of Lucky's hands snakes up to wrap in my hair, and he groans as he pulls, bowing my back as he begins to grind his cock deep into me . . . and lets out a long, satisfied groan.

"Please," I choke out, squeezing around him, but he's already shuddering into me.

"Sorry," he finally pants against my back. "Losers don't get to come."

I choke again, this time in pure offense, and he laughs as he drops a kiss between my shoulder blades, backing up.

"You know, I forgot he could do that," Beau muses under his breath.

"So did I," Jasper mutters, his voice hoarse.

There's a rustle of fabric, and a soft clash of breaths that makes me whimper helplessly, rocking my hips, but there's nowhere for me to go.

Until someone hauls me off the bench a second later. It's rough and fast, and they toss me over their shoulder so fast that I squeal "Jayk!" before I've even stopped to think.

A heavy hand claps over my ass a second later, and I realize my mistake.

It's my *other* big, giant bully.

"Dom! Dom, I'm sorry, sir. It was the shoulder. You did it on purpose, I—"

He throws me down off his shoulder, and I squeak, my stomach flipping at the sudden drop before my back bounces on the mattress.

"You've done it now, pet," he says above me, though he sounds amused. "Lie back. Put a pillow under your hips, spread your legs, and cross your arms over your head, then don't move, no matter what we do to you. Understood?"

"Yes, sir," I tell him huskily, my heart pattering in sheer, skittish nerves.

Even Dom's funishments scare me.

I move into position fast and as gracefully as possible, trying to buy any goodwill I can. When I cross my wrists above my head, I leave them turned up, open and vulnerable. I arch my back, displaying my breasts as I sink back against the bed, and when I spread my legs, I let my feet slide slowly over the silken sheets, letting my thighs fall submissively wide.

Far too soft and pretty to punish for long, surely—especially over one teeny, tiny understandable mistake.

Even if I still have Jayk's cum on my skin, and Lucky's making a slick, ruined mess of my pussy. I can feel his cum dripping out of me, sliding down the cleft of my ass.

"She obeys you so beautifully," Jasper says softly, a hushed kind of approval in his voice.

Dom snorts. "Sure, Jasper. That's what happens when you don't go soft on your subbies."

Oh. Oh, *no.*

Beau whistles low.

"I . . . beg your pardon?"

I wince at the dangerous, incredulous shock in Jasper's voice, right as Lucky starts choking on his sudden lost, helpless laughter.

"Lucien, shut up," Jasper snaps, and Dom tuts, dryly amused.

"See? Indulgent. Lacking discipline. Now, do you want to continue your game or . . .?"

Jayk starts laughing, too, but none of *them* are naked and laid out ready to be used as an example.

My nipples are sharp, aching buds in the cool air of the room, and I suddenly feel hopelessly exposed. My brutes fall quiet again, but this time, it only takes seconds before I feel hands on me—and only seconds more before I realize my next mystery brute is not alone.

Someone tilts my head to the right, sliding their stiff cock over the seam of my lips. I open obediently, trailing my tongue over the sensitive underside, right as someone draws my left nipple into their hot, wet mouth.

As I gasp, the brute by my head starts feeding me his cock. It's heavy and familiar, and so thick I know exactly who he is this time, but I'm not given the breath to get my gold star before he starts rocking lazily into my mouth.

Another hand moves between my legs, cruelly teasing and toying at the wet mess Lucky left, rubbing it tauntingly into my clit until I'm shivering, and it takes every effort not to squirm.

Generous, coaxing fingers tease my breasts, and my other brute's greedy mouth drifts over my chest to lavish the same hungry attention on the other, while the cock in my mouth grows rougher and more demanding the more my attention is torn.

Suddenly, a hot tongue slips along my pussy, and my muffled cry is helpless.

"Oh, fucking hell," Lucky curses hoarsely, and this time he gets a rough *thump*.

Cool, elegant hands shove my thighs wide as they try to close around the brute's ears, and he begins to lick up every bit of mess Lucky left behind. I can't help the way I arch into his mouth, shuddering, my mind melting over the obscene, avaricious feast he's making of me.

The cock in my mouth is throbbing, heated and delicious, and I can taste him as he starts to drip precum into the back of my throat.

I can hear the fast, slick strokes as the brute by my side fucks his own fist. While he touches himself, he's worshipping my body in sharp, sucking little bites over my breasts. In long, lascivious licks down my stomach. In cruel plucks of my nipples.

That mouth between my legs is panting hot, and it slides up to suckle ruthlessly at my clit.

Tears leak from the corners of my eyes as my orgasm crests again, this time harder, more brutally, until—

"No!" I sob, gasping for air as the cock is finally pulled from my mouth, and the tongue lifts from my stomach, and the mouth pulls away from my clit.

"Please," I moan desperately, and my toes curl in the sheets, "I can't. Please."

Someone swats hard at my clit, and I flinch.

"Jasper," I manage between choppy breaths.

Fingers run briefly over my breasts, and I sob, "*Beau*."

The cock touches my lips again, and I whisper, "Sir, *please*."

Every one of my brutes is touching me in ways that are so exactly *them* that I don't even need to think to guess who they are.

"Better," Jasper murmurs, sounding drunk, and his breath fans cruelly over my pussy. "Wait here."

Then he disappears from between my legs, and I start to tremble, lost and needy. My head drops back against the mattress in miserable defeat.

"Ah, that's rough, beautiful," Lucky says sympathetically. "Classic dominant asshole move. It's a rigged system we're working in, Eden. They set you up to fail and then use your sweet little body as their personal dick depository. They'll never know the betrayal. Sub club for life."

"You literally *just* dommed me, Lucky," I hiss, not sure whether I want to laugh or cry when he chuckles affectionately.

"Oh, yeah."

"Stop talking, pet. If you want anything from us, you let me come down your throat first," Dom orders.

Then his heavy cock pushes into my mouth with careless entitlement, and his wide hands pin me in place as he starts to fuck me with leisurely, self-indulgent strokes.

Beau groans. "I love how she looks while she's sucking cock."

He suddenly lifts up beside me, his breathing ragged, and I hear his hand working over his cock again—this time faster.

"It feels even better," Dom growls, and then his breath sighs out.

His cock pulses, spilling over my tongue, and I choke a little, then moan as I swallow him down. I'm still sucking at his cock when Beau's hand suddenly stops.

Beau lets out a soft grunt, and then hot, thick jets of cum are painting my breasts. I squirm under them, feeling filled and claimed, slick and stained by their hunger, and it only brings mine to a fine, sharp point.

Dom slips out of my mouth, and his thumb brushes my lips.

"Good girl, pet. I know it's been a long day," he tells me softly, and Beau's fingers replace Dom's a moment later.

They're still slick with his cum, and I lick them on instinct as Beau murmurs, "Just one more now, darlin'. Then you're all done. You've done so well."

I feel my final brute move up on the bed, between my quaking thighs.

I'm shaking from head to toe, caught in the dark but not lost there, not anymore. My brutes are all around me, and I know they won't leave—no matter how dark it gets.

"J-Jasper," I sob, and he strokes my hip as he presses his cock gently against my wet entrance.

"I know, sweet girl. I have you. They're right. You've worked so hard for us," he says tenderly.

His heavy cock shoves in hard, and I twist up, gasping. A second later, something scalding hot drips over my breasts, and I flinch, crying out in shock and sudden, startled pain.

Moving his hips in slow, brutal thrusts, Jasper fucks me while I squirm.

My cunt accepts him covetously, even as my hands strangle the sheets over my head. Every thrust stokes me higher, but that burn is . . .

I sob, tears streaming down my face beneath my blindfold.

"Oh, I know. I know it hurts, my Eden," he croons, with heart-breaking, malicious tenderness. "You know what to say if it's too much, but I think you'll like the wax. Just give it a moment."

He pins me by my throat, dripping more wax over me, until it sizzles over my skin, and I have nowhere to escape. My thighs squeeze his hips as his cock claims me spitefully, and I gasp as my burns begin to soak together.

Jasper's breathing is panted, fast, his voice as thick and dark as it ever gets when he's enthralled by a scene. By Lucky.

Or by me.

"Jasper, *please*!" I cry out, my voice breaking as the sweet, hot pain and the brutal, aching pressure start to crash in on me.

Jasper's breath catches on a sweet groan. "You're so lovely when you're soaked in us, sweet girl. You're so lovely when you're ours."

His cock is throbbing inside me with every hard, greedy thrust. He splashes more fire over my chest, down my stomach, and then he leans over me, smearing the wax between us, until we're both coated in the heat and the mess, and I'm squirming helplessly toward my peak.

My cunt tightens around him, and Jasper's hands find mine above my head, his fingers twining through mine.

"Fuck, the things you let me do to you," he groans in my ear, burying his cock in me in deep, claiming thrusts. "You can come now, my Eden. Show me how grateful you are. You've earned it."

His mouth trails along my neck, and his bite is sharp, piercing.

The pain sets off a ruthless, brutal chain reaction, and I come without breathing. I come like I'm fragmenting. Jasper's heat floods me, mixing with Lucky's. Dom and Beau and Jayk are on my skin, their scents still surrounding me, and I shatter apart with every one of them hurtling me over the edge.

When I finally come to, I'm still shaking, and crying, but that's not unusual after a Jasper scene. They're not the kind of tears I used to cry, alone in my pillow next to Henry. Or alone in my cave just miles from here.

These tears come from relief, and joy, and an overwhelming, crushing sense of disbelief that anything—any life—can feel this good.

My brutes move around the room, fetching water and warm cloths, soft blankets and my favorite snacks. They're laughing and teasing one another, making jokes about Jasper lasting long enough to get the job done. Jokes that were already overused nine months ago but they can never seem to resist. My brutes come to settle by me, telling me sweet things and kind things, and drawing me into their arms in generous turns because they know I need it. All of them. Every one.

And when I finally drift drowsily off between them, it's knowing that I have a lifetime of nights just like this waiting for me when I wake.

Author's Note

I'm not crying, you're crying! Oh, man. I can't believe we're actually here. Two years, three books, a novella, and 630k words later, the Brutes of Bristlebrook is complete. These characters have been part of my life for so long now, so entrenched in every day, that saying so long to them now hurts in all the best ways.

Jasper would be proud.

This book in particular was incredibly difficult to write. As you might have guessed, it was hard from a technical standpoint, especially as a debut author, threading everything together until I thought I'd fall apart from how overwhelming it all was.

But from the story point of view, from my characters, that was also hard.

This book, in many ways, is a love letter to people who have been hurt.

To anyone who was told they should have known better. To anyone who was preyed on. To anyone who wasn't heard when they spoke. To anyone who could have used a storm of Valkyries and brutes at their back.

To anyone who couldn't tell who the villain was until it was too late.

I hope you found justice, and peace, and if not, I hope you were able, at least, to find it within these pages.

Consent matters. Supporting the people who need it matters. Being open and willing to grow and learn from our mistakes matters.

This was my debut series, and I'm so proud of it. It tore my soul out of me to write. It pushed me to learn and grow as a person. It drove me to deep dive into places I didn't know existed. Writing, to me, should be an exercise in empathy, and I'm so thrilled and privileged to do this for a living now. I'm excited to keep learning and writing and sharing stories that make me want to laugh and bleed and occasionally turn on the air conditioning.

Starting with the Sinners of Cyanide, a standalone spin-off book to the Brutes of Bristlebrook that I'm planning to release this year in 2025. (No dates confirmed yet!). It will be a shadow book to Entwined, showing all the delicious angst and pain and all the layers of the schemes that were going on in Cyanide while our Brutes were occupied here.

And yes, it follows Heather, Alastair, Mateo, and Bentley, my morally grey crew. It won't be a why choose (it will be MF and MM), but it will have all the same bromance, found family, and deep platonic intimacies that our Brutes had.

Finally, I'm grateful to you, my reader. Endlessly grateful. Thank you for giving this life to me. You made it possible for me to do all of this.

So thank you.

WANT MORE?

DAY DEATH:
A BRUTES OF BRISTLEBROOK
PREQUEL NOVELLA

OUT NOW ON KU, PAPERBACK, & FULL-CAST AUDIO

One night. Six stories. Total nuclear annihilation.

THE BRUTES

Tonight was meant to be about kink. Our lives are a nightmare of last-minute deployments and near misses, and we needed the break.

Instead, *we* broke. The whole world broke.

But as city after city is blown apart, and with a club full of civilians to protect, we have to pull it together and get them to safety. No matter how we're feeling. No matter how many family members are disintegrating into ash. We have a job to do, so we'll be each other's strength.

Even if it means walking into bomb-fire together.

EDEN

I'm alone.

Please, someone forgive me for what I have to do.

I don't think I can.

ACKNOWLEDGMENTS

Okay, starting the acknowledgements crying. That's a good start. Cool, cool, cool.

I have so many people to thank. It takes a village to create a book, and this one took at least a village to get over the line, and I'm so incredibly lucky and humbled to have these people in my life to help me.

First, I'd like to thank my designers, Artscandare (main series covers) and Justine at JAB Design Studio (who did my special edition covers). You ensnared (see what I did there?) people from the get go—there are so many people who never would have picked up this series if not for you, so thank you.

To Jessica at Fervent Ink Editing and Andrew H. for doing my editing, well, you saved me from a lot of embarrassment. A LOT. You went above and beyond to get this book out the door and I can't stop gushing about you. Thank you for catching my Aussie-isms and my silly typos.

To my agent, Susan, you have been absolutely wonderful. Thank you so much for everything you do. Every email from you makes my day.

To Avery Caris, JF Harding, Jason Clarke, Teddy Hamilton, Sebastian York, Rose Dioro, Connor Crais, Robert Hatchet, and Gregory Salinas, thank you so much for bringing my characters to life with so much care and empathy. You've opened up the world of this series and made these characters so tangible and human, and that is a talent and a skill I'll live in awe of forever.

To my betas. Shannan, you make me snort laugh every time you dive into my doc, thank you for being my hype person. Bree, you have been a cheerleader and a champion and I value every word. To Jess, Chels, Julia, Kristie, CiCi, Paris, Stephanie, Lou, and Chelsey, I am in awe of you. Thank you for giving me the privilege of your time and thoughts, thank you for your empathy and kindness in your feedback. You've cheered me on and hyped me up and this book is so much better for your input. Thank you.

To my book wives, Letizia Lorini, WH Lockwood, LH Blake, and Heather Garvin, you remind me constantly that I'm not alone and what a strange world we live in. Thank you for our chat, and for your friendship, because you're all too talented, fun, and special not to have in my life.

To my PA, Tegan, who has been doing an incredible amount of behind-the-scenes work. If it weren't for you, I never would have had the space to be able to write. I love you so much, and for anyone reading, look up Your Story Enchanted, for the most incredible bookish candles and swag you've ever seen.

To Char, who is a total force of nature. You're a total force of nature. Thank you for managing my Facebook group, but even more for protecting my peace. I owe you so much.

To A.K. Blythe, my writing buddy, who leaves me constantly in awe and screaming jealous profanities at my screen over your prose, thank you for your friendship and patience and for cheering me on at every step. You're a superstar.

To my Lisa, who deserves the world. I might not be able to deliver that but, as promised, Jayk is yours. Treat him well. Or ride him like a cowboy, whatever works. Your fierce friendship, loyalty, and big heart should be studied.

To my fiancé, Daniel. You're the best of every brute, and I love you with everything. Thank you for being an incredible father to our son and a partner to me in every way. Without you holding down our life, I couldn't have done this at all. I adore you.

To my sister, Nicky. I'm very lucky to have a pretty spectacular family, who all support me so much, but Nicky is there for the books as much as for me. She's there for every event, every late-night phone call, every plot discussion, and breakdown. I don't think there's anything I can do to make it up to you, but if you think of anything, let me know.

Finally, to my Elisa. There are no words, and I don't even know where to begin with this. I know I'm already sobbing. My book doula.

My dear, dear friend. You've been there as my alpha, my socials support, my confidant, and my plot unraveller. You've been there for every draft and every moment I second guessed myself. You lifted me up when I was exhausted and hurting, and it's your love for these characters and series that made me fall back in love with them too. Your compassion and empathy and piercing intelligence are an absolute privilege to have in my life. I could write an essay on how grateful I am to you—you're well aware of my wordiness—but instead I'll just say thank you.

And we did it.

About the Author

After spending her career publishing other writers' wonderful words, Rebecca Quinn decided to unleash her own. Turns out, she's a little debauched. Rebecca loves writing inclusive, character-driven why choose romance with heart, humor, and kinky heat—or romance with bromance, as she calls it.

Rebecca lives in a coastal town south of Sydney, Australia. She spends her days cuddling her young son and her fiancé, getting far too invested in her DnD campaigns, drinking too much wine, playing board games, and—of course—reading as many novels as she can get her grabby little hands on.

If you want to keep up to date with the next books in the series, bonus content, new series, filthy memes, and ridiculous chats, come get Quinnky with me on my socials, or sign up to my newsletter via my website.

www.ingramcontent.com/pod-product-compliance
Lightning Source LLC
Chambersburg PA
CBHW031726180726
48283CB00005B/1398